ENCOUNTERS UNFORESEEN

ENCOUNTERS

UNFORESEEN

1492 Retold

Andrew Rowen

ALL PERSONS PRESS
NEW YORK, NEW YORK

All Persons Press
New York, New York
First published in 2017 by All Persons Press

Encounters Unforeseen: 1492 Retold
Copyright © 2017 Andrew Rowen
All rights reserved.
Interior Maps and Illustrations by David Atkinson.

Permissions and Credits on pages ix–xi, 490–491
Library of Congress Control Number: 2017911346
ISBN13: 978-0-9991961-0-6

Cover and Book Design by Glen Edelstein, Hudson Valley Book Design
Cover Illustration by Robert Hunt

To my late mother, who taught me to listen to the voice and soul of each person, and my father, who taught me to make up my own mind.

CONTENTS

LIST Of MAPS
AND ILLUSTRATIONS

All maps and illustrations are from the fifteenth and sixteenth centuries other than those designated by an asterisk, which have been drawn by David Atkinson.

HISTORICAL NOTE

This novel dramatizes the history leading to Columbus's first encounters with Native Americans from a bicultural perspective, fictionalizing Native American beliefs, thoughts, and actions side by side with those of Europeans. The history is presented through short stories alternating among three historic chieftains of the Taíno peoples of the Caribbean and a Taíno captive and comparable stories of Columbus and Spain's Queen Isabella and King Ferdinand. The narrative portrays the life experiences each protagonist brought to the encounters and then his or her astonishment, fears, and objectives in 1492 and 1493. The focus extends beyond Columbus's voyage of "discovery" to depict the entirety of the encounters from the Native American perspective, including the Taíno "discovery" of Europe, when Columbus brings the captive and other Taínos back to Spain, as well as the chieftains' reactions to the abusive garrison of seamen Columbus then leaves behind in the Caribbean. I seek to explore how and why Taínos and Europeans each made decisions and to avoid the traditional Columbus- and European-centric focus of most histories of the events, including those critical of Columbus and colonialism. The Taíno protagonists are neither merely victims nor statistics, but personalities and actors just as the Europeans.

The outcome we know was uncertain or indiscernible to the participants, and I have tried to present their thoughts and actions from youth through 1493 as they would have lived them day to day, often enveloped in confusion or chaos, without imposing the historical conclusions of a history written with hindsight or inventing an overarching story plot typical of traditional fiction. Throughout, I have sought historical validity and considered first primary sources written by those who witnessed the events, knew the participants, or lived in the sixteenth century. Each participant's thoughts and actions are presented consistent with my interpretation of the historical record to the extent one exists or fictionalized in a manner I believe likely could have occurred, with the methodology noted below.

The Taínos had no written history, and the only contemporaneous written accounts of the encounters are by the conquering Europeans, reflecting the conquerors' knowledge and perspective and sometimes lacking credibility. The pre-1492 stories of the Taíno chieftains—Caonabó, Guacanagarí, and Guarionex—and the Taíno captive depict the few events known to have occurred, including the rulers' ascensions to power, their marriages, and a religious prophecy of genocide. Within this framework, the stories are fictionalized based on descriptions of Taíno culture in the writings of contemporary Europeans (such as Peter Martyr d'Anghera, Bartolomé de Las Casas, Gonzalo Fernández de Oviedo, Ramón Pané, and Columbus himself) and twenty-first-century anthropologists, archaeologists, and linguists. Commencing October 12, 1492, the stories are constructed by extrapolating from the conquerors' day-to-day accounts of the encounter (to the extent credible), including Columbus's *Journal*, the biography written by his son Ferdinand, and Las Casas's *Historia de las Indias*, what the Taínos then experienced—fictionalizing the conquered's account to mirror the conquerors'.

With respect to the Europeans, vastly more is known, but the historical record is incomplete and, as to youth, sparse. The stories of Isabella's youth and Columbus's youth and early adulthood are almost as fictional as the pre-1492 Taíno stories and are similarly constructed on the basis of what is known of contemporaneous Castilian, Genoese, and Portuguese society. The passages regarding Columbus's pre-1492 ocean-sailing experience are founded in but a few sentences in primary sources, the validity of which historians debate, and are fictionalized in part based on other sources indicating the conditions and purposes for which similar voyages occurred in the fifteenth century. Following youth, the stories of Isabella and Ferdinand reflect the record provided by court chroniclers and official documents, as do the Columbus stories commencing with his voyage, but events and thoughts are fictionalized with a specificity that far exceeds this record.

The novel also seeks a rounded presentation of European history by portraying both the larger Atlantic world into which the participants were born and how the European sovereigns ruled over their very own subjects and subjugated other Old World peoples, closely prelude to encountering Native Americans. A prologue introduces Old World seaborne commerce, based on the European merchant's own account. Stories depict Isabella and Ferdinand's subjugation and Christianization of the Canary Islands, establishment of the Inquisition, conquest of the Islamic kingdom of Grenada, and expulsion of the Jews from Spain, as well as the Portuguese establishment of African trading colonies as they sought to reach the Indies first by circumventing Africa. These and other stories explore the European justifications for conquest and enslavement of other peoples and forced religious conversion of them and religious minorities. They also illustrate the threats to European Christian civilization posed by Islam's spread and chronicle the expansion of European geographic knowledge and dominion. As a result, the novel includes more pre-encounter European stories than Taíno.

I have tried to dramatize thoughts from the participants' perspectives in the fifteenth century, including those of rulers and common subjects, masters and servants, slaves, and concubines. For both Taínos and Europeans, religion was central to the individual's identity and understanding of the world, and the stories present spirits, God, and saints as ever present. Taíno and European societies were both organized by social caste and defined different roles for men and women, and the Europeans practiced slavery. While many of the thoughts related are readily understood as improper and wrong in a modern perspective, frequently it is clear many participants perceived otherwise. Columbus's unspoken thoughts presented during the encounters embody the concepts underlying the European subjugation of Native Americans over the next centuries. I have sought to fictionalize thoughts accurately as I believe they would have been, to avoid—undoubtedly imperfectly—my own embellishment of hero or villain beyond that, and to leave moral and historical judgments regarding Columbus and others as so fictionalized for the reader.

Stories are told from the perspective of the participants' probable knowledge of geography at the time of the story, and all maps presented herein are from the fifteenth or sixteenth centuries, except the four modern maps immediately following this historical note. Taínos and Europeans both believed places existed—sometimes known through religious tradition—that today we know do not exist, and these places are presented as real when the participants would have so believed. The modern maps show the principal Taíno chiefdoms and Hispanic kingdoms existing before 1492, the greater Atlantic world, and the Taíno Caribbean.

Throughout the novel, almost all persons identified with proper names are historic, although historic Taínos known to history by their baptized Christian names are given fictitious birth names, as are a few historic persons whose name is unknown. Occasionally, unknown—and thus fictitious—relatives of participants are referred to simply by their relationship to the participant (e.g., "Mother"). In a handful of instances, stories include fictitious relatives, intimates, or other minor characters who are given fictitious names in order to facilitate the narrative's continuity; these few persons are identified as fictitious in the list of Participants or the Sources sections provided at the novel's end. The conventions used with respect to the language and spelling of names of persons and places; the measurement of time and distance; the assumed ages of the Taíno participants; the words *Taíno*, *Caribe*, *Lucayan*, and *Indian*, and various Christian religious terms; and fictionalization are set forth under Conventions following the Participants list. Taíno words (other than proper names) are italicized and translated when first introduced and then compiled at the end in the Glossary of Taíno Words. Parenthetical phrases or footnotes in the narrative occasionally identify historic persons or peoples unnamed in the narrative, when historic persons lived, or the modern names or locations of historic places.

The historical record is conflicted often—with primary and secondary sources disagreeing as to what occurred and why—and to preserve the novel style I present only my interpretation. For readers interested, the Sources section lists by story the primary and secondary sources relied on, occasionally noting my reasoning and contrary interpretations. The stories often incorporate words from or paraphrase the primary sources, with the objective of best capturing the participants' intent and fifteenth-century perspective. To preserve the novel style, these incorporations are not designated by quotation marks, but the Sources section indicates the chapter, section, paragraph, and/or date of the primary sources relied on, as well as acknowledging those who have graciously permitted such usage.

The novel ends in September 1493, as Columbus prepares in Spain for his second voyage and the chieftains consider what to do with the garrison remaining on their territory. During the period presented, the violence done by Europeans to Taínos consists of isolated events. But the conceptual framework has been set before the maelstrom, and it remains for future novels to explore the horrific story of the systematic slaughter, religious contempt, servitude, slavery, and utter collapse of human well-being and dignity that followed.

August 3, 2017   Andrew S. Rowen

PRINCIPAL CHIEFDOMS IN HAITI AND
THE DOMINICAN REPUBLIC BEFORE 1492

Anthropologists and historians debate the locations and boundaries of the
chiefdoms, and the locations above are consistent with those proposed by Irving
Rouse. See Rouse's *The Tainos: Rise and Decline of the People Who Greeted
Columbus* (New Haven: Yale University Press, 1992).

PRINCIPAL KINGDOMS IN SPAIN AND
PORTUGAL BEFORE 1492

ATLANTIC WORLD MAP
(with places mentioned in
this book)

GREENLAND

ICELAND

L'Anse aux Meadows

Galway
Bristol • London

Savona • Genoa
Rome • Smederevo
Seville • Segovia • Granada
Lisbon

Kaffa
Oranto • Istanbul
Gallipoli • Athens • Chios
• Jerusalem
Cape • Mediterranean Sea
Carthage

Cape Blanco
Arguin
 Río de Ouro
Dakar

Shama • El Mina

Cape Cross

Cape Padrone
Mossel Bay

Cape of Good Hope

2000

Miles

0

Madeira
Porto Santo
Canary
Islands

Cape
Verde
Islands

Cape Bojador

Cuba
San Salvador
Jamaica • Haiti • Turks and Caicos
• Dominican Republic
Puerto
Rico • Guadeloupe

Corvo
Flores

Graciosa
Faial • Terceira
Pico • São Jorge
São Miguel

Santa Maria

AZORES

Porto
Santo

Madeira

Ilhas
Deserias

MADEIRA and
PORT SANTO

Lanzarote

Fuerteventura
Gran
La Palma Tenerife Canaria
La
Gomera
El Hierro

CANARIES

THE TAÍNO CARIBBEAN
(with Taíno names for islands
mentioned in this book)

Island names are based on Julian Granberry and Gary Vescelius's *Languages of the Pre-Columbian Antilles* (Tuscaloosa: University of Alabama Press, 2004) and other sources. Aniyana (Middle Caicos); Ba We Ka (Caicos bank); Baneque (Great Iguana); Boriquén (Puerto Rico); Caicos (North Caicos); Guanahaní (San Salvador); Haiti (Dominican Republic and Haiti); Manigua (Rum Cay); Samoete (Crooked, Fortune, and Acklins Islands); Utiaquia (Ragged Islands); Wana (East Caicos); Yamaye (Jamaica); Yuma (Long Island). Cuba abbreviates a longer word.

NOTE ON DATING OF STORIES

If the historical record indicates a specific or approximate date for an event or events central to a story, that date is noted in the story's title—without parentheses. If the historical record is conflicted or silent as to the date of the central events dramatized, or if the central events are fictional but an historical context has been described as of a specific date, the story's title indicates a possible date or the date of the historical context—in parentheses. If history provides no guidance or context, the story is left undated.

PROLOGUE: 1455

CA' DA MOSTO
Land of the Budomel (North of Dakar, Senegal, Africa),
April–May 1455

A solitary caravel, dispatched by Prince Henrique of Portugal and flying the colors of his nephew the Portuguese king Afonso V, sailed southward in the Ocean Sea along the west coast of Africa, its lateen sails emblazoned in red with the square cross of the Order of Christ. Its owner, the pilot, and a young merchant stood together on the stern deck and studied the shoreline some miles east, comparing it to their chart based on voyages of previous Portuguese traders. The ship cruised rapidly, propelled by steady northeasterly winds that blew offshore to sea—permitting it to run with the wind without tacking—and a strong current that swept south along the coast. The pilot estimated they had coursed more than sixty miles south of the Río de Senega, which separated the great desert of the north from Guinea, the tropical land to the south.

The three men agreed they had arrived at a Wolof kingdom ruled by a local chieftain the Portuguese referred to as "the Budomel," "Lord Budomel," or simply "Budomel," with whom the Portuguese had traded for over five years. There was no port, just a beach suited for landing abreast the open ocean and sheltered from the south-bound current. The pilot summoned the ship's black slave, Pedro, who confirmed their arrival. Pedro had been purchased by previous traders farther north along the coast and then trained by Prince Henrique's men to serve as an interpreter with the Budomel and other Wolof chieftains.

The ship's owner, Vicente Dias, served as its captain to protect his investment, and he directed the pilot and crew to tack the ship toward shore slowly, alert for shoals. They lowered the sails and anchored well outside the surf breaking on offshore sandbars, a few hundred feet from the beach.

The merchant, the Venetian Alvise da Ca' da Mosto, was excited that his objective—trading with the Guineans—at last was at hand. Prince Henrique had charged him with the voyage's success, and he and Henrique would share its profits equally. This expedition was his first for Henrique and, if pleased, the prince likely would sponsor others.

Ca' da Mosto's woolen shirt, breeches, and jerkin were finer than Dias's, and his silver neck chain dangled a jeweled pendant to draw attention to his greater stature. But Ca' da Mosto was in his early twenties and exercised his authority respectfully and often deferentially. Both Dias and the pilot were older men and more experienced sailors, and they might not abide by instructions affecting the ship if they disagreed substantially. Both were Portuguese, as was the crew of some twenty men, and Ca' da Mosto's ability to converse with the two older men casually in Portuguese, no less to reason with them over a point of controversy, was limited. He was a foreigner to their kingdom and mindful that his instructions matched their view as closely as possible.

Ca' da Mosto descended into the caravel's hold to inspect the condition of his principal cargo, seven horses. The air below reeked of their sweat, excrement, and fodder, the stench aggravated by the stifling heat and humidity. They had sailed with ten horses, but two had died from the heat and one had been thrown overboard after breaking a leg when the ship lurched. Ca' da Mosto inspected them carefully, aware the Budomel had paid handsomely for horses in the past. The seven remained healthy, and their harnesses, the woolen cloth from Genoa, the silk from Mohammedan kingdoms of the north, and the iron cooking pots had survived undamaged.

He returned to the deck and ordered that Pedro be taken ashore to announce their arrival to the Budomel. Ca' da Mosto had grown fond of Pedro, who was but a teenager and quick to understand. Prince Henrique had interviewed him sometime before and judged he had the facilities with language, conversation, and commerce necessary to be an interpreter. As with other slaves, Henrique had required his conversion to Christianity, and Pedro had been baptized in memory of one of Henrique's deceased older brothers. There was little risk Pedro would flee when ashore. The Budomel would not permit it, as the Budomel also relied on Pedro to accomplish the trade. Pedro understood his role, boarded the caravel's rowboat, and was ferried by two seamen through light surf to the beach, where Wolof tribesmen were watching, waiting, and then vanished with him into the forest.

As they awaited the Budomel's reply, Ca' da Mosto reflected on his incredible journey to achieve this remote beachhead. They had departed Sagres Bay at Cape St. Vincent (Portugal) in March and sailed the Ocean Sea more than five hundred miles southwest to Porto Santo and Madeira, islands donated by the Crown to Prince Henrique, where Ca' da Mosto had dined on beef and honey. Henrique had granted a gentleman of Milanese descent hereditary governorship of Porto Santo for settling it.[*] The caravel then had traversed more than three hundred miles south to the Canary Islands, anchoring at Gomera and Hierro where Christians had settlements under Castilian sponsorship. He had eaten but barley toast, goat, and goat's cheese, as the settlements had little other produce. The islands were inhabited by fierce tribes of brown-skinned idolaters who worshipped the sun, moon, and planets and resisted Christian invasion of their homeland, although the Castilians frequently captured them for enslavement and sale in Lagos, Seville, and Aragón. Finally, they had run another five hundred miles south to Cape Blanco (Mauritania) and followed the African coast along the great desert (the Sahara), passing Henrique's trading post at Arguin Island (Mauritania) where the local peoples[†]—more darkly brown skinned than the Canarians—lived a harsh nomadic existence and practiced Mohammedanism.

[*] Bartolomeu Perestrelo.
[†] The Azanaghi or Tuareg.

Arab merchants from the desert's interior frequented Arguin to trade slaves, gold, and spices for horses and European wares. The desert had ended at the Río de Senega, where the kingdoms of the black peoples began, but Mohammedanism had crossed the river to claim souls among the Wolof, rather than Christianity.

Soon, Lord Budomel entered the beach from the forest mounted on a horse and dressed in a cotton robe falling to his ankles, followed by fifteen mounted warriors and over a hundred foot soldiers bearing spears. Ca' da Mosto and Dias understood the show of force—the trade, and their men's safety onshore, were subject to the Budomel's grace. The caravel was equipped with crossbow, sword, and cannon, but they were hopelessly outnumbered ashore.

Ca' da Mosto descended into the rowboat with Henrique's representative, a scrivener who would monitor the trade and Ca' da Mosto closely. The Budomel dismounted as Ca' da Mosto arrived at the beach, and the two men embraced. Through Pedro and hand gestures, Ca' da Mosto expressed Prince Henrique's esteem for the Budomel and their special seaborne trading relationship, and the Budomel expressed that the visit was his honor and that he held the same esteem for Henrique. Ca' da Mosto presented a silver washbasin as an intimate gift, and the Budomel reciprocated with an ivory comb.

That evening, in a village nearby, Lord Budomel hosted Ca' da Mosto and his officers to a feast of fish, fowl, kidney bean, fruit, and palm wine. The Budomel reminisced about Portuguese traders he had known, and they discussed the competing overland desert trade routes through Timbuktu and Wadan by which Arab merchants transported gold and slaves north on camels.

With a rapport established, Ca' da Mosto described his horses and their harnesses in detail, as well as his wool, silk, and iron pots. He offered to trade all the horses and harnesses and most of the other goods for slaves. The Budomel replied he would pay one hundred slaves for that and invited Ca' da Mosto inland to visit his principal village for pleasure and to understand the Wolof while the slaves were gathered. He also presented Ca' da Mosto with a beautiful Wolof girl, twelve years old, to take for his chamber when he departed. Ca' da Mosto reflected that one hundred slaves was a bargain for but seven horses and harnesses and some cloth and pots, and he accepted, including the visit inland. The Budomel reflected that just one hundred slaves was a bargain for the same.

In the morning, Ca' da Mosto instructed the scrivener to have the ship readied for slaves and that the girl be taken aboard and kept near his cabin. He and Pedro set off inland with the Budomel. They saw elephants, great serpents, and brightly colored parrots, and Ca' da Mosto enjoyed the Budomel's hospitality. Like the sovereigns of Hispania, Lord Budomel continually moved his court from village to village to impress his rule over local chieftains. Ca' da Mosto learned that the Budomel frequently warred with other chieftains, much as Christian princes did among themselves. The spoils of these wars included the slaves Ca' da Mosto was to receive—men, women, and children of other chiefdoms the Budomel had vanquished.

Lord Budomel invited Ca' da Mosto to visit his mosque to observe evening prayer and sought an explanation of Christianity. Ca' da Mosto studied the Budomel and his noblemen praying, murmuring to the sky and then bowing to kiss the earth, and sensed that his host's faith was not as absolute as the Arabs to the north, but more a matter of custom and unification with his local chieftains. Ca' da Mosto explained some articles of Christianity and, after they had discussed them for a few days, challenged his host, comfortable that the Budomel's curiosity signaled that a debate wouldn't affect the trade.

"Your faith is false on many grounds. Mine is true and holy."

"Your faith does appear to be good," the Budomel said with a laugh. "It could be no other than God that bestows you such riches, skills, and knowledge."

"More's at stake than wealth," Ca' da Mosto warned, concerned for his host's well-being. "You should consider conversion so your soul attains salvation."

"But God is a just Lord," the Budomel responded, shaking his head. "My people are better able to gain salvation than yours. God has given us almost nothing in the world, so he will give us paradise hereafter." The Budomel declined conversion, yet Ca' da Mosto perceived he would have embraced it but for fear of losing his power as chieftain.

Pedro also appreciated the Budomel's hospitality, particularly since the Budomel addressed him as Malik, his name before the

Christians had purchased him. Malik reciprocated, hailing his host with the proper Wolof pronunciation, as the "Damel." Malik had grown up with giraffes and elephants, and, while Ca' da Mosto went about examining the Wolof's customs, Malik excused himself, sometimes to worship spirits and his ancestors in the forest. As he prayed, Malik remembered the ancient Wolof proverb that a log stuck in a river doesn't turn into a crocodile, and he wondered whether he would ever believe in Christ.

As Ca' da Mosto visited the Wolof, Dias supervised the bolting of ankle chains on the caravel's deck and in its hold and took responsibility for Ca' da Mosto's Wolof girl. Ndey dreaded the caravel and the crew. She had never seen such a sinister being—its body was enormous and its three appendages towered to the sky—and she feared the portholes on the bow were its eyes and that it would eat her. She had never met pale men, nor men so fully clothed, and she feared their paleness meant they were of the dead, evil spirits returning to visit the living. They leered at her body and, as men of other tribes, were dangerous. But they didn't touch her, as she was for their own chief. They hung a wool cloth to make a tiny enclosure for her in the crawl space between their chief's cabin and the stern.

Dias brought the caravel close to shore when the slaves had been gathered. Lord Budomel's soldiers herded the vanquished Guineans—men, women, and a few children—through the shallows at low tide, and the crew hauled them aboard and shackled them, some where the horses had been corralled and dung rotted, swarming with flies in the heat. As Ndey, they were terrified by the immensity of the structure and thought the pale men were evil spirits. They had no inkling where they were being taken or whether they were about to be executed or eaten. A discharge of the caravel's cannon augured that death at the devil's hand was imminent.

After formally parting from the Budomel, Ca' da Mosto boarded the ship, and it entered the swells of a turbulent Ocean Sea, causing the slaves further terror. Dias set the course south to trade the remaining goods and explore for gold. Ca' da Mosto went to his cabin, a tiny room to starboard below the stern deck and above the hold, adjacent to the tiller attached to the rudder, which was manned by two seamen. He found the girl inside, apparently nourished and unmolested, and was pleased. Upon returning to the deck, he asked Pedro her name.

As the sun set, the caravel sped through rising swell at a brisk pace. The crew prayed and sang a hymn to the Virgin Mary, a version of "Salve Regina," seeking the Virgin's protection of the ship during the night. After the moon rose, Ca' da Mosto retired to his cabin and, by candlelight, entered notes of the Wolof visit in a log. He bade the girl join him.

Ndey entered his cabin resigned and prepared to fulfill the Damel's gift. Before her seclusion aboard the ship, Ndey's mother—weeping—had instructed her on what to do and what it meant for her future. The Damel had decided her fate. She would not be given to a neighboring chieftain to forge an alliance or to one of the Damel's generals in reward for a battle victory. She had been given to a pale-skinned chieftain and would be taken far distant to lands unknown. She would not be married to him, but she might bear his child. She might be forced to worship his gods and renounce her own. He might discard her at any time in some hostile land. She shouldn't dream she had any choices to make.

Still weeping, Mother had tempered this. He appeared to have tremendous wealth and power. Mother had instructed that if she pleased him, and if his customs were as the Wolof's, she would not want or be bound. Like the other pale men, he stank from the lack of bathing and constant wearing of garments in heat, but he appeared more refined. Ndey stood meekly before Ca' da Mosto, terrified.

To Ndey's surprise, he knew her name. He caressed her face once, took her goatskin from her waist, and then removed his own garments and motioned for her to lie before him. With the pilot walking the deck above, the tillermen adjusting the tiller just steps away, and the cries and moans of the vanquished peoples rising from the deck and hold below, Ca' da Mosto entered her. She felt pain and cried aloud. When he was done, he fell asleep and Ndey returned to her crawl space, passing the tillermen who grinned meanly at her. Ndey wiped the blood and his seed from her crotch as her tears began quietly, and then she wept and trembled uncontrollably. She knew she would never see Mother again.

Above, on the stern deck, Malik chose a place to sleep. In the moonlight, he looked down at the slaves, stupefied by all that was new and terrible. Some pale men said interpreters became freemen after four voyages, but Malik wondered if that always occurred. He remembered when he had been captured by a Mohammedan chieftain like the Budomel and then sold to Henrique's Christian slave masters and transported by ship to the slave market at the quay in Lagos. That quay was this cargo's fate, too. Prince Henrique would give a few of them as gifts to other lords and to Christian bishops, and the rest would be sold, husbands, wives, and children broken apart according to the wishes of the buyers.

Malik watched as many of the slaves succumbed to seasickness and lay chained in their own vomit, urine, and excrement. He reflected on how the Christians and Mohammedans both worshipped the same god and thought the other infidels and fit to burn in hell. He wondered whether this hell could be worse than what he witnessed below. Clouds then shrouded the moon, and it began to rain.

I
1455—1460,
CHILDHOOD, LESSONS, LEGACY

CAONABÓ
Aniyana (Middle Caicos, Turks and Caicos, Caribbean)

Caonabó lay naked on a bed of fronds cut from surrounding palm trees, intently studying the gourds floating among the ducks in the pond below, all but three gently blown by the wind. He had observed the duck hunt many times, but today he focused carefully on its method as he would participate for the first time. He marveled at the stealth and cunning involved, doubted whether he could achieve it, and pondered whether the hunted's soul remembered the hunter.

In the pond, Caonabó's father and two servants were submerged to the chin, peering through eyelets carved in gourds that masked their heads and presence. Father had ordered the servants—his *naborias*—to fill the pond with gourds fallen from the calabash tree that morning, and some twenty true ones now floated among the birds. Father stared directly along the water's surface at a duck but a yard before him, extended his arms underwater beneath it, and shot his hands upward to clutch its feet and yank it under. A second duck immediately dived to follow the doomed duck in search of fish, and one of the naborias seized it underwater. The other ducks remained stationary, unconcerned with the gourds floating or stalking about them.

Caonabó studied where the two ducks had vanished and watched ripples quietly emanate to lap and wash out against the pond's embankments, grimly aware that death befell the ducks beyond his vision and mesmerized that the hunt nevertheless would continue. Underwater, the ducks struck their bills to bite and flapped furiously to escape, but Father swiftly broke his duck's neck and tucked it under a cord strung about his waist. The naboria stuffed his in a cotton net to drown. Father, in thought, honored Yúcahu, the spirit of *yuca* (yucca or manioc), the sea, and male fertility, fatherless and the most important spirit in daily life.*

Mother, Father's first wife, sat calmly on her knees on the fronds beside their son, her back upright and hands in her lap, reflecting her stature, grace, and elegance. She was naked except for a married woman's *nagua* (loincloth) strung in front below the navel, a cotton headband, and jewelry, and sunlight flickered through the forest to dance lightly on her olive-brown skin and long, black hair. She was heavy with child and irritated by the scruff of the forest underbrush and hovering mosquitoes. But she ignored the discomfort and turned slowly to sit on her thigh to better watch Caonabó study the hunt, concerned that he remain attentive and confident. He was her first-born, just eight years old, and she knew him to be strong and clever and eager for his first try. She sensed his impatience with the pace of Father's advance to the next prey and whispered to him that it was important to move very slowly.

Father and the naborias continued to hunt, slowly drifting among the unsuspecting ducks and silently striking, seizing more than a dozen before those remaining grew wary and took flight. The men removed their helmets, waded from the pond, and laid the kill on the forest floor for Caonabó to examine. Caonabó approached, and the ducks' glazed eyes stared back at him, as if seeking retribution. He wondered if their souls had departed.

Father motioned for his son to sit as he and the naborias taught how to catch a duck's feet underwater and snap its neck. The naborias let on that ducks sometimes got away and that one wanted most of all to avoid being bitten, particularly on the butt or, worse, the penis. The older naboria spun a story of an odd Lucayan† on a

---

*More fully known as Yúcahu Bagua Maórocoti, yucca being an excellent source of starch and the sea the source of fish.
†From the Taíno word meaning "island people," of the Bahamas or Turks and Caicos.

neighboring island who got so tangled up wrestling with an enormous duck that the bird nipped off a bit of his rump. Everyone laughed. Caonabó felt a surge of blood at his temples, exposing his anxiety about achieving manhood.

After the lesson, children and other villagers wandered over to wish Caonabó success in his own hunt. He greeted them proudly, particularly the younger girl Onaney. Father's fourth wife brought Caonabó's infant sister to say hello, and he took her in his arms to show her the dead ducks. But Father soon ordered that those interested hike north through the woods to a tidal pond adjacent to the sea. Caonabó followed Father and, when they arrived near the pond's embankment, they sat again, this time alone.

"There's more to learn than stalking the ducks slowly and grabbing their feet." Father waited for Caonabó to respond, but the boy's eyes betrayed uncertainty, and Father continued. "It's important to consult the spirits." Father unleashed a cotton pouch from the cord about his waist and withdrew his *cemí* of Yúcahu, a triangular rock statuette smaller than his hand carved with Yúcahu's image—a being with eyes glaring forward and an enormous mouth wide-open, ready to plow earth, its legs folded underneath like a frog's on the statuette's base, its back arced at the rear, and its prescient forehead at the triangle's top. "You know Yúcahu. Why do we honor him?"

"He helps us grow yuca for *cazabi* [cassava bread] and catch fish."

Father nodded in approval. "The spirits live with us. Some are fruitful, some destructive. We honor them to obtain the alliance of the fruitful spirits and the forbearance of the destructive." Father lifted the cemí toward his son's gaze. "Yúcahu is the supreme fruitful spirit, and we consult him for guidance in farming, fishing, and hunting—like whether we should hunt at this pond. Hunting and the sea are dangerous, and we also want his protection." He stared directly into Caonabó's eyes. "Have you spoken with Yúcahu about your hunt?"

"No." Caonabó shrugged his shoulders. "I didn't know I should, yet." His eyes blinked.

Father smiled. "Communications with spirits are often led by myself as *cacique* [chief] or our village *behique* [shaman]. But it's also important for each person to consult our spirits directly. You should consult Yúcahu right now, before your hunt. Honor him. Seek his alliance for a successful hunt and your and our men's protection."

Caonabó tried to do so, but he felt awkward communicating through thought rather than speech and was unsure how Yúcahu would hear and respond.

Father anticipated this doubt and addressed it unequivocally. "Yúcahu is present, both in the stone and all about us. He hears you. That doesn't guarantee your hunt's success, which depends on your skill." Caonabó blinked again, realizing that success remained his responsibility.

"You will lead," Father continued. "Stand still whenever a bird becomes suspicious, and remain still until it's unconcerned. Understand?"

"I already know this."

"The naborias filled the pond with gourds this morning. Remember, the ducks must believe your helmet is being blown by the wind—that it's not you. Stay where the pond is shallowest so you can walk on the bottom, and walk no faster than the real gourds are blown by the wind." Caonabó blinked yet a third time.

Father ordered the villagers present to come no closer. Mother and Father's fourth wife knelt together on fronds laid by their naborias, and Onaney hid behind a palm tree. A naboria brought Caonabó a small helmet carved for him that morning and placed it over his head.

Caonabó understood his birthright was to lead, and he respectfully asked Father's men to don their helmets again and follow into the pond. Father stepped closely behind him and soon whispered with condescension that, if he went too fast, there would be nothing to hunt. Father sharply criticized his path—unless they entered the pond upwind, the ducks would be spooked by the subsequent movement of their helmets. Caonabó slowed and change course, gradually arriving at the reeds by the pond's edge, where he felt the mud ooze between his toes.

Caonabó peered intently through his helmet's eyelets to sight at least a dozen ducks downwind to the west, as well as gulls, sandpipers, and a few flamingos. The birds were wandering to fish and eyeing him and the men, and he shortened each step forward to mere inches, invigorated that he was now a predator. He felt the sun disappear behind clouds as the water lapped his belly, reappear when his shoulders submerged, and then vanish again when his chin dipped in the water, whereupon he identified a prey.

Father and the naborias were relieved the approach had been accomplished, and the naborias identified their own ducks and began to spread out to deeper areas. The men's traditional haircut kept their black hair short above the ears but left untouched a few strands at the back, and these emerged from the helmets to trail lightly behind on the water's surface. They watched Caonabó closely, certain they would have to strike immediately after the boy failed to bring his bird underwater cleanly.

Caonabó inched forward until his prey floated just feet before him. Its eyes stared into his own, and he was astonished that it failed to recognize his presence and the violent end he intended for it. An urge to strike surged within him, and he impulsively honored Yúcahu again. He inhaled deeply and slowly glided his arms underwater beneath the duck's belly and, without pause, quickly lifted his hands to grab the feet. He got them! The duck lunged upward, its legs extended, and Caonabó fought desperately to hold on, successfully pulling the bird underwater. But the duck thrashed and turned to bite, with terrifying strength and viciousness! It burst to the surface, quacking hoarsely in defiance, and Caonabó heard the resounding crack of many wings flap at once. Dozens of birds bolted into flight, and he panicked that there hadn't been time for the others to snare prey.

Suddenly, the duck went limp, and Caonabó felt Father by his side. He stood upright, sputtering and panting, and removed his helmet. Father grinned. Caonabó accused Father of breaking his duck's neck, and Father and the naborias chuckled. Caonabó quickly realized the naborias had killed ducks, too. Father told him to catch his breath and honor Yúcahu and that he had stalked and captured the duck himself. Skills for breaking the neck would be learned over time as he grew older.

The hunters walked to the embankment with their prey. Father smiled to his wives, and they waved and congratulated Caonabó, as did Onaney. Caonabó was unsure whether to show pride, but he wanly acknowledged the onlookers with a return wave. He gazed at his duck's inert body and, to his surprise, realized he held neither remorse for killing it nor fear of its soul and, above all, that victory invigorated him.

Mother stood—her red shell necklace, bracelets of tiny stones, and gold earrings proclaiming her paramount status—and a litter composed of a reed mat drawn between poles was brought to carry her back to the village. She sat on it, and naborias hoisted her above their shoulders and began the journey home, first south through the forest and then along the southern shore from which tidal flats caked with salt extended more than a mile out to sea.

As she rode, Mother surveyed the desolate expanse of Aniyana. Scrub bush, marsh, mangroves, and beach rose lowly from the sea, leading inland to forest and minor gardens of yuca and sweet potato, with myriad birds and plentiful fish, turtle, lobster, and mollusk, but with slight hills and no mountains or rivers. The windswept flatland baked in the sun. She had come here from Haiti as a girl, given as a bride to Father by her parents. Her mother's brother ruled the *cacicazgo* (chiefdom) of Maguana in Haiti, a fertile plain farmed with varied crops and surrounded by mountains.

Mother remembered the beauty and magnificence of Haiti— mountains coursed by streams cascading through forest, field, and glen to enormous valleys and plains verdant with crops and nourished by rivers surging to the sea—a land filled with warmth and cold and tremendous enchantment. It was the cradle of civilization, where men had first come from the earth to populate it. Haiti's caciques ruled in prosperity and feasted, sang *areítos* (songs), and danced with an unrivaled sophistication and culture—which was not attainable in this outpost of Taíno society. Mother was not bitter, for Father was the most powerful cacique of these islands and they prospered. Her life was free of need. But she knew Caonabó was fit and meant to lead and, in time, would return to Haiti to seek his uncle's cacicazgo. This was Mother's birthright. Mother's womb, and the wombs of her mother's younger daughters, bore the succession of potential Maguanan caciques.*

She glimpsed behind and was amused to find her son suppressing a grin to hide his elation. He had caught his duck, and that was

---

*Matrilineal succession.

enough for him this day. Father soon would begin his education to pursue his greater destiny.

Father ordered that Mother's naborias cook the ducks for dinner that night for all villagers who wished to eat. The hunters, and Caonabó, could have their share, but no more.

Yúcahu.

CRISTOFORO
Genoa, (March 1460)

Eight-year-old Cristoforo woke to his mother's touch and command, alert to learn his parents' customary instruction on the day's chores. He heard roosters crowing nearby and, in the distance, the murmur of the morning's first prayer chanted in the neighboring monastery.

"Put on your warm clothes, promptly," she ordered. "You're going to port with Father, and it'll be cold in the wind." She laid his wool shirt, trousers, and coat on the cot. She shook his younger brother, Giovanni Pellegrino, asleep on the same cot, and told him to rise quickly, as well. "Hurry, and you'll see the donkeys that are coming."

As he dressed, Cristoforo gleaned that a lesson was involved, not so much a chore. He grew curious to understand but wary that Father would judge his performance nonetheless. He gazed from a window to the narrow street two stories below, which curled between homes and shops of three or four stories on either side. The sun had yet to rise over the hills to the east, and the cobblestone walkway was dark and damp. He overheard Father descend to his workshop on the home's ground floor to wake his teenage apprentice.

Domenico Colombo's business had suffered over the past few months, and he instructed the apprentice to pack most of the unsold woolen cloth they had woven in sacks for shipment. He stepped outside briefly to check the weather, bracing against the cool March air. At forty-one, he was relieved much of the inventory would be sold that morning.

Genoa's fortunes, and those of Domenico and its ordinary citizens, were subject to the ambitions and jealousies of its noble merchant families and foreign princes, who frequently fought for control of its politics and commerce, establishing and breaking alliances without apparent scruple to that end. Two years before, a patriarch of the Fregoso family—Domenico's political patrons—had abdicated Genoa's dogeship in favor of the French king for protection from the Aragonese, and the French king now ruled Genoa through an appointed governor.* The Aragonese had blockaded the port in opposition to the French, but the blockade had withered upon the Aragonese king's death,† and the Fregoso patriarch then had died attempting to reclaim his authority from the French. Control of the city so changed often, sometimes accompanied by street battles, a recurring chaos that invited plague and injured commerce.

Domenico called above to his wife to hurry the breakfast. On the second floor, Susanna set biscuits and leftover fish on the dining table and summoned Cristoforo and Giovanni to eat, and Domenico and the apprentice joined them. Susanna reminded the boys to say their prayers—which they did perfunctorily—whereupon Domenico instructed that the apprentice would mind the shop while he showed Cristoforo how cloth is sold to the merchant families.

---

*The Duke of Calabria, Jean d'Anjou.
†Alfonso V, died 1458.

Cristoforo now grasped Father's intent and was intrigued. He understood weaving, but he had never seen Father trade with a nobleman.

"Who are you meeting?" he asked.

"A Centurione," Domenico responded, referring to one of Genoa's leading families. He warmed to his son's inquisitiveness and intent blue-green eyes, but he noted the innocence and naïveté still betrayed by the boy's reddish hair, pink cheeks, and freckles.

Shortly, two donkeys arrived tethered in train, their hooves clattering on the cobblestones, and Domenico greeted the Centuriones' donkey driver. Cristoforo helped cinch the sacks of cloth to the baggage saddles, and, scarcely without pause, the driver started to lead the donkeys uphill to the city gates of Sant'Andrea, looming high above. Cristoforo fell in line behind Domenico at the rear and waved good-bye to Mother and Giovanni.

Father and son passed the Colombo's small garden and the neighboring monastery, a hymn now resounding within. They entered the old city through the stone gate's archway and began the descent to the port, their progress slowing as the traffic of people and animals and the number of shops open for business quickly grew. Cristoforo listened to Domenico stoutly greet acquaintances, and Domenico encouraged Cristoforo to greet them forthrightly, too. Domenico occasionally stopped to shake hands, inquiring whether a relative survived an illness or where a child was now living. By chance, Domenico met his friend the tailor and reminded him that Cristoforo's cousin Giannetto soon would be old enough to apprentice to a tailor. Cristoforo recognized that Domenico might arrange his own apprenticeship as a weaver in just a few years.

They came to the doge's palace and its open plaza, where Cristoforo and Giovanni sometimes waited to watch noblemen riding in to meet the doge, and Cristoforo studied those lounging or lurking about. Domenico hailed two men on horseback, requested that the donkey driver halt, and took his son's hand to meet the riders, agents of the Fregosos. Some years before, Fregosos had appointed Domenico as warder of a city gate for brief terms, which eventually expired without reappointment. Domenico asked the riders how the family elders fared, reaffirmed his loyalty, and beseeched the riders to pass on his greetings. Cristoforo perceived that Domenico held ambitions beyond his trade and mused whether they had been frustrated.

Resuming the descent, father and son strode alongside the high walls of St. Lawrence's cathedral. While Cristoforo and Giovanni frequently wandered in the streets about it, they had never prayed inside, as the nobility did. As always, Cristoforo saw beggars huddled in the shadows of its walls, destitute and imploring passersby for alms. The street now teemed with people, and father and son filed slowly by shopkeepers selling spices, perfumes, gems, and wares imported from foreign lands. There were street stands with pepper from the Black Sea, oranges from Andalusia, mastic from Scio (Chios, Greece), ivory and gold from Alexandria and Tunis, and iron tools and weapons from other kingdoms.

Domenico met an acquaintance who was a silk weaver and halted their walk again to inquire how his business had withstood the city's recent turmoil. Cristoforo observed a shop where slaves were sold, packed with young women seated, shackled, and motionless, their pale skins like corpses in the shop's inner darkness. He wondered who had brought them there and where they would go. He pointed them out to Domenico, who surmised that they were from the Balkans, purchased by Genoese traders from the infidel at Scio to be sold as chambermaids to Ligurian nobility. Domenico knew they also would serve as concubines.

The donkey driver recommenced the path to port, and they soon entered the square by St. George's palace, embraced a strong wind pushing dark clouds from the southwest, and trod through the densely crowded fish market toward one of the shorter piers, where Cristoforo beheld the entire harbor. Ships' masts crammed the skyline as if a dense forest, and a cacophony of cracking ropes and rigging and cawing seagulls filled the air. The largest merchant ships and the Genoese navy were anchored in the bay of the harbor, their hulls slowly undulating in the waves. The port bustled with men toiling, including carpenters crafting booms, sailors repairing sails, and blacksmiths molding anchors. Beggars and orphans foraged the garbage heaps of the fish market for scraps of food.

They strode onto the pier, passing a few small boats, and the driver brought the donkeys to rest beside a small, single-masted caravel. Two sailors were lowering crates of iron tools into its open hold below the pier. One of the sailors hollered that they were expecting wool cloth and would sail just miles down the coast to Rapallo and Lerici as soon as loaded, and father and son waited as the sacks of cloth were pitched atop the tool crates. Cristoforo had imagined a more distant destination and a larger ship—and perhaps an opportunity for his carrying their sacks of cloth on board. Domenico remained silent, and Cristoforo suspected he also was disappointed.

The driver led them off the pier and through the port to its principal quay, where the largest carracks in the harbor were tended, and stopped beside a three-masted carrack flying the crest of the Centuriones. Its deck rested some feet above the quay, and before it stood the young nobleman Domenico sought for payment, dressed in an exquisitely tailored wool coat. Domenico gritted his teeth, bitterly recognizing that the thread of the coat's cloth was finer than his own, probably woven in Milan or perhaps even London. Domenico pulled Cristoforo aside, adjusted his collar, and sharply instructed him to speak courteously and agreeably as the family was an important customer—and could remain so when he grew older.

Cristoforo studied his father salute the young nobleman and grandly affect pleasant conversation, remarking that it was a pleasure to find him healthy, a blessing spring approached, and an accomplishment that the wool cloth was already stored on the smaller vessel. Cristoforo was surprised Father acted as if the two men were friends. The nobleman was much younger and wore elegant accoutrements, including a silk scarf, leather gloves, and a gold chain and pendant that hung about his neck. A servant kept his horse nearby. Cristoforo pondered whether the nobleman's wealth exceeded that of a thousand men like Father, and he felt awkward when Father nudged him forward to introduce himself.

"This is Cristoforo, my eight-year-old," Domenico interjected, before Cristoforo could speak.

"Good morning, sir," Cristoforo said, raising his voice.

"Have you ever seen a merchant ship this big?" asked the nobleman, foregoing any formal greeting with the weaver's boy. "It'll sail for València and Flanders tomorrow morning."

"No, sir."

"Your father's cloth isn't bound there, but you can go aboard for a moment to watch the cargo stowed—if you wish."

"Yes, I'd like to." Cristoforo's eyes glimmered, his eagerness transparent. The ship was far larger than any boat he had ever boarded. "Thank you."

"Yes, thank you." Domenico added, smiling broadly.

The nobleman hailed a teenager standing nearby on the deck above. "Escort this boy about the ship, briefly." The noblemen turned to Domenico and replied, "My pleasure," indicating with a nod that their conversation was finished.

Cristoforo ascended the plank to the ship's main deck, and the two boys recognized each other, possibly from church or simply around the neighborhood, but realized they were not acquainted. Antonio introduced himself, boasting with assurance and pride that he was the assistant to the trader who would manage the voyage on behalf of the family and had been to sea twice before. He led Cristoforo toward the bow and forecastle.

Cristoforo gazed upward along the masts to where the highest booms were wrapped in sail and then downward along the ropes— some tautly stretched from the masts like a spider's web—back to the bulwark. He scanned the deck, where sailors walked, stood, and sat, all purposefully engaged in some task to ready the ship to sail. He sensed enormity, design, alignment, energy, common purpose, and resolve, and was smitten by them.

They arrived at a stairwell descending into the hull, where— Antonio explained—sailors and a few tradesmen were lowering the merchant cargo, including finished silk cloth, barrels of olive oil and fine wine, jars of mastic, and crates of glassware. The sailors also were loading the crew's provisions for the voyage, barrels of cheap wine and crates of salted pork and hardtack (baked wheat biscuit). Two men sat at a table nearby, Antonio's master—the trader employed by the merchant family—and the ship's captain. The trader shrewdly inspected each piece of cargo loaded and accounted for it in a logbook. The captain greeted Cristoforo heartily and asked if he was a new ship's boy and then laughed without waiting for an answer, advising him to come back in a few years' time. Cristoforo was surprised how deeply the wind and sea had wrinkled, crusted, and faded the captain's skin and clothing.

The boys continued to the bow and forecastle, and, for the first time, Cristoforo gazed back across the entire ship from bow to stern, startled. While from the quay it appeared a large structure, he now realized the ship was small for the number of sailors on board, not much longer than three or four houses on the street where he lived, and that it would be tiny on the sea beyond the harbor. He asked Antonio where he and the crew slept and ate, and Antonio explained there was a cook and firebox on deck and that each sailor just ate and slept where he wanted, typically on deck. It could be very hot or cold, sometimes awfully wet.

Antonio's master called and ordered him to return to the table to inventory the load. The boys returned to the stairwell, and Cristoforo watched Antonio count and complete the logbook as sacks of silk were loaded. They descended into the hold to monitor that the sacks were properly secured, and Cristoforo gazed forward and aft, impressed at the thickness of the arched beams from which the hull had been constructed. He was shocked that the sailors followed Antonio's stowage instructions.

When the trader returned, the boys climbed to the stern castle, and Antonio related that the captain typically stood there when commanding the crew. Cristoforo gazed into the wind, observed the sailors working below, and marveled at the importance and prestige of directing them. An old sailor sat on a barrel nearby, and Antonio made an introduction.

"Cristoforo, this is the pilot who will navigate the ship when it sails tomorrow morning."

"It's brisk today, isn't it?" said the pilot, shaking his head. "It's nice the merchants think we'll sail in the morning, but that isn't necessarily so."

"Why not?" Antonio asked. Cristoforo was surprised that a sailor would disagree with a nobleman.

"The ship can't sail directly into the wind." He rose slowly and motioned for the boys to follow him to the rail. "This wind bears directly over the bow. The sails must catch wind for the ship to move forward, and they won't do that unless the ship points at least thirty-five or forty degrees off the wind."

The pilot saw Cristoforo didn't understand. "If the wind holds its present course and force tomorrow morning, the ship would have to be pulled to face directly across the harbor to sail on its own, an impossible course with all the other ships anchored there, and the wind's too strong to bother asking the crew to row us out of the harbor. It'd be simpler to wait patiently for the wind to shift or abate, which it always does." The pilot turned to Antonio. "But don't worry. If we can't sail in the morning, we can drink the wine."

Antonio grinned, and Cristoforo saw it was safe to grin, as well. The pilot smirked and continued. He pointed to the masts and booms above and asked Cristoforo, "Can you see the birds perched there?"

"Yes." Cristoforo puzzled over what came next.

"Do you know the four things the birds tell us sailors?"

Cristoforo shrugged. "No."

"When they fly away, you know where land is. When they dive, you know fish can be caught. When they hunker down, as they are now, you know a storm's coming."

After a long pause, Cristoforo was led to ask, "What's the fourth?"

"When your ship's sinking, they tell you good-bye." The boys laughed.

With that, Antonio took Cristoforo back to the quay and Father. Cristoforo realized Father had been paid because he stood well apart from the nobleman, who was surrounded by others seeking favor. Father urged him to thank the nobleman again, and Cristoforo called and waved but wasn't noticed. They started home.

Domenico asked what he had done on board, and Cristoforo recounted the tour from bow to stern with enthusiasm. Domenico listened, but his mind quickly drifted to anxious reflections on his trade, the nobleman's fine wool coat, and how, since his youth, the market for Genoese wool had declined to become purely local.

When they arrived home, Susanna had the three boys' lunch of the remaining fish laid on the table.

"What did you do?" she asked.

Cristoforo related the walk to port and that he'd been invited aboard the Centuriones' carrack. He noted that the pilot doubted the ship would sail the next morning and tried explaining why.

"What did you learn?" Domenico interrupted.

"It's important to be polite and respectful of the nobility," Cristoforo knew to respond. He paused, reflected, and faced his father. "I'd like to learn to read and write."

Genove la Superba, engraving from the Nuremberg Chronicle of 1493.

PRINCE HENRIQUE OF PORTUGAL (HENRY THE NAVIGATOR)
Raposeira, Southern Portugal (Spring 1460)

Prince Henrique had chosen to build his palace and exercise his governorship in the small village of Raposeira, which lay nestled in a valley of forest, grassland pastures, and farms, a serene oasis sheltered from strong northern winds by a ridge on its northern edge. He had remained unmarried and celibate his entire life, free from a king's preoccupation to father a male successor, and Raposeira was removed from the daily life of King Afonso V's court, which resided in northern cities and towns. Instead, it was central to places that had become important to Henrique's goal—and he believed destiny—of establishing a Portuguese maritime empire under his control and bringing Christian salvation to the heathens in the lands possessed or reclaimed from the infidel.

The port of Lagos was some miles east on Portugal's southern shore, where ships were built, captains and crews recruited, and voyages dispatched and unloaded under Henrique's authority and license. To the west lay Cape St. Vincent, the windswept plateau on mortally high cliffs jutting defiantly into the Ocean Sea where the coast turned north. All ships sailing between the Mediterranean Sea and France, England, or other points north rounded the cape. Just east of Cape St. Vincent lay Cape Sagres, an equally forlorn sister plateau jutting south, and then—closest to Raposeira—Sagres Bay, where ships frequently took refuge from the winds and Henrique had established a small village, the "Infante's town," to service them.

The prince was keenly aware of the geographical significance of Cape St. Vincent, recognized since the time of ancient mariners and geographers as the western endpoint of the earth's landmass, "terra firma," which stretched through Europe to Jerusalem and then to the Indies and Cathay. Ptolemy (ca. AD 100–170) had taught that the land from the Cape to the farthest point in Asia known to him stretched across half the globe, and the scriptures held that Jerusalem lay at terra firma's very center (Ezekiel 5:5). Terra firma also extended south of the Cape into Africa, with Egypt, Libya, and other Moham-medan kingdoms bordering the Mediterranean and Ethiopia farther southeast and Guinea southwest, their southern limits unknown to Henrique. Beyond the Cape to the west lay the vast Ocean Sea, whose extent was unknown, as well, and its forbidding inhospitality perhaps rendered it unknowable. For centuries, men had referred to it as the Sea of Darkness.

While aging at sixty-six, Henrique rose early for breakfast and was briefed by his secretary as to developments at Afonso's court and the known whereabouts of the ships sailing under his license. He learned that a few Genoese carracks en route to London had harbored in Sagres Bay to shelter from an approaching storm, and he dispatched a messenger inviting their ranking merchants and captains to dine with him there. He would ply them for news of Liguria and entice them to trade at his colony on Madeira. If the weather held, he would worship at the village's small church.

After breakfast, Henrique and his retinue mounted their horses and departed, passing through countryside Henrique frequently had hunted in his youth. He was strong and tall, with dark hair closely cut, and his black cape fluttered southward in the breeze. He enjoyed the ride and the memories it evoked, and his thoughts wandered over the course of a lifetime that had grown increasingly focused and purposeful and, he sensed, neared its end.

In his thirties, he had sponsored the colonization of Madeira and Porto Santo and encouraged captains that the Sea of Darkness could be sailed south along the African coast. Sailors had feared the north-easterly winds and southern currents encountered there would make return impossible and that the earth became uninhabitable toward the equator. Aristotle (384–322 BC) had taught the earth was a globe and warned that the sun bore so excessively on the earth's equatorial zones that they were a burning zone. St. Augustine (AD 354–430) had believed that water alone covered the earth's southern portions. But, with Henrique's prodding, crews could now be recruited to continue south toward the equator to explore for the point at which the Guinean coast turned east to Ethiopia and the Indies. Henrique believed his success was due to the choice of younger men as merchants and captains, such as Ca' da Mosto, because they were better able to question or ignore the ancient learning.

At fifty, he had presided triumphantly at the quay at Lagos to witness one of his ships unloading a cargo of African Mohammedans who would receive baptism and salvation in Christ in return for a lifetime of servitude. The pope asserted responsibility for the salvation of all men and authority to regulate their relations, including their conquest and enslavement, both among Christians and between Christians and unbelievers. Henrique was permitted to conquer non-Christian territories held by Mohammedans and heathens, and the permission to conquer Mohammedans had always included permission to enslave them. But Pope Eugenius IV had indicated (1434) that enslavement of heathens who wished to become

Christians was forbidden because heathens, unlike Mohammedans and Jews, didn't affirmatively deny Christ.

The Guineans purchased by Henrique's mariners did include heathens, and Henrique and King Afonso had pushed Eugenius to reverse his position to allow their enslavement, too. They had also persuaded Eugenius's successor, Pope Nicholas V, to recognize Henrique's zealous efforts to convert men to Christianity by granting Portugal exclusive jurisdiction through all of Guinea south of Cape Bojador (Western Sahara) (1455), precluding Castilian and other competition. A year later, Pope Calixtus III had clarified that this exclusive jurisdiction and permission extended not only to points south of Bojador but all the way to the Indies.

Toward the end of the ride, Sagres Bay came into view, and the men bore the full force of the wind. In the distance, the Ocean Sea churned with whitecaps surging south in a fury that would terrify any sailor. Henrique understood this terror and grasped as well as any prince that, before underwriting or enlisting on a voyage, merchants and sailors had to be convinced the ship, the provisions, the route planned, the experience of the captain and his pilot, and the risks and rewards of the intended trade were sound and that they and their merchandise wouldn't perish.

In his youth, most sailors had feared sailing out of sight of land for any significant length of time. But Henrique had promoted the development of navigational and shipbuilding know-how and geographic knowledge under his schooling at Sagres, and many seamen now were comfortable sailing modern caravels far at sea. His crews had discovered, or rediscovered, the Azorean archipelago, nine islands lying between eight hundred and twelve hundred miles west of Lisbon, far distant and remote in the Sea of Darkness.

The Genoese merchants and captains had been entertained in the small town's only tavern. Henrique's arrival was announced, he entered, and they knelt. He bade them rise in a calm, gentle tone, and they presented an ivory carving of the Virgin purchased in Carthage as a gift on behalf of the patriarch of the Genoese family for whom they sailed. The merchants and captains knew some Portuguese, and an interpreter finished each thought when necessary.

Henrique put them at ease with pleasantries, and they feasted on beef, squid, and, although Henrique abstained, fine Madeiran wine. He invited them to discuss the doge, the pope, the French, the Aragonese, and the advance of the infidel Mehmed II west from Constantinople, which Mehmed had conquered seven years earlier (1453).

The eldest merchant grittily summarized the march of Mehmed's army into Serbia. "The butchering horde took Smederevo without a battle [1459], leaving the entire kingdom to be plundered. All say the rape of the Hungarians follows."

"Do the colonies at Pera, Phocaea, and Scio still function?" Henrique asked, referring to the Genoese trading colonies remaining within Mehmed's conquered territories.*

"They do," replied the merchant, with transparent unease. "Subject to Mehmed's grace. The annual tributes they pay him are steep."

The grim specter of Mehmed's advances and the might of his armies cast a pall on the conversation for some moments, as he and other Mohammedan princes now ruled from Serbia to Athens to Constantinople to Jerusalem to Alexandria, and then across Africa and into Hispania's own kingdom of Grenada. To lighten the discussion, Henrique cordially shifted the topic to Liguria and the pope, and, after learning what he could, promoted his island and Guinean possessions.

"My Madeiran wine rivals your own and can fetch good prices. The island's timber and sugar are readily accessible to port." He turned to his secretary.

"The strength and endurance of our black Guinean slaves is unsurpassed," the secretary chimed in. "They can command the highest prices of any, and the cargoes available are limited only by the ships to be dispatched." The merchants listened carefully and promised to inform their patriarch. When the meal was over, and gracious salutations complete, Henrique departed.

The sky was ominously dark, blanketed to all horizons with massive thunderheads sweeping rapidly south. Henrique's staff cautioned that he return to Raposeira, but he instructed them to wait as he worshipped at the village church. He was fond of the small

---

*Pera, the town north of the Golden Horn at Constantinople (Istanbul); Phocaea (Foca), a town east of Constantinople along the Aegean coast; and Scio (Chios), the Aegean island nearby offshore Phocaea.

church's austerity and berth above the sea, the most fitting site to pray for the safety and success of his crews and ships. He rode from the tavern to the church with his horseman and personal servant, buffeted by strong winds. The church friar was surprised to receive them in such weather, and Henrique invited his horseman and servant to shelter and worship inside.

Henrique prayed for the Lord to guide his mariners to shelter from the approaching storm and, ultimately, to achieve his lifelong quest—to reach Ethiopia by circumventing the southern limit of Guinea in order to locate the reputed sovereign of the Christian Indians many believed to reign there.* He beseeched the Lord to grant his ultimate aspiration, that the Christian kingdoms of Europe and Ethiopia then unite and surround and defeat the Mohammedans to retake Jerusalem.

Henrique's personal servant, a Guinean who had been baptized in Lagos years before, mimicked his master's devotion and prudently recited a prayer to Christ, too. He had long since forgotten his introduction to Mohammedanism. As he prayed, he fought to suppress his incredulity that the prince believed worshipping Christ was a just return for a life of servitude and his bitterness that the prince's men merely used Christ as an excuse for gain. For all their piety, the ships Henrique dispatched to Guinea were packed with merchants, soldiers, and slave masters but few priests or monks. The servant recalled the spirits of his youth and prayed for his father and mother, brothers and sisters, and wife and children, whom he missed dearly.

The gale howled fiercely about the church, reminding Henrique of the Lord's awesome power over earth and man and that he conferred both life and death. In the beginning, the Lord had blessed man's creation and the very earth to live on, separating terra firma from the seas, lighting the sky with the sun, moon, and stars, and providing man beast and fish to eat, all in but six days. Yet when man had sinned, he had destroyed them all, flooding terra firma beneath the seas again, leaving only Noah, his sons, and their wives to replenish the world. When man had sinned again—seeking to build a tower to Heaven—the Lord had punished them all a second time, scattering them into many nations and tribes throughout terra firma,

---

*The legendary kings titled the Prester John.

confounding them to speak different languages so as to be unable to communicate. He shattered Henrique's ships and drowned the crews whenever that fit his purpose.

Henrique requested that the service be closed. The three men said farewell to the friar and stepped into the tempest. Henrique looked south over Cape Sagres at the enormous expanse of gray ocean undulating ceaselessly to the horizon as if an inferno of cold, boiling water. With trepidation, he turned west to behold Cape St. Vincent jutting into the sea. The ocean swept past it with an immense force, massive swells, froth, and spray violently contorted by the wind. The current curling around the Cape was extraordinary, as if Job's serpent dragon Leviathan were rapidly advancing on its prey just below the ocean's surface. To the northwest, a wall of rain approached.

Catalan World Map, 1450.

Henrique had seen this countless times before, but it never ceased to astound him. The Ocean Sea held the fury of hell! It was the Ocean Sea, not the cliffs of Cape St. Vincent, that ruled their juncture and defiantly ended the habitable world. No caravel would be safe in this tumult during daylight, no less the dark of night. Aristotle, Seneca (ca. 4 BC–AD 65), and other ancients had thought it possible to sail west from Cape St. Vincent to the Indies. But no man who witnessed this hell could seriously contemplate such a journey, no less venture so far from land.

II
1460s, YOUTH

CAONABÓ
Journey from Aniyana to Haiti

Before sunrise, Caonabó rose from his hammock inside Father's
caney (the chief's house, constructed with wood beams, reed or palm
siding, and a thatched roof) to find himself standing before Mother.
He felt tears welling and averted his eyes. He had grown to a young
man, thirteen, and now would journey to Maguana, Mother's homeland in central Haiti, to compete with cousins to be chosen as Maguana's next cacique. He had never been there.

Mother had watched him sleep, having anticipated this day for
years with pride and sadness. She knew he would cry and hugged
him tightly to cherish him. He now stood tall above her, with the
thin, muscular frame and rapt black eyes of a hunter. But he was still
her boy, and she whispered that she and Father loved him and would
think of him always. His younger brothers would join him when they
reached manhood. Caonabó searched for words but didn't find them
and simply told Mother he loved her, too.

Mother let go of her hug. "Uncle will care for you. Remember
you owe him obedience and loyalty. Reciprocate his generosity." She
handed him the stone cemí of Yúcahu that had been her mother's
and whispered with a penetrating intensity, "Remember Father and
myself and your brothers and sisters. Honor our spirits."

Caonabó remained at a loss for a significant response and replied merely that he would always do so. Mother gently kissed his fore-head and wistfully told him to join Father to eat. She cried when he left, recovering when Caonabó's many brothers and sisters awoke and called for her.

Father's village lay nestled beside forest, more than twenty *bohíos* (ordinary houses or homes, constructed like caneys but smaller) encircling two plazas and a *batey* (ball court) where the ballgame was played, with Father's caney astride the larger plaza. Caonabó met Father there as he supervised the preparations for the canoe journey to Haiti. The crewmen had gathered for a substantial breakfast of cazabi and fish while their wives readied the provisions, filling gourds with fresh water, wrapping smoked fish in wet leaves, and packing a reed basket with sweet potato and more cazabi. Naborias departed the village, hauling baskets of salt for trade in Haiti north to the ocean beach that harbored the larger canoes.

Caonabó shared in the crew's breakfast and sensed their admira-tion for Father. The afternoon before, Father had spoken to him of his conduct and future, including the importance of developing traits worthy of a cacique, particularly virtue, and the appropriate balance between harmony and competition in seeking to be chosen. Father rarely was intimate, and more rarely acknowledged fault. But Father had shared his experiences, the mistakes he had made when seeking his own anointment, and explained—in perhaps the last conversation of their lives—that Caonabó undoubtedly would err, as Father had, and would need the perspective and flexibility to correct himself.

Father scanned the tidal flats to the south, now intently focused on the journey itself, and remarked to the crew that the weather was suitable for the voyage, which would take a full day and night.* The wind was mild, the sky overcast so the sun wouldn't bake, and the hurricane season well past. The crew had masterful experience in making the journey, which it did frequently in the drier months when the weather was more predictable. Its leader was Father's most trusted younger lieutenant, a *nitaíno* (nobleman) well versed in the crossing and, if necessary, hostilities. At the meal's conclusion, the leader led the crew in invoking Yúcahu for the journey's protection.

*About 120 miles.

Confident in their prowess, the crewmen said good-bye to their families without ceremony and left for the northern beach, where they would push Father's greatest canoe into the sea and load it.

Caonabó said good-bye to his friends. He would miss them, particularly Onaney, of whom he had grown fond. She was eleven, and they had walked alone along the salt flats at dusk the day before.

"Will you remember me, Caonabó?" she had asked.

"Of course," he had answered.

"I will soon be old enough for marriage."

While eager to respond, he had chosen silence, to learn what she proposed.

"And my father won't delay to arrange it. No one expects you'll return to Aniyana."

"That's not true. I can return whenever I wish."

"You won't return if you're chosen Maguana's cacique. Or when you marry the daughters and sisters of Haitian caciques."

"I will take as wife whom I wish, whether chosen as cacique or not."

She had gazed into his eyes, inviting him to her, and he had kissed her softly and then passionately as the day ended.

Caonabó's brothers and sisters joined him in the plaza. Little Manicoatex, three years old, asked if he was going as well, and Father laughed. Caonabó embraced them one by one, overcome by the recognition that the strongest bonds of trust and loyalty lay within family. Father and Mother began the hike to the northern beach, and, with melancholy, Caonabó departed with them, carrying Mother's Yúcahu cemí in a small pouch. As they walked, Father imparted final advice.

"There may be cousins who make fun that you're Lucayan, not Haitian. Don't let that bother you—either their attitude or your own concern that you aren't their equal. You are the equal of your cousins born on Haiti, and you have the ability to be selected cacique. Uncle certainly will see it that way. Mother is as Haitian as your cousins' mothers."

"Father, I'm proud of who I am. I won't be cowed."

"It's also important to appear moderate. If you're teased about being Lucayan, don't overreact. Simply ignore it. Seek your goal firmly, but avoid friction."

"I understand, but I will let others know I'm their equal."

Father didn't press further to avoid appearing overly concerned.

They arrived at the beach, and Caonabó beheld the great canoe floating in calm, shallow water, sheltered from the ocean by coral reefs offshore. It had been carved and burned from the trunk of a single tree and stretched more than forty feet in length, with benches for the oarsmen and ample space for provisions and passengers. Father and Mother embraced him cheerfully for the last time, and the leader bid him sit at the canoe's midpoint, behind a satchel of gifts to be dispensed along the journey. In unison, the crew hunkered against the heavy hull and pushed it forward to gather speed and momentum, whereupon they jumped aboard as Caonabó waved good-bye, exhilarated. They sped east to vanish into the channel separating Aniyana and Wana (East Caicos), heading south to cross the great undersea bank, the Ba We Ka (Caicos Bank), a turquoise shallow that extended many miles south toward Haiti. The canoe coursed first toward two tiny cays some twenty miles south (Big and Little Ambergris Cays).*

Caonabó had been on the ocean countless times before, traveling among the neighboring islands and trolling the Ba We Ka, which teemed with fish, lobsters, and rays. He knew that Haiti was an island amid many islands surrounded by an encompassing sea on a flat earth. The heavens ascended above, the sea and underground caves descended below, and the sea and the heavens converged on the horizon where spirits could pass from one to the other. His home, Aniyana, and other Lucayan islands (the Bahamas) stretched northwest from Haiti. Cuba and Yamaye (Jamaica) were to Haiti's west, and far west of Cuba lay a great landmass where men wore clothes. To Haiti's east lay Boriquén (Puerto Rico) and then a chain of islands—including Matininó, Guanín, and Carib—extending south to another great coastline. Spears tipped with the stingray's poison tail lay in the canoe's hull in case they encountered Caribe warriors.

Haiti was the center of this universe. Caonabó marveled with humility that he would now live there and that the caves where mankind had lived before emerging to populate the world were in the center of Haiti itself. His noble people—the Taínos—had emerged

---

*Cay is derived from the Taíno word for island.

from the Cacibajagua (the Jagua Cave) in the mountain of Cauta.*
The rest of mankind had emerged from the cave of Amayaúna (without merit, value, or importance).

Every hour, the crew rested and drank water, and, before midday, they entered the passage between the two southern cays and ceased paddling to eat. Caonabó understood they could return to this shelter if it stormed before nightfall, but they would not thereafter—regardless of the peril. The leader studied the sky, wind, and surf farther south and silently consulted Yúcahu and Guabancex, the female spirit of hurricanes and storms, and her herald Guataúba, a male underling who ordered wind and rain. He invited the crew's and Caonabó's opinions and, hearing no objection or concern, decided to continue to Haiti.

"How often do you turn back?" Caonabó asked.

"Not often," the leader responded. "But you can't make a mistake. The decision must be free from pride."

Caonabó nodded, wondering if his pride was transparent.

"It also must be free of undue fear. How tall are the waves, how strong is the gale, does the sky reveal the spirits will have them grow or shrink or storm? Those are the questions to be answered."

The men recommenced paddling, with a few taking turns to rest in the hull, and the canoe left the shelter of the cays to enter the ocean. It rose and fell on large waves blown west by a strengthening wind, and the water grew dark as the ocean deepened.

When the canoe surged upward, Caonabó gazed about to landless horizons far distant and recalled with pride how the Taínos had first ventured from the Cacibajagua onto the land and then braved the ocean. Before his recognition as the Taínos' ancestral leader, a young Guahayona had led other men's wives out of the cave and ventured by canoe into the sea, tricking his cacique into joining but soon throwing him overboard. Guahayona took the women to the island of Matininó and left them there, to live without men except for small portions of the year, and then continued alone to the island of Guanín to gather its *guanín* (gold alloyed with copper and silver, with a shiny reddish hue and scent of copper). He found a beautiful young woman, Guabonito, in the sea, and, while she would not sleep with

*The Jagua being a tree species from which Taínos extracted dye for body paint.

him, she bestowed more guanín on him, healed his disease (syphilis), and showed him how to be virtuous. Guahayona then returned to the mountain of Cauta and, in recognition of his learning and respect for the spirits, was anointed ruler. Caonabó pondered Guahayona's valor and search for wisdom and mused whether Guahayona's journey and fortune foretold his own.

The rhythmic rise and fall of the canoe and swish of paddles dipping the sea lulled Caonabó to recline and slumber in the hull, which sheltered his nakedness from the wind. The wind's howl and the splash of cold spray roused him as the afternoon waned, and, with apprehension, he listened to the crew discussing the weather. The gale had strengthened, and wave and spray curled into the hull, forcing the crew to bail with calabash gourds. Land wasn't visible in any direction, and Caonabó recognized his dependency on the leader's judgment and recalled the wrath of Guabancex. But there were no storm clouds, the canoe held a firm trajectory and balance, and the leader remained silent. The sun set in a fiery array of purple and gold, and Caonabó studied the night's darkness envelope the eastern horizon, the stars rise from the sea to the heavens, and a crescent moon cast a silver coating on the undulating sea. He admired the crew's mettle to venture at night and dozed on and off for hours.

Twilight's faint halo revealed Haiti low in the distance, and, when he woke, Caonabó was astonished by its immensity across a great sweep of the horizon. He had learned that Haiti had a spirit within, an enormous female beast that nourished the Taíno people who dwelled there. The canoe was approaching the beast's backside, her eyes far beyond the eastern horizon and her rump beyond the western. The beast gradually grew from a gray sliver to an enormous, mountainous coastline partially covered in lush, green forest. At dawn, they passed through a strait between imposing cliffs and a small island swarmed by birds (Cabo del Morro and Isla Cabra, Dominican Republic). Caonabó spied fishermen in canoes floating in a calm bay and smoke rising from villages inland, and the leader landed the canoe ashore at the mouth of a great river surrounded by beach and mudflats (Río Yaque, Dominican Republic). They had arrived in the cacicazgo of Marien, four nights' journey overland to Uncle's home in Maguana. Fishermen and naborias who transported fish and other goods inland crowded the beach.

The leader recognized acquaintances, and they offered Caonabó and the crew cazabi and papaya juice from Marien. Caonabó shared the remaining fish from Aniyana and related news of Father's settlement, startled and gratified that he could speak to these people as he spoke to Father's subjects on Aniyana. The leader traded the Aniyanan salt for pottery and gold jewelry, and, after resting some hours, he and Caonabó departed up the Yaque with a single crew member in a small canoe, leaving the goods acquired with the crew on the beach.

The river cut through a mangrove swamp into an enormous plain, bordered by mountains to the north. By dusk, gardens of yuca, *mahisi* (corn), and sweet potato lined the riverbank, stretching as far as Caonabó could see on either side, with mountains rising to the south to form an enormous fertile valley. The cultivation of the fields astounded Caonabó, rows upon rows of large dirt mounds planted with yuca and carefully mulched, weeded, and irrigated by water channeled from mountain streams. He recognized cotton and fruit trees, and the leader pointed out a patch of tobacco. They passed villages on the Yaque with twenty or thirty bohíos each, with hundreds of people and throngs of children at play. Taínos of all ages bathed in the river. The Yaque curled frequently, and, at each turn, Caonabó expected wilderness to begin—but it never did, as every turn revealed a new settlement.

The leader eventually brought the canoe to rest at a village where he was known. The local cacique greeted Caonabó with cazabi and juice and invited the visitors to share his caney for the night. At dusk, they feasted on sweet potato, turtle, and iguana, and Caonabó offered a shell trumpet made on Aniyana as a gift. After nightfall, Caonabó lay in a hammock, too excited to sleep, yearning to understand the calls of the parrots, the gurgle of the river, and the scents of the verdant gardens rising from Haiti's backside.

In the morning, Caonabó and the leader bade the cacique, the last crew member, and the river Yaque farewell and started the journey south through the valley and then over the mountains to Maguana.

They now strode through villages and fields on foot, greeting and greeted by villagers, glancing into people's bohíos, listening to their daily lives. Caonabó glimpsed yuca being shredded and baked to cazabi, trees slashed and bled for rubber, and tobacco rolled to smoke.

They came to foothills on the valley's southern edge and began to climb, arriving by midday at a pass to rest in a thicket of palms. The cacique of a nearby village offered a traditional meal of pepper pot—peppers and other vegetables stewed with *hutia* (a cat-size rodent) and bird in a large turtle shell. Caonabó gazed toward the mountains they would cross, a region strewn with rocks the leader called the Cibao, and was shocked by its remoteness. In less than a day, he had traveled from the most populated villages to the most splendid wilderness he had ever seen. He and the leader commenced traversing it, climbing up and down hills and ridges but gradually ascending until dark, passing through fields of wild, tall grass growing from hard, stony ground and groves of trees blooming orange or red flowers and tall pines. The air grew cooler, and, at dusk, they arrived at a village where again the leader was known.

As they retired for the night, Caonabó asked the leader, "Have you ever thought to remain in Haiti—if that pleased my father?"

"No. My wife and children are on Aniyana. Your father is the source of my nobility."

"But if you didn't have family or concern for your nobility?"

"Like yourself? I'd remain."

Caonabó recalled Onaney's prediction. "Would the Haitians accept you?"

"They've always been friendly and generous to me. It may depend as much on yourself as them."

Caonabó fell asleep contemplating the rustle of the highland grass and the scents of pine resin and cold stone. They occupied the next two days much as the first, continuing south to Maguana. Mist enveloped the mountains at dawn, which the hot sun quickly burned away. They hiked until sunset, villagers freely offered meals when they passed, and local caciques shared their caneys for the night. On the final night, they rested at a village where the local cacique owed allegiance to Uncle and had played with Mother as a girl. He embraced Caonabó and praised Mother, and Caonabó remembered Father's final assurances and realized that he did belong in Haiti, to be known as Mother's son.

In the morning, Caonabó and the leader descended into the fertile valley of Maguana and, after some hours passing through crop fields and gardens, they arrived at Uncle's village, teeming with more people than Caonabó had ever seen together. The leader brought Caonabó to Uncle's caney, which stood astride an enormous plaza, and remarked that Uncle's batey field was the largest in all of Haiti.* For an instant, Caonabó remembered Father's esteem that Uncle had more than two dozen wives, most of them born in distant villages, each marriage arranged to maintain or extend Uncle's authority in the wife's native village and territory. Caonabó grew apprehensive, preparing himself to meet a paramount Haitian cacique for the first time and anxious that he meet Father's and Mother's expectations of his conduct. Uncle was summoned, and Caonabó trembled.

From the caney stepped a large, late-middle-aged man. A guanín medallion hung upon his chest displaying a double rainbow—one rising above the flat earth and one descending below—proclaiming the bearer's caciqual authority and responsibility to influence the spirits for the benefit of his people and to bridge spiritual and temporal life. His ears and nose were adorned with gold, and a cotton belt embroidered with pearl was wrapped around his waist. He slowly lifted his arms in a sign of friendship and said in a deep voice, "Welcome to Maguana, my nephew." He paused momentarily, scrutinizing Caonabó and searching for something of ceremonial significance to say, but memories and affections for his sister crowded his thoughts. Chuckling with emotion, he simply proclaimed, "You do look like your mother."

---

*Corral de los Indios, San Juan de la Maguana, Dominican Republic.

Gonzalo Fernández de Oviedo's sketches of a bohío and caney, sixteenth century.

GUACANAGARÍ
Marien, Haiti

Eight-year-old Guacanagarí was relieved to be excused from his father's lessons on conduct and joined his two older sisters and younger siblings swimming at the beach late one afternoon. They found a spot where the ocean waves slipped partially through the off-shore coral reefs to break ashore, and Guacanagarí carried a broth-er—a toddler born of one of Father's younger wives—into the surf. The youngster screamed with delight as waves tumbled before them and surged past. Heitiana, the oldest sister, warned Guacanagarí to stay in the shallows as the child hadn't learned to swim. Soon, she called all the children to the beach, where they sat as their naked bodies dried in the breeze and hot sun, and then announced it was time to return home for dinner. It would be dark that night as the moon had waned, and the village would prepare for nightfall earlier than usual.

Guacanagarí obeyed Heitiana with trust and affection, regardless that it was he who might rule one day. The children slowly mean-dered behind her from the beach, and Guacanagarí and his second sister, Butiyari, each bore siblings on their backs. They crossed an embankment where the forest began and encountered two sentries on duty, teenagers just older than Heitiana, armed with spears, an arrow sling, and a shell trumpet for warning the village of an attack. The sentries nodded deferentially to acknowledge Guacanagarí as of the caciqual family, and he put them at ease with a wave of his hand. Heitiana and Butiyari, both pretty, began to flirt with them.

Guacanagarí listened and recalled overhearing Father and Mother discussing his sisters' marriages. Heitiana was now a woman and Butiyari soon would be, and Father, Mother, and Uncle would marry them to important subordinate caciques, not Uncle's soldiers. Guacanagarí studied Heitiana's and Butiyari's grace in their innocent tease and realized that the soldiers appreciated the attention well beyond the flirtation.

The toddlers squirmed on Guacanagarí's back as the conversation extended, and he released them on the ground and turned to scan the sea, as if a sentry himself. Uncle ruled the territory of Marien from the coastal village inland behind him (now Bord de Mer de Limonade, Haiti). To the north, directly off the beach, fishermen hauled in nets, lines, and hooks, just as they did every day, supplying the village with food. In the distance to the west, a darkly forested, mountainous cape (Cape Haitien, Haiti) majestically rose to tower above an expanse of intervening farmland and beach, as if to herald the importance of the territory. To the east, a mangrove swamp jutted into the sea, obscuring the coastline beyond. Guacanagarí sensed order, tradition, permanence, beauty, and peace.

The sentries' watch continued to nightfall, when they would retire to the village until dawn. Heitiana ended the conversation, and Guacanagarí and the children tramped behind her through the forest to the village, which was well organized with many streets and a clean-swept central plaza. She handed the children over to their nurses in the plaza and joined Mother to supervise naborias cooking dinner on a fireplace before their bohío.

After dinner, Guacanagarí and his sisters relaxed at the bohío's door while the younger children were laid to sleep in their hammocks. A small fire smoldered inside to repel mosquitoes with its smoke, and cooking fires dwindled throughout the plaza, casting an amber hue that gradually diminished to points of orange glow from dying embers. They had been taught to return to the bohío at night. While one's soul lived on in another place after death, spirits of the dead haunted the forest—apparitions like the living but without navels— and stalked about at night. Heitiana noticed Guacanagarí staring into the darkness and understood he was frightened by the spirits that might be lurking.

"We're safe here."

"I know that." Guacanagarí was annoyed. "I'm not scared. I know the spirits are there and was thinking of them, but that doesn't mean I'm scared. They have their place and we have ours."

"I didn't say you were scared." Heitiana and Butiyari grinned. "Tomorrow, after you've finished what Father sets for you, we can teach the younger children to play at batey."

Guacanagarí and his sisters talked until Father came to sleep and then all retired.

Unbeknownst to Guacanagarí and the sentries, beyond the mangrove swamp and their sight, a dozen canoes had rapidly plied the ocean that afternoon, approaching the swamp from the northeast. The crews were Caribes from a homeland they called Turuqueria (Guadeloupe), more than seven hundred miles away. There was a deliberate ferocity in their appearance, their black hair uncut and uncombed and their naked olive-brown skin painted with red and black stripes. They had arrived at the swamp before dusk's last light, located a small rivulet channeling through the mangrove root in which to hide their canoes, and found shelter on mudflats deep within—where they had slept undetected. Some of them had raided the village years before.

These warriors woke before dawn to eat, invoke their spirits for victory, and tip their arrows with poison. In the faintest twilight, they dragged their canoes into the ocean and circled west to the beach where the children had played the afternoon before, careful to avoid the smack of their paddles against the hull, particularly when landing. They pulled the sterns of their canoes ashore to permit a rapid escape and spread apart to enter the forest at intervals to advance upon the village aligned in an arc. But they quickly halted at the forest's edge when they heard voices.

The two sentries had returned to their post and were eating breakfast and chatting, speculating whether Heitiana and Butiyari would return that day, their weapons and trumpet set on the ground. Caribe bowmen silently aimed and shot their arrows, which pierced the sentries' chests, and they toppled, gasping hoarsely. Caribes rushed to strangle them and muffle any cries, and the sentries suffocated in excruciating pain.

The Caribes advanced quietly and rapidly on the village in search of their prey, young women or girls to be captured for use as wives, concubines, or slaves. At the village edge, they howled a war cry in unison to terrify the sleeping Taínos and then charged with spears and *macanas* (heavy wooden clubs) into the bohíos, spearing or bludgeoning those men who rose. They seized the women and girls they found desirable, dragging them from the bohíos to haul them to the beach. Bowmen dispersed along the village perimeter to shoot those Taíno men who were able to give chase.

Guacanagarí woke in terror at the sound of the war cry, lost his balance, and fell from his hammock to the ground, cringing at the clamor of footsteps charging toward the bohío and his brothers and sisters screaming. He peered desperately in the semidarkness to discern Father's dark shadow rising to meet the onslaught and the shadows of Mother and Father's other wives rushing to shelter his siblings. Invaders crashed through the doorway and attacked Father, hurling him to the ground and thrusting a spear to pierce his heart, which he deflected but which sank deeply into his thigh. Guacanagarí was trampled. He heard Mother and the other wives shrieking, and he rose to help Father, who shouted that Heitiana and Butiyari must be protected.

In that instant, Guacanagarí grasped the meaning of the chaos and what was at stake, and he lost fear for himself, consumed with the terror that he must save his sisters or lose them. He recognized Butiyari screaming and charged through the doorway into the plaza to behold Father's naborias struggling to wrest her from a Caribe warrior dragging her toward the forest. Suddenly, one of the naborias shrieked and bolted upright, gasping and holding his chest, pierced by an arrow that had flown unseen from the forest. But the other naborias held their grip on Butiyari, and other villagers joined the fray to bludgeon the Caribe. He toppled and released Butiyari, and she fell to the ground, bleeding from the groin.

The Caribe warriors fled as quickly as they had attacked, vastly outnumbered by the villagers now awake and ready for combat. Guacanagarí began to run with other men toward the sea. He had not seen Heitiana, and that terrified him. But, before he reached the forest, one of Father's naborias restrained him and warned him the battle was for men and that he must return to Father. The naboria stood firmly between him and the forest.

Guacanagarí returned to Father and Butiyari, who were carried into a bohío where Mother and the village behique, together with Father's other wives, attended them. The women stopped their bleeding with cotton cloth. Father gasped for Heitiana. A naboria responded that she was not yet accounted for, and Mother wailed uncontrollably.

The sun finally rose on the village. The reed of plundered bohíos, pieces of shattered furniture and utensils, personal vestments, jewelry, and torn hammocks lay strewn on the ground as if a hurricane had swept through. At the shore, the men had watched the Caribes escape, apparently with over a dozen captives. During the morning, they were identified by their absence, including Heitiana. Some were married, some unmarried, and some but girls. Some were nitaíno, some commoners, some naborias, and Heitiana was of the caciqual family. The entire village had been violated. A number of villagers had died responding to the attack, including the two sentries. One Caribe had been killed and some wounded, who were unable to escape. They were tortured and executed.

Mother knew Guacanagarí loved Heitiana and feared for her fate, and she held him to console him. "Guacanagarí, listen to me—Heitiana will not be killed. She will survive to serve the Caribe as a wife or concubine." Mother reflected on what she had been taught as a girl, and told her son before he heard it from others. "If Heitiana has daughters by the Caribe, they also will become wives or concubines. If she has sons, they will be eaten."

"Maybe she can escape?" Guacanagarí asked. "Can't we follow them to rescue her?"

"No. No one escapes the Caribe. Their brutality makes rescue impossible." Mother sought to foreclose any hope. "Guacanagarí, we will never see Heitiana again."

"If no one escapes from them, how do you know they eat boys?"

"We've known that for generations."

In the following weeks, Guacanagarí did reconcile himself to losing Heitiana forever. There were young children in the village who had lost their mothers, and he was humbled by their misfortune. Father and Butiyari slowly recovered. Uncle's authority was never publicly criticized, but his esteem suffered greatly. This was the second attack during his rule, and his own sister's child had been seized.

One morning, Father invited Guacanagarí to observe as he assisted Uncle as a member of Uncle's council of elders in the routine administration of the village and cacicazgo. The elders sat on wooden *duhos* (ceremonial seats) in the plaza, and Guacanagarí listened as commoners and naborias reported on the yuca and fish harvested over the past week and presented baskets of cazabi, smoked fish, and fruit. Uncle distributed the food among the villagers, with fishermen receiving cazabi and fruit, farmers receiving fish, and the sentries, woodworkers, and other craftsman receiving a bit of all. He allocated greater delicacies, such as bird and iguana, to the caciqual and nitaíno families.

Father taught his son as they walked home afterward. "It's a cacique's responsibility to provide for all his people. In return, the people owe him absolute loyalty. You saw that Uncle provided food for all?"

"He gave people different things. Some got better food than others." Guacanagarí studied Father's reaction.

"That's correct. Uncle gave each person the food he lacked. He also recognized the nobility of the nitaínos and gave them delicacies. All present were satisfied with the result. All have food. None hunger." Father appreciated his son's perception and kindness. "Would you have done differently?"

Guacanagarí shrugged. "No, if you think it's fair."

"It is. Uncle is known to be fair and generous."

Guacanagarí gathered his thoughts before continuing. "My friends say some people think Uncle isn't a good leader. They say other tribes laugh at us because we can't protect our women."

"The Caribes raid other cacicazgos, too." Father was stern. "Uncle is a good cacique. And he is both your uncle and your cacique, so you owe him unquestioned loyalty. He's called a cohaba ceremony. He and the local caciques will consult the spirits to consider better ways to defend the village."

"What'll they find out?"

"People have ideas. We could have more sentries, guarding all night. But Uncle could decide that kind of thing himself. The Caribes pass along Haiti's northern coast before attacking us. Uncle's cohaba might consider whether we should ask caciques to the east to warn us when the Caribes pass, and what we should offer those caciques in return."

Within a few weeks, Uncle's subordinate caciques in Marien's largest villages arrived for the ceremony. Together, Uncle, the village behique, and the caciques began to purify themselves before invoking the spirits, remaining celibate and abstaining from meals for a few days other than drinking tea brewed from the plant whose juice was used for soap. They grew physically weaker, releasing the constraints of ordinary perception to achieve better communication with the spirits, and, on the eve of the ceremony, they induced themselves to vomit any food remaining within by placing a ceremonial stick—carved from the rib of a manatee—down the throat.

The following afternoon, finely carved wooden duhos were arranged in a semicircle inside the bohío at the village edge, where Uncle stored his cemís, and a cohaba table set before them, its carved base depicting a behique squatting with his hands on his knees, the tabletop balanced atop his head. Guacanagarí approached at a distance to spy the village behique preparing the cohaba powder, a powerful narcotic, on the table-top, crushing pods of the piptadenia tree and other ingredients, where-upon Uncle and the caciques entered the bohío. Soon, Guacanagarí overheard Uncle raise his voice in a speech and tone weirdly contorted, seeking a direct communication to attain the spirits' wisdom. The caci-ques responded, in tones similarly contorted, frequently loudly and with intensity, debating with Uncle what had been revealed.

The ceremony continued well into the night, and Guacanagarí returned home, resigned to learn its result the next day. As he lay to sleep, he imagined himself grown, leading the ceremony as cacique. But he was haunted by his final conversation with Heitiana and his fear of men's nighttime spirits. He realized he should have feared men instead.

Cohaba table, duhos, and vomit sticks.

ISABEL
Segovia, Castile (January–June 1465)

In January 1465, thirteen-year-old Isabel stood awaiting her older brother, the Castilian king Enrique IV, in the great Hall of Kings of the majestic alcazar in Segovia, where the nobility had pledged allegiance to their father decades ago. She shivered, as cold winter winds swirled around the castle's lofty promontory above the ravines carved by two rivers that joined far below.

Above her, displayed on the walls of the great hall, loomed the gold effigies of over thirty Castilian rulers—kings and a few queens—both great and undistinguished over past centuries. Isabel was humbled to be in their presence. She gazed up at them and wondered what struggles they had surmounted to achieve and maintain their crowns. She admired that some had fought valiantly to establish and expand

the boundary of the Castilian kingdom during the Reconquista, the
Christian reconquest of Hispania from the Mohammedans who had
invaded from Africa in the eighth century. She mused whether the
queens had commanded the respect of their husbands and noblemen.

With honor but little remembrance, Isabel studied the visage most
recently sculpted, that of King Juan II, her father, who had died when
she was a young child (1454). She recalled overhearing others chide
that Father had been a weak king and fallen subject to her mother's
counsel and ambition, executing at Mother's insistence a nobleman
who opposed her influence.* Whether Father's weakness was true
or not, Isabel was heartened to think of Mother, Isabel of Portugal,
once queen and now queen dowager. Mother had loved Father, and
her love and care for Isabel and Isabel's younger brother, Alfonso,
remained boundless. Mother had been Father's second wife and
had born Alfonso within a year prior to Father's death. Yet, in spite
of Mother's ambition for their infant son, Father's chosen successor had remained his son Enrique—born to Father's first wife† and
then nearly thirty years old. Father's will had left the small village of
Arévalo for Mother, to which Mother had retired—dejectedly, Isabel
knew—from court with herself and Alfonso.

For an instant, Isabel proudly recalled that her own lineage
included not only the Castilian royal family above her but the English,
through both Mother and Father, both descendants of King Edward
III, and the Portuguese, through Mother, as Mother's mother, Isabel
de Barcelos, was an aunt to Portugal's King Afonso V and sister-
in-law to the renowned Prince Henrique. But Isabel's pride quickly
vanished as she was overcome by the grim reality that her brothers, King Enrique and young Alfonso, now were in opposing camps,
openly hostile to each other. Uncertainty, chaos, and fear were enveloping Castile and herself. She now lived at Enrique's court in Segovia alone, separated from Mother and Grandmother, whose love and
counsel she dearly missed, and under heavy guard.

King Enrique—her guardian—now claimed as heir and successor
his Queen Juana's daughter, also named Juana, not yet three years old.
Prior to little Juana's birth, Enrique had been childless for his entire

---

*Álvaro de Luna, executed in 1453.
†María of Aragón.

life, both in and out of wedlock, including for more than a dozen years of barren marriage to a prior wife,* whom he had divorced for failure of child, and a half dozen years of marriage to Queen Juana before her pregnancy. Isabel pondered that his own servants jested behind his back that the childlessness was his fault—owing to a deformed member—and scorned that he was a blasphemer with young men and boys. Whether these rumors were true or not, she found him a strange man indeed, withdrawn, reclusive, and brooding, and much of what she had seen of his court had shocked her. The women of the court—including even the queen and her attendants—wore scant clothing, and it was obvious the attendants frolicked with the court prelates and noblemen.

Enrique had summoned her and Alfonso to court prior to little Juana's birth. Isabel had attended the girl's baptism as a sponsoring godmother and dutifully recited the customary oath recognizing the child as heir to the Castilian throne. But some nobleman since had alleged that Enrique himself had invited a cohort[†] to the queen's bed to produce an heir, intent on precluding the nobility from passing the kingdom to Alfonso before Enrique's death. Last year, noblemen promoting Alfonso—including the powerful archbishop of Toledo, Alfonso Carrillo—had forced Enrique to recognize Alfonso as heir instead of little Juana. When Enrique continued to deny the child's illegitimacy, they then had required him to release Alfonso, but not Isabel, to their custody.

Isabel overheard counselors greet Enrique in the alcazar's throne room on his arrival from a city palace, where he had resided since entering Segovia some nights before. Their speech was indiscernible at the distance she stood, but she strained to understand their voices' verve and tenor, whether revealing decisiveness, fear, loathing, or something else. Alfonso's proponents recently had criticized Enrique severely for religious depravity in tolerating the Mudejar,[‡] Jews, and heretical Christians living in Castile, and they had forced the appointment of a commission to recommend reforms for the kingdom's governance. But Enrique had rejected the commission's

---

*The Aragonese Blanca of Navarre.
[†]Beltrán de la Cueva.
[‡]*Mudejar* refers to Muslims living in a Christian kingdom, practicing Islam while vassal to a Christian sovereign.

recommendations—including election of noblemen to the Cortes, enlargement of the king's council, and restrictions on royal taxation—in their entirety, furious that the recommendations were but a manifesto to eviscerate the Crown. Just days before, he had renounced Alfonso as heir, accepting that warfare could follow.

Isabel waited for Enrique to settle at work, and then entered to greet him, permission for a sister's informal audience being unnecessary. He was dressed plainly in a dark wool hunting coat and trousers, as if to proclaim disdain for sovereignty rather than celebrate it, slouching over a table set by his counselors with letters and orders for his signature, resting his large head in his puffed hands, and, at forty years old, weary and dejected. He gazed up at her, and she caught that his eye appreciated her womanly figure.

"How are you, my sister?" He studied her intent blue eyes, plump cheeks, and auburn hair, parted at the forehead to curl back over the ears and fall to the shoulders upon a wool shawl wrapping an amber, long-sleeve dress cut squarely above her breasts.

"I'm lonely here, my lord."

"I'm lonely, too, most of the time." Enrique hid an anger that welled within, a rage that noblemen who filled his court, shared his bread and wine, and offered him gracious salutations daily had entreated young Alfonso to challenge succession. He was vexed how much his sister understood of the commission recommendations, the approaching confrontation, or Alfonso's intentions. "A king can be lonely even though people fill the room." He paused and smiled. "If you took a husband, you wouldn't be lonely."

"I have the Lord." Isabel smiled in response, aware that Enrique had and would promise her in marriage solely to achieve an alliance that gave him advantage over Alfonso's proponents or, as Mother and Grandmother had warned, simply to remove her from Castile. Years ago, at different times, he had sought to marry her to each of the legitimate sons of King Juan II of Aragón, marriages that would have been appropriate to her stature and taken her from Castile. But Enrique had broken the arrangement for the younger son, Fernando, as alliances shifted, and the elder son, Carlos, had died. Enrique had also offered her to the English king Edward IV and, when Edward declined, introduced her to Queen Juana's older brother, the widowed Portuguese king Afonso V. Isabel was now a woman, and any marriage could be consummated promptly.

"So you do. We all have the Lord, although it's frequently difficult to discern how he dispenses his grace."

"How's the queen?" Isabel asked, aware Enrique cared nothing for the queen except her womb.

"She's healthy," Enrique replied perfunctorily, as he was unsure. "She sends her love."

"And the princess?" Isabel continued, maintaining a facade of loyalty but pausing slightly to signal the last word was chosen advisedly.

Enrique noted the acknowledgment of little Juana's hereditary entitlement and scrutinized the blink of Isabel's eyes and the purse of her lips, certain of her insincerity. "She's healthy, as well. Any word of Alfonso?"

"As you know, I have none, my lord," Isabel lied. Her heart swelled that Alfonso was Mother's child as well as Father's and had been her companion throughout childhood. She would embrace his ascension to the throne and decry its usurpation by an illegitimate.

Isabel recognized Enrique wanted to attend to other business and that he knew she knew it to be a crisis. For a moment, she sensed that, as ever, he appeared to believe that little Juana was his child, and she remembered that he was the king their father had chosen, decades her senior, and that important noblemen yet supported him, warning that his crown could not be usurped prematurely regardless of successor. But she scorned and pitied that he was neither a good nor powerful king. His shabby dress and demeanor invited disrespect rather than loyalty. He cared little for worship, and his failure to lead in faith undermined his authority. He insulted every Christian by ignoring Christian tradition, sometimes wearing Mudejar clothing and eating as they did by reclining on the floor, and he employed Mudejar soldiers rather than Christian for his own protection. He had failed—as had Father, she confessed—to complete the Reconquista by driving the infidel from their last bastion, the kingdom of Grenada on Hispania's southern coast.

At the same moment, Enrique studied Isabel and knew he enjoyed her company but could never trust her. Alfonso's claim was also her own. Discussing the current situation would result in nothing but friction between them, and he ended the audience as quickly as it had begun. "We should dine and hunt together later this week, if there's time."

"That would be my pleasure, my lord."

Isabel was relieved. They had greeted each other, affirmed civility, and parted without hostility, and she was free to pass the time outside his presence, although his informants filled the alcazar. She strolled from the throne room to the alcazar's chapel and sat alone, longing for a kind word or embrace from Mother and Grandmother. But she realized neither could help anymore. Mother had grown mad, believing her castle in Arévalo haunted by ghouls and demons, including the ghost of the nobleman Father had executed to satisfy her. Grandmother was close to death. Isabel gazed to the altar cross depicting Christ and would talk with him.

The queen sends her love! For a moment, Isabel was overcome by contempt for Juana, whose frivolity, coquetry, and moral laxity she despised. Her education had been entrusted to Juana, and she had suffered for years to feign attention to Juana's lessons on how to dress for and please such suitors that the king might choose for her. The contempt was mutual. Ignoring Christ's presence, Isabel gloated at the rage Juana must have felt when Enrique recognized Alfonso as successor and forsook her daughter. She exulted that, two years before, the queen had miscarried a baby boy. Juana now had lost two purported heirs to the throne! But Isabel's eyes quickly reverted to Christ, and she was certain he didn't approve all her thoughts. His serene visage forgave her.

Yet her anger continued to simmer. Juana's lessons weren't the only lesson at fault—far from it! An entire lifetime of education—lessons from Mother, Grandmother, and tutors in Arévalo—had schooled her to be but a wife to the most powerful prince she could marry! She'd been taught to read and write, faith, the glory of Hispania and the Reconquista, and how to sew. But she hadn't been taught court politics, how a king ruled noblemen, or that the motives of noblemen were rarely pure—simply because she was a girl. Archbishop Carrillo had always sought her well-being—insisting that she live with Mother rather than Enrique—and now championed Alfonso's succession to the throne, but this protection and promotion served the archbishop's own empowerment. The commission had sought to eviscerate Enrique's authority, but the evisceration was designed to apply to any king hereafter, including Alfonso—for the nobility's permanent benefit. Her lessons on the glory of Hispania hadn't taught that noblemen thought they had the right to influence succession for their own ends.

Isabel pondered what her lessons had taught, and she realized that the conflict between her brothers now invoked appeals to religious concerns, fears, and hatreds that had smoldered and flared in Hispania since her birth and for centuries before. She averted her eyes from Christ's stare, uncertain he approved of what was happening.

The commission had proposed that all Jews and Mudejar live in separate quarters within one year and restrictions on their employment. It also advocated the establishment of an inquisition to punish Christian heretics, intending that it be directed only against Jews who had converted to Christianity, the *conversos*. Isabel had heard one of Enrique's confessors* preach that, for their betrayal and murder of Christ, the Jews should be barred from official positions and decent occupations and their property and synagogues seized, and that all conversos were heretics, secret Judaizers denying Christ, thereby deserving punishment. But Enrique had rejected these visions. As Father and kings before, he had recognized the Jews as the Crown's direct subjects, entitled to the Crown's direct protection. He accepted the views that a converso who erred in faith was no different than a longtime Christian—an "old Christian"—who so erred, and that any inquisition should be directed at both with the purpose of teaching the heretic the salvation of conversion, not punishment. Isabel realized many Castilians were moved by the confessor's harangues and favored these commission recommendations and that Enrique's rejection of them diminished his popularity to Alfonso's advantage.

Isabel's gaze returned to Christ, and she asked him what was right and true, regardless of the insincerities of men. Revulsion rose within her—surely his response—to the bald assertion that all conversos were heretics. It belied his and the pope's instruction to bring and welcome all to the faith and effectively meant that Jews could never

---

*The Franciscan friar Alonso de Espina.

achieve salvation. Many of her friends were children of conversos. The scriptures taught that the son shall not bear the iniquity of the father.

⊡   ⊡   ⊡

Below Isabel, in the valley just north of the city, Fray Tomás de Torquemada, then forty-five and prior of the Dominican convent of Santa Cruz, was also speaking with Christ, sensing his presence and seeking to emulate him and strive for his perfection.

Fray Torquemada had been introduced to the Dominicans as a teenager by his uncle, a cardinal raised in a converso household, and had embraced an austere abstinence ever since, never eating meat, wearing no linen undergarments, and worshipping in a bare cell, where he slept on a plank. He had administered his convent for ten years with the same austerity.

Fray Torquemada often gazed up to the city of Segovia—teeming with the impious, swindlers, prostitutes, and Jews—to remind himself of the actions and teachings of Christ. He adored that Christ had thrown the animal keepers and money changers from the temple so that God's house not be desecrated with merchandise and thieves. He revered that Christ had taught the apostles he came to earth not to bring peace but with a sword, to set son against father and mother against daughter, for a person who loved his father or mother more than Christ was not a sufficient believer. He raged that Christ had warned the Jews of the Day of Judgment—whereafter nonbelievers would burn in hell's furnace forever—but the Jews had sought to stone him to death and then delivered him to Pilate. For Fray Torquemada, heaven and hell, and this sword and final judgment, were ever present, as real as his cell and convent. He was incorruptible from this perception and in his belief in Christ's teaching that those with a pure heart would be blessed in seeing God.

As Isabel and Fray Torquemada worshipped, so did Professor Hernando de Talavera—to the northwest in Salamanca. At thirty-five, Professor Talavera was the chair of moral philosophy at the university at Salamanca, a post he shortly would resign to pursue monastic life by entering the Hieronymite order as the prior of a small monastery nearby. He had been raised in a converso family and had studied St. Augustine and the same gospels as Fray Torquemada.

Talavera also sought to strive for Christ's perfection so that he might see God. He embraced that Christ had taught the two greatest commandments were to love God with all one's heart and to love thy neighbor as thyself. He was inspired that Christ had preached one should love his enemies and that God meant for the sun to rise on both the evil and the good. He venerated that Christ had protected the adulteress from being stoned, warning that no man who had sinned should cast a stone, and then told her to sin no more. Professor Talavera cherished St. Augustine's teaching that God had made every soul and body and that faith was a matter of choice rather than birth.

Over the next few months, Enrique's and Alfonso's supporters prepared for war. In June, standing on a platform set in a field near Ávila, noblemen led by Archbishop Carrillo removed a crown from a straw effigy of Enrique, pronounced Enrique deposed, threw the effigy on the ground, and then hoisted Alfonso, eleven, to the platform and acclaimed him king of Castile. There were then two kings of Castile, and the kingdom disintegrated into civil war.

Guarionex
Hurricane, Magua, Haiti

At dawn, a village behique studied the fiery red, orange, and purple glow of the clouds to the east, the direction from which hurricanes arrived, and grew alarmed. He warned the village cacique, who studied the sky and easterly wind. The weather did not appear extraordinary. But it rarely did before hurricanes, and the cacique decided they should walk to the beach to inspect the sea in the large gulf on Haiti's eastern shore (Bahía de Samaná, Dominican Republic).

When they arrived, the easterly wind remained mild and the sea calm. But the water's surface appeared strangely unctuous and without its typical ripple. It was a matter of judgment, but the behique thought the tide was higher than normal. A fisherman advised that dolphins had been jumping, which usually preceded storms. Another related that there had been a few sudden, brisk squalls since sunrise, vanishing as quickly as they had come. The cacique decided it would be prudent to warn his superior Cacibaquel, the paramount cacique of Magua, to prepare for a hurricane if the wind rose significantly, and smoke signals were dispatched to be relayed from village to village west through the cacicazgo.

Guarionex sat with Cacibaquel, his father, in their village's central plaza, studying the clouds marching west. Magua lay almost entirely inland but for a few villages on the eastern gulf, comprising most of the immense fertile valley through which the rivers Yaque and Camú flowed, and their village lay among the Camú's tributaries on the valley's southern side (La Vieja Vega, near La Vega, Dominican Republic), nestled in the foothills of the Cibao. They had grown concerned with the weather by midmorning and, upon sighting the smoke signals, Cacibaquel retired alone to the ceremonial bohío where he kept his cemís to seek Guabancex's forbearance and Yúcahu's protection.

Guarionex recognized his father's frequent consultations with the spirits comforted their people. In his late teens, of small, slender stature, Guarionex had experienced hurricanes and knew the risks inland were different than at the coast. The mountains surrounding the valley partially diffused the wind and its destruction, but the valley created an equally mortal risk of torrential flooding from the rainfall. The spirit Guabancex had an underling, Coatrisquie, who brought mountain floods, and Cacibaquel and many Maguans often sought to appease him as well as his mistress.

Guarionex joined his wife, Baisi, and young son, Yomabo, outside Cacibaquel's caney, awaiting his father's next instruction. Naborias were preparing a substantial meal, foreseeing the weather would preclude cooking thereafter. Baisi was with child, and Guarionex whispered to her that he sensed a hurricane would arrive and, when it did, she should rest in the caney's center. He admonished Yomabo to stick close to her.

The sky darkened ominously during the afternoon, and the wind shifted to the northeast and rose to a gale. The paramount and local caciques living on Haiti's coastlines recognized a hurricane's unmistakable approach. They ordered fishermen to drag canoes safely inland and urged their subjects to shelter in caves before nightfall, if available. The paramount cacique of Higüey, at Haiti's southeastern tip, ordered his subjects near the ocean to evacuate inland.

Guacanagarí's uncle, who ruled the northwestern coast, reminded villagers that those in sturdy bohíos should share them with neighbors less fortunate. The cacique of the Ciguayo, who governed from a village in the mountains on Haiti's northern coast, admonished his people to beware of rock and mudslides and overhanging trees. Haiti's most powerful ruler, the Xaraguán cacique whose cacicazgo comprised much of southwest Haiti, counseled his subjects that their ancestors welcomed them for the duration of the storm in the caves where they lay entombed.

Inland, Cacibaquel summoned his nitaínos, behique, and Guarionex to his ceremonial bohío. Guarionex entered to find Cacibaquel's cemí of Guabancex sitting atop the bohío's table, her arms swirling counterclockwise in a frenzied circle about her face.

"Guabancex will rage," Cacibaquel said. "Dispatch messengers along the rivers and larger tributaries to warn those living there to take shelter in bohíos above the flood plain and to bring cazabi sufficient for a few days." Cacibaquel let the nitaínos depart and turned to teach his son.

"I've honored Guabancex for the many seasons she's spared us, but she will remind that her mercy isn't permanent." He studied Guarionex. "We now must seek her favor to storm hardest on the sea and spare our people grave harm."

"We should honor Yúcahu, as well."

"Yes, and I have. But Guabancex is upon us, so I will direct my thoughts to her. When her floods pass, I will honor Yúcahu as we heal our people. If you become cacique one day, you may decide how best to please the spirits yourself."

By dusk, villagers throughout Haiti entered the bohíos or caves where they would endure the storm. Torrential rain came after nightfall, swept harshly by the wind. On Haiti's northern and eastern coasts, the waves rose horrifically and surged beyond the beaches and mangrove swamps to wash lowland fields. The tempest howled relentlessly through the entire island, uprooting and snapping trees as if merely bushes everywhere, including in the mountains of the Cibao.

After midnight, in Magua's great valley, the gale began to damage bohíos, sheering away reed siding, ripping off rooftops, and breaking beams to flatten them, with the debris flying to wound those inside and forcing them to seek shelter with neighbors. The streams and dry washes quickly filled and breached their embankments, and the rivers Yaque and Camú rose dangerously. Guarionex and his immediate family; his brothers, sisters, and their families; and his father and father's wives, huddled together in the caney as the wind roared about it, seething through the reed walls. They shuddered from both cold and fear. The thatched roof creaked and heaved upward, and Guarionex grimly surmised that, if they lost it, the rest of the structure would shatter quickly. He admired Baisi, who sat quietly holding Yomabo, his head buried in her swollen breasts. The youngster and other children were sullen and silent, terrified that the wind's extraordinary howl forebode immanent destruction.

Dawn came darkly, and Cacibaquel and Guarionex emerged naked outside the caney into the hurricane, hunkered low in crouches to maintain their balance. Cacibaquel stepped first toward the plaza, then to the stream, and then back to the caney, and he decided they could stagger through the onslaught. Guarionex studied his father and proudly reflected that Cacibaquel's august spirituality belied a commensurate fortitude and bravery not often recognized. Father and son struggled side by side against ferocious gusts of wind, sheets of rain, and hurtling debris to inspect the village stream, which spilled through streets and gardens into bohíos on lower ground. They visited bohíos to ascertain their subjects' safety and shout encouragement. They stood for a moment in the central plaza to survey the valley below and grimly watched the great river breaching its banks.

Soon, a messenger from a village in the valley struggled uphill to report, and Cacibaquel offered him sanctuary, cazabi, and rest in the caney. There were drownings near the Camú, including mothers and children. Many bohíos had collapsed, injuring entire families. There was significant flooding of the yuca fields astride the rivers.

Shrieks pierced the din close outside, and Guarionex struggled into the storm to assist a neighboring family into the caney. Their bohío had flooded, and, soaking wet and shivering, they huddled gratefully with the caciqual family. Most were unharmed, but an older man and woman limped badly and were bleeding, injured by flying debris, and Cacibaquel's wives attended them.

Finally, by midday, the rain diminished and the wind abated into gusts, occasionally severe but not sustained. Cacibaquel's naborias blew shell trumpets to summon his and Guarionex's closest nitaínos to meet in the plaza. One nitaíno reported that people were severely injured in the bohíos in the lowest portion of the village, to which the men descended rapidly. Guarionex beheld the nightmare—the lifeless bodies of a mother and two children pinned by the skeleton of a collapsed bohío to drown in a depression filled with water. There was nothing to be done for them, and the men continued downhill to discover a man and child clinging to a tree by a flooded dry wash, dazed and shivering, trapped by rushing water. Guarionex helped rescue them. Countless similar rescue efforts continued to nightfall.

The weather was balmy the next dawn, and caciques throughout Haiti reviewed the loss of life and destruction. Guarionex's village had suffered more than a dozen dead or missing and many bohíos were destroyed. There were four that were severely injured, including the two elderly people who had sheltered in the caney. One of Cacibaquel's brothers-in-law, the local cacique of a mountain village, had been crushed by an uprooted tree and died. But Magua's food supply, while damaged, remained sufficient. The yuca fields closest to the great rivers had been washed away, as had beds of pineapple and fruit trees, but most productive capacity remained intact and would be shared with the unfortunate.

Guarionex listened and learned as Cacibaquel attended to the dead and injured. The funerals were held within days, and the dead, commoners or naborias, were buried in the cemetery near the village. Cacibaquel presided and offered personal words for each decedent—adult and child—thanking each for his or her contribution to the lives of others and the natural order. He sought to solace the grievers by setting their misfortune in a greater context, explaining that Guabancex's wrath itself was part the natural order and brought their loved ones not an end, but a transition. Their souls lived on, and they would be remembered and honored.

After the funerals, Cacibaquel asked Guarionex to join him in his ceremonial bohío, where they sat alone on duhos. "I think you're ready to assume responsibility for my brother-in-law's funeral." Cacibaquel saw his son was startled. "You've watched me do them for years, as well as moments ago."

"Won't his relatives find it a slight?"

"Not at all. You're ready, you may be cacique one day, and there's much for me to do here."

"I won't do it as well as you would."

"But you'll do it well. Sincerity is more important than experience at a funeral anyway, and you've had that since birth. You must comport yourself as if a cacique, with unquestioned authority and power, which will comfort and flatter the grieving. A cacique's subjects must see his resolve to provide for them—and to reconcile the spirits of fertility and destruction—never falters."

Guarionex soon departed for the mountain village, proud to perform a funeral service. Over years, Cacibaquel had delegated him important assignments—communicating with local caciques, commanding troops when frictions arose, and allocating food among their subjects—but this was the first task that required him to articulate thoughts on the meaning of Taíno life. He believed, and he knew his father believed, that wisdom—of both spirits and men—was the most important attribute of a cacique and that his remarks at the funeral must please both.

When Guarionex arrived, the brother-in-law's head had already been severed from his corpse, releasing his soul from the body so that it might travel to Coaybay, a place where souls of the dead went. At the funeral, Guarionex comforted the grievers, relating that the decedent had led a virtuous life and that his soul's journey thereafter would be pleasant. The head's flesh soon would be burned off and the skull preserved in his memory and to provide his family guidance in the future. Guarionex assured the grievers that the decedent's soul would be available to counsel them always. The decedent was then interred in a grave lined with wood sticks, as if in a bohío, and buried with food and some possessions, wrapped in cotton. His first wife chose to be buried with him and, heavily sedated and wrapped in cotton, she was lowered by her nitaínos to his side and the grave covered. All paused as she reunited with her husband.

Guarionex explained that the decedent and his wife were well provisioned for their next journey and departed knowing their neighbors had the resolve to rebuild their village greater than before. Seeing the grievers satisfied, Guarionex completed the ceremony by honoring Yúcahu and Guabancex. He fought to banish from his thoughts

the vision of being acclaimed as a wise cacique, a vanity inappropriate in the spirits' presence.

A few days later, after returning home, Guarionex watched his father
finish the decisions relating to the hurricane. Each of the four severely
injured had been treated by the village behique, who induced cohaba and
then sucked on the injured's body to extract the infirmity within. Cacibaquel and his council now examined each to determine whether he or she
could long survive without others' significant support. If not, Cacibaquel
would order the injured abandoned in a secluded place or strangled.

Guarionex observed as his father listened and asked many questions, thoughtful and dispassionate. The council deliberated, and
then Cacibaquel ordered that one should live and three be abandoned or strangled. As his father spoke, Guarionex stared at the
ground, breathless with the knowledge that each of the injured had
been Father's friends, or the children of Father's friends, for many
years. Cacibaquel gazed at his son and reflected that, in one's youth,
one did not truly understand that one's soul continued upon death.

Guabancex.

ISABEL AND FERNANDO
Death and Marriage in Castile, 1468–1469

At the end of June 1468, Isabel rose at dawn in her childhood bedroom in Mother's tiny castle in Arévalo, with exhilaration, pride, and foreboding. King Alfonso—as the fourteen-year-old was now addressed—had freed her from Enrique's custody in Segovia the prior autumn, and, after reuniting with Alfonso and Mother, Isabel had discarded the pretense of neutrality in her brothers' war to openly support Alfonso. Her freedom and honesty had then invigorated her, but she now realized her decision grew fraught with increasing uncertainty and peril.

Enrique had persuaded many noblemen to abandon Alfonso's rebellion, and Alfonso's supporters appeared to be losing enthusiasm. Castile's common subjects were weary of the conflict—they had been taxed to support troops of both her brothers, commerce had dwindled when townships became embattled, and vandals now roamed the countryside looting with impunity in the absence of royal authority. The Toledans had been the latest to defect to Enrique, and Archbishop Carrillo now urged that Alfonso promptly muster troops in Ávila to reverse this betrayal. She would ride to Ávila at Alfonso's side that morning, departing Arévalo more quickly than intended because of the onset of plague, with young and old succumbing around the town in recent weeks.

Before breakfast, Isabel entered Mother's chamber to find her wan and exhausted after a night of ghostly terror, having barely slept. They strolled hand in hand from the castle to the small church close by, set on a steep embankment overlooking a western river ravine that, together with an intersecting eastern river ravine, served as the town's principal defenses on three sides. The church had been converted from a mosque during the Reconquista and renamed in honor of St. Michael, the leader of the army of God who confronted Satan and threw him from Heaven. Isabel recalled her childhood fondness for the quiet repose and sanctuary she found within, well removed from the murmur of village life. She prayed with Mother for Alfonso's victory and safety, for salvation from the plague, and for Grandmother, who had died two years earlier.

Later that morning, Mother's Castilian and Portuguese staff served bread, honey, and ham, and Isabel bid Mother a tender, optimistic good-bye, sharing none of her doubts about Alfonso's success. While customary for women to ride mules, Isabel had enjoyed the speed and agility of a horse since youth, with Mother and Grandmother's approval, and she donned a prince's breeches beneath her dress and joined Alfonso and his guard in the castle plaza. They mounted to ride south, passing in single file through a narrow gate in the southern wall that completed the town's defenses, slowly entering a main street of the Jewish *aljama*.

As many Hispanic towns, Arévalo had significant Jewish and Mudejar quarters, and its homes were largely of Mudejar design, reflecting construction during the period of Islamic conquest. The street wound narrowly between houses of two and three stories and bustled with people working and shopping. Tailors, cobblers, blacksmiths, and merchants sold goods from their homes. Wash hung drying on cords strung above. Adults and children all stopped to watch the royal party pass, many leaning out of doorways and windows. Isabel smelled fires cooking lunch, almost as if she were inside their kitchens. She waved modestly with cheer and dignity to all she passed, regardless of her belief that the Jews were peoples of lesser stature. The riders crossed an open square, and Isabel sighted young mothers chatting, infants slung on their hips. The women waved their infants' hands, and Isabel smiled warmly and waved back. Men saluted and praised Alfonso. They understood the sovereign protected their community.

Within moments, the riders entered the street that divided the Jewish and Mudejar quarters. While the Jews and Mudejar dressed differently and had their own religious languages, they spoke the same speech in daily intercourse. Activity on either side of the street was the same. Merchants of both communities sold goods to buyers of both communities. The Mudejar women wore veils. Isabel continued to wave and smile. There were no Mudejar praises for Alfonso.

As she rode, Isabel recalled being taught as a girl in St. Michael's church of Christ's Second Coming. When the infidels were defeated and Jerusalem retaken, he would return to earth to sit as king of all men, and the world in its present form would be consumed in fire. The souls of all men, then living or dead, who believed in Christ would be united in bliss in a renewed world, purified by fire and glorified by Christ's presence. But the souls of men who didn't believe in Christ would burn in hell forever. The Jews and Mudejar could convert and be baptized, and they would be admitted to Heaven. But if they didn't, they would suffer this eternal damnation.

Isabel searched for the synagogue and mosque where these villagers worshipped. She couldn't discern the synagogue, but the mosque was clearly revealed by its diminutive minaret, and the riders rode directly past it. Isabel beheld it cautiously, apprehensive of the presence of the devil. But she confessed she could neither see nor feel evil. The Mudejar women simply were preparing lunch, babies also slung on their hips.

The riders progressed beyond Arévalo's outskirts, entering verdant fields of wheat and barley, and Isabel reflected that, on Christ's return, the Mudejar and other Mohammedans would receive their just punishment for denying him and conquering Hispania. But the thought of the Jewish mothers and babies burning disturbed her. She reflected on the awesome severity of the punishment and said a prayer that the mothers and babies convert.

At dusk, the small party arrived in the tiny village of Cardeñosa, nestled in a shallow valley in the grassland mesa some miles north of Ávila, and the patriarch of the village's leading family offered Alfonso and Isabel his home and beds for the night. The simple decency, loyalty, and adulation of this common man and his neighbors—farmers, herdsmen, and their womenfolk—touched Isabel. They rejoiced to meet Alfonso and herself. They did hold Alfonso to be their king and herself an important princess, and they looked to Alfonso to protect them—from hunger, disorder, and lawlessness—in return for that loyalty. That evening, their host and his brethren offered their finest meal and, after dining, she and Alfonso lodged in the stone cottage and quickly fell asleep, exhausted from the ride.

Isabel woke before dawn to roosters crowing, and their host provided breakfast and courtesies as they awaited the king's rising. The guard began to ready the horses. As the morning grew long, Isabel wondered at Alfonso's absence, and Carrillo became impatient and dispatched Alfonso's steward to wake him. The steward summoned others, and then Carrillo. A commotion ensued, and Isabel rushed to Alfonso's bedside to discover, in horror, that he remained motionless even after shaken. Carrillo implored her to leave immediately, fearing Alfonso stricken with plague, and a doctor was summoned urgently.

Isabel obeyed, stunned by the abrupt onset of Alfonso's illness and frightened his condition was grave.

The doctor arrived, found Alfonso's mouth black, and applied leeches over his body to bleed him. As the day passed, he neither regained consciousness nor died, but the dreaded corpuscles signaling the plague did not rise on his body. Some whispered it was poisoning, not pestilence. As night fell, Isabel cried to herself. She loved him, he was the only family she could rely on, and Enrique held her in rebellion. She prayed desperately for his survival. But he weakened through the night.

There was no improvement during the second day, and, by the third, Isabel recognized death was at hand. She wiped her tears and grimly acknowledged Castile was in chaos and that civil war had wronged most everyone. Fear, assault, and even rape and murder invaded daily life. Her hosts, and thousands of Castilians like them, simply longed for a ruler—whoever it might be—to provide law and order.

Isabel was shocked to perceive the Lord's design emerging from her brother's death. She and Alfonso had lived in close proximity and intimacy as brother and sister, but the Lord would take Alfonso's life and spare her own. Father's will provided she would rule after her brothers if they failed to produce a legitimate heir—and he would deny them such through impotency and death. His intent was unmistakable, and she recognized as never before that she yearned to be queen of Castile and should fight to achieve that with her utmost determination.

Upon Carrillo's advice, Isabel wrote noblemen and townships throughout the kingdom that King Alfonso was dying and that she was the sole and legitimate heir to Castile. Alfonso died on July 5, and Isabel retired with advisers to a monastery in Ávila to consider how she should become queen.

"You must succeed Alfonso immediately," advised Carillo. "Crown yourself as he did. Continue the contest to unseat Enrique."

"My lord, the odds of prevailing seem slim," she responded. "The few queens in our history have risen to the throne upon the deaths of their husbands—reigning kings. I'm a maiden."

"You need not be. King Juan of Aragón has offered Fernando in marriage if you pursue the rebellion."

"You shouldn't attempt to continue Alfonso's rebellion," others cautioned. "You'll never win. You're a woman alone, and Alfonso wouldn't have won anyway. You should strike a deal with Enrique instead, recognizing his rule so long as he recognizes you as his successor and disinherits the bastard Juana."

"But will Enrique honor the bargain?" Isabel asked. "Or will he wait for our loyalists to disband and then marry me outside the kingdom when there's no one left to object?"

Isabel had always followed Carrillo's advice, but she now felt confident to decide her actions alone as the Lord guided her, having witnessed years of court intrigue. She despaired that her advisers, supporters, and friends—together with her detractors, absolutely everyone!—denied her ability to make decisions as a ruler simply because she was a woman, regardless of her native acumen and accumulating experience. Few perceived or appreciated her ambition and resolve—traits admired in princes, not princesses.

Isabel reflected some weeks and then received word Brother Enrique desired a truce and would absolve her and others of treason. She shuddered to wage war against a brother duly anointed at their father's direction. Few to whom she had written had responded to offer support, and she recognized most of them doubted her ability to unseat Enrique and would, as a matter of political calculation, accept his amnesty. Rejecting Carrillo's advice, she authorized her advisers to negotiate a truce recognizing herself as Enrique's successor, perceiving it the surest route to achieve her ambition to rule as queen over a kingdom controlled through history by men.

To Isabel's delight, there were now rumors that Queen Juana had been unfaithful again and was pregnant, and Isabel's advisers worked tirelessly to ensure the rumors spread throughout the kingdom, casting further doubt on little Juana's legitimacy and building consensus that Isabel's succession could never be usurped. Isabel reflected that her own purity and abstinence, and her devotion, offered a clear alternative to the depravity of her brother's rule, and that she must adhere to and publicly display that purity and devotion always.

⊟   ⊟   ⊟

Fernando, prince of Aragón and king of Sicily, was in Catalonia leading his father's troops in battle against Catalan rebels and their French supporters when he received word of the death of

King Alfonso, whom he had never met. The rumor was that one of Alfonso's champions had poisoned him, secretly remaining loyal to Enrique. Fernando brooded that Alfonso had been forced to rely on insincere noblemen, lacking the father and mother's protection and tutelage that Fernando had enjoyed since birth.

At sixteen, Fernando was of modest height, with brown eyes, dark hair worn to the collar, and a nimble, athletic frame. His royal stature was forthrightly proclaimed by clothing of unsurpassed quality and elegance, including a bejeweled jerkin and fine leather boots, and a sword at his hip inherited from predecessor kings of Aragón. When but ten, he had been recognized by the Catalans as heir to Catalonia in one moment and then disclaimed the next, to be entrapped, besieged, and assaulted for weeks with Mother—Queen Juana Enríquez of Aragón—in Gerona's fortress deep within Catalonia. He had beheld the bloodshed, suffering, and deaths of their defenders, only to be rescued by then-allied French troops because Father—King Juan II of Aragón—did not have the wealth or army to rescue them himself.

Fernando had fought with Father and Mother since then to subjugate Catalonia, hunting, battling, incarcerating, and executing rebels against Father's rule, and learning many lessons, some rude or unpleasant. Alliances and pledges of allegiance couldn't be trusted. Retreat sometimes was the best course of action, regardless of humiliation. The glory of the Crown of Aragón and the righteousness of its causes themselves were not sufficient for military victory. Justice should be brutal, vindictive, and exemplary. Mother had died that winter, and Fernando now grimly understood the Catalan rebellion hadn't been crushed but had grown stronger. The rebels had elected the French king's surrogate as their ruler,* and, were the French to provide the rebels greater support, Catalonia could be lost and Aragón's interests in its Mediterranean possessions, including his Sicily, jeopardized. Aragón desperately needed an alliance with Castile to defend its interests.

As Isabel reposed in Ávila's monastery, Fernando speculated what she would decide. He had never met her either. She hadn't been

---

*René d'Anjou (René le Bon), who opposed Aragonese domination of Genoa and Catalonia, uncle of the French King Louis XI and father of Jean d'Anjou.

involved in any political or military action he knew of and appeared simply to be waiting for marriage. Would she name herself queen and seek a husband to fight and defeat Enrique? Father had offered himself to her in marriage many times, and now offered marriage and troops precisely to that end—regardless of the desperate need for troops in Catalonia. By mid-September, Father's spies and frequent communications with Archbishop Carrillo provided the disappointing answer.

As King Enrique and Isabel prepared to meet to seal their truce, Fernando met Father at Cardona in Catalonia to review their military situation and Castile. Fernando listened as Father intently revealed his next move, aware that Father—then seventy and close to blind— never gave up.

"Isabel has been weak or misinformed by her advisers," Father began. "Enrique will never honor the promise that she succeed him, and he'll rid her from Castile by arranging a marriage that takes her to live with a foreign prince. To become queen, Isabel needs a husband who lives in Castile and is fit to replace Enrique as king, either now or later. That's you." Juan studied his teenage son. "Isabel's supporters still need us, and they know it. Do you understand the marriage terms we must offer them to secure her hand?"

Fernando waited deferentially for Father to continue.

"Carrillo and the others will demand that we agree that she, you, and your children of her live in Castile. That's how she rules when she becomes queen and how Carrillo and the others derive their future power. They'll fear diminished influence if she moves to Aragón, and they won't tolerate rule from afar." Juan paused to gauge and invite his son's reaction.

"If—or may I say, when—I inherit Aragón, I'll need to rule it from afar."

Father pondered silently for a moment, and Fernando worried that Father perceived him as presumptuous.

"You'll also have to agree to recognize Enrique, just as Isabel intends," Father continued. "Thereafter, you'll have to tread carefully between obedience to Enrique and ensuring Isabel becomes queen. If she doesn't, you won't become king of Castile through her." Father slapped Fernando on the knee to emphasize the point.

"And assuming she does become queen, her Castilian supporters won't allow you the full power of a king in Castile. I don't
know what they'll demand in the marriage contract at this time,
but they'll want to retain through Isabel, and perhaps directly
themselves, constraints on your authority in Castile in favor of
their own."

"We could promise Carrillo and others important positions when
I rule," Fernando interjected.

"Which you will have to live with for some time, perhaps forever."
Juan frowned. "Perhaps not."

Fernando puzzled over whether he as husband would dominate
Isabel to eviscerate these constraints.

Juan was ahead of his son. "You'll dominate her as husband
to wife, but that wouldn't free you entirely from the noblemen's
constraints. Remember, now that young Alfonso has died, I and then
you have our own claim to the Castilian throne on Enrique's death—
as Enrique's closest living male heir.* This isn't the time to argue this
point—if we so much as mention it, the Castilian noblemen won't
marry her to you in the first place! But—remember this—the time to
assert it is on Enrique's death."

Father asked Fernando to embrace him, and they dined on
roasted wild boar.

In the morning, Fernando rode back to fight the rebellion. Before
departing, he knelt in filial obedience before Father, seated on the
Aragonese throne. Father made certain his son understood the
intended result of the marriage. "When you inherit Aragón, Aragón
will rule Castile from Castile."

◻ ◻ ◻

In September, Isabel met Enrique to agree upon the truce, relinquish-
ing her claims to the throne until Enrique's death in return for recognition as his successor. The truce terms provided that both Enrique's
and Isabel's consents would be required for her marriage. Enrique's
marriage to Queen Juana would be dissolved, and the queen and her
daughter sent back to Portugal. But, yet again, Enrique did not concede that little Juana was not his daughter.

---

*As descendants of Juan I of Castile.

Isabel went with Enrique's court to live in Ocaña and soon confessed to herself she had been wrong to trust her brother. Enrique failed to dispatch the queen and little Juana back to Portugal. He formulated terms for Isabel's marriage to Portugal's Afonso V, which Isabel rejected, but Afonso V sent representatives to Ocaña to negotiate the marriage, regardless.

Isabel had already grasped the singular merits of marriage to Fernando, and her informants had confirmed his valor. He was already a king, a general, and prince to the remainder of Hispania except Portugal. His throne and future thrones were of lesser wealth and power than her own rightful throne, so her own resources and power would exceed his. They were the same age, and he was well proportioned, healthy, and athletic. It was said he was devoted and worshipped daily, well spoken to whomever he addressed, and compassionate to those in need. He drank little. He also was experienced and potent in bed—there were two women who shortly would bear him children. Isabel was not shocked or dismayed. Most every bishop or prelate she knew, and every king or prince except Enrique, had fathered children outside wedlock. She knew she desperately needed not only a king to achieve the throne but a son to maintain it.

In November, Juan II dispatched his principal minister to Ocaña to seek Enrique's consent for Isabel's marriage to Fernando, knowing full well that it would be denied. The true purpose of the mission was to negotiate Isabel's marriage terms with Carrillo and other noblemen loyal to her. Isabel waited nervously alone as the minister conducted these negotiations secretly with her counselors at night, after excusing himself from court.

By February, the negotiations achieved marriage terms acceptable to Juan II and the Castilian nobility loyal to Isabel, which recognized Isabel as heir to Castile and by which Fernando made various capitulations. Fernando would obey King Enrique until his death. He would respect the Castilian bishops and nobility and their privileges, including Carrillo. He and any children from Isabel would live in Castile. Castilians alone would be appointed to office, and he would honor Isabel's choices. They would sign orders as prince and princess jointly. He would not conduct war in Castile or with his father without Isabel's consent, and, when he became king, he would prosecute the war against the infidels to reclaim the remainder of Hispania for Castile. Upon consummation of the marriage, Isabel would receive 100,000 gold florins and the revenues of various towns in Sicily and Aragón. Fernando himself would give Isabel his mother's ruby-and-pearl necklace worth 40,000 gold ducats and an additional 20,000 gold florins.

For their support and treason, a number of Isabel's counselors would receive titles to townships or public offices, as well as gold payments. Papal approval was required for the marriage because Fernando and Isabel were second cousins,* and the prelate who conferred the papal dispensation would receive, in addition to gold, a bishopric.

Isabel anguished that Fernando would find his capitulation demeaning and think she had chosen all its terms, which she had not. She wrote him a short note, responding to a note he had sent and her first communication to him. She ended the note indicating it came from the hand that would do that which Fernando ordered.

In March, Fernando received Isabel's note and the agreed capitulation, which he signed. Alfonso, his first known illegitimate son, had been born sometime before. Given the meager state of Aragón's treasury and the need to finance the Catalan war, the monetary payments were a steep burden. He studied the last sentence of her note carefully. Was it merely a feminine pleasantry? Was she indicating she would assume the traditional role of a queen as wife? Did she mean she didn't embrace his capitulation and would provide her own interpretation?

Fernando reflected that he knew nothing of Isabel's character. While his life had been led in battles and Cortes for all to see, hers had been close to invisible. He understood she was of medium height, with a cheerful face, pink cheeks, and blue-green eyes, plump and healthy, and that she was as proficient with a horse as any man. It was said she enjoyed the company of the devout, never drank, cared for the victims of brutality, and longed for the Reconquista's completion. But there was little else to indicate how she would rule as a queen.

Juan II also signed Fernando's capitulations but refused to make any monetary payments or forward his wife's necklace until he saw

---

*Sharing Juan I of Castile as their great-grandfather.

Isabel was truly committed, which he indicated meant she had to break from Enrique and leave Ocaña. Isabel anguished.

Enrique left Ocaña for Andalusia in May and, before departing, again asked Isabel to marry Afonso V. She again refused, exulting that her deception remained undiscovered and trembling that it remain so. Furious, he indicated that, on his return, he would arrange another marriage, but he forbade her leaving Ocaña or entering marriage commitments before then.

With trepidation, Isabel realized there were no compromises left to pursue with Enrique. One night, she prayed to the Lord, no longer for guidance, nor for blessing of just her treason, but for her very safety and, with two counselors, mounted on horseback and stole from Ocaña. She had never felt such fear or exhilaration. As they rode, and as her escape proved undetected, the Lord again revealed to her that he was with her. She went to live with her mother in Madrigal.

Enrique by then had sought her marriage to King Louis XI's brother, and threatened Madrigal's officials if they permitted Isabel to marry another. Juan II received word of Isabel's flight and dispatched the necklace and 20,000 gold florins. Isabel was charmed to wear the necklace, and she and Carrillo dispensed some of the florins to Madrigal's officials.

In August, Isabel entered Valladolid, safely within the territory of her supporters. Confident in prevailing, she publicly wrote Enrique explaining that she would marry Fernando, justifying her actions, and seeking his consent. Enrique did not respond and began to return north with troops. In October, disguised as a muleteer, Fernando and a few advisers stole from Aragón into Castile north of Valladolid, escaping entrapment by noblemen loyal to Enrique.

Isabel, then eighteen, and Fernando, then seventeen, met for the first time at about midnight on October 14 in the home of Juan de Vivero, the husband of Carrillo's niece. Carrillo was present with other counselors. Isabel's supporters advised that Fernando be required to kiss her hand in deference to her greater stature as heir to a greater throne. She rejected that as unfitting both a king and a husband.

Before Fernando was ushered in, Isabel's heart pounded with excitement and anticipation, having awaited this moment her entire life. She wanted to please Fernando, for him to love her, and for their marriage to be happy and blessed with at least a son. She also wanted him to respect her authority. She agonized how to balance the two desires. She was eager to see the man she would sleep and share her life with. She prayed that the meeting would go well and resolved to keep it personal, not involving sovereign matters. At this moment, those matters were for Carrillo.

Before he entered, Fernando felt a tension in his chest almost as keen as when he prepared for battle. He had won the hand of the princess of Castile. But he knew close to nothing of her, and he had wondered for months what the last sentence of her note really meant. He was anxious that he not appear proud, overbearing, or arrogant, but he feared acting in any way subservient or revealing the weakness of Aragón. He would not act learned or wise, for she may have been far better schooled. He would show his stature simply, for he was proven in battle, court, and the bedroom. He wanted her to love and obey him. He, too, resolved to avoid sovereign matters.

Carrillo ushered Fernando in and the teenagers met. They looked into each other's eyes for the first time, and, after a lifetime of frequently contemplated or proposed marriage, cheerfully greeted each other. With calmness and authority, Isabel asked Carrillo and advisers to sit apart as she spoke to Fernando, which had been his intent regardless. Fernando was confident to lead a dignified flirtation with any woman, and Isabel gaily acquiesced.

Two hours later, Fernando left. Isabel was enthralled with him and their rapport, which she judged genuine. She could not sleep. She thought he was handsome and was delighted she would share her bed with a husband her own age. As he rode away, Fernando was flush with accomplishment. She was charming, astute, clever, and worthy in every respect. He thought she was feminine and attractive. He could not yet determine the meaning of her note.

The wedding ceremonies and festivities lasted several days. When it came time to join them in marriage in Vivero's home, the papal dispensation of consanguinity had not been obtained. The pope had already granted one for Isabel's marriage to Alfonso V, and Enrique had warned him not to approve another for marriage to Fernando. Archbishop Carrillo falsely proclaimed the dispensation in hand and married them regardless. Isabel's supporters were jubilant. Then followed an afternoon and evening of music, dance, jousting, and other celebration, soaked with wine and other spirits.

As the evening wore on, Fernando and Isabel went to the bridal chamber on a floor above the raucous revelers and, with witnesses at the chamber door, Fernando and Isabel consummated their marriage as the revelers cheerfully waited. Fernando then gave the blood-stained sheets to the witnesses, who displayed them to the revelers—who offered thunderous applause above the blare of trumpets and pound of kettledrums.

III
1470S, ASCENSION

CRISTOFORO
Scio (Chios, Greece), (1470–1474)

At dawn in May 1474, two ships bound for Scio slipped slowly from Savona's harbor into the Ligurian Sea some twenty-five miles west of Genoa, a warship and a merchant vessel bearing carpenters, weavers, and traders. A scion of Genoa's Spinola merchant family commanded each vessel. Cristoforo stood on the deck of the merchant ship, enlisted as a common seaman and assistant to a Spinola trader. Near twenty years old, Cristoforo had grown tall, sturdy, and handsome, retaining his red hair and pinkish complexion. Years before, Domenico had enrolled him in the small grammar school run by the Genoa wool weavers' guild, and he knew to read, write, and draw, as well as arithmetic and a little Latin, the language of the scriptures and their ancient heritage.

After conquering Constantinople, Mehmed II had spared the Genoese colonies at Scio and Lesbos in return for receiving annual tributes, as well as the Venetian colony at the Negroponte (Euboea). He had since subjugated Lesbos (1462) and, irked by continued foreign presences within his Aegean empire, in 1470 he had directed a substantial expansion of his fleet and invaded and subjugated the Negroponte. The Sciots had dutifully sent caulkers to assist the fleet expansion. But, with the specter of their own subjugation looming, they also prepared to defend themselves, petitioning the pope and the Genoese for assistance.

The Spinolas and other Genoese merchants were roused by the appeal and bent on expanding their trade with Scio, rather than forsaking it. Scio served as the world's principal source of mastic and a key source of Genoa's slave trade. The Genoese sold mastic gum, harvested from Scion mastic trees, to Christians and infidels through-out the Mediterranean and Europe for use as a digestive medicine, cure for rheumatism, and breath freshener or perfume for the women of their courts and harems. Year-round, Mehmed's armies sold war captives—of any people, skin color, or religion—in the large slave market in Scio, and the Genoese resold them to purchasers—of any people, skin color, or religion—throughout the Mediterranean.

Cristoforo waved farewell to Domenico, who stood on the quay, having relocated to Savona some years before with the family, now seven—with two more surviving sons, Bartolomeo (b. ca. 1461) and Giacomo, and a daughter, Bianchinetta. His weaving business hadn't met their budget in Genoa. Collectives and factories of weavers in Milan and other foreign principalities produced finer-quality cloth at lower prices, and Domenico had worked longer hours to produce more cloth only to earn less. He had started an additional business as a cheesemonger. He also sold wine and recently had opened a tavern. Cristoforo had assisted him dutifully, sailing as a passenger on small boats along the coast of the Ligurian Sea to inspect, purchase, and retrieve shipments of raw wool, cheese, and wine.

Cristoforo now carded wool and often referred to himself as a wool merchant. He hadn't apprenticed to become a weaver when attaining the age permitted by the guild. Whether disappointed by this or not, Domenico understood from the merchants to whom he introduced Cristoforo that his son was courteous, well spoken, and affable, possessing the aptitude to become a trader.

As the ship gained speed, the captain laid a sheepskin chart of the Mediterranean on his table and, together with his pilot, began to navi-gate the route to Scio, more than twelve hundred miles distant. They set the compass coordinate for sailing the first half hour, measured by the run of an ampolleta (a sand clock), and, when the sand had run, reckoned the distance traveled in light of the shoreline or their sense of the ship's speed and entered the ship's estimated position in the ship's log. A ship's boy promptly turned the ampolleta and called a prayer or psalm for all to hear, and the captain or pilot adjusted the compass course for the next half hour. The process and prayers would continue day and night, every half hour, until they anchored safely at Scio.

Cristoforo had learned the mechanics of sailing—how to catch the wind, tack, run against or with the wave—when retrieving Domenico's shipments on smaller boats, and he was ready and eager to do whatever was now commanded, be it raising, trimming, or reefing the sails, bailing the bilge, or washing the deck. He was assigned a shift for the entire voyage, each of the crew's two shifts working four hours and then resting four except for two two-hour slots that allowed the shifts to exchange time slots every twenty-four hours. They would sleep in their clothes and all would be summoned to duty when necessary if the sea grew rough. The captain would lead a prayer to the Virgin every dawn seeking her protection for the upcoming day. Every evening before sunset, the crew would sing "Salve Regina" or another hymn seeking her protection through the night.

The ships sailed the coast south beyond Rome, and Cristoforo eagerly embraced the new and unknown. He had ventured beyond the Ligurian Sea but once, and the experience had taught him more about captains and crews than distant seas. Father's loyalty to Genoa's Fregoso family had assisted Cristoforo's enlistment on a warship their ally* dispatched to capture another warship off Tunis. Most of the crew had succumbed to fear while off Sardinia and refused the chase, demanding reinforcements before they continued. But the mission leader had continued south toward Tunis regardless, deceiving the crew at night with Cristoforo's assistance by misaligning the ship's compass to feign that the ship was sailing north. At dawn, the crew was stunned to behold Cape Carthage on the horizon. Cristoforo had learned crews did expect—short of mutiny—the right to disapprove a course they felt jeopardized their safety and that a captain's deception was a means for managing them.

----

*René d' Anjou.

As they approached Sicily, Cristoforo gazed across the starboard rail to the western horizon, far beyond which lay the Pillars of Hercules* and the Sea of Darkness. He recalled learning, as every Genoese child, that long ago the city's Doria merchant family had sponsored the Vivaldi brothers to sail to the Indies and Cathay to trade for gold and spices.[†] Marco Polo, the legendary Venetian, already had ridden there overland,[‡] but the route was arduous and required passage through kingdoms of the infidel, which the Dorias sought to avoid. Sadly, after sailing beyond the Pillars, the Vivaldis were never heard from again, and the Genoese still debated why. Ever practical, Domenico always said their ships likely foundered in a storm or on unseen shoals. Others claimed the ocean boiled and the air burned their skin when they turned south along Africa's coast, as it was so hot there that people had to lie in streams up to their necks during the day to survive. A few concluded the crews were eaten by people, landing on an island where the men had heads like dogs, ate snakes, and hissed like them. As many, Cristoforo wondered whether the Vivaldis had survived and reached the Indies after all, but just couldn't get back because the winds or currents were too contrary.

Cristoforo's excitement grew when the ships navigated the Straits of Messina between Sicily and the mainland, and he observed the captain and pilot plotting the course across the Ioanian Sea, reckoning to achieve Cape Matapan at Greece's southern tip. He overheard the pilot expound to officers of the watch where the winds blew from or to shore, how the sun's heat affected the wind's strength, and when the Lord caused storms. He befriended the pilot and sought his wisdom, learning that seamen tempt disaster if they proceed when the weather is uncertain. The ships encountered strong winds in the Ioanian Sea and were buffeted by waves more severely than Cristoforo had experienced. At dusk, he sang the "Salve Regina" with greater conviction than before.

The expedition passed Cape Matapan, traversed the Laconian gulf, veered north past Aristotle's, Alexander's, and now Mehmed's Athens, and sighted Cape Sounion, where Cristoforo beheld the

---

*The promontories of the Rock of Gibraltar and Jebel Musa, Morocco.
†The voyage of Ugolino and Vadino de Vivaldi, financed by Tedisio Doria, 1291.
‡Marco Polo's journey to and residence at the court of Khubilai Khan, 1271–1295.

Temple of Poseidon high atop its cliffs. He understood Poseidon to be but a false god of the ancients and that it was the Lord who moved the sea—not a god of the sea itself. But he allowed there was logic to the ancients' pagan worship given the sea's awesome ferocity. The expedition veered east to Scio, and he listened to the captain recount stories of sailing the Aegean as a boy, anchoring at Patmos where St. John the Evangelist wrote the Apocalypse, at Patera where St. Nicholas—the sailors' patron saint—was born, at Cos where Hippocrates had lived, and, of course, at Scio, which claimed itself as Homer's birthplace. Cristoforo marveled that he sailed in lands of prophets, saints, and ancient heroes.

The expedition warily skirted the crags of Scio's Cape Mastika and turned north. A sailor in the crow's nest spied alertly for reefs and a sounding lead was held ready on the bow if the ship entered shallows. They arrived off the town of Scio after dusk and anchored close offshore, to be quarantined. Cristoforo gazed a few miles east to the dark shores of the infidel's Anatolia and then west into the island's small port, which was chained shut for the night. High stone walls encircled the town, once built to defend the Sciots from pirates and raiders, be they Christian, heathen, or Mohammedan, and now serving in defense against Mehmed II. Torches burned atop the walls, a breeze bore the scent of mastic, and the dark contour of Scio's mountains undulated north and south into the distance beneath starry heavens.

The next two mornings, a customs official rowed alongside to inquire about illnesses among the crew, and the captains reported they were aware of none and that the crews were Savonans and Genoese, whereupon the ships were permitted to berth in the harbor and enthusiastically met by Scio's leading citizens. After unloading the cargos, the crews were released for rest.

Cristoforo strolled through the thick city wall at a narrow archway by the port and wandered into the town's central bazaar, which teemed with peoples of many principalities, with skin and clothing of many colors. Mohammedans from Africa, Turks from Anatolia, Tartars from the Crimea, and Christians, Jews, and Mohammedans from the Holy Land bargained with one another to trade foods and wares arriving from ports throughout the Mediterranean and Black

Sea. There were Genoese and others who spoke Ligurian, and there were numerous other tongues, including some Cristoforo did not recognize. The scent of mastic, the sounds of music, and the babel of scattered peoples filled the air.

He came to a narrow alley of brothels serving the harbor and spied crewmates but did not join them, expecting to be offered women later, when assisting the merchants. Instead, he found a small basilica dedicated to St. Nicholas and entered to thank the Virgin for the safe passage from Savona.

He continued outside the city wall to the unprotected village and entered a slave market, far larger than he had ever beheld, and was stunned. Rows and rows of vanquished peoples—Greeks, Bulgars, Bosnians, and Serbs from the west, and Tartars and Circassians from the north and east—were shackled in chains, awaiting their fate. The stench of vomit, urine, and excrement smothered the scent of mastic. A pall of terror and despair engulfed them, their voices mute but for the wail of women and infants and the anguished murmurs of prayers or disbelief. Cristoforo was unnerved to recognize pleas to his own God and Virgin. He beheld families huddled wretchedly together, with fathers, mothers, brothers, and sisters like his own, and he shuddered to imagine Domenico, Susanna, and his siblings—and himself—so vanquished.

Cristoforo was overpowered by the recognition that there was no essential difference between these conquered people—commoners—and himself. But he admitted to himself that he would have enlisted on the voyage to Scio even had he known these peoples were to be the return cargo instead of mastic. He studied a delegation of Genoese traders negotiate a price with Turkish slave masters, puzzling what the amount was and how it compared with the resale price achievable in Genoa.

The next day, the Spinola traders, Cristoforo, and their hosts mounted horses and mules and rode south under a blazing Aegean sun, ascending into orchards of nut trees on arid hillsides. They halted to pray and rest at the oasis of a small church nestled in the shade of tall pines beside a gushing mountain spring.* Both regenerated and refreshed, they wended southwest into the parched mountains

*Perhaps Panagia Krina, Madonna of the Fountain.

and valleys where the mastic flourished, arriving by dusk at a village fortified with thick stone walls near Scio's southern shore but invisible from the sea and enemies afloat. That evening, the hosts served a banquet of fish, rice, vegetables, sweets, and nuts and boasted of the profits that could be obtained by selling mastic in the northern principalities of Europe. They offered a girl to each visitor, purchased at the slave market to serve as chambermaids, washerwomen, and gifts for trading partners.

Cristoforo's girl led him through a narrow, stone alley barely lit along the city wall to a tiny chamber and bid him enter as she undressed. She spoke a few words of Ligurian, learned from previous traders, and dutifully invited Cristoforo to her. He wondered from where she came, how old she was then and when taken from her parents, whether she had brothers who missed her, and the price she had commanded in the slave market. But he quickly remembered she was one piece of the trade, and he welcomed his lust to drown his thoughts and enjoyed his gift.

As the Spinolas pursued their Sciot mastic venture, Mehmed ordered his fleet to subjugate the Genoese colony on the Black Sea at Kaffa, whose trade had already been eviscerated by his control of the Bosporus. Kaffa had served as a principal trading post for obtaining goods from the courts of the Grand Khan of Cathay, including pepper and other spices that were important for preserving, curing, and flavoring meats from rapid spoliation, and it surrendered quickly (1475).

As he discovered the Orient, Cristoforo ceased referring to himself merely as a wool merchant. He came to perceive a larger world in which to seek a greater fortune. The narrow boundaries of the Ligurian Sea vanished into the greater Mediterranean, and to even beyond. The large ships, varied cargos, and lengthy voyage of an organized expedition invigorated him, and he lost any desire to return to Domenico's wool, wine, and cheese business. He was captivated by the adventure of exotic lands in hostile territory, filled with diverse peoples speaking strange languages. He saw for himself that the Dorias' attempt to sail to the Indies was born not of fancy, but to achieve a solution to a merchant's problem. He grasped, as he never had before, the primacy and imperative in life of being the conqueror.

Chios, by Cristoforo Buondelmonti, ca. 1465–1475.

ISABEL
Disorder and Hatred in Castile, 1470–1474

Isabel and Fernando quickly became young lovers, infatuated with
each other's company, and within months, she was pregnant. The

labor pains began one midnight in October 1470, and midwives and witnesses were summoned.

Isabel was frightened but ready, having prayed for a healthy son for months. As the contractions strengthened, she beseeched the Lord for the mercy of a quick delivery. Yet the Lord obliged neither.

Labor was protracted, and, as the pain grew terrible, she asked for a veil to hide her face and struggle. After sunrise, she moved to squat on a birthing stool, terrified that death could claim both her and the child, but firm in her faith that the Lord would not allow it. Fernando and his advisers grew alarmed, and Fernando prayed gravely. He cared for her, and his future succession to Castile's throne through her would be abrogated if she and the child perished.

Finally, before noon in Dueñas north of Valladolid, Isabel gave birth to a girl, whom she and Fernando named Isabel, honoring the maternal lineage from Grandmother. They were disappointed with the sex, but Fernando was immensely relieved and supportive, content to know his wife healthy and fertile and his right to Castile's crown intact. That night, as she cradled her precious firstborn to her nipple, Isabel whispered she would love and stand with her always—regardless of what men thought.

Enrique openly celebrated. He disinherited Isabel for marrying without his consent, obtained a papal dispensation absolving the nobility from prior oaths recognizing her as heir, and, together with Queen Juana, swore to little Juana's legitimacy before Castilian nobility in Segovia's great cathedral. Castile again descended into lawlessness and anarchy as the opposing factions disputed succession.

Isabel and Fernando did not challenge Enrique's right to be king, as Alfonso had, but sought support for Isabel's succession, a struggle that deeply fortified their partnership. A new pope, the Ligurian Sixtus IV, affirmed the legality of their marriage. Isabel impressed the nobility with her Castilian virtue, in striking contrast to her brother. Fernando assisted his father in crushing the Catalan rebellion, and his military stature grew. The Valencian Cardinal Rodrigo Borja, vice-chancellor of the church in the Vatican, convinced Castile's bishops and nobility that Isabel should succeed Enrique, and, in return for his support, Enrique's longtime defender Pedro González de Mendoza was appointed Cardinal de Santa María and known as the Cardinal of Spain. Queen Juana openly lived with another man, eventually bearing him two children, and support for little Juana evaporated.

Isabel did suffer disappointments. As for her husband, Fernando simply frolicked with other women when absent from court, including mistresses in Aragón, and it was almost unbearable to embrace and love him at times, knowing her own intimacy meant so little to him that he readily found satisfaction with scores of others. She swelled with bitterness and jealousy often, ceaselessly studying his expression as he eyed the women who occasioned court—many more attractive than herself—and scrutinizing whether their smiles in return revealed a flirtation, or worse.

As for her kingdom, religious contempt that simmered beneath the veneer of everyday life ominously boiled into violence. In Córdoba, a brotherhood was established to unite "old Christians"— pure Christians, having clean blood, it claimed—against conversos. A blacksmith led it, and he vehemently warned that the conversos sought to secure the best royal and noble offices to usurp control of the kingdom. He harangued that the conversos' conversions were insincere, motivated by the avarice and opportunism that flowed in their Jewish blood, and that they could never become true Christians because their blood would lead them forever to practice Jewish rituals and customs. His brotherhood marched through converso neighborhoods, bearing a statue of the Virgin and seeking to intimidate the residents, and violence eventually erupted when urine allegedly was thrown on the statue. The blacksmith ordered his followers to set fire to converso homes, and fighting and rioting grew to engulf the neighborhood. After the blacksmith was mortally wounded, it spread throughout the entire city. Old Christians ransacked converso houses and shops, raped women and girls, and massacred as many conversos as possible.

Isabel heard reports of the riots, including of women and girls raped and murdered, and was revolted. She was surprised that Enrique, who as king remained responsible for law and order, prosecuted no one. She saw that his inaction emboldened the anti-conversos in Andalusia, where shortly similar riots occurred in Jaén and Seville.

Isabel and Fernando visited Enrique in Segovia over the New Year's celebrations commencing 1474, and Fernando met Enrique for the first time. They feasted and danced, and Enrique publicly acknowledged his love for her and respect for Fernando, as if she would succeed him. But he refrained from recognizing her as successor.

When in Segovia, Isabel summoned Cardinal Mendoza, more than three decades her senior. He and his wealthy, landed family had supported Enrique and sheltered little Juana for over a decade. Yet he now supported her succession, and, when the two met, he explained that the king—or a queen—is meant to rule with absolute authority, whether a good king or not, without dissent from the nobility. Isabel agreed and assured him her first priority and unequivocal passion, when crowned, would be to impose her authority on the nobility and restore law and order in everyday life.

Isabel also summoned Fray Tomás de Torquemada. Years earlier, he occasionally had served as her confessor, and she asked him what he thought of Córdoba, whether the king should have punished the murders and rapists. He replied that the riots that occurred were the consequence of the king's tolerance of heresy, conversos, and Jews over his entire reign and that God meant for heretics and Jews to be punished. Isabel pondered Torquemada's compassion, and a vision of the mothers and babies in Arévalo's aljama flickered through her thoughts. She knew that Christ wouldn't have countenanced murderers or rapists. She realized that Torquemada would want her to be more severe with the conversos and Jews than she then wished.

As their meeting ended, Isabel asked Fray Torquemada to serve as her confessor that day, and they retired to the alcazar's chapel. As she was royalty, he also knelt when Isabel knelt before him. She had grown circumspect on what she now confessed and to whom, and she did not confess whether she wished Enrique's death or knew with certainty that Enrique was not little Juana's father. She confessed that she had danced at the New Year's celebrations.

As the friar left, Isabel determined to seek another confessor.

Guarionex
Cacibaquel's Cohaba Ceremony

Guarionex sat in a grove of fruit trees listening to his father, Cacib-aquel, and two of Cacibaquel's oldest friends, the village behique and the cacique Guamanacoel, pass the afternoon discussing any-thing that came to mind. Father gradually had delegated Guarionex responsibility for the daily administration of Magua, and, with the day's work done, Guarionex relaxed, content to catch the conversa-tion but not participate. The trees shaded them from the afternoon sun, and the talk wandered between the tribal and the personal, as well as the practical and the philosophical, a serious but informal union punctuated with occasional humor reflecting the three older men's long friendship.

Guarionex gazed at Father and reflected that he had aged. He was neither frail nor infirm, and his wit and perception remained keen. But he had grown slender, almost gaunt, and he spoke and walked slowly as the elderly man he now was. Father's delegation to Guarionex of routine duties had been and remained Father's choice, yet it was a wise choice because Guarionex had the ability, patience, and desire to perform them, and Father no longer really did. Father frequently directed conversation to the spiritual as opposed to the practical, focusing on larger meanings and, perhaps, anticipating his soul's next journey. To Guarionex's amusement, he did so now, directing the discussion to the explanation of the origin of the sea, and his two friends eagerly followed.

"I remember watching it taught to grandchildren," the behique said. "Youngsters can't imagine killing their fathers. Teenage boys aren't at all surprised. Teenage girls see it as a story about their broth-ers, not themselves."

"The guidance to our boys is obvious," Cacibaquel noted. "Death follows rebellion. Stealing is wrong. Learning proper conduct heals. Bones of the dead are food for the living. My son, what do you think?"

Guarionex was caught off guard by the request to participate but not the question itself. He had pondered the explanation many times, seeking its guidance on proper conduct. Yaya, the supreme spirit to whom all others answered, had learned that his son Yayael rebelled and plotted Yaya's death. So Yaya smote Yayael first, and placed his bones in a gourd to remember him. When Yayael's mother opened the gourd to visit her son, the bones had turned to fish and she planned to eat them with Yaya. But the boy Deminán Caracaracol and his brothers came to steal the fish because they were hungry. Deminán had been born in adversity, with syphilis, and dropped the gourd in fear of Yaya's return. It shattered, releasing a great flood on the earth, creating the sea and the fish in it and sweeping the boys away. Deminán and the boys grew hungry again and asked another man for food but offered him nothing in return. The man was insulted and spat on Deminán, who grew sick, almost to death. Eventually, Deminán overcame the adversity of his birth and his misfortunes. He learned proper reciprocal conduct and built his home and prospered and his sicknesses healed.

"For me, I understand from it that it's best to avoid confrontation when possible, to solve matters by reciprocating courtesy and compromise," Guarionex replied. "One must be industrious and productive and make one's own opportunities for oneself and for all, both giving to and receiving from others."

The older men agreed and debated it further, and Guarionex was glad to be released from the conversation. As the afternoon waned, Cacibaquel proposed hosting a cohaba ceremony to honor Yúcahu for the cacicazgo's tranquility and seek guidance for future prosperity. As the older men discussed this, Guarionex excused himself, knowing they would enthusiastically arrange the ceremony themselves.

It was an honor for a subordinate cacique to be invited, and, when the time came, each arrived with his own display of power and authority. Some were born on litters, others arrived with splendid gifts, and a few entered with an escort of warriors. They did not bring wives. Cacibaquel offered bohíos for accommodation, whereupon they remained celibate and fasted for seven days.

Guarionex was invited to participate, and, as the ceremony commenced, he watched Father place his cemí of Yúcahu on the cohaba table and praise him, honoring him for years of bountiful yuca crops and protection from Magua's enemies—the Caribes and other Haitian caciques who harbored ambition for Maguan territory.

Father inhaled the cohaba powder through his nostrils using a hollowed stick shaped like a Y and sat down, gazing sideways at the earth. Soon, the hallucinogen overcame him, his eyelids drooping and his arms and legs relaxing limply. One by one the caciques, the behique, and Guarionex inhaled the cohaba.

Guarionex felt a rush, as if thousands of tiny bubbles were streaming through his limbs and head, and then pleasant contortions, as if waves were rising and ebbing through his entire body. He could see Father and the others, but he sensed time and space suspended about them, and he slumped on his duho to await the spirits.

Father stood and gazed upward toward the heavens, addressing and imploring Yúcahu in a murmur, and frequently an occasional wild cry, that Guarionex did not understand, posing questions to Yúcahu and receiving replies. One of the behique's assistants sometimes portrayed the replies, uttering through a long, hollow blowpipe that extended from behind the cohaba table through the bohío's wall to the assistant sitting outside. Guarionex could not judge the time passing. Father eventually addressed the assembled caciques and recounted what he had learned from Yúcahu in a voice they could understand. Guarionex would remember Father's words that moment for the rest of his life.

"Yúcahu has told me that those who remain alive after my death will rule for a brief time before a clothed people arrive to overcome them and kill them, and they will die of hunger."

Guarionex and the caciques were stunned. It wasn't a warning to prepare for an unknown enemy. It appeared a prediction of what would occur.

The caciques thanked Father for this sacred communication but sought explanation. Father replied that Yúcahu had divulged no more and revealed simply what Father had related. The caciques questioned what Yúcahu meant for them to understand and whether Father's literal interpretation was correct.

"Is this a prediction for Magua or for all of Haiti?"

"Or all peoples emerging from the Cacibajugua?"

"Do these clothed people kill us all or do we starve? With all respect, Cacibaquel, this revelation seems unclear or ambiguous—or misunderstood."

The caciques asked Father to consult Yúcahu again, to seek clarification and meaning, which he did—several times. But Father indicated that the subsequent communications simply confirmed the first, no more, no less. The caciques remained incredulous and ceased puzzling the meaning to challenge whether Father's revelation was even valid.

"None of our spirits have ever warned of this. Why now? What has changed? I know of nothing."

"The clothed peoples on the western and southern shores harbor no ambition for our land! We trade peacefully with them. Who can these people be?"

After what Guarionex perceived as a very long time, Cacibaquel concluded the ceremony, and the caciques retired to their bohíos in the moonlight, annoyed that Father's revelation had been incomplete or confused.

In the morning, Guarionex woke to find that Father had returned to the ceremonial bohío. Guarionex grew anxious. It was not his place to criticize Father or the ceremony, even privately, but he was entitled to question the revelation's meaning. He strode to the ceremonial bohío, where Father sat on a duho, alone, wan, and vanquished. Guarionex sat down next to him and spoke softly.

"Father, permit me a question about your communication with Yúcahu. If I succeed you as cacique, what do I do with it? How do I act upon it?"

Cacibaquel stared at the ground, pondering, and they sat in silence a few moments.

Guarionex continued. "If it was a warning, as opposed to a prediction, then I could direct our people to prepare to defend themselves. But if it was a prediction, was Yúcahu clear that everyone would die—or were some to survive, giving all a reason to defend themselves?"

"Yúcahu gave me no guidance on how to respond to this enemy," Cacibaquel responded softly. "When you succeed me, you may decide to do with these clothed people what we could do with any enemy—either fight for victory, including their total annihilation, or negotiate a truce or compromise. There was no suggestion of simply succumbing, none. That would be unthinkable." Cacibaquel recalled his son's conception of Deminán. "Deminán's civility, generosity, and willingness to compromise are not boundless. He understands to go to war for his people."

"I understand."

Cacibaquel reflected further. "More fundamentally, Yúcahu spoke to me. When you are cacique, you may ask Yúcahu these questions yourself, and he may answer you—perhaps differently. Other caciques certainly will seek their own advice." He pondered a moment. "Yúcahu's communication to me was clear."

"Father, the Caribes don't wear clothes. The peoples we trade with on the distant southern and western shores* do wear clothes, and some have far superior military strength. But we haven't suffered attacks from them before, and they would have to come very far with multitudes of men to launch an attack. The Caribes steal a few women from Haiti every year, but they don't come to conquer, and the logistics of such a conquest of Magua, no less Haiti, seem insurmountable. I see no practical risk regarding this prediction."

"Nor do I. I, too, was surprised by it. But the reason we ask for Yúcahu's guidance is precisely because of the want of men's vision."

"I understand. I intend to ask these questions of Yúcahu myself at the appropriate time. We must continue to be mindful of Caribe attacks and help other caciques directly affected to repel them. We must be watchful of the clothed peoples to the south and west when we trade for guanín and other goods with them. That will be our policy." Guarionex sat in silence with Father for a few moments longer and then excused himself.

⊡   ⊡   ⊡

Within a few seasons, Cacibaquel grew infirm and died, and, as he had wished, Guarionex succeeded him as cacique of Magua. The principal caciqual families of Haiti attended the funeral and recognized Guarionex's accession. Guarionex eulogized his father eloquently, praising his spirituality, wisdom, and bravery, and commending that peace reigned when Haiti's caciques possessed such virtues. The audience included a young Guacanagarí, attending with his uncle, and Caonabó, representing with cousins their uncle who was too elderly

---
*Central and South America.

to make the journey across the Cibao. All appreciated the sentiments expressed, and none, except Guarionex, gave a passing thought to Cacibaquel's strange cohaba revelation.

Deminán Caracaracol.

KING AFONSO V AND PRINCE JOÃO OF PORTUGAL
Ptolemy, Toscanelli, and Marco Polo, 1474

Following Prince Henrique's death in 1460, King Afonso V continued to dispatch mariners in the quest to circumnavigate Guinea beyond the points achieved by Ca' da Mosto to reach the Indies and locate the Christian kingdom of the Prester John. The mariners soon discovered that the Guinean coast rounded to the east and Afonso and his counselors rejoiced. A mariner also set up a trading post on Guinea's southern shore at Samma (Shama,

Ghana),* where African traders brought gold panned and mined inland to the sea.

By 1473, voyages crossed the equator for the first time,† and Afonso believed his ships had progressed east beyond the longitude of Tunis and, perhaps, even Alexandria. However, the mariners also reported that the Guinean coast turned sharply southward. By 1474, the mariners had traveled more than three hundred miles south from the bend in the African coastline (at Bioko, Equatorial Guinea), and the coast was not reverting east toward the Indies. The feasibility of the Guinean route to the Indies remained unproven.

Court cosmographers and geographers recognized that the mariners' reports of Guinea challenged and refuted the established wisdom of Aristotle and St. Augustine. Aristotle's warning that the equatorial zone was uninhabitable was plainly false. Thousands and perhaps millions of people inhabited the earth below the Saharan desert, including at the equator. Trees, vegetation, beasts, and man thrived in the humid heat—which was not unbearable. St. Augustine's warning that the southern portions of the globe were covered with water was equally false, as the continuing southern projection of the Guinean coastline demonstrated.

But Ptolemy remained revered. He had taught that the inhabited land of the earth known in his day covered only a quarter of the earth's surface. He believed this known portion stretched largely in the northern hemisphere east from the Canary Islands halfway round the earth to Sēra (perhaps Luoyang, central China) and Kattigara (perhaps Indonesia, southern Vietnam, or southern China) in the Indies, as well as from Thule (Iceland) in the north to somewhat below the equator in Libya (Africa). The Ocean Sea covered the remainder of the Northern Hemisphere, stretching west from Cape St. Vincent and the Canary Islands halfway round the earth to the Indies without interruption save islands. The rest of the world was unknown. He had estimated the circumference of the earth at the equator to be about 20,700 miles, implying an uninterrupted sailing distance at Lisbon's latitude from Lisbon west to the eastern most point of the Indies known to him of more than 8,000 miles.

---

*Fernáo Gomes.
†Fernandes, Esteves, and Po.

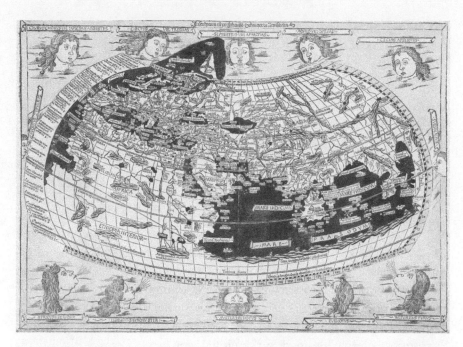

Ptolemy's world map in his second projection. Ulm edition of 1482.

With the Guinean coast stretching southward rather than east to the Indies, Afonso and his counselors grew receptive to reconsidering whether the Ptolemaic calculation of the breadth of the Ocean Sea was exaggerated and sailing directly across it to the Indies was feasible. Afonso learned from a cleric in his court that a reputed Florentine physician Paolo del Pozzo Toscanelli believed exactly that. At Afonso's instruction, the cleric wrote Toscanelli for an explanation.

By training a physician, Toscanelli had devoted much of his life to studying astronomy, mathematics, and geography, including writing a text designed to modernize Ptolemy's geographical conclusions.[*] He had also participated in his family's trading business, which, prior to Mehmed II's conquest of Constantinople, imported pepper and other spices sourced from the Indies at Kaffa on the Black Sea. He had studied—as both a geographer and merchant—Marco Polo's account of his lengthy overland journey from Venice to the court of Khubilai Khan near Cambalu (Beijing) in the province Cathay and Marco's

---

[*]Lost to history.

identification of an island named Cipangu (Japan) lying 1,500 miles offshore east of the Indies. Toscanelli believed the lands in the Indies described by Marco Polo constituted an eastward extension of land beyond Ptolemy's Sēra and Kattigara measuring almost a sixth of the earth's surface, thereby substantially lengthening the extent of the Indies across the Northern Hemisphere beyond that known by Ptolemy and likewise shortening the sailing distance across the Ocean Sea from Portugal to the Indies. The existence of Cipangu off the Indies' eastern coast further shortened that sailing distance.

In June 1474, Toscanelli responded to the cleric with a letter and chart,* extolling the riches of the Indies and the possibility of sailing westward to them. The chart dramatically challenged the Ptolemaic conception of the breadth of the Ocean Sea, reflecting an uninterrupted open sea sailing distance from Lisbon to Quinsay of less than 6,000 miles, much shorter than the Ptolemaic calculation. Astoundingly, it indicated that the journey might be broken by harboring at Antillia—the lost island in the Ocean Sea to which it was said Portuguese clerics had fled in the eighth century to escape the invading Mohammedans—and Cipangu, making the longest landfall to landfall distance less than 3,500 miles.

Afonso and his advisers reviewed the letter and map and found Toscanelli's reliance on Marco Polo inappropriate and the conclusion incredible and not worthy of superseding Ptolemy. As virtually all learned men, they believed Marco a charlatan and self-promoter. His account teemed with stories of kingdoms of fabulous riches and sophistication; brutal tortures and conquests; exotic customs, enormous harems, and sensual concubines; liberal tolerance of multiple religions; and peoples who ate human flesh. It also frequently glorified Marco's own stature at Khubilai's court.

To Afonso's gratification, the exploration of the Guinean coast also was proving a tremendous success irrespective of achieving the Indies. By the end of 1474, substantial quantities of gold were being obtained at Samma, augmenting the Crown's prestige and military strength. Afonso appointed his son Prince João, then nineteen, to administer the overseas expansion in Guinea, giving particular attention to the importation of gold.

---

*The latter lost to history.

Regardless of the breadth of the Ocean Sea, Afonso, João and their advisers, as Toscanelli himself, continued to share with Aristotle, St. Augustine, and Ptolemy—and most everyone living on terra firma—an unequivocal belief in the following fact: the Ocean Sea stretched from Europe to the Indies.

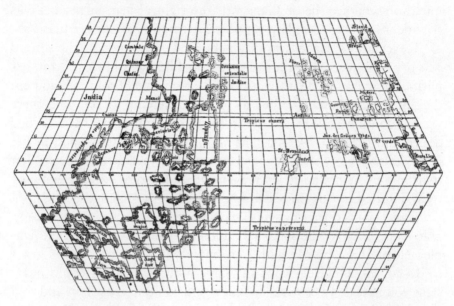

Toscanelli's chart of 1470s, as reconstructed in Justin Winsor's *Narrative and Critical History of America* (Boston & New York: Houghton, Mifflin and Co., 1889).

Isabel and Fernando
Succession in Castile, Segovia, 1474–1476

King Enrique IV died after midnight December 12, 1474, in the alcazar in Madrid attended by Cardinal Mendoza, a priest, and a few advisers. A note was dispatched that night to Isabel in Segovia, which she received on December 12. Archbishop Carrillo sent a letter to Fernando in Zaragoza, where he was assisting his father at the Aragonese Cortes, which Fernando would receive December 14.

Then twenty-three, Isabel quivered when she read the note, not from surprise or elation, but from recognition that the final step to achieve her crown was at hand and demanded swift resolution. There were two other claimants to the throne whom she feared would seek it. The first, little Juana, still claimed to be Enrique's legitimate heir, and, while Queen Juana had been discredited, there remained noblemen who might espouse her claim in intrigue with foreign princes. Isabel received a notice from Enrique's counselors to wait for a determination whether she or Juana was the rightful heir, but Isabel was confident her own Castilian supporters would prevail over Juana's.

Nevertheless, Isabel's stomach churned with anxiety. The second was her own husband—the father of her child, her only lover, and her partner in seeking the Crown since their marriage. From the moment they first met, they had acted as one in sovereign affairs, and there was no doubt he expected to be crowned king when she was crowned queen and that he deserved that honor. But she feared—and in her heart knew—he wished to be crowned with her at his side, rather than him at hers, and to be recognized as Castile's king in his own right, entitled to rule on her death instead of their daughter.

Isabel winced that her husband's deepest desires were unacceptable—not only to the Castilian noblemen but to herself. She was pleased to share power with him but would not rely on his grace to do so. His children from any later wife or mistress could never steal young Isabel's crown. She knew she couldn't trust him and that any delay in her coronation risked his interference with her claim. She recalled her flight from Enrique at Ocaña and again resolved to seize the initiative over the man then most important to her. With trepidation that she risked Fernando's rage and perhaps more, and with Bishop Mendoza's secret concurrence, she ordered that she be anointed the next day, December 13. She dispatched her own message to Fernando announcing Enrique's death but withholding that she would be crowned queen in his absence, knowing Fernando soon would understand it as betrayal.

On the morning of December 13, dressed in black in mourning, Isabel rode on horseback from the alcazar to the church of St. Michael in Segovia's central square, where a funeral was held for Enrique and his standards lowered. After changing into a royal gown bedecked with jewels and gold, she mounted a platform at the church door and Fernando was proclaimed king consort and Isabel queen proprietor, signifying that her children would inherit Castile on her death, not Fernando. She swore on a Bible to aggrandize Castile, honor its clergy and nobility and their privileges, promote the common good, and maintain justice throughout the realm. Those present, her close supporters, pledged allegiance to her as proprietary queen and to King Fernando as her husband, whereupon she entered the church to pray that God direct her to fulfill her duty justly and wisely. She emerged to mount a horse as queen and, in accordance with Castilian tradition, parade through the city preceded by a sole horseman, an advisor who held an unsheathed sword aloft,* an ancient symbol of the ruler's authority to punish those who disobeyed.

Fernando received Isabel's announcement of Enrique's death on December 16 and left Zaragoza on December 19 in a torrential rain. On December 21, he received an adviser's letter describing Isabel's coronation. She had been queen for a week! Fernando was stunned. Isabel had indicated nothing of this. For over five years, they had struggled together to attain the throne, and, without forewarning, she had arranged the culminating public ceremony to involve her alone and to bar his right to succeed her! Fernando had never heard of the sword of sovereign authority drawn before a queen and was enraged at the usurpation of male authority. He bitterly recalled her very first letter to him and berated himself for having been taken a fool.

Fernando's advisers harangued that a woman had no authority to be crowned without a king and that Isabel's insolent, preemptory seizure of the throne revealed sinister motives of her own advisers. Fernando's capitulation did not address Fernando's status as king in the event of Isabel's death, and Juan II reminded his son of their own claim to Castile's throne and insisted that a lawyer immediately join Fernando in Segovia. While Fernando's capitulation reflected Isabel's right to inherit Castile, under Aragonese law a woman could not inherit as queen and the throne passed to the nearest related male heir. Fernando's advisers now plotted to assert, for the first time, that this principle also applied in Castile and that Fernando was independently king as Enrique's closest male relative. Isabel was queen by virtue of her marriage to Fernando, and Fernando would inherit Castile if Isabel died first.

---

*Gutierre de Cárdenas.

As Fernando approached Segovia, Isabel braced for confrontation and resolved not to waver in the supremacy of her claim. The intent of Fernando's capitulation was clear enough, as was the Castilian precedent that a woman could inherit the Castilian throne. She would not be usurped, ignored, or discarded as women had been throughout history! If the marriage faltered, Castile was her kingdom, alone. She understood better than anyone the daunting odds of successfully ruling without a husband and believed in her ability to retain him. To please him, she ordered extraordinary preparations in Segovia to welcome him to his kingdom.

On January 2, 1475, Fernando rode into Segovia to be met with extravagant honors and celebrations. His native caution intuited acquiescence in the ceremonies planned. He swore to protect Castile's laws as king, and the nobility present pledged their allegiance to him as the queen's husband the king. Fernando and Isabel met warmly in public, and he feigned appreciation of the honors.

That night they dismissed every chambermaid and attendant from their bedroom and fought alone. Fernando spoke to her as he never had before.

"You betrayed me, lying as a whore, despicable as Judas."

Isabel gazed at the floor, stealing herself. "Fernando, I received a warning to wait for a determination whether Juana was heir, but Mendoza and Carrillo advised me to take the Crown swiftly."

"Juana's supporters will name a price to be bought!" Fernando shook with anger. "And that isn't even the point. Your own note to me didn't say a word about your seizing the Crown alone!"

"Fernando, should I have risked that a note disclosing my intention be intercepted by those against us? Mendoza and Carrillo wanted it this way—it wasn't my decision." She looked into his eyes, as if lovingly. "Fernando, I did it for our kingdom—yours and mine. Nothing has changed between us. We will share power as king and queen, and you will be obeyed as king, I standing at your side."

"You should stand at my side! Your acceptance as your kingdom's queen is due as much to my presence and ability as your own!" He turned away. "You still lie, now to my face. You've named yourself proprietor, leaving me as the queen to your king, subject to the jest and scorn of everyone in this castle and throughout the realm. You yourself have scorned me, you've humiliated me, you've breached our understandings, and you've poisoned our love."

"Fernando, I've done none of those, and my love for you is as constant as ever." Isabel shed a few tears. "The ceremonies crowning both of us were simply those agreed to when we married. I made no choices in them. They were as agreed before—agreements critical to the Castilian noblemen. I can't imagine a greater risk to our rule than violating them—the noblemen would swarm to assist Juana if they saw your heirs apart from me could inherit Castile."

"For five years, we've done everything together—in unison. You had time to wait to be crowned—in unison!"

"I've done what we both needed to be done to secure our rule of my kingdom." Isabel shed a few more tears. "Fernando, I would never seek to demean or dishonor you. I am wife to your husband. But Castile is my inheritance. Your advisers' arguments that Castile is yours over mine are false and have never been discussed before now." Isabel wiped her tears and frowned sternly. "You know they are false."

Fernando could not stomach being upbraided by a woman. "I know that a king rules in his own right and that the sword of justice is borne before a king not a queen. Even your own counselors are shocked how you've demeaned me." Fernando clutched Isabel by the shoulders and shook her. "We will change the ceremonies so I am king in my own right. If not, I leave for Aragón."

For the true whores! Isabel screamed to herself. She repressed the urge to gloat that his Aragonese lovers weren't queens, perceiving this the worst moment to upbraid his manhood. This was about her supremacy, not her jealousy.

Isabel began to cry and then lost control of herself and sobbed. "Fernando, nothing has changed, absolutely nothing. We have become king and queen as intended. If you leave, where are we then? I'm a queen without a husband. You're a king without a kingdom."

Fernando fought the urge to strike her. Aragón was a kingdom, a proud kingdom, and he would be its king. He gazed at their bed and despised that it reeked of Castilian supremacy.

Wife and husband stared grimly at each other. Each knew she had mistrusted him, and rightly so, and each knew she had been faithless, as he would have been—and that she had prevailed. Each asked God to redirect the actions of the other. They slept apart.

Their struggle continued for two weeks. Isabel repeatedly felt weakness and asked herself if she had erred and should relent. Regardless of his baseless legal position, her husband genuinely felt demeaned and deceived. Many of the Castilian noblemen who advised her were duplicitous. They demanded she maintain the position taken to safeguard their own entitlements. But they sympathized with Fernando because they, too, secretly felt she had usurped male prerogative.

Isabel surmounted her doubts, maintained her resolve, and asked God for the wisdom to retain both her kingdom and her husband. Fernando recognized that returning to Aragón accomplished nothing but squandering his opportunity to be king of Castile. Both remembered that they and their kingdoms were strong together, weak apart. Fernando humbled himself to return to Isabel's bed, and her love and devotion began to mollify him.

Mendoza, Carrillo, and Juan II understood even more clearly that their own interests and both kingdoms would suffer if the couple failed to reconcile, and a mechanism was devised to dissipate the couple's ill will. Cardinal Mendoza and Archbishop Carrillo would arbitrate whether a woman could inherit alone and submit their resolution to the Castilian noblemen then present.

Fernando soberly recognized that his father's vision of Aragonese control wasn't achievable and that he had no alternative. He had learned many times to retreat or disengage when the battle couldn't be won, and he consented to this solution, bitterly recognizing the outcome was foregone and waited merely articulation of a rationale. Isabel argued to the arbitrators that, since the couple yet had only a daughter, it made sense to allow a woman to inherit alone. While they listened to Fernando's lawyer, the two Castilian leaders and the Castilian noblemen quickly ruled for Isabel and their interests, and Fernando ruefully concluded the matter by agreeing to abide by their decision, spared the ignobility of merely submitting to his wife. Adjustments were made to the terms of Fernando's capitulation, some in Fernando's favor, some not, and recorded in a concordia. Isabel's relief was incomplete as she knew Fernando remained displeased, and, in future months, she would grant him authorities beyond those agreed.

▣ ▣ ▣

After her coronation, Isabel had asked Cardinal Mendoza to recommend a new confessor for her, an educated person who could also serve as a religious adviser and administrator. Mendoza suggested Hernando de Talavera, the converso Hieronymite friar, vouching he was of the highest devotional, intellectual, and moral fiber. Talavera had resigned teaching moral philosophy at the university at Salamanca and served as the prior of a large monastery in Valladolid.

Isabel summoned him, and they spoke. He condemned heresy and believed it essential for Hispania that it be eliminated. But he thought heresy best fought through teaching and education, not threats or punishment. Isabel tested his thoughts on Córdoba.

"Should my brother have punished the murderers and rapists?"

"They were sinners, and God's judgment on their souls will be most severe."

"I understand that. But I'm asking what the king should have done to them on earth."

"A sovereign must emulate and demonstrate God's perfection, to the extent worldly achievable. That includes punishing sinners for temporal crimes."

Pleased by the response, Isabel asked Talavera to take her confession, and they retired to the alcazar's chapel. As she knelt, he sat on the bench before her, and she suspected he had never administered confession to royalty. She gently advised him of his mistake. "We should both be on our knees."

"No, Your Highness, I will be seated as you kneel because confession is God's tribunal, and I serve him here."

Isabel perceived the older man was neither imposing an order nor asking approval. He appeared, without aggression or ego, simply to be reminding her that God was supreme and that he would receive her communication on his behalf. He did recognize that she was God's instrument on earth.

Isabel appreciated the friar's view of proper sovereign conduct, intellectual approach, and apparent virtue. She understood he lived ascetically and humbly, as had the founder of his order St. Jerome, and was chaste. Unlike Mendoza, he had no troops, amassed wealth, or possessions, or children, but simply an ever-present communication with God, and he appeared resolute in that outlook. He did seem worldly and practical, able to negotiate with those who did command troops or wealth. Unlike Fray Torquemada, he appeared compassionate.

As she knelt before him, she decided that he would be her confessor. But it was premature to confess any impolitic thought to him. For this confession, she chose simply to confide that she quarreled with her husband sometimes.

⊡ ⊡ ⊡

In the spring of 1475, Archbishop Carrillo and several other Castilian noblemen found themselves disappointed with their appointments. They agreed upon an alliance with Portugal's King Afonso V, whereby they would assist if little Juana, Afonso's niece, succeeded to the Castilian throne and Afonso married her, thereby acquiring control of Castile. Recognizing that war was inevitable, Afonso, then forty-three, wrote Isabel and Fernando demanding they relinquish the throne to Juana, then thirteen, and forewarning that he would marry her to defend her claim to the throne. Isabel bitterly rued that, for all the torment she'd endured for crowning herself without her husband, she had been proven right for fearing noblemen would entreat young Juana to take it herself.

Isabel and Fernando rejected the ultimatum, and Fernando prepared to go back to war, this time as king of Castile to defend its independent existence. Isabel raised their army. They dispatched letters throughout the kingdom, criticizing the disloyal noblemen and rallying support. Isabel frequently rode by horseback from town to town to make their preparations. Afonso and Prince João were not deterred and invaded Castile with fifteen thousand troops, whereupon Afonso was betrothed to Juana and they declared themselves king and queen of Castile, although the marriage was postponed for failure to obtain papal dispensation.

The strain was too much, and, at the end of May near Ávila, Isabel miscarried a child. As she writhed in pain, the witnesses determined the fetus a boy—a future king of Castile never to be—and the pain became agony. Fernando was apprised and devastated. Both found their faith tested by God in every aspect of their lives and implored him to reveal how they had failed. In their despair, their union grew unqualified and indivisible.

Fernando now recognized that their kingdoms' perpetual union was essential for each. Acquiescing to Isabel's supremacy, he wrote a will with Talavera's assistance just days before going into battle, specifying that he should be buried permanently wherever Isabel was buried and entrusting her and his father with guardianship of his illegitimate children and their mothers. Regardless of the laws of Aragón, little Princess Isabel was to inherit Aragón and Sicily on his death so that Aragón, Sicily, and Castile would remain under one rule.

Isabel recognized the exigencies of war and woefully accepted the necessity of arranging a truce with the emir of Granada Abū l'Hasan for one year,* shamed and humiliated to make the very compromise with the infidel she had contemptuously scorned as a girl. She sought to disrupt Afonso's supply of African wealth and ordered Portuguese shipping and trading posts plundered for gold. As her father, she asserted Castile's prior right to most of Portugal's African possessions, including navigating in the seas of Guinea to obtain its gold and slaves, as well as sovereignty over the Canary Islands and her intent to subjugate them. She provisioned the Castilian armies and sometimes went to the battlefront, occasionally wearing armor, with tremendous impact on the troops' moral and fortitude.

CRISTOFORO
Lagos, Lisbon, London, Galway, Thule, and Vinland, (1476–1477)

In the summer of 1476, Cristoforo enlisted on a trading expedition to Flanders and London organized by the Spinolas and di Negros to sell Sciot mastic, spices, and oriental wares. Five ships were fitted, and Cristoforo sailed as a common seaman on one that recruited part of its crew in Savona.

---

*Abū l'Hasan 'Alī ben Nasr ben Saád.

As the Genoese ships entered the Pillars of Hercules, Cristoforo gazed through a sultry mist north to Spain, south to Africa, and west to the enormous horizon and the end of the known world. Almost twenty-five, he was thrilled to be on the Ocean Sea for the first time and marveled at its enormity. On August 13, the expedition came abreast of Lagos, but a short sail to Sagres and Cape St. Vincent. As every sailor, Cristoforo knew tales of Prince Henrique and his African exploits, and he grew pensive sailing along the prince's coast toward the Cape, captivated by the mystique of the renowned waters.

The French King Louis XI then supported Portugal in its war with Castile, and Louis had authorized a French corsair known as Louis Coulon to patrol Portugal's southern coast with a fleet of warships, with orders to attack Castilian and Aragonese vessels. As a mercenary, Coulon was entitled to the booty seized, and he thought the Genoese expedition too grand a prize to slip by, regardless of nationality. He ordered his crews to intercept them, chain their hulls to his fleet's own, and then board and plunder, killing resisters.

The Genoese fiercely defended their cargos and honor, and the battle raged from morning to late afternoon, with the decks of both fleets littered with dead and wounded. Cristoforo was terrified, and, when fire engulfed his ship, he grabbed an oar and jumped to the sea. Two other Genoese ships, and a few of the corsair fleet, sank before two surviving Genoese ships broke free and fled east, leaving hundreds of sailors, Genoese and pirate, desperately floundering, deserted six miles offshore, nearly all to drown.

As the frenzy of drownings concluded in silence, Cristoforo grimly assessed that his first passage on the Ocean Sea would be his last, despairing that the tide would sweep him farther to sea. But he praised the Lord that he remained alive and beseeched continued mercy as he swam toward the coast, propped by the oar. After sunset, shivering cold, dehydrated, and exhausted, he crawled onto a beach near Lagos. The summer heat engulfed and restored him, and, as never before, he thanked the Lord for his grace.

Fishermen on the coast watched the battle, and, moved by the plight of imperiled seamen, one offered Cristoforo water and a biscuit. He sheltered at the beach for the night and, at dawn, walked to Lagos to wander its quays and markets, which bustled with activity and brimmed with African wares, gold jewelry, and slaves. He marveled that he stood at the center of world exploration—but a day after nearly perishing anonymously on the Ocean Sea as countless seamen since Creation.

Cristoforo learned that the surviving Genoese ships had safely harbored at Cádiz and soon rejoined them. He discussed with the Spinolas and di Negros that he work for their agents in Portugal and secured a position on a vessel bound for Lisbon. After rounding Cape St. Vincent, he arrived Lisbon by autumn and went to live in the city's significant Genoese enclave, where members and agents of Genoa's trading families resided.

◻ ◻ ◻

Undaunted, the Spinolas and di Negros reassembled the plundered trading expedition. Additional ships were fitted in Genoa by December 1476 and sailed to meet the two surviving ships in Lisbon, where Cristoforo rejoined the crew. The reconstituted fleet departed for London in January 1477, again bearing mastic, spices, and other oriental cargo.

The northern Ocean Sea was tempestuous and inhospitable in winter, and Cristoforo learned how ships and crews bore a relentless wind and swell as a matter of routine. He perceived milestones when the ships entered the British Ocean (English Channel) and, in February, slipped into a large estuary (Thames estuary) on England's eastern coast, twelve hundred miles from Lisbon and grateful for the shelter. He marveled as the ships slowly made their way up the river to London, sailing when possible, assisted by the tide when rising, and towed from the river's banks by men hauling ropes when necessary, eventually to dock at a quay in the large city by a customs house, near the fortress where the English kings sometimes resided (Tower of London), downstream from an enormous stone bridge spanning the river (London Bridge).

The city was cold, wet, and shrouded by cloud. The mastic and other cargos were unloaded, Cristoforo was paid for his service, and, as the crews began loading fine wool cloth and other merchandise for return to ports south, he departed into the city, reflecting on Domenico's struggles to earn a living, now bound on his own exploration.

He ambled along the city wharfs and found inexpensive shelter in a cold, broken tenement by the wharfs with other seaman seeking work. At night, he ate and drank in the sailors' pubs and, using gestures and a few words similar in Ligurian and English, learned when the next Bristol-bound ships would sail. He found employment on one, and the passage took him to England's western coast, where he was astounded by a ferocious tide as the ship navigated another large estuary (Severn estuary) to slip with the rising sea into a river gorge (the Avon), winding to a large city invisible to seaborne invaders and pirates. The ship berthed astride an imposing fortress wall, the quays heaped with wood, grain, salt, and wine awaiting delivery to Thule (Iceland) when winter thawed.

Cristoforo again frequented the wharfs and sailors' pubs to learn of ships sailing, and, by late winter, he enlisted on a small English expedition bound for Thule, a voyage that typically took two weeks, depending on the seas. The ships first coursed the Celtic Sea to Galway (western Ireland) to harbor and water before the nine hundred and fifty mile open-sea crossing, docking at piers directly beside Galway's imposing city wall. Cristoforo was surprised to see a man and woman with features he believed were traits of people from the Indies—including slanted, as opposed to rounded, eyelids—sitting nearby in two small boats. He studied them, wondering how they had arrived in Galway.

When off duty, the crews entered the town to feast and drink at its pubs, most to visit whores, and nearly all—including Cristoforo—to pray at St. Nicholas Collegiate Church for the Virgin's protection of their crossing to Thule. As he drank with his mates, Cristoforo listened to their banter and boast. While unable to understand most of it, he recognized a story he had heard as a boy. As the tale went, centuries past (sixth century AD), an Irish abbot, St. Brendan, had fasted forty days and nights—three at a time—and then departed in a wood-framed, ox-hide boat westward to find the Promised Land of the saints, trusting God as his helper, sailor, and helmsman and with fellow monks as crew. Cristoforo recalled how the Genoese spoke of the Vivaldi brothers and discerned that his mates had similar affections for their own story, too.

The expedition soon departed northwest and the wind grew brutally cold, the deck treacherously slippery, and rain and spray froze on the seamen's clothing. Cristoforo was on deck when the lookout sighted Thule's southern coast. Mountains capped with snow and glacier stretched as far as he could see into the interior and came forward to fall, sometimes precipitously, to a coastal flat-land—often a weird, brusquely deformed plain of gray and black volcanic rock and ash, other times verdant pastureland. The vessels navigated west along the southern shore and turned northwest to a mountainous peninsula (like Snæfellsnes), where they anchored at a secluded pastureland with a tiny natural harbor (like Bjarnarhöfn). There was no town, only a road, an open field, and a small church nestled between the harbor and snow-covered mountains. Within days, merchants arrived by ship and horseback to purchase the expedition's cargo in return for stock fish (dried cod) and whale and fish oil, destined to feed and light the English cities.

When the crew rested, Cristoforo listened as best he could to his crewmates relate tales of their prior voyages to Thule and of Thule's legendary mariners, including one Eiríkur Thorvaldsson Rauda (Erik the Red). Cristoforo gleaned that Eiríkur had been an outcast, expelled from Norway and then Thule, leading him to explore Greenland farther west, which he decided to colonize and bestow its ill-fitted name to attract colonists. Cristoforo deciphered that Thule's merchants had once traded with Eiríkur's colony in Greenland.

Cristoforo prayed daily in the small church. He reflected that items he took for granted—such as wood for cooking, warmth, and building homes and ships—were dear in this place. He realized there were few people to buy goods, they were poor, and, while Domenico struggled in Genoa, the struggle here for existence alone was far more brutal.

When the expedition raised anchor to return to Bristol, Cristoforo studied the western horizon. He understood that the Greenland of the fabled Eiríkur was beyond it and, likely, other islands that could be visited or discovered. He saw the Ocean Sea was navigable at this extreme latitude, just as at Lisbon. But at this latitude the Ocean Sea was fierce and more hostile and, in winter, the sun orbited above the horizon fewer hours, rendering navigation—and all existence—more difficult. He gazed at the sea swishing below the hull, remembered his swim at Lagos, and reflected that even a short immersion in these waters meant death.

Unknown to Cristoforo, beyond Eiríkur's Greenland lay lands previously visited by Europeans but forgotten or misunderstood. After Eiríkur colonized Greenland (AD 985), his son Leifur and others explored shores west of Greenland previously sighted by its colonists (commencing AD 1,001), discovering sites they named Helluland, meaning Stone-slab-land (Baffin Island?), Markland, meaning Woodland (Labrador?), and Vinland, meaning Vineland (Island of Newfoundland and farther south?). A colony was established at Vinland (L'Anse aux Meadows?). It lacked food and suffered internal discord and likely was abandoned within twenty years, perhaps owing to recognition that the native people could and would easily fight to eliminate it. Greenlanders continued to travel to Vinland for perhaps two centuries to obtain wood and fur. Eventually, Thule's Greenland trade itself died for lack of profit, and Greenland was largely abandoned by Europeans in the fifteenth century. The Norsemen and their European successors thought of their colonies as northern or polar European islands, not envisioning themselves in the Indies or another possibility. While some European cartographers added Greenland to world maps, Greenland and lands beyond typically were not recognized as "Indian," but as extensions of northern European coasts.

European portion of Nicholas Germanus's World Map, ca. 1467–1474, reflecting Germanus's addition of information relating to northern Europe to Ptolemy's second projection.

ISABEL
Guadalupe, Castile, 1477

By April 1477, Isabel and Fernando had reduced the Portuguese incursion into Castile to border areas, and Isabel rode south to Seville to compel the submission of disloyal Castilian noblemen while Fernando continued to prosecute the war. Her entourage bore Brother Enrique's body to inter it next to his mother's in the Hieronymite Monastery of Santa María de Guadalupe deep in the mountains in the center of her kingdom. The monastery's icon of the Virgin—known as Our Lady of Santa María of Guadalupe—was venerated by pilgrims from throughout Hispania. More than three feet tall, the icon was held to have been entombed with St. Luke and, over centuries, passed to Hispanic clergy who buried her when fleeing the infidel in the eighth century—only to be revealed centuries later by the Virgin to a local herdsman.

Isabel came as a pilgrim herself. She had given birth to but one child in almost eight years of marriage and ached for a son, knowing that critical to establishing her dynasty, regardless of young Isabel. She had visited Guadalupe and worshipped its Virgin before, and she now sought to redouble her pleas for a son after years of disappointment.

She entered the monastery accompanied only by her guard, knelt in the shrine before the Virgin icon, and praised the Virgin for the magnificent example of her purity and perfection, a life without sin at any time. Church doctrine held that, upon conception by her parents, Saints Joachim and Anne, and before her birth and baptism, God had preserved Mary free from original sin in light of her destined immaculate conception of Christ. Isabel prayed that she, too, be blessed with a son.

She also addressed the Lord as his servant, promising to be guided by his will as he revealed it in her conscience. With doubt and trepidation, she paused to consider her own imperfection and reminded him that, unlike the Virgin, she ruled a kingdom on earth, and it was her duty to do that necessary to protect it from usurpation by a foreign lineage.

Isabel arranged for Enrique's body to be entombed with a royal funeral service. She knelt before him and, as never before, appreciated the anguish he must have felt over the absence of a male heir—and, as far as she was concerned, any heir. Queen Juana had died the previous summer, forgotten and deserted, and Isabel mused that the Lord did not favor a queen who failed to produce a male heir. The affections she sometimes had held for Enrique swelled within, and she thanked him for rejecting and crushing the noblemen's gambit to usurp the Crown's power and glory.

As she knelt, Isabel also brooded on her own husband's philandering and fertility. He had fathered a son and daughter with other women before their marriage and at least two daughters since. Isabel had grown accustomed to bitter jealousy, and to repressing it. She resolved to insist that both girls born after their marriage be placed in a convent, never to know of their father's identity.

Santa María de Guadalupe.

But Isabel reflected proudly on her marriage. She had avoided a loveless dynastic coupling and wifely subservience to an aging sovereign in a foreign principality or culture—who might well have been ugly, lecherous, impotent, perverted, ignorant, untutored, ill mannered, decrepit, weak, or even faithless. She had achieved instead an independent and mutual sovereignty at home with a Spaniard who, regardless of marital infidelity, was none of those things— who was her own age, handsome, devout, and a warrior second to none—and, above all, was loyal and devoted to her sovereignty and their child. This sovereign loyalty mattered far more to her than marital loyalty. Royal documents and coins minted bore a phrase proclaiming their sovereign equality, "Tanto Monta" ("one and the same, without difference"). She also did love him and recognized he did love her to the extent he was capable. The result was beyond her girlhood expectations, albeit not perfect.

CAONABÓ
Succession in Maguana

Caonabó's uncle lay in his hammock most of the day, attended by naborias, and he recognized death approaching and that the time had come to choose his successor—upon which he had reflected considerably since Cacibaquel's death. Villagers throughout Maguana were satisfied Uncle's family aligned the spirits for their benefit, and the only issue was which family member would replace him. The son of his sisters best suited to rule normally would be selected, but, if none were worthy, one of his own sons might be chosen, as had occurred with the selection of Cacibaquel's Guarionex. One morning, Uncle bid naborias carry him by litter to the secluded bohío where he stored his cemís, and they left him there with a gourd of pineapple juice to consider his final decision, alone but for the presence of Yúcahu. Uncle pondered about Caonabó.

Of his sisters' children, Caonabó undoubtedly was the most distinguished and accomplished choice. He had proven himself in war and in peace, both as a clever general and as a just leader. The issue was not ability but acceptance by others. He was aloof, sometimes perceived by many as pompous or arrogant, although Uncle understood him otherwise.

Caonabó had proved a superior warrior at an early age, when Uncle had dispatched him with troops to the southern coast to defend Caribe wife-raiding attacks. Rather than waiting to repel a raid, Caonabó attacked first, tracking the course of Caribes spied at sea to their nighttime encampment ashore, routing them as they slept in predawn twilight, and taking no prisoners. The effectiveness of being the aggressor, which was not the Taíno custom, and his singular, impassive resolve to annihilate the enemy, had impressed all. He had vanquished Caribes many times, and his personal bravery in combat was renowned.

Uncle had invited Caonabó to participate with the elders in council, and Caonabó had comported himself well. His own thoughts were always sound, yet he was able to accept someone else's ideas as better. He genuinely appreciated that peace had reigned among the Haitian caciques for many years, with but a handful of frictions settled through discussion or minor skirmish. While raised on simple Aniyana, he had come to understand the more complex Managuan society, where food was shared among peoples of different occupations. Inevitably, there were disputes over who was entitled to work which land or fish which area, and, while infrequent, misdeeds had to be punished. Caonabó appreciated the cacique's responsibility to resolve these disputes and impose fair punishments to preserve harmony.

His demeanor was caciqual. Caonabó had exhibited a self-assurance that he was destined to be cacique from the day Uncle first met him as a teenager, and he now comported himself with a confident expectation that all should and would follow his every command. Uncle saw his sister's hand in this. Caonabó's naborias and soldiers adored him and would make any sacrifice he asked—as their honor. Almost thirty, he had taken only a dozen wives, each but one having been chosen wisely to augment his stature. For his first wife, he had returned briefly to Aniyana to marry Onaney, with whom he shared many thoughts. She was clever and also had adapted well to Maguana.

Uncle took a sip of pineapple juice and sighed that his nephew did have shortcomings.

Caonabó's conduct and display at ceremonies always exceeded that of his peers. His entrance, attire, and accompaniments—be they warriors, gifts, or food—were always the most conspicuous, often ostentatious. Uncle didn't understand what drove this—was it an insecurity born of his humble upbringing on Aniyana, a belief that ceremony itself augmented authority, or simply poor judgment? He made too much of ceremony and cared too little for the goodwill of his peers, and Uncle had told him so many times, warning that family members thought him arrogantly bent on upstaging them.

More worrisome, Caonabó often was a stranger and mystery to his family, friends, and subjects. He had learned and observed Maguanan custom and tradition appropriately, yet many people, including Uncle, doubted he truly appreciated them, as opposed to merely craving power. He participated ably in spiritual life, including the cohaba ceremony, and he understood the spirits. But Uncle doubted that Caonabó sincerely believed that Yúcahu and other spirits affected destiny, as opposed to men. He was primal more than spiritual, concerned with domination and survival more than purity and goodness. There was a risk in anointing such a person, as disregard of the spirits inevitably would bring misfortune on Maguana.

Uncle had agonized over these fundamental concerns for months, debating whether leadership or spirituality was more important for a cacique, and he now asked Yúcahu to guide his thoughts to the conclusion. He recognized Caonabó might not support the anointment of another person and, in that event, Uncle would have to order him to return to rule Aniyana, forsaking his military prowess.

Uncle took another sip of pineapple juice, spoke softly to Yúcahu, and then resolved in favor of leadership and that Caonabó be anointed. He called for a naboria to summon his nephew before him.

Caonabó entered the bohío deferentially. "Uncle, what can I do for you?"

"You can worship the spirits with conviction. You can appreciate Maguanan custom. You can embrace modesty."

Caonabó was uneasy, unsure whether he had erred and of Uncle's purpose. "Uncle, I do and I will."

"And you shall rule Maguana as my successor."

Caonabó flushed with triumph and fought to conceal it, but Uncle understood and smiled broadly, whereupon so did Caonabó. The nephew knelt to embrace his uncle, who remained seated, thanking him for his confidence and guidance for years. Caonabó recalled standing before Mother the morning he left Aniyana, and his eyes misted.

"This isn't a matter of thanking me, Caonabó. Remember to honor Yúcahu."

◻ ◻ ◻

Within months, Uncle's eyesight and hearing failed, and he no longer cared to rise from his hammock or even eat. One morning, he summoned Caonabó beside his hammock to murmur that the time for transition had come and contentedly bid his graven nephew to embrace him a last time. Uncle's first wife convened the entire family in the caney, and Uncle affectionately whispered his blessing for the future, whereupon both were taken by litter to the secluded bohío to receive water—which Uncle declined—and cohaba. They sat reflecting on their long journey together through decades of marriage, understanding Uncle no longer provided to others what he took from them.

Uncle's wife placed the cemí of Yúcahu in his hand, and he remembered that, with Yúcahu's protection, he had received Maguana from his uncle decades ago and would now pass it to his nephew. His wife watched him weaken in the afternoon heat and, as the sun set, offered him water for perhaps the last time, which he refused. As the moon rose, she helped him inhale the cohaba. His body succumbed to the narcotic, and his last vision was of his spirit passing through a rainbow.

Caonabó rose anxiously in his bohío before dawn, prepared to wait perhaps days as Uncle lingered, but a messenger soon arrived to report that Uncle had died. The village behique came, together with Uncle's nitaínos and other village elders, bearing Uncle's feather crown and guanín medallion pendant to consummate the transition of authority in a simple ceremony prelude to Uncle's funeral. Solemnly, the behique set the crown on Caonabó's head and hung the pendant about his neck, and Caonabó assumed responsibility for interpreting and influencing the spirits for the benefit of his people. For an instant, he remembered Father teaching him years before how to seek and achieve this moment and, to his surprise, he was engulfed not with pride but awe, gratitude, and a recognition that, regardless of triumph, he had made mistakes as Father said he would. Messengers were quickly dispatched throughout Haiti to announce Uncle's death.

Caonabó understood that neither his crown nor pendant assured he would be a powerful ruler and that the funeral ceremony was his first step to that end. He dressed in his finest jewelry and ornaments—his head bearing a new crown decorated with golden eyes and brightly colored feathers—and greeted each guest in the plaza at Uncle's caney, which was now his own, his warriors standing nearby.

Guarionex was the first to arrive, hoisted on a litter by naborias and trailed by a band of nitaínos, all unarmed, his acclaimed spirituality so heralded. The two men were about the same age, acquaintances from prior caciqual gatherings and neither friend nor enemy, neighbors with a common boundary which each watched carefully but without animosity. Guarionex extended his sympathy and congratulations and presented an amulet that had been Cacibaquel's. Caonabó was moved by the intimacy, particularly since the giver's stature far exceeded his own. As he would with each cacique, Caonabó reciprocated with a finely carved wooden mask, adorned with golden eyes, ears, and lips, representing Caonabó's most personal offer of his own soul in friendship to an equal.

The Higüeyan cacique arrived next with his nephew Cayacoa and warriors, and presented a collection of feathers of many colors—azure, jade, hazel, onyx, turquoise, and others—plucked from parrots of the eastern peninsula. Caonabó promised he would include a few in his crown. They were followed by the cacique of Marien, to the northwest, and Guacanagarí. Caonabó had met both before and understood that Guacanagarí, while younger than himself, already had half a dozen wives and was perceived the successor to his cacicazgo. The Ciguayan cacique and a nitaino named Mayobanex then entered, their bodies painted black with charcoal, their warriors armed with bow and arrow. Caonabó couldn't speak their language, Macorix, and an interpreter joined when he greeted them, complimenting their people's military prowess, wary that the Ciguayans sometimes fought with their neighbors.

The cacique of Xaraguá, the most esteemed Haitian cacicazgo, made the last entrance, preceded by both nitaínos and warriors and accompanied by a few nephews and nieces, including Behecchio and his younger sister, Anacaona, as well as other girls Anacaona's age—ten or eleven years old. He greeted Caonabó solemnly, presented a cotton belt delicately inlaid with gold, and introduced Behecchio, who had just married for the first time. Caonabó afforded Behecchio great dignity, knowing through informants that he was the likely successor and well aware that neighboring Xaraguá was larger than his Maguana and could muster far more warriors. He showed Anacaona equal attention, as her beauty and charm were already spoken of throughout Haiti—and captured his eye instantly. Caonabó expressed his pleasure the girls had come, and the Xaraguán cacique promised Anacaona would sing for him.

The village behique presided over Uncle's burial at the village perimeter, together with—at her election—his first wife, heavily sedated by the cohaba. Caonabó spoke before their chamber was covered, praising Uncle and his peaceful relationships with those present. As he concluded, to Caonabó's surprise, the Xaraguán cacique rose to offer an areíto lauding Caonabó's anointment and the peace that had existed between Xaraguá and Maguana and throughout Haiti for generations. Caonabó graciously indicated he was honored.

The Xaraguán girls advanced together to form a line before the assembled, their soft, naked skin radiating the warmth of the sunlight, and a lone drummer began a solemn and austere beat to which they began to dance. Anacaona stepped forward to sing alone. Womanhood was approaching, and all present realized the rumors of her allure and presence were not only true but understated. In unison with her chorus, she lifted her arms gently to one side above the shoulder, as if gently blown by a breeze, and then let them gracefully fall in an arc, swaying her hips to cross behind them and then replicating the motion on the other side, whereupon she began her story. She sang that Deminán had been born with disease, swept by flood, spat on, and sickened to near death, but had never given up. He had desired merely to live in peace and harmony with all, and eventually learned how. All present prayed that Yúcahu would lead Caonabó to achieve that goal for his people.

She finished, and there was silence. It was impossible for a man not to want her.

At Caonabó's invitation, the caciques returned to the central plaza for a traditional feast and games of batey. His naborias offered *chicha* (corn beer), *uici* (yuca beer), intoxicating herb drinks, and tobacco to all. Caonabó recognized that each ruler present could be an ally or enemy, and he moved among the crowd to befriend each and his potential successor. The Xaraguán cacique moved similarly, silently judging each man's mettle and ambition, as he knew they all would seek his niece's hand in marriage. Guarionex approached the Ciguayans, his neighbors, and offered his own welcome in broken Macorix to Mayobanex, whom he had known for years. Guacanagarí approached Behecchio, eager to establish a relationship with the potential successor to Marien's most formidable neighbor.

Caonabó soon announced the commencement of the batey, and everyone removed to the perimeter of the plaza, revealing the boundaries of the ball court, which stretched perhaps a hundred yards in length and thirty yards in width, bounded on all sides by a slight ridge of earth and cornered with stones. Xaraguáns would play the Higüeyans, Maguans the Ciquayans, and so on, throughout the afternoon. All understood batey was to be played with full aggression without impacting the gathering's goodwill. The caciques and their successors bet on their teams, wagering jewelry or exotic items, and occasionally played themselves.

Anacaona watched the men compete. Throughout Haiti, batey was played as much by women and girls as men and boys, and she was disappointed women of the visiting cacicazgos were not present to field teams. She was a good player. She studied the caciques who had just complimented her and wondered if her uncle soon would bid her sleep with one or more of them when they visited Xaraguá. Uncle certainly would arrange for her to marry one of them.

As the afternoon waned, Caonabó invited Guacanagarí to play and the Maguanans took the field against the Mariens. Each selected the best players of his cacicazgo present, almost twenty men a team, and Caonabó's behique ceremoniously presented Guacanagarí with the large, firm black ball, compacted from the gum of rubber trees mashed with reed, to begin the game. Before beginning, Caonabó and Guacanagarí commended their opponents.

As they spoke, Guarionex studied both men, musing silently over the choice presented. There was a pride in Caonabó that challenged harmony and an innocence in Guacanagarí that embraced it. As the teams lined at opposing ends of the court, Guarionex resolved it would be Yúcahu's victory, and a sign of providence, if Guacanagarí's team won. If his team lost, it would be Guabancex's victory, and a sign of misfortune, and it would be necessary to pray for Guabancex's forbearance more regularly the following year and to proceed cautiously, as the spirits might not be in alliance.

Guacanagarí put the ball in play by kneeing it, and it bounded high in the air toward the Maguanan team. The Maguanans' objective was to hit the ball back while in the air, using any part of the body except the hands. It was acceptable for the ball to bounce before returning it, perhaps a few times, and for members of the same team to pass the ball among themselves before returning it, but the serving team would win a point if the ball rolled to the ground without bounce, and either team would win a point if the other team drove it out of bounds.

A player on Caonabó's team brusquely jutted the ball with his shoulder to return it, and players from both teams rushed to gain advantage on its fall, one of them bounding high to strike it with his head. They exerted every limb, muscle, and joint of their bodies except the hands, and the great bounce and speed of the ball caused them to leap, dive, and contort to attack it at many angles. The players were panting within minutes and exhausted before the game's end, which would occur upon a team's winning a set number of points.

When play became rough and a player hurt, Guacanagarí graciously inquired whether he was injured but Caonabó did not, and Anacaona wondered whether Guacanagarí would be the kinder husband. He was slightly shorter than Caonabó, but with more graceful movements, more tutored in conduct and, while not a cacique, confident he would be.

But she would not get to play that day, and Anacaona's thoughts wandered from the game. She puzzled over which of the caciques had best understood her areíto and would be most interested in her thoughts, which were as worthy as the thoughts of any boy she knew. She pondered whether men so much older would even listen to her.

She surprised herself with the realization she would care more that a husband shared his power than listened.

The Maguanans won the batey, and Guacanagarí congratulated Caonabó. Each was aware that Anacaona had been watching, and each glanced to see whether she remained watching. But by then she had been introduced and was talking to Guarionex.

ISABEL
Seville, Castile, 1477–1478

In July, as Fernando remained occupied to the north, Isabel approached Seville determined to fulfill her duty as queen to cleanse it and Andalusia. The region's lawlessness was renowned and seemingly perpetual. Its nobility fought among themselves and with the Crown, its religious groups simmered with hostility, the seafaring merchants from Palos and neighboring coastal towns paid scant attention to royal requirements, and criminals flourished. Seville itself was her kingdom's largest city and a substantial port, teeming with over forty thousand old Christians, conversos, Jews, and Mujadin crowded in densely packed neighborhoods, with communities of foreign merchants—including Genoese—and a significant population of African slaves, imported from Guinea by the Portuguese and the merchants of Palos and other towns.

Isabel affected a captivating display of her royal authority by entering the city on an ornately decorated barge, floating down the river Guadalquivir past cheering crowds to the city's central bridge, where she was welcomed officially by Enrique de Guzmán, the Duke of Medina Sidonia and Andalusia's most powerful nobleman, together with other noblemen, clergy, and representatives of the Jews. She explained to Guzmán that she, and soon the king, would remain in Seville for an indefinite period to rid the city and Andalusia of both tyrants and criminals. Guzmán thought to himself that a woman's resolve was insufficient to deal with Seville without a husband. She completed her arrival by parading triumphantly through more applauding crowds to Seville's great cathedral, where mass was held, and finally to its magnificent alcazar, where she would live and install her administration for over a year.

Isabel was determined to cure Seville by administering justice quickly, severely, and omnipotently. She held a public audience in the alcazar's great hall every Friday to hear civil and criminal cases, presiding on a platform above the petitioners, surrounded by clergy, judges, and royal officials, and directing her staff to resolve cases promptly. She often resolved them herself, determining guilt or innocence and punishment, comfortable in pronouncing the severest corporal punishments without qualm or need to consult the Lord. As she intended, word spread quickly that her justice was awesome, fierce, and unforgiving.

Thousands of Sevillians fled the city to avoid her severity, and the bishop of Cádiz publicly appealed for clemency. Within days, Isabel pardoned those guilty of civil wrongs, if they made fair restitution, and all criminals except heretics. As she intended, word spread of her compassion. Thousands who had fled returned.

Leading nobility quickly realized the queen viewed her authority as absolute—with or without a husband present. Rodrigo Ponce de León, the Marquis of Cádiz, had allied with Afonso V in the Portuguese war, and he approached Isabel to apologize and submit to her sovereignty. Enrique de Guzmán had fought against the Portuguese but retained crown property seized in the hostilities, and he approached Isabel to relinquish it. Both men's private armies had fought each other, and Isabel reconciled each to the other, seeing it essential for domestic tranquility. She comforted Seville's Jewish community by forbidding injury to them and reaffirming her duty to protect the Jewish aljamas in their property and possessions against attack.

Fernando arrived in September. The couple had been separated for long periods during his extended visits to Aragón and tours on the battlefield, and they enjoyed their reunion. They made love in the alcazar, surrounded by its exquisite arches, facades, gardens, and pools, oblivious to her Castilian sovereignty and his infidelity. Isabel soon declined an invitation to board a ship to experience the Ocean Sea because she suspected she was pregnant. They delighted when that became apparent, and they prayed for the birth of a son, believing that the single most critical want of their kingdom.

As they awaited the child, the sovereigns witnessed that daily life in Seville and Córdoba was continuously rent with agitation and hostility directed at their converso populations. They recognized that achieving law and order required reducing these tensions.

In Seville, Fray Alonso de Hojeda* charged that many conversos secretly practiced Jewish customs and rituals—failing to baptize their children, secretly inviting rabbis into their homes on the Sabbath, and never confessing—and were amassing great fortunes on usurious loans. He advocated that an inquisition be established directed solely at the conversos. Torquemada agreed, arguing that such an inquisition was the only solution to rout the heresy that abounded and protect the faith. Inquisitions had been implemented in Europe to root out heretical sects and dissenters and subjugate conquered peoples, and Aragón and Sicily already had papal authority to conduct one.

To the contrary, Mendoza and Talavera—himself a converso and now often Fernando's confessor as well as Isabel's—cautioned the need for further study of the converso situation. They recommended that, instead of an inquisition, an attempt be made to better educate the clergy on proper adherence to Christian ritual and observance.

Isabel and Fernando listened. For them, there was one true religion, and the Jews were mistaken to deny Christ's divinity. Heresy was a terrible religious crime, and they feared failure to punish it could injure the faith, both by losing the soul of the heretic to the devil and by releasing the heretic to infect others. Yet a person became a Christian through baptism and faith in Christ's divinity, and they had learned that the denial of any person's ability to become Christian violated Christ's own teachings—the baptism of any man, including of a Jew to become a converso, prevailed over blood, race, and nation to make a new man. The child growing in her womb reminded them that the Lord afforded every child the opportunity of salvation.

The worldly situation complicated the spiritual, as their kingdom's governance and commerce included both conversos and Jews. The royal bureaucracies employed conversos in important positions and contracted with Jews, and Jewish merchants frequently provided loans to the Crown in return for protection. Castile's leading Jew, its chief rabbi Abraham Seneor, was Castile's chief tax gatherer. But the general populace was anti-converso and anti-Jewish, and Isabel and Fernando feared their consolidation of control over the kingdom

---

*Prior of the Dominican convent of San Pablo, currently the site of the Church of Magdalena.

could be impaired, and the social hostilities would continue to boil, if they failed to achieve law and order in a manner that quelled these prejudices. Prior rulers had exhorted the Jews to convert many times, typically under threat of confiscation of property, restriction of freedom or livelihood, or physical harm—to the satisfaction of the general populace.

The sovereigns decided they wanted more than anecdotal evidence of Hojeda's and Torquemada's charges—that thousands, if not all, conversos practiced Judaism—and appointed a commission, chaired by Mendoza, to review what should be done. Seville's Jews themselves viewed the city's conversos as Christian, as traitors to their own belief. Mendoza reported the evidence was overwhelming that conversos in Andalusia failed to practice proper Catholic worship and ritual, but he remained uncertain whether the cause was a failure of Catholic education generally in Andalusia as opposed to the Judaizing efforts of Jews or a few bad conversos.

With a secretiveness that shrouded their intention, Isabel and Fernando determined two courses of action, both intended to assimilate the conversos in Catholic society and reduce the social turmoil occasioned by anti-Jewishness. They authorized Mendoza's campaign of religious education, and a legion of clerics under Talavera and the bishop of Cádiz's direction would arrive in Seville to teach its Christians—particularly conversos—proper Catholic worship. As an alternative, they also sought the pope's authority for an inquisition in Castile directed at the conversos. The pope had been in favor of an inquisition established in accordance with historical precedent—subject to papal control—since Isabel's coronation. But Isabel and Fernando would defer implementing this inquisition pending the results of the education effort, thereby deferring the inquisition's punitive nature while warning the conversos to improve their practices. Deferral bought time to strengthen their control of Castile and conclude the Portuguese war before risking a policy that would trigger converso opposition.

At the end of June, Isabel gave birth to a healthy son, named Juan after both grandfathers. Seville, as well as all of Castile, Aragón, and Sicily, and even Barcelona, erupted in tumultuous celebrations. The prince who would become the king proprietor of all Spain had at last been born. Old Christians, conversos, and Jews alike believed that God had shown mercy on Spain.

In October, the sovereigns and their two children departed Seville. Fernando and Isabel continued discussions with the Holy See regarding the terms of a papal bull authorizing the inquisition. Fernando was firm: the inquisition had to be an authority of the Castilian crown, not the papacy. Its administrators had to be appointed and compensated by the sovereigns and answer to them, and the fines and property confiscated from those found guilty of heresy had to inure to the inquisition and thereby to the sovereigns. Fernando viewed the potential inquisition, if implemented, as a means for imposing royal authority and securing revenue in Andalusia.

In November, Pope Sixtus IV issued his bull Exigit Sincere Devotionis, authorizing Isabel and Fernando to conduct an inquisition in Castile to extirpate the heresy among those who had converted from Judaism and those infected thereby. The sovereigns were pleased the inquisition could be directed solely at the conversos and at rich and poor alike because the overwhelming popular sentiment demanded those targets. The pope did disappoint in one respect, however. Traditional church doctrine held that a person whose conversion had been absolutely forced—such as on threat of death—had never truly become a Christian and therefore could not be guilty of heresy, and the bull appeared to recognize that an inquisition would not be directed at such a converso. The sovereigns knew this limitation would disappoint the general populace and wondered how such a converso would be identified and how many might be so exempted. While the bull's authority to conduct the inquisition extended throughout Castile, perhaps neither sovereign then had a grand vision of its use beyond Andalusia. Fray Torquemada did.

Isabel understood the inquisition so authorized would take a step she once thought inappropriate. If implemented, it would be directed only at former Jews, not at a single old Christian who disregarded his religion. But a converso could be innocent, it was less than a law subjecting every converso to a subservient status, and the sovereigns' converso advisers and supporters presumably would not be affected.

Through nine years of marriage, Isabel and Fernando had made important decisions jointly, and, with the overwhelming press of objectives to accomplish, they had developed a sharing of authority where one sometimes took lead responsibility. Isabel now sometimes deferred to Fernando on military strategy and, when the separate interests of Aragón were significantly implicated, on its foreign policy. But the decision to defer or implement an inquisition in Castile, dealing with the most fundamental issues of faith, conduct, heresy and justice, was for and by them both and within the ambit of Isabel's strongest convictions. At this time, Isabel chose to continue to rely on Christ's love rather than his sword.

GUACANAGARÍ
Gold Homage, Marien

One afternoon, after completing Uncle's responsibilities for the day, Guacanagarí sat in the shade of a tree with his aging Father and Uncle, discussing difficult caciqual decisions and the consequences for the cacique's soul when it departs the body on death.

"If a man has been good to others and promoted peace and tranquility, his soul departs to travel on a path that is full of joy," Uncle began. "If he has treated others badly, his soul's path will be dark and dreadful. So where will a cacique's soul travel when, for the good of his people, he instills fear in them or commands that they harm others?"

Guacanagarí politely paused to reflect on the question, although his initial reaction was that the answer was obvious. "It's the cacique's responsibility to defend his people and territory from Caribe attack and any other enemy—such as encroachment by Caonabó or the Xaraguáns. War or fighting for that purpose are justified and don't prevent the cacique's soul from attaining the path of joy." He reflected that the answer was not entirely obvious. "There may be times when attacking an enemy first is necessary for protecting one's people. That's justified, as well. Sometimes, maintaining one's authority requires frightening a subordinate cacique to compel loyalty, and that's justified—particularly if it helps one rule without dissention."

"One should be mindful to use force or threats only to the extent necessary, not more, and it's not always easy to decide what's necessary," Uncle cautioned. "Guacanagarí, indulge me for a moment in simple questions. If a storm arose and a Caribe raiding party were passing at sea, not intent on attacking, would you allow it to come ashore for shelter?"

"Of course not. If they came ashore, you'd kill them on the beach. That's protecting your people. There's no issue."

"If, instead of the Caribes, it was Caonabó in the canoe, would you let him ashore?"

"Of course, Caonabó isn't an enemy. While he may not be a friend, he may visit Marien peacefully. It'd be unthinkable, and a conclusive strike on one's soul, to prevent him from coming ashore. Preventing him—or for that matter any person other than an enemy—from landing in distress would be wrong, and would be condemned by all. What's more, when he came ashore, Caonabó would be in your debt, and you'd strengthen the protection of our southern border by such an act."

"Now, let me pose a real question, where perhaps the answer isn't as obvious," Uncle continued. "Suppose there were a hurricane that floods villages on our common border with Caonabó but which owe allegiance to him, not myself. In their distress, we offer them our fish. Can we withhold the fish unless they pledge their allegiance to us?"

"Of course not," Guacanagarí responded without hesitation. "Taínos offer food to friend and stranger alike, freely, whenever people meet. It'd be unthinkable to withhold food from those in distress for an advantage. But, after receiving it, the local caciques might offer us allegiance in reciprocity. They might not, and offer something else in return." Guacanagarí reflected for a moment. "I think it'd be acceptable conduct, after supplying them food, for you to suggest to the local caciques that you'd be gratified by their allegiance."

"I agree," Uncle replied. "But remember that our cacicazgo has never been as powerful as our neighbors, at least in my lifetime."

"Caonabó would view the suggestion as aggression," Father warned, interrupting.

"He would." Uncle gazed at Guacanagarí to ensure his attention. "We usually are better off responding to aggression than initiating it—even when our own aggression would be acceptable conduct. You'll have to make your own judgments, and it's important to appreciate that peace and harmony should be disturbed only for the most extraordinary objectives or concerns."

Guacanagarí grew circumspect, as Uncle had struggled his entire life to raise their cacicazgo's esteem and failed, and Guacanagarí knew this failure largely reflected that Uncle himself was perceived as less consequential than other caciques. Uncle wasn't feared as a warrior, admired for his wisdom, or appreciated as an exceptional taíno, a good man. Guacanagarí suspected Father understood this, but Father had never countenanced any such criticism. Guacanagarí had grown impatient to address Marien's stature himself as time marched toward his near-certain anointment.

The men were silent for a moment, and Guacanagarí's impatience welled and emboldened him. "I believe our esteem would benefit if I established my own military and spiritual reputation."

"It would," Uncle observed.

Guacanagarí advanced, as if thinking aloud, although the thoughts had preoccupied him for a long time. "I think I might lead a substantial squad of warriors around Marien, reviewing the coastal villages and their preparations for Caribe attack, and then march inland to meet our subordinate caciques in the mountains. I could also lead this year's gold homage. Both events could be made conspicuous, and the troops and gold homage would be in border areas watched by the Xaraguáns and Maguanans."

Uncle and Father glanced at each other, surprised.

"Marching with a squad of troops isn't customary, but I think it can be done without appearing menacing," Guacanagarí added. "Everyone knows we need to improve our defenses against Caribe raid."

"Leading troops along the coast is one thing," Father responded. "But taking troops inland would be perceived much differently. There's no risk of Caribe raid there, and Caonabó or the Xaraguáns might misconstrue it as a belligerent gesture, although I understand you don't intend that."

"I have no intention of changing or even risk changing our peaceful relations with neighbors. But I do want them to understand I'm comfortable with military action."

"I think you'd do better to establish your spirituality rather than a militancy," Uncle indicated. "Leading the gold homage in exemplary fashion is a fine idea. Guarionex's stature is principally due to his reputation as a wise Taíno versed in our spirits, not as a warrior. Your civility and generosity are well known, and you're not known as a warrior."

"Uncle, I have no intent or desire to be perceived as militant, but I should be respected as one who is not afraid to be a warrior when necessary."

"If the issue is your stature, I think the most pressing opportunity isn't leading troops or a gold homage, but whether you can secure Anacaona in marriage."

"The Xaraguáns know of my desire, our desire, to do so—as well as everyone else's." Uncle and Father nodded agreement. "But to secure that marriage, I must augment my stature."

Uncle realized his nephew's thoughts were not casual or tentative or wrong and that his own energy to advance his cacicazgo was fading sharply. "Let me study with the elders the idea of your peacefully marching on the borders with soldiers. But I commend you to lead the annual gold homage." Uncle looked to confirm Father's concurrence. "I understand you will dig conspicuously close to our border with Xaraguá, as your focus is to impress its cacique."

Guacanagarí led the annual gold homage when the rainy season began. Streambeds in the mountains bore gold dust and nuggets, which were gathered easily when the water flowed, and, as tradition, caciques throughout Haiti bid their male subjects halt work to dig for a few weeks. The gold obtained was embedded in amulets, face masks, and other objects to animate a soul or spirit.

Guacanagarí and the village behique invoked the homage with a cohaba ceremony, whereupon they accompanied hundreds of their subjects—fasting and celibate—into the highlands to villages bordering Xaraguá, where they were sheltered by local caciques. They dug with their hands in the mud of streambeds for twenty days—still fasting and celibate—trusting the spirits would receive their purity favorably and lead them to the gold, just as Guabonito had bestowed guanín on Guahayona when celibate.

As the men dug, the behique ambled through the neighboring countryside searching for spirits, and, when villagers showed him a tree moving its roots, he induced cohaba to speak to the spirit within, which revealed itself as an assistant to Yúcahu. Guacanagarí ordered woodworkers and an artisan to carve the spirit from the tree and inlay his eyes, ears, and nose with gold found in the homage. Pleased with the result, Guacanagarí dispatched a messenger bearing the cemí as a gift to the Xaraguán cacique, with the explanation that the spirit had revealed itself as Guacanagarí led the gold homage in a border area, attesting to the unique relationship between their two cacicazgos.

⊡   ⊡   ⊡

Uncle weakened and died within a few seasons. Many of his subjects were saddened, as on the loss of any cacique, many were relieved, hopeful of more exemplary leadership. Messengers were dispatched to invite the paramount Haitian caciques to the funeral ceremonies.

Guacanagarí arranged gifts of a face mask for each cacique, splendidly adorned with an unusual amount of gold, and lined the village central plaza with a row of warriors—never dispatched to the border areas—as he awaited his guests. Mayobanex and Cayacoa, now anointed as their cacicazgos' rulers, were unable to attend but sent subordinate caciques. Guarionex and Caonabó arrived with a few nitaínos but without any display of warriors. Behecchio came as his uncle's representative and explained his uncle was too old for the journey. Guacanagarí waited in vain for a compliment of his prior gift. Behecchio was accompanied by a few nitaínos, but not girls to sing and dance. Anacaona hadn't come.

Isabel, Fernando, and João
Treaties at Alcáçovas, Portugal, 1479–1481

In January 1479, King Juan II of Aragón died at eighty years, whereupon Fernando and Isabel became its king and queen. All of Hispania except Portugal was united under one rule, posing a formidable opponent to any foreign prince with contrary intentions.

In February, the Portuguese Cortes authorized the Duchess of Viseu Beatriz of Portugal, Afonso V's and the late Queen Juana's sister-in-law and an aunt to both Juana and Isabel, to seek a peace treaty with Isabel. Isabel met Beatriz alone in the Castilian town Alcántara at the border to discuss Juana's fate and peace and pardon terms. Isabel could not secure an acceptable agreement on Juana's parentage or elimination as an heir to the Castilian throne, and after a week she and her aunt gracefully handed the negotiations to representatives, including Prince João on behalf of Afonso. In September, two treaties were executed in Alcáçovas, Portugal.

The first treaty resolved the dynastic issue, extinguishing Afonso's and Juana's claims to the Castilian throne and offering Juana, then eighteen, the choice of marrying Prince Juan, then one, on his maturity or entering a nunnery. Juana chose the nunnery, believing the marriage would never happen. The treaty also provided for the marriage of Princess Isabel, then almost nine, to Prince João's son Afonso, then four, on their maturity to further solidify the kingdoms' perpetual peace.

The second treaty, the Treaty of Alcáçovas, lamented the great evils and disservice to God occasioned by the wars following King Enrique's death and, at God's recommendation and order, reinstated the perpetual peace that had been declared between Castile and Portugal in 1431. Isabel and Fernando looked forward to heal their kingdom, not behind to punish. The peace terms reestablished the kingdoms' boundaries as those existing on Enrique's death, and the disloyal Castilian nobles were pardoned, prisoners released, and financial claims extinguished.

This treaty also resolved the outstanding disputes regarding Guinea and ocean island claims in Portugal's favor. The possession of and trade in Guinea and the islands of Madeira, Porto Santo, the Azores, and Cape Verde, as well as others known or to be discovered or conquered from the Canary Islands down toward Guinea, were Portugal's with the exception of the Canary Islands—acquired or to be acquired—which were Castile's. Castile thereby recognized Portugal's right to Guinea and, effectively, to circumnavigate southern Africa to the Indies. The Castilian sovereigns agreed they would forbid their subjects to traffic in Guinea or Portugal's islands without consent of the Portuguese sovereign and punish those who did.

With peace secured, Isabel returned to Toledo and, in November, gave birth to the sovereigns' third child, Juana, named in memory of Fernando's mother.

Prince João, then twenty-four, had managed Portugal's Guinean trade in his tutelage and had been outraged by Isabel's disruption of it. Following the treaty's adoption, he and Afonso ordered Portuguese captains traveling to Guinea to capture unlicensed foreign vessels found in those waters and throw their entire crews overboard.

João understood far better than Isabel and Fernando that the treaty's concession of Guinea to Portugal conferred an exclusive route to the Indies. In 1481, he successfully sought a bull from Pope Sixtus,[*] confirming the prior papal bulls obtained by Prince Henrique conferring Portugal's exclusive right to traffic in Guinea and, in addition, clarifying that Portugal's southern territory lay below the southernmost point of the Canaries and west of and in the vicinity of Guinea. But João would live to learn he had not understood enough.

ANACAONA
Succession in Xaraguá

The paramount cacique of Xaraguá ruled his territory from a village on a dry agricultural plain east of the innermost point (Port-au-Prince) of the great gulf on Haiti's western coast. Farms stretched east and west from the village for miles, surrounding two freshwater lakes[†] and the great saltwater Lake Hagueygabon (Lake Enriquillo). The village drew its water from a large stream that tumbled north from the mountains on the southern coast and was siphoned to irrigate the fields, which were cultivated year-round. Women were practiced in cooking fine dishes for great feasts where guests were entertained by areítos that recorded Taíno culture, religion, and history. Civility, discourse, and beauty were understood and appreciated, as was the general peace that had reigned for generations.

Anacaona sat with her older brother, Behecchio, on duhos in the plaza before Uncle's caney, the largest in Haiti, sipping papaya juice, waiting to be summoned. They had grown up together, children of the same mother, and had always been close friends and confidants. Behecchio enjoyed and trusted Anacaona and appreciated her sharp intelligence, uncommon presence, and mystique as Haiti's most

---

[*]Aeterni Regis, June 21, 1481.
[†]Guacca and Yainagua (Trou Caïman and Etang Saumátre).

beautiful woman. Anacaona recognized that Behecchio was fit to rule Xaraguá, and that he was not only the customary choice but an excellent choice. He led warriors, inspired the loyalty of the subordinate caciques, and demanded the respect of Xaraguá's neighbors. They each appreciated that women were rarely selected cacique—only if a man cacique died and one of his sisters was then the only good choice—and that Anacaona would be fit to rule in that event. It was Anacaona through whom the family possessions—its cemís, duhos, canoes, and stores of cotton goods—would pass by custom, not Behecchio.

Uncle had called a council of the subordinate Xaraguán caciques and a cohaba ceremony next month to discuss succession and Anacaona's marriage. Presumably that was what he wanted to discuss today, perhaps to tell them his decisions, perhaps simply to ascertain their views. The time for resolution had come. Uncle was growing infirm. Behecchio already had taken almost a dozen wives. Anacaona had been initiated to womanhood in a traditional ceremony over a year before, and many women her age were already married. Uncle had offered her as a nighttime gift to important visiting caciques a number of times now, and she also had chosen her own partners and was ready for marriage.

Behecchio took Anacaona's hand. "Succession and marriage decisions are practical. If they think I'm fit to rule, they'll simply follow custom and choose me. It wouldn't be a criticism of you." Anacaona nodded and shrugged, and Behecchio continued. "Your stature makes your marriage an opportunity to forge an important alliance. If Uncle listened to you, who would you want to marry?"

"Before I answer, who do you think I should marry?"

"The obvious choices are Guarionex, Caonabó, and Guacanagarí. Caonabó and Guacanagarí are neighbors, so a marriage to either would secure peace along the common border. Caonabó is the stronger, more important to neutralize. Guarionex isn't a neighbor, but an alliance with him could neutralize Caonabó."

"Who should I want to marry? Who do you want me to marry?"

"From Xaraguá's viewpoint, the best marriage is with Caonabó. But I will support your preference, whoever it is. There are differences in these men that would affect your happiness—and your own exercise of authority."

"Behecchio, I want to hear your thoughts on these men. You know them, and I don't. They have many wives, and they're all older than you, no less myself. Uncle has never asked me to sleep with any of them."

Behecchio was amused Anacaona sought more information before revealing her views. "Guarionex is the most thoughtful and cultured. Perhaps he would understand you best and you would enjoy his company the most, as well as his confidences, and through his confidences have influence. The marriage understandings must include that you be the principal wife in function, if not in affection. But his territory is farther away, and your continuing access to Xaraguá would be less. Caonabó is the best warrior, as we all know, but he would appreciate your culture less, and I'm not sure you would influence his thinking. Guacanagarí is cultured and would appreciate you, and you might be able to exert control over him more than the other two."

"If the choice were mine, I wouldn't choose Guacanagarí. He doesn't have my stature, or Xaraguá's stature, in any respect. I want to marry only a cacique of the greatest stature." Anacaona paused, confirming by his expression that Behecchio agreed. "You say that I must be the principal wife in function, if not affection, and I agree. As to commanding affection, I will handle that myself. But being the principal wife is not enough. I must be entitled to bring Xaraguán nitaínos and naborias to my husband's caney, beholden to my exclusive control." She paused again to stare directly into her brother's eyes. "These older men will pay attention to me only if I have authority and power independent from them, and that must come from my retaining authority and power in Xaraguá."

Behecchio stared directly back. "Assuming I'm chosen cacique, you will retain access to Xaraguá and the family possessions. Your child will succeed me if worthy. These are not only custom, but my agreement with you. It must be understood that your husband has no authority in Xaraguá. I will not choose as my successor any child of yours if that is your husband's design. Xaraguá is and must remain independent and supreme."

"I agree." She kissed his forehead.

"So, who do you want, Caonabó or Guarionex?"

"Let's see what Uncle has to say first."

Behecchio burst into laughter.

Within moments, Uncle summoned Behecchio into the ceremonial bohío to advise him that Uncle would recommend to his council that Behecchio succeed as cacique, whereupon Uncle congratulated Behecchio and dismissed him. He summoned Anacaona to tell her Behecchio would be the chosen successor and that Uncle would recommend to the council that she be married to Caonabó. Anacaona explained the marriage conditions she thought were important, and Uncle indicated that he had already thought of all of them and a few others. He congratulated her and consoled her that, regardless of Behecchio's selection, he had never doubted her ability to rule Xaraguá.

CRISTÓVÃO
Marriage in Lisbon, (1479)

In 1477, Cristoforo returned from Thule and made his home in Lisbon, taking jobs as an agent arranging shipments for the leading Genoese merchant families doing business there. He learned some Portuguese and become known in Lisbon as Cristóvão Colombo or simply Cristóvão Colom. In Savona, Brother Bartolomeo decided at sixteen to become Cristoforo's assistant in Lisbon rather than apprentice as a weaver. Domenico was confident his two sons would complement each other. He recognized Bartolomeo as the shrewdest of his children, more careful and astute with people than Cristoforo and harsher and less trusting.

The brothers lived in a small room near the port in Lisbon's commercial district (Baixa), surrounded by the bustle of Portugal's burgeoning African trade and close to the shipyards. The Crown buildings for administering the trade and collecting the gold were but a few minutes' walk, overlooking large plazas abreast the quays and piers where ships berthed to load and unload. Merchandise arriving and departing lay everywhere, including slaves held in pens awaiting evaluation of their age, health, and strength necessary so buyers and sellers could negotiate prices.

Cristóvão decided they would go into business making maps for sale to mariners. They purchased parchment and paint and became accomplished at their trade, particularly Bartolemeo, producing charts of the Portuguese coast, the Mediterranean, and the Ocean Sea. Bartolomeu—as he then became known—minded the business when Cristóvão traveled with the shipments he arranged.

The brothers enjoyed Lisbon and, following Domenico's example, worked tirelessly to establish themselves. The city's neighborhoods were home to many foreign peoples—merchants from Venice, England, and Flanders, and Arab and black Mohammedans from Africa—and its hillsides gracefully descending to port reminded them of home. They explored the old city, the Alfama, climbing its steep, narrow streets to sit on the hillside outside the walls of the Alcáçova (Castelo de São Jorge), built by the infidel in the eleventh century, where the king resided when in Lisbon. They ventured past Restelo (Belém) to watch ships departing north and south into the Ocean Sea, stopping to pray at the small chapel of the Santa María de Belém established by Prince Henrique for mariners.* They gazed at the sunset over the horizon and, infrequently, saw ships dip beyond it en route to the Azores, more than eight hundred miles west.

Cristóvão began to seek an advantageous marriage. He purchased finer clothing with his modest earnings and began to attend church services at the Convento dos Santos west of the commercial district, which boarded widows and daughters of the knights of a Christian military order. Every Sunday, he studied the women and girls as they came to mass and, when service recessed, followed them into the convent's gardens overlooking the Tagus River where they were available to meet suitors. One Sunday, he approached a woman who looked about his age, beyond the norm for a woman's marriage, and introduced himself in the broken Portuguese he had acquired, with confidence and bravado.

"I'm Cristóvão Colombo, a Genoese merchant and cartographer, and it would be my privilege and pleasure to talk with you." The woman smiled and nodded, indicating she would entertain more of his advance. "I now live in Lisbon, near the port, and have just returned from exporting goods from Scio and exploring the seas at

---

*A tiny predecessor at the site of the Convento de Jerónimos, *Belém* being Portuguese for Bethlehem.

Thule. I've fought pirates off Cape St. Vincent and sank four or five of them before my ship succumbed."

Filipa Moniz Perestrelo was shy, an elderly twenty-six or so, and flattered by the attention, conscious that charm would be necessary to offset an absence of beauty. She knew the suitor sought her background and was eager to tell him.

"I'm Filipa Moniz Perestrelo, of noble stock through both my father and mother. My father was Bartolomeu Perestrelo, the nobleman of King João I's household to whom Prince Henrique conferred hereditary governorship of the island of Porto Santo. Father passed away when I was young. He had fought with Henrique in Africa and his ancestors hailed from Piacenza, north of Genoa. My mother is Isabel Moniz, Father's third wife, born of a noble family established for centuries in the Algarve on our southern coast. My brother Bartolomeu has assumed the governorship of Porto Santo, and Mother and I visit the family possessions there often."

Both remained interested, Cristóvão keenly so. He began to tell some humorous stories of his travels. Filipa enjoyed his cheer, and he enjoyed her trusting simplicity and warmth. He asked if he could talk with her the following Sunday, and she gaily agreed. She told her mother Isabel.

Cristóvão and Isabel investigated further. Cristóvão inquired with agents of the Spinolas and di Negros, and they confirmed Filipa's nobility, although they noted that the family was not wealthy. The Perestrelos were known to the king and court, particularly since some of their women had born the archbishop of Lisbon's children. Isabel's chief of household conferred directly with the same Genoese families, and they related that Cristóvão was nobody, his parents were nobody, and he worked as a merchant's agent and common seaman and made maps when unemployed.

Isabel met with Cristóvão directly one Sunday. She asked whether he enjoyed hunting on horseback and dancing at court and to see his family crest. He told her that he had no inherited wealth but that his ancestors were distinguished. He described his business and travels. Isabel's chief of household investigated his habits in Lisbon, and Isabel was comforted that he was religious, well spoken, never swore, and rarely drank, and that he did earn a living.

Cristóvão asked Brother Bartolomeu whether he thought the potential match worth pursuing. Bartolomeu said Cristóvão could do no better and that it was a long shot. Cristóvão shouldn't dare request a dowry or that would sink it. If the marriage were landed, servants would cook his food and wash his clothes and he might live as a merchant on Scio. He might even meet Prince João.

Cristóvão agreed. He liked Filipa, as well. She spoke to him as if they were of equal status. He recalled how inconsequential Father was to the Genoese nobility.

Filipa soon asked Isabel's consent if Cristóvão proposed marriage. Isabel angrily refused at first, admonishing that the marriage was beneath their lineage as Cristóvão had no noble heritage whatsoever. But she recognized Cristóvão was an able conversationalist, unfortunately boastful, but always pleasant and engaging to everyone. He could be introduced at court. He could learn to dance at banquets with Isabel's friends and even at the prince's court. Isabel also recognized that, if Cristóvão proposed, it likely would be the only offer Filipa ever received. She allowed the courtship to continue.

The courtship frequently was interrupted as Cristóvão traveled to arrange shipments for Genoese merchant families. In July 1478, Cristóvão shipped to Madeira to purchase some sugar for Paolo di Negro as agent for the Genoese nobleman Lodisio Centurione. Lodisio advanced Paolo funds for the full purchase price and Cristóvão purchased the sugar in Madeira in advance of receiving most of the funds from Paolo. When Paolo failed to deliver the remaining funds, the transporting ship left for Genoa with only that portion of the sugar paid and Lodisio brought claims in Genoa against Paolo. Cristóvão was called to Genoa in 1479 to testify as a witness.

Before departing Lisbon, Cristóvão proposed to Filipa, and she and her mother consented. Cristóvão and Filipa found shadows in the convent gardens and embraced. His heart pounded with satisfaction that he had achieved a tremendous advancement. Her heart pounded that, while others might scorn, she would be married and bear children and attend the king's court with a husband.

Cristoforo testified in Genoa as a citizen of Genoa in the sugar shipment matter on August 25, 1479. In the days preceding, he reunited with his family in Savona. Domenico and Susanna were aging, and

Domenico had reverted simply to weaving. They were pleased to hear of their boys' successes as business agents and mapmakers, and they were astounded to learn of Cristoforo's engagement to a woman of noble birth. Cristoforo accurately described Filipa's charm, but Domenico and Susanna concluded to themselves that Filipa must be unusually unattractive or pregnant, probably both. Cristoforo's parents and siblings didn't have the means to travel to Lisbon for his wedding. This was convenient for him, since he didn't want them to attend. He gave a portion of his savings to Domenico, and, on August 26, Cristóvão sailed from Genoa for Lisbon.

In the autumn, Cristóvão and Filipa were married in her convent's church in a simple, sparsely attended ceremony. That evening, Cristóvão made love to her and consummated their marriage. For both, their nakedness and warmth dispelled the constraints of class and origin, and of wealth and want, and they were happy together and with their union. Neither then expected more of the other. They each looked forward to Cristóvão's success in exploiting Moniz and Perestrelo contacts to better himself and to dancing at Prince João's court.

IV
1480 — 1485, AMBITION

CAONABÓ AND ANACAONA
Marriage in Xaraguá

Caonabó released his naborias to return home and sat motionless alone upon a log astride a creek in the Cibao's foothills, intent on immersing himself with the great beast of Haiti on which he had now lived for almost two decades. He shut his eyes, savored the creek's soft gurgle, the scent of the glade's ferns, and the coolness hovering above the water, and waited for the beast to grow accustomed to his presence. The birds soon returned to the surrounding trees and then alighted in the streambed. Caonabó raised his eyelids a sliver.

Some thirty paces upstream stood a heron, as motionless as Caonabó, its gray legs rising as slender sticks among the reeds where it stood. The bird spied Caonabó's eyelids flicker and they studied each other carefully. Each spotted a small frog resting on a stone in the creek between them, and Caonabó wondered whether the heron would hunt. Perhaps it felt too distant from the frog, he too close, or the frog too small. After a few moments, the heron began to move about, skirting the frog while apparently searching for other prey, making its motion obvious and feigning disinterest. The bird came within striking distance and turned to face the frog, which was well aware and prepared to jump. But the heron's eyes darted back and forth between the frog and Caonabó many times.

The stalemate lingered, and Caonabó reflected that critical judgments—whether to attack or retreat, whether one was safe or vulnerable, and whether another was friend or foe—frequently were difficult to make. He felt his soul rejuvenated and stood to depart, whereupon the heron took flight and the frog dived into the creek, and he thanked Haiti for the serenity of the past few moments and her wisdom.

When he reached the village outskirts, his closest nitaínos awaited to advise him excitedly that a Xaraguán nitaíno waited at the caney, bearing a message he would not reveal. All agreed it must be the response regarding Anacaona, and they reminded Caonabó to be gracious whether he had won or lost. Caonabó assured them he would be—Anacaona's hand was but one of many means to maintain friendship with Xaraguá. But he churned inside.

Caonabó hailed the nitaíno from the plaza and walked slowly to greet him. Neither sought an audience in solitude or to engage in pleasantries, and without much ado the Xaraguán informed Caonabó that his offer to marry Anacaona had been accepted provided he agreed to certain understandings.

Caonabó glowed triumphantly, his nitaínos cheered him loudly, and the news immediately spread throughout the village. No one—including himself—could have envisioned this accomplishment two decades before.

The Xaraguán terms were not surprising, and Caonabó and his nitaínos realized they were not worth negotiating because the Xaraguáns would remain firm. Maguana's western border would be secure from encroachment, the alliance would have unequaled strength on Haiti, and Caonabó's stature and influence would rise in manner not otherwise achievable. Messengers departed for Xaraguá that afternoon to communicate Caonabó's acceptance, bearing ceremonial stone axes for Behecchio and his uncle as gifts and, for Anacaona, a red shell necklace of Mother's made on Aniyana.

As dusk approached, Caonabó dismissed his nitaínos, dispatched his children and naborias to the river to bathe, and spoke alone with his nine wives. He told them that his relationships with them had

not changed and that they must welcome Anacaona as an honor to
the household. He then dismissed eight of them, leaving Onaney and
himself alone.

She had been crying, and he held and kissed her.

"This changes nothing between us. My love for you remains as
always, born on Aniyana and constant since."

"I understand it's a tremendous honor for you, Caonabó."

"I'm honored. My rule is strengthened. That's the point." He
gazed away. "Anacaona will become my principal wife in public and
at public ceremonies, and you will have to step aside." He watched
her grimace and gazed into her eyes. "But our bond is unchanged."

"Our bond shouldn't change!" Onaney replied in a hoarse whisper. "Her nobility doesn't mean she'll care for you. Her areítos might
be wise, but that doesn't mean she will understand you. There is no
one who has stood with you as I." Tears returned to her eyes. "Your
entire life!" She bit her lip. "Caonabó, the beauty of the stingray and
the spider belie their venom."

"You once predicted I'd never return for you. I brought you
here—for your entire life." He held her some moments longer and
then indicated she was dismissed with another kiss.

◻ ◻ ◻

Behecchio and Anacaona, together with their mother and Uncle,
began arranging the wedding ceremonies—particularly the secluded
bohío at the village's perimeter for the abstention rite and the thoughts
to be expressed in the areítos sung. Mother tutored Anacaona on
the intimate aspects of being one of many wives, about commanding
a husband's affection while maintaining harmony with the others.
Mother assured her that she was the most beautiful woman in Haiti
and the cleverest, and that she should simply rely on her own instincts
and Caonabó would be smitten. They had heard reports of Caonabó's first wife, apparently his favorite, an unimportant but clever
Lucayan born on Aniyana, undoubtedly to be jealous. Mother promised Anacaona her intellect and nobility would absorb Caonabó's
attention, sundering his bond to the Lucayan.

Anacaona retired to be shuttered alone in the secluded bohío the
day before the wedding, and Uncle and Behecchio met the ranking

guests as they arrived at the central plaza. A Cuban cacique, a trading partner from Cuba's eastern tip, entered first, followed by Caonabó's friend Cayacoa from Higüey, Guarionex from Magua, and Guacanagarí's brother, who came as his representative. Caonabó, nitaínos, and warriors entered last with naborias bearing food and gifts, and the celebrations erupted—all present except Anacaona—with a feast and games of batey continuing into the evening. Uncle circulated among his guests, assuring each cacique that the marriage did not affect their own special relationship. Caonabó did the same.

Alone in her bohío, Anacaona listened to the din of conversation and laughter and rehearsed in her mind the following day, when she would start to win both her husband's affection and respect. He would understand not only that her womb bore a Xaraguán ruler but also that she would remain nigh such a ruler herself.

In the morning, her nitaínos dressed her in her wedding attire—gold and guanín jewelry on her ears, wrists, and ankles, a flower garland in her hair, and Caonabó's gift of the red shell necklace. For the last time, she was otherwise fully naked, without a nagua. Caonabó was dressed by his nitaínos, with his crown and gold jewelry and red stripes painted on his back, symbolizing male fertility.

Uncle solemnly announced commencement of the marriage ceremony. The ranking caciques were escorted to stand before the door of the secluded bohío, in which Anacaona remained, while Caonabó stood apart with Uncle and Behecchio to watch, together with the other guests. Cayacoa started the abstention rite, shouting for all to hear that he was entering the bohío to have sex with Anacaona and then abruptly charging into the bohío. For a few seconds, Cayacoa and Anacaona stood motionless side by side, hidden from the crowd's view, and Anacaona then shouted for all to hear that she would not have him, and he stepped back outside. Guacanagarí's brother then yelled that he would have her and bounded into the bohío. Anacaona shouted that she would not have him, either, and he stepped back outside. The Cuban cacique then shouted and entered the bohío. Anacaona had been given to him for a night months before, and they smiled at each other, remembering. He wished her good luck, and she shouted that she would not have him either. One by one, each of the other caciques entered the bohío and each was similarly repulsed.

The last cacique to perform was Guarionex, and the crowd grew silent as he took his turn. Guarionex spoke calmly, indicating that he would have Anacaona, and entered the bohío slowly, gracefully. Anacaona gazed at him, breathlessly aware that she was in the presence of the perhaps the greatest Taíno then living other than Uncle, whom Uncle had rejected as a husband for her. Guarionex gazed back at her, younger than his oldest children, and recognized she probably was the most beautiful woman in Haiti. Their eyes met and they smiled. Anacaona then shouted that she would not have him, and he stepped outside the bohío.

Anacaona waited a moment and then burst from the bohío, shouting that she was strengthened and invincible. The guests applauded wildly. Amid the uproar, Anacaona recognized Caonabó standing just feet away, and they beheld each other for the first time since Cacibaquel's funeral. She was mesmerized by his height, adornments, and presence. Astonishment and pride flushed through her, as she realized he was the right choice and that there could have been no other. He was mesmerized by her beauty and poise and instantly sensed he wanted her as his own, regardless of her status. A rush of victory, conquest, and lust shook him.

The ceremonies reverted to the plaza. Xaraguán mothers and girls sang areítos to Yúcahu and Attabeira, Yúcahu's mother and the spirit of female fertility and fresh water, to bless Xaraguá, Maguana, and the marriage. As all anticipated, Anacaona sang and danced alone. She enthralled the gathering with her serene calm and confidence, as well as the beauty of her voice and nakedness and dance, uniquely sensual and sophisticated. She sang of Guabonito and her gift of guanín to Guahayona and explained that, for years, Anacaona herself had wanted to give Caonabó her own gift of the womb that bore the cacical family. The areíto continued with a prayer that she and Caonabó would be fertile and explained that their child might rule both cacicazgos. Caonabó listened carefully. He understood the words, and he understood the uncommon directness and independence of the young woman he was marrying. He remembered the heron and frog in the stream in the Cibao and wondered which he was. Caonabó and Anacaona were then joined in marriage.

The villagers feasted and partied into the night. Toward the end, Caonabó and Anacaona said farewell and, hand in hand, left for the secluded bohío. As they walked, they spoke alone for the first time, and Caonabó complimented her areíto.

"I make them up all the time," she said with a laugh. "It was nothing, but I hope you really liked it because that's what's important to me."

They entered the bohío, and she offered him a small gourd with pineapple juice. As he sipped, she stroked his arms and chest. "Have you ever been wounded in your great battles?"

As he responded, she approached intimately and took the gourd from his hand and began to remove his caciqual belt, placing the gourd and the belt on a duho to the side of the hammock where they would sleep. "You're incredibly strong."

He looked down at her, and she wrapped her arms around his neck, kissing him and pulling their bodies gently together. He felt her supple body and was taken with desire. He lowered himself backward into the hammock, pulling her on top, and they made love with growing passion until he was spent. She lay on him, and they felt as one.

They smiled at each other, kissed, and talked into the night. As he slumbered, she began to sing to him softly, continuing her own areíto of Guabanito. Guabanito returned to Guahayona after he was anointed cacique and consented to marry him. She agreed to stay as long as he continued to make her happy.

CRISTÓVÃO
Births of Diogo Colombo and an Idea, Porto Santo, (1480–1481)

After their wedding, Cristóvão, Filipa, and her mother, Isabel, sailed from Lisbon six hundred miles southwest in the Ocean Sea to Vila Baleira on Porto Santo's southeastern shore, the island's port and largest town, where they took up residence in family possessions. The island stretched barely eight miles, with volcanic mountains at its northeastern and southwestern tips, lower grassland in between, steep cliffs on the windswept northwestern coast, and a lovely beach stretching more than six miles on the protected southeastern shore. Cristóvão's father-in-law had imported livestock that grazed the grassland.

Filipa was pregnant and she gave birth to a son they christened Diogo in Vila Baleira's church.* The delivery was difficult, and Filipa

---
*Ingreja de Nossa Senhora da Piedade.

never fully regained her prior strength and vitality. When Filipa was able, she and Cristóvão carried Diogo on walks south along the great beach.

Cristóvão continued to work as an agent for Genoese merchant families and began to build his business from Vila Baleira. He passed through Madeira—visible from Porto Santo—frequently and shipped from there or Lisbon to the Canary Islands, less than 350 miles south of Madeira, and to the Azores, whose largest eastern island, São Miguel, was 950 miles northwest of Madeira. Madeira had abundant timber, sugar plantations, and vineyards. Slaves from the Canaries and Africa had been imported to work its plantations, and Madeira and Porto Santo were key watering and refitting stations for Portugal's Guinean gold and slave trade. When in Lisbon, he stayed with Bartolomeu, who continued the mapmaking business.

Cristóvão sometimes explored Porto Santo with one of his brothers-in-law, Pêro Correia da Cuhna, and was drawn to the rocky cliffs and crags on the northwestern coast. Pêro related he had found carved driftwood cast there in a westerly wind and speculated that it had been blown from unknown islands. Pêro had also retrieved driftwood he believed to be bamboo cane and explained that others, including Prince João himself, had seen similar driftwood. Ptolemy believed bamboo was grown in the Indies, and the speculation was the canes had originated there.

Isabel and Cristóvão enjoyed each other's company and occasionally discussed the exploration of the world, and she gave him her deceased husband's private papers, maps, and nautical possessions. Cristóvão was surprised how outdated the maps were—in just his lifetime, the Portuguese had discovered Guinea's extension south beyond the equator, the archipelago of the Cape Verde Islands, and the most distant Azorean islands.

Cristóvão began to amble the cliffs along the northwestern shore alone, gazing at the sunset over the western horizon and contemplating his future and the astounding enormity of the Ocean Sea. Almost thirty, he was confident that he had advanced beyond his father by profession and marriage. But he wondered whether he was satisfied to be a merchant's agent. He reflected that the nobility, wealth, or glory of his father-in-law, or more substantially of Marco Polo or the Eiríkur the Red spoken about in Thule, or even of the Vivaldi brothers, derived from their voyages, discoveries, or settlements. He recognized that his own position would achieve neither nobility nor great wealth, and he dreamed that discovering his own island—like Scio or Porto Santo—would achieve both.

As he traveled as a merchant's agent, Cristóvão grew more than accustomed to ships, sailing, and the ocean. He began to study them keenly, with as much interest as the cargos he was employed to deliver and the profits to be had thereby, assimilating information about the channels, currents, and weather of the ports he visited and the seas he sailed, derived both through his own observations and stories told by sailors and island residents. He shipped on caravels, carracks, cogs, galleasses, urcas, and other vessels and came to appreciate their relative merit—the tonnage of cargo they floated, the degree they sailed into the wind, their maneuverability in the shallows at port, and their seaworthiness in the swell and storm at sea. He began to study navigation and the measurement of location and distance by degrees of latitude and longitude, curious to understand the ancient and modern estimates of a degree's length and the earth's circumference.

As every sailor, Cristóvão came to understand how quickly comfort and safety could descend to peril on the Ocean Sea, and his faith in his God became resolute and beyond doubt. At sea, he sang to the Lord at dawn and dusk, he prayed to the Virgin when the sand clock turned every half hour, and he invoked her when the fury of the Ocean Sea broke upon the deck and threatened to shatter the ship. A mariner's rhythm rooted within him, with the Lord as compass, and he confessed and took communion often and prayed at tierce, vespers, and other offices—whether at sea or ashore.

When Cristóvão shipped to the Azores, sailors told of unusual pine trees and dead bodies with non-European features swept onto the rocks and of carved wood plucked from the sea. When he shipped to the Canaries, he heard that rafts and boats topped with houses had been found blown ashore on the African coast. Sailors and fishermen on both archipelagos claimed that other islands could be spotted when sailing west, but Cristóvão was skeptical, understanding that even experienced mariners frequently—wishfully—mistook clouds or haze on the horizon for landfall. He heard that the winds at the westernmost Azorean islands, Corvo and Flores, were predominantly from the west or southwest,* perhaps rendering sailing further west difficult for an extended period. He saw for himself that the winds at the Canaries blew to the southwest,† and the current flowed southwest off to sea, every season he visited, facilitating sailing west. He recognized the Ocean Sea was more benign at the Canaries than to the north at the Azores, and far less tempestuous than at Thule.

In Lisbon, Cristóvão and Bartolomeu shared the geographical knowledge acquired from Cristóvão's travels and Bartolomeu's ongoing contacts with pilots and mapmakers. Together, they wondered where the lost Antillia should be located on a map of the Ocean Sea. The tradition was that seven bishops had embarked from Lusitania in the eighth century to escape the infidel's conquest and preserve Christianity, settling on Antillia and burning their ships so their congregations would not be tempted to return home. The island lay perhaps no more than 750 miles west of the Azores. Perhaps it lay west of the Canaries, considerably south.

"Men don't know where Antillia lies," Cristóvão said. "But it'll be possible to find it since it was found before." He studied his younger brother and, for the first time, revealed to another what he had been dreaming. "It may also be possible, if the weather permits it, to sail all the way west to the Indies. We know the Indies exist, too. Marco Polo lived there."

Bartolomeu shrugged. "The distance is too great, regardless of the weather. No ship could be provisioned for such distance."

"I've heard other mapmakers say the ancients believed it could be sailed—that Aristotle and Seneca taught it was but a few days' sail from Hispania to the Indies."

"Cartographers have always claimed that, but men have tried and failed."

"Bartolomeu, they say Seneca prophesized that the Ocean Sea would be sailed to discover new worlds beyond. Some claim a John Mandeville has written in recent times‡ that it's possible to travel completely around the earth."

---

*The prevailing westerly winds.
†The permanent trade winds.
‡1356–1366.

Bartolomeu realized the discussion was not just about geography and waited.

"We could be the discoverer of Antillia or other islands. We could be the discoverer of Seneca's prophecy."

By early 1481, Cristóvão learned from a Florentine agent in Lisbon that King Afonso had received advice from the Florentine physician Toscanelli that the Indies could be reached by sailing west. Cristóvão obtained and reviewed a copy of Toscanelli's letter and was captivated—not only by the geographic conclusions but the description of the destination, which resembled what he had heard of Marco Polo's accounts.

According to Toscanelli, the Indies were ruled by one prince—a Grand Khan, meaning king of kings—who lived in the province of Cathay in a fertile land of spices and gems. The splendid city of Quinsay (Hangzhou), meaning the City of Heaven, was situated near the coast south of Cathay in the province of Mangi (south China), with an enormous circumference of one hundred miles, ten marble bridges, and a multitude of treasures. Farther south was Zaiton (Quanzhou), the world's busiest shipping port, where every year a hundred shiploads of pepper passed. The island of Cipangu lay to the east 1,500 miles, with temples and royal houses roofed with gold. The Grand Khan's ancestors had craved intercourse with Christians and requested the pope to send teachers of the faith, but none had reached them—yet.

Cristóvão decided to write Toscanelli himself. Toscanelli responded, enclosing a copy of the original letter and map and acknowledging Cristóvão's grand desire to travel west to the source of spices. Cristóvão wrote back with further questions and Toscanelli again responded, explaining that the voyage would take him to rich and powerful kingdoms eager to know of Christianity and that the novelty of the voyage would confer honor and inestimable gain and the widest renown among all Christians, befitting the great courage of the Portuguese nation.

ISABEL, FERNANDO, MEHMED II, AND ABŪ L'HASAN
Otranto and the Emirate of Grenada, 1480–1481

Isabel, Fernando, and Christian princes throughout Europe believed Mehmed II, emperor of the Ottoman Empire, was intent on their overthrow and the elimination of Christianity. Mehmed had conquered Constantinople in 1453, when but twenty-one years old, besieging the city for two months and entering it after his army and navy had breached the defenses. As his troops looted, butchered, raped, and enslaved, he had advanced through the carnage to the magnificent church Hagia Sophia to celebrate its first afternoon prayer to Allah and pronounce its conversion to a mosque, the Ayasofya, to be heralded by his people as "the Conqueror" ever since. He had stood as Conqueror before the Parthenon on the Acropolis in Athens in 1458 and converted it to a mosque, as well. By 1480, his empire extended from Trebizond at the southeastern corner of the Black Sea (northern Turkey) into Europe through the Balkans to Serbia's Smederevo.

In July 1480, Mehmed dispatched an armada of over one hundred ships bearing eighteen thousand troops, seven hundred horses, and considerable cannon from Vlore in Albania to cross the fifty-mile straight in the Adriatic Sea to attack the kingdom of Naples at Otranto, then ruled by Fernando's cousin, an illegitimate son of Fernando's deceased uncle King Alfonso V of Aragón. The Turkish cavalry surrounded Otranto and demanded surrender, whereupon the town's citizens would be spared, whether they remained or departed, and permitted to continue to practice Christianity. The offer was rejected, and the Turks crushed the defenders, beheading every priest and slaughtering more than ten thousand men. Those spared were offered the choice of converting to Islam or death, and eight hundred men who refused conversion were beheaded and their corpses left for the birds and dogs. Eight thousand prisoners were shipped back to Albania for slavery, together with gold and other booty.

Christians everywhere perceived Otranto's slaughter and loss as God's punishment for their societies' faithlessness, greed, promiscuity, and blasphemy. Isabel and Fernando ordered daily prayers throughout their kingdoms to assuage God's anger. They feared Mehmed would use Otranto as a base to conquer their own kingdom of Sicily, which was largely unfortified.

The emir of Grenada, Abū l'Hasan, was pleased by Mehmed's advance to Otranto, as were his Muslim subjects and the Mujadin under Catholic rule in Castile, Aragón, and Portugal. Over the past centuries, the Christian Reconquista had reduced the Islamic emirates of al-Andalus* to his small kingdom, and Abū l'Hasan's predecessors had built the Alhambra fortress in the city of Grenada as a final mountain refuge following retreat from their palaces in Córdoba and Seville. To preserve even this refuge, his predecessors frequently had humbled themselves to offer tribute and vassalage to achieve truce with the Christians. But Grenada's frontiers had not shrunk under Abū l'Hasan's rule, and it had been the Castilian rulers, Enrique and Isabel, who had sought assurances of mutual nonaggression, preoccupied with other opponents.

As Isabel and Fernando fretted, and Abū l'Hasan rejoiced, in Istanbul Mehmed planned an invasion of the Italian peninsula. Mehmed believed there was but one God and that the Prophet Muhammad alone had received God's last and true revelation. Mehmed tolerated the presence of infidels and nonbelievers, both in his conquered territories and his personal life, permitting peoples who did not oppose him and who were loyal subjects to continue worshipping as they were accustomed. But he believed the notion that a man had been God—and stories of a holy trinity, incarnation, and resurrection—was a ridiculous heresy, denying Christians an equal station on earth. He fervently held that, just as there was one God, on earth there must be only one empire, one true faith, and one emperor, himself.

But Mehmed would not live to achieve that destiny. In May 1481, he became ill suddenly and died at forty-nine, perhaps poisoned by his son, born to a Christian slave, and successor, Bayezid II. Isabel, Fernando, and other Christian princes now took their turn rejoicing—before grimly pondering what Bayezid next intended.

ISABEL, FERNANDO, DORAMAS, AND TENESOR SEMIDAN
Gran Canaria, Canary Islands, 1477–1483

Following the Treaty of Alcáçovas, Isabel and Fernando sought to reinvigorate the Castilian conquest of the Canary Islands, the first step in the creation of an overseas empire. The seven islands held fertile land for sugarcane and would serve as a trading base for African gold and slaves north of Guinea. Since colonization commenced (1402),

---

*The Moorish word for Hispania.

the three islands with the least population—Lanzarote, Fuerteventura, and El Hierro—had been subjugated. But settlers had been unable to overpower resistance in the four more populated islands—Gran Canaria, Tenerife, Palma, and Gomera—and those remained under control of the local peoples except for a harbor and garrison on Gomera. A Castilian noble couple of the Herrera and Peraza families held the hereditary governorship of the subjugated islands and Gomera, exacting tribute from the locals and exporting sugar, wine, dyes, and slaves. They utilized those subjugated to slave raid in the four unconquered islands.

The peoples native to the seven islands spoke different languages, observed similar but different customs, and were not organized as one nation or tribe, engaging in little navigation even among the seven islands. They lived in caves and stone huts, herded goat, sheep, and cattle, and farmed wheat and barley. Their skin was olive, the same color as the coastal peoples in Africa on the same latitude, and European court geographers and cosmographers theorized the local peoples' descent from Noah as originating in one of the lost tribes of Israel or some Muslim sect.

In 1477, Isabel and Fernando dispatched a squadron of soldiers to subjugate Gran Canaria, expecting little difficulty because the locals' weaponry consisted of wooden clubs, spears, darts, and stones and, other than a small, clothed ruling class, the locals usually went naked or wore only loincloths. The squadron landed on the island in June and began construction of a stone garrison. The two chiefs—*guanartemes*—then ruling the island recognized that the construction meant the Castilians intended to invade, settle, and subjugate their peoples, and they resolved to destroy the garrison. The more powerful chief, Doramas, was chosen to lead an attack, and he ascended a peak to pray to Acoran, his people's supreme god, for victory.

Isabel and Fernando had considered the status of the peoples to be conquered, their conversion to Christianity, and the consequence of resistance. The sovereigns' aim was to subjugate the heathen Canarians to the Crown's authority and entreat them to convert as free people—as vassals of the Crown directly subject to the sovereigns' control, not as the slave property of the conquering military governor or his commanders. St. Augustine had taught that the conversion of another person should be accomplished by persuasion, not force. The Catalan theologian Ramón Llull (ca. 1232–1316) had argued that crusades were to be led by spiritual knights seeking to convert by logic, reason, prayer, and love. Pope Sixtus IV recently had reaffirmed (1472–1476) the doctrine that enslavement of heathens on the path to Christianity was forbidden and warned that pirates and merchants who enslaved would be excommunicated. Isabel and Fernando readily accepted the doctrine's application to pirates and merchants who slave raided without any concern for the locals' conversion, and they would order the manumission of Gomerans enslaved and sold in Castile by Hernán Peraza, the heir apparent to the Herrera-Peraza title, and others. But they had sought and would obtain an interpretation of church doctrine that Canarians who did not convert or appear on the path to conversion upon the sovereigns' conquest—resisters—could be enslaved.

The Castilian commander foresaw Doramas's attack and sent a messenger to advise Doramas of the following "requirement": that the garrison had come in the name of the Castilian sovereigns to place Gran Canaria under their Christian protection and supremacy and to invite the inhabitants to adopt Christianity; if the inhabitants accepted submission as the sovereigns' vassals, they would not be harmed and could remain secure in their families, lands, and possessions under the sovereigns' protection; if they refused, they would be killed.

Doramas scorned and rejected the requirement, his people having repulsed invasions of Castilians, Portuguese, and the ancients since time forgotten, and he led his armies to attack at dawn the next day. His attack was fierce, and each side took heavy casualties, yet his armies failed to dislodge the garrison. The Castilians established a permanent mission (Las Palmas). They built a fort and started a war of raids to subjugate the island, destroying crops, seizing livestock, and killing those who resisted.

Doramas and his people continued to fight back, and Isabel and Fernando's conquest stalled. The Canarians were expert at drawing their pursuers into ravines to inflict an avalanche of rocks on them, and the Castilian mission suffered lapses in leadership. Isabel and Fernando learned that ruling an overseas colony was more difficult than commanding court in Castile as the overseas governor effectively was on his own and could not be supervised. In 1480, the sovereigns appointed Pedro de Vera, whose military and practical judgment Fernando trusted, as governor of the islands to reinvigorate the conquest. Hernán Peraza was brought to Castile and tried for the murder of the islands' former commander, but pardoned by Fernando in return for participating in the islands' conquest, as well as punished—at Isabel's insistence—by being required to marry, and return to the Canaries with, one of Isabel's attendants, Beatriz de Bobadilla,* a vivacious teenager who had caught Fernando's eye and perhaps much more.

Fernando and Isabel soon recognized their method for conducting the conquest did not effectively motivate their soldiers. They had compensated the commanders and troops with wages, funded by the church's sale of indulgences to penitents ensuring their admittance to heaven. But wages alone appeared insufficient incentive for facing death. The troops shied from the bloody task of rooting Doramas and his warriors from Gran Canaria's mountainous regions. The sovereigns decided to revert to the traditional incentive of the Reconquista, awarding the conquering commander hereditary title to a portion of the land conquered, with the conquered people working the land and paying him tribute, and encouraging the troops and others to settle by awarding them territory, labor, and tribute in return for assisting the locals' conversion.

Doramas watched Pedro assume command and convinced Tenesor Semidan, who had become ruler of Gran Canaria's smaller chiefdom, to join in an overwhelming attack marshaling all their troops. Pedro marched foot soldiers and mounted cavalry onto the plain of Tamaraseck (near Arucas) to meet Doramas's massively larger army. The battle drew heavy casualties on both sides, but Doramas was killed and beheaded, not appreciating that spears and stones were no match for mounted troops and firearms outside mountainous terrain, regardless of troop count.

A truce followed, and, as winter came, the Canarians planted their crops and Pedro arranged for their mass baptism, whether they comprehended it or not. Isabel and Fernando invited Doramas's successor to court in 1481 and greeted him and his noblemen as they

---

*A different person from Isabel's childhood friend of the same name.

might a lesser European prince, promising them and their subjects' freedom from enslavement and free movement within Castile—as any Castilian subject—in return for submission to vassalage and conversion to Christianity.

Tenesor was captured in 1482 and brought with a wife as royalty to meet the sovereigns in early 1483. After being feted at court and embraced by Fernando, he pledged vassalage and was baptized Fernando Guanarteme. King Fernando granted him some fertile land in his former kingdom. Fernando Guanarteme returned to Gran Canaria to assist the Castilians in the baptism of his subjects and the conquest of the island and, later, of the peoples on Tenerife. He convinced his noblemen on Gran Canaria to surrender, arguing resistance would result only in their destruction and that, upon surrender, the Castilians would continue to recognize them as nobility.

Fernando Guanarteme did not convince everyone, and many viewed him as a traitor. As Doramas before, many Canarians refused to surrender to conquerors or forsake their religion. Pedro's Castilian troops, together with local troops from the islands of Lancerote and Fuertaventura, marched through the island conducting a *tala*— seizing or burning herds, crops, and food stores in areas where the Canarians still resisted to starve them into submission and slaughtering most who resisted. Those captured were either executed or enslaved, including for sale in the slave markets in Seville and València. Innocents sometimes were killed in reprisal for attacks on Castilian troops to demonstrate that resistance was futile. Some Canarians chose to jump from high cliffs in suicide rather than forsake their god for Christ.

By 1483, Gran Canaria was fully subjugated. Land was allotted to the conquering troops and to Fernando Guanarteme, his nobility, and loyal followers, who were integrated into the island's new society. One of Fernando Guanarteme's daughters was married to the son of a Castilian nobleman.

Isabel and Fernando had learned to quash native resistance brutally, to use subjugated native troops in battle with those resisting—thereby dividing the natives to conquer them, and to integrate the native nobility into Castilian society through marriage and continued recognition of their nobility.

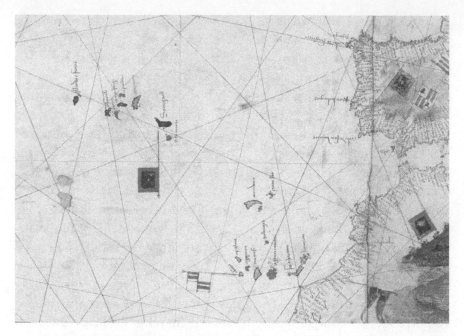

Canary Islands, Madeira and Porto Santo, and Azores, a portion of the Cantino
World Map of 1502.

JOÃO AND KING ANSA
Mina de Oro (Elmina, Ghana), 1481–1482

Prince João was crowned João II after his father, Afonso, died of the
plague in August 1481. He promptly sought to reinforce his claim on
the Guinean trade.

In João's view, the treaty at Alcáçovas, Sixtus's confirmatory bull,
and his own order to throw trespassers overboard were not enough to
ensure monopoly. He proposed to his Cortes that a fortress and permanent military presence, as well as the first Oriental church, be established near Samma (Shama) in the gold-trafficking region on Guinea's
southern coast (Gold Coast, Ghana). His advisers dismissed the idea
as impractical owing to the distance involved and the diseases men
suffered when trading there. He dismissed their advice, noting that the
possibility of converting even one soul to Christ was worth the effort.

João chose as the project's leader the nobleman Diogo d'Azambuja, an older man with administrative experience who had fought

against Castile, and ordered that the fortress be established peacefully, with the consent of the local Guinean ruler. D'Azambuja recruited one hundred craftsmen, an initial contingent of five hundred soldiers to ensure consent, and experienced captains, including one Bartolomeu Dias. In December 1481, the expedition departed Lisbon in a dozen ships, with the building materials loaded in two enormous urcas. The fleet arrived offshore Anomansa, a small coastal village east of Samma, by mid-January 1482, and d'Azambuja dispatched word to the local ruler—a king the Portuguese referred to as Caramanca—that he would debark the following day.

King Ansa, the paramount King of Edina,* observed the fleet was of unprecedented size and was pleased. His people, an Akan tribe, traded gold mined in local hillside tunnels and Guinea's interior to other coastal kingdoms, obtaining in return slaves to work the tunnels, farm, and do other labor. Ansa also had traded gold to the Portuguese for almost a decade, obtaining cloth, iron, and slaves the Portuguese purchased from the Wolof (Senegal) or Beny (Benin, Nigeria). The trade with the Portuguese always had been profitable and peaceful, and they valued gold more dearly than others. They had never sought to claim his land as their own.

But the pale men who landed at the beach the next morning didn't resemble previous traders. Some were finely dressed noblemen. Others obviously bore concealed weapons—and there were far more of them than necessary to accomplish any trade. They gathered at the foot of a large tree, hoisted their king's shields on it, and set a table with a wooden cross in the shade of its limbs, and their apparent prince sat in a high chair, waiting.

King Ansa grew angry and fearful. He knew the hidden arms, the shields, the cross, and the prince's throne were not about trade. But he hid distrust and alarm and ceremoniously led his warriors, armed with spears and bows and arrows, onto the beach to the beat of drums and other instruments.

D'Azambuja rose and advanced to greet him, whereupon Ansa pronounced, "Peace, peace," in Akan, and d'Azambuja's interpreter translated. Greetings to and from King João continued some moments.

---

*Kwamena Kweigya Ansah I, ruling 1475–1510.

"King João has always appreciated that King Ansa loads the Portuguese ships rapidly when they call here," d'Azambuja began, waiting for the interpreter to translate. "King João wishes to reciprocate this love and invite you and your people to embrace Christianity so that your souls may be saved. If you receive the baptismal water, the eyes of your soul will see clearly and João will regard you as friend and brother and help you in all your need. As a token of João's esteem, he has dispatched myself and other noblemen to trade merchandise never before seen in Guinea."

D'Azambuja studied King Ansa's reaction as the interpreter caught up, but Ansa neither smiled with pleasure nor winced with concern.

"If you permit, King João wishes to build a fortress here to house these riches and my men," d'Azambuja continued. "It would be the base for future merchandise trafficking and available to defend you and your people. It would be an honor for a Guinean king to have it built, and João has selected you over King Bayo of Samma because of his high esteem for you and the love you have shown. You would become powerful in this land and the lord of your neighbors."

King Ansa watched d'Azambuja's gestures as he spoke, reflecting with trepidation that Portuguese weaponry was far superior to his warriors' own. When d'Azambuja finished, Ansa gazed at the ground to collect his thoughts.

"I appreciate King João's gracious concern," Ansa responded through the interpreter, pausing to raise his eyebrows and linger on the words chosen, "with my soul and well-being. I do deserve that. For years, I have fairly traded with João's people. I'm surprised by your arrival. Previous Portuguese traders have been ill dressed and ragged, desirous of quickly trading and then returning to their homes. But you come with many people, including noblemen bedecked in finery, and now ask to establish a residence."

Ansa gazed directly into d'Azambuja's eyes, commanding that he listen.

"This profoundly disturbs me. You and your men should depart. Men of nobility always require things on a lavish scale and would not endure the simplicity of my kingdom. Friends who meet occasionally remain better friends than they would be if neighbors. The human heart is like the waves of the sea crashing upon a rock, whereby both the wave and the rock are damaged by the contact. I do not wish to disobey King João. To the contrary, I believe peace, trade, and openness to learning of King João's god would better flourish if you depart."

The men on the beach—black and white, minimally and fully clothed, and armed—paused in silence for d'Azumbuja's reply, gripping their weapons.

D'Azambuja stared steadfastly back at Ansa. "King João has sent me here because he desires peace and closer friendship with you. João trusts you to allow and assist my men to live without harm in a strange land where we will depend on assistance for food and survival. João is fair and immensely powerful. My men and I are the least of his subjects, and we fear him more than death itself. We will strictly perform João's command that peace and concord be maintained."

King Ansa again paused to consider the situation. He reflected that perhaps there could be a benefit from the proposed relationship and that, regardless, his people on the beach could be slaughtered if he did not accept. After a moment, he replied curtly, "I will permit the fortress to be built so long as peace and truth are kept. If not, I and my people can easily depart this village and leave you unassisted."

Ansa stepped back to signal the meeting was over. He chose not to commit to learning about Christianity. He suspected that d'Azambuja, having obtained permission to build a fortress, did not truly care about the response. King Ansa would continue to worship his own gods and the spirits of his ancestors who kept watch over the living. He left the beach to a drumbeat.

On the following day, d'Azambuja's men commenced preparing for the fortress's construction on a low rock tableau on the sea. Some of King Ansa's subjects attacked them because the site chosen was holy ground for their spirit worship. D'Azambuja rushed to quell the disturbance, rebuking the builders and distributing gifts to the attackers. The construction proceeded on the same site, and the fortress wall was completed within twenty days. But the gifts were insufficient. King Ansa's subjects remained unhappy, quarrels continued, and d'Azambuja soon decided to burn Ansa's village. He said he was establishing peace firmly.

The Portuguese quickly built a church near the tree where d'Azambuja's chair had been set, and Mass was said daily for the soul of Prince Henrique. The church graveyard steadily filled as jungle diseases beset them. The fortress and settlement were named São Jorge da Mina and grew rapidly as King Ansa's people traded gold for slaves—most bought by the Portuguese from the Wolof and Beni—who in return produced more gold.

Many Europeans came to believe that Mina was the Ophir from which King Solomon had annually imported gold. Mina augmented João's stature among Christian princes, and many of his subjects now wondered whether it was their own king—not Fernando of Castile—who would retake Jerusalem from the infidel.

The fort at Mina de Oro, taken from the Cantino World Map of 1502.

ISABEL AND FERNANDO
Inquisition, 1480–1483

By 1480, Cardinal Mendoza and Fray Talavera's two-year campaign to bring conversos to the faith was viewed by all as a failure. There was little change in the rituals and practices of Catholicism in Andalusia, and Seville's leading conversos were openly dismissive that an inquisition would be initiated.

In September, Isabel and Fernando issued an edict accepting the pope's 1478 bull and establishing an inquisition of the conversos in Andalusia, explaining that they were appointing two Dominicans as inquisitors for Seville in furtherance of preserving the faith, saving souls, and punishing bad Christians, as well as clearing the reputation of good Christians. Their edict quashed the issue whether the inquisition could apply to those whose conversions had been absolutely forced, stating simply that conversos hadn't been pressured or forced. The sovereigns expected the inquisitors, whom Torquemada approved, would be zealous and uncompromising. But, when the inquisitors published the edict in Seville, they found themselves ignored.

Affronted, Isabel and Fernando ordered all Andalusian noblemen to support the inquisitors. The Sevillian conversos became alarmed, some began preparations to emigrate to Portugal, Grenada, or Africa, and thousands fled Seville to reside in Andalusian towns controlled by Guzmán, Ponce de León, and other noblemen, many of whom took pity and gave shelter. In January 1481, the inquisitors responded by advising the nobility to seize and deliver the conversos who had fled and their property to the prison in Seville, warning the nobility they risked their own excommunication, trial as heretics, and property seized if they harbored heretics. Years earlier the nobility would have scorned and punished such a demand from two friars, but Isabel and Fernando's authority to discipline powerful nobility—and over the inquisition itself—now could be ignored only at the risk of grave peril. Many conversos returned to Seville.

The inquisitors gathered evidence and, by February, the first six men and women were charged, arrested, and imprisoned in Fray Hojeda's monastery and their properties sequestered. Their identities were not publicly revealed, nor were they informed of the witnesses against them. They were given a nonpublic audience before the inquisitors, afforded the opportunity to confess, judged guilty of heresy, and then taken to Seville's great cathedral, where Hojeda pronounced the sentence—burning at the stake—whereby they would be reconciled to Christ. Soldiers marched them to a field outside the city walls, the Tablada, and tied them to stakes, where they were given a final opportunity to repent and receive mercy—strangulation before the fires were lit. None accepted Christ, and they slowly expired in horrific agony, their flesh roasting from the feet up, their lungs suffocating in billows of smoke.

Within days, the inquisitors alleged that three of the wealthiest conversos in Seville had conspired armed resistance to the inquisition.

Their property was confiscated and they, too, were burned at the stake.

Few people witnessed these spectacles as the plague had returned to Andalusia, and Sevillians were reluctant to leave their homes, no less gather with strangers publicly. Perhaps fifteen thousand persons would die of the plague in the following months in Seville alone, a third of the city's population.

As the plague raged during the summer, the inquisitors traveled from town to town, congregation to congregation, refining their operating procedures and augmenting their staff to include fiscal assessors, lawyers, and clerks. They instituted the practice used in prior inquisitions of affording a term of grace in which a converso could repent and reconcile to Christianity—and during which every Christian had a duty to provide incriminating evidence. A converso who denounced heresies within the grace period would be reconciled to the church and required to serve penance—such as payment of fines and wearing a yellow robe emblazoned with an X and a conical hat (a sanbenito and coroza) for months. Those failing to denounce themselves were accused and tried, bearing the burden of proving innocence and forfeiting a fraction of their property to witnesses for the inquisitors. Conversos quickly came to understand that the result of trial audiences almost always was conviction.

The inquisitors wanted the conversos to fear not only damnation and the inquisitors but their neighbors—friend or enemy—and family, who might act as informants. Fear of thy neighbor was meant to extend the inquisitors' limited reach, with mass denunciation and reconciliation the principal objective, not trial audiences, and during 1481 most Sevillian conversos chose denunciation. Perhaps three hundred in total were burned at the stake—a number and spectacle dwarfed by thousands of diseased, dead bodies taken by the plague to be burned, buried, or simply decay throughout the city and its environs. But the inquisitors instilled fear in every converso and implicated every old Christian's duty to provide evidence, and this fear vastly exceeded their actual reach. Some conversos wrote Pope Sixtus IV to decry the arbitrariness and cruelty of the proceedings.

There was other converso resistance, and Isabel was deeply affronted by an anonymous pamphlet circulating in Seville that asserted Judaism was superior to Christianity and could be practiced concurrently. She directed Talavera to respond, and he wrote a vitriolic counterattack refuting the doctrinal errors of the heretic, explaining Catholic doctrines and practices were irreconcilable to Judaism—the synagogue of Satan—and admonishing that heretics deserved punishment. He remained steadfast to the principles that a true convert was as much a Christian as any other, and that Jews and Mudejar never baptized were not heretics. Yet, while he had opposed the inquisition, he now warned that Christ was armed and God's justice was cruel and vengeful. Isabel drew comfort from her confessor's publication, particularly his characterization of God's justice.

In 1481, Fernando requested papal permission to increase the number of inquisitors in Andalusia and began to implement the inquisition in Aragón based on preexisting papal authorization. Pope Sixtus IV responded by expressing his disappointment with the Andalusian inquisition, criticizing the behavior of the inquisitors. In reply, Fernando indicated his displeasure with the criticisms, and the pope granted Fernando's request, including the appointment of Fray Torquemada as an inquisitor.

But the pope's discomfort hardened, and he published a bull publicly charging that the inquisition in Aragón was not motivated by faith and the salvation of souls but by lust for wealth, indicating that the identities of witnesses could no longer be kept secret and sentences rendered were appealable to Rome. Fernando responded that he would not implement these changes, and Isabel sent the pope her own handwritten letter, explaining that the sovereigns were motivated by faith, not wealth. The pope soon withdrew his conditions and authorized the inquisition in Aragón on Fernando's terms.

Isabel and Fernando were pleased by the process of the inquisition and proud of it. The mass reconciliations and repentances confirmed the beneficence of their endeavor—the saving of souls and aggrandizement of Christianity throughout their realm. The burnings at the stake and other punishments confirmed the endeavor's righteousness—the purification of their realms and the faith. They came to perceive that both conversions and reconciliations under threat of force were true, at least from the perspective of Christ's teachings. For them, there was but one true faith to which a man could rightly believe, whether or not he arrived at this belief on his own initiative.

With papal approval, Isabel and Fernando appointed Torquemada Grand Inquisitor in charge of Castile's inquisition in 1482 and, following papal approval for Aragón's inquisition, of Aragón's inquisition, as well. In 1483, Isabel and Fernando took steps to separate Jews from the rest of Andalusian society by expelling most of them from Andalusia. They understood that the inquisition and this expulsion contributed to the economic dislocation of Andalusia and all Spain and thereby financial injury to everyone. But they felt this dislocation a necessary price to achieve a purer faith, and they appreciated the inquisition as a source of Crown revenue.

They had a use for this revenue. Each now felt destined as the Lord's servant to pursue the completion of the Reconquista, to which they had now turned their full energy.

CRISTÓVÃO
Voyage to Mina, (1482–1483)

Cristóvão learned King João was commissioning a fleet to resupply Mina. Filipa's health was declining, doctors were unable to identify the cause or cure, and it was an inopportune time to leave her. But Cristóvão recognized he needed more accomplishment to be noticed at court and merit an audience with the king, and the credentials of having sailed to Mina and met with d'Azambuja were enticing. He longed to visit the source of gold, to confirm for himself that the earth could be sailed below the equator, and to investigate how best to sail west on the Ocean Sea. He explained the importance of participating on the voyage to his family and shipped to Lisbon to enlist on it as a common seaman, leaving Isabel to nurse Filipa and raise Diogo.

After departing Lisbon, as his ship coursed south, Cristóvão attempted to estimate the length of a degree upon the earth,* and thereby calculate the circumference of the earth, by estimating the distance between two points of known latitude. He confirmed for himself that one degree was 56.67 Roman miles (or 52.1 modern

---

*That is, 1 degree of 360 degrees.

statutory miles), shorter than Ptolemy's estimate* and, Cristóvão believed, the same as estimated by the Arab geographer Al-Farghani (Alfraganus, ninth century AD). He concluded the earth's circumference was about 20,400 Roman miles (or about 18,800 statutory miles), almost 10 percent shorter than estimated by Ptolemy.[†]

He grew excited when the fleet passed the Canaries, pleased that the winds and currents continued to flow southwest offshore as he remembered and thrilled to enter seas new to him. He was astonished by the enormous cloud of dust rising above the African desert, captivated by the desert's abrupt termination at the Río de Senega, and roused in anticipation of Mina as the fleet veered southeast and the days and nights grew hotter. Lookouts sighted sirens swimming in the sea, and he peered to behold their faces, observing they did not resemble women as much as sailors said.[‡]

At night, the heavens revealed new constellations, including a southern cross spoken of by mariners returning from Mina. Cristóvão remembered as a boy being taught in church that the Lord held the earth aloft and that the heavens were the earth's roof, extending just over the earth's Northern Hemisphere. The ancients had taught that the heavens were a sphere encircling the entire globe, and he realized the ancients were correct and the church wrong. He pondered that men in Europe stood toe to toe to men in Cathay and that rain fell in opposite direction onto the earth, and he confessed astonishment how the Lord made it work. He was enthralled when the coastline fell away to the east and, at dawn, the ships sailed into the rising sun.

Cristóvão's heart pounded as he beheld the landing and beach at Mina, which thronged with people, almost all black. João's castle sat tiny and alone, remote and nigh inconsequential, the only European structure within hundreds of miles. Cristóvão believed he had crossed the equator[§] and verified for himself that Aristotle, St. Augustine, and common knowledge were all wrong—thousands of people lived there.

In the blazing sun, Cristóvão and crewmates supervised local slaves unloading the vessels' cargos into the fortress. He listened to their speech and surmised their language held no words common to

---

*That is, 62.5 Roman miles, or 57.5 modern statutory miles.
[†]That is, 22,500 Roman miles, or 20,700 modern statutory miles.
[‡]Presumably seals.
[§]Actually, five degrees north.

those he spoke. He prayed at Mina's church, where the graveyard was full, and reflected that Europeans frequently died there. He overheard the soldiers departing warn their replacements of the horrors of the post—terrible food, no wine, swarming insects, wrenching diseases, and diarrhea—and some of its marvels, such as beasts and serpents of the jungle and slaves that worked and died in the gold tunnels. The gold was King João's property, but each man had hoarded and hidden his own stash, which, for those who survived, justified the hardships endured.

Cristóvao had no cause or standing to meet d'Azambuja, but he succeeded nonetheless, introducing himself much as he had to Filipa, but with greater sophistication, approaching after church to recount how the trade at Mina compared to that at Scio and Thule. He learned of Caramanca, the local king, and observed at a distance when he met with d'Azambuja outside the fort, each man accompanied by his own guard. Cristóvão was impressed by the Caramanca's dignity and the respect d'Azambuja afforded him when together. But he sensed neither friendship nor esteem of either man for the other, a relationship drawn by commerce and weaponry alone.

One day, Cristóvão accompanied João's traders north beyond the fortress into the jungle on a trail astride the river, passing the villages and farms of King Ansa's people and spying women sifting the river's sands for gold dust. They came to a hillside where King Ansa's slave masters were supervising the excavation of a tunnel, a narrow shaft descending steeply into the earth. One by one, slaves crawled into the narrow shaft and vanished, returning minutes later with a sack of dirt that was emptied and sifted for gold to be brought to the fortress for trade. The traders remarked that the slaves were worked to exhaustion and frequently died. The mosquitoes swarmed, and Cristóvão and the traders soon retraced their steps to the fortress and the relief of sea breezes. Some of the traders grew sick—first feverous, then shivering and vomiting in agony, and finally falling into a coma and dying (malaria). Cristóvão realized that disease posed more risk to João's settlement than the local people.

The ships soon were loaded to return home with departing troops and João's gold, which was carefully accounted—other than the private stashes—by royal scriveners. The fleet sailed first for the Cape Verde islands, where it harbored and watered, and then north toward Jesus Christo (Terceira, Azores) to achieve Portugal's latitude in one tack, sailing to the west of the Canary Islands and Madeira.

Cristóvão spent his time off duty on the port rail peering west, particularly at sunset. He observed that the wind and currents west of the Canaries continued to bear southwest. He searched for Antillia and St. Brenden's islands and clues to decipher whether Antillia and the Cipangu of Marco Polo and Toscanelli were at the latitudes he passed. He mused that neither the church nor the ancients knew all truth, that the Lord's design for all things remained to be fully revealed, and that his own observations would find explanation within that design.

At night, he prayed for the health of his family—in Porto Santo, Genoa, and Savona. Filipa likely was dying, and he felt guilt for leaving her and Diogo to face her death without him. Giovanni Pellegrino had died the previous year, and he prayed for Giovanni's soul.

Cristóvão gazed across the moonlit ocean and realized he had changed forever and no longer cared to be a merchant's agent. He was now certain his life was to pursue a greater calling—the discovery of islands to the west and, perhaps, a western route across the Ocean Sea to achieve Cipangu. He would seek nobility, wealth, and fame that way. Bartolomeu already understood and would assist. Isabel and Filipa would believe it dangerous and crazy. Domenico would find it utterly foolish, squandering a business that could prosper for a dream or illusion. Domenico would say that dreams and illusions were for noblemen, who could survive their failure, not a weaver's son.

The vast expanses of ocean before him and heavens above united in darkness at an indistinct and seemingly infinite horizon. Cristóvão reflected that the ocean's beauty belied its mercilessness, and he startled himself to admit that death upon it no longer frightened him. He accepted the Lord could choose that fate for him rather than reward any of nobility, wealth, or fame—just as the Lord might take Filipa early and had taken Giovanni.

Cristóvão gazed upward to the heavens. He would trust in the Lord and pursue his noble destiny.

Isabel and Fernando
Reconquista Resumed, 1482–1485

With the Inquisition established, Isabel and Fernando remembered their dream, glory, and duty to complete the Reconquista. Their truces with Grenada's Abū l'Hasan—extended multiple times during the Portuguese war—had facilitated the war's resolution, and it had been convenient to ignore his refusal to pay tribute. But excuses for a truce no longer existed, and Mehmed II's slaughter at Otranto and his empire's ambitions reminded them of the justice and imperative of their duty. They appreciated that the hardship of this duty also would be well rewarded by the Granadan kingdom's enormous wealth—substantial cities, ports, fortresses, and palaces filled with gold and silver, fertile cropland, orchards, and vineyards, and new vassals.

Regardless of the ongoing truces, for centuries noblemen of the Hispanic and Granadan kingdoms had often raided the other's neighboring towns for gold, horses, food, and other booty anyway, taking prisoners fit for sale as slaves or to be incarcerated indefinitely until exchanged for prisoners taken by the other, proclaiming the murder and plunder fulfilled a duty to God. In 1481, shortly after Christmas, Grenadan soldiers raided the Castilian town of Zahara, seizing the town's mayor and his wife, slaying their small garrison, looting, and abducting many inhabitants back to Granada for sale as slaves. Isabel, Fernando, and most Castilians were incensed, perceiving the attack as substantially exceeding that fit to respond to Ponce de Leon's most recent looting, thereby breaching the truce.

In early 1482, Isabel and Fernando declared the resumption of Holy War against Grenada, requesting the nobility to proffer soldiers and arms and bear expenses. For centuries, the Reconquista had rewarded nobility participating with the hereditary governorship of lands reconquered and the vassalage of the vanquished Mohammedans. The Reconquista, perhaps as all wars since Creation, also included as reward for the troops participating the clothes, food, horses, and other possessions they looted from the vanquished.

In February, Ponce de León led the reinstituted Holy War's first engagement, penetrating twenty miles south of the frontier to capture the town of Alhama, slaughtering more than eight hundred residents and seizing more than three thousand to be sold into slavery or held prisoner. The corpses were thrown over the town walls to be fed upon by dogs. Abū l'Hasan counterattacked and trapped Ponce de León's soldiers within the town. But Ponce de León's former rival Guzmán came to his rescue, and Abū l'Hasan retreated, whereupon Ponce de León's troops came to blows with Guzmán's troops over the division of Alhama's loot.

Fernando and his army ceremonially entered the town, accompanied by prelates to attend to its Christianization. Alhama's mosques were promptly converted into churches, and Isabel—then pregnant—provisioned the prelates with the necessary religious sacraments and prayer books for the new churches. Pope Sixtus IV had given the sovereigns a large silver cross, and it was hung on Alhama's tallest minaret. Consistent with prior centuries' practices, the sovereigns offered the ordinary houses and gardens of the vanquished to those Christians willing to settle in Alhama, and the houses filled with younger Christian families seeking their first home. Settlement was encouraged with an exemption from taxation and a pardon for murderers and other criminals.

Regardless of her pregnancy, Isabel tirelessly organized Andalusia for an extended war, exhorting her noblemen and subjects of their duty to enlist and provisioning food, weapons, and ammunition. The sovereigns planned their next attack further north, at Loja. Isabel went into labor in late June while attending a war council. She soon delivered her fourth child, María, named in the Virgin's honor, and, after an excruciating thirty-five hours, another daughter, stillborn.

Isabel would not countenance the war's delay. The next day, Fernando marched from Córdoba toward Loja, deep into hostile, mountainous territory. His army met the fierce guerrilla resistance of local Muslims who would rather die than lose their homes and succumb to Christians, as well as a fierce counterattack by Abū l'Hasan. Fernando's troops were routed, and he narrowly escaped death while in hand-to-hand combat. Some Castilians felt that the stillborn had been a bad omen. Others, as Isabel, believed the Lord tested one's faith and perseverance. The Muslims of Loja felt Allah had answered their prayers and come to their defense.

Abū l'Hasan's natural heir was his son Boabdil, but Abū l'Hasan had left unclear whether he would name Boabdil as successor or choose another son. While Abū l'Hasan was fighting the Castilians, Boabdil anointed himself emir,[*] exploiting discontentment with the escalation of hostilities with Castile. Similar to Castile just years before, there were now two emirs of Grenada, and a civil war commenced between father and son that would sap the emirate's strength.

Castile's own strength to wage war was less than the sovereigns admitted. Their kingdom had been at war, either internally or externally, for almost twenty years, and their subjects were exhausted by the taxation supporting that. Isabel and Fernando searched for new revenue sources. The Inquisition provided some. They imposed an additional tax on the Jews and Mudejar. They secured Pope Sixtus's bull proclaiming a crusade of Holy War against the kingdom of Grenada for which churches were authorized to sell indulgences. Soldiers could purchase absolution from sins incurred in battle and martyrdom if killed, and ordinary worshippers could purchase salvation.

Isabel and Fernando understood the war would take years to prosecute. In 1483, Boabdil was captured and released on his agreement that Castilian troops could pass through his territory to attack his father. Grenada's religious leaders condemned the release and advised continued loyalty to Abū l'Hasan and, when he became ill, to Boabdil's uncle al-Zagal. In 1484, while Fernando was attending the Aragonese Cortes, Isabel directed their armies to cut a tala from the frontier south to the coast west of Málaga to destroy Grenada's most fertile cropland, burning the food supplies supporting the infidel troops and undermining the populace's support of their rulers. In 1485, Ponce de León besieged Ronda and, despite a zealous defense, inflicted severe devastation to the town.

Fernando offered the Rondans surrender terms traditional of the Reconquista, being two choices: exodus, with safe passage to Africa or the city of Grenada, or submission to become the sovereign's vassals, as the Mudejar in Castile, with the right to practice their religion and live under Islamic law. The town's mayor and

---

[*]Taking the name Muhammed ben 'Alī, or Muhammed XII.

leadership—with whom Fernando discussed and quickly agreed the truce terms—were entitled to be resettled with their possessions in the outskirts of Seville in homes confiscated from those found guilty of heresy by the Inquisition. Their fortresses and villas near Ronda were awarded to the Castilian noblemen who fought the engagement.

In December 1485, having returned north to winter at Alcalá de Henares, Isabel and Fernando celebrated the birth of their fifth child, Catalina. While the Lord had seen fit to deliver her but one son, Isabel honored the Virgin for providing yet another delivery where mother and child survived.

ANACAONA
Birth of Higueymota

As her time approached, Anacaona consulted Attabeira frequently for a safe delivery and the health of her child. When contractions began, she rose from her hammock and, with a handful of her closest nitaínos and naborias, left the caney. They walked to a secluded spot by the village stream, where Anacaona had selected a tree with a branch low enough for her to grasp in her hands and hang in a wide squat below, her feet resting gently on the ground.

Alerted, Caonabó chose to walk alone in his subjects' yuca fields. He, too, honored Attabeira for Anacaona's safe delivery, as a Taíno and grimly aware that his prestige would wane if Anacaona were lost.

As the contractions strengthened, Anacaona hung from the branch and thought of her baby. She had decided on names for the child, with Caonabó's consent. It would be a Xaraguán name and would not reflect the word *caona* (gold) in either Caonabó's name ("Golden House") or hers ("Flower of Gold"). Behecchio would approve. After hours of pain, Anacaona gave birth to a healthy baby girl and the news immediately spread throughout the village. Her name was Higueymota.

Anacaona's nitaínos and naborias washed her and the infant in the stream. Caonabó joined them there, knelt to embrace his exhausted wife, and then beheld the child in the arms of Anacaona's nitaíno, also beaming with pride. Caonabó carried Anacaona, herself carrying Higueymota, back to the caney, and a wan Anacaona announced her name to those present. A number of Caonabó's subordinate caciques were in the village, and they were invited to give their own names for the child.

As the moon rose high, when others slept, Anacaona heard Higueymota's tiny, precious cry, and the nitaíno brought the infant to be nursed. Anacaona cradled her babe to her nipple and, as the babe sucked, whispered that there was no rush, as Anacaona would be there forever. She delighted that she had born a child to whom the family possessions would descend in Xaraguá and, perhaps, Maguana.

As with all Taíno infants, when Higueymota was but a few weeks old, Anacaona and naborias gently bound a wooden slat wrapped in cotton against her forehead to flatten it.

Attabeira.

CRISTÓVÃO AND JOÃO
Audience and Review, 1484–1485

Cristóvão returned to Porto Santo from Mina to find Filipa severely ill, and he brought her and the family to Lisbon to see doctors in a last attempt to find a cure. He and mother-in-law Isabel prepared little Diogo for Filipa's death. With brother-in-law Pêro's introduction, Cristóvão wrote King João and was granted an audience to discuss maritime discovery, the Perestelo and Moniz lineage worthy enough for such access.

João's transition to authority following his father's death had not been seamless. In 1483, he had executed the kingdom's most powerful nobleman,* allegedly for plotting treason with the Castilian king Fernando. In 1484, during a private moment in the royal living chambers, João himself stabbed and killed his brother-in-law for suspected disloyalty.

But João had remained constant in his enthusiasm for the circumvention of Guinea. In 1482, he had funded and dispatched Diogo Cão on a voyage further along the Guinean coast to discover its southern terminus. Cão reached a southern latitude of approximately thirteen degrees (Angola) and set a stone pillar dedicated by João to St. Augustine to mark the achievement. In 1484, João had appointed a committee of accomplished theologians, mathematicians, and cosmographers—the Junta dos Mathemáticos—to review and assimilate navigational knowledge learned in his discoverers' voyages, chaired by Bishop Diego Ortiz de Vilhegas and including João's Jewish physician Master Rodrigo, an expert in astrological instruments used for ascertaining longitudinal position.

Ecstatic for the audience, Cristóvão purchased finer clothing. He and Bartolomeu debated their strategy, and Cristóvão was unequivocal. He would bring a map of the Ocean Sea—resembling Toscanelli's— to depict the eastern extent of the Indies and Cipangu, the intended destinations. But he wouldn't reveal their intended departure point, either the Cape Verde islands or just below the latitude of the Canary Islands in Portuguese waters, where the winds and currents were

---

* The Duke of Braganza.

favorable. This viewpoint—their own, practical knowledge—would be shared only if and when a voyage were commissioned. If revealed earlier, João might simply usurp the idea by entrusting a native Portuguese mariner to implement it without the Colombos.

Cristóvão, wrought with anxiety, traveled to meet João. He had never ventured on a voyage of discovery and now would propose one. He had little education and no family crest other than by marriage, and he would be surrounded by those who had both. He lived in modest circumstances and would now seek to impress those who lived immeasurably better. He had never met a doge in Genoa, but would now speak with the king of Portugal.

Upon his arrival, João's secretary ushered Cristóvão to the entrance to the meeting room, where João and Master Rodrigo were waiting. João invited him inward, Cristóvão knelt, and, after brief pleasantries, João invited him to present.

"I am a Genoese merchant and have lived in your kingdom for eight years and married into the Perestrelo family long known to the Crown. In the Genoese merchant tradition, I have sailed much of the known world arranging shipments of merchandise and become expert in navigation. I've sailed to the Levant at Scio and witnessed with my own eyes that the infidels imperil trade from the Orient. I've sailed to London and Galway and as far north as Thule, and understand the northern Ocean Sea." Cristóvão studied João and perceived the slightest perk of his eyebrows. "I've trafficked in your possessions in the Azores and Madeira, and with the Castilians in the Canaries, and understand these waters, as well. Most recently, I have served your Lordship on a voyage supplying d'Azambuja, with whom I conferred regarding Mina's trade." He paused, confident he had captured a king's attention. "I deeply admire your monumental effort to circumnavigate Guinea and pray often that you succeed."

João studied Colombo, unmoved by the flattery but surprised by the content and polish of his delivery. João remained silent, signaling Colombo to continue.

"I requested this audience because my experience has convinced me there is a more direct route to reach the Indies. It is directly west across the Ocean Sea. The coast of the Indies is not so far from our coast as men have thought. Marco Polo also reports that the island of Cipangu lies east of the Indian coast, making the Indies even easier to achieve. Other islands may be discovered en route—perhaps Antillia—making the open sea distances even shorter, but that's not necessary to achieve Cipangu."

"How do you know Cipangu even exists?" Rodrigo asked. "You believe Marco Polo?" Rodrigo glanced at João, puckering his lips, intimating disdain.

"The Venetians are excellent merchants. When they say they've found an island, we Genoese tend not to doubt it." Cristóbal glanced at Rodrigo, preparing to address his skepticism. "The Venetians have made many discoveries."

"No learned man believes Marco Polo," Rodrigo replied. "But assuming Cipangu exists, what's the distance to it and how long's the sail?"

"I don't know the distance or sailing time, but the evidence is overwhelming that the distance is short. I've sailed the Azores and learned of unknown pine trees blown upon them from the west. Dead bodies of Tartars or Mongols have washed up, as well, presumably from Cathay." Cristóvão turned to João. "Bamboo and carved wood have drifted onto the western shores at Porto Santo, Madeira, the Canary Islands, and the Cape Verde islands, and I understand you have seen the bamboo yourself. Even before Marco Polo, Aristotle and Seneca said it was but a few days sail to the Indies."

João reflected that Colombo was quick-witted, confident, and puffed up with his own ability.

"And what of Ptolemy?" Rodrigo asked. "Have you studied Ptolemy?"

"Not directly. In my travels, I've found one can't trust all the ancient learning." Cristóvão faced João again. "As you and your father have shown, the equatorial zones are habitable and their discovery has procured great wealth for the kingdom."

"I don't disagree with that," Rodrigo replied. "Aristotle was wrong about the equatorial zones. I suspect he and Seneca also were wrong about the sailing time to the Indies. Ptolemy would have said the distance from Lisbon to the Indies was more than 8,000 miles. How long would it take to sail 8,000 miles in open sea—assuming Ptolemy were correct—and could a ship be provisioned for such a voyage?"

Cristóvão knew 8,000 miles was far beyond the range of any ship and awkwardly searched for words. He hadn't read Ptolemy, or for that matter Aristotle or Seneca, or even Marco Polo, and he sensed they suspected that. He responded to Rodrigo. "I believe Cipangu or least other islands are far closer to Hispania than Ptolemy had knowledge of—as that alone can explain the carvings, driftwood, and dead bodies." He turned back to João. "It has been brought to my attention that his Excellency your father received the advice of a Florentine physician—Paolo del Toscanelli was his name—that the distance was far shorter than men believe. He said the distance from Lisbon to the city of Quinsay in Cathay was but six thousand miles and that Cipangu and perhaps Antillia lay in between. This advice confirms that Cipangu should be reached before Cathay."

Surprised, João and Rodrigo looked at each other and remembered the letter, which had not been pursued. João reflected that Colombo had come prepared to cite authority for his plan.

"We examined that and have never found even Antillia," Rodrigo replied. "The king receives many suggestions how best to advance his discoveries. But six thousand miles of open sea still is much farther than ships travel today. Your own open sea voyages have been far, far shorter—even to Thule. It would take months at sea to travel that distance, even with the most favorable winds. How could a ship survive that long without harboring to reprovision itself?"

"As I said, the evidence points to islands further west. Prince Henrique colonized the Azores well before he discovered Corvo and Flores farther west. My father-in-law, in the Italian merchant tradition, discovered Porto Santo for Henrique decades before that. Other foreigners have discovered islands for the Crown. I believe I, too, can discover islands further west for you, and that it will allow a voyage through to Cipangu and Cathay. Once the route is established, it will be quicker to the Indies than circling Guinea." Cristóvão paused for emphasis. "I have never been a dreamer—I am a Genoese merchant. I believe Toscanelli wrote that the longest open sea distance to Cipangu, if one harbored at the Azores and found Antillia, would be less than 3,500 miles."

Rodrigo shook his head in disbelief, and there was an awkward silence.

João asked Cristóvão his opinion of the current exploration of
the African coastline and whether he thought it soon would yield a
route to the Indies. Cristóvão described his own voyages to and from
Mina, his conference with d'Azambuja, and the gold-mining operations at the settlement, all with a detail demonstrating his knowledge
of navigation, seamanship, and commerce. He turned to Rodrigo.
"In the circumnavigation of Guinea to reach the Indies, it's no more
rationale to guess that a coastline will turn east and then north than
to guess that an island will be found in the sea."

"Perhaps." Rodrigo frowned. "But the consequence of guessing
wrongly is quite different—the loss of the ships and the expedition."
He paused, and Cristóvão perceived the trace of a smirk. "The death
of the crews."

"Putting aside the geographic wisdom of your idea, what is it you
request of me?" João asked.

"Your Lordship, I would request that you fund and sponsor perhaps two or three caravels under my command to sail west
equipped and victualed for one year. The captains could be of your
selection. If islands or land are possessed, I would be knighted and
entitled to hereditary governorship of them, as my father-in-law on
Porto Santo, and a portion of the resulting profits."

João and Rodrigo glanced at each other, startled by the terms
proposed. João hesitated momentarily, puzzling whether the brazenness was knowing or untutored. He politely responded he would
consider the idea although the terms suggested were unacceptable. He
sent his salutations to Pêro and Isabel. Cristóvão knelt and expressed
his gratitude for the audience and was ushered out. Rodrigo quickly
remarked to João that the idea was fantastical—without a shred of
cosmographical support—and the terms suggested equally absurd.
João laughed at the reliance on the petty Venetian merchant's account
of the so-called Cipangu.

But João recognized Colombo was experienced with the Ocean
Sea and, while boastful, uneducated, and a charlatan, more intelligent and eloquent than João had expected. Colombo was not wrong
to compare the unknowns of circumventing Guinea and crossing
the Ocean Sea. João asked Rodrigo to convene the Junta to review
Colombo's proposal.

The Junta did so, including affording Colombo and his brother an audience to advance their argument. Colombo's idea was as old as Aristotle's and Seneca's speculations, neither novel nor untested. The Crown previously had authorized numerous attempts to explore the Ocean Sea to the west. In 1452, King Afonso had authorized Diogo de Teive to sail west from São Dinis* to find Antillia. He had found nothing after sailing five hundred miles, but discovered Corvo and Flores—which obviously weren't Antillia—on his return. Afonso had authorized an explorer† to find St. Brendan's islands in 1462 and another expedition to find Antillia in 1475,‡ each to no avail.

The Junta was certain that the breadth of the Ocean Sea from Portugal to Cathay—which they knew existed—was far longer than Toscanelli believed, based on their own estimates as well as Ptolemy's. Even assuming Cipangu existed, the sailing distance from Corvo and Flores—the farthest western points known to them—to Cipangu exceeded by multiples any distance ships then sailed without landfall. The success of such a voyage would depend entirely on the fortuity of discovering intervening islands or shores.

Filipa died as Cristóvão awaited his answer. Isabel, Cristóvão, and little Diogo buried her at the Church of Carmo in the valley below the Alcaçóva. The funeral barely befitted nobility, as neither Isabel nor Cristóvão had resources. Cristóvão had secured little work as a merchant's agent since his voyage to Mina and incurred debts that would require significant effort to repay.

The Junta reported to João that the voyage was fantastical, and João understood to reject it. He also expected a discoverer seeking a hereditary governorship to bear the expense and risk of the ships, voyage, and colonization. Yet, until the circumvention of Guinea was proven, he wanted the flexibility to reconsider Colombo's offer—which few other men, if any, would dare make. João summoned Cristóvão to communicate the rejection graciously in person so he not harbor bitterness. Cristóvão left deeply disappointed.

Cristóvão had heard rumors his idea was the butt of jokes and mockery as ridiculous around João's court and grew deeply

---

*Now Faial, a central Azorian island.
†João Vogado.
‡Fernão Teles.

distrustful. At times, he fumed that the Junta's learned men had dismissed him as an ignorant, uneducated charlatan and rejected his idea and geographic argument as frivolous on that basis alone, without the slightest consideration. Other times, he raged that the Junta held prejudices against the Genoese and were against him, not his idea, which they embraced and would usurp by dispatching their own Portuguese to implement it. But he recognized the king and his advisers held a firm belief that the circumvention of Guinea would prove successful and a deep commitment to it, regardless of how seriously they had considered his proposal, and that it would be necessary to find another sponsor.

Cristóvão and Bartolomeu agreed they would depart for Castile to convince King Fernando and Queen Isabel to be that sponsor. The Castilian sovereigns' eagerness to expand their meager overseas possessions in competition with King João was known to all. Andalusia's mariners were competent to sail the voyage. There was a substantial Genoese community in Seville, including representatives of many of the merchant trading families Cristóvão had worked for since boyhood, and he calculated they might provide assistance, support, and a source of livelihood. Filipa's sister lived in Huelva, in the heart of seafaring Andalusia, and she was the woman best suited to help raise Diogo, as well as the traditional choice. He knew he would be treated like Domenico if he sought support for his voyage in Genoa.

As the brothers prepared to depart, Bishop Vilhegas urged João to arrange Portuguese mariners to effect Colombo's plan, sailing from the Azores. João began to consider whether yet another westward attempt was worth the effort, perhaps to find Antillia or another great island or mainland less distant than Cathay, employing an experienced pilot from the Azores. Colombo's experience at sea was sufficient, but there were Portuguese subjects, both noblemen and experienced sea captains, better qualified to be leaders and administrators of a voyage to discover and claim new possessions—and they all would be satisfied with lesser compensation.

V
1485 — 1490, FAITH

BAKAKO'S FISHING LESSON
Guanahaní (San Salvador?, Bahamas)

At sunrise, five-year-old Bakako squatted with his father and younger brother, Yuni, as well as his grandparents, uncles, and cousins, waiting for his mother and aunts to prepare breakfast outside their small bohío. Father, grandfather, and the uncles were all fishermen, and the day started early before Guanahaní baked in the sun. As Lucayan Taínos, they worshipped Yúcahu, and, when the men went to sea, the women tended yuca, sweet potato, and maize in small gardens. Their tiny village of a few bohíos lay between a long sand beach that rimmed a portion of the island's leeward western shore (Long and Fernández Bays) and flatlands with occasional hills and bluffs extending inland, covered with forest, bush, grass, and scrub, all nourished by a number of inland lakes.

Bakako listened as the men discussed the weather, concurring that the sea would remain calm. Father turned to him to relate the result. "We'll fish the barrier reef for larger fish—unless the wind rises."

Bakako had eagerly anticipated doing this for the first time. Father had initiated his education just weeks before, teaching him to troll nets and lines in the sheltered waters within the coral reefs that surrounded the entire island. At the barrier, Father and Uncle would hunt with spears instead, and there could be larger fish, and some dangerous ones, barracuda and shark.

After breakfast, Father and Uncle silently invoked Yúcahu's guidance and protection and motioned for Bakako and an older cousin to follow to the sea. Mother warned Bakako to drink often, as it would be hot on the water. At the beach, they provisioned Father's small canoe, climbed aboard, and glided into the serene turquoise waters sheltered from the easterly winds.

Bakako took the bow, Cousin the stern, with Father, Uncle, spears, and a basket for their catch cramped in between. Uncle directed they paddle to intersect the barrier to the southwest, somewhat distant from the village, hoping to fish alone.

"There're larger fish on the reefs, including grouper and snapper," Father lectured. "Uncle and I will stand to hunt, so we can hurl the spears. When we spot a good catch, we'll tell you where to maneuver the canoe. That's your job, to bring us close above the fish, so we can strike."

"It's unusually calm, so you won't have to worry about breaking surf," Uncle added. "When it's rough, the waves churn over the reef, making it difficult to maneuver. They can even dunk the canoe."

"Would sharks eat us?" Bakako asked.

"We won't dunk," Cousin assured him, having fished the barrier a few times. "I've never dunked."

"Bakako, it's the sea that dangerous," Father said. "Don't worry about sharks. We usually stay inside or at the reef, without passing into the open sea. Whatever the weather. A sudden wind or current outside the barrier can drive the canoe to sea. Today, it'd be easy to paddle back. When it's rough, you could be swept away."

"But men paddle to and from other islands. All the time," Bakako responded.

"Yes, adults do, typically in large canoes with many oarsmen. Not children in small canoes, like ours. Uncle and I occasionally fish beyond the barrier—but we never did when we were just boys, alone. Never."

Bakako studied the water swishing across a long arc extending north and south before him, revealing the reefs below. The ocean swelled gently beyond, slight waves marching away, pushed west by a gentle breeze. "Wouldn't it be safer to fish on the other side of the island?"

Father was startled by the observation, perceptive for a five-year-old. "Yes, the winds there blow you back to Guanahaní, not away. But it's harder to fish in the wind."

Father soon directed the boys to stop paddling so the canoe would slow and then to back-paddle when the reef emerged below. He and Uncle grasped their wooden spears and nimbly stood in search of prey.

Bakako peered through the veil of the water's surface and, when its ripple permitted, discerned countless fish darting about the coral. He waited for Father or Uncle to strike or shout to maneuver the canoe. The wait grew longer than he anticipated, and he wondered whether Father had seen them. "There's a lot of fish there," he said.

"Be patient," Father scolded. "We're here for big fish, not small ones."

"You can't hunt small fish with a spear," Uncle added.

After a few moments, Uncle spied a grouper. "Take us sideways, to the right. Slowly boys, slowly."

Bakako and Cousin gently tread their paddles on the starboard side, searching for the prey below, studying Uncle's shadow cast over the water by the morning sun, his arm and spear slowly rising above his head, the spear's tip homing down toward its target.

"Can it see us?" Bakako whispered.

"It sees the hull," Father replied softly. "But it fears only movement."

"Won't Uncle's shadow scare it?"

"Yes, it could." Father flashed a grin to Uncle, embarrassed by his son's talkativeness but proud of his self-confidence and intellect.

Suddenly, Uncle fiercely hurled his spear into the water. Bakako intently peered below. To his surprise, the spear soon rose to the surface off the bow, a large fish impaled and writhing at its tip. The boys maneuvered the canoe to retrieve it, and Uncle demonstrated how to bludgeon and remove the grouper from the spear, placing the fish in their basket.

They fished for hours, occasionally breaking to drink or eat cazabi. Father and Uncle taught a lesson on how the spirits revealed the weather. Other fishermen drifted by, and Father and Uncle shared knowledge of which fish were swimming where. Father decided they would follow the reef north, hoping to find new prey. The basket slowly filled.

Bakako was impressed by the consistency of their success, captivated by the expertise involved and Father and Uncle's patience, confidence, and execution. He marveled at the number of fish caught and their multitude in the sea.

"Father, Grandfather says all fish come from one man's bones? Is that right?"

"Grandfather does say that," Father replied. "All fish are descended from Yayael's bones."

"Do you think that?"

Father hesitated. "The story has a meaning that is true. The bones of the dead become food for the living." He saw his son didn't understand. "Remember, fish have babies, just like people, and only a few fish need to have come from Yayael's bones many generations ago."

Bakako shrugged. "But I don't think it could happen."

"Maybe, maybe not." Father felt uneasy, uncomfortable with too much curiosity. "But you should respect Grandfather's learning."

As the afternoon wore on, a wind gusted and then strengthened, and the slight waves in the open ocean grew, departing Guanahaní. Father waited for the surf to rise a bit and then muttered to Uncle, "It's time for the day's final lesson." He turned to Bakako. "Boys, let's see if we can catch even bigger fish outside the reef. The biggest ones may be out there."

"We can do it," Cousin replied confidently.

Bakako and Cousin paddled forward, gingerly crossing the reef, the water's surface heaving and sinking below them as bubbling water flushed onto and from the reef, seething froth. The canoe entered the ocean, rising and falling on its small waves.

"How far should we go?" Bakako asked immediately, surprised that the swell topped the hull when the bow descended into the trough, even though the waves were small.

Father paused a few moments before replying. "This is far enough. It seems rougher here than we thought—don't you think? The canoe feels smaller. You'd better turn around and get back inside the reef."

Cousin veered the canoe to port, and spray flew over the rim as waves smacked broadside to the hull. The boys struggled to make the full turn, and the tip of a wave spat over the bow, coldly slapping and frightening Bakako.

"Pull harder, boys!" urged Uncle.

Bakako and Cousin swiped their paddles mightily, but the canoe barely moved forward, the wind and small waves pushing it backward. They pulled harder, panting, but to little avail. Bakako felt the awesome power of the sea and recalled he was a child.

Father and Uncle let them struggle a few minutes, and then took their own paddles to propel the canoe safely within the reef, gliding toward home.

Bakako sagged with relief. After hauling the canoe onto the beach, Father grasped him firmly and stared into his eyes. "Remember, when you learn to fish without myself or an adult, stay within the barrier. Always. If you pass beyond, you might never return."

CRISTÓBAL, ISABEL, FERNANDO, AND TALAVERA
Palos, Audience with Sovereigns, and Talavera Commission, 1485–1487

Cristóvão brought Diogo to Grandmother Isabel's pension in Lisbon to say good-bye. Isabel held the four-year-old tenderly between her legs, whispered that his aunt Violante in Huelva would love him, and tearfully hugged and kissed him farewell, heartbroken the Lord had endowed her daughter with poor health and destined marriage to a dreamer. Cristóvão hugged her, and they parted with a bittersweet stare, acknowledging that life hadn't worked out as either planned.

Cristóvão and son trod sadly to the Carmo church to say farewell to Filipa, and the boy cried before her tomb in the family chapel. Cristóvão held him and swore to Filipa that he regretted his absences, thanked her for taking him as husband, promised that their boy would remember her and her lineage, and humbled himself to pray that the Lord bless her for treating him as an equal. He left the church with his son on his shoulder, and the boy slept as they descended the steep hillside to the port and Bartolomeu's shop. Defeat enveloped Cristóvão, the departures from Isabel and Filipa sundering his last ties to Portugal.

That night, as Diogo slept on a mat in the corner, Cristóvão and Bartolomeu agreed to their final preparations. The ship was bound initially for Palos de la Frontera, nearby Huelva, and Cristóvão and Diogo would board before dawn to avoid Cristóvão's creditors, who would be alarmed to spot him embarking with his son. Bartolomeu would remain in Lisbon as Cristóvão sought an audience with the Castilian sovereigns, closing the shop in a practical manner and then sailing to Guinea as he had committed. They eventually would reunite in Castile, likely in Seville where the Centuriones and di Negros had representatives.

Bartolomeu had drawn a map of the world for Cristóvão to present to the sovereigns, depicting the coasts of Europe and Africa to the right, the mainland of Cathay to the left, and, in the Ocean Sea, the Canary Islands east of Cipangu, with Cipangu surrounded by an archipelago of islands. Distances were not marked. The brothers would study the ancient and modern learning to credential their plan in a manner that would be convincing to the Castilian court geographers and other supposed learned men. They had resolved never again to be speechless before experts or perceived as ignorant or uneducated.

Before dawn, Cristóvão and Bartolomeu embraced deeply and parted. Cristóvão and Diego boarded the caravel unnoticed, and by noon the ship was sailing south in the Ocean Sea. At sunset, they leaned on the starboard rail and Cristóvão held Diogo closely, sobered that he alone was responsible for the boy, sad that he hadn't tutored him as Domenico had tutored himself. Cristóvão softly explained that the Lord had made the sun, moon, and stars to circle the earth, with the sun circling to the west to disappear over the western horizon.

In the morning, father and son leaned on the port rail as the caravel rounded Cape St. Vincent, and Cristóvão related that Prince Henrique had once lived nearby. As they passed Lagos, he recounted how pirates had sunk him. When he sighted Cádiz, he explained they were in Castile and that Diogo would call himself Diego thereafter and learn Castilian.

With the tide rising, the caravel crossed the sandbars off Palos, where two rivers met the ocean, and veered north into the Río Tinto, whereupon Cristóvão spied a large white building sitting alone atop a bluff beyond the river marshes. The pilot explained it was the Franciscan Monastery of Santa María de la Rábida, and Cristóvão decided to pray there to honor St. Francis for the safe voyage. The caravel floated up the river to anchor off Palos's church of St. George, and father and son disembarked in Castile. With Diego at his side, Cristóbal Colón—as he would be known in Spain—set off along a dusty road winding south upon the river bluff to the monastery.

A porter met them at the monastery's gate, and Cristóbal requested bread and water for his son, whereupon the porter led them inside to a dining room. Cristóbal let on that they had departed Lisbon where he had dealings with King João, and the porter, surprised by the visitor's importance, alerted the senior churchman present, Fray Antonio de Marchena, who came to introduce himself.

Marchena administered La Rábida and other Franciscan monasteries. He also had a keen interest in cosmography and astronomy and was acquainted with the ancient and modern learning regarding the earth's geography. He was surprised to learn Cristóbal had sought some ships to sail westward to the Indies and indicated that he would be interested to hear the whole story, inviting Cristóbal and Diego to stay the night and providing a cell.

After vespers, the two men sat alone and Cristóbal recounted the discussions with João. Fascinated, Fray Marchena probed the evidence introduced to support the plan, and Cristóbal recited the accounts of driftwood, dead bodies, and Marco Polo, and boasted of his travels on the Ocean Sea. Marchena asked if he had read Ptolemy or Cardinal Pierre d'Ailly, and Cristóbal admitted he had not. Marchena advised that there were learned men who believed the sailing distance between Spain and the Indies was short, and Cristóbal confirmed he knew that. As the night grew long, the two men felt the growing warmth of a strong mutual respect and trust.

They continued their conversation the next day. The friar was taken by the Genoese's practical experience and his enthusiasm, wit, and strong faith. Cristóbal was taken by the friar's learning and grasp of the idea. Cristóbal revealed that he intended to seek an audience to present his idea to King Fernando and Queen Isabel. As the day passed, he confided more and more of the plan and, by evening, he drew Bartolomeu's map of the world from his sack to explain it.

Marchena was astounded his visitor was so bold to produce a map to present to the very king and queen, and he offered to help seek the sovereigns' audience in Córdoba. Cristóbal, humbled by the confidence and support of a learned man, perceived his chance encounter with the friar a sign of destiny. Marchena also offered to guide him to the geographical learning that supported his plan and to provide Diego board and education at La Rábida while Cristóbal pursued the audience. An enduring bond between the two men was established.

Within days, Cristóbal took Diego by ferry to meet Violante in Huelva, to whom he explained his situation and intent to depart for Córdoba. Violante welcomed her nephew into her home, pleased that he could be educated at La Rábida. With Marchena's endorsement, Cristóbal wrote the royal council requesting a sovereign audience. Marchena advised a response would take time, as Fernando and Isabel were preoccupied with the assault on Ronda.

Palos and Huelva, and the neighboring Moguer, were sailors' towns, where most men either fished or shipped on commercial voyages through the Mediterranean or along the European coast. They proudly held the sea was their domain, not the sovereigns', and had trafficked for decades in gold and slaves from Guinea in violation of King Enrique and Isabel's recognition of Portugal's rights to Guinea. They regularly concealed their trade to avoid payment of crown taxes and had even plundered Portuguese vessels for slave cargos. Word spread quickly from tavern to tavern that a Genoese boarding at Rábida had petitioned the king to sponsor a voyage west into the Ocean Sea, and an elderly resident of Palos, Pedro de Velasco, came to Rábida to introduce himself to Cristóbal.

Pedro had served as pilot on Diogo de Teive's voyage discovering the westernmost Azorian islands, Corvo and Flores, thirty-three years earlier. He recounted that, after discovering the two islands, d'Teive had sailed to a latitude of approximately 51 degrees, equivalent to the southern coast of Ireland. They had failed to sight land there and had turned back because the season was late. But the sea was relatively calm regardless of stiff westerly winds, indicating a large sheltering landmass to the west. Pedro encouraged Cristóbal to pursue his plan.

⊟ ⊟ ⊟

Cristóbal left Diego with Violante and departed for Córdoba to await the royal council's response. His savings had dwindled and he lived day-to-day on support from Marchena, Violante, and new acquaintances in the Cordovan Genoese community, all while maintaining the pretense of being a successful merchant's agent. He turned to study ancient and modern geographical texts to amass evidence that the distance from Hispania to the Indies was shorter than Ptolemy's estimate, to prove that terra firma—Cape St. Vincent overland to Cathay, and then to Cipangu—stretched far longer than presently understood, thereby resulting in an Ocean Sea—Cape St. Vincent to Cipangu—far shorter.

Cristóbal read works Marchena suggested, including Cardinal Pierre d'Ailly's *Ymago Mundi* (Description of the World, ca. 1410) and Aeneas Sylvius Piccolomini's *Historia rerum ubique gestarum* (Universal History, ca. 1450), jotting down notes of key points helpful to his argument in the margins of the texts.* The former confirmed Cristóbal's belief that the earth's circumference was about 18,800 miles. Cristóbal also marginally noted his own observations—bodies blown ashore, climate, and the like—integrating his experience with these authorities. He studied copies or recountings of John Mandeville's *Travels* (ca. 1360), Marco Polo's *Il Milione* (Travels of Marco Polo, ca. 1298), and Ptolemy's *Guide to Drawing a Map of the World*—the *Geography*—for the first time.

The modern French theologian and cosmographer Cardinal d'Ailly was clear: the Ocean Sea had far less breadth than Ptolemy thought because Ptolemy had underestimated the portion of the earth being terra firma. The Cardinal believed that the distance of terra firma from the Orient to Cathay alone—excluding Europe—was half the globe, so the Ocean Sea was far shorter than half the globe. He cited as proof that King Solomon's mariners had spent three years sailing from the Red Sea to Ophir in India and back. He responded to the tradition that Jerusalem was in terra firma's center (Ezekiel 5:5) by explaining that it was in the center of the Promised Land, but not the center of terra firma.

---

*The "postils."

The cardinal found support for his conclusion in a biblical prophet—the Jewish sage Esdras (ca. last decade of the first century AD)—who had taught that the earth was one part water and six parts land. The cardinal argued that the distance from Hispania west to the Indies was consistent with that proportion. He credentialed Esdras by noting that St. Augustine had endorsed Esdras as a prophet, and Cristóbal was taken by the simplicity and sanctity of Esdras's teaching.

Cristóbal also discovered that Ptolemy's predecessor Marinus of Tyre (ca. AD 100) had estimated that terra firma extended farther than Ptolemy thought—five-eighths of the globe's circumference as opposed to just one-half. As Ptolemy, Marinus had not understood the extent of the Indies discovered by Marco Polo nor the existence of Cipangu. Cristóbal decided to assert that the Indies unknown to Marinus, Cipangu, and other adjustments added about one-fifth of the globe more to terra firma than Marinus's estimation, resulting in a breadth of terra firma and Cipangu of almost six parts of the globe, and a breadth of Ocean Sea between the Canaries and Cipangu of about one part. This matched and was confirmed by Esdras's prophecy.

Taking these arguments, Cristóbal achieved proof for roughly 4,000 miles from the Canary Islands west to Quinsay (Hangzhou) and 2,700 miles from the Canary Islands west to Cipangu, disregarding any islands lying east off Cipangu. The longest open sea sailing distance from Europe to the Indies was thus at most 2,700 miles, a distance clearly traversable by well-provisioned modern caravels. As Esdras had prophesized, the Ocean Sea extended 2,700 miles over a globe with a circumference of 18,800 miles.

⊡   ⊡   ⊡

During the summer, the royal council met with Colón to discuss his request for a sovereign audience and denied it. Marchena and Colón appealed. Through friendships at court, Marchena eventually arranged an audience with the sovereigns in January 1486 at their winter court in Alcalá de Henares. The friar offered Cristóbal advice regarding his presentation: the king and queen were deeply engaged in the highest endeavor of a Christian prince—casting the infidel from the realm—and it would be sensible for Cristóbal to commend that and explain his proposal's import to the Catholic faith, particularly to the queen.

Cristóbal spent most of his remaining savings to purchase a velvet silk cape and fine woolen garments for the audience, befitting a successful merchant meeting his sovereign. On January 20, he was ushered into the salon in the sovereign's residence in Alcalá de Henares to meet Isabel and Fernando and some advisers. His heart pounded, but less so than with João, his mind crammed with a presentation—and arguments and counterarguments—well rehearsed.

Cristóbal knelt and Fernando bade him rise. Isabel handed Catalina to her nurse and invited him to speak, indicating she understood that he had sought to convince King João of a proposal to sail west to Cathay but that João had denied him. He nodded and replied that he had married nobility in Lisbon but had no continuing relationship with King João or Portugal, his wife having died. He related his experience and then revealed his plan.

"The Portuguese are splendid mariners, but the route circumventing Guinea is not proven, and, if proven, it will be much longer than west across the Ocean Sea. The wealth of Cathay is astounding, and the sovereign to reach it first will realize tremendous gain. Islands may be discovered offshore to Cathay to facilitate trade with the Grand Khan—much as the Genoese colony in Scio facilitates trade with the Orient to the east. Islands or mainlands may be possessed yielding gold in quantities surpassing João's Mina."

Cristóbal turned his gaze directly to the queen. Her visage was harsher than he had imagined, her eyes confident of an ability to discern and judge. "For centuries, the Grand Khans have sought Christian emissaries to teach them Christianity, and it will augment your glory to be the sovereigns that bring the Tartars and Mongols to the Faith. You may use the riches from the trade to complete the Reconquista, further multiplying your fame, and for which I pray fervently every day." He turned to the king, whose frame was shorter and leaner than his own, and gauged Fernando's piercing stare, revealing an intent to scrutinize both man and plan. "The wealth will surpass that required for the Reconquista. It will fund your retaking Jerusalem."

"My friend João is astute in maritime discovery," Fernando drily noted. "What's your plan, and why's it feasible?"

"My plan is to sail due west," Cristóbal responded, inferring by the steel of Fernando's gaze that, in spite of Marchena's advice, expressions of faith would not move the king. "My calculations indicate that Cipangu may be achieved in five or six weeks' afloat, assuming favorable wind and current." Cristóbal paused to draw Bartolomeu's map from a pouch, laid it on the floor before the sovereigns, and waited as they studied it before resuming. "The distance to Cipangu is no more than 2,700 miles, and islands may be encountered before then. This is longer than an unbroken sail from the Cape Verde Islands to Lisbon—which sailors do frequently—but it's feasible. Cathay is just over 1,000 miles from Cipangu thereafter." He paused again, encouraged that the map intrigued them, and then finished. "Aristotle and Seneca said the Indies were but a few days' sail from Spain. It's more than a few days—it's a few weeks. The prophet Esdras taught that the Lord created the earth to be one part water and six parts land, and my calculations are consistent with that prophecy."

"I thought Ptolemy believed the distance far greater," Fernando replied. He turned to Luis de Santángel, one of the advisers present.

"Ptolemy calculated the Ocean Sea covered half the globe," Luis replied.

"Ptolemy lived over a millennium ago and didn't know the extent of terra firma as we know today," Cristóbal responded. "He didn't know how far east Cathay extended or that Cipangu existed." For an instant, he recalled Master Rodrigo's reaction to being told that Ptolemy was wrong. "Ptolemy wasn't wrong as to what he knew, he simply didn't know what we know today." Cristóvão perceived Isabel's eyes flicker, perhaps impressed with his prescience.

"The Portuguese have tried to sail west before and never succeeded," Fernando replied. "What's different in what you propose?"

"They have tried to find Antillia, not sail to the Indies by reaching Cipangu. João understands that the circumvention of Guinea has not achieved the Indies, and I suspect he will try westward again." Cristóbal wouldn't reveal his understandings of the wind and current at the Canary Islands or that the Canaries would be his departure point. He held his breath, waiting for Fernando to probe.

Fernando was disappointed by the response's brevity but didn't press, perceiving it calculated rather than unintended. He focused more on the warning as to the stakes involved. "We are engaged in Holy War. What are the resources you request were we to approve this plan?"

"My voyage will require three ships with experienced crews provisioned for a year."

"Why a year if Cipangu is so close?"

"Your Majesty, one can never predict what trials the Lord destines in the Ocean Sea, particularly where unexplored. He may bring winds and currents that are contrary or unanticipated. As I said, the voyage should take but a few weeks in each direction, but a mariner must be very cautious. This I know from experience."

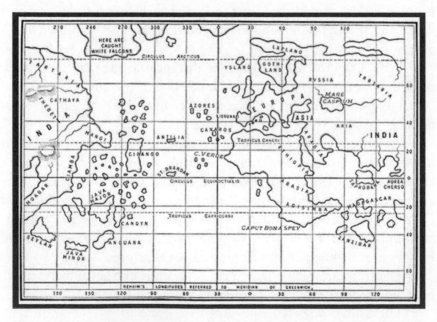

Martin Behaim's 1492 world globe reduced to a Mercator projection.

The sovereigns permitted their advisers to ask questions, which focused as much on the mercantile potential as the geographic considerations, as none of the advisers had the geographic sophistication of João's Junta. As the audience drew to an end, Isabel asked the final questions.

"Do you still have family ties to Portugal?"

"No, Your Majesty. My only child, my son, is with me, living with relatives in Huelva." Cristóbal added, "My mother-in-law is at the end of her life, in a pension in Lisbon."

"How old is your son?"

"Five years."

"Doesn't all knowledge indicate this idea is fantastical?"

"Your Majesty, I have sailed to islands that were unknown to men before my birth, some discovered by Italian merchants much as myself. The prophets foretell that this can be done. I believe it's the Lord's wish that it be done, that Christianity be brought to Cathay." Cristóbal discerned a slight nod of Isabel's head, likely unintended. "The Lord needs instruments to that end—myself and a willing sovereign."

The sovereigns thanked Colón for his proposal and dismissed him.

"We barely have the funds necessary to reclaim Grenada," Fernando said, addressing his wife and advisers. "The council rejected the idea as senseless. If we sponsor this and fail—which seems more than likely—it would be a wasteful diversion from the war."

"Which we can't afford," Isabel agreed. But she had liked Colón. He appreciated that knowledge came from the scriptures. He was self-taught and unafraid to challenge prevailing wisdom. While obviously a commoner, he was not afraid to express views contradicting the men of the royal council, who frequently thought they knew better than her. "But, even though chimeric, we should study the proposal before rejecting it."

Fernando concurred. Colón had impressed him enough to study the plan. The sovereigns directed Fray Talavera to chair and select a commission to study Colón's proposal and advise the sovereigns' response. Fernando asked for a copy of Ptolemy's *Geography*.

Colón was permitted to live and travel with the sovereigns' court pending the commission's decision. The sovereigns' chief accountant took pity on him, seeing him penniless, and arranged food and shelter. In April, the court headed south to Córdoba, resting at Guadalupe for three days, and Cristóbal prayed to the renowned Virgin.

After arriving in Córdoba, Cristóbal was joined by Bartolemeu—Bartolomé in Spain—and they restarted the mapmaking business. Together, the brothers read and reread the learned works they obtained to demonstrate the soundness of their plan, and Bartolomé recorded his own notes with Cristóbal's in the margins of the same books, consolidating their knowledge. Cristóbal also bought and sold books and worked for the Genoese merchant houses, locally and in Seville. He lived at the edge of poverty.

Cristóbal now had achieved introductions to the sovereigns' senior advisers, including Talavera and Cardinal Mendoza. Cristóbal's wit and courtesy impressed some, and his boastfulness and self-assurance put others off.

◻ ◻ ◻

One impressed was Luis de Santángel, who appreciated the commercial benefits that would result from a successful voyage, and Luis and Cristóbal became friendly. Luis was the leader of a wealthy, prominent converso family that had converted from Judaism in response to the pogroms of 1391, as well as one of Fernando's closest confidants, serving as chancellor of the royal household in Aragón and as Aragón's comptroller. Luis had directed the family's mercantile, seaborne operations in València and Barcelona, trading with the Genoese and Portuguese, and served as a farmer of royal customs.

It was rumored that Luis had lent support to converso conspirators who had assassinated the chief inquisitor for Zaragoza* in September 1485, and some said the conspiracy had been hatched at the home of Luis's uncle in Zaragoza's aljama, just a few blocks from the crime site. Within two years of the murder, two of Luis's relatives would burn at the stake for complicity in it and adherence to Judaism, including Luis's uncle whom Fernando's father had knighted for military service against the Catalans decades before. Two more Santángels would burn at the stake soon thereafter, and two more would flee abroad to escape that punishment.

Having been baptized, Luis had no choice but to prove his Christianity whenever questioned, and he feared the attitudes and actions

---

*Pedro Arbués.

of members of his extended family would expose him to charges of
heresy. He understood that Fernando protected him, his wife, and
children from the Inquisition Fernando controlled, and he served
Fernando with utmost loyalty.

⊡ ⊡ ⊡

In March 1486, João authorized Fernão Dulmo, the captain of
Jesus Christo (Terceira, one of the Azores), and a partner* to discover islands or mainland west of Jesus Christo, sailing at their own
expense in return for a hereditary donation of lands discovered and
reasonable titles of honor. João agreed to send troops if lands discovered required subjugation of the inhabitants.

During the summer, a second expedition led by Diogo Cão (1485–
1486) returned from Africa, although Cão had died. The captains
reported that Cão had placed a second stone pillar almost twenty-two
degrees south (Cape Cross, Namibia) and that the southern projection of the coast was slanting east. João and the Junta grew excited
and, in October, João engaged Bartolomeu Dias to explore past this
second pillar. Dias had sailed to Mina and served as superintendent
of Lisbon's royal warehouses and as patron of a royal warship, the
São Cristóvão. The Crown would fund the voyage of two ships and
a supply vessel and pay Dias an annuity.

⊡ ⊡ ⊡

Talavera was slow to convene his commission to study Colón's proposal. Given its unlikely prospects, there was no urgency. He had
many responsibilities, dominated by the tasks to oversee the church's
financial contribution to the Granadan war and its establishment in
conquered territories, as well as serving as Isabel's and often Fernando's confessor. He believed the Reconquista and the evangeliza-
tion of the sovereigns' kingdoms to the Catholic faith were the most
important tasks the Lord destined for him and devoted the spring,
summer, and fall of 1486 to them.

Cristóbal's hope for prompt review faded and he became anxious
he was wasting his time, if not his life. But he traveled with the court
as it moved north to winter in Salamanca, where Talavera—now

---

*João Afonso do Estreito of Madeira.

bishop of Ávila—finally established the commission. Talavera chose royal advisers, scholars, and mariners, including cosmographers and geographers from the university at Salamanca and Rodrigo Maldonado, the sovereigns' senior adviser who had negotiated the Treaty of Alcáçovas.

Talavera and Maldonado appreciated their kingdom's competition with Portugal to secure wealth and new Christian subjects through overseas conquest. They remembered that the Treaty of Alcáçovas effectively gave João an exclusive right to circumvent Guinea to reach the Indies and that Castile's opportunities for empire were constrained. They understood the sovereigns' difficulties in subjugating the Canary Islands. Talavera recalled St. Augustine's teaching—that water covered the globe's Southern Hemisphere, not land antipodal to the Northern Hemisphere's terra firma*—and he puzzled over whether this teaching implicated a voyage west in the Northern Hemisphere. Talavera and Maldonado would be pleased if Colón's proposal actually were achievable. Talavera called the commission's first meetings that November.

The geographers on the commission thought Colón's assertion—that only 4,000 miles separated the Canary Islands and Cathay—was absurd. They felt geographic knowledge had advanced beyond the biblical prophecies and ancient theories on which Cardinal d'Ailly relied. If one accepted Ptolemy, it was more than twice that distance. If one accepted Eratosthenes (ca. 276–195 BC), it was almost 10,000 miles.

The mariners on the commission were just as skeptical. Every sailor knew stories of dead bodies, carvings, and debris of sunken boats washed ashore. Who could possibly proclaim from where they had floated? Colón had told the sovereigns bodies of Tartars had washed onto Flores, but they likely were just drowned fishermen from Faial or Jesus Christo.

Talavera invited Colón to present his proposal to the commission in the university's audience chamber and, when he entered, the two men greeted each other courteously. The bishop observed that Colón didn't appear cowed in the slightest, perhaps hiding anxiety well, but more likely entirely convinced he knew truth. It was obvious he lived on meager resources.

---

*An "antipode."

Cristóbal began his presentation extolling the wealth of the Indies and its use to complete the Reconquista and recapture of Jerusalem. While many on the commission perceived pandering, the bishop did not rush to that judgment, and he saw an underlying faith in the Lord. As all expected, Cristóbal presented Bartolomé's map and explained that Cipangu could be achieved within four or five weeks' sail and other islands possibly sooner, drawing support from Esdras, Aristotle, Seneca, and Cardinal D'Ailly—as well as Marco Polo—and reconciling Ptolemy and Marinus of Tyre.

"Marco Polo wasn't a geographer—he was a merchant," interrupted a geographer, quickly revealing the geographers' collective distaste for Marco Polo. "His descriptions of places he boasts of visiting provide no indication of latitude or longitude, only days traveled between places and estimates of mileage and direction. But you rely on him to conclude terra firma is more than fifty percent greater than Ptolemy's analysis!"

Cristóbal was prepared. "Aristotle, Esdras, Seneca, and Cardinal D'Ailly all would say Ptolemy's estimate of terra firma is too short. None relied on Marco Polo. One might view Marco Polo's observations as corroborating them." He shied from invoking Toscanelli, apprehensive João's rejection of Toscanelli rendered his view unpersuasive and that João would view the Toscanelli correspondence as Portugal's property.

The geographer persisted. "Other than Marco Polo, who writes of your Cipangu?"

"I believe Marco Polo was the first."

The geographers began to murmur in disappointment. Some chortled that Marco Polo was also the last to so write. Cristóvão fought to conceal the blush that crept over his face, stricken by a revulsion to ever mention the Venetian to geographers again.

A second geographer spoke. "Putting aside the fact they are Portuguese possessions, wouldn't it be best to sail from the Azores? Flores and Corvo are considerably west of the Canaries."

"As all recognize, the Azores are Portuguese. I'm committed to sail for King Fernando and Queen Isabel. King João certainly can be expected to attempt to sail from the Azores, if he hasn't done so already. He might also attempt from the Cape Verde Islands."

Cristóbal resolutely withheld divulging his plan to sail from the Canaries, lest it be usurped.

The room became silent, as the assembled remembered their accountability either way for their determination. If they lightly dismissed Colón and King João succeeded in an attempt sailing west to Cathay, the sovereigns would remember their failure.

"There's no need for the Azores," Cristóbal continued. "My plan is based on sailing from Castile or its possessions alone."

"Suppose you're correct as to Cipangu and the distance to it," a mariner interrupted. "Commencing a voyage into 2,700 miles of uncharted ocean is fraught with peril. If the winds and sea are adverse you will never make it there, correct? And if you do make it, how will you ever get back?"

"These are questions every mariner rightfully asks. My experience with the Ocean Sea is that, over an extended period, one can find the right wind to make progress, in almost any direction. The ships will need to be provisioned for one year's sail."

"Your drinking water won't last half that long," another mariner interrupted. "And the crew will toss you overboard well before then to return home—if they still can. Even if you convince this room that Aristotle's or whoever's observations justify an attempt to cross the Ocean Sea, how will you recruit a single man whose life depends on it?"

Cristóbal sensed hostility and was affronted, certain his experience at sea dwarfed that of the mariners present. Talavera perceived the condescension and watched Colón respond in a manner he and many other commissioners found arrogant and evasive. Soon, the bishop wearied that the frictions weren't producing new information, and he introduced another issue. "How many ships do you need, and what are the rewards you request?"

Cristóbal replied without hesitation. "I request the sovereigns sponsor three ships and crews. If I discover or acquire islands or mainland, I would be knighted and entitled to their hereditary governorship and a portion of their profits in perpetuity. If I don't, the sovereigns have lost the expense of the voyage."

Talavera was astounded, as were the other commission members, and the room was silent. Cristóbal anticipated the surprise and unabashedly addressed the reward's justification, reviewing the genius, expertise, and courage involved and—above all—the wealth and aggrandizement of the faith to be attained. As Colón spoke, Talavera cringed at his own assessment of Colón's religious sincerity, disturbed that Colón appeared but an adventurer. Talavera would not entertain or discuss these terms. He indicated the committee would consider Colón's presentation and dismissed him.

When spring arrived, the sovereigns returned to Córdoba to commence the campaign to take Málaga, and the commission completed its review in Córdoba after Fernando departed for the battlefield. It unanimously recommended that Colón's proposal was not feasible. The expense of the effort would be a waste, Castile's wealth would not be increased, the sovereigns' reputation would be tarnished, and the crews likely would perish.

Pending the sovereigns' final review, Talavera authorized a small sum dispensed to Colón in reimbursement of his expenses at court. Cristóbal's utter disappointment was transparent to all. His boastfulness had made many enemies at court, and they mocked his ideas and failure.

GUACANAGARÍ, MAYOBANEX, AND GUARIONEX
On the Border of Marien, Ciguayo, and Magua

Ciguayan fishermen were trolling along Haiti's northern coast when they spotted Caribe canoes far offshore speeding west. They alerted the local cacique, who dispatched smoke signals to be relayed west to their cacique Mayobanex at his highland village and farther to Guacanagarí in Marien. Mayobanex received the warning that day and departed to the coast with his most experienced general and warriors, and Guacanagarí would receive it the following morning, concerned but pleased for a valid opportunity to lead warriors.

Mayobanex encamped at the coast in the evening, too late to sight the raiders, and his general, a short, elderly man, studied the ocean current through the night. He viewed hunting the Caribes as similar to hunting a shark whose fin surfaced and then vanished. Each was capable of traveling a certain distance from where sighted—the Caribes being significantly affected by the surf. Each returned to familiar hunting grounds—the Caribes to villages nestled in forest close to the sea, permitting surprise attack and quick escape.

Mayobanex rose before dawn and dispatched his swiftest scouts ahead west along the coast to inquire of local caciques whether their subjects had noticed anything unusual—perhaps a freshly broken campsite, smoke in an uninhabited area, or the sound of paddling at night. Late that evening, after trekking the entire day, Mayobanex entered a coastal village, where the local cacique reported two fishermen missing. The general questioned him. Were the fishermen healthy? Were they expert at sea? The cacique affirmed they were both. The sea claimed fishermen occasionally, but the Caribes executed anyone they encountered to prevent exposure of their position. Mayobanex had a premonition of their presence and honored Yúcahu to reveal more.

Guacanagarí then stood atop the high plateau beyond the Yaque on Haiti's northern shore (Cabo del Morro), having transported his troops there by canoe in but one day. He gazed east into the nighttime gloom over the ocean, proud of his troops' readiness and eager to prove their mettle. He recognized Mayobanex likely was closer to the Caribes and honored Yúcahu to reveal the enemy to him first.

Yúcahu answered neither man the next day. Their scouts' vigil seaward was futile, and nothing was learned from the local caciques. They continued to trek toward each other, each retiring at night with a premonition of failure—that shortly he would learn that a raid had occurred and, in Guacanagarí's case, that Mayobanex had vanquished the Caribes alone.

Both men and their warriors converged to meet the next afternoon in a small village in a border territory between their two cacicazgos and Guarionex's Magua. Guacanagarí knew enough Macorix, and Mayobanex enough Taíno, for simple conversation, and the local cacique interpreted when necessary. Guacanagarí greeted the older Mayobanex deferentially, remarking that it was an honor to witness feared Ciguayan warriors in the field with their bows and arrow. Mayobanex was surprised to meet Guacanagarí so far east so soon and complimented his troops.

After dinner, as daylight faded, one of Mayobanex's scouts entered the village with the report all had sought—in a nearby village, the scout had heard reports of whispers in a mangrove thicket and, upon investigation, surmised at least a hundred warriors camped within. Mayobanex bid his general propose a plan to Guacanagarí.

"Tonight, I will dispatch scouts to study where our warriors should be positioned to attack at dawn's twilight, marking the positions with *cocuyos* [fireflies as large as beetles]," the general advised. "If the Caribes hear us, they will flee, so it may not be possible to get so close."

Guacanagarí showed no reaction. "That's a sound plan." He was startled by the expertise involved and hesitated, doubting his scouts should accompany Mayobanex's, anxious that being led was preferable to erring. "Your scouts should plan for both our troops."

As the stars rose, the local cacique invited Guacanagarí and Mayobanex into his caney to rest. Their warriors slumbered in the village plaza.

Mayobanex steeled himself for the violence of the impending battle, embracing a warrior's bravado, righteousness, and belief in invincibility. Guacanagarí also struggled to harness these feelings, but was overcome with a despondency that the battle—any battle—was a failure of human beings to achieve harmony. He was vexed that his goal of establishing a military reputation was at hand, yet he was neither proud nor eager nor content. For an instant, he doubted Yúcahu, Yaya, and other spirits—why had they conceived a world with violence? He was not cowardly, and he quickly quashed his doubts to resolve steadfastly that he would be the warrior. But it was not truly him. He was a Taíno. Uncle had been correct.

When the moon was high, Mayobanex's scouts departed to reconnoiter the Caribe encampment and found trails leading to the ocean on either side of the mangrove thicket, which opened to the sea on a beach where the canoes would be lying. They left a small cotton sack of cocuyos glowing at each trailhead and returned to the caney. The Cigueyans would align along on the western path to storm the Caribe encampment, the Mariens along the eastern to charge the beach to attack Caribes fleeing.

As the moon descended, the Cigueyans and Mariens crept through the forest to the cocuyos and stationed themselves, invoked Yúcahu a last time and, when the general waved a cocuyo sack, shrieked their war cries and charged, the Cigueyans raining a volley of arrows into the Caribe encampment. Guacanagarí relished that ambiguity had vanished, the imperative of victory overwhelmed, and the fear of death scalded his soul to dispense death first.

The battle was fought hand to hand in the emerging twilight. The ferociousness of the Taíno attack terrified the Caribes, and they were unable to launch their arrows in a coordinated volley. Mayobanex stood with his troops in the center of the engagement, bearing a spear, and gouged the chest of his first attacker. Warriors with macanas stood by his side and mightily crushed the bones and skulls of other attackers who threatened him. Cries of agony replaced war cries as men on both sides writhed with wounds and in death. At the beach, the Mariens intercepted the Caribes as they fled, preventing even one canoe from escaping, and then circled inward from the beach, clubbing and spearing Caribes devastated to realize they were encircled. Blood covered the encampment and beach.

As victory became apparent, Mayobanex faced the surviving Caribes and raised his hands above his head, his bowmen ready to fell any attacker. The survivors dropped their arms, and the Taíno warriors dragged those not wounded to the beach to await their fate, tortured the wounded to death, and speared and bludgeoned the eyes and testicles of the dead so their spirits would be unable to return.

Guacanagarí surveyed the gore and death, and, for a moment, pride engulfed him. He and Mayobanex agreed the winner at batey would have the privilege of executing those taken captive.

The next day, the captives were tied to trees at the plaza's perimeter so Mayobanex and Guacanagarí could interrogate them before the assembled villagers and troops, although the Caribes understood neither Macorix nor Taíno. Mayobanex approached to stand before the Caribe with the fiercest appearance, demanding answers. How many more attacks would come? How many Taíno women had he raped?

The captive, close to death from exhaustion and dehydration, did not reply. Mayobanex moved to the next and continued. How many Taíno boys had he eaten? No answer.

Mayonbanex turned to offer Guacanagarí a turn. Guacanagarí knew the interrogation's purpose was not information but to instill pride and fear in the Taínos present of Mayobanex's rule and, if Guacanagarí wished, his own. He remembered his last evening with Heitiana and her kindness in comforting him that they were safe from the nighttime spirits. She had been wrong and wronged, and vengeance for her seizure was now at hand. But remembrance of her serenity and gentleness, of her exemplary Taíno peacefulness, burst through his thoughts, and Guacanagarí responded simply, "There's no need to belabor this. Your questions have been well put. These captives shall be put to death."

That night the local cacique's wives mustered the greatest feast they had ever prepared, and chicha and tobacco were shared by all. The warriors found women to lie with, and, for those warriors too shy, women took them directly.

Mayobanex and Guacanagarí spoke alone. The local cacique owed to Guacanagarí a portion of his naborias' food production in tribute, and Guacanagarí agreed to share some of it with Mayobanex in the future in return for Mayobanex's agreement to protect the area from Caribe raid.

The batey was played the following afternoon, with the warriors from Marien and Ciguayo taking the field against each other as Guacanagarí and Mayobanex watched. The play was vigorous and fair, and the Ciguayan team won. With the villagers cheering wildly, Ciguayan warriors then took turns executing the Caribe captives one by one. Mayobanex's general watched contentedly, and memories of spearing sharks in his youth flickered through his thoughts.

◻ ◻ ◻

Guarionex had heard through informants of the successful Caribe massacre and dispatched a messenger inviting Mayobanex to visit with him before returning home. The traveling distance was short, the men had been friends for years, and it presented an opportunity to discuss their cacicazgos' relationship and the other Haitian caciques. Mayobanex was happy to accept and made the journey over the coastal mountains to arrive at Guarionex's village, known now as Guaricano, within two days, arriving at dusk. The two men knew enough of the other's language for informal conversation and were assisted by an interpreter.

After sunset, Guarionex offered his friend a fine meal and, as customary, village women danced before them in firelight and sang a short areíto praising the friendship of the Maguan and Ciguayan peoples and the peace between them. Both men had heard areítos to such effect many times.

"Our peoples are different," Mayobanex remarked. "The areíto has described our peoples as friends, but there have been times of hostility. We haven't led our people as peacefully as the areíto boasts."

"Taínos compose areítos to record our history, knowledge, and beliefs," Guarionex responded. "But they're also informed by the spirits. You might say the peace spoken of is aspirational, the spirits' own thought revealed, regardless of men's shortcomings."

"At this time, we do have peace throughout Haiti." Mayobanex gazed at Guarionex to initiate serious discussion. "Has Caonabó's marriage to Anacaona affected you?"

"I had feared Behecchio would begin to exert influence over Caonabó at my expense. Perhaps he has influence in ways I don't understand, but my relationship with Caonabó hasn't changed. Anacaona appears to be a wife in Maguana, not a cacique. Caonabó has proved as strong a ruler in peace as he is a warrior."

"I've been surprised, as well," Mayobanex replied. "But I was more concerned with Caonabó than Behecchio, afraid that Caonabó would be emboldened by the alliance to take his own liberties with you."

"I watch that carefully. Caonabó has brought all his brothers from Aniyana, and some have been given subordinate villages to rule. There is a young brother, Manicoatex, who's now a reputed cacique of a village directly on my border. Caonabó's principal general, Uxtamex, has a reputation for crushing disloyal subordinate caciques, burning their caneys to the ground. But Caonabó has never threatened my border."

Guarionex recalled Anacaona standing before him, refusing his symbolic demand to mount her. "Caonabó won Anacaona. But she seems a Xaraguán first before all else. Her people adore her and I suspect many Maguanans adore her, too. Perhaps she has more cunning than either her brother or husband. If there were a person to rule both Maguana and Xaraguá, I suspect it would be her. To her credit, she is Taíno."

Stars began to glimmer in the east and the two men quietly smoked tobacco for some moments. Mayobanex remembered his interrogation of the Caribes and chose his words carefully. "I see Guacanagarí as weak. He shies from ceremony displaying his power."

Guarionex was mindful Guacanagarí had proven a friend. "Did he need to display his power beyond the victory? Guacanagarí is Taíno."

"'Taíno.'" Mayobanex twitched his eyebrows. "Anacaona and Guacanagarí are both 'Taíno.' You yourself are said to be the wisest Taíno living. For you, what's the essence of this?"

"You know the meaning in everyday conversation. *Taíno* simply refers to a good man, just like *caribe* refers to a strong or brave man. But both words have larger meanings. A man is Taíno when he aspires to prosper in harmony with the prosperity of others, both giving to and receiving from them, with devotion to the spirits and without confrontation except if necessary."

"That's what I've always understood. But, as caciques, we both understand confrontation sometimes is necessary." Mayobanex studied his friend's expression. "I suspect you think my Ciguayans go to battle too quickly."

Guarionex laughed and hugged Mayobanex's shoulder. "We do think that. But you're Taíno, my friend. While we differ on when force is necessary, you do believe in peace otherwise. That may not be said of the Caribes."

Guarionex pointed to the stars rising on the horizon. "Taínos understand that rare things come from the heavens beyond the horizon. The guanín Guabonito and Guahayona gathered came from the heavens beyond horizon. So do the aspirations of our areítos."

A memory of spying Caribes at sea flashed through Mayobanex's thoughts, and he mused that Caribes also came from beyond the horizon.

FERNANDO
Málaga, 1487

As spring arrived, the sovereigns believed they had the military advantage to conquer Málaga. Al-Zagal now ruled from Grenada's

Alhambra, and his nephew Boabdil, whom Fernando had fought, captured, and released for a second time in 1486, now lived just minutes away on a neighboring hill. The sovereigns' use of Boabdil had born fruit, as Al-Zagal and Boabdil's loyalists fought and murdered one another daily, sapping the emirate's strength.

In April, Fernando marched with an enormous army, well-equipped with heavy artillery and siege equipment, to surround Vélez Málaga, miles east of Málaga. Fernando demanded Vélez Málaga's surrender on much the same terms offered the Rondans, and its Mohammedan leaders accepted.

Fernando then demanded Málaga's surrender and directed an Aragonese fleet to blockade its port. Málaga's leaders asked Boabdil for relief but he advised surrender. Neither Al-Zagal nor the North African principalities appeared willing to assist, either, and Málaga now stood alone.

But its leaders had anticipated and prepared for this very battle. The central city had garrisoned a squadron of North African soldiers for its defense and was well fortified with two formidable castles, the Alcázaba on the plain and the Gibralforo above it atop a steep hillside, the latter commanded by a veteran general known as al-Zegri. Fernando sought to pay al-Zegri a bribe of gold bullion to surrender his fort, but he refused. The civilian leadership, as well as the general populace, believed defending their faith and customs was worth the ultimate sacrifice. With popular support, the leadership rejected Fernando's surrender offer, and Málaga's residents fled within the forts, hoarding food for an extended siege and burning the homes abandoned near the fort to deny attackers strongholds.

Fernando's army commenced the siege, unleashing continuous cannon fire on the fortresses' walls, and Fernando soon recognized the Málagans' determination to defend their city and life. Castilian cavalry rushed the walls to breach them, but, to their surprise, Mohammedan troops rushed from their fortresses to engage on the open terrain. For days, opposing soldiers fought hand to hand, and any yard or foot gained by the Castilians was paid for dearly in blood. Slaughter became both participants' objective, not prisoners. Fernando realized that his enemy was prepared to die simply to achieve the blood and death of Christians and the vengeance of its God. He understood his troops had a more limited resolve—to face death so long as the great spoils of Málaga appeared achievable. As the summer heat surged, the wind bore the stench of the fallen, unburied bodies of both opponents upon both of them, and Fernando asked Isabel to come to Málaga. Her presence at the battle-field, her charity to the wounded, and her exemplary devotion would fortify the troops' morale.

Isabel arrived with Princess Isabel, their lady attendants, Cardinal Mendoza, and Bishop Talavera, and visited the troops and their field hospitals, exhorting the glory, privilege, and duty of the conquest. The army's morale did improve. The queen also expressed her resolve to the enemy. The pope's silver cross, first displayed in Alhama, was raised before the fortress walls for defenders to behold and fear. The church bells destined to be installed in the mosques when converted were pealed for them to hear.

Isabel and Fernando dispatched messengers again proposing surrender. But the Málagans feared Isabel and Christ no more than Fernando. Al-Zagal did order a battalion to breach the Castilian encirclement and deliver supplies to the beleaguered defenders. But Boabdil sent troops provisioned by Fernando to intercept them, and Al-Zagal's troops retreated.

Inside the fortresses, July and August brought hunger. Almost all the food stored had been consumed and the soldiers and citizens—men, women, and children—resorted to eating the flesh and hides of their dogs and asses and the leaves and bark of trees. The North African soldiers plundered Jewish households for their last supplies. Old and young began to die. Some citizens could bear it no longer and left the fortresses to surrender themselves into slavery. An African prince sent messengers bearing Fernando and Isabel gifts and imploring that they be merciful when they took Málaga. Fernando honored the messengers but explained that mercy had been offered but its time had passed.

In August, Málaga's civilian leaders in the Alcázaba offered to surrender the city in return for their people's submission to the sovereigns and freedom to leave—just as the sovereigns had agreed for Ronda and Vélez Málaga. Fernando replied that, after three months of war, those terms were not available. The Málagans had a singular choice: enslavement or death.

The civilian leaders consulted their people and replied that, unless the sovereigns guaranteed their liberty, they would kill every Christian captive held in Málaga, burn the city and their possessions to the ground, and die to the last man attacking the Christians, leaving Fernando and his troops with but blood for their spoils. Fernando replied that, if one Christian captive were harmed, every Málagan would die. Málaga's leaders, with the support of most of their people, eventually chose enslavement.

The Castilian army entered the city, disarmed the remaining Málagan soldiers, released the surviving starved Christian captives from their jails, secured as loot the entire possessions of the city, and brought wheat for everyone to eat. The Málagans were herded into corrals and al-Zegri placed in irons, and Fernando and Isabel entered the city after the dead were burned.

Fernando gazed across the splendor of his conquest and the squalor of the vanquished and was reminded of the cosmology of the Sicilian abbot Joachim de Fiore, which he had studied as a boy. The abbot had postulated that God's plan for history was divided in three ages—the Age of the Father, which had already passed, when God was first revealed; the current age, the Age of the Son, which had started with the incarnation of Christ; and a final age, yet to come, the Age of the Spirit. Christ would then battle the Antichrist and a last emperor would reconquer Jerusalem, whereupon the world would end cataclysmically and be reborn with heaven on earth, and with Christianity spread to all people of the world. Fernando had been taught this last emperor might be a king of Aragón.

Fernando and Isabel awarded one-third of the population as slaves to the conquering troops. They retained one-third as their own slaves to compensate for the campaign's expenses, and Luis de Santángel augmented the war chest by selling many. They exchanged the lucky remaining one-third with the infidels in Africa for the release of Christian prisoners. As incentive for the Málagans to hand over all their jewels and gold, Fernando promised they could ransom themselves from slavery by raising an enormous sum within the following year, with the jewels and gold deposited as down payment. The enormous sum was never raised and the Crown kept the deposit.

The sovereigns gave special gifts of slaves: Pope Innocent VIII received one hundred of the African soldiers; Fernando's sister, Queen Juana of Naples, one hundred maidens; Queen Leonor of Portugal, fifty maidens; and each of the principal Castilian noblemen who had participated in the siege, as well as ladies of Isabel's court, up to one hundred slaves each depending on their prestige and contribution to the victory. The sovereigns' Jewish tax collector Abraham Seneor was permitted to purchase the freedom of over four hundred surviving Jewish residents, further augmenting the war chest. Some conversos who had fled the Inquisition were burned at the stake.

As they consolidated their conquest, the sovereigns summoned Colón to Málaga. The Talavera commission's conclusion did not surprise them but, as King João, they were reluctant to dismiss him entirely. Castile's opportunities for overseas expansion were limited and, if they dismissed him, Colón might sail for another sovereign, including Henry VII of England, Charles VIII of France, or even João.

Fernando and Isabel told Colón that the Reconquista remained their greatest concern and highest duty. They could not divert attention or funding to his plan. However, they would consider it in the future when the war was concluded. The sovereigns could see the pain in Colón's face as he listened and that his plan was his life and its limbo a purgatory. They authorized their accountant to disperse Colón funds for his subsistence at court while he awaited the war's end.

Cristóbal interpreted the rejection as a test of his faith. He had come to believe that the Lord intended for him to achieve his voyage. As he walked through the battlefield and conquered city, he studied the smoldering funeral pyres of slain Christians and infidels and the masses of infidels held in corrals pending their sale, and he realized the king and queen truly were engaged in a Holy War of transformative proportion. The sovereigns appeared sincere in their belief that the Lord directed them to pursue their war first and in their promise to reconsider his voyage. Cristóbal decided he would wait in Castile for their change of heart, but not exclusively.

Cristóbal returned to Córdoba and dispatched Bartolomé back to João's court to plead again for a voyage and, if that failed, to proceed to the court of King Henry VII in England.

Cristóbal learned of João's authorization of the voyage west from Jesus Christo and that it had utterly failed. Dulhmo had sailed west into the northern Ocean Sea in wintry March and encountered fierce westerly winds, made little progress, discovered nothing, and limped back to port with the crews ragged and sails torn. The expedition's futility was said to be the butt of ridicule on Lisbon's wharfs. Cristóbal took solace that his observations of the winds and currents—at both the Azores and the Canaries—remained unperceived and relished the outcome. He also learned that yet another explorer, Bartolomeu Dias, had sailed from Lisbon to attempt again the circumnavigation of Guinea.

CRISTÓBAL
Beatriz, Dias, Henry VII, and baby Fernando, 1487–1488

Beatriz Enríquez de Arana was born to a peasant farmer and wine presser in the hills west of Córdoba, orphaned at an early age, and raised by a devout grandmother and aunt who taught her to read and write. When these ladies also died, Beatriz was raised by her mother's cousin Rodrigo de Arana, together with Rodrigo's son Diego. Beatriz was unmarried and in her early twenties when Cristóbal returned to Córdoba from Málaga—about fifteen years his junior. Cristóbal and Diego de Arana had become acquaintances at a Genoese apothecary, and she had flirted with Cristóbal on a number of occasions.

In October 1487, Bishop Talavera authorized further stipends for Cristóbal to remain at court. But Cristóbal's idea had now been considered and at best deferred by two kingdoms, and he realized its prospects were quite uncertain. He slept at night alone in poverty. Little Diego lived in Huelva with Violante, Bartolomé in Lisbon, Filipa and Susanna had departed, and Domenico yet survived in Genoa. Cristóbal reflected uneasily that Domenico would have scorned Cristóbal's abandonment of the merchant's career he had once achieved. Domenico had raised and supported five children, and Cristóbal couldn't support his one. His voyage could secure nobility, wealth, and fame but, if the Lord so designed, he would spend his entire life without ever achieving it.

One afternoon, after meeting at the apothecary, Cristóbal and Diego de Arana passed by Rodrigo's house, where Cristóbal met Beatriz in the garden. They chatted. Cristóbal enjoyed her intellect, and her literacy was unusual for a woman of her status. He saw her faith and was pleased. He told her of his voyages on the Ocean Sea and his meetings with João, Fernando, and Isabel, and she listened intently and appeared to understand his enthusiasm for his idea. Beatriz was younger than Filipa had been when Cristóbal first met her.

Beatriz listened to Cristóbal boast about his accomplishments and saw beyond the boasts to an inner excitement and faith that she found rare and captivating. Regardless of his obvious poverty, he was handsome and extraordinarily well self-taught. She told him of her youth and upbringing. She had no parents to decide her marriage and was free to do as she wished. He listened and told her about Filipa's death and little Diego.

As the afternoon passed, Cristóbal was smitten by her sensuality and understanding. He realized he wanted her even though she had no title or connection that would benefit him. He reflected that securing another favorable marriage undoubtedly would improve his prospects for a voyage. But that didn't preclude being with, or being seen with, Beatriz. Noblemen of all courts of all nations and peoples had their concubines, including João, Fernando, Cardinal Mendoza, and even St. Augustine.

Beatriz was captivated by Cristóbal's commanding presence and accomplishments and by their genuine rapport. It was obvious he wanted her. She liked him, and she made that clear.

Before dusk, Cristóbal kissed her hand, and they agreed to meet again. Soon, he came again to the garden and they talked of faith and family and enjoyed each other's company. He spoke of his life on the Ocean Sea without boasting, allowing that the Lord's wind and weather ultimately determined the outcome of a voyage, not men. He poured out his bitterness that men of wealth and status disparaged his ideas although they themselves were ignorant. She peered through the rage to discern whether he truly liked her or merely sought her guardian's wealth or her bed in comfortable accommodations. He sought to embrace and she halted him, disclaiming any interest in a brief encounter for the sport of it, studying whether he was sorrowed or merely unfulfilled. He promised he was sincere. She reflected that perhaps she would make him love her. If she bore his child, perhaps he would stay. Perhaps he would marry her.

One evening, Cristóbal came to the garden, and they talked late into the night. His voyage slipped from his mind, and her fear of the risks of their relationship slipped from hers. He pressed and she invited him in. Quietly, he undressed and made love to her, and they whispered close to dawn, excited to be together beyond facade or pretense, separated only by a paramount relationship to God. When they rose, her servant prepared them lunch and Beatriz said he could stay.

As Beatriz and Cristóbal became a couple, Bartolomeu Dias's expedition to circumvent Guinea progressed south past Cão's last stone pillar (Cape Cross, Namibia). The weather became stormy and his two ships—the flagship São Cristóvão and the São Pantaleão— sheltered in a small bay (northwestern South Africa) for five days, whereupon Dias decided to proceed. The ships sailed west from the sight of land to escape unfavorable winds and current and, for thirteen days, drove southwest. The sea and air grew colder and the crew fearful. Eventually, they discovered more variable winds and Dias ordered the ships to tack due east to find the coast.

Cristóvão dispatched a letter to King João offering to return to Portugal if João would reconsider Cristóvão's plan.

Dias failed to achieve the Guinean coast within a few days. Surprised, exhilarated, and fearful, the crews of the São Cristóvão and São Pantaleão veered the ships north. Eventually, they sighted the coast of Guinea stretching west to east and, on February 3, 1488, they disembarked in a bay where black-skinned inhabitants were herding cattle (Mossel Bay, South Africa). They offered prayers to the Lord and Virgin and gifts to the inhabitants, who refused them. An altercation occurred, and an inhabitant was killed by crossbow.

Beatriz concluded she was pregnant, as they had suspected for some weeks. Cristóbal and Beatriz prayed to the Virgin for her and the baby's safety.

In mid-February, Bartolomeo Colombo presented the Colombo's map of the world to King Henry VII in England. Bartolomeo indicated to the king that his brother, Cristoforo, would be present but was discussing the same with King João in Portugal and King Fernando and Queen Isabel in Castile. The brothers would sail for the first sovereign to offer sponsorship. King Henry VII did not pursue the offer.

Dias continued to sail east along the Guinean coast, and it began to turn northeast. In March, he placed a stone pillar dedicated to St. Gregory on a promontory (Cape Padrone, South Africa). Soon, his officers requested that they turn back due to the harsh weather, unknown seas, and hostile inhabitants. Dias's orders required him to consult the officers as to important decisions, and the ships landed to consider the question. The officers voted to turn back and signed a document attesting their decision. Dias convinced them to sail two or three more days, promising to turn back if they did not change their minds.

On March 20, 1488, King João responded warmly to Cristóvão's letter, inviting him to Lisbon and assuring that he would be protected from any actions in Portugal instigated by Cristóvão's creditors.

On his return voyage, Dias followed the coast of Guinea, which he had not seen, arriving at a tremendous plateau visible from the sea from a great distance (Cape of Good Hope). Dias left his last stone pillar there, dedicated to St. Philip.

Over the summer, Bishop Talavera did not reauthorize a stipend for Cristóbal, perhaps neglectfully. In August, Beatriz bore their son, whom they christened Fernando in honor of the king. Beatriz's relatives had accepted her relationship with Cristóbal, and the child was welcomed with love regardless of his illegitimacy. After baby Fernando's birth, Cristóbal secretly shipped to Lisbon to advance new discussions with João.

Bartolomeu Dias sailed into Lisbon in December 1488, having discovered that Guinea could be circumvented. Cristóvão was invited to be present when Dias related his success to King João. Cristóvão gleaned that, instead of proceeding to the Indies, Dias's crew had refused him. But João beamed triumphantly that his own insight and perseverance had born fruit. Cristóvão perceived the assembled advisers and nobility were mocking him, that João's warmth to him had dissipated, and that João would never reconsider his plan. Cristóbal stole out of Lisbon to return to Beatriz in Córdoba, his vision and aspirations devastated yet again.

Cristóbal reasoned that João's success should reinvigorate the Castilian sovereigns' appetite for his plan—as their only alternative to reach the Indies. But the sovereigns' interest remained their Holy War. Cristóbal confronted the dreadful truth: he had now spent much of his adult life pursuing an idea he knew was true but which other men denied and which had brought him to poverty. At thirty-seven, he was failing rather than achieving, wandering rather than progressing, descending rather than ascending, and begging rather than commanding. When he returned to Beatriz, she welcomed him with support and love.

Isabel and Fernando
Rebellion in Gomera, Canary Islands, 1488–1489

In 1488, Isabel and Fernando learned that Hernán Peraza, whom they had pardoned for murder in return for participating in the Canaries' conquest and marrying the enticing Beatriz de Bobadilla, had been killed in a native rebellion while ruling Gomera. Some said that Hernán had treated the Gomerans cruelly, as or as if slaves. They had resisted his domination, frequently rebelling, and then killed him as he met his Gomeran lover Iballa in a cave. Beatriz and her two children had barricaded themselves from massacre in the small, square tower (Torre del Conde) where they lived at San Sebastián, the island's tiny eastern harbor, and had been rescued by Pedro de Vera.

Soon thereafter, the sovereigns heard from Lanzerote's bishop that Pedro and Beatriz had inflicted cruel punishments and enslavements in reprisal for Hernán's death. Many Gomerans had been executed regardless of participation in the revolt, some after torture. Others had been thrown overboard while being transported between islands or disemboweled or dismembered. Pedro and Beatriz had sold the wives and children of the slaughtered into slavery at Palos and other ports in Andalusia, ignoring the bishop's warning that enslavement of Christians was unlawful.

Isabel and Fernando ordered an inquiry into the enslavements by their religious advisers, which would continue over three years. Pedro responded that the Gomerans were infidels. Beatriz argued that they were not Christians—they had never been baptized, went naked, and were polygamists. It was determined the bishop was correct, where-upon Fernando ordered the slaves manumitted and their purchasers repaid by Pedro and Beatriz. Pedro was recalled from the islands to serve in the Reconquista and replaced by his key lieutenant, Alonso Fernández de Lugo.

ISABEL AND CRISTÓBAL
Audience, Jaén, 1489

In 1489, as the sovereigns' army slowly claimed Grenadan territory from al-Zagal, Fray Marchena suggested that Cristóbal approach prominent Andalusian merchants with his plan, rather than waiting on the sovereigns any longer. Cristóbal understood that merchants could not bestow hereditary titles to lands discovered but realized the sovereigns' reconsideration was too uncertain. The French king Charles VIII had expressed interest in evaluating the plan, but his convincing was no more likely than Fernando and Isabel's and easier for Bartolomé to pursue. Cristóbal took Marchena's advice and sought sponsorship first from Enrique Guzmán and, when rejected, from the Duke of Medinaceli, Luis de la Cerda.

The duke had substantial maritime businesses and lived in a castle on the Bay of Cádiz at Puerto de Santa María. He invited Colón to visit and they discussed the voyage from a mercantile perspective.

Puerto de Santa María invigorated Cristóbal. He had starved for ships and the ocean, and ambling about the bustling quays of the small port reminded him of his true vocation, relieved him of the scorn he perceived at court, and turned his nightmare back to a dream. He even met a one-eyed sailor who confirmed that lands could be achieved sailing west from Ireland.

The discussions culminated in the duke's agreement to sponsor three ships and crews for a year provided the sovereigns' consented. Cristóbal moved to reside at the castle as a member of the duke's staff to organize the expedition. After five years of rejection, he was ecstatic with the achievement, vindicated that he had shown his detractors wrong, and humbled that the Lord had recognized his faith. He drew up specifications for the ships and provisions.

Yet, when the duke requested the sovereigns' consent, they denied it! In May, Isabel summoned Cristóbal to meet her at the episcopal palace in the village of Jaén, where she and much of the court were encamped while Fernando and his armies bore down on al-Zagal's troops nearby. Cristóbal warily reckoned that the sovereigns had disapproved the duke's venture in order to sponsor him themselves. There simply could be no other cause for precluding a private venture they could tax and that expanded Castilian influence in competition with João.

Cristóbal rode a mule east from Córdoba into the hill country to Jaén, where a spectacular precipice hovered high above the village, emblazoned with a large cross. He gazed up to it and implored the Lord that his faith was pure and had never wavered and that there was no occasion to test it further. He was eager to bring the faith to the Indies if the Lord so destined. He entered the palace and was ushered into an audience with Queen Isabel, Cardinal Mendoza, and Bishop Talavera.

The queen thanked Cristóbal for making the journey and informed him of her and Fernando's decision. "Cristóbal, you can't pursue your voyage with the duke because the king and I are still interested in it. Al-Zagal's elimination is the Holy War's final battle and, when we're victorious, Boabdil will submit the city of Grenada as vassal. Although we're not ready to commit to it, your plan then will be reconsidered." Isabel smiled cheerfully. "I understand this may come as a disappointment, but you should be hopeful instead."

Cristóbal's body froze, his breath stopped, and his temples pounded as he searched for words, utterly aghast and bewildered. He had anguished five years in the queen's court to hear this—a voyage denied without a voyage committed! He bit his tongue, smothered his rage, cried to his Lord, and gazed to the floor to collect himself. Heartbeats passed. Slowly, he recognized the queen sought to encourage him as much as she could, and that he had no other ready option.

Cristóbal turned from the floor to the queen and responded in a measured voice. "Your Majesty, my extreme disappointment in the absence of your firm commitment is surpassed by my desire to serve you and the king. I understand the importance of the Holy War and the glory of your victory. I assure you that my enterprise will achieve even greater glory for you and the king. You will bring the faith to the Indies and retake Jerusalem."

Bishop Talavera peered into Colón's eyes to discern his sincerity. Cardinal Mendoza studied his composure to comprehend whether he was resourceful or crazed. Accustomed to flattery and pandering, Isabel ignored both and saw an extraordinary resilience and fortitude that touched her deeply.

With her business done, she sat on a throne and sought information, with Colón standing before her. "Cristóbal, as I remember you've been to Mina."

"Yes, Your Majesty."

"Do you think Mina is the Ophir where King Solomon obtained his gold?"

"Your Majesty, it's possible, but I think not. According to the scriptures, Solomon and Hiram's ships sailed from Eziongeber on the Red Sea. I believe they sailed east toward Cathay to achieve Ophir. I would hope to find Ophir in the Indies sailing west."

Cristóbal was startled by what came next. It appeared the queen simply wished to talk. At that moment, she indicated Cardinal Mendoza and Bishop Talavera could excuse themselves, and they departed, leaving Cristóbal and Isabel in the company of only guards and attendants.

The queen paused for a moment to reflect, and Cristóbal perceived she became more serious. "Cristóbal, if men could enter it, where is the Earthly Paradise of Adam and Eve to be found?"

"Your Majesty, there're different theories. Sir John Mandeville believes it lies in the Indies at the earth's highest point. He says its spring, which waters the Tree of Knowledge, separates and flows underground the length of terra firma to emerge as four great rivers— the Ganges in the Indies, the Tigris and Euphrates near the Orient, and the Nile in Ethiopia and Egypt. Cardinal d'Ailly agrees."

Isabel smiled. "And you'd hope to find it by sailing west, as well?"

Cristóbal nodded. "You've understood my plan well." He studied the queen, and she appeared amused to hear more. "When Marco Polo returned from Cathay to Venice, he sailed west on the Ocean

Sea from Zaiton [Quanzhou] to Ormus [at the Strait of Hormuz]. If you sponsor my voyage, and if I reach Cathay, it'd be possible for me to return that way, too. I wouldn't do that, because the distance between Cathay and Spain is far shorter. But Mandeville himself discusses circumventing the entire globe."

"Cristóbal, your confidence in your plan is very high." She stared directly into his eyes. "Why? So many disagree."

Cristóbal gazed directly back. "As Your Majesty, I have faith in the prophets and scriptures. Esdras says water is only one-seventh the globe and that—together with evidence I've accumulated over decades at sea—is proof enough for me. For Bishop Talavera's commission, I have offered far greater support and reasoning and answered innumerable misconceptions and superstitions. But, in the end, I believe it has been revealed by the prophets and confirmed by the evidence I have seen."

As he spoke, Isabel was captivated by his apparent sincerity on this point. She also perceived a haughty scorn and disrespect for the Talavera commission. She reflected that, like an adventurer, Colón boasted of his experience, relied on unlearned sources such as Mandeville and Marco Polo, pandered as to Jerusalem, and was transparent in his lust for nobility and wealth. Yet she found him to be fundamentally different from an adventurer. He possessed both a geographical idea and an enormous ego and vanity to establish that the idea was correct. He was committed to risk his life in reliance on his faith in the Lord, the prophets and scriptures, and his own sailing observations—rather than a brash calculation of the risk and reward a mere adventurer would make. His faith was sincere and true, independent of his open lust for nobility.

"Are you certain of this Cipangu? Bishop Talavera told me members of the commission said even Sir Mandeville doesn't speak of it."

"Yes, Your Majesty." Cristóbal gazed to the floor.

There was a moment of silence. "When you face danger on the Ocean Sea, to whom do you pray?"

"As most Christian sailors, I pray to the Lord and the Virgin. Frequently, I pray to St. Francis of Assisi, as well."

"Why?"

"As Your Majesty knows, St. Francis was a merchant and the son of a merchant. But the Lord called him for other purposes—to follow the scriptures faithfully, live ascetically, and brave hardship. St. Francis trusted God to lead him. He understood that, with faith and adherence to the gospels, God would lead him to his destiny regardless of the struggle."

"You should understand that I do understand struggle and have since childhood. I frequently pray to the Virgin. I often reflect on the teachings of St. John the Evangelist—that the devil must be vanquished before Christ comes again. The king and I are responsible for leading the struggle to vanquish the devil from Spain."

As she spoke, Cristóbal was astounded by the queen's choice to discuss her faith with him. He nodded but was speechless. Isabel smiled and spoke softly. "I do understand that you view me as part of your struggle. You should understand that I must pursue my struggle first and nothing can impede its achievement." She reflected and then sought to lighten the conversation. "Cristóbal, have you ever encountered sea monsters or dragons at sea?"

"I've never seen the Leviathan of Job or Isaiah. But I've witnessed enormous crocodiles in Guinea. Sometimes the sea churns with little wind, and crews fear their ships are being hunted, particularly at night."

"Does that frighten you?"

"Mariners must always be alert, prepared. Pliny the Elder teaches that the seas bear such nutrition and are so spacious that beasts can grow to monstrous proportions. He reports that the seas off the Indies are filled with whales as large as three acres, sharks seventy-five yards long, and lobsters six feet long. He says the eels in the Ganges grow to three hundred feet. Jaws of monsters have been found spanning over sixty feet."

"Cristóbal, if you don't return from your voyage, who will care for your sons?"

Cristóbal felt awkward addressing the queen regarding his unmarried relationship with Beatriz. He also felt remorse at not having considered her question fully. "My elder son is being educated at the Franciscan monastery in Palos, and my younger son, Fernando, is with his mother in Córdoba. Diego sometimes stays with my sister-in-law in Huelva." He chose to go no further.

Isabel pressed no further. Courteously, she indicated that she needed to attend to other business. She rose and he knelt. For a moment, both recognized a mutual respect and a bond of faith and resolve. Cristóbal hesitated, and then sought to reinforce a final point. "Your Majesty, remember that Marco Polo explains that the Grand Khan dispatched messengers to the pope requesting to learn of Christianity. To my knowledge, the Grand Khan awaits a reply."

"Do not lose hope. The king will vanquish al-Zagal in short order." She invited him to stay at court and instructed the sovereigns' accountant to provide food and that necessary to alleviate his poverty. The accountant wrote the duke that a voyage wasn't likely to come off but, if it did, the queen would grant the duke a participation.

Al-Zagal surrendered to Fernando in December 1489, and his subjects became Mujadin on the previously established terms. Boabdil then held the city of Grenada alone, and, while he had agreed to be the sovereigns' vassal, he advised them in 1490 that he could not, or perhaps would not, deliver the city to them, explaining that many of his subjects would rather die than surrender. He led troops south to retake territory lost, attempting to occupy a strip of land to the coast so aid from North Africa could be received. But Fernando blocked the gambit and, in September, Fernando's army marched a tala through the farmland supporting the city to burn its crops and orchards so the city would hunger.

The sovereign's conquest of Grenada was not completed expeditiously, Cristóbal's voyage was not reconsidered promptly, and, in 1490, Cristóbal returned devastated yet again to Beatriz's solace in Córdoba.

VI
1490 — AUGUST 2, 1492, DESTINY

CRISTÓBAL
Forgotten, 1491

Ignored and inconsequential, Cristóbal anguished as the sovereigns married their firstborn, Isabel, to João's son, Alfonso, with extravagant ceremony, sparred with Boabdil for over a year, and replenished their treasury as their inquisitors exorcized the realm. He sat with Beatriz and little Fernando in Beatriz's garden in Córdoba, reading the scriptures and cosmographies. He returned to Huelva and Palos to spend time with Diego, Violante, and the friars at La Rábida. He visited the duke in Puerto de Santa María and watched the ships sail in and out. He called on the leading Genoese merchants when he passed through Seville. The sovereigns forgot about him, his funding lapsed, and he relied on these hosts to survive.

In summer 1491, he met Beatriz de Peraza de Bobadilla, Hernán Peraza's widow, who had come to Seville and Córdoba to answer for the massacres and enslavements of Gomerans committed after Hernán's assassination. She was intrigued by his boasts of royal audiences and sponsorship, amused by his wit, and warmed by his handsome physique, although his poverty and absence of nobility precluded a marriage. She enticed him with her beauty, sensuality, and, while she had little appreciation of its irresistible and unique charm to him, her stewardship of a Canary Island. Cristóbal was smitten by all three, a tantalizing respite to his misery. She sported him briefly and then departed.

Cristóbal's degradation and defeat now overwhelmed him and, by autumn, he bitterly concluded he had squandered seven years waiting on the sovereigns for naught but condescension, scorn, ridicule, mockery, contempt, prejudice, and injustice. He raged that his extraordinary experience and studies—Scio, Mina, Marco Polo, Esdras—dwarfed that of other mariners but was dismissed as ignorant by those themselves ignorant of geography and the sea. He beseeched the Lord for the explanation for his punishment and understood the Lord was displeased with his self-importance and boastfulness.

Woefully, Cristóbal decided to depart for France to meet King Charles VIII and reunite with Bartolomé. In Córdoba, he told his first Beatriz that he would return to see her and little Fernando when he could. He traveled to Huelva and Palos to tell Diego, Violante, and the friars of La Rábida of his plans and to determine where Diego should then live.

He was greeted at La Rábida by a Fray Juan Pérez, who was shocked by the decision to depart since the surrender of Grenada appeared certain and Fray Marchena and others had faith in the voyage. Fray Pérez had served the queen as an accountant years before and offered to appeal directly to her. Cristóbal held little hope but appreciated the offer, and Pérez wrote the queen a letter warning of Colón's departure unless she interceded.

Isabel, Fernando, and Cristóbal
Reconquista Completed, 1491–1492

In spring 1491, Fernando's army marched again through the farmland in the valley below the city of Grenada to burn whatever remained fertile and surrounded the city to wait for Boabdil's submission. The king was accompanied by Prince Juan and the sovereigns' nobility, who came to witness the Reconquista's glorious finale. A small city of white tents was erected in the valley to accommodate everyone. Princes throughout Europe sent troops, the papal nuncio to Spain arrived to represent Pope Innocent VIII, and Queen Isabel and

Princess Juana joined in June. The city's conquest would be revenge for the loss of Constantinople.

A fire swept through the tents in July and Princess Isabel's young husband—King João's heir—died in a riding accident in Portugal. The king and queen wore black in mourning but did not waver. In place of the tents, a city of traditional buildings was built in the shape of a cross and named Santa Fe (Holy Faith), demonstrating the Castilians intended never to leave. Merchants set up shops, and Princess Isabel, in mourning, and her younger sisters soon arrived.

Fernando's and Boabdil's troops engaged daily, and it became apparent many of the city's defenders were prepared for a brutal struggle to a bitter end. The sovereigns desired Boabdil's surrender without the slaughter of Málaga and to receive a functioning city with the magnificent Alhambra intact.

Hunger—of Grenada's soldiers, citizens, and their children and animals—gradually became the ever-present focus and panic of daily existence in the city. As food and medicine dwindled, Boabdil met with civic leaders, many of whom recommended surrender, and he commenced secret negotiations with the sovereigns. By the end of November, agreement was achieved and surrender set for the day of the Epiphany, January 6, 1492. While the terms encouraged Mohammedans to emigrate, including free passage to Africa for three years, both sides anticipated most of the population would remain, and those remaining were guaranteed freedom to practice Islam. Mosques were protected from conversion and homes from confiscation. Mohammedan captives were to be released rather than enslaved. Jews who did not convert to Christianity were required to emigrate. Central to the surrender, Boabdil would receive his own territory, estates, and privileges.

As the surrender negotiations progressed, the sovereigns developed plans for the conquered territory and its integration into their realms. They chose Cardinal Mendoza's nephew the Count of Tendilla to serve as the territory's governor and, subject to the pope's approval, appointed Bishop Talavera to become the first archbishop of Grenada, responsible for conversion of the Mohammedans who remained. Talavera requested that the Mujadin who converted be exempt from the Inquisition for forty years, believing that the time necessary for men to shed their daily customs associated with a former religion. The sovereigns noted the concern, Isabel pondering her confessor's misgivings regarding the Inquisition, Fernando his confessor's loyalty.

The sovereigns also reviewed the expansion of their realms beyond Spain. They received their commander in the Canaries, Alonso de Lugo, and discussed his plans to conquer Palmas and Tenerife. After Hernán Peraza's death, efforts had been made to achieve peace treaties with individual chiefdoms on these islands, with some success. But Pope Sixtus IV had discontinued the sale of indulgences for Christianization of the Canaries and the conquest would have to be funded otherwise. De Lugo proposed the funding come from selling into slavery the inhabitants who refused peace treaties.

Isabel had summoned Colón to Grenada after receiving warning of his departure for France, and the sovereigns advised him that his plan would be reconsidered in January by a new commission, again chaired by Bishop Talavera. Cristóbal forlornly accepted yet further delay and took the opportunity to renew acquaintances with supporters, including wiling away hours with Luis de Santángel.

Luis was then administering, with Bishop Talavera, the Crown revenue to fund the war. He remained mindful of the imperative of retaining Fernando's grace. Over the past four years, four more of Luis's extended family had been arrested, convicted, and either penanced or burned at the stake, with substantial properties confiscated. Inquisitors had exhumed a deceased relative to convict her so her estate could be seized. Luis himself had been arrested in 1491 and admitted to some error, marching in a procession in penitence wearing a sanbenito.

But Luis continued to serve the king and queen with genuine devotion. He appreciated that Fernando and Isabel had transformed Aragón and Castile from bickering, crime-ridden, weak principalities to rank as one of the leading powers of the world, and he believed God—of whichever religion he truly believed—had blessed the Spanish people with their leadership, energy, and competence, unequalled among the rulers of Europe. The kingdoms were now ruled by one king and queen to whom the nobility respectfully answered. The kingdoms' roads, and the streets of their cities and villages, were safe to travel and transport merchandise. The sovereigns' son Prince Juan was their undisputed successor and now rode with Fernando into battle. Alliances had been arranged to counter the French: Juana, now twelve, was engaged to a son of Maximilian, the Holy Roman emperor; María, now nine, was engaged to the prince of Capua; Catalina, now six, was engaged to the eldest son of King Henry VII of England, Prince Arthur; and, had João's son not died, Princess Isabel's marriage to him would have united Hispania's Christian kingdoms, perhaps forever. Castilian and Aragonese merchant ships, including of the Santángel family, plied the Mediterranean and the Ocean Sea in competition with the Portuguese, Genoese, and Venetians. The Canaries would be subdued to facilitate trade with Africa and expand Spain's wealth and power.

Within the city, there were religious protests and disturbances as the surrender terms became known, and surrender was accelerated to January 2 to preclude resistance and Boabdil's murder by his own people. At dawn, Isabel and Fernando rode from Santa Fe with their senior prelates, nobility, and troops to the plain below the Alhambra in three separate processions, the first led by the very adviser who had borne the sword of sovereign power at Isabel's singular coronation, accompanied by Bishop Talavera. Fernando, accompanied by Prince Juan and a daughter, led the second. Isabel, accompanied by her remaining daughters, Cardinal Mendoza, and Count Mendoza, came last.

Isabel gazed forward at her husband and was overcome by their achievement. The Lord had destined their marriage to attain this moment, testing them severely for over a decade before their faith persevered. He had been loyal to this destiny and her crown, and his military leadership had secured victory. This was their joint triumph.

As he rode, Fernando remained alert to the military situation, wary of an attack by renegades or religious militants. He also was overcome with their triumph and glanced back toward his wife. He knew that her will had been indomitable. He was the general, and he was destined to be the greatest king in Christendom and, perhaps, to retake Jerusalem. But she was the Lord's truest and most steadfast servant and more than his equal. This was their joint triumph.

Boabdil left the Alhambra and proceeded downhill to surrender to Fernando and Isabel. Bishop Talavera continued with Count

Mendoza and troops uphill to enter the Alhambra at a side gate, and the troops dispersed within. Talavera beheld the Alhambra's great mosque and, accompanied by others, he entered it to conduct the Alhambra's first mass. He and Count Mendoza then marched with troops farther downhill to enter the military fortress jutting high above the valley below, penetrating through an array of inner gates, courtyards, and ramparts to reach the Alhambra's tallest tower, where they gazed across the plain to Santa Fe in the distance. Mendoza bid the troops raise the pope's silver cross for all to behold.

From the plain, the sovereigns and their assembly watched it rise and glitter in the sun and shouted tumultuously. Fernando fell to his knees. The Castilian army shouted over and over, "Castilla. Castilla. For Don Fernando and Doña Isabel," and then sang "Te Deum Laudamus." Isabel trembled and teared, awash in victory. She had accomplished as the Lord's servant what her father, brother, and centuries of predecessors had been unable to do. His justice and vengeance now triumphed.

Cristóbal marched in Isabel's procession, astounded by the enormity of the pageant and the glory the queen and king achieved as God's instruments. He remembered that the queen had brought him to this moment, and his admiration for her burst through him. He sensed the Lord now heralded her approval of the voyage, but Boabdil's departure in despair, utterly vanquished, reminded him of his own defeats. For an instant, he beheld a vision of Scio's slave market and the possibility of his own utter vanquishment.

But the splendor of his queen's smile and tears dispelled his angst, and Cristóbal swelled with conviction that he, too, was the Lord's instrument, destined as she to fulfill the Lord's design for mankind in a fundamental way. With a steadfastness that utterly belied his circumstances, he fervently prayed for the Lord to lead the king and queen to understand that.

CRISTÓBAL, ISABEL, FERNANDO, AND LUIS DE SANTÁNGEL
Reconsideration of Colón's Voyage, January–May 1492

The sovereigns waited some days before ceremoniously entering the Alhambra and, as attacks by fervent Mohammedans remained a concern, for weeks they typically would work in the Alhambra by day and return to Santa Fe by night. The entire court labored to install Castile's administration in the newly conquered territory.

Bishop Talavera did make time to consider Colón's proposal promptly. He organized a new commission to reexamine the voyage's feasibility, including as members some of the leading nobility and prelates present such as Cardinal Mendoza and the papal nuncio to Spain. The only newly discovered geographic information since the prior commission's review was Bartolomeu Dias's circumvention of Guinea's southern tip. Many feared time was short before João achieved the Indies and established a trade monopoly.

The commission quickly reviewed the same geographic arguments as before. Ptolemy's analytics persuaded some the voyage was impossible to sail, and St. Augustine's views were so interpreted by others. A few believed it had been so long since Creation that it was unlikely that significant new lands would be found. Proponents quoted Aristotle, Seneca, and Esdras, and the papal nuncio himself observed that St. Augustine was great for both learning and holiness but had not been a cosmographer.

Cristóbal definitively proposed the terms on which he would sail. He was to be knighted admiral of all islands and mainland discovered or acquired on behalf of the Crown, a hereditary title in perpetuity, meaning he would be the Crown's lord over maritime matters in these jurisdictions. He also would become viceroy and governor of these lands, such offices also hereditary in perpetuity, signifying his authority extended over nonmaritime matters, as well. He would share one-tenth of all profits derived from gold, spices, and other merchandise of whatever kind obtained in these lands, with the sovereigns entitled to the remaining profits and bearing the cost of outfitting the vessels and crews. He would have the option to underwrite one-eighth of the cost of vessels and to share in that portion of those vessels' profits, too.

Talavera was offended and disgusted by this proposal. Colón was expecting the extraordinary simply for the council to approve the voyage's feasibility, and the excessive recognition and compensation sought substantially diminished the commission's appetite to do so. Many members found the foreigner's demand for an important Castilian title of nobility outrageous.

Colón's supporters implored him to soften his terms and strike a deal. He responded he would not do so, having suffered seven years of scorn by most everyone but the queen, and that two other kings were interested in sponsoring the voyage. He believed he was no longer but a merchant and negotiation no longer appropriate. The Lord had destined that he achieve the voyage—with Fernando and Isabel if that was their destiny or with another sovereign if not. He refused to negotiate a single term, and his supporters cringed.

With João's advantage looming before them, some members of the commission were inclined to confirm the voyage's potential feasibility, but the majority was not. Talavera promptly delivered the majority's conclusion to the sovereigns. He also explained he agreed with the majority but had no objection to proceeding with the voyage as a matter of commercial risk if appropriate terms could be agreed. The king and queen understood the majority's view that sailing west to the Indies was a fantasy, and they also found Colón's terms pretentious and incredible. They had pressing matters to resolve regarding Grenada's administration and were weary of further discussion. One January morning, they summoned Colón and told him they would not sponsor his voyage and that he should depart from the court.

Cristóbal was astounded to be denied. Breathless, he gazed at the floor, betrayed beyond comprehension by the queen's rejection. He recovered slowly, and, for a brief moment, Cristóbal and Isabel stared into each other's eyes. Isabel knew she had led him on and let him down and that the time for final separation had come. Her eyes betrayed no sympathy or warmth to the proposal, though her heart held much for him.

Colón departed his audience and, with Fray Pérez, promptly left by mule for Córdoba, oblivious to most about him, the weight of his denial, failure, and poverty—and the utter waste of seven years— crushing upon his consciousness. Yet he had admitted the possibility of the result and steeled himself for it and his resolve was unbroken. As the mule trod slowly toward Córdoba, his misery was tempered by release from the endless futility of Castile and a determination to succeed in France.

Santángel learned of the rejection immediately and also was astounded. He spoke to Fernando, who was irritated to be discussing Colón's proposal yet again.

"Your Majesty, putting aside the geography, this decision makes little mercantile sense. If Colón finds nothing, he gets nothing—neither wealth nor title—and all the Crown loses is the expense, which is an inconsequential trifle in comparison to the war. It's a pittance compared to the cost of Princess Isabel's wedding two years ago." He paused, but refrained from contrasting it to the expense of the king's considerable wardrobe, no less the queen's enormous one. "If he discovers some island—even be it but another Canary Island—the Crown might find enduring profit. If he achieves a route to Cathay before João, either directly or through new discoveries, the Crown would achieve extraordinary trade and wealth."

"You believe he can sail to the Indies across the Ocean Sea?"

"No. But I know merchants take risks that frequently pay off. The Duke of Medinaceli was ready to underwrite this, and he's no one's fool."

Fernando shook his head, unwilling to spend more time on the topic. "Talk to the queen."

Luis met with Isabel, who also was irritated to be discussing Colón again.

"Your Majesty, the cost of this voyage is little, and I can arrange that it be borrowed. Sponsoring Colón will not interfere with your consolidation of the conquest. If he finds nothing, he gets nothing. Your reputation and glory have never been greater, and Colón's failure would not diminish them. João and his father tried this voyage many times and failed without any injury to their reputations. They failed for two decades in Guinea, and look where they are now—they're almost upon the Indies. The greatest threat to your reputation is that you refuse Colón and he then successfully sails for another, which is precisely what he will do."

"What does the king think?"

"I believe he's willing to engage Colón if you are. A possibility of achieving new discoveries before João should be pursued."

Isabel and Fernando spoke briefly, quickly agreed, and dispatched a messenger to catch Colón to bring him back to court. For the second time that day, they were relieved to be done discussing the proposal—which they believed held scant or no prospect—so they could turn to other business. Colón was found but miles from Santa Fe and brought to Santángel, who informed him that the sovereigns would sponsor his voyage on his terms, except they would not fund the full cost of the voyage. Cristóbal came undone and wept, raptured and stupefied by his fortune's reversal. He was profoundly grateful to Luis for his intervention. He found a chapel and knelt for hours, honoring the Lord for answering his prayers.

By the end of April, crown advisers and Fray Pérez on Cristóbal's behalf negotiated written documents regarding the arrangements. Ancillary to his hereditary title and offices, Colón was granted judicial authority over civil and criminal cases with power to punish delinquents and to resolve disputes regarding the profits owing him. In sum, he was titled to islands and mainland possessed on behalf of Castile and delegated executive, administrative, military, and judicial power—including to impose the death penalty—in those lands, with profits inuring to the Crown and Colón.

The sovereigns thus conceded entitlements exceeding those typically granted other maritime explorers. But they retained more for the Crown than retained in the Reconquista or the conquest of the Canary Islands. Neither land nor vassals subjugated would be shared with nobility other than Colón. The sovereigns would retain the lion's share of any profit, rather than a mere slice by taxation. In the unlikely event something were found, the venture was theirs and Colón's alone.

In the Alhambra on April 30, the sovereigns signed the title grant knighting Colón contingent upon his discoveries. They provided him a passport to present to those he met confirming their authorization to send him over the ocean seas towards the regions of India for mercantile and religious purposes. They furnished a number of letters introducing him to foreign princes, one addressed to the Grand Khan and others with the name of the prince left blank, expressing their greetings to the recipient and that Colón was authorized to speak on their behalf.

The sovereigns shied from publicizing Colón's claims that countless peoples would be brought to the faith and scoffed at his frequent boasts that the voyage's profits—if the voyage ever returned—would fund the recapture of Jerusalem, and they did not require Colón to enlist missionaries on the voyage. The arrangements also did not mention slaves as merchandise. Later that summer, the sovereigns would authorize Alonso de Lugo to subjugate Las Palmas, welcoming the inhabitants who had agreed to peaceful alliances as the sovereigns' free vassals and conducting a military conquest of the others, with those captured sold into slavery to fund the conquest after deducting one-fifth of the proceeds as Alonso's share.

The sovereigns' advisers set about financing the voyage inexpensively—from the Crown's perspective—and incentivizing its prompt readiness in light of the race with João to achieve the Indies. The town of Palos recently had been ordered to provide the Crown two equipped vessels for one year because its mariners had violated Portuguese ships or waters. On April 30, the sovereigns issued a decree to Palos ordering that these two vessels be manned and provisioned within ten days of the town's receipt of the decree, ready to depart on Colón's order to where he directed in the Ocean Sea. The decree indicated that Colón would pay the crews four months' salary in advance at customary rates and prohibited Colón or the ships from sailing to Mina. Sovereign orders were issued suspending prosecution of criminals who enlisted to sail, requiring carpenters, merchants, and others to provide Colón goods and services at fair prices, and suspending taxes on such transactions.

Santángel gave and arranged loans covering other expenses, including from his friend the Genoese merchant Francesco Pinelo,* who lived in Seville and had provided financing for Gran Canaria's conquest. Indulgences were sold. Cristóbal found another Italian merchant to fund a portion himself—Juanoto Berardi, who also had participated in financing Canarian conquests and its slave trade. Cristóbal had met a shipowner in Puerto de Santa María—Juan de la Cosa—interested in participating in the duke's proposed voyage and decided to procure the third ship from him. The financiers and shipowner were comforted that additional Canary Islands might be discovered regardless of achieving the Indies.

As the time came to depart Grenada, Cristóbal pondered the guardianship arrangements—whether he returned from the voyage

---

*Francesco Pinelli in Italian.

or not—to be made for Diego, then almost twelve, and the need to provide the guardian, be it Violante or Beatriz, appropriate resources. Little Fernando, then three, of course would remain with Beatriz. In early May, Isabel appointed Diego as a page to Prince Juan with an annual salary, although Diego would remain with the guardian selected until later called to court.

Within days, Cristóbal left for little Fernando and Beatriz in Córdoba. Beatriz and the Arana family were amazed, ecstatic, and immensely proud Beatriz's lover had reached agreement with the king and queen to be knighted upon his discovery of foreign lands. After years of contributing to his support, they expected to become part of his court. Cristóbal asked Beatriz to care for Diego in his absence so the two boys could be together, relying on Diego's salary as page for his support, and Beatriz happily agreed. In Bartolomé's absence, Cristóbal asked his friend Diego de Arana—Beatriz's second cousin with whom she had been raised—to act as the voyage's alguacil, the quartermaster in charge of drinking water, discipline, justice, and punishment, trusting loyalty over experience.

In mid-May, Cristóbal embraced Beatriz and held little Fernando dearly. Then forty, he understood as well as any man his mortality on the Ocean Sea. He recognized the weather and currents west of the Canaries were unknown and that there was no assurance easterly winds blew across the entirety of the Ocean Sea to Cipangu. He knew it was his conjecture and boasts alone that islands lay east of Cipangu. He promised Beatriz and little Fernando he would return and discussed with Beatriz what to do if he didn't.

Cristóbal reflected that the struggle to convince the sovereigns had been but intellectual, religious, political, and financial. He departed for Palos to convince experienced seamen to sail with him, a matter of life and death.

Isabel, Fernando, Abraham Seneor, and Isaac Abravanel
Expulsion of the Jews, 1492

With the Reconquista accomplished, Isabel and Fernando reflected together on Torquemada's admonishment that heresy wouldn't be eliminated in their kingdoms until they eliminated its root cause, the presence of the Jews. Over the past year, Torquemada had extended the Inquisition's reach to publicly prosecute both conversos and Jews for the alleged ritual crucifixion of a young Christian boy, securing confessions from multiple witnesses by rack and water torture regardless of the absence of a record of a child missing or the identity of his parents. Torquemada had achieved both the Jews' burning at the stake and resounding public outrage at the Jewish involvement in the alleged crime.

Yet each sovereign still believed as St. Augustine and Talavera that a Christian became such upon baptism and belief regardless of his father, mother, people, nation, or skin. Isabel had always asserted she was the Jews' protector and tolerated their separate existence. Fernando had always relied substantially on Jews and conversos to administer Aragón. Together, they had just relied significantly on Jews to finance the Reconquista—and, in particular, on two men, Abraham Seneor and Isaac Abravanel.

Abraham, Castile's head rabbi and leader of its aljamas, had known and supported Isabel for decades—since when she stood alone upon Brother Alfonso's death—and had served as the sovereigns' head tax collector and treasurer of the militia,* as well as Torquemada's tax collector in his hometown. Isaac came from a wealthy Castilian family that had fled to Portugal in response to the 1391 pogroms. After serving as a principal financial adviser to King Afonso V, Isaac had fled back to Castile in 1483 to escape punishment for allegedly conspiring with Castile, and then rebuilt his career supporting Isabel and Fernando, farming taxes and serving as treasurer for Cardinal Mendoza's family and, since 1491, acting as Isabel's personal financial representative. Isaac also had devoted years to writing philosophic commentaries on the Old Testament, which would become renowned. He believed he was a descendant of David and felt passionately that Jews who abandoned Judaism either lacked reason or had insincere motives and that conversos were insincere opportunists, traitors to their religion and people, and enemies of God. He judged the Inquisition gave conversos what they deserved as traitors and should have anticipated. Perhaps both men believed the Inquisition was not directed at their people but at conversos solely because they

---

*The Hermandad.

were Christian religious criminals. Both had amassed fortunes they believed would continue to buy their and their people's protection.

Regardless of her beliefs and these attachments, Isabel had grown weary of the continuing strife occasioned by the Jews' presence, whosoever's fault. After a decade of decisions dictating the fate of thousands of people, she now had the conviction to contravene her ancestors' approach and devastate an entire people. Fernando recognized that the Jews' expulsion might be used to strip their wealth at least as effectively as extorting payments from them to remain in Spain. They both may have foreseen their course of action years earlier and simply shied from it to not disrupt the Jews' financial contribution to the war effort or avoid the economic dislocation occasioned by the departure of Jewish merchants and professionals. But the triumph at Grenada confirmed to them their destiny as the Lord's servants—as well as their absolute authority and power—to take the action they would take.

When they decided, Isabel and Fernando did focus on Christ's teachings and their duty to prepare the world for his return. They chose a path that preserved according to the church and in their perception the voluntary choice of each individual regardless of his father or mother—a choice of conversion to Christianity or exodus.

On March 20 in Santa Fe, Torquemada issued an order of the Inquisition directing the bishop of Gerona to expel all Jews from his diocese in Catalonia by July 31. Closely following, on March 31 in the Alhambra, the sovereigns signed an Edict of Expulsion providing that all Jews had until July 31 to depart their realms under penalty of death and confiscation of all property. The Edict explained that communication between Jews and Christians continued to harm Christians regardless of segregation of the aljamas, the expulsion of the Jews from Andalusia, and twelve years of inquisition. Conversion was welcome, and Jews who converted would be exempt from the Inquisition for an extended period of grace. Jews who did not convert had to sell their homes, farms, and animals and could take their portable property, but not gold, silver, or other money. The church would undertake a special evangelical effort to convert those willing.

Fernando wrote principal noblemen that he and the queen had

been persuaded to adopt the Edict by the Inquisition and had done so preferring to save their souls above profit. He signed a similar edict applicable to Aragón alone explaining that he and the queen acted at the request and persuasion of Torquemada.

But the sovereigns refrained from publishing the Edict, and Fernando awaited Abravanel's and Seneor's demand for an audience. While some Jews may have anticipated it, and while Torquemada's abiding hatred was known, the two Jewish leaders were shocked the sovereigns had issued the Edict on their own authority without consultation. They sought the audience with Fernando, which he granted in the Alhambra, and Abraham brought his son-in-law who had succeeded as Castile's tax collector.

"Your Majesty, our people have proven their love and loyalty to you and the queen over and over again for decades," Abravanel began. "We have financed your greatest conquest and faithfully and devotedly administered your and your fathers' and grandfathers' affairs for decades, in fact centuries. Our people love Spain and Your Highness and the queen." He hardened his tone. "But we must love our God first. We have come to plead whether things might be done differently to avoid this draconian choice of renouncing our faith or leaving your kingdom, which also has been ours as your loyal subjects." Abravanel refrained from criticizing the choice as cruel, unlawful, unjust, and anti-Jewish, believing such unpersuasive to the king. Nor did he challenge that a voluntarily choice had been offered, as he perceived it had been.

"Your loyalty and devotion have always been deeply appreciated," the king responded. "They've also been handsomely rewarded—as your homes and estates attest. The queen and I urge that you and your families convert and remain as our loyal subjects. You will save your souls—although I understand you do not yet see that. You will retain your titles, offices, and privileges—and your wealth. You will also benefit the kingdom and all our people as many of your followers will convert and remain, as well."

"Your Majesty, we seek a solution that permits us to worship our God," Abravanel replied. "We are wealthy and prepared to make such payment as is necessary."

"We may discuss payments, but your conversion is important.

Your conversion and that of your families. That will serve best to guide your people at this juncture." Fernando stared intently into Abravanel's and Seneor's eyes, silently communicating a threat of personal consequences to their families, belying the notion that—as for Spain's Jewish leadership—their own choice was voluntary.

"Your Majesty, let us determine what payment we may offer, and then we will return to discuss it again."

The king indicated he would continue to delay the Edict's publication while they did so and dismissed them.

Abravanel and Seneor promptly appealed to the sovereigns' advisers and noblemen to intercede on the Jews' behalf, including Cardinal Mendoza, Ponce de León, and Luis de la Cerda, but the appeals were for naught. They determined to offer the largest payment of gold they could raise to achieve the Edict's rescission, perhaps 300,000 ducats. Fernando listened to their offer in a second audience but did not commit. A third audience arranged, Fernando rejected the offer, indicating that regardless of his views the queen had also issued the Edict.

As a last resort, Abravanel and Seneor obtained an audience with the queen.

"Your Majesty, expulsion of the Jews serves no purpose," Abravanel began, believing he could talk more forcefully with a woman. "You must understand we are indomitable and God's chosen people and can never be destroyed. You must realize that God punishes those who punish the Jews. If Your Majesty goes through with this edict, you risk God's wrath, as well."

Isabel contemptuously embraced the confrontation and responded forcefully. "The Jews became a relic of history when Christ was born. I'm not seeking to destroy you or your people, but I will bring my kingdom to serve God by your conversion or removal, and God will reward me for it."

Abravanel and the queen, two familiar persons of absolute faith, glared at each other, astounded at the other's inability to see truth. Abravanel also was astounded at the cruelty the queen's faith justified.

After a long silence, Isabel tired of the confrontation, which itself reinforced her conviction in her righteousness. "This is the king's decision, too. I can't compromise." She reflected that God's will had manifested itself in both her and Fernando's hearts, and she softened and sought to bring her two acquaintances to her God. "Isaac and Abraham, I entreat you to be baptized and offer you the highest honor and ceremony if you do. Christ's love and salvation awaits but your acceptance."

"I will never worship Christ." Abravanel grimaced, visibly wrought with scorn that anyone—even the queen—could even suggest that he would forsake his God and people for earthly benefit. Abraham demurred.

The Edict was broadly published at the end of April, and the Jews anguished. Centuries of heritage and wealth—homes and estates cherished, businesses built and passed through generations, farms and orchards plowed and nurtured, and revered synagogues and cemeteries—were to be lost forever. Rich and poor began to sell their properties, and prices plummeted. Homes were sold in return for an ass for transport to the coast. Vineyards were sold for cloth to bundle what could be carried. A substantial transfer of wealth from one people to another was brutally accomplished.

The initial panic in the aljamas soon was replaced with a messianic resolve. The rich helped the poor to arrange their affairs and, when their properties were sold, to make their exodus. Some believed the sea would part to permit their emigration. They knew robberies and extortion lay ahead wherever they landed, and adolescents twelve years and older were married so each girl had a husband for protection.

Upon its publication, Spain's old Christian population largely rejoiced and most European princes hailed the Edict as effecting divine punishment. Jewish leaders attempted to arrange destinations that would accept their people. After negotiation, João agreed to receive them only temporarily for an entry fee per head, and perhaps half of Castile and Aragón's Jewish population went first to Portugal. João permitted the very wealthiest to remain in Portugal permanently in return for substantial payments. England and France refused their admission. Some Christian principalities in Italy and Greece agreed to receive them permanently, the motive being an expectation that the emigrants would add to the wealth and knowledge of their new home, rather than a religious duty to love thy neighbor or enemy. Bayezid II, the emperor of the Ottoman Empire, openly welcomed the Jews, desiring to increase the number of taxpayers and economic considerations. Some Jews departed for the Islamic principalities of North Africa.

In June in Guadalupe, Cardinal Mendoza baptized Abraham Seneor and his son-in-law in the Monastery of Santa María de Guadalupe, with Fernando and Isabel attending as sponsors. They took the name Coronel and continued to serve the Crown with distinction. Thousands followed their example to convert, gratifying the sovereigns that the edict had accomplished its objective.

Isaac Abravanel never contemplated baptism for an instant. Fearing reprisal, his grandson was removed from Spain. Luis de Santángel repaid Isaac an outstanding loan to the Crown and Isaac made other arrangements to export some gold. On July 30, he and his family and followers sailed for the Italian peninsula and ultimately found permission to disembark in Naples.

As July 31 approached, Spain's roadways crowded with Jewish families, most trudging toward the sea or Portugal. The July 31 date was not rigidly enforced, and many ships sailed from Cádiz on August 2.

But the deadline for departure was not permitted to slip much. Torquemada's order of March 20 prohibited Christians from communicating with or assisting Jews in any way after August 9. Violators would be excommunicated or perhaps worse.

CRISTÓBAL
Recruiting Crews to Traverse the Sea of Darkness,
Palos, Moguer, Huelva, Summer 1492

On May 23, Cristóbal and Fray Pérez walked from La Rábida to the plaza outside the church of St. George overlooking the Río Tinto and delivered the sovereigns' decree requiring the town to provide two ships by June 2. A notary read the decree aloud to the town's mayors, councilmen, and a few citizens gathered, and the mayors consented to its terms. The sovereigns' decree requiring carpenters, merchants, and others to assist provisioning the ships was read aloud in Moguer later that day.

Palos requisitioned the two ships in Moguer. The first was owned by Juan Niño of Moguer and, as the town's central cathedral, named for the town's patron saint, Santa Clara. Sailors called it the *Niña*. The *Niña* was a three-masted caravel with lateen rigging, approximately seventy feet long on deck bow to stern and twenty-one feet at her deck beam (the widest width), able to load fifty-three tuns of wine (perhaps 250 gallons per tun) and with a draught of six feet. The second was also a three-masted caravel, slightly longer and larger, capable of bearing sixty tuns, and square-rigged except for the poop (stern) mast, which was lateen rigged. Cristóbal Quintero of Palos owned it, and sailors called it the *Pinta*. Cristóbal inspected the ships carefully and was satisfied.

Cristóbal had contacted his acquaintance from Puerto de Santa María, Juan de la Cosa, who owned the third ship, and it sailed to anchor in the Río Tinto. It was a three-masted nao built in Galicia—sailors called it the *Gallega*—and larger than the *Niña* and *Pinta*, able to transport one hundred tuns of wine. She stretched more than seventy-five feet on deck bow to stern and approximately twenty-six feet at the deck beam, had a draught of seven feet and, like the *Pinta*, was square-rigged except for the stern mast. Cristóbal appreciated she would transport more goods to trade than the caravels but would be less maneuverable in unknown waters. Unlike the *Niña* and *Pinta*, she had a sizable stern castle fit for his cabin and administration of the voyage and, above it, a small poop deck. He chose her as his flagship, where he would serve as captain general of the fleet and captain of the ship, and he invited Juan to serve as her master, directly in charge of the ship and crew at all times. Cristóbal renamed her the *Santa María*.

Juan de la Cosa had enlisted a portion of the crew for the *Santa María*, largely Galicians and Basques of Spain's northern coast, the ship's and his native home. Cristóbal and Fray Pérez started visiting the plazas of Palos, Moguer, and Huelva, seeking enlistment to achieve crews for the three ships combined of about ninety men. Cristóbal explained to everyone he met that he was authorized by the king and queen to sail the Ocean Sea to Cipangu and the Indies, where the houses were roofed with gold. Those who enlisted would achieve riches and glory.

By June 2, regardless of the sovereigns' decree and these entreaties, not a single resident of the three villages had enlisted. Scant few had even heard of Cristóbal Colón. When word spread, people learned that he was a Genoese boarding at La Rábida, without a business or even home of his own and with no money other than that which the sovereigns had awarded him. When he departed the plazas, those whom he had buttonholed murmured that there was no land to the west because the Portuguese had searched many times and failed. Some exclaimed that it would take two years to sail to the Indies, others that it would be impossible to return, and many warned those who sailed would never return. Most concluded Colón was a talker, boaster, and dreamer—nothing more.

Cristóbal grew more aggressive with his promises of gold, but to no avail. He reintroduced himself to Pedro de Vásquez, the aged mariner who had sailed for Diogo de Teive forty years earlier, and Pedro remained supportive and joined in the plazas to promote enlistment. But fathers advised sons and sons-in-law not to be deceived by the promises, warning that the Genoese was crazy and the voyage futile. Residents began to jest about Colón and scorn him to his face. Juan Cabezudo, who had rented a mule to Friar Pérez for his journey to Santa Fe, was ridiculed for having done so. Cristóbal Quintero, the owner of the *Pinta*, made no secret that he thought the voyage vain and doomed to fail. Alonso Pardo, the public scribe in Moguer who embargoed the *Niña* and *Pinta* for the voyage, recognized that many villagers held it to be death for Colón and all those who went.

Frays Marchena and Pérez advised Cristóbal to focus his efforts on convincing a leading mariner to sail so others would see validation and endorsement. They vouched that the villages' most reputed mariner was Martín Alonso Pinzón and promised an introduction when his ships returned from Rome, where he was delivering a shipment of sardines.

Martín Alonso Pinzón was a few years older than Cristóbal and one of the wealthiest men in Palos. He and his younger brothers and two sons and the husband of one of his three daughters were all accomplished mariners. Martín regularly sailed the Mediterranean and the European and African coasts of the Ocean Sea, including to the Canaries, and owned ships. He had been widowed and remarried and was esteemed by his neighbors for great skill, judgment, energy, and courage as a mariner and for having fought valiantly against the Portuguese. His younger brother Vicente Yáñez Pinzón, then about thirty, also had a growing reputation as a sea captain.

When he returned from Rome, Martín heard the news of the Genoese soliciting a voyage west into the unknown on behalf of the queen and was amused by the promises of gold booty. But Martín would not lightly dismiss a royally sponsored voyage and, when Fray Marchena inquired, Martín readily agreed to meet Colón in Pedro de Vásquez's home to hear the proposal.

Cristóbal arrived bearing a pouch containing the sovereigns' letter of introduction to the Grand Khan, the passport, and Bartolomé's map, and Pedro invited the two men to sit at his kitchen table. Cristóbal greeted Martín warmly, commending that he had heard much of the Pinzón reputation from Pedro and Fray Marchena.

"I understand you've just returned from Rome. Did you sail by the Barbary Coast to Sardinia and return by Catalonia?"

"Yes." Martín realized that Cristóbal understood the mariner's route for the voyage in summer. "The winds were favorable."

"Is the pope as frail as they say?"

"They say he's waning—but I understand they've said that for some years. Speculation abounded as to his successor. Do you have a Ligurian insight?"

Cristóbal smiled. "I'm just a merchant and an observant Catholic—I wouldn't know."

"I've heard you are more." Martín smiled in return. "They say you've convinced the queen to command us to provide two ships to sail into the unknown."

"Yes, I have. And I come today because I want to convince you to sail with me, to explain how it can be done, and the wealth attainable upon reaching the Indies."

"Good. I'm honored to serve my king and queen. I'm also interested in wealth." Martín raised his eyebrows. "I'm also interested in my life."

"For some years, I've sought a sovereign to sponsor a voyage west to the Indies. I have sailed to the Orient at Scio, to the northern seas at Thule, and to the equator at Guinea, as well as the Canaries, the Azores, and other islands—in fact, I lived on Porto Santo for a spell. I know the Ocean Sea as well as most men—save perhaps you and your family—and each of King João and King Fernando and Queen Isabel have considered my plans. I left João when it became clear he would pursue the circumvention of Guinea. Fernando and Isabel have agreed to sponsor three ships. I have the letter of introduction they gave me to deliver to the Grand Khan—the ruler of the Indies—and the passport I may present to persons I meet." Cristóbal laid the two documents on the table before Pinzón and Vásquez.

Martín picked them up and studied them. He had never held a document signed by the king and queen, no less met them. He handed the documents to Pedro and hid his surprise that a foreigner—apparently but a seafaring merchant—had dealt personally with his own king and queen.

"It's now almost certain that João will achieve Cathay by circumventing Guinea—it's only a matter of time," Cristóbal continued. "The first sovereign to reach Cathay will have the opportunity to seek a monopoly on the trade, and Fernando and Isabel want to be first by sailing west, beating João. Have you read Marco Polo or Sir John Mandeville?"

Pinzón and Vásquez shook their heads.

"The wealth of the Grand Khan's kingdoms is incredible. The houses are roofed with gold, and the cities are more splendid than you've ever seen or could imagine—the greatest in the world. One's named Quinsay, which is a hundred miles round with twelve thousand bridges. Another's Zaiton, the world's largest port, filled with thousands of vessels departing to all directions filled with pepper and other spices. The island of Cipangu lies off the coast and overflows with gold, gems, and pearls. The Ophir of King Solomon will be found somewhere. The king and queen will find riches if they reach these places first—and so will their mariners."

There was silence. Cristóbal asked, "Martín, may I ask where you have sailed?"

"To all parts where you have sailed, I suspect. I've been to Guinea and to the north, not as far as Thule, but to Flanders. I've sailed the Mediterranean, as well, not as far as Scio. I've sailed the Canaries many times. I've fought the Portuguese at sea."

"That's a lot of experience. I assume you believe as I that the

Ocean Sea is navigable at every zone and hour,* weather permitting?"

"Yes. The Ocean Sea is navigable that way." Pinzón reflected for a moment, realizing that Colón did have the experience to pose the central question debated by mariners in his lifetime, succinctly. "Why do you think the Indies are achievable sailing west? The distance is said to be over 10,000 miles. Isn't that impossible? Aren't you relying on islands to be found in route?"

Cristóbal removed Bartolomeo's map from the sack and laid it on the table. He watched Pinzón and Vásquez comprehend it.

"Where did you get this?" Pedro asked.

"My brother and I painted it."

Martín was startled by the map's quality and accuracy as to the European, African, and Mediterranean coasts and that Colón had the ability and knowledge to produce it. "Is this what you presented to the king and queen?"

"Yes. Let me explain. The distance from Cape St. Vincent to the Indies is sometimes estimated to be more than 8,000 miles. On the basis of the scriptures and geographers, I believe that estimate is substantially exaggerated. It also doesn't account for either the Canaries or Cipangu. The distance between the Canaries and Cipangu is much, much shorter—perhaps 2,700 miles or 750 leagues.† To respond to your question, I don't rely on finding Antillia in between the Canaries and Cipangu. But that's possible. I believe there also are islands east of Cipangu making the open sail even shorter."

Cristóbal let Martín and Pedro study the map for a moment and then drew his hand to the map to slowly trace the coast of the Indies with his forefinger, north to south. "The Grand Khan lives here in Cathay, inland a bit. Quinsay is near the coast in Mangi. To the south is Zaiton." He pointed to Cipangu. "Cipangu lies perhaps 1,500 miles east of the coast. I don't know the latitudes north or south to which it extends, but it does straddle 28 degrees north, the zone where the Canaries lie." Colón slowly moved his finger east to the Canaries. "I will sail from Gomera, after provisioning the ships for a year—far more than necessary."

The men were silent for some moments, studying the map closely.

---

*Latitude, categorized by "zones" of habitability, and longitude.
†In sum, 1 league equals 4 Roman miles, 1 Roman mile equals about 0.92 modern US statutory miles, and 1 league thereby equals about 3.68 modern US statutory miles.

"I would've thought you sailed from the Azores," Pedro remarked. "They lie much farther west than Gomera. That's where I sailed from. We found weed in the sea to the west, and it was only winter's approach that caused us to turn back. Land must have been close."

"The winds at Corvo and Flores blow east, sometimes strongly," Cristóbal responded. "After I left King João, he sent an expedition of Portuguese west from the Azores to find the mainland of the Indies, but they were blown back—as I would have predicted. In the Canaries, the wind and current flow southwest across the sea."

Martín again was startled. Colón had more than a map. He had a mariner's sailing plan. "You didn't tell João you'd sail from the Canaries?"

"They are Castilian, of course. If I had sailed for him, I probably would've departed from the Cape Verde islands, where the conditions are similar to the Canaries. But João's mathematicians never believed my estimation of the distance."

Martín reflected on his own sailing experience. "You're correct that the wind at the Canaries blows southwest often. I've seen it myself. But does it always? Are you sure about the current?"

"The wind never blows just one direction—at least anywhere that I've been. But the wind in the Canaries does regularly blow southwest in all seasons and the current, as well, and the current doesn't shift—as far as I've seen."

"How do you know these winds and currents will take you all the way to your Cipangu?"

Cristóbal stared into Martín's eyes. "I don't know that. That's the unknown here. That's why I need an experienced captain such as yourself."

"The unknown is also the distance, no matter how favorable the winds and current." There was silence as each man thought to himself.

"Cristóbal, are you a sailor or a merchant or a mapmaker?" Martín refrained from adding "dreamer."

"I'm a merchant expert in the sea and mapmaking. I need a captain more expert than I to sail this voyage under my command."

"Are you a geographer?"

"I've studied geography to the extent necessary to arrive at this map. I've studied Ptolemy, Aristotle, Seneca, Cardinal d'Ailly, and Pliny, among others."

Martín had heard of some of them, read none of them, and wasn't impressed the slightest. He reflected for a moment. "How many days do you think it'll take to cross? How many to return?"

"Aristotle, Seneca, and Cardinal d'Ailly said the sail is but a few days. I know that to be wrong—if that were the case, mariners would have crossed centuries ago. But, assuming the wind and current remain favorable, I suspect three to four weeks, which is easily achievable. To return, it may be necessary to tack substantially to the north to find more variable winds if possible. But that remains to be determined in light of the winds and seas found. I can't predict the route back."

Martín reflected that the last answer was honest. He sought to learn more about Colón, to engage in conversation to discern mettle and actual experience. The three men drank sherry together, Colón sparingly. They swapped stories of ports visited in the Ocean Sea and the Mediterranean, of storms, shipwrecks, and pirates, and of commerce in gold, spices, and slaves. Martín determined that Cristóbal's knowledge of the Ocean Sea was genuine, not boast. Cristóbal understood Martín's objective. As the afternoon waned, they began to respect each other. It was too soon for friendship. Martín ended the conversation by thanking Cristóbal for the explanation and indicating he would consider the voyage.

In the following days, the two men met a number of times, usually walking together in the streets of Palos or on the road to La Rábida. They met once in Martín's home, where Martín introduced Cristóbal to his brother Vicente, and the three men reviewed the map together and discussed the calculation of the distance involved.

Neither Pinzón brother was convinced by the map or Colón's calculations or Marchena's or Vásquez's endorsements or the views of Aristotle, Seneca, or any other authority. But the brothers had been on the Ocean Sea and, as Colón, seen carved driftwood and abandoned boats and heard stories of Antillia and other islands to the west. For them, it was obvious that unknown islands might be discovered in the Ocean Sea regardless of the distance to Colón's

Cipangu. The brothers were confident they had the know-how and wherewithal to decide when to turn back and safely return if neither islands nor Cipangu were found. The king and queen would pay them regardless.

One day, as Cristóbal and Martín strolled toward La Rábida, Cristóbal pressed for an answer whether Martín would captain the *Pinta* and Vicente the *Niña*.

"What will you do if you fail to achieve landfall as you expect?" Martín asked. "If I accept, what should I tell the sailors I recruit?"

Cristóbal reflected carefully, with a fleeting remembrance that Bartolomeu Dias's crew had forced his return. "Before we answer that together, what is your own commitment in this regard?"

"If Vicente and I sail, we will sail west so long as the men are healthy and the provisions are sufficient to return." He paused for emphasis. "And so long as they don't throw us overboard."

Cristóbal was satisfied. "We should tell recruits the approximate distance and an expectation of some weeks' duration. You may say that I expect landfall in about 750 leagues' sail, but make no firm promise."

"Courage and faith in this scheme will be tested well before you achieve 750 leagues. It's sailable, but you will have to deal with the men's terror when it boils."

The two men halted to face each other. Each man knew not a single seaman had enlisted since Pinzón's return from Rome and that his imprimatur was essential for recruitment. Each knew the crew recruited would look to Pinzón, not Colón, for when to turn back if landfall was not attained when promised.

"If I accept, what's in it for me?" Martín asked.

Cristóbal had long awaited this moment, despairing it would be necessary to offer a portion of his financial entitlement. "Martín, I've already negotiated the arrangements with the king and queen—as you know. There's wealth beyond comprehension to be found. We must find it, and when the sovereigns behold it and are astounded, their gratitude will lead them to compensate you grandly for your contribution. I will support you heartily."

Martín grimaced, staring into Colón's eyes, clearly expressing dissatisfaction, but silent.

Cristóbal stared back and, sensing Martín had already decided to sail, firmed the tenor of his voice. "There are no more participations to be awarded. You must trust me."

Martín paused, not to think, but for emphasis. He had already concluded that the adventure would profit him in stature, if not gold, regardless of a direct participation, and he extended his hand. "Colón, I will rely on that promise."

The men continued to La Rábida silently, overcome by the recognition that they would explore the unknown in union. When they arrived, Diego was sitting in the trees outside the monastery, waiting for his father. Martín met him for the first time and reflected that Colón did have a reason to live other than his voyage.

With that agreement, Martín and Vicente Pinzón visited the plazas of Palos, Moguer, and Huelva to recruit their friends and neighbors, promising to take them out of their misery and achieve gold and glory in the Indies. Juan Niño, owner of the *Niña*, agreed to serve as her master, his younger brother Pero Alonso agreed to serve as the pilot of the *Santa María*, and a younger Niño agreed to serve as a ship's boy on the *Niña*, as well. Cristóbal Quintero, owner of the *Pinta*, reluctantly agreed to accompany the ship as seaman and a relative agreed to serve as its boatswain. A third Pinzón brother agreed to serve as the *Pinta*'s master. There were other brothers, in-laws, and cousins. A surgeon was recruited for each ship. Notwithstanding the suspension of criminal proceedings against recruits, Cristóbal enlisted only four criminals—Bartolomé de Torres, who had murdered a town crier, and Juan de Moguer, Pedro Yzquierdo, and Alonso Clavijo, who had sprung Bartolomé from jail and been sentenced to death, as well. Almost all of the crews were Spanish, with a handful of Portuguese and Italians, including a Genoese seaman, Jácome el Rico, beholden to Francesco Pinelo and the other Italian financier.

Each ship had a few lombards (cannons) and falconets (swivel guns), but soldiers were neither provided by the Crown nor recruited. Cristóbal enlisted an interpreter to sail on the *Santa María*, Luis de Torres, a converso knowledgeable in Arabic, Caldaean, and Hebrew—the Arabic potentially useful with the Grand Khan. The Crown sent Pedro Gutiérrez as its observer, Rodrigo Sánchez de Segovia as comptroller of the fleet to monitor the trade, and Rodrigo de Escobedo as notary and clerk. In addition to selecting Diego de Arana as quartermaster, Cristóbal also brought three personal attendants: Pedro de Terreros, his domestic; Pedro de Salcedo, his young page; and Juan Portugués, a black servant sold by the Portuguese on the Canaries. When enlistment was complete, the *Santa María* had a crew of about forty, including the sovereigns' representatives and Cristóbal's attendants, the *Pinta* over twenty-five, and the *Niña* short of twenty-five.

In July, Cristóbal and the Pinzón brothers provisioned the ships. The *Santa María* stored most of the goods they expected to interest the Grand Khan, principally wool cloth. Trinkets, beads, and hawks bells were stowed to trade with less advanced peoples encountered en route, perhaps on Cipangu's outer islands. The ships' sails were painted with crosses. Cristóbal arranged banners for the expedition to be emblazoned with a common mark—a green cross bearing a crown at the end of each arm, one crown overlaying an *F* for Fernando and another overlaying a *Y* for Isabel.

As July waned, the roads to Cádiz and Puerto de Santa María teemed with the exodus of Jewish families forced to sail by the month's end. Eight thousand households departed from Cádiz alone. It was this exodus—the Jews' suffering, the ships they departed on, and the property they left behind—that captured the region's and the kingdom's attention, not the *Santa María*, the *Pinta*, and the *Niña* or the ninety men that would sail them.

No preparations were more important than the Virgin's blessing of the voyage. On August 2, Fray Marchena led La Rábida's annual celebration of its patron the Virgin of Miracles, Santa María de La Rábida. The crews of the three ships, their families, and their friends, neighbors, and other pilgrims worshipped the monastery's small statue of the Virgin and her baby Jesus, said to have been carved on behalf of St. Luke and given by the bishop of Jerusalem to the parish of Palos. The sailors confessed their sins, received the Eucharist, and prayed that the Virgin protect their ships. All realized this was no ordinary voyage. To their understanding, the Sea of Darkness had never been traversed by one who had lived to tell it.

That afternoon, the sailors and their families returned to the intimacy of their homes to part and, after dinner, gathered before St. George's church to board the ships.

Cristóbal ate supper with Diego at La Rábida. He reflected that he had good ships and crews and that, with a handful of exceptions, the crews would be loyal to Pinzón and Juan de la Cosa first. It would take time before the crews trusted him, and many never would relinquish their jealousy of the Genoese. While he held the royal authorization, not Pinzón, it would be treacherous to make any significant decision affecting the voyage's safety that Pinzón opposed. Cristóbal's wariness of the crews' loyalty to the Pinzóns rivaled his respect for the ferocity of the Sea of Darkness.

Santa María de la Rábida, with an altarpiece rendition of the three ships at her feet.

Bakako's Sentry Duty
Guanahaní (San Salvador?, Bahamas)

Twelve years old, Bakako typically assisted Father fishing unless ordered by the village cacique to do sentry duty on Guanahaní's southern shore, a chore that rotated among older boys every few days. Until recently, Bakako had much preferred fishing. While not yet a man, he now was an accomplished fisher, and Father trusted him with all aspects of the daily routine except he was not old or strong enough to handle the barrier reef or open ocean without an adult. He felt maturity and accomplishment when fishing and looked forward to the day he and his brother Yuni fished the barrier alone. Sentry duty was monotonous in comparison. Friendly traders canoed routinely between Guanahaní and neighboring islands and, less frequently, islands farther south. There had not been a Caribe raid in his lifetime.

But, in the past few weeks, a girl from another village had visited a number of times to flirt as he stood guard, and they had become friends. Bakako had invited her to visit again and, to his satisfaction this morning, the village cacique ordered him to serve. Mother gave him a pouch filled with fish wrapped in wet leaves and a gourd of water, and he retrieved his spear and shell trumpet. With a wave to Father and Mother, he set off southward more than three miles to spend the day at a knoll on Guanahaní's southernmost point, hiking first along the long beach astride his village and then on a beaten trail winding up and down a gentle bluff.

Bakako began his assignment as he strode, studying the ocean southward and sighting fishermen already at sea and a large canoe departing Guanahaní south, presumably to trade on Samoete (Crooked, Fortune, and Acklins Islands). He now well understood the safety provided by the neighboring islands to the southwest and had sheltered once with Father on Yuma (Long Island), when a sudden, northeasterly squall had driven them from Guanahaní when hunting shark beyond the barrier. His remembrance of the day and night he and Father had spent in the ocean, engulfed in storm at the precipice of death, still terrified him and—he understood—had made him a more prudent fisherman.

Bakako soon passed the last village on his route and walked alone, wondering as always why he bothered to bring the spear. He had never used it, and he had never seen an adult Guanahanían use one other than in a ceremony. People from other islands rarely attacked Guanahaníans. He had been taught of the danger of attack by Caribes from Cuba, Bohío,* or Carib itself. People said their appearance, ferocity, and brutality were atrocious—they had but one eye and an animal's snout, and they beheaded and drank the blood of their enemies. But neither Father nor Grandfather had ever seen one.

By midmorning, Bakako arrived at the watch post at the island's southern tip and spied a large cloud bank on the eastern horizon, canoes approaching from the southeast—probably from Samana (Samana Cay), and fishermen all about. Canoes never approached from the east, as there were no islands there, only ocean, and that was the direction of hurricanes. Bakako sensed the tremendous expanses of the heavens and the ocean about him, the enormity of the distance to the horizon in all directions, and the glow of the sun that enveloped Guanahaní. He reflected on his solitude and the peacefulness and warmth about him. If Kamana came, it would be in the afternoon. The canoes in the ocean before him were Lucayan, and he lay down in grass under a grove of trees to shade his naked body from the sun and fell asleep.

As the sun reached its highest point, a flock of green and red parrots flew overhead and alighted in the trees, and their caws awoke him. The great cloudbank had advanced toward Guanahaní, and a dark thunderhead rose at its core to a colossal height, presaging a storm but not a hurricane. Bakako marveled at Guabancex's power. He mused that his spear, and the spears of an army of Lucayans, and even the spears of an invasion of Caribes, were utterly inconsequential in comparison to Guabancex's power. The devastation she could unleash vastly exceeded the harm men could do to other men.

Bakako realized the fishermen and traders at sea soon would distrust the weather and make for shore, and he ate lunch, wondering if Kamana would visit in advance of a storm. She lived in a small village on the eastern coast and was a farmer's child, slightly younger than him. Her smile and slender body were pleasing, and she would

*A Lucayan reference to Haiti (i.e., the Dominican Republic and Haiti).

become a beautiful woman. She was beautiful already. She was humorous and clever in thought and conversation. Bakako knew she wanted to see him because she came. He wondered whether he had been direct enough that he wanted her to come, too. He gazed at the path leading from the knoll toward her village and it was empty. He decided to slumber again, not because he was tired, but because he preferred that to the empty path.

Shortly, he caught the sound of children running toward the knoll, and he stood and grasped his spear, as if he had been alert on duty. The children burst into view—Kamana's two younger brothers—and Kamana soon followed, bearing a little sister on her hip, smiling and waving, and accompanied by her cousin, who was helping with the child care. Bakako greeted the boys as they swarmed onto the knoll and then Kamana and the cousin.

"I thought you'd come," Bakako said.

"We come almost every day because I don't know when you'll be here," Kamana replied. "We don't talk with the other sentries. We just go swimming."

"We shouldn't swim today. There's a storm coming and the current is ripping, even within the barrier."

"My father said we couldn't swim, but I can take them to the beach."

"Let's go. It'll be out of the wind."

Bakako led his visitors off the knoll to a small beach close by on the western shore. Kamana warned her brothers to go no further than ankle deep into the sea and placed the little girl on the sand, handing her a shell to dig with.

"We brought you some cazabi we baked with our mothers yesterday," Kamana said, unwrapping a cloth and offering Bakako a piece. "Our village is preparing for our cousin's wedding tomorrow, and the mothers and aunts are bickering over the preparations." The two girls laughed.

"Are you going to be in the ceremony?"

"Yes," Kamana answered. "We've been included in an areíto as birds." Both girls laughed again. "We get to coo every few verses. Occasionally, we get to say words like people, as well."

Bakako laughed. "What's it about?"

"It's just the normal wedding areíto. The bride and groom get married and will have babies on Guanahaní like the birds do. We've been practicing it a lot over the last few days."

"Let me see your part."

The girls giggled. But, after hesitation, Kamana looked to her cousin and nodded. "I will if you will."

After some whispering, the girls both slowly rose.

"We'll do the last verses, where we get to be human beings," Kamana said whimsically. Bakako thought nothing of it at the moment, but he would remember the innocence of Kamana's face when she said these words for the rest of his life.

The girls began to sing and dance tentatively, but they quickly gained confidence and glanced to see whether their nakedness charmed Bakako. They sang of Yúcahu's protection and nourishment of Guanahaní and how he and Attabeira would provide for the marriage's fertility.

Bakako watched Kamana dance and felt a compulsion to have her he had never experienced. She was more than fun and clever. She was sexual and enticing. Her spirit brimmed with lust.

Bakako clapped when the girls finished. They sat down again, Kamana very close to him. After a few moments, he shifted his position so their shoulders touched, and she did not move away. They spoke of their mothers and fathers and growing up, who they were, who they both knew, who won and lost at batey, and so on. The wind kept rising and, after some time, Kamana called the boys in from the water's edge, so all sat huddled in a circle. She asked, "When were you last at a ceremony?"

Bakako gazed at her and guessed she was asking because she already knew. When a fisherman didn't return from the sea, there was a ceremony, a funeral of sorts, although there was no body.

Kamana saw his hesitation and did know, and touched his arm. "You don't need to talk about it."

"A cousin, last year."

"I heard about it. I've also heard you are an expert fisherman. You should be careful."

At that moment, muffled in the wind but clearly present, the children heard the low rumble of distant thunder, and Bakako realized the thunderhead was now but a few miles offshore. "So should you. You better leave before the storm hits. It'll be hard to walk in the rain with all the children. I should be on duty again in a few days, and we can talk again then." Bakako helped herd the boys from the beach to the knoll, where he said good-bye to all of them.

For a brief moment, Bakako and Kamana looked into each other's eyes and stopped breathing, acknowledging their yet-unconsummated bond. With a wave, and with her sister on her hip, she turned into the wind to return with the children to her village.

Bakako had much farther to go and watched Kamana until she disappeared beyond the ridges to the east. He knew Father and Mother would seek to arrange his marriage to the child of a prosperous family, and perhaps he should want that. Kamana's father and mother undoubtedly would seek the same for her. But they were both children of ordinary people and, if their parents failed at other marriages, maybe their parents would arrange one between them. Bakako reflected he would be very happy with that and that someday he would be a prosperous Guanahanían fisherman.

There was an enormous thunderclap, and Bakako gazed east to the vast ocean. Heavy rain fell and soon would engulf him. The sea boiled like a pepper pot, with waves and spray rolling to crash offshore on the barrier and penetrate within. Cousin, and fishermen from the beginning of time, had perished in such fury. He retrieved his spear, shell, gourd, and pouch and started home.

Bakako realized that Guabancex was present about him, watching and, perhaps, warning. The ocean to the east was for spirits, not men.

VII
CROSSING THE SEA OF DARKNESS

PALOS TO SAN SEBASTIÁN, GOMERA, CANARY ISLANDS,
August 2—September 9, 1492

After supper, Cristóbal and Diego retired to their cell at La Rábida and lay together on a cot in dim candlelight, holding each other dearly. Cristóbal had arranged for a friar and muleteer to take Diego to Beatriz in Córdoba the next day. He brooded he was leaving his son motherless in a foreign land. Diego was old enough to understand his father might never return, and their eyes misted. When the boy slumbered, Cristóbal kissed him good-bye and quietly left to meet Fray Pérez to walk by the stars to Palos, where the friar administered a final communion in St. George's church, and Cristóbal joined his officers and crews aboard the ships.

Before dawn on August 3, the anchors were pulled as the tide began to ebb and the ships floated down the Río Tinto toward the ocean. After sunrise, they passed La Rábida and the murmur of friars chanting prayer stole across the water to envelope them, and the crews honored the Santa María de La Rábida again. Cristóbal waved to Diego and Fray Marchena, who had descended the embankment to say their last good-bye. The ships entered the final tidal channel alongside a cargo boat bearing Jews to exile. By 8:00 a.m., they crossed the sandbar to enter the Ocean Sea and bore southwest in strong breezes for the Canary Islands.

Cristóbal exulted to be at sea, the home he had lost for over seven years, liberated from the ignominy and impotency of pandering to royal officials and rejuvenated to be in command of what he knew—ships and sailors. His fleet was well provisioned with the necessary staples: hardtack; salted meat and fish; cheeses; rice; chickpeas, lentils, and beans; honey and molasses; raisins and other dried fruit; garlic, oil, and vinegar; almonds and other nuts; and water and wine. He discerned Martín's *Pinta* was the fastest sailor, Vicente's *Niña* the most nimble and seaworthy, and his *Santa María* the slowest. He was pleased by the competence of the *Santa María*'s crew as they worked the ship.

As captain general of the fleet, Cristóbal quickly established working relationships over the sovereigns' representatives and the *Santa María*'s officers. Pedro Gutiérrez, the sovereigns' observer, had served as a butler preparing the king's dais and dining table and was a competent and affable gentleman. Pedro let it be known that he played cards with the king and, whether or not that was true, Cristóbal recognized that Pedro served as Fernando's eyes. Rodrigo Sánchez was the Crown's comptroller responsible for accounting the gold and goods obtained on the voyage and assuring the sovereigns received them. Rodrigo was from Segovia, where many Crown functionaries resided, and Cristóbal learned that Rodrigo had been dispatched to Ronda for a number of years after its capture to assist in its governance and integration into the realm. Rodrigo de Escobedo also hailed from Segovia, where he had worked as one of the queen's secretaries for a few years. This Rodrigo—Isabel's eyes—was responsible for drafting correspondence to the Grand Khan or other princes and administering the formal ceremonies whereby the Castilian crown took possession of lands discovered. While the crews might perceive these men as important at the sovereigns' court, Cristóbal knew otherwise.

Juan de la Cosa, the ship's owner, also served as its master, and Cristóbal had been impressed by his skill and enthusiasm for the voyage when in the duke's employ at Puerto de Santa María. Pero Alonso Niño, a native of Moguer in his midtwenties, served as the pilot and second-ranking officer, and Cristóbal quickly appreciated that he was a veteran sailor with expertise and judgment. Juan and

Pero Alonso would rotate as the officer of the watch every four hours, responsible for directing the sailors and ship's boys in their daily tasks. Chachu, a Basque, was the boatswain, the lead seaman responsible for the ship's daily maintenance. Cristóbal's orders would be communicated to the *Pinta* and *Niña* by shouts, hand signals, flags, signal lanterns at night, and, infrequently, when the sea was calm, the Pinzóns' visitation aboard the *Santa María*.

Privacy was neither expected nor possible aboard ship, and Cristóbal also quickly became acquainted with every sailor and ship's boy. The ship's boys cooked one hot meal a day for everybody before noon, using a firebox middeck, and everyone served himself in a wooden bowl, eating with his hands. A table sometimes was set with a slab of meat or fish from which everyone piked a portion using his own dagger. Breakfast and dinner were served cold, each sailor snatching a biscuit and cheese or honey and some raisins or nuts. Cristóbal's steward and page prepared and served his meals. Each man enjoyed a rationed mug of wine a day. All peed over the rail, and, to poop, one sat on a board suspended overboard for all to see, using a common rope to wipe—which then dangled to wash in the sea.

As the ships sailed southwest, Cristóbal retired to his cabin and commenced writing a log on paper sheets to report on the voyage addressed in the name of Christ directly to the king and queen. He had suffered and surmounted years of rejection and scorn, and, with confidence in his destiny, he composed a prologue defining the voyage's purpose and sequence in history. He proclaimed that, after ending the Grenadan war, subjugating the infidel, and expelling the Jews, the sovereigns—as enemies of Mohammedans, idolatries, and heresies—had commanded that he go to India to deliver the sovereigns' embassy to the Grand Khan and other princes and investigate their disposition and conversion to Christianity, traveling not east overland but by sea to the west, where it was uncertain anyone had ever gone. He promised to record the entire voyage punctually, including everything he saw and experienced, and prepare a nautical chart and book locating the lands and seas discovered by latitude and longitude and their winds. He reminded the sovereigns of the titles and concessions they had conferred upon his discovery.

Cristóbal's voyage soon lost its grandeur. Three days from Palos, the *Pinta*'s rudder jumped its gudgeons in heavy seas, and the ship began to leak heavily. Martín fixed it, but it dislodged again the next day. The ships then were becalmed and further delayed. When they finally approached the Canaries, Cristóbal sailed the *Santa María* and *Niña* to Gomera, where he sought in vain to trade the *Pinta* for a better vessel, and Martín took the *Pinta* to Gran Canaria, where he also failed to do the same. Cristóbal had anticipated the assistance of his amour Beatriz de Peraza de Bobadilla, then Gomera's governess, but she was off the island. While Cristóbal projected cheer and optimism to maintain the crews' morale, they grew restive and perceived the sprung rudder, the becalmed seas, and the fruitless delays as bad omens, signs that the Lord disfavored the voyage.

On August 24, an inauspicious three weeks after departing Palos, Cristóbal sailed from Gomera to reunite with the *Pinta* on Gran Canaria, coursing to the south of the neighboring Tenerife—which remained under control of its native population—and leaving Pedro Gutiérrez and some sailors on Gomera to secure supplies for restocking the ships. That night, Tenerife's tremendous volcano (Teide) erupted fire and smoke, signaling to the crews of the *Santa María* and *Niña* that the Lord outright condemned the voyage. When they arrived Gran Canaria, neither the *Pinta*'s trade nor fix had been arranged, and the crews of all three ships murmured that the ominous portents were relentless.

Cristóbal ignored the murmur, started the *Pinta*'s repair, and refit the *Niña* with square rigging to run more securely with the easterly wind he expected. While it cost another week, the *Pinta* finally was fit and the ships departed back to Gomera, and the food, drink, and other provisions arranged by Gutiérrez were loaded. Additional wood was stowed for cooking, repairs, and communicating by firelight and smoke signal, and a few goats and pigs were corralled on the foredecks for fresh meals.

Beatriz had returned to San Sebastián, Gomera's tiny port, and hosted Cristóbal at a banquet in her stone tower, and they renewed their acquaintance. He remained eager for her affections and island. But, as to the island, she had sighted Alonso de Lugo as her next marriage, although Alonso was then off preparing the invasion of Palmas.*

At long last, as dawn broke on September 6, Cristóbal and his crews took confession at the Church of the Assumption in San Sebastián. In spite of the omens, the crews continued to trust their captains. None had deserted. Cristóbal bade Beatriz farewell and boarded the ships with his men.

Unfortunately, the wind was feeble and they floated aimlessly outside the harbor between Gomera and Tenerife. The volcano continued to erupt and the crews grew anxious again, searching for an answer as to why the Lord repeated this sign. Their angst grew as the calm and the eruption continued through the next day. But, at 3:00 a.m. on September 8, the northeast wind on which Cristóbal had designed his voyage arrived. Slowly, over a month after departing Palos, the three ships began to proceed west, sailing to the north of Hierro.

Hierro was the last known island in the Sea of Darkness and its southern tip at 28 degrees north delineated the southern boundary of Castile's possessions agreed with Portugal in the Treaty of Alcáçovas in 1479. The king and queen had advised Cristóbal that the voyage best not deviate south of this parallel in light of the treaty's uncertain application to points west. The crews watched Hierro and the fire atop Tenerife fall from the horizon on the afternoon of September 9.

The queen, at Cristóbal's suggestion, had offered a modest life pension to the sailor who first sighted land—10,000 maravedis per year, equivalent to a sailor's typical annual earnings—and every sailor was eager to win it. But the crews sang "Salve Regina" with unusual conviction that evening, and a pall befell them as many anguished whether they should have listened to their fathers, mothers, wives, and friends.

Cristóbal understood his crews expected—as his own promise— that land would be achieved by 750 leagues sail. He feared the actions they might take if that promise were not met and resolved to under-report to them the distance he estimated the ships sailed each day. They would be less frightened if the voyage's duration was prolonged and comforted that return to Hispania was shorter. He would be

---
*Northwest of Gomera.

able to continue further west if he actually needed to exceed 750 leagues to reach Cipangu. Cristóbal understood that each ship's pilot would make his own estimate of distance traveled, but Cristóbal's reported estimate would serve as the estimate by which his promise was judged and he would answer to no other.

As night descended, sailors placed glowing embers and pine resin in iron lanterns hung at the stern so the ships could sight themselves better at night and remain together. Those on duty worked in moonlight, those off duty lay to sleep, and ship's boys turned the ampolletas every half hour and called a prayer. The ships ran swiftly and competently due west in strong wind.

Cristóbal remained on the stern deck late into the night, monitoring the course. The *Niña* and *Pinta* ran before him in the sea, their lanterns' fires glowing in the wind and appearing and vanishing with the rise and fall of the ocean swell. The wind smacked his back and whistled about him, surging the *Santa María* forward, with the bow plowing waves overtaken with the sound of a deep, melodic swish. The vast starry heavens about him descended in the far distance to meet at the horizon with the Sea of Darkness, which stretched landless, immense, and supreme in every direction. He prayed to the Virgin to watch over Diego, Fernando, and Beatriz in Córdoba and to carry his ships safely through the night.

Cristóbal understood that he then stood alone in the presence of the Lord. He trembled to recognize that he had led his entire life for this moment. He thanked the Lord for this achievement and, envisioning himself as the Lord's servant and instrument, prayed that the voyage succeed in finding islands and mainlands and that his noble destiny be fulfilled.

SEA OF DARKNESS,
September 10—October 9, 1492

The fleet sped west in strong winds. By Cristóbal's private estimation, they achieved 60 leagues on September 10, 40 on September 11, and 33 on September 12, which he reported to the crews as 48, 32, and less than 30.

Soon, the sailors grew silent and downcast, afraid that the conditions were unknown and the portents bad. On September 13,

Pero Alonso and the pilots on the *Pinta* and *Niña* were surprised to discover at midnight that their compass needles no longer aligned with the polestar, but deviated to its west, and that at dawn the needles deviated to its east. Cristóbal admitted his own bewilderment. After nightfall on the fifteenth, the crews witnessed a marvelous flame of fire fall from the heavens to the sea, apparently but four or five leagues distant. The next day, the ships encountered extensive banks of green and yellow weed floating in the sea,* and all grew alarmed there were hidden shoals. On the seventeenth, the weed grew thick as stargrass, tangled with long stalks, shoots, and fruit. Some dreaded they were sailing above drowned continents or approaching another world. The compass deviations from the polestar grew worse at night only to vanish by dawn. Some murmured that the vain Genoese had lured them into unknown danger.

Cristóbal tried to cheer his crews, expounding that the weed was well known to the Portuguese and others—Pedro de Vásquez of their own Palos had seen it before. Martín and Vicente added their reassurances. Cristóbal professed the weed was a good omen, allowing that it probably had drifted from islands close to the west or south from the Azores. He also reflected on the compass deviations and comforted the pilots that they were caused by the polestar itself, not the needles—the polestar wasn't stationary above the northern pole, but orbited in a small circle above and around it. Cristóbal observed that the breezes were temperate and pleasant—the conditions as agreeable as springtime in Andalusia—and advised the crews to temper their concerns.

The crews were fortified by these observations, the murmurs quieted, and alarm dissipated to wonder and curiosity. To everyone's surprise, they discovered tiny crabs living in the weed. Cristóbal asked that one be retrieved, and it was placed on a table for observation. As it crawled about, he warranted that such creatures didn't live far from land—indicating land was certainly near—and ordered that it be preserved for the queen, who would be interested. He soon observed that the breezes were sweeter and purer the farther west they sailed and that the sea was as calm as the Guadalquivir. Some crewmen deduced that the sea had become less salty by a half. The *Pinta*'s crew saw a great flock of birds

---

*The Sargasso Sea.

flying west, and Martín shouted to Cristóbal that land was close.

On September 19, there was a windless, drizzling rain, encouraging all that a landmass certainly was near. Sailors peered intently south, west, and north to sight Antillia or the St. Brendan islands, but did not sight them. The *Santa María*'s crew dropped a sounding lead to ascertain the depth, but two hundred fathoms of line did not touch bottom. Cristóbal pronounced there were islands beyond the northern and southern horizons, but that it best to continue due west to achieve Cipangu, which remained far off.

The next day—the eleventh since Hierro disappeared—some cormorants and other birds flew by, reinforcing many sailors' belief land was near. Before dusk, Cristóbal sat on a stool at the door of his cabin, alone with his personal attendants, who reclined informally and comfortably on the deck at his feet. He sought to gauge their judgments on the morale of the *Santa María*'s crew, turning first to Pedro de Terreros, his steward.

"How's the crew holding up? What are they saying?"

"They're disappointed you didn't change course toward the islands that seem nearby." Pedro esteemed his master, perceiving a remarkable bent to understand the physical world and every situation confronting him and an openness to listen to all persons to achieve that understanding. "They've heard the Portuguese follow the birds to discover land and thought you should've done the same. We've been out of sight of land far longer than usual and they're scared." Pedro glanced away. "They think your decision to continue west was foolhardy."

"I understand," replied Cristóbal. "I expected that. But it would've been a mistake to search for islands and then not find them—that would've further dismayed them and diminished our stores in vain. It's more prudent to pursue the course I'm certain of, west to Cipangu." He turned to his page, Pedro de Salcedo. "What've you overheard?"

Pedro, but fifteen, looked to Cristóbal like a father. "The Basques and Galicians whisper that you have deceived them and are risking their lives just to become a gentleman."

"Is that all? Do they plan to do something?" Cristóbal reflected. "Does this involve Juan de la Cosa?"

"No. It's only sailors' grumbling. I've heard no plan to do anything. Juan wasn't involved."

Cristóbal turned to his servant Juan Portugués. "Any thoughts?"

Juan had served masters before and found Cristóbal's interest in his thoughts unusual and gratifying. He replied in broken Castilian, acquired by necessity, not choice. "They scared, strange things see, scared head to toe. Far land. Men no meant here. Don't know going." Juan gazed at Cristóbal's feet. "Don't share gold like you. Special voyage you, no special them, no want die for."

"I understand."

Juan studied his master and reflected that Cristóbal was prepared to die to achieve his Cipangu.

On September 21, the weed grew even thicker, the breeze light and variable, and the sea calm. This day, the weed inspired the crews' fright—that its thickness would impede their progress, their ships would founder on unseen rocks, and they would perish weeks from land. The voyage's favorable easterly wind now became a curse—it rarely blew toward Hispania and would prevent their return home, prisoning them to perish in the weird weed-bound sea. Some sailors expressed their alarm directly to Cristóbal, without concealing their simmering distrust of him. Cristóbal entreated them to be patient, to consider that they had accomplished the greater part of the voyage already, and to reaffirm their faith in the Lord that they would succeed.

Unexpectedly, the wind reversed itself and during the next two days gusted strongly from the southwest or northwest, sometimes pushing high seas, surprising Cristóbal but solacing the crews' angst. Many were overjoyed and their mutterings and complaints ceased. Cristóbal reflected that the Lord had assisted him with the contrary wind just as he had assisted Moses by sending signals to the Jews that Moses would deliver them from Egypt.

September 24 brought more birds. This day, the birds inspired dread, as countless birds had been sighted without land appearing. The *Santa María*'s crew cursed that they were suicidal, madly risking their lives to follow an insane foreigner who was set on dying on a vainglorious scheme that all learned men knew ridiculous. Sailors huddled in small groups, lamenting whether the time for talk was over and if the best course was to heave the Genoese overboard at night, excusing that he had slipped while sighting the polestar. They reasoned no one would demand an accounting or bother to investigate since he was a foreigner.

Cristóbal's steward, page, and servant kept him informed. He continued to implore the crew to remain patient. But he now also warned that the sovereigns would treat them harshly if they abandoned the voyage at this stage and that there would be punishments for those who hindered it.

The next day, Martín brought the *Pinta* close abreast the *Santa María* and, facing each on the ships' stern decks, Cristóbal and he discussed Cristóbal's map, agreeing they had come far enough to be among the islands that lay east of Cipangu. The ships drew apart at sunset, with the *Pinta* in the lead. Soon, Martín shouted that he had sighted land to the southwest. Sailors on the *Pinta* stampeded to the port rail to peer southwest and began to cheer wildly and sing "Gloria in Excelsis Deo," and the crews of the *Niña* and the *Santa María* heartily joined them. Overwhelmed by triumph and relief, Cristóbal fell to his knees to praise the Lord. As night descended, the ships veered southwest, and sailors proudly reflected on the wisdom of enlisting on the voyage, eagerly anticipating the riches the next days would bring.

But, as the sun rose the next morning, the horizon was but sea in every direction, and all woefully recognized the sighting had been but squall clouds or imagination. Cristóbal quietly directed the pilots to revert to the western course and, recognizing the crews' profound dejection, proclaimed confidently they would achieve the Indies. He reminded that they had not yet sailed 750 leagues from Hierro and that he had not expected landfall this early. He announced that thereafter a false sighting would disqualify the proclaimer from later winning the queen's pension.

On October 1, Pero Alonso estimated they had sailed 578 leagues from Hierro, the *Pinta*'s pilot estimated 634, and the *Niña*'s pilot 640. Cristóbal's private estimate was 707 leagues, but he publicly embraced Pero Alonso's. By October 2, Cristóbal believed they had achieved the longitude of Cipangu, and, the next day, Martín advised searching for it rather than continuing west. Both grew irritated, Cristóbal perceiving an inappropriate insistence in the tone of Martín's shout, and Martín a disdain inherent in Cristóbal's refusal to do so.

When he retired that night, Cristóbal's private estimate of the distance traveled exceeded 750 leagues and, despite his self-assured demeanor, he feared they had missed Cipangu. Incredibly, they had now sailed for three weeks without sight of land, and he pleaded emphatically to the Lord to reveal it. But he continued to reject the pleas to tack north or south to follow the birds, reasoning it would be more certain to proceed to the Indian shore, which eventually had to be reached. The crews were furious.

At dawn on October 6, the crews woke with the knowledge they would surpass 750 leagues from Hierro that day—based on the Genoese's own proclaimed estimates. Cristóbal ignored this milestone and exhorted the sailors to attend to their duties. That evening, landfall having failed, Martín recommended they veer southwest, but Cristóbal declined to do so. Martín simmered, and there were whispers of mutiny among the crews.

At dawn the next day—almost a month from Hierro—the *Niña* discharged its lombard and raised its flag, indicating landfall at last had been achieved. The crews peered west to clouds on the horizon, pining to discern Cipangu, only to recognize forlornly as the day progressed that this sighting, again, was false. Cristóbal sensed the crews simply would not tolerate the western course, or his disregard of Martín's advice, any longer. Large flocks of birds were sighted flying southwest, and, with reluctance, he consented for two days to follow Martín's recommendation that the ships sail in that direction. Herons, ducks, and other land birds soon filled the sky and the crews rejoiced. Martín felt vindicated.

On October 9, with the wind and sea calm, Cristóbal requested that Martín and Vicente join him on the *Santa María* to discuss their alternatives. While the crews were now content with the birds flying about, he knew the slightest ill portent could sway them to fury. He brought Martín and Vicente to his tiny cabin, where they spoke alone, save for Cristóbal's steward, page, and servant, who sat outside to serve their needs and guard against eavesdroppers.

"It's no longer easy to calm my crew," Cristóbal began. "I believe we are among islands and perhaps close to the mainland right now— landfall could appear on the horizon as we speak. But it's only a matter of time before my men demand we turn about." Cristóbal paused to judge the Pinzóns' reactions. "We must go on, at least some days, until we achieve the Indies as promised the king and queen."

Vicente responded quickly. "We must go on. Our water and stores are sufficient to go forward and return to Hispania if necessary. I'm able to control my men."

Cristóbal looked to Martín. Both remembered their conversations in Palos. Both recognized that Martín could end the voyage simply by telling the crews that he felt its abandonment necessary for their survival.

Martín considered the riches and glory within their grasp and was steadfast. "We can't turn around now. We remain well provisioned and the weather has been optimal—far more favorable than any voyage I can remember. At this point, there's not sufficient reason to forsake the sovereigns' mission. But we must find land quickly! My word won't calm the men's terror much longer, and then they'll conclude they've fulfilled their duty regardless of what I say. No man has ever lived to tell of sailing this far from land, or even remotely as far." He gazed at Vicente. "I've known our crews' fathers, mothers, wives, and children all my life, and this can't be their final voyage."

Martín grew stern and condescending, betraying contempt for Cristóbal's relative inexperience at sea. "Let's speak frankly—you don't know the distance to the Indies. This map has always been but a mariner's educated guess. It is critical that we now sail simply in that direction where the signs of land are most convincing—be it north, south, east, or west. Today, as we speak, birds appear to be flying southwest to roost, and that's our best sign of land at this moment."

Cristóbal looked to the deck, withholding a response to this lecture on matters he felt he fully understood, repressing the urge to remind Martín that it was Cristóbal's knowledge alone that had bought them to this precipice of triumph. "We'll continue southwest as you said. What's important is what we communicate about this meeting. I suggest we tell the crews that we have agreed to sail a few more days to investigate the signs of imminent landfall."

"I agree." Martín also stepped back from confrontation, repressing an enmity for Colón that surged within. "And, if we encounter dissent, we should warn that it constitutes mutiny."

Martín and Vicente returned to their ships to advise their crews that the voyage continued for some days. Cristóbal remembered Bartolomeu Dias's experience at the tip of Guinea and reflected that, as it always had been, the voyage was in the Lord's hand.

LANDFALL,
October 10–12, 1492

Before dawn on October 10, stronger winds arose and forcefully propelled the ships southwest and, as the day progressed, the seas grew rough. Birds flocked about. Cristóbal plead to his Lord for land, anticipating the northeasterly wind and heavy seas would renew the crew's panic that return to Hispania was hopeless.

Cristóbal's attendants shared that foreboding. His steward Pedro scrutinized the *Santa María*'s officers closely for whispers or unnecessary conversations with crewmen. The page Pedro and servant Juan hung close to Cristóbal's quarters, reluctant to wander among the crew, grimly reconciled that as Cristóbal's men they would share in his fate if the crew took matters into their own hands. Defending their master seemed their only defense.

The Crown representatives considered their responsibilities. Pedro Gutiérrez reflected that his duty was to stand with the Genoese unless the voyage turned hopeless, regardless of the personal consequences. But he perceived it unlikely he could be found delinquent of that duty if the Genoese failed to survive to attest to that delinquency. Rodrigo Sánchez and Rodrigo de Escobedo felt the same and resolved to retreat as mere observers if an altercation occurred.

Diego de Arana, cousin to Cristóbal's mistress, resolved to defend Cristóbal to whatever end befell him, as Cristóbal's knighthood was Diego's path to fortune. Pero Alonso was torn. He had grown to admire the Genoese, but he would not be thrown overboard simply for the sake of loyalty. Juan de la Cosa felt all eyes upon him. Cristóbal had relied on him to recruit much of the *Santa María*'s crew and they in turn trusted him to safeguard their lives. He resolved that he would not instigate an altercation, but if it came he could not oppose it.

At midday, the entire crew was present on deck as the watches rotated. Sailors studied the landless horizons and witnessed the imposing, whitecapped swells marching west. They cursed the distance they had come from Hierro, despaired that the stores remaining were insufficient to return, anguished that return would be impossible anyway, and swore that they had been duped to enlist. Together, a group of sailors approached the stern deck, where Cristóbal stood with his attendants and the Crown representatives. He had prepared to engage them.

"Those retiring from duty should get some rest, for soon we shall achieve landfall. I have discussed the route with the captains of the *Pinta* and *Niña,* and we have decided the best course is to follow the birds southwest. You can see land birds in the sky, and you undoubtedly heard them all last night."

A sailor spoke. "You have misled us. We have gone far beyond 750 leagues to find nothing."

A second continued. "Our provisions have reached the point where we must stop and return home if we can. We demand we go no further."

"I've determined, together with Captain Pinzón, that we've not yet reached that point," Cristóbal replied. "When we do, we'll turn around if land isn't found, perhaps in a few days. But not now, and that is my order. That's our duty to the king and queen. I command those on duty to take their watch and those off duty to retire."

The men did not disperse. A sailor replied. "We've done our duty to you and the king and queen. We have no duty to die in vain for a scheme that has not borne out."

Cristóbal directed Pero Alonso to order a sailor to send smoke signals to advise the *Pinta* and *Niña* to quarter so the *Santa María* would close with them. Cristóbal continued carefully. "I do not ask that, and I have never asked that. The Lord has shown you signs that land is near, and all three captains have agreed that. It would forsake your tremendous efforts to give up now. We have the stores to proceed further and return to Hispania, and it would be treason for you to demand return now. Captain Pinzón is agreed on this." Cristóbal searched for more words. "There is no rebellion on his ship or on the *Niña.* You are alone in demanding your shameful retreat. It's useless to complain. I will go on until I find the Indies."

Strong winds whistled about the *Santa María*'s masts and rigging and spray careened over her rails onto the men confronted on her deck. The men were silent for a moment.

Cristóbal hunted for a remark to wind down the confrontation. "I have two sons in Spain myself. Those on duty should take their posts, and the rest should retire. Soon we'll all be rich, and this moment will never have happened."

The sailors glared at themselves exasperated, realizing an appeal to Pinzón or any other action would accomplish nothing. Slowly, a sailor departed to sleep in the hull, followed by a second and third, and gradually they all disbanded. The Crown representatives, Pero Alonso, Juan de la Cosa, and Cristóbal's attendants were stupefied in relief. When the *Santa María* arrived by the *Pinta*, Martín shouted above the wind that they all would fulfill their promise to the queen.

On October 11, the seas were the roughest yet encountered, and the ships took waves across the deck. But the portents were terrific. The *Niña* spotted and retrieved a green branch with red berries intact, fresh as if just cut. The *Pinta* found a piece of carved wood and another plant and the *Santa María* yet another green branch. Sandpipers were sighted. All realized that abandonment of the voyage now would be foolhardy, forsaking almost certain landfall for but an unknown passage home of tremendous length. After nightfall, Cristóbal reminded his crew that the Lord had favored the voyage with temperate weather and admonished them to be on lookout for shoals that night. Those off duty couldn't sleep and all hands came on deck seeking to be first to sight land and win the queen's pension. Cristóbal offered a silk jacket to that sailor, as well. He redirected the course due west, and no one objected.

Cristóbal stood on the *Santa María*'s stern deck, peering at the horizon. For a moment, he thought he saw a faint light flicker in the far distance, as if a tiny candle penetrating haze. He averted his eyes for a moment and then peered again, continuing to see it. He called Pedro Gutiérriez to look with him, and Pedro confirmed he saw a light. They called Rodrigo Sánchez to look, as well, but he saw nothing. Cristóbal decided that he was unsure of a sighting and that the *Santa María*'s lombard should not be discharged.

Soon, one of the pardoned criminals, Pedro Izquierdo, shouted from the forecastle that he saw a light, and Cristóbal's page Pedro advised Izquierdo that Cristóbal had already seen it. The light vanished and the ships continued west for some hours. The moon rose at the stern of the ships, with the *Pinta* in the fore and the *Santa María* in the rear.

At about 2:00 a.m. on October 12, a young seaman serving lookout on the *Pinta*, Juan Rodríguez Bermejo,* shouted that he sighted land to the northwest. Martín hurried to the bow and clearly identified low-lying sand cliffs glimmering in the moonlight about two leagues distant. He shouted in confirmation, and the *Pinta*'s lombard was discharged. Martín ordered most sails lowered and brought the *Pinta* to quarter so the other ships would close. The *Pinta*'s entire crew peered at the cliffs. Sailors fell to the deck praising the Lord, weeping and embracing one another.

The shot of the lombard echoed east and the entire crews of the *Niña* and *Santa María* bolted to the rails to peer west, praying that the sighting be true. Their prayers were met. Cristóbal beheld the landmass and fell to the deck to adore the Lord and wept. Sailors cheered, cried, embraced, and sang a hymn to the Virgin for watching over them.

Some who had protested came to kneel before Cristóbal to apologize and ask his forgiveness. He replied that he exonerated all. But, as he spoke, he knew it was a lie, simply a prudent response to retain each sailor's allegiance for the journey then beginning. In truth, he would never forgive those he perceived had belittled, insulted, or mocked his Genoese origin or common status, the wisdom of his voyage or his intelligence, the purity of his motives or faith, or the quality of his seamanship. He did forgive, and would never begrudge, only those he perceived had but succumbed to fear of death at sea, which he understood beyond expression.

Cristóbal ordered most sails lowered and the *Santa María* quartered abreast the *Pinta* and *Niña*. He repressed his growing distrust of Martín and shouted across the turbulent sea to congratulate him for sighting land. Cristóbal directed that the ships quarter until dawn,

---

*Sometimes known as Rodrigo de Triana.

when they could identify the presence of shoals and determine how to reconnoiter the landmass for a suitable anchorage.

Few of the crew, if any, could sleep as they awaited sunrise. They now felt safe and anticipated glory and riches.

Cristóbal forced himself to rest briefly, to be as alert as possible at dawn when directing a landing in unknown waters. But he could not stop himself from rising to scan the landmass for a harbor teeming with ships or a city with temples roofed with gold.

VIII
LUCAYAN ISLANDS

Arrival of Unknown,
Guanahaní, October 12, 1492

Bakako's father woke at the first light, placed a few sticks on the bohío's smoldering fire, and stepped outside to examine the weather. The ocean was windswept and very rough, the sky dotted with clouds but not stormy. He decided to fish within the coral barrier with his sons and returned inside to shake the hammock where Bakako and Yuni slept, now together with their little sister Abana. The children rose to join the rest of the larger family outside the bohío as the women prepared breakfast.

On the eastern coast, near the village of the island's paramount cacique,* the first fishermen to inspect the ocean were shocked to see three unknown objects far at sea to the southeast, apparently approaching. They appeared small at that distance, but—whatever they were—the fishermen knew they were large, likely enormous. The objects buffeted on the sea and rose high into the sky. One fisherman pronounced they were sea creatures. Another exclaimed they were spirits from the heavens. A third warned they were Caribes riding unknown beasts. The fishermen quickly returned to the village to warn the cacique.

---

*At Pidgeon Creek, where a narrow straight connects a long, slender inner bay to the ocean.

Guanahaní's paramount cacique was a prudent, middle-aged man, quite youthful in appearance. He trusted the observations of these particular fishermen and quickly summoned his behique and a party of nitaínos to accompany him to the shore. The commotion woke the entire village and a rumor spread that Caribes were attacking. The cacique and his entourage rapidly climbed a bluff overlooking the ocean and were astounded. To the southeast, illuminated by the sun's first rays streaking across the horizon, three objects of gargantuan proportion were speeding west to pass Guanahaní's southern tip, close outside the surf breaking on the southern reefs. They appeared to have long bellies stretching across successive waves and tremendous tentacles waving in the sky, puffing with pouches like the throats of croaking frogs. They were inexplicable.

The cacique and his nitaínos feared the sightings might be Caribes, beasts hunting, or evil spirits, but the cacique cautioned they could also be friendly spirits—in which case it would be wrong to offend them. He quickly decided battle preparation was urgent and dispatched messengers throughout Guanahaní, directing all women and children to proceed inland for safety and all men and older boys to prepare to engage an enemy. He assembled under his command a small contingent of men best suited to act as warriors to track the sightings along the southern shore, ready to lead any battle, and instructed that hostilities should begin only upon his order, strictly as a last resort.

It took but minutes for a runner to cross Guanahaní to Bakako's village. The village cacique and behique met him at the plaza and, at first, were not convinced of the urgency. The messenger panted about extraordinary beasts or spirits at sea yet was unable to describe them. But when he mentioned a Caribe raid, the village cacique quickly understood and exhorted his villagers to obey their paramount cacique's direction.

Bakako's mother, aunts, and grandmother clamored in pandemonium to gather Abana and the other children. Mother stole a moment to embrace Bakako and Yuni and anguished whether they were young enough to accompany her inland. Father perceived Mother's want and nodded disapproval. Mother urged him to watch over their sons, embraced him, and departed with Abana and Grandmother inland toward Guanahaní's great freshwater lake, silently invoking Yúcahu's and Attabeira's protection.

The village men and boys followed their cacique, toting spears and trotting south along the path Bakako took to his watch post. They rose atop the gentle hill and scanned the southern sea but could not discern Caribe war canoes in the heavy surf. They quickened their pace and Bakako and Yuni ran beside Father, keenly aroused by the emergency, proud to be with the men, awestruck they might use spears other than for fishing, and wondrous of the unknown that would be encountered.

Soon, the cacique shouted for the party to halt, outcries pronounced the unknown's discovery, and Bakako and Yuni beheld it, astonished. To the south, three enormous beasts swam with the sea west outside the barrier reef, pitching in the swells. Bakako thought they had wings like a bird, touching the sky.

The cacique brusquely asked his men for silence and spoke to his behique. "I can't tell whether these things are fish or bird or beast! There're no fins, no duck's feet, no paddles. They're swimming faster than the current, almost as fast as warrior canoes. They could be bearing men."

"Their heft and height are incredible!" the behique observed. "They must be spirits! We've never seen fish, birds, or beasts of this size, and none of our history tells of it. They're not of the earth or the sea we know. They must come from beyond the horizon, where spirits reside."

"What if they can crawl onto land or fly above us!" a nitaíno shouted. "Maybe they're coming to eat us!"

"We don't know that," another replied. "Maybe they're just passing by."

The cacique implored his behique to consult Yúcahu for what they should do, and the men and boys hushed as the behique communicated. After some moments, he advised, "I believe Yúcahu favors letting these enormities reveal themselves as they intend. We should take action only in response. If they're spirits from beyond the horizon, it'd be foolish to dishonor them, whether they're good or evil."

The villagers watched the enormities swim beyond Guanahaní's southern tip, still outside the barrier reef, and then turn north to enter the less turbulent water in Guanahaní's lee.

"They're looking to come ashore!" the cacique grimly observed. The villagers sobered in trepidation of confrontation and, as the enormities came abreast where they stood, studied the tentacles and billowing pouches.

"It's as if they've harnessed wind like a bird," the cacique continued.

"They've aligned Guabancex and Guataúba to their advantage," the behique agreed.

"Look at their bellies!" a nitaíno exclaimed. "There're spirits or men riding them! They're tiny at this distance, but you can see them moving about."

The cacique squinted at the bellies of the enormities and saw the apparitions of men stirring. "We must prepare for Caribes! They may be attacking on beasts or boats we've never seen." He dreaded that his small band would confront this unknown alone and desperately scanned all directions. To his relief, a large party of Guanahaníans with spears was approaching north along the path, tracking the enormities' advance.

Soon, Guanahaní's paramount cacique and his warriors arrived, and the village cacique submitted to his command. Bands of other Guanahaníans converged from the east, and all joined to track the beasts—be they that—north. By midmorning, the beasts arrived west of Guanahaní's great beach and slowed, having discovered one of the barrier reef's few deep passage channels. The Guanahaníans studied them carefully navigate inside the barrier, revealing a terrifying hunting instinct and intelligence. It became easy to identify the men or spirits pacing on them as they advanced toward the beach.

Bakako watched with amazement as the beasts came to a standstill within the tranquil bay. He studied their bellies—there were no scales like a fish, no skin like a ray or shark, and no shell like a crab—they appeared instead to be made of wood, like a canoe. He marveled at the height of their arms or wings—but there were no feathers and the appendages resembled tree trunks draped in rope. Men or spirits on each beast heaved an enormous spear tied to a thick cord into the water, and Bakako immediately recognized the intent to secure the beasts in the sea. Just as canoes, the beasts then quietly adjusted their float in accordance with the current.

Bakako harkened to the sounds echoing across the water. There was a flapping sound—like cloth blowing in the wind—as the great billowing pouches shrank upward to fold into arms held horizontal in the sky. There was a cracking sound when cords snapped against the tall arms, as when nets were thrown into a canoe's hull. There was a thwacking sound as waves lapped the enormous bellies, just like upon a canoe. Astounded, Bakako heard the men or spirits talking in a tongue unknown and undecipherable.

Guanahaní's paramount cacique summoned the village caciques on the beach to review the situation. Whether spirits or men, these beings certainly weren't conducting a surprise attack as would Caribes—they appeared to be coming to introduce themselves. The cacique asked for a duho and sat to consult Yúcahu, who advised treating the visitors deferentially, be they good or evil. It would be wrong to raise a spear against this honest entrance, and it would be unwise to provoke spirits possessed of perhaps fearsome power.

The Guanahaníans discerned that each beast—be it that—trailed with a large cord a small beast, about as long as a canoe but shaped more like an open shell. Perhaps these smaller objects also were beasts, but Bakako thought of them as strange canoes. The men or spirits descended into them and, pulling strange paddles sideways, propelled these three canoes—be they that—toward the beach.

Bakako raptly scrutinized the men or spirits approaching. Some paddled, others sat, and one stood at the bow of each canoe holding a spear draped in cloth. They were massive beings, appropriate to the enormous beasts they came from—much taller, broader, and heavier than Guanahaníans. Bakako couldn't determine whether they wore cloth or paint or had strange skin over most of their bodies. Whatever, they bore many different colors. They didn't appear to come from the world he knew, and, as they came closer, Bakako took fright they were spirits. Perhaps they were dead, hiding the absence of navels in cloth so they might stalk among the living.

"These appear to be men, but larger," Father tensely observed.

"They don't look like Caribes, either," Bakako's uncle responded. "They're pale as the dead, there's hair on their faces, and they paint themselves like parrots. They're savages!"

"We don't know whether they're friend or enemy, spirit or man," the village cacique hoarsely warned. "Let's wait before judging."

The Guanahanians grew breathless with dread. Most retreated from the water to the forest's edge to watch from a distance. Father ordered Bakako and Yuni to hide behind trees and prepare to run inland to find Mother if trouble arose. The paramount cacique ordered his warriors to stand a moderate distance from the apparent landing spot.

As the three canoes arrived at the beach, Bakako recognized that the men or spirits appeared of different ages, including elders and youths. Their foreheads were round for failure of flattening. The three standing were more powerfully colored. Bakako now guessed that these three might be caciques and that perhaps these beings were men, after all, decorated in exotic cloth.

Bakako studied the man—be it that—standing at the bow of the first canoe. He appeared older, with gray hair atop his scalp and upon his chin. Scarlet cloth wrapped his shoulders, accentuating his pale skin. When his canoe grounded, he stepped out onto the sand, clutching his spear and its cloth under his arm. He cupped his pale hands above his head, looked to the sky, spoke in an unknown tongue to his spirits or fellow dead, and walked onto the beach.

POSSESSION, GUANAHANÍ,
October 12, 1492

Cristóbal fell to his knees, engulfed in triumph and tears, and kissed the sand, praising and adoring his Lord. The sovereigns' representatives, the interpreter Luis de Torres, and some crewmen armed with sword and crossbow disembarked and joined him on their knees, weeping and praising the Virgin for having delivered them. Martín and Vicente arrived on the *Pinta*'s and *Niña*'s launches, each captain bearing the banner of the expedition, and they, too, dropped to their knees, crying with jubilation.

Cristóbal rose to his feet, wiped his tears, and unfurled the banner bearing the sovereign's royal standard. He was stunned by the beauty of the setting—the peaceful arc of the soft, white beach separating the turquoise shallows of the sheltered bay from a lush, green, moist forest. He glanced up and down the beach and perceived a multitude of people scrutinizing him, all men and most with spears, astounded they were entirely naked. Their skin was olive—like the heathens of the Canary Islands, much lighter than the Guineans—and many had painted themselves with red, black, or white designs. Memories of the scant clothing of Canarians and Guineans flickered through his thoughts, and Cristóbal was satisfied that the distance of the naked peoples from his crews was sufficient for safety—so long as the crews remained alert. He overheard the people's whispers and guessed that their language, as the Guineans', would lack words common to the languages he knew. He grasped these people were not of the Grand Khan's court and that the site was not Cipangu, suspecting instead that it was an outer island to the Indies' mainland.

Cristóbal summoned his crews to stand before him on the beach and addressed them, praising the beneficence of the Lord in bestowing the discovery upon himself and the sovereigns and proclaiming the island named San Salvador (Holy Savior) in the Lord's honor. He requested that Rodrigo de Escobedo and Rodrigo Sánchez step forward before the peoples watching to state the formal declarations whereby San Salvador became the possession of King Fernando and Queen Isabel of Castile and, when subjugated, its inhabitants their subjects.

Escobedo stated—in a solemn voice loudly directed to all peoples on the beach—that no Christian prince had yet asserted sovereignty over the island and that the Castilian sovereigns thereby were free to do so. Cristóbal surmised the naked men watching had no comprehension of what was occurring. He felt superior over their nakedness and ennobled to be the Lord's instrument to bestow Christian civilization upon them.

Escobedo pronounced that Cristóbal Colón and his men had arrived in the name of King Fernando and Queen Isabel of Castile to confer these princes' and the church's protection over San Salvador and invite its inhabitants to Christianity so their souls would achieve eternal salvation—if none objected. Cristóbal listened to the silence of the naked men and expected no objection. He was relieved his landing had not provoked hostilities, as he had no soldiers to properly fight. He understood the naked peoples were ignorant of both the consequence of their nonhostility and the tremendous spiritual benefit he would confer on them. Cristóbal raised his voice to be heard up and down the beach, declaring to both peoples that he heard no objection to the imposition of the sovereigns' sovereignty.

Guanahaní's paramount and subordinate caciques observed these rituals with wonderment and bewilderment, listening to the strange tongue and intrigued by the frequent gestures to the heavens. As Bakako, they guessed that the pale being leading the ritual— be he a man—was a cacique accompanied by nitaínos following his commands. The beings repeated a mysterious rite or invocation, lifting a hand to the forehead, then to the chest, and then to one shoulder and across to the other. The caciques puzzled over from where these beings had come, what they were doing, and what they would do next. The paramount cacique anxiously pondered whether they wished to stay.

Escobedo announced that Cristóbal Colón was now the viceroy and governor of the island, entitled to be addressed as an admiral, and solemnly requested the affirmation of the crews present. The men were ebullient and readily affirmed, and many from the *Pinta* and *Niña* took the opportunity to thank Cristóbal and plead his pardon for any past insult or disobedience. As before, Cristóbal said he forgave everyone.

Martín congratulated Cristóbal as heartily as the others but was galled to affirm Cristóbal's nobility, jealous that land's discovery was due to his plea to change course southwest. He seethed that Cristóbal's remarks offered him no credit for anything whatsoever—it was an outrageous injustice and ingratitude! Without Martín's participation, there would have been no crews to sail in the first place; after landfall failed at 750 leagues, no crews to continue; and no land found!

Cristóbal turned to the naked peoples to introduce himself and his men and to determine where exactly he had arrived. He took a few steps toward the forest and raised his free hand, intended as a gesture of peace. The paramount cacique approached with reciprocal steps, raised both arms as a gesture of friendship, and spoke in a language unlike any Cristóbal had ever heard. Cristóbal greeted him in Castilian, judging him no older than thirty, unaware he was the peoples' leader.

The two men realized they could communicate only by gesture. With smiles, softer words, and hand movements indicating openness and the absence of weapons, each assured the other that harm was not intended. Both peoples perceived an offer of friendship extended, and Cristóbal and the paramount cacique advised their men bearing arms to refrain from using them. The paramount and subordinate caciques advanced to meet the visitors, and the Guanahaníans waiting at the forest's edge crowded onto the beach to congregate about them. The caciques were astounded how much cloth apparently covered the visitors' bodies. Cristóbal was astounded that the naked peoples—now standing beside him—had no shame, embarrassment, or even awareness of their nakedness.

The caciques were eager to introduce themselves and offered water and cazabi to the visitors. One presented Cristóbal with a gourd of water, which he sniffed closely before taking the slightest sip. Diego de Arana tested it, as well. Finding the water sweet, Cristóbal and his crews drank freely, and the Guanahaníans were gratified. The Castilians examined the cazabi, guessed that it was much like unleavened bread, and, after tasting small morsels, began to eat heartily—their first fresh breadstuff in weeks. The Guanahaníans were delighted.

Bakako and Yuni left the forest edge to meet Father and join a crowd examining one of the visitors, fascinated by the cloth that hid most of his body and the absence of body paint. He wore a necklace with a strange, wood ornament or cemí, like two sticks crossed. His face was hairy, like a hutia, with tangled locks upon his chin and cheeks.

Bakako touched the cloth on the visitor's chest and legs and discovered it to be heavier than cotton. He rubbed the material where feet would be and found it strangely firm. After hesitation, he touched the skin of the visitor's arm—it was pale, moist with sweat, and warm, as if the visitor were human. With trepidation, Bakako softly touched the hair on the chin and the visitor turned to him and smiled. Someone handed the visitor a gourd of water, and Bakako saw the visitor's teeth, tongue, and thirst were those of a man.

The crews felt honored and amused by this groping, perceiving the wonderment at their clothing and skin a flattery, an admiration of superiority. But, as the sun's heat rose, the visitors began to sweat profusely, and Bakako and others wondered whether the burden and discomfort of wearing cloth was borne to hide deformities such as a tail or, worse, the dead's absence of a navel. Bakako studied the youngest visitors on the beach—perhaps just years his senior—baffled whether they simply were ashamed of their bodies. The paramount cacique and his subordinates grew suspicious that the unnatural body coverage hid weapons or unknown powers.

Naked men congregated around Cristóbal, seeking to touch him, too, but reservedly, now cognizant of his authority. Rodrigo Sánchez carried a sack of gifts for the inhabitants, and Cristóbal plucked a red skullcap from it and, with a flourish, gave it to the people's leader. The paramount cacique was honored, recognizing that the gift—as the giver—came from beyond the horizon and was thereby imbued with precious significance. Cristóbal handed a small, round hawk's bell to a second man, demonstrating how it tinkled when shook, and a glass bead necklace to a third, showing how to make it glimmer in sunlight. All were charmed. Cristóbal distributed similar gifts to many others, and the Guanahaníans reveled that the gifts came from beyond their known world.

Cristóbal noticed that the men had broad, flat foreheads and some bore scars. He pointed to the scars, shrugged his shoulders, and asked slowly in Castilian what caused them. The cacique responded in Taíno that they were suffered repelling invaders. Cristóbal pointed to the sea, bit his teeth, and made a hand motion suggesting a shark. A nitaíno understood and waved his head in denial and asked a warrior to display his spear. Cristóbal understood that men had caused the wound. A wounded man pointed across the sea, and Cristóbal inferred that an enemy raided from neighboring islands.

Cristóbal asked one of his sailors bearing a sword to step forward and draw it from its sheath. The Guanahaníans watched the sailor pull a silver stick thinner than a spear from an appendage at his hip and hold it upright to the sky, flashing in the sunlight. A nitaíno stepped forward to touch it and, unaware of the blade's sharpness, cut himself. The Guanahaníans clamored with surprise and Cristóbal told them in Castilian that this object was a sword. Many stepped forward to touch it—this time more carefully—impressed by its sharpness and, despite its thinness, its unusual strength.

The paramount cacique grew silent, acknowledging that he hadn't appreciated the extent of the visitors' weaponry. Cristóbal asked a sailor to reveal a knife, and many admired when the visitor drew it from a sheath on his leg. The paramount and subordinate caciques glanced warily among themselves, confirming that the unnatural cloth did indeed conceal weapons.

The Guanahaníans soon graciously offered fish and fruit. Cristóbal observed that the fish was fire charred and well cooked, and his sailors enjoyed it. He could not identify the fruit, but found it succulent. The paramount cacique and his subordinates grew comfortable with the visitors, in spite of their weapons. They presented Cristóbal with a gift of dry leaves (tobacco), which he graciously accepted without understanding its use. After conferring among themselves, the caciques dispatched messengers inland to instruct the women that it was safe to return with the children to their villages.

As the afternoon waned, Cristóbal recognized that his crews were exhausted, many not having slept for a day, and ordered that all return to the ships for the night. While suspecting men could remain ashore safely, he could not be certain of that or allow it. He indicated by gesture to the naked men around him that he and the crew would return in the morning.

As the launches pulled from the beach, some Guanahaníans followed them into the water, swimming beside them. Others followed in canoes. They brought skeins of cotton, brightly plumed parrots, and spears, and sought to exchange them for more of the beads, bells, caps, and other items they had seen. Cristóbal and his men were amused, as well as surprised at the trade terms these people accepted—a few glass beads could be exchanged for a large skein of cotton. The Guanahaníans were equally surprised—for an ordinary cotton skein, they could obtain an object from beyond the world.

Bakako and Yuni asked Father's permission to swim to the visitors' canoes, but he forbade it. Father reflected that, as for his own children, it was too early to conclude these visitors were not Caribes bent on capture. Father hinted that, if the visitors remained overnight, Father and Uncle might trade with them the next day and bring the two boys along.

Canoeists approached the three large beasts—be they that—with caution. Their enormous hulks and appendages loomed far higher into the sky than any bohío ever built. The notion that the visitors were human and had built these things seemed incredible. Many feared the beasts' graceful inertness belied their true spirit, which would awaken with fearsome brutality.

After sunset, the Guanahanían canoeists and swimmers returned to the beach. Sailors stood as lookouts on each ship. In the twilight, Cristóbal turned to his journal, which he had missed recording the previous day and night. While exhausted, he was exuberant and keen to memorialize the triumph of landfall.

Before writing, Cristóbal reflected with conviction that the Lord must have destined that he be the first to discover land and, with bitterness and jealousy, that it would be intolerable in light of their fickleness and disobedience that a crew member receive the queen's pension or, worse, that Martín receive credit for the discovery. The flickering light he thought he had seen on October 11 had been followed soon by actual landfall, and Cristóbal carefully recorded in the journal Gutiérrez's confirmation of this sighting.

Turning to October 12, envisioning Queen Isabel and King Fernando listening as he wrote, Cristóbal explained the expedition had achieved the first landfall at an island and that he had achieved the natives' good friendship through exchange of trifles. He reported the natives were poor and went entirely naked, with handsome bodies and good countenances, and that they painted themselves in colors. They knew nothing of iron or arms, save wooden spears, and they suffered attacks by people who came from the mainland to take them as slaves.

Cristóbal reflected to himself that the territory possessed had none of the wealth expected of Cipangu. He wrote that the island's peoples appeared to belong to no religious sect, permitting their easy conversion to Christianity, and should make good servants. He was invigorated that the exploration for new lands would commence at dawn and planned to capture six young men with apparent intelligence and geographic knowledge to serve as guides and interpreters.

FROM THE HEAVENS, GUANAHANÍ,
October 13–14, 1492

Bakako, Yuni, and Abana were too excited to sleep. As the waning moon rose, they overheard Father and Uncle discussing their plans to join the village cacique trading with the visitors the next day.

"Is Father letting us come?" Yuni whispered.

"I can't tell," Bakako responded.

"Can I come, too?" Abana asked.

"No," Yuni replied. He wondered, "Will they still be there tomorrow?"

"I don't know," Bakako reflected. "They must have approached by night and could leave at night, like spirits. But I think they said they would stay."

"Are they spirits or men?" Yuni asked.

"I don't know. They don't swim like fish or live on other islands or come from caves. They must come from the sky. I've never heard of men coming from the sky."

"Where are their mommies?" Abana wondered.

"Who knows," Yuni answered. "I saw one of them take a piss."

"So did I," Bakako affirmed. The boys chuckled, and Abana broke out laughing. "Maybe they're both man and spirit. Maybe they call upon spirits we don't know about."

"Are they nice?" Abana asked.

"I don't know," Bakako replied, conscious of repeating himself. "Probably."

The children detected the muffled whispers of villagers sneaking from their bohíos to steal quietly through the forest to the beach to spy on the visitors. Father and Uncle decided to do so, and, after considering the danger, Father consented that the boys come along, leaving Abana to sleep with Mother. They quietly slipped out of the bohío and, in the moonlight, slunk along the short path through the forest to peer south into the bay.

The enormous hulks floated silently, their tall appendages enveloped by the starry heavens, their bellies silver in the moonlight. Small fires glowed at their tips. They had shifted position with the tide. A few men or spirits stood on them, but the rest had vanished, perhaps asleep or risen to the heavens for the night. After a few moments, one chanted a soft areíto, barely audible over the surf. Father whispered that the beings would remain in the morning, and the four returned to the bohío. Throughout Guanahaní, its peoples eagerly awaited dawn.

At the first light, Cristóbal rose to inspect his ships and scan the beach where the naked peoples already gathered. There were now women among them, also entirely naked, and Cristóbal was astonished the women walked among their men without shame or concern, and the men apparently without lust. He remembered that Adam and Eve beheld their nakedness only after falling from grace and pondered whether these people were so simple as to be untainted with evil. He realized his sailors would quickly succumb to temptation and lust, and he brooded whether peaceful relations could be jeopardized, damaging the prospects for these peoples' peaceful subjugation.

At dawn, the crews of the three ships rose to behold the men and women ashore. After morning hymn, some crudely jested they had achieved paradise and could not wait to go ashore.

The Guanahaníans listened to the areíto drift across the water and their distrust of the enormous hulks subsided, as it appeared the pale visitors lived within. Men embarked in canoes or simply swam to greet the visitors, seeking to obtain objects from the sky. They clambered up the hulks' sides, often assisted by visitors, and congregated on the decks. They beheld the hulks from within and were astonished, some by the enormity and others by the realization that the hulks were wood, inanimate, and had been carved from trees.

The Guanahaníans graciously offered cazabi and water. Cristóbal traded trifles with them, intent that every person be satisfied. Crewmen also traded, perceiving the terms extraordinary and relishing the bargains achieved. The Guanahaníans cared little or nothing what they traded to obtain an object from the sky, and, after obtaining it, they quickly jumped back into their canoes or the bay to return to home, without lingering to study or admire the visitors. The crews perceived them simple, timid, and backward. Cristóbal recognized that cotton was of value to the sovereigns and determined to forbid sailors to trade for gold, spices, or cotton except as he approved on behalf of the sovereigns and to punish offenders.

After breakfast, the village cacique, Father, Uncle, and others loaded their parrots, cotton, and other trading items into a canoe, leaving just enough room for Bakako and Yuni to nudge aboard, and paddled abreast of the largest hulk. Cristóbal noticed the boys and warmed to a fleeting recollection of his sons. He motioned for the boat to come alongside and the men to mount aboard. Bakako looked to Father, who ordered him and Yuni to remain in the canoe. Cristóbal came to the rail, gazed down at Bakako, pointed to the boat, and shrugged his shoulders.

Bakako trembled that he had done something wrong. The visitors' cacique pointed to the canoe again, raised his eyebrows as if to ask a question, and spoke in his strange tongue. Bakako did not understand, but he sensed an attempt to learn the word for canoe. Bakako spoke in Taíno. "Canoa. It's a canoa."

Cristóbal recognized the boat was carved from a single trunk like those at Mina and was taken by its seaworthy design. He smiled, pointed, and replied. "Canoa. Canoa."

The village men murmured with appreciation, and Father quivered with both fear and pride. He gulped anxiously as his son then pointed to the hulk.

Cristóbal responded in Castilian. "Ship. It's called a ship."

"Ship," Bakako replied in Castilian, smiling. "It's called a ship."

Cristóbal noted the boy's intelligence. Bakako studied the side of the "ship," trying to determine how the wood before him held together, for it was in different pieces and there were no cords. He examined the large vertical slab of wood descending into the water at the tail of the "ship" and puzzled if it served as a fin.

Cristóbal observed that a few of the canoeists, including their leader, bore a gold piece through a nostril or earlobe. He pointed to his own nose, to the leader's gold nosepiece, and then shrugged, asking in Castilian what it was. The village cacique understood the question as a compliment and explained in Taíno that it was gold jewelry, which many of his people wore. Cristóbal responded in Castilian that gold was what he wanted most, and he would trade generously for it. Rodrigo Sánchez brought forth the sack of gifts and Cristóbal pointed to the nosepiece and then to the sack and then to the nosepiece again.

The cacique and his men nodded they understood. They were surprised that jewelry was of such interest. Cristóbal offered the

leader a large, red skullcap in return for the nosepiece, and the cacique cheerfully accepted.

Cristóbal held the nosepiece aloft with one hand, waved his
other hand across the entirety of San Salvador's coastline, and
shrugged his shoulders, asking in Castilian whether the piece came
from Guanahaní. He repeated the gesture, very slowly.

The villagers conferred among themselves for some time. All
knew the answer was no, as Guanahaní had scant gold, but they
suspected the visitors would leave to trade elsewhere once this was
understood. Some felt this would be a disappointing result, others
that it was the best outcome. The village cacique responded in Taíno
that it came from islands south, where a grand cacique had much
gold. The cacique pointed south, touched the gold piece Cristóbal
now held, and pointed south.

Cristóbal pointed to himself, pointed south, pointed to the cacique
and his party, and pointed south again, and asked in Castilian whether
the cacique and his men would lead Cristóbal south to the gold.

The villagers murmured among themselves again. Some feared
that the visitors indeed had come to capture Guanahaníans, perhaps
by guile rather than force. The cacique ignored Cristóbal's request
and simply pointed to the gold piece and waved his arms across the
southern horizon to assure him that gold would be found there.

Cristóbal traded for the villagers' remaining gold pieces, and they
returned to shore. Father obtained a hawk's bell, and a visitor gave
Bakako and Yuni each a glass bead, which they proudly displayed to
friends.

Sailors took turns ashore and found the island's large freshwater
lake and an abundance of wild cotton. Most everyone they met,
including the women, offered them cazabi, fish, fruit, and water. For
the first time, the sailors stood side by side with the women, and most
interpreted the women's friendliness and nakedness as invitations.
But the women fled with fear when the sailors sought to touch them.

That night, Cristóbal reflected on the attributes of San Salvador's
peoples, including their olive skin and temperament. He worried he
had deviated south of Hierro regardless of the sovereigns' contrary
instruction,* and he observed in his journal that the Guanahaníans'

*San Salvador is 3.5 degrees south of Hierro.

skin was the color of Canary Island heathens—as should be expected because San Salvador was on the same latitude—and that they were docile. He indicated that, while San Salvador had some gold, he would not lose time on the island and planned to leave the next day to find Cipangu.

As Cristóbal wrote, the island's paramount cacique met in council with his subordinate caciques and their behiques. They knew the earth was composed of the sea and land, with the heavens above and the underworld below, and agreed the visitors did not live within the sea or the underworld and did not come from lands known, including the great land to the southwest, where men did wear cloth. They debated, and most agreed by process of elimination, that the visitors had come down from the heavens. All agreed, whether spirit or men, the visitors had or could direct awesome power, and, while they appeared friendly, it was too soon to know.

At dawn on October 14, Cristóbal, Martín, Vicente, and crews boarded the ships' launches and rowed north along San Salvador's coast to explore before departing. Cristóbal sought to determine where a fort might be built and capture the guides and interpreters.

As the launches passed, naked peoples swarmed to the shore, fell to their knees, and gestured at the sky, imploring the visitors to come ashore and trade gifts from the heavens. Cristóbal and his crews were flattered by the apparent adulation. An elderly man swam to the boats and climbed aboard. Others shouted that the visitors came from the heavens and exhorted that they be brought cazabi and water. Cristóbal and his men inferred that these peoples believed they had come from Heaven.

As the visitors explored, Bakako, Yuni, and Abana sat on the beach watching the "ships" in the bay, planning to swim to them later. Guanahaníans from all over the island had come to behold the novel beings, and Bakako and Yuni met friends to whom they proudly displayed their beads from the heavens. Bakako thought of Kamana, and, as if the spirits had heard his thoughts, her shadow soon appeared on the ground before him. He looked up to her.

"I hoped to find you here," Kamana said. "I didn't want to come all the way here and see every Guanahaníian but you."

"I was just thinking of you. Really."

Kamana smiled, introduced herself to Yuni and Abana, and sat down with them. Abana studied her and wondered about her relationship to Bakako. Kamana asked, "Have you met the visitors?"

Bakako related the last two days with excitement and showed Kamana his object. "It's from the heavens."

"Is that what the behiques say?" Kamana doubted. "It looks like a pearl."

"I have touched the visitors myself and paddled to that hulk, which they call a 'ship.'" Bakako pointed to the *Santa María*.

"A 'ship'?" Kamana laughed.

"Yes," Yuni replied. "Their cacique told Bakako that himself."

Kamana looked into Bakako's eyes. "You touched and spoke to them? You should be careful." She paused and reflected. "Everybody is saying they come from the heavens. Is that true?"

"Probably."

"But I heard they have hair on their faces and smell badly from sweat because they're covered in cloth. They apparently don't bathe, and their face hairs are full of sand and crumbs. They eat, drink, piss, and poop like men." Kamana paused. "They want to lie with the women."

"That's correct," Bakako reflected. "But, wherever they come from, they are knowing and powerful. Their so-called ships are made from trees, and they are carved in unknown ways to make them enormous."

Bakako and Kamana chatted comfortably and decided to walk north with Yuni to see where the visitors had paddled. Bakako walked Abana to the path through the forest and sent her home, disappointed again. Bakako had obtained Father's permission to swim to the ships if other Guanahaníans did so. The three children began ambling north, and, before noon, they saw the visitors' canoes returning south. Many Guanahaníans swam to greet them.

Bakako turned to Kamana. "We're going to swim out to them and see them closeup. Want to come?"

"I didn't talk about that with my parents." Kamana looked to the beach. "I have to leave soon to help my mother."

"Wait here and we'll be back. You should hold our weird pearls." The boys handed Kamana their objects.

Bakako and Yuni waded into the gentle surf and waited for the visitors' canoes to approach so they could easily intercept them and, together with others, swam to meet them. Bakako discerned that there were Guanahaníans riding in the canoes, all young men or teen-age boys not much older than himself and, as the distance narrowed, Bakako led Yuni to swim in the path of the canoe bearing the caci-que. They waved to the visitors, and, to Bakako's surprise, the visi-tors ceased paddling and motioned for the boys to climb aboard. Bakako and Yuni glanced at each other, unsure whether to accept, but Bakako reflected that the other Guanahaníans aboard satisfied Father's permission. There was scant time to decide, and Bakako let the visitors pull Yuni and himself aboard.

The cacique smiled at them, and Bakako wondered whether he remembered they had met. Bakako asked the Guanahaníans what was happening, and they indicated they had been invited to visit on the great hulks where they would receive gifts from the heavens. All were excited. Bakako and Yuni realized they were the youngest Guanahaníans aboard—Yuni by quite a few years—and this thrilled and frightened them even more.

The cacique's canoe soon pulled aside his ship and Bakako, Yuni, and the other young Guanahaníans climbed onto it. The visitors offered them some food, a dried meat like hutia but not as spicy, and motioned for them to sit on the deck as Admiral—as they addressed him—met them one by one. Bakako studied as other Guanahaníans were led sepa-rately to Admiral, who sat on a strange duho on a ledge above.

When it was Bakako's turn, Yuni also rose, and the boys didn't know whether Yuni should come, too. Admiral waved both forward to stand before him. Both trembled.

Cristóbal concluded immediately that the younger boy was too young and addressed only Bakako. Cristóbal guessed he was about Diego's age and wondered if it was the same boy he had seen the day before.

Cristóbal pointed to himself and said, "Admiral," and then pointed to Bakako's mouth, indicating that he should repeat.

Bakako responded, "Admiral."

Cristóbal thought he recognized the boy's voice. He pointed to Bakako and shrugged his shoulders.

"Bakako."

Cristóbal repeated, "Bakako." Bakako smiled and nodded.

Cristóbal pointed to the tall appendages looming above and said, "Mast," and then to the wood on which they stood and said, "Deck."

Bakako repeated, "Mast. Deck."

Cristóbal spoke quite slowly. "In the name of Christ and King Fernando and Queen Isabel."

Bakako slowly repeated the strange sounds as best he could, and Cristóbal was satisfied with the boy's memory, facility with language, and composure.

Cristóbal pointed to the island. "Guanahaní."

Bakako nodded and repeated, "Guanahaní," with the proper inflection.

Cristóbal stood and slowly waved his hand across the seaward horizon and shrugged, asking in Castilian for the names of neighboring islands. Cristóbal pointed to Guanahaní again, repeated its name and waved seaward again, shrugging his shoulders.

Bakako understood and replied, "Samana. Manigua [Rum Cay]. Yuma. Saomete." He thought for a moment, considered the most distant lands, and waved across the southern horizon. "Cuba. Bohío. Yamaye [Jamaica]. Boriquén [Puerto Rico]. Guanín. Matininó. Carib."

Cristóbal was satisfied with the apparent geographic knowledge, and indicated to Juan de la Cosa that Bakako should be taken. He would be the last chosen of seven. Cristóbal ordered the mainsails unfurled, the anchors hoisted, and, as the ships got under way, that those natives not selected be dispatched overboard so they could swim ashore. Those seized were to be restrained.

Bakako and Yuni became alarmed as visitors climbed cords high above to let an enormous cloth drop. They were frightened as cloths unfurled on the other two ships, as well. They were horrified when the visitors pulled the cord that held the ship in the sea, for they understood the visitors meant to depart. They were terrified when the men on deck brandished their sharp weapons and encircled them, barking unknown threats or commands. They were violated when the men brusquely pushed them to the deck and made them kneel on their hands and knees.

Yuni started to cry, holding close to Bakako. A visitor clutched Yuni by the hair of his scalp and yanked him to his feet, and Yuni screamed. Bakako rose to defend his brother, but another visitor kicked Bakako hard in the stomach and shoved him back on his knees, where he curled in pain. Yuni shrieked in terror.

Visitors led Yuni and some others to the rail of the ship and pointed for them to jump overboard, and the others quickly did so. Yuni shook his head that he wouldn't and called to Bakako. Bakako screamed that he jump and escape. A visitor clutched Yuni and slapped him hard in the face, shouting and pointing to the sea. Bakako winced with rage at the slap and tried to rise but was kicked again, this time hard in the face. Bakako implored Yuni to jump, but Yuni froze, and a visitor picked him up and threw him overboard. The visitors tightened the circle about Bakako and the remaining Guanahanians, waving their weapons occasionally to show they were prepared to use them. Bakako peered through the rail of the ship to glimpse Yuni swimming to shore, wailing in panic.

The breeze began to fill the mainsail, and Cristóbal and Pero Alonso navigated the *Santa María* toward the passage in the barrier reef, followed closely by the *Niña* and *Pinta*. Bakako saw Yuni rise on the beach and run desperately into the forest toward home. He shuddered with dread as he beheld the barrier reef slip past as the ship entered the ocean, scorched by a vision of Father warning him to remain within.

Cristóbal ordered a running southwest and Juan de la Cosa directed the crew to unfurl the remaining sails. Bakako watched with incredulity as they filled with wind. He was aghast at the speed the ship quickly reached to depart Guanahaní. Soon, he could see the entirety of the island. It grew smaller, and the Guanahanians stared at one another, dreading their doom—unsure whether they would be enslaved for life, eaten, or simply slaughtered. In anguish, Bakako honored Yúcahu and pleaded for protection.

As the island grew distant, the visitors encircling the Guanahanians relaxed their guard and motioned for them to sit. A boy not much older than Bakako brought them more water. Bakako watched the visitors withdraw their weapons entirely and their cacique Admiral then approached to speak.

Admiral held his gold piece aloft, waved to the sea, and shrugged his shoulders, asking in Castilian the direction to the nearest island filled with gold. The Guanahaníans murmured among themselves and quickly pointed southwest toward Manigua, the nearest large island. Bakako studied how quickly the ship veered in that direction.

Admiral smiled and spoke softly in his strange tongue to each Guanahanían, communicating goodwill and friendship, inviting them to be comfortable. Admiral then left them alone unguarded, free to stand, sit, or lie as they pleased. Soon, Bakako listened as Admiral led the visitors—now his captors—in an areíto. As night fell, the captors gestured for the Guanahaníans to lie on the "deck" to sleep. Bakako realized that was how the captors slept themselves, as they appeared not to know of hammocks.

That evening, Cristóbal recorded in his journal that the naked peoples were unskilled in arms and it would not be necessary to build a fort. He was aware of the sovereigns' concern with the grounds for enslavement of Canary Island heathens and indicated that, were the sovereigns to so order, Guanahaní's peoples could be brought to Castile or kept as captives on the island because fifty men could subjugate them to do all that one wished.

On Guanahaní, word spread that the visitors had taken captives. In shock from the violations, Yuni clutched Mother. Mother wept that her son had been captured and she would never see him again. Abana clutched Mother, frightened by Bakako's capture, Yuni's terror, and Mother's despair. Kamana was stunned her chosen had been taken. Father gasped in anguish that he should have known better than to let the boys swim to these spirits or men from the heavens. Father now realized they were evil.

SEARCH FOR GOLD AND CIPANGU,
October 14–25, 1492

Bakako lay huddled on deck with his fellow Lucayans watching with astonishment as the captors—be they spirits or men—worked their ship at night. He gazed up the towering masts to the great cloths stretched tautly by the wind before the stars and understood the wind pushed the ship forward. He felt the ship sway side to side with tremendous inertia, tipping to a far greater angle than a canoe yet springing back to right itself. It creaked and moaned continuously as it lurched, as if speaking to Guabancex and Guataúba to please them. At intervals, a young captor rose to chant an areíto to the spirits.

Cristóbal rose at dawn and directed his page Pedro and servant Juan to gather the captives for breakfast and instruction. The sovereigns' representatives and some armed seamen attended, as well. Cristóbal sat on a stool with the Guanahaníans kneeling before him. They were shocked by the color of Juan's skin and studied him closely.

Cristóbal offered them hardtack and honey and showed them how to smother the biscuit with the honey. Bakako and the others enjoyed the taste. Cristóbal asked Sánchez for some coins and then placed one on the deck and said, "Guanahaní." He placed another on the deck and pointed to their destination.

Bakako understood. "Manigua."

Cristóbal handed Bakako the remaining coins, waved across the entire horizon, and pointed to the deck, and Bakako began setting the coins down to represent the islands neighboring Guanahaní. One of the captives, a tall teenager named Yutowa, had traveled extensively and adjusted the coins' placement to reflect his estimation of actual distances. Quickly, the Guanahaníans mapped much of their known world.

Cristóbal pointed to the gold piece he had obtained and then to Sánchez's sack, gesturing that he wanted the sack filled with gold, as well as many other sacks. Slowly, he pointed to the Guanahaníans, to the sack, to the gold, and then to Guanahaní and spoke in Castilian. "I will return you to Guanahaní after you take me to trade for sacks of gold and find gold mines." He repeated the motions. Bakako surmised Admiral's intent and told his brothers they would be returned home if they filled a sack with gold—and they were shocked by the daunting improbability of achieving this.

Pedro and Juan glanced at each other, to the Guanahaníans, and then to their master. They knew the Admiral's promise was a lie. The captives would be taken to Castile, regardless of how many sacks were filled with gold. Juan wasn't surprised by the lie.

Cristóbal understood the Guanahaníans' dejection. He gave each a hawk's bell and invited them to enjoy more biscuit and honey. He spoke softly, gesturing to ask if the roll of the ship sickened them. He took them on a brief tour of the *Santa María*, explaining the sails and the tiller and showing them a compass and ampolleta. He evaluated them further and chose three to transfer for use on the *Pinta* and a fourth for the *Niña* when the ships next anchored. Cristóbal decided to retain Bakako, Yutowa, and one other for himself.

As the ships approached Manigua, Bakako and his brothers discussed escape. They knew their captors didn't understand Taíno, and they spoke openly among themselves to not arouse suspicion with whispers. They knew Manigua had scant gold—no more than Guanahaní—and that Admiral wouldn't be satisfied. But they were confident that the Maniguans, as Taínos, would assist and shelter their flight. Bakako and Yutowa now knew the Castilian word for *gold*, and they assured Admiral with gestures that the Maniguans wore large gold bracelets on their arms and legs—well worth Admiral's visit. Cristóbal later recorded in his journal that he suspected these assurances were nonsense, invented that they might escape.

The ships anchored off Manigua at sundown on October 15, and the transfer of captives to the *Pinta* and *Niña* was accomplished before nightfall. That evening, Maniguans brought their canoes aside the ships to meet the visitors, and Bakako trembled as he contemplated jumping overboard into one of them. The shore was quickly reachable, and the captors would have difficulty pursuing in darkness.

Bakako anguished that if he remained aboard he would never see his family or Kamana again. He feared harm regardless of what he chose, either by remaining or if he was caught fleeing. He wasn't certain the captors would harm him if he remained, and he sensed they wanted to use him. They had hurt and captured him, but perhaps Admiral's promise to return him to Guanahaní was sincere. They had hurt Yuni but let him go. Admiral had directed the Guanahaníans' capture, but Admiral also had fed them.

As the moon rose, the third captive on the *Santa María* stood and entreated Bakako and Yutowa to join in him in escape. Bakako shuddered with indecision. Yet a day before, he had rashly climbed aboard Admiral's canoe to be captured! Should he now rashly jump overboard to be caught and brutally beaten? A vision of Yuni frozen motionless overcame him, and he felt a timeless inertia envelop and suspend his thoughts and seize every muscle.

The third captive called to Maniguan canoeists close by, who responded they understood and were ready, and the captive abruptly bolted overboard, whereupon the canoeists quickly pulled him from the sea and began paddling furiously to shore. Bakako fought desperately to muster his courage to flee. But the ship's deck erupted in commotion as the captors jumped into their canoe to give chase, and Bakako realized it was too late. Bakako watched the Lucayan canoe ground ashore, proud that it was by far the faster boat, and saw his fellow Guanahanían vanish into the forest with his liberators. Suddenly, Bakako felt the harsh grip of pale hands wrench him to the deck, and he winced in pain—both body and soul—as he and Yutowa were brusquely shoved into the ship's hold for the remainder of the anchorage at Manigua.

At dawn, Cristóbal named the island Santa María de la Concepción in honor of the Virgin and debarked with Escobedo and Sánchez to make the declarations rendering it Castile's possession. Naked peoples met Cristóbal on the beach, and he observed that they were the same as the Guanahanías—sharing similar speech, the same skin color and nakedness, and poverty in possessions. They had little gold but jewelry, and Cristóbal soon returned to his ship intent on sailing to a larger island west, having interpreted gestures of those he met as indicating the larger island held a gold mine. But, before departing, the Guanahanían aboard the Niña jumped ship, also escaping in a canoe of assisting Maniguans.

Bakako listened to the pandemonium from the darkness of the Santa María's hold, tortured again that he remained captive while the daring of two brothers had achieved freedom. He heard shouts and scuffles as sailors seized another canoeist to replace the captive lost. To his amazement, Bakako listened as Admiral gave this man gifts and then set him free, apparently hoping the man would speak well of the captors' kindness to those onshore.

Cristóbal sailed that noon toward the larger island, and, as Manigua grew distant, he released Bakako and Yutowa from the hold and gave them food and water. Cristóbal pointed toward the destination, to which Bakako responded, "Yuma," grimly aware that he was safe when he helped Admiral.

The ships overtook a man in a small canoe. Cristóbal brought him and his canoe aboard, offered him bread, honey, and drink, and discovered that he possessed Castilian coins and beads traded on San Salvador. Cristóbal admired the ability to traverse significant distance across ocean in such a small craft, and he gained confidence that these peoples, and in particular his captives, did know the geography of their islands and traveled among them.

Cristóbal gave the canoeist trifles and, that evening, released him on Yuma to spread good word—apparently successfully. In the morning, the Yumanians led sailors to Yuma's lakes, helped fill the ships' water barrels, and graciously ported the barrels back to the ships on their backs. Cristóbal envisioned the opportunity to exploit them and, having honored the spiritual powers, named Yuma Fernandina. He explored briefly, but found no temples, bridges, or port teeming with ships—no gold mine or any gold except jewelry.

But Cristóbal remained convinced he had attained Marco Polo's Indies, now referring in the journal to his exploration of the Indies and the peoples as Indians. With optimism, he interpreted gestures by the Yumans—confirmed by Bakako and Yutowa—that there was a king living at the island or city of Saomete who wore clothes, possessed much gold, and ruled over all the neighboring islands. Cristóbal sailed east toward Saomete as Bakako and Yutowa directed, pronouncing in his journal that the lands discovered were the best, most fertile, and temperate in the world. Cristóbal named Saomete Isabela, and, when he debarked, almost every Saometean fled in fear. Cristóbal and his sailors searched in vain for the lord, and he now found it necessary to prohibit his crews from looting.

Cristóbal recorded in his journal that the local people he did meet spoke of two large islands to the south named Cuba and Bohío and that many large ships and seafaring people visited Cuba. Confidently, he wrote this Cuba was Cipangu and that he would travel there and to Bohío to find gold, as well as to the mainland and Quinsay to present the sovereigns' letter to the Grand Khan, requesting a reply and returning with it.

Cristóbal sailed for Cuba at midnight on October 24. As he lay to sleep, he anxiously recognized that he had yet to find an Indian ship or merchant or commercial port. The sovereigns were not alone in expecting material wealth from the voyage. He had so promised each crewman, particularly Martín.

CAONABÓ
Maguana

Caonabó was bathing with Anacaona, Onaney, his other wives, and their younger children in the village stream when a naboria came to alert him that a nitaíno had arrived from Aniyana. It was the hurricane season, and Caonabó quickly surmised that the news would be grave, for there was no other cause to risk the open sea crossing. He whispered to Onaney that he would learn what had happened before summoning her.

Caonabó returned to his caney and, as he expected, found that the nitaíno waiting was the leader of the crew who had brought him to Haiti decades before, now thin and wizened with age. Caonabó was moved by the constancy of the elderly man's service, bridging Caonabó's youth and reign. The nitaíno had returned him to Aniyana to marry Onaney, carried Manicoatex and other brothers to join him in Haiti, borne the news of Father's death, and taken Caonabó's eldest son born of Onaney back to Aniyana to compete to be its cacique one day. Caonabó still thought of him as the leader and embraced him.

"How are you, my friend?" Caonabó asked. He stared into the leader's eyes, asking to receive his report.

"Your mother has passed away."

Caonabó flushed with relief that the news wasn't of his son but grimaced as a memory of Mother shot through his thoughts and triggered a thump of his heart. "How did it happen?"

"She asked for a secluded bohío."

Caonabó envisioned Mother resolutely alone, content to die, sustained till the final moment with memories of her family, including himself. At Father's death, she had chosen to remain to watch over Father's children and other wives rather than to be buried with him. Caonabó recalled her strength on the day he first had departed Aniyana, admiring that she had dedicated that strength to Father's family every day since.

The leader handed Caonabó a small sack. "She wanted you to have these."

Caonabó opened it and pulled out a stone amulet, recognizing that it was Father's. He also found a small round of gourd, darkened and hardened from decay. It was curious and he studied it, soon realizing that it was a child's helmet with two carved eyelets, and he was overcome by the remembrance of lying next to Mother before donning it for his first duck hunt. The thoughtfulness of the gift heartened Caonobó that Mother had possessed her wit and memory until the end.

"Thank you for coming," Caonabó remarked. "You shouldn't have—in the hurricane season."

"The sea was unusually calm. It was easy, particularly since I no longer take an oar. There's a younger nitaíno who now leads. I'm just brought along to consider the weather."

"How's my son?"

"He has taken wives and is well thought of. Your youngest brother continues to rule, and can be expected to for many years."

Caonabó dispatched a runner to summon Onaney, and she joined to learn the news. The three sat in the plaza, served a meal by naborias, and Onaney eagerly plied the leader for information of their son, his wives and children, her parents and siblings, and everything Aniyanan. Caonabó listened contently, pleased that his boyhood home remained as he remembered, reminded that Taíno life endured changeless over the march of time. That night, he bid Onaney sleep with him, and they revisted what they had learned and were happy.

In the moonlight, Caonabó retrieved the small gourd mask and studied it. "I wonder why she kept it all these years."

"As opposed to discarding it or giving it to you sooner?"

"Yes."

"She wanted you to remember it as her final message."

"What's the message?"

"There's no gold in it, as in your name. But it's you, regardless, and the memory of you she carried through death. Youthful, proud, free, brave, eager to be the hunter and conqueror. I can't think of a better mask to remember you by."

Caonabó was proud to be this remembrance. He kissed and held his first wife closely. "It's now yours."

In the morning, after breakfast, Onaney returned to the leader his sack, now stuffed with gifts for her son and others on Aniyana. Caonabó offered to accompany him to the pass atop the first mountain range on the route north and arranged bearers and a litter to accompany the entire journey.

The leader declined to ride as they climbed into the mountains, retracing a portion of the journey they had taken together decades before. He proudly recalled leading a boy who now ruled their people. They came to rest at the pass, where he gazed north over the mountains he would cross.

"Do you miss the sea?" he asked. "You must. It was in your blood."

"Yes, I miss it often. Both the beauty and terror of it." Caonabó admired the mountains. "But I've grown to love the mountains, as well. They have a different beauty. They have protected my people."

"So has the sea, from the beginning of time. The sea has protected our people from whatever lies beyond."

IX

CUBA

TO CUEIBA (AT BAHÍA DE GIBARA) AND WEST,
October 26—November 11, 1492

At sunset on October 26, Bakako and Yutowa sat at Admiral's feet next to the page Pedro and servant Juan, studying a chain of low, scruffy islands and reefs to starboard. Admiral sat on his duho. The steward Pedro stood at the rail and asked Bakako, "What's the name for these islands?"

"Utiaquia (Ragged Islands)," Bakako replied. He continued slowly in Castilian. "One, two days Cuba." He thought and clarified. "Canoa."

Cristóbal noted the statement of duration and understanding of speed and distance and appreciated Bakako's civility and intellect. The boy appeared to be learning his role, perhaps accepting his fate.

Bakako and Yutowa remained naked, and Cristóbal didn't insist otherwise. The two Pedros had offered them shirts and pants, and they had found them physically comfortable to wear. But they weren't pleased to do so because hiding one's body was not the custom of their people, and they viewed it an embarrassment. The crews continued to wear their wool shirts and pants day and night regardless of the heat, often for protection from the sun and wind but otherwise in accordance with Hispanic custom.

Cristóbal addressed Bakako in words and gestures. "When we arrive at Cuba, you will speak for us. You will tell the people we are good. You will say we harm no one. You will say we just trade for gold." He pointed to Bakako, toward Cuba, and to himself and his gold piece, and then signaled using his hands and fingers that Bakako would walk ashore in Cuba to vouch that Admiral and his men wanted gold in peace.

Cristóbal convened the *Santa María*'s crew for evening hymn. He named the islands to starboard the Islas de Arenas and the crew sang "Salve Regina." Bakako and Yutowa sang in Castilian, parroting the words and mimicking young Pedro as he gazed upward to conjure the heavens. Bakako now understood the areítos invoked the captors' spirits—Lord, Christ, and Virgin—and the cemí shaped as a cross. He perceived that Admiral consulted these spirits often and reverently. He sensed that young Pedro was not so worshipful and that Juan participated in invocations only perfunctorily, perhaps to mimic Admiral just as Bakako.

On October 28, the ships reached Cuba, and Cristóbal debarked at a river mouth to possess the territory, naming it Juana in honor of the prince. But the inhabitants fled.

Cristóbal was captivated by the territory's hills and mountains, which reminded him of Sicily, and the herbage on the beach close to the surf, indicating calm seas. He observed the palm trees had larger leaves than those in Guinea. Bakako and Yutowa explained that Cuba was an island, and Cristóbal was impressed that the river mouth could serve as an excellent port. He searched for where the Grand Khan's ships anchored to trade and suspected it was but ten days' sail to the mainland.

Following the Guanahaníans' suggestion, the ships sailed west to locate the territory's king, eventually anchoring at another river. Cristóbal named it Río de Mares (Río e Bahía de Gibara) and dispatched a launch with Bakako at the bow. Bakako called to the people ashore to announce he would land with men who were good. But the inhabitants—of a cacicazgo they called Cueiba—fled.

The sailors landed and examined the first deserted houses they reached, finding fishing gear and face masks stored within. Cristóbal had ordered that nothing be touched or taken. He wondered whether the face masks served for worship or decoration and concluded that the dwellings of the territory were of finer construction than those previously encountered, reflecting a greater civilization of the peoples closer to the Indies' mainland.

The expedition continued northwest, and Martín deduced from the Indians aboard the *Pinta* that the shore they skirted indeed was the Indies' mainland and that "Cuba" was a city lying four days' journey inland. Cristóbal and Martín conferred excitedly, Cristóbal pronouncing they were almost upon the Grand Khan and Martín countering they were abreast an enemy neighboring kingdom, at war with the Khan. Whatever, Cristóbal eagerly resolved to dispatch an embassy inland to meet the ruler at "Cuba," and the ships returned to harbor at Río de Mares. He chose Rodrigo de Xerez, who had led an embassy to meet a Guinean king, and Luis de Torres, the converso conversant in Arabic, to lead the mission. Bakako would serve as interpreter and, if one could be enlisted, a local inhabitant as guide.

Cristóbal entrusted Rodrigo and Luis with the sovereigns' letter of introduction and instructed them to search out and advise the territory's king that the Castilian sovereigns had dispatched Cristóbal's expedition to establish friendship and offer their favors. Using Bartolomé's map, he briefed them on the geography of Cathay and Mangi and directed that they ascertain the ships' present location on the mainland in relation to Quinsay and Zaiton. He cautioned Bakako to be certain the king understood Cristóbal came as representative of Fernando and Isabel, not the Grand Khan—who might be an enemy.

Bakako listened carefully to understand as much as possible. He comprehended nothing of the geography, the Grand Khan, or Castile, but he knew he was to travel for his captors into the interior of Cuba, an island, and he sensed this would be his only moment of advantage. He spoke slowly to Admiral in his bare Castilian. "You gold, we Guanahaní."

Cristóbal was startled and remembered his promise. "Yes. That's correct." He nodded affirmatively.

"No. No. I Cuba, we Guanahaní." Bakako shook his head vigorously. He studied Admiral to see if the distinction had been understood, and then repeated it slowly with hand gestures, emphasizing the word *Cuba*. "I Cuba, we Guanahaní."

Cristóbal gazed at the boy, appreciated his mettle, and recalled boyhood in the alleys of Genoa. Cristóbal was now the merchant prince on the quay, not the boy, and he took a mercantile approach—instinctively without hesitation—realizing that a second promise was no more a lie than the first, and replying, "Certainly, you will return to Guanahaní."

Prior to dispatching his embassy, Cristóbal sent men ashore at Río de Mares on November 1 to attempt again to establish relations with the inhabitants, but they fled again. Cristóbal would not be denied. He dispatched Bakako in the bow of the launch, and Bakako shouted ashore that he brought men who were good, harmed no one, and were not from the Grand Khan. Fearfully, Bakako dived overboard and swam ashore where two Cubans waited to escort him into a nearby bohío for interrogation, promising he wouldn't be harmed and soon released.

"Where are you from?"

"Guanahaní."

"Who are these beings, and why are you with them?"

"They're from the heavens, and they don't speak or understand Taíno. They appear to be spirits or men with powerful spirits. Their cacique is named Admiral. They are not Caribes, and this Admiral says he's not a cacique but the nitaíno of a cacique and a cacique wife. I don't know. They call their supreme spirits Lord, Christ, and Virgin." Bakako reflected a moment on the second question. "I'm with them to help them find gold, and they will return me to Guanahaní."

"Have they hurt you?"

"I didn't want to help them, and they beat me twice. But they haven't hurt me since, and they haven't hurt anyone we've met ashore. We've traveled to Manigua, Yuma, and Samoete, and, when they find or hear there's no gold, they just depart. Their vessels are extraordinary, and they have extraordinary weapons. They could kill many people, but they haven't—at least so far."

"What do they trade in return for gold?"

Bakako lifted the hawk's bell strung on a cotton strand about his neck. The two men studied it. They offered Bakako some cazabi and water, and Bakako's increased comfort with them brought him—urgently—to confront the questions he had so far repressed, which now overpowered him. Should he beg for their shelter and bolt into the forest? If so, could he ever return to Guanahaní?

For a moment, Bakako loathed both his terrible, impetuous decision to board Admiral's canoe at Guanahaní and his cowardice in not fleeing into the night at Manigua. He sensed these Cubans would shelter him from Admiral's chase if he ran. But dread swelled within him that their shelter—unlike the Maniguan Lucayans'—could mean servitude or worse. Even if the Cubans did treat him kindly, he doubted that he could ever find a ride on a canoe journeying to Guanahaní. He had forsaken his best chance to escape—flight now would be to the unknown, not home! Bakako suppressed the urge to plead for shelter and wanly chose to rely on Admiral's promise as the only practical hope of seeing his family again.

The Cubans questioned Bakako about other items obtainable from the pale beings and then released him. The village inhabitants who had fled returned, and, soon, canoes surrounded the ships to trade for objects from the heavens.

Cristóbal prohibited his sailors from trading for anything but gold so the inhabitants would understand the expedition sought only gold. He was disappointed that those he met lacked even gold jewelry, but he deduced from gestures that within three days merchants would arrive to trade. That night, Cristóbal related in his journal that he had arrived before the mainland between Quinsay and Zaiton, about 100 leagues distant from each other, among a people at war with the Grand Khan.

Rodrigo de Xerez, Luis de Torres, and Bakako departed inland the next morning, accompanied by a local Cuban. They walked many miles for over a day, passing through numerous small villages and fields of a crop unknown to Rodrigo and Luis, which their guide called mahisi. Bakako announced in each village that the two pale men were not of the dead but good people from the heavens, and the villagers responded by offering cazabi and water, reverential treatment, and shelter. The embassy eventually arrived at a large village of more than fifty bohíos and a thousand people (near Holguin), who received them solemnly. Its cacique hosted them in his caney and provided ornate duhos for Rodrigo and Luis to sit on, and his wives and naborias prepared a ceremonial feast. Men came forward to touch Rodrigo's and Luis's hands and feet to ascertain if flesh and bone, and women brought gifts of cotton cloth, finely carved wood, and stone jewelry. The cacique invited them to stay at least five days.

Rodrigo and Luis beheld the thousand naked people about them, showed appreciation for the courtesies, and wondered at the elaborate ceremony. But they noted there was no city and that the inhabitants appeared to lack any written word. There was no point in presenting the sovereigns' letter of introduction. Rodrigo asked Bakako to inquire of the Grand Khan and Quinsay and Zaiton, but could not discern if Bakako, no less the territory's king, knew of the Khan or these places or any geography of the Indies. After a night in the caney, Rodrigo and Luis indicated they would return to their master, whereupon the cacique decided to accompany them.

As he waited return of the embassy, Cristóbal ordered each ship careened, with two ships always left afloat for security from the Indians. He sighted the polestar and, regardless of the considerable voyage south from San Salvador, recorded in the journal that the fleet was at a latitude of 42 degrees north, not only north of Hierro but north of Lisbon. He explored in the launch with Yutowa and deduced from gestures and conversations with inhabitants that a great quantity of gold and pearls could be obtained to the southeast on the island of Bohío, where apparently there were ports with large ships and merchandise. He also inferred that there was a people who lived far away who had but a single eye or a dog's snout and ate men, drank their blood, and cut off their genitals. He recorded in his journal that the land was most fertile, producing yams (sweet potato or yucca), plentiful cotton, and thousands of fruits that would be profitable.

The crews had more time for casual contact with the inhabitants than on islands previously visited. Sailors learned how the inhabitants rolled dry leaves into a short tube that they lit to inhale the smoldering fire's smoke, alleviating tiredness. Some Cuban women's fear that the pale beings were of the dead or other spirits receded, and a few accommodated and enjoyed the sailors' lust for them. The sailors were humored that neither payment nor marriage was expected.

Cristóbal didn't interfere, reflecting not only that it was the universal habit of sailors but that it appeared consensual and not an impediment to his trade or future subjugation. He didn't discuss it in the journal as inappropriate to relate to the queen.

The embassy returned late on November 5. Rodrigo and Luis reported that the territory's king had warmly received the sovereigns' salutation and his people harvested great quantities of cotton all year-round and possessed fertile lands for crops and many fruits and herbs. But the king and his peoples were poor and there was no city. Undaunted, Cristóbal hosted the king and his party for dinner aboard one of the ships, accorded him great honor, and invited him to stay aboard for the night. Cristóbal also offered that the king return to Castile to meet King Fernando and Queen Isabel. The cacique cordially enjoyed dinner but, after hearing the invitation to meet Admiral's caciques, asked to be put ashore and didn't return.

Cristóbal had spent almost ten years convincing a sovereign to underwrite his ships, and the failure to readily locate Quinsay and Zaiton did not diminish or alter his resolve to find them. His faith that the Lord had destined him to reach the Indies was unshakable, and he reflected on the journey's greater purpose in the journal that night, expressly addressing his sovereigns. He wrote he was convinced the inhabitants of the lands possessed would become Christian as soon as missionaries spoke their language. He trusted that the sovereigns would bring this large nation to Christianity, just as they had destroyed heresy and evil.

Cristóbal decided that captives should be taken from the mainland near Río de Mares because their homeland was better suited for future colonization than the islands visited to the north. They would be taken to Castile for training in language, faith, and custom so they might be resettled in Juana, much as the Portuguese had done with Guineans in their trading posts. He decided to capture women as well as men, believing the Indian men would be less likely to flee on resettlement in Juana if they had their women and that the Indian women would teach Castilian men and women their language.

On November 11, Cristóbal ordered the seizure of five young men who had come aboard the *Santa María*. Bakako watched with utter surprise, fright, and remorse, recalling his assurances of safety days before. The Cubans shouted to Bakako, pleading to know what was happening and why he had led them to this. Soon, they disparaged him, and Bakako was ashamed to be among them.

Shortly, Cristóbal dispatched armed sailors ashore. They captured seven head of women and three small children, who timorously greeted them at the door of their bohío. The women and children were hauled aboard the *Santa María* and made available to the Cuban men just captured. Bakako was astonished and ashamed again—some of the women were already married. One of their husbands—and the father of the children—canoed to the *Santa María* and begged to be allowed aboard to reunite with his family. Cristóbal consented. Bakako implored Yúcahu to understand that he had no role in this.

Cristóbal recounted in his journal that the natives lacked religion, did not know evil, and believed the Christians came from the heavens. He observed that, unlike in Guinea, the Indians all spoke one language, and reflected to himself that this would facilitate subjugation. Remembering Scio, he promised the territory's cotton easily could be sold in the great cities of the Grand Khan to be discovered without sending it to Spain, together with commodities from Spain and Eastern lands—which now lay to his west.

Bakako found a spot below the lantern at the stern to hide and lie for the night. He reflected that Admiral's courtesies and charities belied ruthless oppressions. He heard the Cuban women and children crying and the men murmuring plans to escape and grimly pondered that they hadn't been seized to serve as guides or interpreters but to return with Admiral beyond the horizon. He invoked Yúcahu again to ask what dreadful event would next follow, whether the Cubans' fate foretold his own, and if he would ever see Kamana again to take her as wife. Clouds then shrouded the moon, and it began to rain.

EAST TO BANEQUE (GREAT IGUANA ISLAND?),
November 12–22, 1492

Promptly following the Cuban captives' seizure, the three ships sailed east to find Baneque (Great Iguana Island), which Bakako indicated was three days' journey by canoe. A Guanahanían captive aboard the *Pinta* had assured Martín that Baneque possessed much gold, and, regardless of the failure of prior assurances, Martín was so convinced. Cristóbal and Martín now believed Bohío would prove to be Cipangu but agreed Baneque should be investigated first.

November 14 brought contrary winds and then high seas, impeding reaching Baneque. Cristóbal diverted along the Cuban coast and discovered a large bay (Bahía Sagua de Tamano) with many islands, which he concluded were the islands sometimes depicted on world maps at terra firma's eastern edge. He decided to evaluate the region's commercial potential for a few days, delaying the exploration for Baneque. Martín considered the decision foolish because Juana hadn't yielded gold, and his pride rankled as he submitted to it despite Colón's inferiority as a captain.

Cristóbal set about his evaluation and the inhabitants fled. He discovered mastic and aloes, ordered the Guanahaníans to dive for pearls, and envisaged a site for a fort if profitable trade developed. He directed his crews to construct a large wooden cross to mark the new possession, as had become his custom as the voyage continued. He completed his evaluation by November 18, but did not sail to Baneque that day as it was Sunday, and he preferred to worship on Sundays rather than explore.

Martín's impatience with the delay to Baneque's exploration swelled, aggravating his contempt for Colón's conduct of the voyage. He fumed that he and his crews had risked their lives on the promise of gold and that the extended time Colón spent planning Juana's future subjugation and commerce—in the absence of gold—was predictably selfish and Genoese, as its benefits would inure only to the sovereigns and Colón.

On November 19, Cristóbal at last directed that the fleet sail east toward Baneque. But the wind was easterly and the seas high by the next day, and he again determined that Baneque wasn't attainable. He considered withdrawing north to the island of Isabela but feared its proximity to San Salvador and that, if taken there, Bakako, Yutowa, and the other Guanahaníans would jump ship. Two of the Cuban men already had done so. Cristóbal chose to withdraw back to Cuba. Martín raged.

Two days later, Cristóbal sailed for Baneque yet again, and gave up yet again when the wind shifted. After midnight, the wind veered to allow passage, but he continued toward Cuba regardless, the *Santa María*'s lanterns burning so the *Pinta* and *Niña* would follow.

Martín exploded. He was as certain of Baneque's gold as he had been that sailing southwest would achieve landfall. Neither Colón nor the sovereigns' representatives could stop him and his crew from trading for their private stores of gold if he continued to Baneque alone. Furious, he weighed this opportunity against the crime of desertion, his thoughts racing through the injustices he had suffered and the excuses available. The Genoese manically viewed every achievement of the voyage as conferred by the Lord on him alone and would credit himself alone to the sovereigns—regardless of his promise to recognize Martín's contribution!

Quickly, Martín convinced himself he had the right—as his ship's captain and recruiter of the crews—to direct the *Pinta*'s voyage to achieve the ends for which he and his crews had sailed when consistent with the sovereigns' objectives. And he relished that when he obtained the gold on Baneque he would confront Colón from a position of strength! With the gold in hand, none of the crews from Palos, Huelva, and Moger would testify that he had deserted the Genoese.

Martín also reflected that the sovereigns might not accept his excuses and that he could be hanged.

Martín felt the favorable breeze quicken and made his decision, ordering the *Pinta*'s crew to spin the ship east to Baneque. The crew was shocked at their captain's disobedience and feared they would be held accountable. But they understood the objective, disdained the Genoese, respected and adored their captain, and followed his order.

Cristóbal and Pero Alonso eventually understood the *Pinta*'s diversion, and ordered the *Santa María*'s crew to raise additional lanterns signaling that Martín redirect south. With relief, they recognized the *Niña* continued southward.

The crews of the *Santa María* and the *Niña* watched the *Pinta* vanish from the horizon on November 22 and realized Martín had deserted, an offense meriting the severest punishment in any fleet or navy. Cristóbal was mortified beyond expression before all. His command had been openly disobeyed by his first-ranking officer and the man singularly responsible for recruiting most of the crews. The disloyalty encouraged the disloyalty of the crews of the *Santa María* and *Niña*.

Cristóbal hid his rage and anxiety, recoiled from acknowledging the disloyalty, and let on to the crews of the *Santa María* and
Niña that he didn't know whether Martín had mistakenly continued
to Baneque as originally planned. He appreciated that Vicente and
the *Niña* remained with him and that it was essential to retain this
loyalty, if it be that.

Vicente understood Martín's rage and rationale. He felt all
eyes upon him and, like Colón, publicly assumed that Martín had
misunderstood the signals. Vicente anguished that Martín's rash
confidence of Baneque's gold might lead to the entire family's miser-
able dishonor.

Sailors on the *Santa María* and *Niña* were dumfounded and
frightened. Both Cristóbal and Martín believed Cipangu near. While
the voyage had not yet achieved the gold or civilization promised,
its ambition remained intact and worthy. They were far distant from
home—to their knowledge, as far over the Ocean Sea as men had
ever been—and three ships provided comfort if misfortune took one.
Two ships provided the narrowest resort.

The sovereigns' representatives huddled among themselves.
They weren't surprised that a captain from Palos and his crew were
disloyal to the Crown, and they knew the sovereigns would deal
with it severely. They suspected the Pinzóns hoped to demonstrate by
Vicente's loyalty that the family continued to support Colón as necessary, and they agreed that would hardly merit leniency for Martín.
His greed and jealous conceit had jeopardized the voyage's safety,
regardless of the merits of Colón's command.

Cristóbal's domestic, page, and servant watched their master and
were moved by his discipline to forbear insult, withhold rage, and
confront adversity, and knew it born of a long familiarity with all
three. His fortitude to venture entirely alone was astonishing, as he
dissembled even to them the cause of Martín's disappearance.

Bakako watched and understood that the pale beings had friends
and enemies among themselves, just as Lucayans did. Bakako had
now lived with them for over a month and witnessed them eat, drink,
sleep, laugh, disagree, and argue like Lucayans. While he hadn't seen
one die, Bakako now understood they lived far more like men than
spirits.

EAST TO BARACOA,
November 23–December 5, 1492

The *Santa María* and *Niña* returned to Cuba near Puerto del Príncipe, and Cristóbal explored for two days. On November 26, the ships sailed east to attempt Baneque again, as well as toward Bohío, which the Indians said lay beyond Cuba's eastern tip. Cristóbal studied Cuba's coastline trail southeast into the horizon and summoned Pero Alonso, Bakako, and Yutowa to discuss Bohío's exploration. He asked, "Where do we sail for gold on Bohío?"

Bakako spoke in Taíno, for Yutowa alone. "I'll try to dissuade him again."

Bakako addressed Admiral in broken Castilian, accompanied by gestures. "We not know. More gold Baneque. Bohío people bad. Enemy Lucayans."

Cristóbal remembered the wounds he had seen on Guanahaníans. "People on Bohío harm Lucayans?"

"Bohío people Canibas. Same Caribes. One eye. Take Lucayans. Eat Lucayans."

"'Canibas'? You say 'Canibas'? Are they people of the Grand Khan?"

"I no know," Bakako replied, shrugging his shoulders, bewildered to be asked constantly of the Grand Khan.

Cristóbal gleaned elatedly that "Caniba" sounded to him like "Grand Khan." He summoned the sovereigns' representatives to listen to the conversation, to hear the word spoken by Bakako. "How do you know the 'Canibas' have one eye?" Cristóbal pointed to Bakako. "Have you—Bakako—seen 'Canibas'?"

The question surprised Bakako. "No."

"How do you know the Canibas eat Lucayans?"

"Canibas take Lucayans. Lucayans no home."

"Have you—Bakako—seen them eat Lucayans?"

"No," Bakako countered. "Bakako eaten see Lucayans eaten."

Cristóbal nodded he understood but continued. "Do Canibas take Lucayans to do work, to be servants or slaves?" Cristóbal pointed to Juan Portugués.

Bakako didn't know the Castilian words *servants* or *slaves*, but surmised Admiral's inquiry nevertheless. Bakako now realized that, in Admiral's tongue, Bakako was a "servant" or "slave." He replied, "Canibas eat Lucayans."

Cristóbal proudly turned to Pero Alonso and the sovereigns' representatives. "The Canibas must be subjects or soldiers of the Grand Khan who enslave Lucayans."

Bakako sought to make a practical point. "Bakako Yutowa no talk Canibas Admiral Christians good. Canibas eat Bakako Yutowa. Yes gold Baneque. No gold Bohío."

Cristóbal suspected Bakako was lying, seeking to convince him to sail to Baneque simply because it was significantly closer to Guanahaní.

The *Santa María* and *Niña* continued southeast along the Cuban coastline, and Cristóbal observed a number of large rivers and potential harbors he felt worthy for colonization. On November 27, they entered one of them to explore, and a multitude of inhabitants came to the shore. As the ships approached, the inhabitants shouted, raised their spears, and gestured that the visitors should depart. Bakako explained to Admiral as best he could that the Cubans thought Admiral's men were Canibas and would attack if an embassy disembarked. Regardless, Cristóbal sought to establish peaceful trading relations and, suspecting Bakako and Yutowa would flee if sent ashore, dispatched armed sailors instead. The inhabitants fled. Cristóbal departed and continued farther east to discover another harbor before sunset. But its inhabitants—who referred to their cacicazgo as Baracoa—also fled.

That night, Cristóbal reflected on the beneficence and severity of the Lord. While there had been obstacles that tested his faith, he appreciated that the Lord had shown mercy on the voyage often. The crews of the *Santa María* and *Niña* remained loyal despite Martín's desertion and, while gold remained elusive, they had been spared the debilitating disease and death experienced by the garrison at Mina. In his journal, he recorded that the rivers of Juana—unlike of Guinea—were safe to drink and that, thanks to God, none of his crew had become sick on the entire voyage except for one preexisting condition. He promised his sovereigns Juana would hold infinite things of great profit and that they would have cities built for traffic with all of Christendom, convert the natives to the faith, and restrict admission to the territory to Christians.

⊡ ⊡ ⊡

For the next week, the *Santa María* and *Niña* took refuge in Baracoa from rain, thunder, and strong winds, and Cristóbal named the site Puerto Santo. Sailors explored nearby villages, and, when the inhabitants fled, investigated the deserted bohíos to find heads of men in baskets suspended from house posts. Many believed this confirmed the Indian captives' assertion that there were men who ate men. Cristóbal believed otherwise and, in his journal, explained that the heads were of some family founder or venerated ancestor.

On a Sunday, Cristóbal asked his page Pedro to gather the Cubans aboard the *Santa María* to be taught the Lord's Prayer. Bakako and Yutowa could recite it already, and Cristóbal felt it was time to teach Bakako the meaning. Pedro gathered the Indians to sit on the main deck, where a small cross portraying the crucifixion was set on a table before them, along with Cristóbal's own small statuette of the Virgin. Cristóbal asked for a volunteer among the crew to lead the instruction, and an older sailor was honored to do so. Cristóbal climbed to the stern deck to watch, together with his servants and the Crown representatives, as dark thunderheads marched west in the sky.

The sailor pronounced in Castilian that there was one God, the Lord, and gazed and pointed to Heaven. He explained the Lord had a son, Christ, and pointed to his image upon the small cross, which depicted blood oozing from wounds on his hands, ankles, and chest. The sailor concluded that Christ was the son of God born of the Virgin Mary, and he raised the statuette of the Virgin holding the baby Jesus. He glanced at Cristóbal to ascertain whether more should be said, and Cristóbal thanked him.

The Cubans grimly studied the cemí of the human being, frightened that it foretold their future. It depicted a man almost naked, more like themselves than their captors. His forlorn countenance and wounds were ominous, and it was obvious he was dying. Their captors' invocation of it portended doom.

Bakako studied the cemís carefully, having observed them in Admiral's cabin and heard Admiral invoking them. Bakako remembered

Yúcahu and Attabeira and puzzled whether Admiral's spirits were as kindly and helpful.

Cristóbal and the sovereigns' representatives were impressed by the apparent eagerness of the Indians to understand. Cristóbal's servant Juan pretended to listen, as he knew Cristóbal expected his devotion.

Cristóbal addressed Pedro and Bakako from the stern deck. "Now, together, teach these Indians the Lord's Prayer, as Christ taught upon the mountain to his disciples. Speak slowly. I will explain."

The two youths began slowly in Castilian. "Our father in Heaven, hallowed be thy name."

Cristóbal interrupted, addressing all the Indians, but particularly Bakako. "There is one and only one true God."

Bakako understood that false but hid any reaction. The youths continued. "Your kingdom come, your will be done, on earth as it is in Heaven."

Cristóbal spoke directly to Bakako. "Christ died on the cross for men's sins. He rose on the third day to instruct his eleven apostles to teach all nations his Word. Christ will return to his kingdom on earth a second time. The world will then end, and Christ will reign on earth, which will be transformed into Heaven."

Bakako was confused whether the Christ spirit was friendly or vengeful. He couldn't understand how the spirit revealed guidance or helped its worshipper navigate life. The youths continued. "Give us this day our daily bread, and forgive us our debts, as we also have forgiven our debtors."

Cristóbal continued to gaze directly at Bakako. "Follow the Lord's word, and the Lord shall provide for you. If you forgive men their trespasses, the Lord will forgive your own."

Bakako guessed that Christ provided bread to those who honored him. He recalled Mother and Father teaching him to honor Yúcahu for the cazabi they ate. The youths finished. "And lead us not into temptation, but deliver us from evil."

Cristóbal paused on the concepts involved—leadership and deliverance, temptation and evil—and simplified. "Follow the Lord and do good."

Bakako concealed astonishment that his captor thought himself good. Bakako gazed at the cemí of the bloody man, nearly as naked as Lucayans, and trembled to consider how powerful it might be, either for good or evil.

When the lesson finished, the crew met for the Sabbath's hymn and prayer. They sang "Gloria in Excelsis Deo," a ship's boy recited a psalm, and Pedro and Bakako led the crew in the Lord's Prayer. The Cubans were comforted by the areíto, which sounded beneficent and merciful, but understood nothing of its meaning. Cristóbal and the sovereigns' representatives perceived that the Indians appeared ready to accept the Lord as their one true God.

▣ ▣ ▣

That night, Bakako and Yutowa whispered late into the moonlight, debating if the "Christians" worshipped their Christ as an ancestor and whether Christ had been sacrificed in a ritual, with or without his consent, or simply murdered by others. They were confounded.

Not only might the pale men also be spirits, but their spirit Christ was also a man who couldn't be killed permanently.

The next day, Cristóbal, Yutowa, and some armed sailors went exploring up a river in the launch. Cristóbal was impressed that the entire region was cultivated. They climbed a mountain to discover a large village surrounded by crops on a plateau. Its inhabitants fled, but Yutowa beckoned, promising that the Christians were good. Some villagers reappeared. Cristóbal enticed them with trifles, whereupon more reappeared. But gold was not found.

When the sailors returned to the launch, one of the villagers came to its stern, blocking its departure, and addressed Cristóbal at length. The villager raised his voice, others surrounded the boat, waving their hands and spears and shouting. Cristóbal and his crew were surprised, but not alarmed. Yutowa understood the Cubans intended to kill Admiral and the crew.

Yutowa paled and trembled, terrified by the immanent prospect of mortal violence—which was entirely beyond his life's experiences on Guanahaní, or his expectations for human conduct. He grew breathless, paralyzed by the momentous predicament whether to risk his life to save his captor's. For an instant, he succumbed to fear that his only hope to return to Guanahaní lay with Admiral and Admiral's survival. If he stood aside to watch Admiral slain, the Cubans might take him as a captive or naboria or simply kill him, as well. If he defended Admiral, the Cubans certainly would kill him. But, in the next moment, a harmony and brotherhood with the Cubans surged defiantly through him—a compassion for their fear of the pale beings trespassing upon their land, a revulsion toward Admiral's deception and brutality, and a fear that Admiral's men, although severely outnumbered, would slaughter them.

Regardless—beyond these conscious, conflicting thoughts and feelings—the Taíno within him abhorred senseless violence, and Yutowa instinctively stepped forward and spoke to the crowd. He pointed to a crossbow, pulled a sword from a sheath, and warned the Cubans that the weapons could kill them all, and the villagers were frightened and retreated upstream. Yutowa gazed to Admiral, expecting kind words, relieved that bloodshed and death had been adverted on both sides, and stunned by his own pivotal urge to intervene.

To Yutowa's amazement, Admiral then insisted—yet dismissive of the danger about—that peaceful relations be reestablished to facilitate future colonization and commanded that the launch approach the villagers cautiously. Admiral offered soft words and trifles, and trade ensued peacefully. Yutowa's fear melted to bewilderment at the slender proximity of tranquility and violence.

Cristóbal recorded in his journal the Indians were so timid that ten Christians could cause ten thousand Indians to flee. He reflected that Yutowa had trembled like a coward.

As Cristóbal wrote, Bakako and Yutowa lay together on deck, discussing how Yutowa had saved Admiral's life. Yutowa was astounded Admiral and his crew had not appreciated their danger. Bakako was astounded Admiral had not thanked Yutowa. Both were astonished with how little regard the pale men held Lucayan and Cuban weaponry. Both believed Yutowa had acted as a Taíno. Both grimly pondered whether Yutowa simply should have stepped aside to watch.

On the morning of December 5, the *Santa María* and *Niña* reached a point where the Cuban shore turned south and then west (Punta de Maisí). Bakako and Yutowa grimly overheard Admiral and Pero Alonso conclude the northeasterly wind again precluded sailing northeast to Baneque and set a course southeast instead (across the Windward Passage), destined for the island the youths feared and called Bohío and its inhabitants called Haiti. Soon, Cristóbal also became disillusioned, as Bohío quickly came into sight and he realized Bohío could not be Cipangu—which lay much farther offshore from the Indies' mainland than Bohío lay from Cuba.

BARCELONA,
December 1492

Isabel and Fernando had departed Grenada with their children over the summer and brought the court to Barcelona for the winter. They received word that Colón's departure west from Gomera occurred in early September, a surprising delay given his departure from Andalusia in early August. If the Indies were but a few weeks' sail, he might have arrived there. But it didn't surprise them to have heard nothing of it. It was still too early for reports, and they had scant expectation he would arrive there anyway. The demands of ruling their kingdoms relegated the voyage to but an infrequent, fleeting afterthought until December 7, 1492, when they forgot about it entirely.

That morning, an assassin awaited Fernando outside the Casa de Deputacion, where he was hearing grievances and resolving criminal and civil cases of his common subjects. At noon, Fernando finished and, as he descended the casa's steps to the Plaza of Kings, the assassin crept from behind and attacked with a knife, gashing him deeply in the neck and shoulder. The blade would have penetrated further but for Fernando's gold neck chain. He fell to the ground, bleeding profusely and likely mortally wounded.

As the king hemorrhaged, his advisers and subjects mobbed the assailant, stabbing him repeatedly and tearing his limbs to mutilate him, intent on lynching him to death. Fernando fought to retain consciousness, groaning that the assailant's life be spared for an interrogation to identify conspirators. Fernando was obeyed, and the lynching ceased as advisers carried Fernando inside to be saved by doctors or die.

Isabel immediately suspected Catalan dissidents or French agents and ordered soldiers to guard the royal family and prepare ships in case evacuation was necessary. She rushed to the bed where Fernando lay and prayed for him, and she ordered Barcelona's priests to lead her subjects in prayer, as well. Barcelonans assumed with remorse that the assailant was Catalan, and they filled their churches to pray for the king—as well as his and the queen's mercy.

Fernando's condition quickly worsened. Doctors removed cartilage from the wound in a painful operation, and he grew feverish. But he did not lose appreciation of the situation.

The assailant's interrogation revealed he was an elderly Catalan peasant who believed himself the rightful king of Aragón and entitled to kill Fernando. The interrogators found him lunatic and that he had acted alone, and Catalans everywhere felt tremendous relief that reprisals were not due. Fernando publicly attributed the wound as punishment for his own sins and recommended leniency.

The royal council promptly sentenced the assailant to a gruesome public death. The hand that caused the offense was dismembered, the heart and other body parts that assisted the crime were plucked with red-hot pincers, and the onlookers finished the punishment by stoning and burning what remained. It was reported that the queen felt the lunatic deserved mercy and ordered that he be strangled first. Fernando and Isabel were satisfied that the punishment and spectacle were appropriate warning to deter others.

Isabel nursed her husband for days and contemplated mortality, including her own and others. She was forty-one and Fernando forty. Pope Innocent VIII had died in July and Rodrigo Ponce de León and Enrique Guzmán in August. The abrupt turn in the Lord's destiny for her and her husband was shocking. The year 1492 had brought the crowning achievements for which they faithfully had served him, the Reconquista's fulfillment and the expulsion of the Jews. She anguished as to his purpose in their punishment, vexed whether there were important confessions for her to make and restitutions and satisfactions owed others, and wrote Talavera asking that he identify them.

Fernando's fever subsided, and he began to recover. Throughout the kingdom, word was disseminated that the devil had sought to end the king's Christian service and that the Lord had let the act occur to demonstrate the king's indefatigability.

X

HAITI

UNKNOWN ARRIVES ON HAITI (BOHÍO),
Late November–Mid-December 1492

After deserting Colón, the *Pinta* sailed to Baneque, and Martín's certitude and ambition were dashed as he beheld an island much as San Salvador—and certainly not Cipangu. There was no port teeming with ships, the inhabitants were as naked and poor as on San Salvador, and the only gold obtained was earrings and nose rings. Sailors chafed that their participation in Martín's desertion had been for naught.

Martín soon sailed southeast for Bohío, predicting it would be the Cipangu Colón promised. Progress east was slow, hampered by inclement weather and strong contrary winds, but the *Pinta* was a nimble sailor and achieved Bohío's central northern coast in December. There were few harbors sheltered from the winds—none teeming with ships—and the inhabitants fled when the *Pinta* could anchor and the crew debarked. But Martín's confidence resurged—Bohío was enormous and, in the absence of Colón and the sovereigns' representatives, he established that half the gold the *Pinta* obtained would be his, the remainder split among the crew.

Guarionex was at home when a messenger arrived on behalf of a local cacique to alert that unknown pale beings had landed at the cacique's village on the northern coast, borne in a gargantuan

sea creature. The cacique wished Guarionex to understand that the
beings did not appear to be Caribes but spirits or extraordinarily
large dead men, with pale skin wrapped in cloth almost entirely
but for their heads, chests, and hands. Confounding the mystery,
the beings were accompanied by a Lucayan, who shouted that they
came from the heavens beyond the horizon and wished only to trade
for gold. The cacique's subjects had fled, and the beings had then
rummaged through his village to loot the bohíos of gold pieces and
jewelry. But they had not sought to capture women or girls and, after
their pillage, simply returned to their creature and departed east.

Guarionex respected the judgment that spirits might be involved,
not Caribes, and, after conferring with his council, dispatched his son
Yomabo with nitaínos and warriors. He instructed Yomabo to kill
the beings if Caribes and, if not, to study them and establish a trading relationship if it seemed advantageous, whereupon Guarionex
would meet them. Guarionex also sent a messenger to Mayobanex,
warning of the strange beings traveling east and cautioning against
using force because they likely were spirits, not men. Reverence to
achieve their assistance or forbearance might be wise—particularly
if they were evil.

Behecchio and Caonabó soon received word from informants of
unknown beings seeking gold and Guarionex's plans to meet them,
and Behecchio quickly dispatched his own embassy of nitaínos to
the coast. He urged caution and reminded them that, if the beings
sought peaceful trade, the paramount status of Xaraguá should be
acknowledged and the trade secured for it. Caonabó appreciated
that Haiti's gold lay principally in the mountains and streams of the
Cibao separating Maguana and Magua and, after consulting Anacaona, dispatched nitaínos to meet the beings and identify the opportunities and the dangers presented—including the beings' intent in
visiting Haiti.

By mid-December, the *Pinta* anchored in one of the few natural harbors found (Bahía de Luperón, Dominican Republic), a small
inlet about ten miles east of the river Bajabonico in territory bordering Marien, Magua, and Ciguayo. Martín observed that the hillsides
sloping to the shores of the inlet were fertile and populated, and he
dispatched his Guanahanían captive ashore to advise the inhabitants

that he and his men came from Heaven in peace to trade for gold. The captive feared the inhabitants were Caniba and was barely comforted by his escort of armed sailors. But the inhabitants fled.

Undaunted, Martín decided to harbor in the inlet to restock the *Pinta* and explore, hoping the inhabitants would soon return. A small river provided the inlet fresh water, and Martín named it and the harbor the Río e Puerto de Martín Alonso Pinzón.

Río e Puerto de Martín Alonso Pinzón, 1592.

CRISTÓBAL'S FIRST ENCOUNTERS IN MARIEN
(Mole St. Nicolas to Baie de l'Acul, Haiti), December 5–22, 1492

The *Santa María* and *Niña* attained the northwestern tip of Bohío before sunset on December 5 and, the following day, explored an enormous bay nestled in a cultivated valley fertile with crops and fruit trees. It was the day of St. Nicholas's feast, and Cristóbal named the site for the saint. They encountered canoeists who fled. Onshore, the inhabitants fled and fired smoke signals inland to warn of invaders from another world.

While impressed with the land's cultivation, Cristóbal wanly admitted to himself that there was no city filled with temples and lost confidence that Bakako and the other captives knew enough—or were honest enough—to lead him to Cipangu rather than back to San Salvador. Cristóbal questioned Bakako about Bohío again.

Bakako reaffirmed the Caniba lived on Bohío and that they would kill and eat Yutowa and himself if they went ashore. He remained unable to confirm that a Grand Khan lived nearby. He grew increasingly distrustful that Admiral ever intended to return Yutowa and himself home.

On December 7, the ships sailed east along Bohío's northern coastline and anchored to harbor for a week in a bay southwest of a large offshore island. Cristóbal named the bay Puerto de la Concepción (Baie de Moustiques), as it was the vigil before the feast of the Virgin's Conception, and the island Tortuga (Turtle), and commenced Bohío's exploration.

In his journal, he compared Bohío's farmlands, mountains, and valleys to those of Castile and Bohío's temperate but cool weather to Castile in October. He observed that the fish, plants, and birds were like those of Castile. He decided Bohío was suited to colonization on a grand scale and possessed it on behalf of the sovereigns with the name La Isla Española (the Spanish Island), or simply Española.

☒   ☒   ☒

Española's inhabitants continued to flee at each encounter, precluding trading for gold or locating its source. Frustrated, Cristóbal ordered sailors to capture an inhabitant to whom he could confer courtesies and gifts to demonstrate good intentions, and they chased some locals through the forest to seize a young woman wearing only a gold nosepiece and nagua. She shrieked and struggled in terror as they hauled her into the launch and rowed toward the *Santa María*, petrified she was to be raped and enslaved or eaten by unknown Caribes or the vessel itself. The sailors' lust was aroused by her nakedness, and they groped her privates under the guise of restraining her, ripping off her nagua as she resisted. But they crudely understood to withhold from raping or beating her, as Cristóbal's intent was to treat her as an invited guest to be made an ambassador for him among her own people.

The woman was hauled to stand trembling before Cristóbal.

He asked Bakako to comfort her, and she was shocked to behold a boy with olive skin standing naked as herself. Her panic and wailing gradually subsided as she resigned herself to learn her fate.

Bakako spoke softly in Taíno. "What's your name?"

With supreme effort, the woman gathered herself and responded. "Bawana."

"Bawana, don't be scared. You won't be harmed. I'm Bakako. These men have come from the heavens in peace." He sought her confidence. "Bawana, these men don't understand our speech. You can speak freely with me."

Bawana doubted. "Where are you from?"

"Guanahaní, to the north. I'm helping these men find gold. They are good and won't harm you." Bakako pointed to Admiral. "This man is Admiral, and he is their cacique. He will give you gifts."

"Why are you with them?"

"They seek gold." Bakako searched for a credible explanation that would not terrify the woman. "When they find it, I'll be returned to Guanahaní." He wondered how sincere he appeared.

"Daka tiyawo [I am friend]," Cristóbal said, greeting the woman in Taíno. He reverted to Castilian. "I have come on behalf of King Fernando and Queen Isabel of Castile in peace." He touched the gold piece in her nose. "I want to trade for your people's gold."

Bakako translated. "They have come from the heavens in peace. They'll give your people gifts from the heavens in return for gold."

Cristóbal asked Rodrigo Sánchez for a glass bead necklace and then advanced to the woman and gently placed it about her neck. He smiled and stood back, studying her reaction. He remembered Beatriz, Diego, and little Fernando in Córdoba and reflected that the woman appeared closer in age to Diego or Bakako than Beatriz.

Bakako explained. "That's for you—a necklace from the heavens."

Cristóbal requested that Sánchez retrieve a shirt intended for trade at the Grand Khan's court and that Bakako dress the woman.

"Here's cloth to wear," Bakako said. "These men view covering one's body as good, and you should understand that they give it to please you, and for no other reason. It's not a trick, and it won't harm you to wear it, at least to show them you've received it."

Bawana submitted to donning the shirt, embarrassed to conceal her beauty and apprehensive she exhibited a shame she did not feel.

Cristóbal directed that Bawana be given a tour of the *Santa María* and offered food and water. She met and spoke with the Cuban women, who related that they had been held captive by the pale beings for a month and still did not understand their fate. They warned her that the pale beings' lust and evil intent were obvious, and, while they had not been raped or molested, it was simply because the cacique Admiral prohibited misconduct so he could trade for gold. After Bawana appeared to have calmed, Cristóbal ordered Bakako and sailors to restore her to her village. To her surprise, they released her ashore clothed but unharmed.

The next morning, Cristóbal directed Bakako to escort armed sailors to learn if the woman had convinced her people it was safe to meet. Bakako winced in despair, utterly perplexed by his predicament. He was the captive of pale men from the heavens who had dispatched him against his will as their own ambassador to a village of Caniba, who otherwise—but for the pale men's presence—would eat or enslave him.

As he approached the village, Bakako saw the inhabitants preparing to flee. Trembling, he asked the sailors to halt while he approached alone. He shouted in Taíno.

"Please, don't run. The men who took Bawana didn't harm her. They gave her gifts of friendship, and they want your friendship. They come from the heavens and will give you gifts from the heavens. They simply want to trade for your gold jewelry and whatever gold you possess. They will treat you as kindly as they did Bawana."

The villagers stared at Bakako and, in the distance, the pale, clothed beings from another world. Bakako sensed he could prevail.

"You all will receive gifts. No one will be harmed. You'll behold and touch men from the heavens and meet their cacique."

More than two thousand villagers soon decided to trust Bakako and return to their village to meet the sailors. Bawana's husband came to express thanks for her gifts. Bawana then appeared, borne by villagers on their shoulders. Bakako saw she was naked again, but for her gold nosepiece, a nagua, and Admiral's necklace. The villagers offered the sailors water, cazabi, and fruit, as well as parrots, asking nothing in return, and the sailors gave them trifles. Some villagers placed their hands atop the sailors' heads to express admiration. But the gold the sailors procured was limited to small pieces of jewelry.

Cristóbal was pleased with this contact but disappointed with the meager gold obtained, and he concluded the limited gold on Española was imported from elsewhere, probably from mines on Baneque. He remained impressed by the sophistication and civility of the peoples met and convinced that Española was ideal for colonization.

⊡　⊡　⊡

The *Santa María* and *Niña* tacked by moonlight east through the channel between La Española and Tortuga in fierce winds, fortuitously picking up a canoeist traveling in the rough waters mid-channel on the morning of December 16. Cristóbal pacified him with gifts and deposited him like Bawana at a beach on La Española to spread goodwill.

More than five hundred inhabitants soon filled the beach, and some swam or canoed to the *Santa María* and freely gave their gold earrings and nose rings to Cristóbal. The inhabitants' cacique arrived on the beach, accompanied by numerous attendants, and Cristóbal, Bakako, and Diego de Arana took the launch to meet him. Cristóbal found him young—perhaps twenty-one years old—and the most sophisticated ruler he yet had met. Bakako explained that the pale men thought gold could be found on Baneque and the cacique agreed and indicated the route there.

Cristóbal invited the young ruler and his attendants for a Spanish dinner aboard the *Santa María*. The cacique carefully tasted morsels of stale hardtack and smoked, dried meat and sipped the Andalusian wine, and then passed them to his nitaínos for their sampling.

"I have come from Castile in Europe as representative of its King Fernando and Queen Isabel," Cristóbal said. "They are the greatest Christians sovereigns in Europe and the world."

Bakako had heard Admiral speak of his paramount caciques and was convinced of their existence, but he still could not understand where Castile was, although the Cubans were bound for it. He summarized the intent of Admiral's remark to the extent he understood it. "These men refer to their cacique as Admiral. Admiral says he himself answers to a paramount cacique and a wife cacique. Admiral says he has come from Castile across the water, where the two caciques live."

The cacique and his nitaínos were astounded in disbelief. The cacique turned to Bakako. "Are you sure you understand him? His caciques must live in the heavens beyond the horizon. What land is he referring to? How far away?"

Bakako turned to Admiral and asked the questions on behalf of the cacique, which were the same questions that still mystified him. "Fernando Isabel heavens? Fernando Isabel Castile? Bohío Castile canoa?"

Cristóbal was not surprised by the cacique's questions but that Bakako still was unable to answer them. He had explained to Bakako many times that the Christians did not come from Heaven—as he believed the Indians imagined—but from land across the Ocean Sea. He turned to Bakako.

"Guanahaní and Bohío are in the Indies. Castile—where King Fernando and Queen Isabel live—is in Europe, across the ocean. Castile is land, not Heaven. Christ the Lord is in Heaven. Fernando and Isabel are on earth."

Bakako turned to the cacique and his nitaínos. "Admiral says he comes from Castile, which is another land beyond the horizon. He says he and his caciques live in Castile—a land called Castile."

Bakako looked to the deck, and Cristóbal and the cacique and their respective advisers were silent and crestfallen, frustrated by their mutual inability to communicate. Bakako and the cacique could not decipher where Admiral and his pale beings fit within the world and its history, and the references to Cipangu and the Indies were bewildering. Cristóbal was certain he had arrived at islands offshore of the Indies but believed his inability to decipher the precise location was due to the Indians having different names for places or little knowledge of geography. He briefly succumbed to a frustration vividly echoing that he had felt when unable to make Bishop Talavera's commissions understand. He reflected that these peoples were clever, but that the inability to converse with them rendered confirming the proximity of the Grand Khan's court as difficult as convincing the Castilian nobility that the Ocean Sea could be sailed.

After dinner, the cacique and his nitaínos departed, gratified by the hospitality they had received, regardless of the staleness of the strange food.

That night, Cristóbal reflected on Española's future subjugation. He wrote in the journal that the inhabitants were gentle and without religious sect and that the sovereigns would readily make them subjects—as he already considered them—and Christians. He explained he could march over the entire island because its peoples had no skill with arms and were so cowardly that a thousand would flee from three Castilians. He concluded that the inhabitants were fit to be ordered about and made to work, plant, build towns, and everything else required, as well as to be taught Castilian custom and to wear clothes.

⊡   ⊡   ⊡

On December 17, Cristóbal, Diego de Arana, and Bakako met a local cacique and his nitaínos on the beach. As they talked, a large canoe arrived from Tortuga and the canoeists debarked to greet Cristóbal. The local cacique grew angry and shouted at the canoeists to go away. He rose to throw water at them and then stones, whereupon the canoeists departed. The cacique sought to demonstrate he held a favored relationship with the pale beings and handed a stone to Diego, but Diego declined to throw it. The cacique promised to bring Cristóbal more gold.

⊡   ⊡   ⊡

The young cacique previously hosted for dinner on the *Santa María* returned to the anchorage on December 18, borne by his subjects upon a litter and bearing a few gold pieces. He and his nitaínos canoed to the *Santa María*, which was decorated with banners for the feast of the Annunciation of our Lord, and joined Cristóbal in the feast. After exchanging gifts, the two men resumed their prior conversation about Castile and its sovereigns, with Bakako interpreting.

Cristóbal showed the cacique and Bakako a gold coin depicting King Fernando and Queen Isabel, clothed and crowned. As they studied it, Cristóbal again related that Fernando and Isabel lived on land at Castile, which Bakako translated. Cristóbal asked Escobedo to display the expedition's banner and explained that the royal coat of arms displayed the sovereigns' earthly power and the cross the Lord's Heavenly power. Bakako was unable to understand and merely reiterated that Castile was land.

Regardless, the cacique was impressed by the banner and construed its significance for his nitaínos, which analysis Bakako did translate for Admiral. "Fernando Isabel powerful send Admiral from heavens no fear."

Bakako realized the cacique had not understood Admiral's remarks, and suddenly his own failure to comprehend his situation burst as a terrible, sinister revelation through his thoughts. He himself had failed to acknowledge or ignored Admiral's deception for weeks now, ever since the Cubans' seizure! Admiral was clear on two points, and always had been: Castile was as earthly as the coin, and the Cubans were being taken there. And that's precisely where he and Yutowa were being taken, too! Admiral had lied to the Guanahaníans from the beginning.

The cacique disembarked before nightfall and lombards were discharged, delighting everyone, whereupon the cacique vanished into the forest borne by naborias on his litter. Cristóbal deduced in conversation with an elderly nitaíno who lingered that gold could be found on numerous islands located within one hundred leagues and that there was one island that was entirely filled with gold. Cristóbal considered taking the nitaíno captive since he appeared to know the precise sailing directions to these places, but refrained from doing so because the nitaíno was an important counselor of the young ruler. Cristóbal explained in the journal that he now considered the inhabitants of Española the sovereigns' subjects and that it wasn't right to offend them.

॰   ॰   ॰

On the same day, sailors erected a large cross in the central plaza of a neighboring village. Cristóbal believed the inhabitants prayed to and venerated it.

॰   ॰   ॰

On December 20, Cristóbal sailed east along Española's coast to anchor, in his view, at the greatest harbor he had yet discovered (Baie de l'Acul, Haiti). He named it Mar de Santo Tomás as the day was the vigil of St. Thomas, noting in his journal that the harbor was better than any seen on voyages to England or Guinea. He was moved by the fertility and cultivation of the enormous valley surrounding the bay, the height of the encircling mountains, and the density of the population.

While fearful, none of the inhabitants fled and, over the course of two days, Cristóbal and his crews were greeted by a number of local caciques and thousands of their subjects, who freely offered food, water, and gold pieces. Canoeists surrounded the *Santa María* and *Niña* and clambered aboard. Cristóbal dispatched sailors to honor caciqual invitations that he couldn't accommodate. He ordered that trifles be given freely to all in return for their gifts and wrote in his journal that it seemed right to give mutually, particularly since the Indians were now Castilian subjects.

Cristóbal recognized that word of his arrival and objective had preceded him. News had spread through Marien's villages that the pale beings were not Caribes, their vessels were not beasts, and they could be met without danger. Villagers still debated whether the beings were spirits or men, and many remained concerned they might be evil.

Unknown to Cristóbal, Guacanagarí's scouts had tracked the two ships since their arrival at the Haiti-Tortuga channel, and Guacanagarí had received reports of the various encounters for a number of days. After the ships anchored in Marien's great bay on December 20, Guacanagarí reviewed the situation with his council, and it resolved that Guacanagarí should investigate the desirability of establishing a favored relationship with the beings. Guacanagarí had learned through informants that Caonabó, Behecchio, and Guarionex were meeting other pale beings to the east, and the council was intrigued that this new arrival provided Marien's own opportunity.

On Saturday, December 22, Guacanagarí dispatched a canoe with a principal nitaíno to invite Cristóbal to meet in his village, now named Guarico. He sent as a gift a face mask inlaid with gold and woven to a tightly knit cotton girdle quilted intricately with fish bones. It took time for the invitation to be understood. But Cristóbal soon gathered that Guacanagarí was the paramount cacique of the local area and all of the territory of Española he had just explored. Cristóbal accepted the invitation for the next day, regardless of his aversion to leaving port on a Sunday.

GUARIONEX'S, CAONABÓ'S, ANACAONA'S, AND BEHECCHIO'S FIRST ENCOUNTERS, *Mid-December 1492–Early January 1493*

At dusk, Guarionex's son Yomabo and his nitaínos gazed down the hillside to the small inlet where the enormous, solitary hulk floated in tranquil water. Guarionex had instructed him to study the beings closely—to discern how they behaved among themselves, if they slept or disappeared at night, and whether they consulted spirits if not spirits themselves. Yomabo observed the beings shuffle slowly upon the hulk's belly, apparently cooking food on a fire lit upon the belly itself and lounging about as would a squad of warriors waiting to eat—far more like men than spirits.

The beings gathered on the hulk at sunset and sang an areíto, frequently gazing to the sky, and Yomabo assumed it spoke of spirits to whom they worshipped. At nightfall, many lay down on the hulk's belly, apparently to sleep without hammocks, and Yomabo studied their bodies in the moonlight, which neither rose to the heavens nor disappeared but remained motionless as men. Some of the beings did vanish into the hulk's belly, and Yomabo guessed they remained inside—but he could not be certain they had not departed. Occasionally, one would rise and chant in the darkness, and Yomabo concluded they frequently sought to confirm their spirits' alliances. They urinated and defecated into the bay—just like men. At dawn, they sang another areíto. Yomabo then led his nitaínos down to the inlet and arranged for a local cacique to paddle them to the hulk.

Martín's captive studied the canoeists and advised that men of authority were approaching, and Martín welcomed them aboard. Yomabo expressed salutations on behalf of Guarionex and offered Martín and crew cazabi, fruit, and water. Martín reciprocated with hawks' bells and other trifles and gave the visitors a tour of the ship, which astonished them. Yomabo cautiously and respectfully touched Martín's clothing and pale skin and guessed that—were Martín a man—he was older than Guarionex.

Yomabo then turned to Martín's captive and questioned him, in the nature of a polite interrogation. Where were the pale beings from, what did they want, and where were they going? The captive was well versed in the answers given continuously over the past two months.

Yomabo surmised that a relationship with the beings would be beneficial, glanced at his nitaínos for concurrence, and offered Martín Guarionex's friendship and agreement to trade gold at the inlet. Martín expressed his eagerness.

Within a day, to Martín's surprise, he received embassies of each of Caonabó and Behecchio asking similar questions and promising much the same.

⊡ ⊡ ⊡

Within days, Guarionex assembled his council to receive Yomabo's report. His son and the nitaínos described the clothed beings and warned that Caonabó and Behecchio had sent embassies to meet them, too.

Guarionex began his inquiry. "You say they worship spirits continuously?"

"Father, that would be my guess," Yomabo replied. "At intervals, one calls a chant. At other times, they sing, frequently gazing toward the heavens."

"Are they fearful?"

"I'm not sure we could tell. But I doubt it. They seem brave to be so far from wherever they come from."

"Men are fearful and worship often for that reason. Spirits are not, and worship less." Memories of honoring Guabancex before hurricanes flashed through his thoughts. "You say their bodies remained on their vessel during the night."

"Yes. Many of them. Some vanished inside."

"The spirits of the dead walk out at night. So, should we conclude these are not the dead—as they didn't walk out?"

Yomabo nodded his head in agreement but also shrugged his shoulders in bewilderment, as did some of the council members.

Yomabo equivocated. "Their skin is pale like the dead."

"You say they come from the heavens, or at least from beyond the horizon."

"Yes. The Lucayan said that many times."

"Spirits travel to the heavens and back freely, but not bodies." Guarionex pondered and looked to Yomabo. "Perhaps it's just the Lucayan who believes they come from the heavens. Did the pale beings' cacique confirm they come from the heavens?"

"I think so. But all communication was through the Lucayan." Yomabo shrugged his shoulders again. "The only words we understood were the Lucayan's."

"I thought the beings were traveling east. Isn't it possible they came from the far western or southern shores—which are beyond the horizon?" There was silence. "Maybe the Lucayan is just mistaken they come from the heavens or is too simpleminded?"

"The goods they possess are extraordinary—nothing like what we obtain from peoples on the western or southern shores."

"So, it's possible they are spirits." Guarionex was transparent with his doubt. "At minimum, their alliance with spirits seems extraordinary. But, if men, they must come from land." There was more silence as Guarionex reflected. "Why do they seek gold? Are they engaged in a homage, purifying themselves to find gold and communicate with the spirits, as we do?"

Yomabo and the nitaínos peered at one another, and Yomabo replied. "We didn't find out why they seek gold. But the Lucayan didn't mention a homage. They didn't appear to be purifying themselves."

"Gold is the only thing they want?"

"The Lucayan indicated gold was their only trading objective. They're searching for a place they call 'Cipangu.' According to the Lucayan, when they obtain gold, or find none, they will depart."

"Are they good or evil?"

"Father, we can't tell yet, but there's no indication they're evil."

Guarionex reflected for a moment and then directed Yomabo to collect as much gold as possible in a few days and return to the inlet as he had promised the pale beings' cacique.

"We must act quickly in case these beings are worthy of a relationship.

We have lots of gold to trade. But undoubtedly Caonabó and Behecchio will tell them they possess it, as well." Guarionex tempered his enthusiasm. "We also must be cautious. If they do come from the heavens, they must be spirits and, whether friendly or unfriendly, we must then determine how to assuage them. It's too soon to assume only good will come of them."

☒ ☒ ☒

In Maguana, within days of Yomabo's report to Guarionex, Caonabó, Anacaona, and Caonabó's council met with their own embassy and received a similar report, as did Behecchio in Xaraguá from the Xaraguán embassy. All three also learned from informants in Marien that additional pale beings had landed on its coastline, also seeking gold.

Caonabó questioned his chief emissary and an informant from Marien. "You each say these beings are accompanied by Lucayans. Are the Lucayans with them voluntarily or as slaves?"

Anacaona mused on her husband's Lucayan heritage and his experience brutally extracting information from captives taken on the battlefield.

"The Lucayan didn't admit to being a slave," the nitaíno responded. "But my impression was that he was with them only temporarily, to help lead them to gold."

"Did he seem under duress?"

"We couldn't tell. But I think we should assume so."

"The beings in Marien are said to have Cubans with them, including women," the informant interjected.

"Do they force the women to lie with them?" Anacaona interrupted. "Have they enslaved them to fornicate?" Anacaona looked to Caonabó, startled.

"I don't know," the informant replied. "But the Mariens are meeting and trading peaceably with these beings. I haven't heard a report that their women are being captured, raped, or otherwise molested."

Caonabó gazed at his nitaíno. "You say they are not Caribes. If not, what's the risk they will war like Caribes?"

"There was no way to discern this in our meeting," the nitaíno responded. "Perhaps their friendliness is a ruse. Their skin is as pale as the moon, and they may well be evil spirits of the dead."

Caonabó pondered, gazed at each of Anacaona and the nitaíno, and thought aloud. "If they are of the dead, I suppose it would be impossible to kill them?"

Anacaona mused on her husband's savvy in warfare and remembered it was unequaled.

"What weapons do these beings possess?" Caonabó asked.

"They appear to have powerful weapons with which we have no experience," the nitaíno responded. "The weapons propel arrows an enormous distance, far exceeding the range of our arrow slings. Some boom, more piercing than a thunderclap, propelling stone at incredible speed."

Caonabó raised his hand to emphasize an importance to his next question. "Do they want only gold? Or do they want to possess our land where gold is found?"

"They appear to be traders," the nitaíno responded. "There was no suggestion they want to stay on Haiti."

Caonabó made his decision. "We have access to the gold they want. It's too early to say whether these beings are friendly or unfriendly. But we can't let Guarionex establish an exclusive trading relationship—or Guacanagarí, no less. Until it proves unwise, we should invite them into the Cibao to show them we are the trading partner they want."

"They've arrived in Magua's influence," Anacaona cautioned. "It'd be appropriate to coordinate with Guarionex, particularly since we and these beings must cross his territory to meet."

"I'm not concerned with Guarionex's reaction. I have the warriors to conduct myself in the Cibao as I wish."

Anacaona reflected silently that the Taíno approach would be to compromise the discordant caciqual interests into harmony, and she so cautioned her husband.

"We and Guarionex both have access to the gold, and ultimately these beings will recognize that. There's no need for a dispute with Guarionex. Shouldn't we deal with the beings side by side with Guarionex, as well as the Xaraguáns—who also have gold-bearing streams?"

Caonabó thought for moment—well cognizant that his wife was

Xaraguán first—and consented and asked her to coordinate with her brother. Caonabó dispatched nitaínos on his behalf inviting the pale beings to meet in the Cibao south of the Yaque to trade for the Cibao's gold. The Maguans and Xaraguáns could attend, too.

▣   ▣   ▣

Soon, Martín received invitations inland to trade for gold from Haiti's paramount caciques and was ebullient, gripped by the expectation of wealth far exceeding that of his ancestors and neighbors in Palos. He, his captive, and some sailors followed Caonabó's and Behecchio's guides and warriors south from the inlet across the river Bajabonico onto a trail through a beautiful, high pass (at Los Hidalgos) over the coastal mountains. The dark bloom of the forest mesmerized the Castilians as they climbed, and the fertility of the vast valley into which they descended enchanted them. They slept in a lovely village by a mountain stream and, the next two days, strode through farmland on the valley floor to ford the Yaque and ascend into the Cibao, arriving at a village where they met many hosts.

Caonabó's and Behecchio's nitaínos and Yomabo presented Martín with more gold than he had collected in the entire prior eight weeks, both jewelry and unworked pieces. He reciprocated with a silver cup and trifles and, through his captive, promised them he would remain in the inlet to continue trading for gold for some weeks. At dusk, the local cacique invited Martín to stay in his caney, and made bohíos available for the crew. The cacique offered Martín a pretty daughter for the night, a gift he graciously accepted and enjoyed, as well as sisters and nieces for the other pale men.

Martín soon returned to the *Pinta* and continued to barter for gold during the remainder of December, amassing a considerable quantity. His disappointment in not finding Cipangu, and his crew's concern about the desertion, were forgotten. At long last, the voyage had triumphed.

One day, after listening to Yomabo give another report of the pale beings, Guarionex retired alone to his ceremonial bohío. As Caonabó and Behecchio, he was comforted the pale beings appeared uninterested in remaining on Haiti after completing their trade. But their clothing vexed him. He could not extirpate from memory the evening decades before when, in that very bohío, father Cacibaquel had divined Yúcahu's dire prediction of their peoples' extinction. Guarionex studied his cemí of Yúcahu and resolved, as he had decades before and ever since, that consultation with Yúcahu as to that prediction served no practical purpose.

TO GUARICO,
December 23–25, 1492

Cristóbal woke on December 23 to find the wind weak and the sea becalmed. As the sun rose, three messengers arrived on behalf of Guacanagarí to guide the *Santa María* and *Niña* to Guarico, and Cristóbal apologized to them through Bakako that the ships couldn't sail that day, although he was eager to come. He arranged for an embassy led by Rodrigo de Escobedo to accompany the messengers back to Guarico to deliver the apology to Guacanagarí in person. Over the past month, Cristóbal had grown increasingly disturbed by his men's conduct—their wont for egregious trading terms, lust for women, and disrespect of the honor due caciques and nitaínos—and Rodrigo was one of the few he still trusted to behave properly.

Countless Mariens visited the *Santa María* and *Niña* during the day. More than a thousand came by canoe. Over five hundred simply swam. Five local caciques brought their households, wives, and children. They swarmed over the ships' decks, sharing cazabi, water, and fruit freely, and bearing cotton skeins and parrots as gifts. They brought substantial gold jewelry and, for the first time on Cristóbal's voyage, substantial pieces of unworked gold. Cristóbal now suspected that Española—not Baneque—possessed the gold mines he sought and ordered that something be given to all, believing that well spent. In his journal, he expressed his prayer that the Lord's favor help him find the mines.

Bakako witnessed the Haitian multitude meet and marvel at Admiral. The Bohían caciques not only desired Admiral's company, they competed for it. Two months had elapsed since Bakako's seizure and, while missing his family dearly, he now intuited he was participating in an extraordinary event that dwarfed his existence as a Guanahanían fisherman.

Bakako pondered—for the first time—how life as Admiral's servant compared to being a fisherman. As Admiral's servant, he had met and spoken with Bohían caciques of far greater stature than Guanahaní's paramount cacique—with whom he had never spoken. Admiral had captured him and others, lied as to their release, sought to couple men and women against their will, and, twice, set men to beat him—and the threat of punishment for disobedience, no less escape, was ever present. But, since the early days of captivity, Bakako had not been harmed, and Admiral had treated him kindly, almost as if he were Admiral's own son, with a sternness born of absolute authority but mixed with compassion and occasional cheer. If Admiral were human and not spirit, he nevertheless was an exceptional human, endowed with an energy and dedication to his purpose that was extraordinary. He did treat each captive courteously so long as the captive fulfilled the function he commanded. He did afford the Bohían caciques and nitaínos honor.

Bakako reflected contemptuously that Admiral's subjects were neither kind nor exceptional, and most repulsed him. They treated everyone they met—captive or not, even the caciques and nitaínos—as inferior in ability and stature. Bakako considered that Admiral was likely no different at heart but merely dissembled to achieve his objective of finding gold. Bakako pondered whether trust in Admiral was warranted, convinced that the other pale beings couldn't be trusted.

Rodrigo returned to the *Santa María* in the moonlight, while Mariens still crowded the deck. He reported that Guarico was the largest village they had yet discovered—with thousands of inhabitants, many streets, and a central plaza cleanly swept—and that Guacanagarí was the most powerful lord. Guacanagarí had invited them to stay the night and, when Rodrigo declined, graciously had escorted him back to the launch, affording him the courtesy due a nobleman.

With the Indian visitors on deck, Cristóbal, Vicente and their crews barely slept the night of December 23.

◫   ◫   ◫

Cristóbal rose before dawn on December 24, and, with a land breeze permitting departure, the ships sailed from the great bay and turned east along the mountainous shoreline, retracing Rodrigo's route to Guarico. As they sailed, Cristóbal and Bakako spoke with an Indian who had come aboard. Cristóbal asked, "Where can gold be found?"

Bakako translated, and the Indian answered, pointing east. "Cibao."

Cristóbal shuddered in disbelief momentarily, then elatedly anticipated triumph. "Ask him to repeat that."

Bakako complied, and the answer was the same. "Cibao."

Cristóbal beamed, caught his breath, and praised the Lord. He raised his hand, summoning Rodrigo. "We've found it. They call Cipangu 'Cibao'!" He pondered Bartolomeo's map. "There's no other explanation—it's nearby to the east. We'll find it in days, and the gold mines—and the cities Marco Polo visited. This Lord Guacanagarí undoubtedly is vassal to the Grand Khan."

Bakako was startled by this revelation, amazed that at last he would meet this great cacique the Grand Khan. Escobedo was dumbfounded, astonished by Colón's resolute fixation on—and perhaps monumental inflexibility to reconsider—his geographical conception that these naked peoples and straw huts closely neighbored Cathay's gold temples and bridges.

The ships progressed slowly in light breezes, and Cristóbal turned to his journal, enthralled that his ultimate objective lay but days ahead. He was taken by the Indians' friendliness, generosity, civility, and adulation, and he wrote that there could not be a better or gentler people in the world. He assured that the sovereigns would rejoice when these peoples became Christian and learned Castilian custom, and he confirmed they spoke of Cipangu, calling it Cibao.

As night fell, the ships approached an imposing rocky promontory where the coast would veer south (Point Picolet, Cape Haitien, Haiti). The breeze lulled and the *Santa María* and *Niña* floated slowly past the promontory, their crews well content to celebrate the Holy Christmas Eve offshore. All were exhausted from two days of trading with the Indians. Each man now hoarded his own stash of gold. Bakako sat with Admiral's page Pedro, listening as Pedro related the story of Christ's birth.

The ships' watch changed at 11:00 p.m. The moon was a thin crescent, and Cristóbal studied the imposing promontory, silver in the moonlight, which he had named Punta Santa (Holy Point). He listened to gentle swells break on reefs closer to shore, instructed Juan de la Cosa to follow Escobedo's route to Guarico, and then retired to his cabin to pray. He yearned for a priest to administer the Eucharist, but was content the Lord heard his prayer and lay to sleep. Juan de la Cosa also retired to sleep, even though it was his watch, and the sailor assigned to man the tiller delegated it to a ship's boy, contrary to Cristóbal's prohibition against such delegation, and dozed off.

◻ ◻ ◻

A line of coral reefs extended east of Punta Santa a few miles toward Guarico, readily evident in daylight under breaking surf in a typical sea, less apparent in a calm lit by a waning moon when the tide is high. Guacanagarí's subjects fished them daily. The *Santa María* had coursed closer to the promontory than the *Niña* and, as the breeze vanished, she drifted toward the reefs as those responsible slept.

After midnight on Christmas Eve, the ship's boy felt the rudder shudder and shouted. Cristóbal awoke in alarm and sensed the hull pivoting rather than undulating in the water. For an instant, he sought solace that he heard no grating or grinding of the hull and that his alarm was mistaken, but just as immediately he acknowledged he couldn't deceive himself. The bow had drifted onto a reef. He rushed from his cabin to inspect the situation, and there was commotion as the entire crew woke to man the deck.

Cristóbal ordered Juan de la Cosa to take the launch and drop an anchor astern of the *Santa María* so those on board could winch the ship backward off the reef, and Juan and other sailors obediently jumped to the launch. But Juan and his mates quickly panicked, terrified they soon would be wallowing beside a sunken ship to drown or be devoured in unknown seas—as Vicente and the *Niña* deserted to join Martín. Juan abandoned his own ship, fleeing toward the *Niña* farther to sea.

When Cristóbal recognized Juan's intent, he felt a rage as severe as upon Martín's desertion, tempered only by the understanding that most men did succumb to terror upon the ocean. It was now a friend deserting, and the desertion now imperiled Cristóbal's own ship.

The commotion aboard the *Santa María* echoed across the flat ocean to the *Niña*, and Vicente immediately ordered sailors to take the *Niña*'s launch to assist the *Santa María*. When Juan arrived, Vicente refused to receive him and commanded that he return to the *Santa María* and do his duty as Colón ordered.

Cristóbal felt the *Santa María* list to its side as the current pushed it further onto the reef and the tide ebbed beneath, crunching the reef into the hull. He cursed that he had lost the opportunity of a ready solution. He prayed for the Lord's guidance, astonished by the abrupt change in the Lord's design for the voyage. He listened to the beams blister in agony and grimly ordered the crew to saw off the main mast to lighten the weight upon the hull so that the two launches might be able to yank the ship free.

There was pandemonium on deck in the moonlight as the mast toppled into the sea with a resounding crack and swoosh. Sailors quickly tethered the two launches to pull the *Santa María* and heaved mightily to apply all possible force. Cristóbal implored the Lord to spare his ship, and the Guanahaníans and Cubans invoked Yúcahu. The heaving and praying were to no avail.

Cristóbal desperately peered into the ship's dark hold as the groaning intensified. He realized the receding tide rendered the hulls' breach inevitable and, when it came, he shuddered as the *Santa María* filled with seawater, stunned that he had now lost two of three ships. The memory of jumping to the sea off Lagos flickered through his thoughts, and he anguished that there were no Christians ashore. But, for the moment, the *Santa María*'s deck held intact, dry, and walkable.

Cristóbal ordered the entire crew and captives evacuated in the wan moonlight to the *Niña*, stretching *Niña*'s capacity for passengers but safe in the tranquil sea. Castilians, Guanahaníans, and Cubans— men, women, and children—descended into the launches, terrified not only that they achieve safety, but also that it be aboard the *Niña* and not ashore—where the Castilians feared the unknown and the Guanahaníans and the Cubans the Caniba. At the dawn's first twilight, Cristóbal ordered Diego de Arana, Pedro Gutiérrez, and Yutowa to take a launch to apprise Guacanagarí of the disaster. The easterly wind rose with the sun and, recognizing the *Santa María*'s deck soon would collapse in pounding surf, Cristóbal directed his crews to transfer its possessions and storage to the *Niña*.

Guacanagarí received Admiral's messengers and was astounded. The reports he had received described the pale beings as extraordinary, perhaps spirits rather than men. He reflected that men's canoes capsized and men drowned, but not spirits, and that spirits never requested men's assistance. His memory flickered years back to Uncle's advice regarding the actions caciques took when they held advantage over other men. As a Taíno, Guacanagarí knew he would assist these beings because he had no knowledge they were Caribes or evil.

He barked orders that his ablest crews speed his largest canoes to rescue Admiral and the vessel. Naborias shouted calls throughout Guarico, and, as if defending a Caribe raid, Guacanagarí's subjects bolted through the forest to the beach, shoved over a dozen canoes into the surf, and began paddling furiously west with the morning sun low at their backs. They quickly rose to full speed, plying the ocean in a dense congregation with spray flinging wildly from the forward swipe of their paddles. The grunt of the canoeists' exhale resounded across the water.

Guacanagarí rode as a passenger, as did his brother and principal nitaínos in separate canoes. He was astonished by the unpredictable changes in fortune and now calculated that this Admiral's disaster might present an advantage—that he could receive Admiral not only as host but also as rescuer. If these pale beings were peaceful, and if their allegiance beneficial—questions he had to answer first—he might establish a friendship with them exceeding mere trade. His thoughts sped just as quickly as the canoes, and he mused that his relationship with these pale beings might be exclusive, denying access to the paramount Haitian caciques who had ignored Uncle and himself for decades—including at that very moment with the other pale beings to the east! He gazed forward to behold the healthy vessel and was astounded at its size and poise in the sea.

From the *Niña*, Cristóbal beheld the fleet of enormous canoes racing toward him from the east, approaching as rapidly as any vessel he had ever seen. He realized that the Lord Guacanagarí's people would help, and his gratitude swelled. Their canoes surrounded the

Santa María, and there were shouts in Castilian and Taíno as men who had never met hailed one another and, through grunts and gestures, coordinated unloading everything they could into the canoes. The Mariens were astonished by the things they hauled unknown to them—clothing, food, utensils, instruments, chains, barrels, and weapons—and the Castilians were astonished that naked Indians were their saviors. It was obvious the *Niña* could accommodate but a fraction of that retrieved, and Guacanagarí directed his men to transport everything to Guarico.

Cristóbal searched to identify Guacanagarí in the chaos enveloping the *Santa María*. Soon, a canoe approached the *Niña* and Guacanagarí's brother came aboard to introduce himself, accompanied by Yutowa. Brother expressed through gestures and Yutowa that Guacanagarí had arranged for the contents of the *Santa María* to be stored in Guarico under his control and would provide whatever additional help necessary. As Brother spoke, Guacanagarí identified Admiral and was struck by Admiral's noble features, albeit pale. Brother pointed out Guacanagarí to Cristóbal, and Cristóbal acknowledged recognition, respect, and heartfelt thanks by hand waves.

As midday approached, Guacanagarí returned with the laden canoes to Guarico, accompanied by a few clothed beings, and supervised the temporary deposit of the *Santa María*'s contents beside his caney. He ordered two bohíos emptied to serve as a storehouse and placed them under armed guard as the contents were transferred to them. Castilians and Mariens returned to dismantle the wreck itself so that no plank or nail that could be saved was lost, and pieces of the deck, hull, masts, and other remnants were towed by Guacanagarí's naborias to be heaped on Guarico's beach or fields beside the two bohíos.

Cristóbal implored his Lord to explain the meaning of the disaster. He seethed at the disloyalty or cowardice of his own crew to run from the ship rather than save it. Many of them—including the very first man he had enlisted—had meant to desert him on the sinking vessel, an incomprehensible ingratitude and disloyalty! But he confessed to himself that both Vicente and the naked Indian peoples had rescued him from entire loss.

Cristóbal spent the rest of Christmas on the *Niña* in odious proximity to Vicente and the crews of both ships, as well as their Guanahanían and Cuban captives. He fought to disguise his contempt for the sailors who had forsaken him and loathed to recognize Vicente's valor because of Martín's transgression. He feared that Vicente, Juan, and the rest of the crew would sail for Castile without him if he debarked ashore. He anguished that Martín already was sailing home to steal credit for the voyage's discoveries. Beyond bitterness and recrimination, Cristóbal gravely confronted the awesome peril that he had but one ship to cross the Ocean Sea and that he and everyone else would perish if it foundered. Guilt for leaving Diego and little Fernando pricked his soul.

Cristóbal also reflected on Guacanagarí's valor and chivalry and that the gentle peoples of the Indies actually observed the Lord's commandment—they loved their neighbors as themselves.

Escobedo was astonished by Guacanagarí's charity—if the *Santa María* had foundered off the shores of the Mohammedans, Rodrigo and the rest of the crew likely would have been enslaved by now, just as would the crew of a Mohammedan ship that foundered off Castile, and in either case the entire storage looted. Pedro Gutiérrez reflected on how his king had brutally subjugated the naked peoples of Gran Canaria, and Pedro was relieved the Lord Guacanagarí was ignorant of that. Cristóbal's servant Juan reflected how the Christians had brutalized fellow Guineans and Canarians and that the Lord Guacanagarí was promoting his own doom.

Bakako and Yutowa whispered that they were now certain the pale beings were but men. They surmised that the prospect of returning to Guanahaní was extinguished, and they implored Yúcahu that Admiral not leave them in Bohío. The Cubans were forlorn and hopeless, perceiving that terrible fate inevitable for themselves.

After sunset, Cristóbal mustered his resolve to lead his men and summoned the sovereigns' representatives and Diego de Arana to discuss the situation. Cristóbal felt it would be imprudent for the *Niña* to attempt to transport the crews of both ships and the captives to Spain, even if all the Cubans were released. He believed some crewmen instead should be left to establish a temporary settlement at this site as the first step toward the island's colonization. These men could explore for gold, spices, and other riches to recommend the best locations for a town, as well as learn the language and customs of the inhabitants.

All four men agreed with Cristóbal that Española was fit for colonization. Rodrigo Sánchez observed that it had been the Crown's experience in the settlement of Ronda and other reconquered territories that once people saw settlers prospering, many more volunteered, and an initial settlement on Española could serve that purpose. Pedro and Diego attested that many crewmen would beg to stay, lured by the gold. All agreed that a settlement of a significant portion of the two ships' combined crew made sense provided it were peacefully arranged with Guacanagarí.

While likely unnecessary, Cristóbal thought it prudent—as well as typical in the establishment of settlements among unknown peoples—that a small fort be built for the men's protection in the event relations with Guacanagarí deteriorated from that envisioned. He recalled the fort at Mina, realized he could never build such a structure, and reasoned that the Indians' meager weaponry rendered that unnecessary. Anxiously, he pondered whether there was a greater need to protect the Indian women from the crew.

None of the four doubted Cristóbal and crews now had the geographic knowledge and nautical ability to sail to Spain and then return to retrieve the men left behind. Lured by gold, all but Sánchez agreed to remain on Española when Cristóbal departed. That evening, many of the crew also volunteered, and Cristóbal was comforted that there was little risk in his own abandonment ashore. That was provident, as his presence ashore was essential for the settlement's establishment.

GUACANAGARÍ'S FIRST ENCOUNTERS,
Guarico, December 26–27, 1492

At dawn on December 26, naborias paddled Guacanagarí at a stately pace in his greatest canoe to meet Admiral aboard the remaining vessel. Cristóbal, Bakako, and Yutowa watched his regal approach and Cristóbal welcomed him at the *Niña*'s rail, bowing to acknowledge his nobility.

"Your Lordship, I humbly express my deepest thanks, and that of my King Fernando and Queen Isabel of Castile." Cristóbal's tone and expression communicated his gratitude, obviating the need for translation, but Bakako attempted one.

Guacanagarí smiled. "I am honored to meet you. Your greatness has preceded you, and I'm honored to provide whatever assistance you need."

"Guacanagarí like Admiral," Bakako offered. "Admiral good."

Guacanagarí turned to Yutowa, whom he already knew, and smiled again. "I see there are two of you."

Cristóbal was impressed with Guacanagarí's grace and civility. The two men began their first conversation, gesturing frequently to communicate when neither Bakako nor Yutowa could translate or understand, neither man knowing whether the other fully or even partly understood.

Guacanagarí pointed to the reefs where the *Santa María* had foundered and then to Guarico, and gestured as if carrying a load in his arms. "My subjects have placed everything taken from the stricken vessel in or beside two bohíos in my village. I will make more bohíos available if needed." He grasped Admiral's hands in his own. "Do not be disheartened."

Bakako translated the first thoughts. "Food. Sails. Knives. Guacanagarí house. Guacanagarí more house." He couldn't translate the second thought, but Cristóbal gleaned the sentiment of friendship.

Cristóbal opened his arms, looked into Guacanagarí's eyes, and spoke with a soft intensity. "Your assistance and friendship will be remembered and rewarded." Yutowa translated that Admiral was Guacanagarí's friend and Guacanagarí politely listened, surmising Admiral had said more, certain that it was kindly, yet uncertain what.

Guacanagarí pointed to the crew and then to shore. "You and your subjects may stay ashore as long as you wish, and I will assist you in whatever way possible."

"Sailors land," Bakako said. "Guacanagarí friend."

Cristóbal invited Guacanagarí and his nitaínos on a tour of the *Niña* and then served a Castilian meal. Guacanagarí watched canoeists approach and offer Admiral gold, confirming for himself that Admiral coveted it. Through Bakako, Guacanagarí explained there was abundant gold in the "Cibao," and that he had access to it. He boasted that his cacicazgo held gold as well. Cristóbal understood Yutowa's translation to mean that Guacanagarí claimed gold was so abundant that it was valueless to his subjects.

Guacanagarí noticed the Cuban men, women, and children huddled alone. He pointed to them and asked Bakako, "Why are they with these beings? I can tell by their speech they're Cuban."

Cristóbal perceived the question and, without waiting translation, turned to Bakako and replied. "Tell the lord I have been taking them to Castile to learn Castilian language and custom. They will return to Juana."

Bakako despaired that his fate mirrored the Cubans but managed an interpretation.

Pointing to the Cubans and then to the shore, Cristóbal instructed Bakako further. "Tell him we no longer have room on our ship for them, and that we must leave almost all of them ashore."

Bakako winced breathless, his despair descending to dread that Admiral would leave him on Bohío as well, to be enslaved or eaten. "Admiral asks that you take the Cubans ashore."

Guacanagarí nodded graciously toward Admiral. "Certainly, we shall take them." He studied Bakako. "Are they here of their own choice?"

Bakako hesitated, fearful Admiral could understand.

"No," replied Yutowa.

Guacanagarí grew uneasy, uncertain what this meant for himself and his people. But, for the moment, he repressed any fear as premature. After the meal, he offered to escort Admiral to Guarico for the reception arranged prior to the disaster and to review the stricken vessel's possessions. Cristóbal, Escobedo, a despondent Bakako, and armed crewmen boarded the launches and followed Guacanagarí's canoes to Guarico, where thousands of Guacanagarí's subjects waited to behold them. It was Guacanagarí's turn to lead a tour of his dominion, trailed by this multitude. Cristóbal was impressed by the size and orderliness of the village, the villagers' civility, and Guacanagarí's sovereign demeanor among them.

Guacanagarí's wives supervised the preparation of a bountiful feast of fish, fowl, and cazabi. At its conclusion, Guacanagarí washed his hands in water with herbs and offered the same for Admiral.

Cristóbal was impressed by Guacanagarí's propriety and cleanliness, believing it evidenced nobility.

Cristóbal presented Guacanagarí with a shirt and gloves originally destined for the Grand Khan's court. Guacanagarí admired them openly before his subjects, donned them, grinned with approval, and thanked Admiral. Cristóbal reflected that Guacanagarí was as deft in ceremony as any European prince.

Trailed by the multitude, Guacanagarí led Admiral through Guarico's verdant gardens and tree groves to the beach to review his armada of great canoes. He waved his arm across the horizons and explained that his cacicazgo extended as far as one could see and well beyond, including the great bay west of the imposing peak and the mountains inland and to the east. Cristóbal expressed his esteem for the realms.

Cristóbal also decided it was his turn to reveal sovereign power. As the olive- and pale-skinned peoples mingled on the beach, he ordered sailors to retrieve the *Santa María*'s weapons stored in Guacanagarí's bohíos and give the Indians a demonstration. A sailor shot an arrow from a Turkish bow, revealing a fearsome range that the villagers had never witnessed. A lombard and a spignard were discharged, and most villagers fell to the ground in terror of the unknown forces and powers, undoubtedly of spirits. Cristóbal studied Guacanagarí's reaction.

"Your weapons are advanced and powerful," Guacanagarí remarked, unsure how Bakako would translate. His mind now raced in fear and bewilderment, but he concealed his thoughts.

Bakako was too incredulous to translate, stupefied by Admiral's arrogance. Admiral had chosen a celebration of friendship to demonstrate belligerence, no less to the very cacique who had just saved him! Admiral's dismissal that Guacanagarí could destroy him was equally astonishing—only spirits could feel so invincible. Yet Bakako finally rendered an interpretation. "Admiral weapon good."

Guacanagarí searched for words to continue conversation, unsure whether the pale beings were men or spirits, pondering Admiral's brazenness, the brutal force he commanded, and his restraint of the Cubans. While the weaponry was incredible, they were stored in his own bohíos, not aimed at his people. The pale beings hadn't shown hostile intent—they hadn't even intended to visit for an extended period, no less attack. Wouldn't this Admiral—as any Taíno cacique—reciprocate the charity of rescue with lasting friendship? Wouldn't he forbear from using weapons against his rescuer? Couldn't and shouldn't his weaponry be an advantage of their potential alliance, not a threat?

Guacanagarí turned to Admiral. "My people suffer raids from Caribe warriors who live on islands to the east. They steal our women to be slaves and concubines. If they capture our men or boys, they eat them." A recollection of his sister Heitiana's abduction flickered through his thoughts.

Bakako didn't know enough to translate, and Guacanagarí used gestures to make the communication, drawing a map in the sand to show where the Caribes came from.

Cristóbal pondered how to establish his settlement. Advising Guacanagarí he was already the king and queen's vassal and entitled to their protection would likely lead to hostilities. Cristóbal pointed to the sailors holding the weapons and chose circumspect words, recognizing that Bakako's translation would introduce even more ambiguity. "My Lord Guacanagarí, my King Fernando and Queen Isabel can protect you from these Caribes and destroy and enslave them. That is what these weapons are for."

Following repetition and gestures by Admiral and Bakako, Guacanagarí thought he understood, and mused that protection from Caribe raids was desirable. But he was seized by the realization that an alliance with Admiral could command the respect of the other paramount Haitian caciques. Admiral's offer to use weapons against the Caribes alone was suspicious, and the pale beings might yet be revealed to be evil. Regardless, they were so vastly outnumbered that the risk their weapons would be turned on his subjects seemed remote.

"Let's commemorate our friendship," Guacanagarí replied.

Guacanagarí led Admiral and his subjects back to Guarico's central plaza. Before all, he solemnly placed a necklace adorned with gold about Admiral's neck and gave him a face mask finely inlaid with golden eyes, ears, and other features. "This is my gift to you. It indicates I have presented my soul to you in lasting friendship."

Bakako couldn't translate, but Cristóbal understood Guacanagarí's intent to make a strong, intimate statement. As the Indian stood naked before him, Cristóbal realized that Guacanagarí had a regal presence rivaling the most powerful Castilian noblemen, and he perceived Guacanagarí as a vassal to Fernando and Isabel with equal peerage to a Canarian or Guinean king.

"Your Lordship permitting, I plan to stay some days with you before returning to Castile. Is that acceptable?" Bakako translated as best he could.

"That would be my pleasure and desire." Guacanagarí nodded affirmatively.

"It's good you will take the Cubans. When I depart, I also would leave some of my men here. They would live in or near your village and trade gold with you." Cristóbal pointed to his sailors and the ground where they stood and refrained from using the word *settlement*—even though Bakako wouldn't understand it—or mentioning the fort intended. He pointed to himself, gesturing he would leave and then return to trade for more gold. "I will return with others and our trade will increase." Cristóbal watched Guacanagarí consider his gestures and listen to Bakako and grasped that the language barrier had facilitated omission of his true intent.

Guacanagarí was pleased, perceiving an arrangement to shelter the crew displaced by the vessel's demise and facilitate the development of a lasting, exclusive alliance with the clothed men. "I'm happy to accommodate your men as part of our mutual understanding. My people seek to trade and otherwise ally with you and your cacique Fernando and wife Isabel."

Bakako relayed, "Admiral men Guarico. Trade gold. Guacanagarí yes."

Cristóbal surmised Española's initial settlement had been approved and sought reconfirmation. "I am grateful my men can remain. Your people will be protected from the Caribes." Cristóbal evaluated Guacanagarí's reaction carefully as Bakako attempted translation, certain Guacanagarí did not perceive the ultimate intention.

At the day's end, Cristóbal returned to the *Niña*, exhausted. He mused again on the Lord's design for the wreck of the *Santa María*, reflecting that the ship had grounded in the calmest seas while traveling a route already traversed and known to the crewmen who had visited Guarico. He recalled that the swell's lapping on the reef had been audible from a distance and turned to his journal to record the past two days.

Cristóbal concluded for his sovereigns that the Lord's design was to cause the ship to ground so that a settlement be founded. Prior to the wreck, he had never intended to stay long at the site and would have moved on quickly, missing the terrific opportunity to trade for gold now understood. Even after the grounding, the ship could have been saved but for the crew's treachery and he wouldn't have stayed.

He also promised his sovereigns that the entire island—which he believed larger than Portugal—could be subjugated with the men he had because the inhabitants had no arms and were cowardly. The fort to be built was not even necessary for his men's protection, but would acquaint the Indians with the sovereigns' skills and powers, so that the Indians would obey with love and fear. On his return, his men would have found the gold mines and, within three years of colonization, the sovereigns would achieve such profit that they could undertake the recapture of the Holy Sepulcher in Jerusalem— as he had promised in Grenada and to which they had scoffed.

田　田　田

At dawn on December 27, Guacanagarí, his brother, and another relative came aboard the *Niña* to relate they were gathering as much gold as possible and to invite Admiral to dwell longer in Guarico. Cristóbal declined, explaining that he had to return to Castile to report to his sovereigns. He invited them to dine on board.

"I would be honored if my brother and relative Xamabo could accompany you to meet your cacique and his wife," Guacanagarí stated, with gestures and help from Bakako.

"I would be honored to bring them," Cristóbal replied, pleased Guacanagarí understood Castile was land and not Heaven. Cristóbal turned to the brother and Xamabo. "You shall be your Lord's representatives to meet King Fernando and Queen Isabel." Certain Bakako wouldn't understand, he added, "You will pledge your people's allegiance to Fernando and Isabel and, as their subjects, receive their protection of your people."

"Your brother and Xamabo will meet Fernando and Isabel in friendship," Bakako surmised.

Guacanagarí was elated and perceived a substantial accomplishment attained. None of Caonabó, Behecchio, or Guarionex could secure a superior relationship with Admiral's caciques.

As the men dined, messengers reported to Guacanagarí that the other vessel of pale beings had been sighted at a river to the east, and he informed Admiral, who was shocked. Cristóbal drafted a letter, entreating Martín to sail to him to reunite but refraining from asserting that Martín's separation had been wrongful, and Guacanagarí dispatched one of his canoes east, bearing a sailor and the letter.

Cristóbal raged that Martín might simply depart for Spain alone and resolved to establish his settlement quickly. The intended fort would be built with a watchtower and moat beside Guarico's river. The garrison would be provisioned with a year's supply of bread, barrels of wine, the expedition's store of crop seed, most of the weapons and ammunition, and the merchandise intended for trade with the Grand Khan, which could be traded for gold. The garrison would keep the *Santa María*'s launch to explore for gold and find a better harbor for Española's first permanent settlement, likely farther east toward Cipangu's gold mines.

Cristóbal named his settlement Villa de la Navidad and began selecting the men to remain, which was not difficult because many volunteered. He would have no choice but to release the Cuban captives other than one teenage boy named Abasu, who appeared capable of becoming a good interpreter.

In Guacanagarí's Bohío,
December 28, 1492

Cristóbal came ashore on December 28 accompanied by Bakako to discuss with Guacanagarí the crewmen to be left behind and their activity while Cristóbal went to Castile. Guacanagarí was eager to discuss these matters, as well as his relationship to Admiral and alliance with Fernando and Isabel. Guacanagarí learned of Cristóbal's arrival and had him escorted to the finer bohío storing the visitors' possessions, where palm fronds had been woven to cover a portion of the bohío's dirt floor.

Guacanagarí entered the bohío solemnly to present Cristóbal with a necklace bearing a gold medallion, honorific but distinct from the guanín medallions worn by the paramount Haitian caciques, intending the gift be understood as vastly more significant than its gold. Cristóbal was enthralled by its weight and solemnly thanked Guacanagarí for it. The two men sat on ornate duhos, with Bakako at their feet to assist communication and naborias at the door to attend with juice and cazabi. As before, Guacanagarí and Cristóbal gestured frequently to communicate when Bakako appeared unable to understand or translate.

"About forty of my men will remain with you, and I will build a fortress by the river for them to use," Cristóbal began. "We will use the planks of the sunken vessel." Cristóbal saw Bakako didn't understand. "We will make a house for my men." Cristóbal stood and walked to where the dirt remained uncovered and drew a picture of a walled fort with a tower and moat. He pointed outside the bohío toward the planking of the *Santa María*'s hull, which lay broken and scattered in a nearby field.

"This is a house?" Guacanagarí replied, studying the diagram.

Bakako turned to Admiral. "House?"

"Yes. This is a fort where men can go for protection and keep weapons."

Bakako couldn't understand "fort" or "protection" or the statement's underlying sense and remained silent.

Guacanagarí moved his finger along the depiction of the wall and gazed upward. "How high is the wall?"

Cristóbal stretched his hand above his head. "About ten feet."

Guacanagarí touched the depiction of the tower and gazed upward again. "How high is this?"

Cristóbal pointed to a beam high on the bohío wall. "Twenty feet, maybe more."

Guacanagarí had marveled at the construction of the *Niña* and was impressed by the intended structure, realizing that the strength of the wood exceeded the reed of bohíos. But he touched the depiction of the tower and remarked to Bakako that it functioned as a tree or hill for lookouts. He quickly grasped the moat's function. He realized the structure's small size and formidable wall meant for it to be more a refuge than a home, and his admiration faded.

"Why do you need the wall, tower, and ditch?" Guacanagarí pointed to the depictions and shrugged his shoulders.

Cristóbal surmised Guacanagarí's inquiry and answered directly. "For protection of the men and gold. We will keep the gold inside." Bakako now gleaned enough to decipher *protection* and translated for Guacanagarí.

"Protection from whom?"

After translating for Admiral, Bakako gazed at the floor, understanding Guacanagarí's suspicion.

"From your enemies, the Caribes. From others who might take the gold."

Guacanagarí recognized the words *Caribes* and *gold* and didn't wait for Bakako's assistance. "Caribe attacks are infrequent. No Haitian will take the gold." Guacanagarí pointed to the depiction of the wall and then stared into Cristóbal's eyes. "This is how you build a house in your Castile?"

"House Castile?" Bakako relayed.

Cristóbal was surprised, envisioning Mina, but realizing the question focused otherwise. He recalled the walls of Genoa, Scio, London, Galway, and the cities and villages of Portugal and Castile, for century's essential protection from enemy princes, criminals, plague, and the infidel. "Yes. Every village where I come from has a wall for its protection. Every village." Bakako simply nodded yes.

"There are no walls like this in Guarico," responded Guacanagarí. "There are no walls like this in Marien or anywhere in Haiti."

"No Guarico. No Bohío," Bakako said, pointing to the wall's depiction. There was silence, and Cristóbal recognized Guacanagarí understood the wall and moat were intended as protection from Guacanagarí's own people.

For a moment, Guacanagarí pondered that the leader whom he had just rescued held much distrust. The wall and moat indicated Admiral sought at most an alliance, not a true friendship of peoples. But Guacanagarí refrained from expressing disappointment, reflecting that Admiral's fear for his men—vastly outnumbered in a place unknown—was natural.

Bakako waited for Admiral's response, musing that Admiral and his men frequently were selfish, arrogant, brusque, and disloyal— among themselves alone. Admiral's indication that his people lived behind walls in their native Castile was revealing of this nature. Bakako suspected Admiral intended these walls to imprison more captives.

As he considered his response, Cristóbal wondered that the Indians lived idyllically among themselves without walls, in a peaceful state of nature without crime, sin, plague, or war save for Caribe invasion, loving their neighbors as Christians taught but rarely observed. He recalled that the Lord's city would not have walls when Christ returned and marveled that the Indians appeared to achieve that existence on earth while Christians and others failed. But he was certain that the absence of defenses was backward and cowardly, as well as his sovereigns' opportunity. He sought to assuage Guacanagarí and lied again. "We will use our fort to protect you from the Caribes. Together, we will become wealthy trading gold."

Guacanagarí recognized the word *gold* again and responded without waiting translation. "We are pleased that you build the house in Guarico. You can use it as the place where you keep the gold. We can arrange to bring gold from throughout my cacicazgo, as well as elsewhere in Haiti and the neighboring islands."

"House Guarico good," Bakako translated. "Guacanagarí bring Admiral gold Bohío. Guacanagarí bring Admiral gold islands."

Cristóbal guessed Guacanagarí's intent and reflected. Navidad likely was east of the gold mines to be discovered, its shoreline unsuitable for a harbor, and reliance on Guacanagarí for collecting gold from other places—no less an exclusive relationship—was unacceptable. But denying exclusivity risked appearing ungrateful for Guacanagarí's rescue, support, and protection of the settlement, and Cristóbal sought to mislead Guacanagarí yet again. "I'm very grateful for this. We will trade for all the gold you bring us." Bakako so translated.

Guacanagarí nodded appreciation and then stood, beckoning Admiral and Bakako to follow him to the neighboring bohío, in which they had stored much of the *Santa María*'s hardware and equipment. He pointed to various items—including a washbasin, water pitcher, and mirror—and asked how many pieces of gold Admiral wanted for each.

For weeks, Cristóbal had witnessed Indians freely give and share food and their possessions, exhibiting generosity beyond constraint and, to his and his crews' perspective, utter guilelessness. He reflected that Guacanagarí was not guileless and had a mercantile instinct. He responded as Domenico had taught him. "I would have to see the gold pieces."

The men returned to sit on their duhos in the finer bohío. Guacanagarí continued to probe. "Every year, I direct my subjects to cease work, fast, refrain from their women, and travel to our streams to find gold to do homage to our spirits. Do you seek gold for your spirits?"

Bakako struggled. "Want gold Christ?"

"We use gold to trade and for jewelry. King Fernando and Queen Isabel will use the gold for soldiers and weapons to defeat Christ's enemies, the infidel."

"Admiral's cacique and wife will use the gold to fight enemies," Bakako guessed.

Guacanagarí listened to Bakako and was struck by Admiral's reference to Fernando and Isabel. He suspected that the collection of gold was part of the exercise of cacical authority and, perhaps in that sense, similar to a Taíno gold homage. He mused that the pale beings were indeed human, organized in a society with cacical authority like theirs. He was surprised that Fernando and Isabel had enemies. "Who are the enemies of Fernando and Isabel?"

"Enemy Fernando? Enemy Isabel?" Bakako shrugged his shoulders.

"Fernando and Isabel are the supreme Christian princes," Cristóbal responded. "Their enemies are princes of false religions who do not worship Christ and jealous Christian princes."

"Fernando and Isabel fight enemies who dishonor the Christ spirit," Bakako translated, intrigued that the pale men warred among themselves.

Guacanagarí sought confirmation. "Fernando and Isabel fight enemies?"

"Yes." Cristóbal gazed at Guacanagarí's naked body and reflected that Guacanagarí had the same instincts as a European prince. "They have many enemies, but they are always victorious." The bitter memory of seven years' idle wait while the sovereigns struggled to conquer Granada flickered through his thoughts. He added, "King Fernando and Queen Isabel will protect you from the Caribes."

"How many wives does King Fernando have? I have many daughters he could choose."

"Wives Fernando? Guacanagarí girls."

Cristóbal remembered the voyages of his youth as a trader in the Orient and the islands of the Ocean Sea, and Guacanagarí's question and suggestion did not strike him as unusual or presumptuous but as practical and intelligent. He responded respectfully and slowly so Bakako could translate. "King Fernando has one wife. The king and queen make alliances by marrying their children."

"I have sons and daughters for their children. Or myself."

Cristóbal surmised Guacanagarí's direction and shook his head no. "Their children are already married or the marriages arranged."

Surprised to be denied, Guacanagarí pressed further. "King Fernando has only one woman?"

"Fernando one woman?"

"Yes. For purposes of an alliance, there is only one woman, his wife, Isabel."

Guacanagarí was disappointed and there was silence. The two men and the youth studied one another and grinned sheepishly, respectful that each was trying to understand, aware that communication frequently failed, disappointed that they could not fully know each other, and content to be together. Guacanagarí forgot that Admiral wore clothes and Cristóbal forgot than Guacanagarí was naked.

Guacanagarí pointed to the silver cross on Cristóbal's necklace. "Many of your naborias wear that."

"This depicts the cross upon which Christ died. When I return, I will bring men to teach you of Christ so that you may achieve salvation." Bakako understood the thoughts, learned at the Sunday services aboard the *Santa María*, and translated. He recalled Admiral's expectation that he become a Christian and simmered that Admiral and his men neither honored nor respected Yúcahu or other spirits. He yearned to warn Guacanagarí that their spiritual knowledge was incomplete, their assurance of Christ's supremacy arrogant. But it wasn't his role to explain this to a paramount cacique, nor would the cacique give import to what he said.

"Christ is friendly?" Guacanagarí asked.

When translated, the question surprised Cristóbal. "He is supreme, the one true God. He judges each person on death. He has a destiny to be revealed for all the world's peoples." Cristóbal reflected that the Lord tested faith severely at times and that neither *friendly* nor *unfriendly* were appropriate.

Not understanding, Bakako shrugged. He turned to Guacanagarí. "Admiral believes his Christ spirit is the supreme spirit."

Guacanagarí wasn't surprised. Many of Guacanagarí's subjects focused their worship similarly, comforted by that simplicity. He wondered how powerful this Christ was. He didn't feel threatened by Admiral's intent to teach him of this spirit or perceive any consequence of nonbelief. Guacanagarí had no intent of ceasing to honor Yúcahu or any other spirit in favor of this Christ.

Guacanagarí asked his naborias for pineapple juice and cazabi. Cristóbal savored the juice and Gucanagari asked the naborias to fetch a pineapple and cut it open for Admiral's inspection. Cristóbal marveled at the fruit's size. After relaxing a few moments, the men returned to discuss to the garrison and practical issues that, with gestures and Bakako's assistance, they could communicate.

"When I depart, my men will trade for gold with you. They will use the ship's launch to explore for gold." Cristóbal paused for Bakako to explain, watching Guacanagarí deceived as to the exploration's other purpose of finding a site for the permanent colony from which Española's subjugation would be directed.

"I can bring the gold here to your men."

"My men have Castilian food, but they will need you to provide additional food."

"Taínos share food freely, and your men will not hunger."

"I will appoint leaders, and they will befriend you before I leave." Cristóbal maintained an innocent composure regardless of a gnawing apprehension. "I will order my men to behave properly. Their leaders will enforce proper behavior. My men should not steal your women or possessions." Bakako understood and relayed simply that Admiral meant his men would be good.

"I am pleased for that. Who is the leader?"

"His name is Diego de Arana."

"Is he your brother?"

Cristóbal again recalled answering practical questions from diverse peoples when a trader. "He's a brother of my woman."

Guacangarí appreciated this. "Will you leave the men your weapons?"

"Yes. As agreed, my men will defend your people against the Caribes. We will enslave the Caribes." Cristóbal waited for Bakako to translate and watched Guacanagarí's reaction to the explanation for the weapons. But Guacanagarí revealed none.

Cristóbal looked into Guacanagarí's eyes and then asked for his favor. "I want you to protect my men against enemies."

"We have no enemies other than Caribes," Guacanagarí replied after Bakako's translation, gazing directly back into Admiral's eyes. He fully understood Admiral's intent to be that if there were friction between his subjects and Admiral's, he would protect Admiral's. He placed the burden on Admiral to ask for this.

Cristóbal acknowledged Guacanagarí's understanding—as far as it went. "If fights arise between our peoples, I want my men protected."

"Admiral wants you to protect his men from bad Bohíans," Bakako interpreted.

"I will protect your men from harm. That's my responsibility in our alliance."

"Yes," Bakako responded.

Cristóbal was pleased and immensely relieved Guacanagarí did not perceive the intended subjugation of his peoples. He liked Guacanagarí and, with the garrison's protection arranged, sought answers to his key unanswered questions.

"Do you trade with the Grand Khan?"

Bakako translated the question almost verbatim, knowing that Guacanagarí would have no knowledge of this person.

"No." Guacanagarí shook his head. "I don't know of him."

"How far are we from Cibao?"

"Not far. It's to the southeast." Guacanagarí felt uncomfortable, sensing that Admiral wanted to meet the ruler of the Cibao, either Caonabó or Guarionex. "We have access to the Cibao's gold." Guacanagarí changed the subject. "How far from Haiti is Castile?"

"Days canoa, Bohío Castile?" Bakako asked.

"Very, very far." Cristóbal knew that a statement of leagues or miles would not be understood and spread his arms wide to emphasize the great distance. "I believe it will take up two months to return there." He reflected that he was speculating wildly, as the route east had yet to be traversed and its winds, weather, and currents were unknown. Bakako was shocked and translated that it was two moons by canoe.

Guacanagarí was shocked, as well. "The sea exists so very far to the east?"

"Yes."

"Your vessel can travel two moons at sea?"

"Yes."

"Are there islands along the way?"

Cristóbal remembered Talavera's commissions. "Yes." Cristóbal had already considered the route, which passed the Azores.

"When will you return?"

Cristóbal reflected that the time necessary for the sovereigns' approval of a second expedition and its provisioning were as unknown as the duration of the homeward voyage. "I don't know. I hope to return within twelve months." Bakako was startled again, as was Guacanagarí when he heard the translation.

"I hadn't thought so long, but that is acceptable. We will provide your men the food they need until you return and much gold by then."

As the afternoon waned, Guacanagarí and Cristóbal finished their conversation and agreed to meet soon to complete preparations. Guacanagarí offered to host Cristóbal in his caney for the night and the company of his most beautiful daughter.

Cristóbal declined both. He would not sleep ashore lest he be abandoned. He felt his crew had deteriorated into excessive relations with the Haitian women and wanted to set an example of abstinence. While he remained virile, this abstinence wasn't sacrifice. Cristóbal's remaining interest in women had narrowed solely to whether a woman, by marriage or otherwise, would further the pursuit of his enterprise of exploring and colonizing the Indies.

"Do you have wives and children?" Guacanagarí asked.

Cristóbal was surprised but gratified to receive a personal question. "My wife died. I have two sons." Bakako had heard the word *died* in relation to Christ and knew its meaning.

As Bakako translated, Guacanagarí reached to hold Admiral's hands, and Cristóbal received him. Guacanagarí said he was sorry, and no translation was needed. Both Guacanagarí and Bakako were stunned, realizing they now had information—if they understood Admiral properly—that the pale beings did die as men.

"How old are your sons?"

Cristóbal counted with his fingers. "One is twelve—like Bakako—the other four."

Guacanagarí looked at Bakako and then turned to Admiral. "When you leave for Castile, I trust Bakako will remain so that I can talk to your men." Guacanagarí interpreted himself with gestures.

Bakako looked to the ground, breathless to hear the answer.

"No, Bakako will come with me to Castile," Cristóbal replied, scrutinizing Bakako's reaction to the betrayal. "Bakako will meet King Fernando and Queen Isabel."

Bakako was devastated to hear what he already knew. He fought to conceal any emotion whatsoever, avoiding both Admiral's and Guacanagarí's gazes, refusing to express any appreciation to Admiral for this fate, hiding from Guacanagarí the bitterness within, and adamantly avoiding any acknowledgment that he had submitted forever to Admiral's lies and control—albeit resigned he had no choice but travel to Castile.

Cristóbal was prepared to reciprocate sternly any hostile glare to remind the boy of the consequence of resistance, but he caressed Bakako's shoulder instead. "It'll be the greatest honor of your life."

When parting, Guacanagarí offered that his naborias would help Admiral's men construct their fort. Cristóbal expressed gratitude. While it would be but a dwarf to the fort at Mina, he departed for his launch immensely relieved that he had successfully arranged—without hostilities—the first fort by which Española would be subjugated.

But Cristóbal was not content. The discoveries made since landfall on Guanahaní had whetted rather than quelled the bitter memories of his lifetime journey to achieve them. Every day brought new evidence that a vast, unknown, and ever expanding enterprise remained to be pursued. He pined for the gratitude of his queen and king that he had delivered on his promises to them. He craved public vindication that his geographic theory was correct, driven by an abiding contempt for the noblemen who had scorned his common status, and he yearned to expand the discoveries to which he became a wealthy, esteemed nobleman of the Christian world. He lusted for the accumulation of gold, not because his tastes demanded luxury or opulence but as the emoluments of the foregoing achievements. Encompassing all, Cristóbal saw incontrovertible confirmation that the Lord had chosen him for the singular destiny of bringing Christianity to the heathen populations of the Indies and islands of the Ocean Sea.

Guacanagarí was pleased with the meeting and reviewed it with his council. The alliance would augment his and Marien's prestige given the pale beings' superior vessels, weaponry, and knowledge of the heavens, as well as the novel possessions they were willing to trade. He would provide full support to the fort's construction so Admiral perceived the worthiness of a strong relationship. He would allow the garrison to remain after Admiral's return if the relationship proved fruitful.

As he strode to Navidad's beach, Cristóbal felt the gaze, wonderment, and friendliness of hundreds of Guacanagarí's subjects, many who approached simply to behold him. He was moved by their gentleness and generosity and waved to them. But he saw their nakedness as inferior and observed for the countless time that they were timid and cowardly and could be subjugated easily. He wondered how Alonso de Lugo was faring in his military action to subjugate Palmas and relished that military action would be unnecessary to subjugate Española, a far greater prize.

Cristóbal's mind wandered from the carefree naked bodies of the Indians he passed to memories of the slave girls shackled in the shop in Genoa and the stinking slave markets of Scio, Lagos, and Seville. At this moment, he envisioned Guacanagarí and his people would have a different fate, as they were uncorrupted by Mohammedanism, Judaism, and other sects and appeared ready to embrace Christianity.

Instead, they would retain the integrity of their homes and families and be taught to wear clothing and Castilian custom and set to work in Española as the sovereigns' subjects, building Castilian settlers' homes, farms, forts, and churches. He believed this role suited them given the backwardness and inferiority he perceived in them and the benefit bestowed by their conversion. Cristóbal now saw the Indians as human, fit to work as a subjugated people for their natural rulers and conquerors in return for receiving Christian custom and salvation.

As he boarded the launch, Cristóbal reflected on his promise to protect Guacanagarí's peoples from Caribe attack. He continued to view the stories that Caribes ate human flesh as but salacious tales. But he reflected that Caribes, as wartime enemies of the sovereigns' subjects, could and should be enslaved and sold as chattel to slave traders regardless of the validity of these stories—as well as any Indians who opposed subjugation.

FINAL PREPARATIONS AND DEPARTURE,
December 29, 1492–January 4, 1493

Guacanagarí's naborias followed sailors' commands to haul planks, dig the ditch, and do whatever necessary to help construct Admiral's fort. Guacanagarí's brother reprimanded a youth who told Admiral where gold could be found to the east, fearing Admiral simply would go there to obtain the gold himself.

On December 30, Guacanagarí hosted a feast for Admiral at the fine bohío to review the fort's progress and honor their relationship before Admiral's departure. Five subordinate caciques attended, each regaled as Guacanagarí in their finest jewelry and feathered headdresses, and Guacanagarí escorted Admiral by the arm from the beach to their ceremonial reception at the bohío. After dining, Guacanagarí removed his own headdress and placed it on Admiral. Cristóbal removed his necklace to place it on Guacanagarí and gave him a fine woolen cape, boots, and a silver ring.

The next day, Cristóbal ordered the crew to commence the *Niña*'s final provisioning with water and wood, and Guacanagarí directed that his naborias supply the *Niña* fresh cazabi. The crew loaded samples of Española's fruits and crops and some marvelous and exotic trophies for the sovereigns, including green parrots, feather headdresses, javelins, and batey balls. Xamabo brought face masks, gold jewelry, and other gifts on behalf of Guacanagarí for Fernando and Isabel. Cristóbal ordered storage of gold pieces, ceremonial vestments, and powders and juices to make body paint for the captives to wear in Castile. Bakako, Yutowa, and Abasu pondered with trepidation what their function would become when they arrived there.

The canoe and sailor dispatched to find the *Pinta* returned without success, and Cristóbal feared Martín had departed.

By New Year's Day, Cristóbal selected almost forty individuals— roughly equivalent in number to the *Santa María*'s crew—to be left in Navidad, mostly volunteers. Luis de Torres would remain in the event a translator with the Grand Khan was needed. The caulker Lope, the cooper Domingo, the ship carpenter Alonso, and the physicians Masters Alonso and Juan would stay to service the garrison. So would a lombard gunner. The sailmaker Juan would remain to be the tailor, the Genoese seaman Jácome el Rico to watch for the interests of the voyage's financiers.

Cristóbal chose Diego de Arana to be the garrison's captain, to be succeeded in the event of death by Pedro Gutiérrez and, if he also perished, Rodrigo de Escobedo. Cristóbal recognized the selection of Diego as leader would be ill received, as Diego was nigh his relative and lacked any credential for the captainship. But Cristóbal didn't trust Gutiérrez or Escobedo to respect his interest in the gold and other wealth that the garrison might find.

Grimly, Cristóbal acknowledged that he trusted none of them, leaders or crew, to properly pave the way for achieving his and the sovereigns' common interest—Española's peaceful subjugation, without need for troops. The greed, lust, contempt, and brutality in their hearts would simmer and grow following his departure, and the leaders selected lacked the authority, presence, wit, and severity to reign those impulses for long. Transgressions against the Indians could quickly result not only in reprisals against the crew but Guacanagagi's rejection of Cristóbal's friendship and settlement. Cristóbal realized his return was urgent.

Cristóbal summoned those remaining to receive his prayers, advice, and orders, designed to impart his sternest warning. He ordered that they obey Diego. He commanded that they respect and revere the lord

Guacanagarí and his nitaínos and not displease them—for Guacanagarí had saved them and was their host in his own land and kingdom—and that they avoid as death angering Guacanagarí. He cautioned that he expected them to deal sweetly and honestly, earning Guacanagarí's respect, so that on his return Guacanagarí would remain favorable to their relationship. He exhorted that they not commit insults or violence to the Indians or their property, admonishing scandals against the women that would defame Christianity. Envisioning reprisals, Cristóbal directed that they not separate into small parties vulnerable to attack, travel inland unless all together, or leave Guacanagarí's kingdom other than with his representatives and protection. He promised to seek special compensation for those remaining from the sovereigns.

On January 2, Cristóbal came ashore to say farewell to Guacanagarí and instill his friendship and fear. After reminding that the garrison would defend against Caribe attack, Cristóbal directed crewmen to conduct a mock battle between themselves using swords, crossbow, and artillery. They fired a lombard at some plank siding of the *Santa María* heaped at the beach, and the ball blasted it apart and careened far to sea, awing the onlookers. Guacanagarí's naborias assisted the crew in transporting the items stored in the two bohíos to the fort, but, as it was too small hold much more than the weapons and wine, much was deposited in a small bohío and field close by. Cristóbal and Guacanagarí dined together at the fine bohío for the last time.

As the day waned, Cristóbal embraced Diego, Pedro, and Rodrigo, and shipmates departing embraced shipmates remaining. As the final gesture, Cristóbal and Guacanagarí parted affectionately.

Cristóbal stepped into the *Santa María*'s launch to be escorted to the *Niña* by Escobedo. Rodrigo assured him that plenty of gold would be gathered while he was absent but expressed concern that Arana and the others would hoard it as their own, not the king's. Cristóbal had always understood the crews' motivation for enlisting on the voyage, and he advised Rodrigo that his role in Navidad was to ensure the king was served, for which he would be well compensated.

Rough weather delayed departure until dawn on January 4. The *Niña* now bore Cristóbal and Pero Alonso as captain and pilot of the "fleet" of one ship, and Vicente, Juan Niño, and Sancho Ruiz de Gama remained captain, master, and pilot of the caravel itself.

Cristóbal assumed Vicente's berth in the squat hold beneath the stern deck. *Niña* sailed east along Española's coast toward a high peak (Cabo del Morro, Dominican Republic), and Cristóbal spied for a harbor where, on his return, mules, cattle, and other livestock—which the islands discovered appeared to lack—could disembark safely. He named the peak Monte Christi in honor of the Savior and concluded Cipangu lay within Española and, given its proximity to Española, that Cuba was an island, not the Indies' mainland.

Within days, Caonabó, Guarionex, and Behecchio learned through informants that Guacanagarí had permitted the pale beings to construct an imposing structure within Guarico, inviting almost forty of them to live and trade, and that Guacanagarí had dispatched one or two relatives to meet the beings' paramount cacique beyond the horizon. All were astonished that Guacanagarí had upstaged them to establish perhaps a dominant, fruitful relationship with the beings. All were discomforted that the decision to allow the structure was a premature acquiescence that the beings were friendly.

Caonabó's concern ran deep. His experience as a soldier cautioned that, until otherwise proven, one had to assume a potential adversary was unfriendly, and much he heard disturbed him. The beings apparently lusted for women they had not entreated or been given. They entered bohíos uninvited and took things not offered. They had weapons that thundered and smoked to propel stone with fearsome force and range, and a purpose of their structure in Guarico was to protect these weapons.

Caonabó recognized that Guacanagarí had the authority to invite the beings into his cacicazgo and that their harboring temporarily was appropriate given their misfortune. But he doubted Guacanagarí had the ability or judgment to evaluate the risk inherent in harboring these beings permanently.

MONTE CHRISTI,
Early January 1493

By New Year's Day, Martín Alonso Pinzón and the *Pinta*'s crew had amassed more than nine hundred pesos of gold trading with nitaínos of different cacicazgos at the Río y Puerto de Martín Alonso Pinzón. Martín learned through them that Colón and Vicente were trading for gold farther west on Haiti and surmised that one of the ships had been lost. Rumor of a sinking spread rapidly through the *Pinta*'s crewmen, who feared for the safety of their relatives, friends, and neighbors, and all eyes turned on Martín to ask what happened next.

Martín had pondered that question for six weeks. He understood—as well as any man—that attempting the unchartered return across the entirety of the Ocean Sea in his one ship would be foolhardy and that reconciliation was essential, and he resolved to sail west to find Colón. While Colón's forgiveness of the desertion was inconceivable, Martín thought he could wrest Colón's pardon from prosecution. He believed his exploration had yielded the voyage's most substantial discovery of gold, and he would gloat to Colón's face that he had found the gold, that the entire crew relished he had disobeyed a Genoese's instructions, and that they all would wink and smirk in Spain when Martín adhered unstintingly to the story that his separation had been involuntary. Martín appreciated his contention of involuntarily separation was belied by weeks of trading at his cove, and he ordered the *Pinta*'s crew to swear that they had anchored there for but six days.

Before departing to find Colón, Martín decided to seize his own captives, envisioning they would impress the sovereigns if and when he obtained his own audience, and he ordered the *Pinta*'s crew to seize four men and two girls. The Haitians residing and trading in the cove were alarmed, and the families of those abducted were distraught. Word spread that the men seized would be eaten and the girls enslaved as concubines.

The crews of the *Niña* and *Pinta* sighted each other after midday on January 6 and cheered mightily, and those on the *Pinta* realized the *Santa María* had been lost and wondered if crewmates had perished. The *Niña* quartered into the wind as the *Pinta* closed to her, and Martín's heart pounded when he spied Vicente. His gut wrenched when he spied Colón. Cristóbal spotted Martín and prayed that St. Francis grant himself the composure to achieve a working relationship with the traitor. Bakako and Yutowa waved to the Guanahaníans aboard the *Pinta*. Cristóbal ordered that the caravels return to the bay at Monte Christi since there was no other harbor to shelter a meeting.

The tranquility of the bay belied a tumultuous storm of emotion stirring on board the ships. The crews of the *Niña* and *Pinta* grew quiet, apprehensive of the impending confrontation. Bakako and Yutowa grimly observed there were additional captives aboard the *Pinta*, including girls. All studied Admiral's reaction as Martín descended into the *Pinta*'s launch. Cristóbal stood motionless on the stern deck, with a countenance revealing only gravity. As its captain, Vicente greeted Martín when he climbed aboard the *Niña* with a formality unnatural for brothers, designed to evidence an absence of collusion or levity.

Cristóbal and Martín recognized each other icily but professionally, emphasizing to all that orderliness would prevail. Cristóbal ordered Martín to meet in the hold beneath the stern deck, where they sat on chairs given the low ceiling, but feet apart. Vicente and Cristóbal's steward Pedro stood outside, listening but precluding that to others.

Cristóbal and Martín beheld each other and seethed with irreconcilable distrust and hatred. But Martín spread his hands to indicate he had come for reconciliation.

"I come aboard to excuse myself. I parted against my will."

"Your insolence exceeds only your pride and covetousness. Your words are false, your disloyalty brazen, your heart corrupted by Satan."

Martín folded his arms upon his chest, insulted by the association to the devil. He glared into Colón's eyes and beheld a fury as violent as the Ocean Sea—which Martín had met time and again.

"I have come for reconciliation. The weather separated us. No member of the crew will testify otherwise."

"Absurd! No sailor will testify the weather separated you for seven weeks."

"I parted against my will. That is what all will say. And after parting, I found the gold we have sought. I have found hordes of it, over nine hundred pesos. No one will conclude I erred in pursuing a different route than you." Martín studied the scorn written in Colón's face. "You may have some of it."

"Every piece of gold you possess is already the sovereigns'!"

There was silence.

"I can return to Spain myself, with gold for the sovereigns, and they can decide who served them best." Martín glared at Colón. "Or you can pardon me. You discovered neither this island nor my gold. But you may consider my gold a discovery of your voyage if you pardon me."

Vicente sagged with relief upon hearing Martín's claim of the gold found but grimaced at the stances and tone of the two men.

To Cristóbal's and Martín's surprise, he quietly entered the hold, squatting beside them. Cristóbal glared at him, despising him and the loyalty to his brother.

Cristóbal seethed that the Lord was testing his faith yet again, asking that he bear for the countless time insults and ignominies directed by unworthy, ungrateful, and deceitful men. He ached to deny Martín any comfort and relished the thought of placing him in chains. But Cristóbal bitterly understood that he was the foreigner and Martín the crews' true leader.

Vicente interceded. "Martín has returned to your command, and now you must pardon him and his success. We must cross the Ocean Sea in unison, ready to assist each other." Vicente lowered his voice to an urgent whisper, sharpening his tone. "When we step outside, you must affirm to all that you pardoned Martín because he was separated against his will."

There was silence as Cristóbal reflected. The fire in his eyes betrayed that, regardless of anything promised, he would vehemently seek Martín's prosecution on return to Spain. Martín's eyes revealed an equal conviction that, regardless of anything promised, he intended to retain the gold aboard the *Pinta* and claim credit before the sovereigns for its discovery and the discovery of the Indies. But both men were sea captains and grimly understood the fury of the Ocean Sea rendered their hatred inconsequential and that sailing together was essential.

Cristóbal grudgingly nodded agreement, speechless, and gazed bitterly away. Martín was satisfied. Vicente slumped in relief that a pardon would be witnessed by all aboard.

There was another silence. Then Martín asked, "How did you lose your ship?"

"The ship grounded upon a reef well discernible. The owner de la Cosa fell asleep on his watch and fled while the ship's lodging became irreversible." Vicente nodded his head in agreement. Cristóbal added, "We have left forty men for whom I must return."

Martín winced. "How can that be safe? They're among savages, vastly outnumbered, and we are more than eight hundred leagues from Spain. What do I tell their mothers, wives, and daughters? It's a crime to leave them."

"There's little alternative—we couldn't safely carry everyone and our captives in the caravels," Cristóbal responded. "It's also for the better. We have started the first settlement, mostly with eager volunteers."

"We have built them a fort and left them most of the weapons," Vicente added.

"Do you really think these cowardly, weaponless peoples pose risk?" Cristóbal continued.

Martín was silent, but shook his head indicating no.

When their composure returned, the three men stepped outside the hold and the word spread that Martín had been lost and pardoned. Cristóbal recorded in his journal that he had overlooked the falsity of Martín's excuses so that Satan would not impede the conclusion of the voyage. He did take credit for Martín's discovery indirectly, writing that the Lord had miraculously ordered the *Santa María* to ground at the best place to make the settlement near the island's gold mines. He informed the sovereigns that Martín and Vicente were arrogant, greedy, disobedient, unjust, and unruly but that there was no time for punishment.

Over the next two days, Cristóbal explored up the Yaque, finding gold pieces as large as lentils and naming the river the Río de Oro (River of Gold). He spotted some mermaids,* as in Guinea. He learned from Martín's Guanahanían captive of a mountain pass leading south from Martín's cove to the "Cibao" within Española's interior. He also heard of the existence of a large island to Cuba's south named Yamaye and of an island farther east where there were none but women, as Marco Polo had written. He now understood that the mainland was but ten days' journey by canoe from Española and Yamaye and that the mainland's people were clothed.

The ships departed Monte Christi after midnight January 9 to anchor at Martín's inlet a day later. Cristóbal was determined to extirpate any memory of Martín's success at the site and any possibility that Martín could exploit it. He renamed the cove's stream the Río de Gracia (River of Grace), dissembling further as to the pardon and directed that the captives seized by Martín just days before be clothed and released so Martín would have no loyal interpreters or guides in the future. He explained in the journal that these captives were released because they were the sovereigns' subjects on an island

---

*Perhaps manatees.

where the sovereigns already had a settlement and that Martín's treachery was so public he could not hide it. Cristóbal shuddered to consider what use the *Pinta*'s crew had made of the girls. At midnight, the ships raised anchor and sailed east with favorable winds.

The Haitian families at the cove were overcome with surprise and relief when their loved ones returned. The captives quickly removed their clothes. When dawn came, the mothers of the girls took them to the stream to cleanse their bodies, fearing their souls would never heal.

Caonabó, Guarionex, and Behecchio received successive reports that Martín had seized and then released captives, including girls. Anacaona inquired as to the girls' treatment and was revolted. Caonabó couldn't interpret the pale beings' conduct, but his anxiety over their presence in Marien grew.

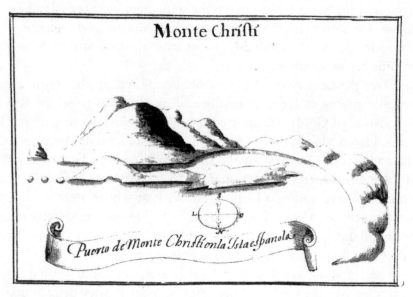

Monte Christi, 1592.

Ciguayo and Samaná, *January 12–16, 1493*

Mayobanex lay quietly in his hammock in darkness, listening to the din of crickets and tree frogs, unable to sleep. For weeks, he had received reports that pale beings with fearsome weapons were trading with the other paramount Haitian caciques and, but days before, that they were approaching Ciguayo in their vessels. As dawn approached, a scout arrived to warn that they were now offshore. Mayobanex waited patiently for sunrise and then dispatched messengers summoning his nitaínos and troops to his village's central plaza.

Mayobanex's first wife, Tuobasu, emerged from the caney, directed naborias to serve her husband juice and cazabi, and joined him.

"The strange beings have arrived," Mayobanex remarked. "I will meet them."

"You should be careful. They may be evil."

"Possibly. But the reports are that they just want gold."

"Then you'll disappoint them. Guarionex and Caonabó have the gold. Will you seek their friendship?"

"I don't know yet. I'll talk to them, peacefully, and ascertain their substance and intent. If I doubt their friendliness, I'll encourage them to pass us by."

"Still, you should be careful. Be sure your men don't provoke a fight."

"Remember, we aren't as timid as our neighbors. If there were a fight, I don't expect to lose it." Mayobanex saw Tuobasu's concern rise. "But there'll be no fight. I'm going myself to ensure a cordial and peaceful encounter."

Mayobanex assembled his nitaínos and troops. They asked whether he desired a litter and he declined. While this was a diplomatic mission, he intended to walk as a soldier, tracking the pale beings as he had stalked Caribes. He waved to Tuobasu and his other wives and led his men into the forest in single file, departing east onto a ridge of coastal mountains and bearing bows and arrows, spears, and macanas.

Soon, they emerged onto open hillside cascading toward the coastal plain, and Mayobanex gazed north into a strong, northwesterly wind to behold the two enormous vessels distant at sea. He was surprised by their speed and admired their apparent dominance over the wind and ocean. By nightfall, the vessels passed the promontory at which Haiti's northern coast veers south (Cabo Francés Viejo) and stalled in the sea for the night. Mayobanex studied them quarter in the moonlight, their fires and enormous cloths flickering in the wind, and marveled when they departed in the darkness before dawn.

Mayobanex's warriors hiked the entire next day, traversing coastal plain during the morning, when sight of the vessels was lost, and ascending into the mountains of the Samaná peninsula during the afternoon, when sight was regained. By evening, the vessels came to rest in the large bay at the peninsula's northeastern tip (Bahía del Rincon). The beings alighted ashore seeking water and the local Samanáns fled.

Cristóbal named the mountainous cape on the bay's northern shore Cabo del Enamorado (Cape of the Lover, now Cabo Cabrón) and, in his journal, compared the cape on the bay's southern shore to Cape St. Vincent in Portugal. He rose early on January 13 and remained at anchor because of unfavorable winds, astonished Española was so large.

Sailors rowed a launch to a beach where they encountered local men with a fearsome appearance. Their naked skins were darkened by charcoal and black paint, and their hair was long, falling on their backs almost to the waist and bundled in hairnets of cord and parrot feathers. To the crew's surprise, these Indians carried bows and arrows designed as those used by Europeans, and the crew bought two of them in exchange for trifles. The crew implored one of the locals to meet Admiral, and, with Mayobanex's scouts watching, he was taken to the *Niña*.

Cristóbal was astonished by the visitor's appearance and ascertained his language differed from the Indians previously encountered because Bakako and Yutowa could not converse freely with him. Cristóbal suspected that the peoples at this site were Caribes. Through Bakako, he attempted a conversation with the Samanán of gestures and singular words, and he inferred that the Caribes lived farther east on an island that possessed significant gold. He also gleaned there was another island east named Matininó where women lived alone, as well as one named Guanín where gold or copper abounded. Cristóbal recalled that Mandeville told of an island where women lived alone east of Ethiopia* and that Marco Polo told of this island and a related island where men lived alone.†

Cristóbal bestowed trifles on the Samanán and dispatched him as

---

*Amazonia.
†Islands of Males and Females.

an emissary back to the beach to spread goodwill, accompanied by seven armed crewmen. When they landed, more than fifty Samanáns armed with bows and arrows and macanas waited at the forest's edge. Their friend the emissary convinced them to disarm, and the crew and the Samanáns met on the beach, where, at Cristóbal's instruction, the crew bartered for more bows and arrows. But soon the Samanáns distrusted the situation and ran to rearm themselves to threaten or attack. The crew anticipated attack and struck first, gashing one Samanán's buttocks with a sword and piercing another's breast with an arrow dispatched by crossbow. The Samanáns fled, terrified by the unknown weapons. The pilot commanding the launch prohibited the crew from pursuing and they returned to the *Niña*, unharmed but unnerved by the first combat hostility of the voyage.

Mayobanex's scouts rushed to inform him of the altercation and smoke signals rose from village to village warning of the pale beings. Mayobanex listened to his scouts carefully, recalling Tuobaso's warning and intent on deciphering the skirmish's cause. He well understood that the terror of men armed and unknown to one another, and in close proximity, frequently triggered violence. Gravely, he resolved to heal the wounds on both sides in the morning, regardless of fault.

That night, Cristóbal wrote in his journal that he was both pleased and sad. His pleasure was that these Indians would fear Christians, including the crew of the Navidad garrison if it explored at this site. He surmised that these Indians probably were the Caribes who ate people or, if not, fearless neighbors to Caribes. He decided to take captives from them, hoping they could lead to the women's island of Mandeville and Marco Polo.

At dawn on January 14, Mayobanex and his warriors arrived at the beach where the altercation had occurred. He met the Samanán who had been invited aboard the vessels and listened to his account of the visit and the cause of the skirmish. Mayobanex visited the bohío where the two wounded men lay, perhaps mortally, and spoke briefly to their wives, thanking them for their husbands' bravery. He promised they would not want if their husbands died and then returned to the beach, intent to meet the beings' leader.

Cristóbal observed men gathering on the beach, including the man previously hosted and a cacique of importance. He realized these Indians intended to renew a peaceful contact regardless of the altercation and dispatched well-armed crewmen to meet them. When the crew debarked, Mayobanex removed his stone necklace and had it handed to the crews' leader as a gesture of peace and security. Unarmed and outnumbered, he and three nitaínos stepped into the launch to meet the pale beings' cacique.

Mayobanex studied the weapons the pale beings carried and realized the swords and crossbows were the instruments that had wounded his subjects. He scrutinized the sweat-drenched cloth that wrapped their bodies and pondered the reason for it. He smelled their pale skin and realized they rarely bathed. He studied the heavy paddles they used and judged that their strange canoe was not as swift as the Ciguayan.

Cristóbal stood with Bakako on the stern deck, studying the cacique as he climbed aboard the *Niña*, his blackened skin shimmering in the sunlight and his lengthy hair and parrot feathers fluttering in the wind. Cristóbal reflected that the ruler comported himself with grace, stature, and confidence, belying his wild appearance and any fear stemming from yesterday's altercation. Cristóbal was confident of winning his friendship with trifles and courtesy—as had been achieved with other caciques over the past three months.

When they arrived before him, Cristóbal welcomed the cacique and his nitaínos and received the stone necklace. He sought with a soft tone and Bakako's assistance to indicate gratitude for the gift and friendship and offered biscuits and honey to all and, for the cacique, beads and a red cap and cloth. Mayobanex responded in his native Macorix and gestures that he valued the gifts and enjoyed the food. He realized the youth spoke Taíno with a Lucayan accent—likely a Lucayan naboria—and resolved to communicate in Taíno as best he could. He suspected the youth was assisting against his will.

Admiral graciously led Mayobanex on a tour of the ship. Mayobanex perceived the courtesy but discerned no attempt by Admiral to address the skirmish. He wondered if the language barrier made apology too difficult, but surmised Admiral felt no sorrow or guilt. He studied Admiral's confident speech and gestures describing his vessel and suspected that Admiral not only felt justified in what had occurred but sought to warn that it could occur again—whenever Admiral so ordered.

Cristóbal held his gold piece aloft. "I seek gold." Bakako said the Taíno word for *gold*, which Mayobanex recognized.

"We have gold, but there is more on the islands to the east." Mayobanex nodded his head affirmatively but pointed east. He reflected that emphasizing the latter point was important if he wished to encourage these beings to leave. "There's much gold on the islands to the east."

"Are you Caribe?" Cristóbal asked through Bakako.

"No. Caribes live to the east." Mayobanex pointed east.

"Do they live on the island Carib?"

"Yes."

"Is the island Matininó east, as well? Do women alone live there?"

Mayobanex recognized the word *Matininó* and was surprised that Admiral appeared to know the ancestral account of Guahayona and his travels. He perceived Admiral's intent to travel east and again chose to encourage that. "Yes. Matininó is east. Women live there alone except when men come to lie with them."

"Is the island Guanín east?" Cristóbal continued. "Is it near Matininó? Is it full of gold?"

Mayobanex now was startled, perceiving that Admiral knowingly sought to follow Guahayona's legendary voyage. His anxiety surged as he reflected that Admiral and his beings might indeed be spirits with power to achieve Matininó and Guanín. But his skepticism to the contrary also swelled, and he questioned whether Admiral and his beings simply were men who misunderstood what they had heard—fools seeking gold in reliance on a faith they did not comprehend. For the third time, Mayobanex chose to encourage Admiral's departure. "Yes. It's near Matininó and overflows with guanín."

Cristóbal was elated, and the men shared more biscuits and honey. Cristóbal interpreted that the cacique was content with the visit. Before departing, Mayobanex promised Admiral that he would return with a face mask embedded with gold to affirm the two men's personal relationship.

The next morning, Mayobanex rose to decide the relationship his cacicazgo should have with the pale beings. He consulted his nitaínos but made the decision regardless of their views. Mayobanex wanted no relationship with the pale beings, preferring that they leave amicably never to be encountered again. He didn't trust them. He dispatched a face mask to fulfill his promise to Admiral but did not return to meet him, deciding instead to wait in a highland village until the beings left the peninsula before returning home.

Cristóbal rose and determined to depart east after meeting the cacique again and taking captives. Relations with the local peoples remained strained, and he named the bay Golfo de las Flechas (Gulf of Arrows) in remembrance of the skirmish. During the day, he received the cacique's face mask and discovered that the Samanáns possessed significant cotton and a chili more valuable than pepper. His crew discovered considerable weed floating in the bay, similar to that encountered midsea on the outward crossing, and he speculated that they were less than 400 leagues from the Canaries.

Four youths came to the Niña and Cristóbal discussed the islands east with them. He was impressed with their knowledge of geography, gold, and guanín and, as the youths tried to depart at dusk, he had them seized. Some were but a few years older than Bakako.

That evening, Cristóbal wrote in his journal that the site would yield fifty caravels of the chili per year and copper likely could be obtained on the islands Carib and Matininó, noting it would be difficult to secure Carib's copper since its peoples ate human flesh. He indicated he would take more captives on both islands, and, past midnight, the Niña and Pinta raised anchor and departed homeward bound.

While proud of the territories claimed, Cristóbal despaired that not a single city, bridge, or golden-roofed temple had been found as proof of the Indies after three months of exploration. He yearned to achieve this proof on the homeward journey by locating the islands spoken of by Mandeville and Marco Polo and seizing captives therefrom.

A scout woke Mayobanex as he slept in a local cacique's caney. He stepped outside in the moonlight to watch fires stoked throughout the village as alarm spread that some youths had not returned from the vessels, which had departed. He wasn't surprised and pondered what fate befell them. Soon, a mother's wail pierced the night.

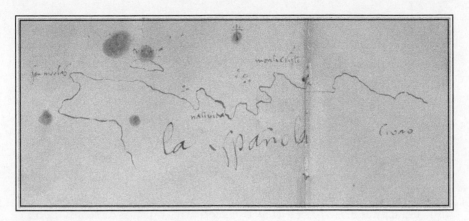

Columbus's map of Northern Haiti, 1493.

MEETING WITH ADMIRAL'S LIEUTENANTS,
Guarico, (January 1493)

After watching his emissary depart to meet King Fernando and Queen Isabel on January 4, Guacanagarí hoped to establish a productive relationship with Admiral's lieutenants that would flourish to become an exclusive trading partnership when Admiral returned. He recognized the lieutenants had neither Admiral's perception nor nobility but understood that neither did the men who captained his own war canoes. He dispatched a messenger to the fort to invite the lieutenants for breakfast the next day.

Most of the crew slept outside the fort, as it was too small to hold them, and some had found women to sleep with in their own bohíos. Diego de Arana interpreted Guacanagarí's invitation as exclusive to himself, as the garrison's captain. But that insulted Pedro Gutiérrez and Rodrigo de Escobedo, who reminded Diego that they were the Crown representatives and, unlike himself, had experience in leadership and meeting foreign peoples.

Diego shied from publicly denying Pedro and Rodrigo and sullenly acquiesced as they strolled together to Guarico's central plaza. Guacanagarí greeted them warmly and they sat on duhos, sharing cazabi and pineapple juice.

Through hand gestures and dirt diagrams, Guacanagarí sought to discuss food, gold, and women. He explained that he presided in the plaza every few weeks to apportion food among his subjects and invited the lieutenants to attend to obtain the garrison's food. He offered the lieutenants plots where the garrison could plant the seed from Castile.

Diego agreed they would attend the plaza but looked to Pedro and Rodrigo for guidance as to the seed. While many of the crew might know enough to tend a small garden, none were farmers, as settlement had never been envisaged, and sailors eschewed labor ashore. Pedro thanked Guacanagarí for the land and pointed to Guacanagarí's attendant naborias to suggest that they do the planting. Guacanagarí worried that the seed was unknown to his people but gestured he would provide naborias to assist.

Guacanagarí indicated that he would bring gold often, to be traded for the items now stored near the fort. He held a gold piece in one hand and his gloves and a hawk's bell in the other.

Diego responded immediately, pointing to the hawk's bell and himself. "I will decide the items traded and receive the gold." Guacanagarí observed that Rodrigo and Pedro were surprised.

Rodrigo spoke, pointing to all three of them and the hawk's bell. "The gold is for Fernando and Isabel. We three together will decide the items traded and receive the gold." Guacanagarí noted Diego's surprise.

"I'm captain," Diego interjected. "I'm responsible to the Admiral."

"I'm Fernando's captain," Pedro countered. "Rodrigo is Isabel's captain."

Guacanagarí couldn't understand the words, but he perceived the situation. He nodded courteously to all three and acknowledged to himself that Admiral's leadership would be lacking or contested and that he would, of necessity, deal directly with all three lieutenants.

Guacanagarí asked a nitaíno to introduce two women who had been standing nearby for this moment. With gestures, the nitaíno explained the elder woman was his wife and wore a nagua, and that the men of the garrison could never touch women wearing naguas. Guacanagarí studied the lieutenants' expressions and refrained from berating them that this prohibition had already been violated, more than once. The nitaíno indicated the younger woman was unmarried and that unmarried women didn't wear naguas and could be touched if they agreed, but only if they agreed. Guacanagarí gaged the lieutenants' reactions and again concealed his disgust, as this prohibition also had been violated. He reflected that perhaps the pale men's attachment to clothing distorted their perception of when women consented, confusing nakedness for consent.

Finished with his agenda, Guacanagarí escorted the lieutenants back to the fort, where he observed the crew at rest and leisure, lying about. Before all, he parted courteously from Pedro and Rodrigo and then, with greater solemnity, Diego. Diego responded with exaggerated adulation of the two men's relationship, unpracticed and inappropriate given their unequal status, and Guacanagarí doubted Diego had the slightest experience with leadership.

Within a few days, Guacanagarí invited the lieutenants to sit with him in Guarico's plaza while fish was distributed to farmers, cazabi to fishermen, and both fish and cazabi to the garrison. He was astounded how much food the pale beings took to eat. Within a week, his naborias planted the seed, observing the commands of a few crewmen. While it sprouted quickly, the pale men made no effort to weed or mulch.

XI

NORTHERN CROSSING

LETTERS TO THE SOVEREIGNS,
January–February 1493

The *Niña* and *Pinta* coursed east by north toward Europe, propelled by an unusual westerly wind. As the sun broke the horizon beyond the *Niña*'s bow, Bakako and Yutowa gathered the Samanán captives to sit before Admiral on the stern deck, where they trembled to learn their fate. Cristóbal offered them cazabi and water, tempering their fears before seeking information.

Cristóbal turned to Bakako and Yutowa. "You say they speak of Matininó, where women live alone, and of Carib, where there are only men. I want to sail to both, and then to Guanín for its gold and copper." Cristóbal pointed to the Samanáns. "Get them to lead us there."

Bakako and Yutowa nodded yes, but Bakako was dumbfounded. He had accepted they were traveling to Admiral's Castile, far beyond the horizon, but never conceived Admiral would visit Matininó and Guanín—as if retracing Guahayona's own voyage. While Admiral's interest in Guanín was obvious, the interest in Matininó was inexplicable given his disrespect for Yúcahu and other spirits. Bakako marveled to behold the venerated places.

Cristóbal pointed east and addressed the Samanáns. "Carib? Is it that way?"

A Samanán pointed southeast.

Bakako responded in Taíno, pointing toward the Samanán and then southeast a number of times. "Admiral is seeking Carib. Have you actually seen or been to Carib?"

The Samanán replied in Macorix and gestures. "No. Never. The Caribes would eat us. But they say it's there."

Bakako understood only "no." There was no purpose in translating, as Admiral would sail there regardless.

Cristóbal redirected the ships southeast, and sailors dutifully adjusted the sails to run with a tail wind over starboard. But Cristóbal quickly detected the crew's reluctance to veer the course from Europe and, within moments, his steward Pedro reported to him substantial murmurs of gloom, discontent, and even hostility. The crew was distraught the ships were leaking at the keel and would barely service crossing the Ocean Sea, no less further exploration. Most of the fleet's provisions had been left at Navidad, and many feared the stores remaining were insufficient. They had thought they were homeward bound.

Cristóbal sensed the hostility himself and, within moments, decided the risk of severely alienating his crew outweighed the validation achieved by finding Carib. When the wind sharpened, he ordered Pero Alonso to reset the course northeast by east, believing that the direct route to Spain.* The crew cheered mightily.

But Cristóbal had not yet given up, hoping the course set would achieve Matininó so he might take yet five or six more captives as proof of the Indies. He turned to Bakako. "Ask the Samanáns whether this course will attain Matininó, or close thereto."

"Admiral seeks Matininó," Bakako said to the Samanáns, shrugging. He completed the thought silently to himself. *Where Guahayona left the women taken from the Cacibajagua.*

Whether they understood or not, the Samanáns obliged the confirmation. But no island appeared as the day waned and, recognizing the Lord meant to deny him, Cristóbal abandoned further discovery. That night, he reported in his journal that they could not have passed more than fifteen or twenty leagues from the islands Carib and Matininó, where women and men lived apart.

---

*Actually, closer to the Artic.

For the next three weeks, the *Niña* and *Pinta* sailed on a starboard tack northeast to north when the wind permitted, sometimes veering farther east or north, occasionally driven southeast on a port tack. Cristóbal sought to escape the easterly winds that had pushed him west from the Canaries to find more variable winds, hopefully including westerlies to push him back to Spain. On January 21, he noticed the temperature growing colder and the nights longer. The next day, the winds fell and the Indians enjoyed bathing in the sea. On January 25, the crew caught a dolphin and a large shark, which all enjoyed since their provisions had dwindled to hardtack, cazabi, sweet potato, and wine. On February 3, Cristóbal dead reckoned that the polestar appeared very high in the sky, as on Cape St. Vincent, indicating they were approaching a latitude of 37 degrees north.* He sought to locate the strong westerlies apparently encountered by Dulhmo.

Each day, Bakako and Yutowa took instruction on Castilian and Christianity from Admiral's servants. Bakako warmed to the Castilian and the art of translation, gratified he had a facility with the pale men's language that exceeded Yutowa's and far surpassed the other Taínos'. He remained cold to the Christianity.

In spite of the temperate weather, some of the crewmen developed rashes, with red sores on their penises (syphilis). They joked and wondered whether the cause was overuse with the Indian women. A few developed more serious rashes on their palms and the soles of their feet, as well as headaches. Martín was afflicted and grew weary. Pain surged, and some perceived the Lord's condemnation.

As they progressed northeast, Cristóbal turned to draft two letters to announce and aggrandize the triumph of his voyage and convince the sovereigns and financiers to underwrite a substantial second voyage to commence Española's colonization. One was designed for broad publication, the other for the king and queen alone, and he intended both to be dispatched to the sovereigns as soon as he arrived in Castile. Unlike the journal, neither would contain nautical information sufficient to permit others to replicate the voyage. Cristóbal would safeguard the journal—which did reveal the route sailed—for his own delivery to the king and queen when they met. He also would

---

*Actually, 34 degrees north.

distribute copies of the public letter for his own promotion of the discovery, first to Luis de Santángel, who would grasp the commercial potential right away.

Each letter began boldly proclaiming unqualified triumph. The public letter declared that he had sailed from the Canaries to the Indies to take possession by proclamation and without opposition of many islands filled with innumerable peoples. The private letter pronounced that the Lord now gave the sovereigns the greatest victory he had ever given any prince. The public letter also rebuked his detractors, noting that the Lord gives triumph over things that appear impossible to those who follow his ways, and proclaimed that all Christendom ought to delight in the potential converts and temporal gains.

In the public letter, Cristóbal explained that the islands discovered were fertile to a limitless degree, particularly Española, having arable land suited for planting, cattle, building towns and villages, and mining gold. The Indians encountered went naked, spoke a common language, possessed no weapons other than canes, and were incurably timid and guileless, generously sharing all they possessed, especially food, and it was unclear whether they recognized private property. But they weren't ignorant and had acute intelligence, and they were good navigators, with canoes of incredible speed. They also weren't black as in Guinea, the sun shining less intensely at the islands' northern latitude. He hadn't found human monstrosities except for an island of ferocious people who ate human flesh and ranged throughout the islands to pillage and loot, and he had discovered an island named Matininó where women lived alone except when they had intercourse with these fierce peoples. As for the Indians' subjugation, they had been given gifts to achieve their affection and induce them to Christianity and the love and service of the sovereigns and the Castilian nation. They knew no creed, were not idolaters, and were inclined to conversion.

Without mentioning the *Santa María*'s demise, Cristóbal explained that he had taken possession of a large town on Española in the best location for the island's gold mines and trading with both the Grand Khan and Spain. He had constructed a fort and left a sufficient number of crewmen there, with arms and provisions for a year and a great friendship with a friendly king who called Cristóbal a brother. Even if this king were hostile, the men left could defend themselves and destroy the land—assuming they knew how to govern themselves. Cristóbal promised he would provide the sovereigns as much gold as they needed—provided the sovereigns lent further assistance—as well as spices, cotton, aloe, and mastic, and as many slaves as they ordered shipped, who would be taken from the idolaters.

Cristóbal remembered his queen, her abiding faith, and their special bond and included in the private letter much the same information, but emphasizing spiritual triumphs and divine and personal aspects. The expedition had placed very large crosses in many harbors discovered throughout the journey. The Lord had ordained the discovery of innumerable peoples and gold mines, and, from Española, would give the sovereigns gold, pepper, mastic, cotton, and aloe, as well as immumerable slaves from the idolaters. When the sovereigns ordered slaves, Cristóbal would send Caribes for the most part. Cristóbal indicated Bakako had taken his friendship, without naming the boy, and related how Guacanagarí distributed food among his subjects, characterizing it as a very singular manner of existence.

Cristóbal also pronounced that, in seven years, he would be able to pay the sovereigns for 5,000 cavalry and 50,000 foot soldiers to conquer Jerusalem, asserting that was the purpose for underwriting the voyage. Subsequent profits would pay for doubling those numbers. He warned against delays—as suffered with respect to the first voyage—and he implored that the church send prelates to evangelize the Indians, admonishing that those the pope provided should be free of greed. Bitterly, Cristóbal reminded the sovereigns that he had languished seven years, borne a thousand indignities, and suffered much hardship to achieve the voyage, which happened due to his importuning them. His purpose was to serve the Lord and them and to bring the business of the Indies to perfection—for which he was due honors according to his service. He requested they seek a cardinalate for his son when they wrote the pope.

As Cristóbal wrote his letters, on February 4, the *Niña* and *Pinta* encountered the northwesterly gale he had anticipated at the Azores and veered east to Spain, with the wind astern. Two days later, Vicente believed they were south of Flores. The wind shifted to the east for two days and progress slowed but, by February 10, Vicente, Pero Alonso, and Sancho agreed they had passed east of the Azores and were approaching Madeira and Porto Santo. Cristóbal disagreed, believing that Flores now lay to the north and that they were 150 leagues farther west.

On February 12, the seas grew high and the weather stormy. Cristóbal and his officers weren't surprised, for that was typical of the Ocean Sea at this latitude in the winter. Cristóbal stored his letters and turned to brave the Ocean Sea.

VIOLENT STORM, OFF AZORES,
February 12–15, 1493

Bakako and Yutowa huddled on the stern deck, helping to tend a signal lantern's fire and coveting its warmth, yet shivering naked in the gale howling from the southwest. Bakako grimaced as an enormous wave curled into the ship below him and broke along the starboard rail, propelling the stern violently upward as the wave crested and then precipitously downward into the trailing trough as the bow jutted to the sky. Sailors on deck clutched masts, ropes, and bulwarks dearly to avoid being swept overboard, and sailors in the hold secured everything movable lest they be impaled as objects careened about. Bakako studied the *Pinta* labor to stern and remembered that, unlike canoes, the pale beings' vessels could shatter and sink. He realized that Guabancex was furiously approaching and honored her, assuring her he hadn't ignored her power and authority.

At dusk, the crew sang the customary hymn to the Virgin with extraordinary conviction. Every man—crew and captive—was bone cold, wet, and hungry. The provisions had dwindled to support but one meal a day. Bakako joined the crew to worship the Virgin. But he had studied Admiral's statuette being or depicting her many times, and he dismissed her understanding of the wind and sea. The memory of Father invoking Yúcahu when the squall drove them west from Guanahaní flickered through his thoughts, and Bakako also honored Yúcahu, pledging reverence surpassing that offered the Virgin so Yúcahu not be jealous.

As night fell, the sea grew more turbulent, and waves and harsh spray swept the deck frequently, drenching all. Admiral's servants offered Bakako and Yutowa clothing and Admiral joined them in the halo of the lantern to study the weather. An enormous lightning bolt forked broadly across the heavens to the north-northeast. Bakako understood that Guabancex's herald Guataúba had arrived, undoubtedly to warn that his master's anger grew severe. Within moments, Guataúba struck twice again, and Admiral explained that the storm would grow worse.

Cristóbal watched the *Pinta*'s lantern disappear and reappear in the tumult and reminded Bakako and Yutowa that maintaining their lantern's fire was essential for keeping the ships together. He ordered sails furled, abandoning forward progress in the darkness to focus singularly on safely floating the towering waves. He esteemed the *Niña*'s seaworthiness and remained on the stern deck most of the night, frequently conferring with Juan Niño as to the ship's integrity and Pero Alonso as to her bearing within the onslaught.

Dawn emerged from darkness slowly on February 13, as thunderclouds blanketed the sky to all horizons, and Cristóbal ordered some sails unfurled. Bakako recognized that the wind had abated slightly but the sea was more tormented, engulfing the *Niña* in a fashion he had never beheld. Enormous pyramidal swells arrived from the west, as if propelled by another spirit, crossing violently and unpredictably with the waves blown by the southwestern gale. Ceaselessly, every wave now curled and crashed onto the deck. The day's only meal—cazabi and sweet potato—was dispensed at midday to the men at their posts, and all gulped it down lest it be lost to the sea.

Cristóbal asked his page Pedro to call out the seamen's verses of Psalm 107. From memory, Pedro shouted above the howl that the Lord raises the stormy wind to lift the waves, mounting sailors to the heavens and dropping them to the depths, melting their souls and reeling them to and fro like drunken men until they cry at wits end to the Lord in their trouble—whereupon the Lord hears them, calms the storm, and stills the waves to bring them from distress to their haven. The crew prayed to the Lord, and Bakako and Yutowa joined them, believing it could only help. They then appealed fervently to Yúcahu, with faith in his greater stature.

Cristóbal feared the hulls would buckle. As dusk arrived, he ordered the sails furled again but for a portion of the mainsail reefed and hung low to leave the ship sufficient power to weave between the cross waves. He observed the *Pinta* had parted considerable distance and pitched and bruised worse than the *Niña*, and he ordered additional lanterns fired so the ships maintained contact.

The storm strengthened into the night, and Cristóbal and Juan Niño determined *Niña* could no longer withstand the beating of the waves to starboard. They ordered Pero Alonso to abandon the eastern course and let the ship run with the wind farther northeast, its high stern bearing the brunt of the sea. The *Pinta* did the same and soon disappeared from sight. The waves broke relentlessly through *Niña*'s rudder port, washing over the deck and crew below. All were freezing numb. All confessed their sins.

At dawn on February 14, the men on the *Niña* and *Pinta* awoke to see the other had vanished. Each crew surmised the other likely had perished and a pall of gloom, despair, and death overcame both ships. Sailors writhed that their private stashes of gold were for naught and bitterly regretted having enlisted upon the Genoese's entreaty of riches. They cursed that the Genoese had cajoled them to continue the voyage when they had wanted to turn back.

Cristóbal had brushed death at sea before and accepted that the Lord gave life and took it according to his design. While Cristóbal felt no charity toward the crew, he confessed that he had promised riches, not death. He ached that death would rob him of the glory of his triumph and the sovereigns of the victory due their support. His detractors would never concede his geographic theory was correct! His nobility would never be acclaimed!

Cristóbal grimly realized he had done all worldly that could be done to save *Niña* and that the only resort was an extraordinary appeal to divine providence. He summoned the crew to prove their devotion by vowing that a pilgrimage be made on their behalf to worship at the shrine of the revered Santa María de Guadalupe. A chickpea was carved with a cross and placed in a sailor's cap with unmarked peas. Shouting to be heard above the gale, Cristóbal gravely explained to the men huddled about him that, if the Virgin heard their vows and saved the ship, the man who drew the crossed pea would serve as the pilgrim to Guadalupe and present the Virgin a five-pound wax candle.

Bakako watched the shivering pale men—far paler now than he had ever seen them—fervently pledge the pilgrimage if selected. Admiral put his hand in the cap and drew the crossed pea. Admiral, and each crewman and captive, prayed fervently to the Virgin that their devotion be heard and rewarded with *Niña*'s salvation. Bakako and Yutowa honored Attabeira in case she could help.

The storm did not abate, and the *Niña* continued to scud with the sea, seemingly doomed on a course northeast to a landless horizon. Cristóbal's faith wavered, and he asked why the Lord had enlightened him as to the certainty of the voyage and crowned it with victory, aggrandizing the sovereigns and squashing his opponents—only to have all hindered by his death!

Cristóbal summoned the crewmen together to prove their devotion again. They gathered numb and forlorn midship to vow a second pilgrimage to the renowned Santa María di Loreto in the Papal States, where it was said the Virgin performed miracles (Loreto, Italy). A sailor drew the crossed pea, and Cristóbal promised to pay his expenses. They pledged a third pilgrimage to the *Niña*'s namesake and patron saint, Santa Clara, at the church of Santa Clara de Moguer, committing to pay for mass and that the pilgrim selected would pray for an entire night. Cristóbal drew first and selected the crossed pea. They vowed yet a fourth pilgrimage to be made together—barefoot and wearing only shirts in the cold—to the first church dedicated to the Virgin they encountered. As the crew worshipped the Virgin, Bakako and Yutowa returned to honor Guabancex, believing the only remaining hope was to assuage her anger, the source of the fury.

As night fell, Cristóbal's faith wavered again. He asked whether the Lord intended to allow the voyage's completion or to humiliate him for his faults so that he not enjoy worldly fulfillment. He cried that Diego and little Fernando would be orphaned in Córdoba without a legitimate mother and that the sovereigns would have no reason to support them, believing the voyage a failure.

As the sea convulsed about the *Niña*, Cristóbal retired alone to his space in the hold and by candlelight hastily composed a final message on parchment to the sovereigns summarizing his discovery, the peoples encountered, and the men left at Navidad. He inscribed its outer fold with the instruction that a thousand ducats be paid to the person who delivered it unopened to the sovereigns, whereupon the parchment was set in a wax cake and sealed in a barrel. The crew beheld the barrel thrown overboard, unaware that the Admiral had prepared for their death and perceiving it an additional measure of devotion.

But the Virgin still did not hear! Driving rain enveloped the ship, and Cristóbal's legs stiffened so he labored walking.

On the *Pinta*, the situation was as dire. Martín tried bravely to lead his crew, but he was feverish. The cold, wet violence of the storm and his hunger compounded his illness. He anguished that he had recruited everyone, their children would be orphans, and their gold would lie on the sea's bottom.

During the night, the sky cleared, the rain ceased, and the wind slowly abated. While the seas remained high, Cristóbal set a course again, east-northeast. When dawn broke, the cold, dazed, exhausted, sleepless, and hungry crews of both ships beheld a navigable sea and were humbled beyond expression. They fell to their knees on the deck, crying and adoring the Virgin for her intervention. On *Niña*, Bakako and Yutowa adored Guabancex, Yúcahu, and Attabeira, as well.

A sailor on *Niña* sighted land. Some thought it Castile, others Portugal, and others Madeira. Cristóbal thought it one of the Azores, where he had never intended to call. Cristóbal realized the hunger and exhaustion of the crew and damage to the ship left no choice but to harbor on Portuguese territory. He considered that there might be occasion to dispatch a copy of his public letter, and he dated it as done February 15. He feared the sovereigns would misinterpret harboring on Portuguese territory as disloyalty and that João might treat it as a willful trespass.

SANTA MARÍA, AZORES,
February 15–24, 1493

Vicente, Pero Alonso, and Sancho peered into the fog toward the landmass, perhaps fifteen miles east-northeast. The wind reversed to blow from that direction, requiring the ship to tack against the wind,

and heavy waves continued to roll from the west. The *Niña* labored
in the swell and failed landfall—to the crews' bitter chagrin. By dusk,
the three recognized the land to be an island, possibly Madeira. The
next day, they sighted another island to the west and understood
that consistent with sailing among the Azores. Yet again the *Niña*
failed to reach landfall, and the crew was distraught. A day later,
the *Niña* navigated dense fog to anchor at the first island sighted,
only to have the anchor chain—and the crew's faith—torn asunder
in the heavy seas.

But, after quartering the night at sea, the *Niña* finally made landfall
at dawn on February 18 and the crew rejoiced. Cristóbal dispatched
the launch and three locals returned on it for the night, bringing chickens and fresh bread, which enraptured everyone. The island was Santa
María, the easternmost of the Azores.

Pero Alonso admitted to himself that the Admiral had been
correct. He reflected on the journey—south from Palos to Hierro,
west to San Salvador, south to Juana, east to Española, and then
last northeast to this site—and was astounded by the Admiral's
uncanny sense of location on the globe earth. Juan Niño and Vicente
were humbled, too. Juan realized that the Admiral had understood
the strengths and weaknesses of Juan's own ship at least as well
as himself. Vicente reflected on the decisions made to navigate the
tempest—as terrible as he had ever witnessed—and confessed to
himself that the Genoese was as good a mariner as Vicente had met,
ruefully acknowledging that the ignoble, conceited, vainglorious,
impoverished Genoese in truth had conquered the Ocean Sea as
no man had before. That night, less charitably, Cristóbal wrote to
his sovereigns in his journal that he had exaggerated the distance
traversed on the voyage to confuse his pilots so he would remain
the master of the route to the Indies.

At dawn, Cristóbal dispatched the three locals back ashore to
fetch a priest to open a nearby hermitage to the Virgin so the crew
could fulfill the fourth pilgrimage vowed. He sent half the crew
ashore, barefoot and without pants, retaining the other half on board
with himself to mind *Niña* until it became their turn. He recalled his
last Mass in Gomera over five months before and yearned for the
Holy Communion.

Cristóbal's yearning was unfulfilled, as he soon learned the townspeople had seized the crew onshore as they marched to the hermitage, suspecting that the *Niña* had been poaching in Guinea. The village leader approached in the *Niña*'s launch but refused Cristóbal's invitation to come aboard to talk, tartly pronouncing that the citizens of Santa María didn't recognize or fear the king and queen of Castile. Cristóbal protested that King João would be offended by this treatment, offered to produce his royal letters of recommendation and passport, and demanded his sailors be released, warning that King João would severely punish the locals and threatening to capture one hundred of them. But the leader departed back to shore and the conflict remained unresolved.

On February 20, the weather worsened, and Cristóbal had no choice but to take the *Niña* to sea with half a crew until the storm abated. He returned to Santa María two days later, and the locals sent two clerics and a notary to make amends and peace—which he accepted—and the crewmen held captive were released and put their pants back on. On February 24, at midnight, the *Niña* sailed east for Cape St. Vincent and then Seville. Cristóbal now brooded the *Pinta* might have survived and that, owing to the insulting delay on Santa María, Martín was already contacting the sovereigns to take credit for Cristóbal's triumph.

To Bayona, Galicia (Castile),
February 14–Early March 1493

At dusk on February 14, the *Pinta* lurched and plunged forlornly in the violent storm northwest of the *Niña*, passing in the ocean between São Miguel and Santa María without landfall, driven farther north. As the sea calmed the next day, the ship returned to sail east, continuing to be tossed by the same inclement weather battering the *Niña* at Santa María. But, by late February, the *Pinta* made landfall at Bayona, a Galician town just north of the Portuguese border, where Castilian ships frequently harbored when traveling to northern European ports.

Martín was seriously ill, perhaps mortally. Large portions of his body were discolored, his limbs occasionally trembled, and his sight and coordination were failing. But his mind often was rapt, and he honored the Virgin for bringing his men—at least a third of them—home. He dispatched sailors ashore to provision and repair the *Pinta* before returning to Palos.

Within days of Martín's arrival, his son Arias and cousin Hernan Peréz Mateos fortuitously sailed into Bayona en route from Flanders to Palos. Arias quickly spotted the *Pinta* and boarded her to share an incredulous and joyous reunion with his father, although Arias was jarred and heart-stricken by his father's condition.

Arias and Hernan listened as Martín recounted the voyage and his fury at the Genoese charlatan. The Genoese had cowered to retreat to Spain when landfall failed at 750 leagues! It was Martín himself who had insisted they sail on! He had redirected the ships' course southwest to San Salvador over Colón's objection and sighted it first! Colón had become lost after San Salvador, leaving himself to discover Española! He had found Española's gold, not Colón! He had recruited the crews in the first place, not Colón! The triumph of the voyage was his, not Colón's!

In early March, Martín dispatched a letter to King Fernando and Queen Isabel in Barcelona explaining that he was the captain of one of Colón's ships and requesting an audience to relate his discovery of the islands and mainland of the Indies.

NIÑA
Second Storm, February 24–March 4, 1493

The *Niña* suffered more tempestuous weather and rough seas en route from Santa María to Cape St. Vincent, with southeasterly winds forcing her course further north. Cristóbal placed a second note in a barrel in case he perished and lodged the barrel on the ship's stern to float from wherever she sank.

After sunset on March 3, another violent storm enveloped the ship, with enormous lightning bolts and thunderclaps. A full moon illuminated the thunderclouds, casting a ghostly hue fitting for death. Cross waves battered the *Niña*, raising her high, dropping her low, and washing her deck with enormous tonnages of sea. Her sails ripped, and she ran bare pole wherever the torrent bore.

But the *Niña* would not succumb. Her occupants pleaded to their god and spirits yet again for mercy. Cristóbal sensed the Lord stalking behind, ceaselessly creating storms to humble him so that he not vainly believe he alone was responsible for the discovery. The crewmen confessed their sins, vowed a pilgrimage to the Santa María de la Cinta on the hill above Huelva, and promised to fast on bread and water for the first Saturday after landfall instead of celebrating with drink and women. Cristóbal drew the crossed pea. Bakako and Yutowa honored Guabancex, imploring her that they revered her kindness to spare them from the last storm.

Land was sighted through driving rain after midnight, and Cristóbal raised what sail remained to take the *Niña* farther to sea, lest she founder on the rocky shore. At dawn on March 4, the crew recognized the Rock of Sintra offshore Lisbon, and, with no other alternative, Cristóbal directed that *Niña* sail into the Tagus and harbor at Restelo (Belém) rather than continue to Cape St. Vincent. He again was humbled beyond expression, recognizing that the Lord had wished to deliver him, after all.

Memories of sneaking surreptitiously from Lisbon to escape creditors and the humiliation of Bartolomeu Dias's triumphal return from Guinea flashed through Cristóbal's thoughts. He anxiously turned from navigating the fury of the Ocean Sea to the jealousies of princes, despairing again that the sovereigns would interpret his harboring in Portugal as disloyalty. He feared João would punish him for sailing to Guinea or south of Hierro or simply take revenge for sailing for Castile.

More immediately, he worried that thieves at Restelo would loot the *Niña* of the gold and other trophies. With trepidation, he wrote João requesting that he be allowed to harbor in the safer area of Lisbon proper, indicating that he had returned from the Indies, not Guinea. He retrieved his letters to the sovereigns and added a postscript to the public letter to indicate that he had harbored in Lisbon due to storms.

ALIENATION, GUARICO,
(Winter 1493)

At dusk, Diego de Arana watched his two women prepare a fish casserole outside the fort. He enjoyed both of them and their nakedness and beauty and was flattered they had chosen to lie and live with him since he was the leader. Both were exciting to mount, particularly the young teenager, and the older one paid attention to his needs like a wife. He missed his wife and daughter in Córdoba and prayed daily for their health. But he judged that neither the Lord nor the Admiral had cause to consider his conduct scandalous—since every sailor and most priests he knew would do the same.

Every man and ship's boy of the garrison had found women to live with and none returned to the fort at night. Most exulted in frequent sex. Diego had reminded them repeatedly of Guacanagarí's instruction to refrain from touching married women or forcing the unwilling and of the Admiral's orders to avoid angering Guacanagarí or inciting jealousies among the Indian men.

Diego reflected that there had been many transgressions. A sailor had enticed a fisherman's wife to lie with him while her husband was at sea and then to desert the husband, angering the couple's relatives. Two ship's boys had quarreled over the same girl and drawn knives to fight, only to be restrained by older sailors. Diego had publicly disciplined them, but quarrels over who claimed which woman continued to arise. Worst of all, one of the Basques had forced himself upon a mere girl, not yet a woman, and her father and uncles had become enraged. Swords and spears had been drawn between the garrison and Indians, and the Lord Guacanagarí had intervened to maintain peace.

Diego's older woman brought him a morsel of the casserole in a spatula. He tasted it and smiled and said "good" in Taíno, and she smiled and returned to the fire. He missed talking to his wife at dinner and wondered what their daughter had done that day. He missed the orderly house his wife kept, the sheets in their bed, the clothing she washed, their visits to church to pray, and the wine and drink he shared with friends at the apothecary. But he recognized he liked this older woman, as well. She, too, was decent and kind and, although they couldn't converse, he was happy to be with her until the Admiral returned. The food she cooked disappointed, but he understood she cared for him in preparing it.

As he awaited dinner, Diego reflected with unease that discontentment had swelled over the food supply. The crew lamented the wine was already spent and that the Indian cazabi, yams, and fish were hardly substitute for beef, pork, chicken, rice, and bread. Guacanagarí had advised repeatedly that the quantity of food he supplied the garrison far exceeded that which the same number of Indians ate. The crew had ignored Diego's orders to tend the plots sowed with Castilian seed, and neither Pedro nor Rodrigo had lent example or authority to those orders. Sailors and Crown officials simply refused to be farmers, and all felt it was the Indians' lot in life to farm for them, as servants for their natural masters. Weeds had overwrought the plots sown.

Worse, the crew had begun to snatch and loot food from the Indians' cooking fires and bohíos. Guacanagarí had explained that his subjects willingly shared food among themselves and with guests and strangers. But Taínos expected food not to be taken unless offered first, and Taínos didn't steal. At Guacanagarí's request, Diego had disciplined the crewmen, reminding them of the Admiral's order to deal sweetly and honestly with the Indians. But the crew had ignored him.

The teenager invited Diego to sit near the fire where she had laid some palm fronds, and the older woman served the casserole. Before eating, Diego crossed himself and said grace, and his women waited and listened, recognizing that he consulted the Christ spirit. They ate together, and Diego remembered his wedding and the first meals his then-young wife had prepared, and how he had enjoyed her company. He missed her and Spanish cooking, which he felt far surpassed the casserole. But he listened to his two women talk, and, while he could not understand, the sound of their soft voices had the same tenor as his wife and daughter, and he found it and them comforting.

With chagrin, Diego reflected that relationships with Pedro, Rodrigo, and the crew were, surprisingly, more aggravating than with Guacanagarí. Every crewman agreed that the reward for remaining in Navidad was hoarding one's own stash of gold. But they agreed on little else.

Pedro and Rodrigo had denigrated his authority from the moment the Admiral sailed and now disobeyed it. They repeatedly denounced his control of the weapons held in the fort. They completely ignored his right to control the trifles now strewn on the field and heaped in the small bohío nearby, trading them openly. It was obvious they intended to take credit with the sovereigns for the gold that actually reached them.

Jácome el Rico, the seaman from Genoa, had complained repeat-edly to Diego that all the gold yet collected remained in the crews' pockets and none had been stored in the fort for the king and queen and the voyage's financiers, as the Admiral had intended. Pedro and Rodrigo had warned Jácome they were responsible for the sover-eigns' gold and that it would be dangerous for him to criticize the sovereigns' collection.

Other than the sovereigns' representatives and Jácome, none of the crew cared one whit about the Admiral's objective that the Indi-ans be dealt with honestly and sweetly to ensure that Hispaniola's subjugation be secured peacefully. Unlike the king and queen, the Admiral, and the financiers, the crewmen would not share in the profits of future colonization. Securing for themselves now the best terms of trade for gold—no matter how dishonestly the Indians were treated—was their only concern. Each man traded broken garbage from the *Santa María*—hoops from barrels, broken pottery, torn sail—for as much gold as he could wrangle. Worse, sailors had begun to loot gold jewelry, barging into bohíos to steal family heirlooms the Indians did not want to trade. Guacanagarí had demanded return of the jewelry taken, but none of the crewmen would relinquish that stolen from an Indian.

Diego realized the more he tried to discipline the men—be it over women, food, or gold—the more they ignored him and gravitated to align with Pedro and Rodrigo or worse, the Basques. The Basque and Galician sailors had rejected both Diego's and the sovereign represen-tatives' authority. Their leader Chachu, the *Santa María*'s boatswain, held sway over his countrymen and most of the ship's boys through boisterous and brazen conduct, openly derisive and contemptuous of Indian food and custom and even disrespectful of Guacanagarí. His band leered at the naked women and took as many as four or five concubines each, who they frequently traded or discarded. They openly mocked the Indians as silly, stupid, docile, and untrustworthy.

As the sun set, Diego and his women finished dinner, and the teen-ager sat close beside him. He knew he would lie with her first. For an instant, he remembered the commandments prohibiting adultery, stealing, and coveting another's woman, and memories of priests' warnings of hell flickered through his thoughts. He worried how he would feel if this girl were his daughter and he one of the Basques. But the warmth of her naked body, and the incredible distance he now sat from any church, priest, and Spain itself, quickly relaxed and comforted him.

To Diego's surprise, Guacanagarí then appeared in the twilight and approached, together with nitaínos. Diego gestured for them to sit beside the dwindling fire and share in the remains of the casserole. Guacanagarí declined, and Diego stood to talk as his women retreated toward the fort, embarrassed to be seen by their cacique living with the pale men.

Through gestures, Guacanagarí indicated that there had been a knifing in Guarico. A sailor had stabbed another sailor over the possession of a girl. Guacanagarí asked what would be done.

Diego pondered and replied with a show of conviction that the wounded sailor should be brought back to the fort for treatment by the surgeon, as well as the assailant for punishment. But he had no idea what punishment to order or whether any of the men who remained loyal would administer it.

Guacanagarí studied Diego and knew he was not fit to govern. He watched Diego's women pretend to busy themselves and reflected that they had no cause for embarrassment. Guacanagarí had offered his own daughters in marriage to the cacique Fernando. The women seemed happy to be with Diego, yet Guacanagarí felt for them. They had sought a powerful cacique from beyond the heavens and his status—as was natural. But he studied their bellies to discern whether they were with child and wondered whether Diego would take them for wives or care for the children after Admiral returned.

XII
LISBON TO BARCELONA

AUDIENCE WITH JOÃO,
March 5–13, 1493

Bakako and Yutowa stood on *Niña*'s stern deck gazing wondrously in all directions. There was a stone house on the embankment by *Niña*'s anchorage, less formidable than the one Admiral had drawn on the floor of Guacanagarí's bohío. Pero Alonso said it was a "church" dedicated to the Virgin.* Hills rose beyond it, dotted with more houses with smoke billowing from their tops. A large road curled along the shore and there were exotic beasts walking it, some led by pale-skinned natives and a few—shockingly—bearing the natives seated atop their carcasses! Bakako studied the beasts, spellbound by their heft and obvious strength—they were far taller and heavier than men, with lengthy, muscular legs and skin covered in fur. Pero Alonso said they were "mules" and "horses." The beasts often pulled large wooden litters rolling like logs—Pero Alonso called them "wagons" with "wheels"—which were laden with food, wood, or things unknown. A tremendous harbor stretched east, filled with a multitude of ships like the *Niña*, many much larger. The largest ship lay anchored close by, packed with weapons butting outward, and a launch approached from it.

---

*Santa María of Belém, the chapel established by Prince Henrique.

Cristóbal and Vicente waited at the *Niña*'s rail to receive it, apprehensive of suffering ill-treatment as in the Azores. Cristóbal was startled to recognize the launch's ranking officer as none other than Bartolomeu Dias.

"I am the master of the royal warship *São Cristóvão*," Dias called courteously across the water. "Your ship bears the flag of the Castilian sovereigns, and I request that your captain accompany me back to the warship to explain your arrival to the king's agents."

"I am Cristóvão Colombo," Cristóvão replied in Portuguese. "I command this ship and, as an admiral of Castile, I will not leave it at the request of such persons."

Bartolomeu did not recollect who Colombo was. "Captain, my request is the harbor's normal practice, honored by all mariners."

"I am Cristóvão Colombo and am now an admiral of Castile." Cristóvão did not disguise his insult that Dias did not know of him. "If you won't come, kindly dispatch your master instead."

Vicente offered to go, but Cristóvão would not countenance that. "I will not send another when I myself will not go. Admirals of Castile die before they surrender themselves."

Bartolomeu restrained himself and pondered a bit, surmising that Colombo's Ligurian accent explained his haughtiness. He brought the launch astride the *Niña*. "Show me your papers."

Cristóvão handed the sovereigns' passport over the rail. "I've come from discovering the Indies and haven't visited Guinea."

Bartolomeu pondered again, subdued by memories of Guinea, his triumphal return, and a subsequent decline in his fortune. He returned the passport and relinquished reluctantly—"I'm satisfied"— and departed to his ship, resigned to tend it while another explorer was acclaimed.

Soon, the warship's captain came to the *Niña* with trumpets, pipes, and kettledrums to fete and honor Colombo. Word quickly spread through Lisbon that the Genoese had reached the Indies and returned with naked Indians to prove it and marvelous trophies. For two days, throngs of skiffs and rowboats surrounded the *Niña*, and noblemen and others clambered aboard to meet Colombo and behold the wonders the ship bore. The Lisboans peered at the captives' nakedness and touched their olive skin and gold jewelry, fascinated that indeed they might come from the Indies since they were not from Guinea. Cristóvão recounted his triumph to old friends and enemies and all who came.

King João and Queen Leonor had departed Lisbon as a plague visited the villages along the Tagus estuary. João magnanimously granted Colombo's request to berth the *Niña* in Lisbon proper, ordered the ship refitted as Colombo directed, and dispatched a nobleman to invite Colombo to meet in the Vale de Paraíso some thirty miles northeast of Lisbon, all at the Crown's expense. Cristóvão feared acceptance would cause Fernando and Isabel to favor Martín if Martín had survived, but João undoubtedly would interpret refusal as an admission of sailing to Guinea. With trepidation, Cristóvão debarked with Pero Alonso, Bakako, and Yutowa, leaving Juan Niño and Vicente to take the *Niña* and the rest of the crew and captives to Lisbon's shipyard quays. With the assistance of old friends, Cristóvão discretely dispatched his public and private letters to the sovereigns' in Barcelona before João might interfere with them.

For the first time, Bakako and Yutowa stood on what Pero Alonso called "terra firma," although it wasn't Castile, and more pale-skinned natives surrounded them to behold and touch. Bakako recalled when the roles had been reversed and he had first touched a sailor on the beach on Guanahaní, puzzling whether the being was man or spirit. Many who now touched poked rather than caressed, and Bakako and Yutowa grew apprehensive that some onlookers were amused by their nakedness. They sensed that those poking sought to determine not whether they were men or spirits, but men or beasts.

Cristóvão entered the small church by the anchorage and knelt at the altar to pay tribute to the Virgin for reprieving his life on the Ocean Sea and to the Lord for the successful voyage of discovery. He recalled kneeling at the same altar more than a decade before to offer prayers for Prince Henrique, and he mused whether his own fame would now eclipse the prince's.

Cristóvão, Pero Alonso, and their hosts mounted mules for the journey east along the river road, and Bakako and Yutowa fell in line walking behind like naborias. The two Guanahaníans smiled and waved in friendship as they passed natives who came to hail Admiral and inspect their bodies. They saw incredible peoples. Many were

pale skinned, others dark, and some olive, perhaps paler than themselves. Many had hair tinted brown as dirt, some black as themselves,
a few light as the sun, and a handful even red. They crossed through a
market and beheld the exotic—huge slabs of meat from beasts; cakes
of biscuit much larger than those stored aboard the ship; baskets,
sacks, and jugs of vegetables, fruits and drink unknown; and unusual
birds caged and clucking. Pero Alonso related that the meat was from
"cows," "pigs," and "goats," the "breads" were like cassava but made
from "wheat," the "milk" was weaned from the teats of the beasts,
and the "eggs" of the "chickens" were eaten for breakfast. Bakako
and Yutowa observed that none of the natives offered them "bread" or
cazabi, but Admiral's hosts traded for it using coins like those Admiral
had shown them.

Soon, Cristóvão bid his hosts halt as they passed the Convento
dos Santos, where he had met and married Filipa. He weaved his
way through a throng of well-wishers to find that the convent and
boardinghouse had closed, but he entered the church remaining and
again knelt at an altar where he had prayed years before. He found a
priest and confessed his sins, particularly of frequently believing the
voyage and discovery were his achievements alone rather than those
of the Lord.

As they waited on Admiral, Pero Alonso pointed to the house he
had entered and again said, "Church." Bakako spied men, women,
and children huddled by the church's walls with their arms and hands
outstretched, greeting passersby. Some of the children approached to
wander among the crowd surrounding Bakako, stretching their arms
and hands to the onlookers. One of Admiral's hosts handed a child a
morsel of bread, and the child retreated to the church to eat it.

Cristóvão returned to his hosts to request that he might visit Filipa's family chapel in the Carmelite monastery. It was along the route
chosen and they agreed, and the mules and Guanahaníans ascended a
gentle hill and coursed through a village home to peoples with dark-
black skin. Bakako and Yutowa smelled strange foods cooking, overheard the natives speaking in a tongue markedly unlike Admiral's, and
discovered men kneeling on the ground to pray to spirits facing east.

The village soon petered into beautiful countryside, forest and
pasture, and the travelers continued to rise gradually to higher

ground. But they soon arrived at another village bustling with people, and then at an enormous wall that wound far up the hillside and even farther down to the harbor. Bakako studied the wall's thick stones as they strode through an archway and grasped that Admiral's wall in Guarico was inconsequential in comparison. It was obvious the natives prepared for ferocious enemies. Bakako mused that these enemies could be beasts, but he realized that he knew enough to be certain they were other pale men.

Bakako and Yutowa emerged from the archway into the most densely populated village they had ever seen (Lisbon) and found themselves in another market brimming with the natives' foods. The view was spectacular. Pero Alonso pointed to a tremendous church set on the hillside before them (Church of Carmo), with a tower rising high to the heavens. The village sprawled into a great valley below, stretching south to the harbor and filled with countless houses. A massive fort (Castelo de São Jorge) stood across the valley on a facing hill. Bakako and Yutowa were dazed by the energy and dynamism of the innumerable natives moving about.

Pero Alonso indicated Admiral's wife lay within and that Admiral would speak to her. Bakako perceived the house the most foreboding structure he had ever seen, displaying from ground to sky stone figures of men and evil spirits, apparently warning—with a realism not achieved in Guanahaní or Bohío—of the Christ spirit within. As at the prior church, natives congregated by its walls and extended their hands to Admiral's hosts and well-wishers. Bakako suddenly realized they were begging for food to eat. He scanned their dirty bodies and clothes and their sullen faces and looked to Pero Alonso, seeking an explanation.

Pero Alonso replied these people were "poor" and sought others' "charity." Bakako pointed back to the food market. Pero Alonso repeated that these people were "poor" and explained that the market didn't give food freely to anyone. Bakako couldn't understand "poor," but he and Yutowa remarked to each other that the pale beings had a most singular way of living.

Inside the church, Cristóvão knelt before the Moniz family chapel, recognized that mother-in-law Isabel now lay there, and spoke to Filipa, assuring her Diogo approached manhood nobly. He asked her forgiveness for his absences, but allowed that it had been the Lord's destiny that he discover the route to the Indies.

When Cristóvão rejoined, the travelers slowly descended a steep hillside into the valley and a labyrinth of streets jammed with merchants hustling to sell countless items Bakako and Yutowa couldn't recognize. They saw "paper" and quill "pens" as Admiral used for "writing," "books" that told stories, "lamps" that burned "oil" to light the night, and countless cemís of the Christ spirit, his mother, and other spirits. Close to the harbor, Cristóvão silently observed when they crossed the alley where he and Bartolomeu had opened the chart shop, and he sensed the Lord meant to remind him of the humility in which he had been born. They continued into the shadows of massive stone buildings, taller than any caney Bakako could remember, to enter an open plaza before the water, where ships were anchored. Black-skinned men, women, and children were huddled together around posts, downcast and almost motionless.

Bakako and Yutowa realized with horror that these peoples were bound as captives, as if Caribes waiting execution but with their wives and infants, and that they were "slaves"—of which Admiral frequently spoke. At the center of the plaza, they passed within feet of the slaves, who studied their nakedness with equal astonishment. Bakako felt his breath suffocate, as if awakening into a nightmare. The plaza reeked of urine and excrement. The men were shackled at the ankles with chains like Admiral used for his ships' anchors, and the women and children were bound with cord. Many gazed and cried forlornly to the ground. Others groaned and pleaded to their spirits in the heavens.

Bakako recoiled from this spectacle and stared forward to the mule Admiral rode. But he couldn't escape the haunting reality, as close to his side stood a girl as beautiful as Kamana with an infant on her hip, with lovely black skin and an innocent face, and with a rope about her neck. Bakako peered into her eyes and beheld a depth of hopelessness he had witnessed but once—in the storms at sea—and she gazed back into his eyes as if to ask what his own fate would be. He longed to shout that he was not with or of the natives. But he averted his eyes forward again, kept his pace, and, instead of shouting, prayed to Yúcahu that she be spared whatever fate the natives intended.

Bakako glared at Admiral, Pero Alonso, and their hosts and perceived that they continued the journey without pause or concern, oblivious to the degradation about them, seemingly because they found it ordinary and commonplace. Admiral did turn to evaluate some of the larger black-skinned men, much as he studied the angle of *Niña*'s sails in the wind. Bakako felt the harsh stare of natives inspecting his arms, legs, body size, and strength.

The travelers turned east along the shore and entered the greatest market Bakako and Yutowa had yet seen. As Pero Alonso explained, they wondered at baskets of "oranges" and "lemons" and sacks of "rice," "wheat," "barley," and black "pepper." They were astonished by the variety of weapons displayed for trade, including not only the daggers, swords, and bows and arrows to which they had become accustomed but "bludgeons," "battle-axes," and shining "armor" worn like clothing. They spied related items Pero Alonso chose not to discuss, including chains and shackles apparently fit for men's ankles and wrists, thick, tapered ropes with lashes that could be used to whip beasts or men, and a wooden piece with holes where a man's neck and wrists could be locked.

By nightfall, the party arrived at a small village (Sacavém) along the Tagus, where their hosts arranged lodging and a hearty local meal. They dined on the meat of beasts—Pero Alonso called it "beef"— which they found tough and heavy and, at the meal's end, "cake," which pleased them. That night, Pero Alonso took them to a room for themselves and showed them "beds," as Admiral had aboard the ships. For the first time, they lay in "wool" cloth from "sheep" and found it kept them warm, although the bed was not as comfortable as a hammock.

They lay in darkness but for the wan hue of a candle, and Yutowa turned to Bakako. "It hasn't been as I expected."

"Nor for me. The houses are tremendous, the villages are enormous, and their know-how to make things is extraordinary. Their beasts are extraordinary and incredibly powerful."

"Yes. But I expected to be amazed by these things—except the beasts. We knew it would be extraordinary before we arrived."

Bakako sensed Yutowa's anxiety and sat upright, as he felt it himself. "I know what you're thinking, and I felt it all day." He paused to express his thoughts carefully. "These people are not a friendly people."

"They don't share food and water with visitors."

"They don't share food and water even among themselves. They don't even share food and water with a child or infant who is hungry unless repeatedly asked. And even then there appear many who go hungry."

Yutowa nodded in agreement. "Our dinner tonight was fulsome. But there are natives outside—you saw them in this very village—who now hunger."

"You saw the hungry outside their 'churches.' Their spirit Christ doesn't see or care to help," Bakako reflected. "It's worse than being unfriendly. They have many 'slaves,' as Admiral would call them."

"Maybe they've won them in battle, and the outcome deserved. Maybe they're born as naborias."

"Maybe. But everywhere the slaves are black skinned. It's as if they chose a different people to enslave. Maybe they're like Caribes in this regard, but unlike Caribes they enslave men as well as women."

The two Guanahaníans quivered silently, each aware they dreaded the same premonition. Yutowa broke the silence. "Do you think that's what they intend for Guanahaníans and the Taínos of the other islands?"

"I don't know." Bakako shuddered. "But we'll learn the answer if ever Admiral returns us home."

Both youths labored to sleep. Bakako was haunted by Admiral's explanation to Guacanagarí that the fort in Guarico was built to defend against Caribes. He trembled at Guacanagarí's horror if informed of what Bakako now knew.

The next day, after trudging through rain, the travelers arrived by evening at the Monastery of Santa María das Virtúdes in a small town nestled among pine forest in the Vale de Paraíso, and King João received them in a local residence. He had been warned that Colombo beamed with pride and insolence and exaggerated the discovery falsely. João recalled his own pride on proving Guinea could be circumvented, and he steeled himself to bide the Genoese's smug rejoinder that India had yet to be so achieved while the route across the Ocean Sea had proven true.

Cristóvão anticipated the king's jealousy and relished it. He judged that, as he had not sailed to Guinea, the king likely would not harm him for fear of a dispute with Fernando and Isabel.

João was overcome by humiliation the moment Cristóvão, Pero Alonso, and the two heathens were ushered before him, realizing that the heathens couldn't have come from Guinea and did possess the skin color often ascribed to Indians. But he concealed his consternation and graciously invited Cristóvão to be seated, courteously inquired of his health and that of his family and sovereigns, and then asked to hear of the tremendous voyage. Cristóvão responded effusively, describing his journey to Cipangu—indicating that the two "Indians" called it "Cibao"—and ballyhooing its gold mines, great wealth, and commercial potential.

João waited for Colombo to express every treasure and splendor and then responded. "I'm delighted your journey has come to such fruition."

"Your Lordship, Cipangu indeed is as I told you."

"I have two concerns, however. First, which we can discuss when you are rested tomorrow, is whether what you have found is Antillia as opposed to Cipangu." João sternly gazed into Colombo's eyes. "The second is that, whatever you have found, I believe it is my possession, according to the treaty between myself and Fernando and Isabel."

Cristóvão was startled. "I assure you it was Cipangu, neither Guinea nor Antillia." Cristóvão pointed to Bakako and Yutowa. "These are Indians, not Guineans, as you can see plainly. Your Lordship, Fernando and Isabel prohibited me from sailing to Mina or any place in Guinea, and I did not. We sailed west from the Castilian possessions at the Canaries."

"So, by the treaty, your Cipangu is mine."

Cristóvão recoiled silently for a moment, aware he couldn't bluff arguments about royal understandings with the king. "Your Lordship, I haven't read the treaty, but I've followed my sovereigns' orders to not sail to Guinea."

"Your discovery is mine." João smiled graciously. "But there is no need for you and I to discuss this. This is for myself and King Fernando and Queen Isabel. I'm sure there will be no need for arbitrators." João dismissed the audience and extended Colombo great courtesies for the night.

On Sunday, March 10, João invited Colombo to participate in Mass at the monastery's chapel, and they celebrated the Eucharist together. Each man's confession was scant in substance if not form. João pondered what riches were at stake. Cristóvão cringed that he not say anything that bolstered Portugal's claim to Cipangu.

After Mass, João invited Colombo and his party to continue the report of their discovery. João ordered an attendant to set a bowl of dried beans on a table and turned to Yutowa to ask in Portuguese and with gestures, "Can you make a map of your kingdoms?"

Cristóvão understood João's design and directed Yutowa in Castilian. "Make a map of the Indies, just as you did the first day on the deck of the *Santa María*."

Yutowa laid some beans in the shape of Bohío. "Haiti or Bohío."

"I have named this island La Española," Cristóvão interrupted. João hid his great displeasure.

Yutowa then shaped Cuba. "Cuba."

"It's now Juana, for the prince," Cristóvão added.

Yutowa continued, depicting Boriquén, Yamaye, and many Lucayan islands. Sadly but proudly, he placed a tiny pea for Guanahaní at the map's northern edge. "Guanahaní."

"San Salvador, for the Savior."

João studied the map. "Which is your Cipangu?"

"It's within Española." Cristóbal studied João's face, but it was impenetrable. Cristóbal turned to Yutowa. "Show him Cibao." Yutowa pointed to Haiti.

"And Cathay?" asked João.

"It lies west of Española, perhaps a few days' sail."

"Impossible. Absolutely impossible. The Indies can't be that close. These islands are consistent with our understanding of Antillia."

After an interlude of some debate—cordial but pointed—João wiped the beans to the side, undoing the map, and then turned to Bakako and gestured for him to draw a map of his kingdoms.

Cristóvão hid his glee. "Bakako, draw your own map of the Indies."

Bakako quickly did so, producing a map of the Taíno world much like Yutowa's and ascribing the same names to each island. Cristóvão glanced at João and confirmed the king was convinced the islands named had been discovered. João suspected the archipelago lay southeast of Jesus Christo, where many had expected Antillia to be found.

João gave Bakako and Yutowa scarlet clothing for their efforts and dismissed the audience, again affording Colombo gracious courtesies. That evening, the king's councilors decried the Genoese's boastfulness and insolence and harangued that his conduct could be said to have triggered an altercation that resulted in his death. João recoiled from murdering Colombo, envisioning a scandal with Fernando and Isabel regardless of the momentary satisfaction it would provide.

On March 11, Cristóvão's party departed for Lisbon, stopping en route to pay respects to Queen Leonor, who was avoiding the plague at another convent nearby, together with her younger brother, Manuel, now heir to the throne. João summoned his council to consider dispatching an armada to the islands Colombo claimed for Castile.

Cristóvão's party rested that night in small town (Alhandra) by the Tagus and chartered a boat to travel by the river directly to the *Niña*. A messenger arrived professing that the king offered pack animals to take them to Barcelona by land, but Cristóvão declined, suspecting instead an attempt on his life, and proceeded by the boat, rejoining the *Niña* the next evening. The *Niña* sailed for Seville when the tide ebbed the following morning.

Unknown to Cristóvão, as the *Niña* rounded Cape St. Vincent, the *Pinta* was not far behind. Martín had learned of Colón's arrival in Lisbon and, without a response from the sovereigns' to his own request for an audience, set sail from Bayona for Palos. Martín was now dying, too debilitated to walk, no less journey to Barcelona, and Arias accompanied him home, armed with an additional charge to lay against Colón—treason with João. Martín raged feverishly that the Genoese would seek his incarceration and that it would be necessary to hide rather than return to the home in Palos. He exhorted deliriously that the gold not be shared with the Genoese.

The *Niña* encountered weak winds on March 14 and failed to advance to Seville. At noon the next day, Cristóbal directed Juan Niño to guide his ship across the bar at Palos, and, in a rising tide, the *Niña* floated up the Río Tinto to anchor off St. George's church.

News of the *Niña*'s return spread rapidly—shouted in streets and markets, borne by ferrymen to Moguer and Huelva, heralded in the towns' churches and taverns—and crowds thronged the embankment at St. George's church. Mothers, fathers, wives, children, friends, and neighbors were overcome with relief and joy that the *Niña* and crew had safely returned, dazzled that lands had been discovered at an incredible distance west, petrified that many of their loved ones had been left there, and desolate and grief stricken that many had been lost and would never return, including the expedition's very captain. But, as the *Pinta* floated into the Saltes hours later, borne by the same tide, and as word spread that those left in the distant lands were well safe, tumultuous celebration erupted.

Cristóbal watched from the *Niña*, proud but entirely alone. He ended his journal reminding his sovereigns that the Lord miraculously concluded the voyage even though many of their household had said it was folly. He hoped it would be the greatest honor of Christendom that first appeared so unimportant.

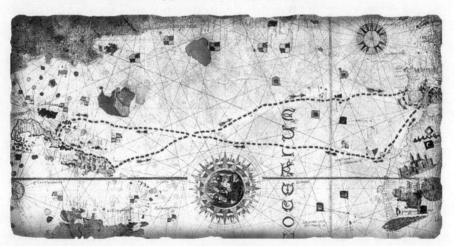

Portion of Juan de la Cosa's World Map, 1500, with the route of Columbus's voyage superimposed.

PALOS, MOGUER, AND HUELVA,
March 15—End of March 1493

Bakako and Yutowa were captivated by the little village, the pretty marshes, and the hillsides about them and realized that the settlement was vastly smaller than the previous one and, for that matter, smaller the Guacanagarí's Guarico. They warmed to the small skiffs lining the riverbank, laden with fishing nets and poles, as well as a few returning from the sea with catch. The village was like their own on Guanahaní, populated by fishermen and their families and woven into the rhythm of the sea.

They studied the natives celebrating ashore, including the women-folk and children who embraced the sailors, all laughing, crying, and hugging loved ones, sharing food and drink, beating strange drums, bellowing into instruments to pipe and honk. Bakako recalled the expressions of his relatives when he and Father returned to Guana-haní after having been blown away, and he realized this celebration was a larger version of the same. He studied the strange dress of the pale women. Their naguas wrapped around the entire body, hiding their buttocks, and their shirts covered their breasts but pulled the breasts upright to bulge forward, some with an opening at the neck to permit peeking in. Bakako pointed it out to Yutowa, and they laughed uproariously.

Skiffs and rowboats surrounded the *Niña* and *Pinta* and villag-ers boarded, bearing bread, meats, and wine. They marveled at the captives and parrots. A launch approached bearing Fray Pérez, and Cristóbal welcomed him aboard with a deep, tearful embrace. Bakako studied this native's dress—a dark robe covering the entire body with a chain hung from the neck bearing a large silver cross— and perceived the native a behique.

Cristóbal now participated in the celebration and, for this moment, felt an acceptance and respect that he had supposed would be reserved only for Martín. Juan and Pero Alonso Niño openly recognized Cristóbal as the leader of the voyage and responsible for its success. But many of the *Pinta*'s crew whispered that the Genoese had sought to sell his discoveries to King João.

Suddenly, the celebrations ashore and aboard the ships ceased, and Bakako and Yutowa scanned the embankment to ascertain why. Two natives, with robes similar to Admiral's friend, stood at the embankment preparing to board a rowboat to be ferried to the *Niña*. Juan Niño shook his head and Bakako heard him warn Admiral, "Inquisitors. We'll have to answer their questions."

Cristóbal recognized the inquisitors' boatman as the muleteer who had escorted Diego to Beatriz seven months earlier. The man cheerfully called to Cristóbal that Diego was with Cristóbal's mistress. He then resumed a somber demeanor, nervous in afterthought whether his cheer revealed an absence of piety.

As the rowboat came abreast, Bakako studied Admiral and his crew and sensed caution and reticence. The two robed natives climbed onto the *Niña*'s deck, silver crosses dangling at their chests, and Bakako surmised by the crews' gravity that these two perhaps held greater authority than even Admiral. They were supreme behiques. They glared at the Taínos' nakedness and greeted Admiral and Juan formally, without expressing the slightest pleasure over their return. Bakako listened closely.

"We come on behalf of the Holy Office," the elder behique began, "to ascertain whether there are any persons present who have converted to the faith from Judaism and, if so, whether they wish to confess to any heresy. Who is the leader of this ship and the neighboring ship *Pinta*?"

"I'm an Admiral of Castile and captain-general of both ships." Cristóbal pointed to Juan. "Juan Niño is the master of this ship and may help with your questions. But I know of no person present who has converted from Judaism."

"Nor I," Juan added.

"Are any present whose parents or grandparents or more distant relatives converted from Judaism?"

Admiral remained silent.

"I know of none." Juan scanned those present and called, "If anyone present has relatives who converted from Judaism, you should step forward." None did.

The younger behique addressed Admiral directly. "We have information that one Luis de Torres—a known converso—is among you. If you are lying, it will be most serious—for you."

"We have sailed to the Indies for King Fernando and Queen Isabel to bring Christianity to the heathens there, and we left a garrison for the initial settlement. Such person is among the initial settlers."

"That's unfortunate."

There was a long silence. The older behique pointed to Xamabo.

"Who are these blasphemous people, and what is their faith?"

Admiral walked to hold Xamabo's hand. "This is a brother of the Indian Lord Guacanagarí, who is a lord of the territories newly possessed by the king and queen. This prince, and the rest, are heathens, but inclined to the faith."

"How do you know they're not Jews or conversos?"

"I have seen they have no sect. I will show you." Admiral asked Bakako to retrieve a face mask from storage. "This is the type of item within their worship. There are no Stars of David or Torahs."

Bakako observed the supreme behiques confer between themselves and Admiral nod to Juan.

"They have fine gold jewelry," Admiral said. He motioned for Xamabo to step forward and pointed to his gold nosepiece. The behiques studied it for a moment. Admiral asked Xamabo for it, and continued. "Their gold is soft and easily cut." With a knife, Admiral split off a significant portion of the nosepiece and handed it to the older behique, as well as a sliver for the muleteer. "You have no concerns on either ship, and this is for your efforts."

The elder behique studied the gold piece. "If anyone here knows of information to the contrary of what we've just been told, it's your Christian duty to step forward and speak." None spoke.

The behiques departed. When they were distant, Bakako watched the sailors scowl and curse Isabel and Fernando and then resume their celebration.

Cristóbal left the Crown's comptroller Rodrigo Sánchez to secure the gold pieces remaining on the *Niña*, as well as the parrots and other trophies, and disembarked with his three attendants, Pérez, and the captives to walk to La Rábida. The captives, led by Xamabo, followed in the rear, waving to natives, who came to greet, examine, and touch.

Martín also disembarked, but with the *Pinta*'s gold, gently lowered prostrate in a blanket by Arias and a few sailors into a launch to be whisked upstream to his villa in the farmlands on Moguer's outskirts.

With Pérez's assistance, Cristóbal dispatched a note to the sovereigns announcing his arrival in Castile and requesting an audience in Barcelona, as well as a letter to Beatriz and his sons in Córdoba, advising that he would see them shortly. Copies of his public letter

heralding the voyage were sent to a number of persons, including
Luis de Santángel, the mayor of Córdoba, and his old patron the
Duke Luis de la Cerda.

Rábida's friars warmly welcomed Cristóbal's entourage into the
monastery, shared their food and water, and provided accommodation.
At dusk, Cristóbal left to ride by skiff upstream to Moguer to fulfill
the overnight vigil and Mass in the Church of Santa Clara pledged off
the Azores. Juan and Pero Alonso Niño and other *Niña* crewmen introduced the Admiral to the church clergy and purchased candles. All knelt
humbly before the main altar, praised the Lord for saving them upon the
Ocean Sea, and offered that Cristóbal would prove the uncompromised
devotion that merited sparing their ship and lives. Cristóbal then prayed
alone as the sun set, and as the moon rose, crested, and fell, through
the owls' hooting and the roosters' crowing, until the sun rose the next
day, continuously expressing this Faith. Juan and Pero Alonso returned
to the church before dawn, together with other crewmen, and together
they celebrated Mass and the Lord's mercy for their lives. All of those
present save Cristóbal also prayed for Martín, who lay dying close by. It
was Saturday, and Cristóbal and the *Niña*'s crew began the fast on bread
and water vowed in the storm off Lisbon.

Cristóbal returned to La Rábida and, later that morning, Marchena arrived. Cristóbal triumphantly related his voyage, revealing his
aspirations for a grand second voyage and, with bitterness, the fail-
ures and disappointments he had encountered, particularly Pinzón's
desertion. He invited Marchena to accompany him on this second
voyage to bring the Indians to the faith. He admonished that he would
seek Martín's prosecution and incarceration. To the latter, Marchena counseled restraint and forgiveness, reminding that Martín had
recruited most of the crew and that the Father forgave those who
forgave the trespasses of others.

La Rábida's friars offered a lunch for Cristóbal's entourage.
Bakako overheard Cristóbal explain his abstention—save bread
and water—to Marchena, and Bakako asked Admiral, "Should my
people abstain, as well?"

"Did you so promise Christ the Lord?"

Bakako hesitated, remembering many prayers, including to
Yúcahu, Attabeira, and Guabancex.

Cristóbal perceived his confusion and simplified. "You may abstain or eat as you wish, for Fray Marchena and his brothers want to share their food with you. Soon you will be baptized, cleansed of your sins, and born again as a child of God into his family." Cristóbal nodded toward Fray Marchena. "Perhaps next Sunday you and Yutowa may watch Mass administered by Fray Marchena and learn of the communion with Christ shared by his family—those who are baptized." Marchena embraced the suggestion and served the Indians the full meal.

In Barcelona, Isabel and Fernando received with utter astonishment Cristóbal's public and private letters and the note of his return. They immediately concluded the Genoese had delivered what he promised and that the voyage they considered a lark potentially had resulted in a triumph of substantial new colonies. They feared João's ambition for the lands discovered and promptly summoned advisers to consider what had to be done to protect Castile's entitlement. They decided—on the basis of Cristóbal's letters alone—that a large fleet should be assembled promptly to transport a considerable number of colonists to commence subjugation and thwart João.

The Duke Luis de la Cerda was angry. He immediately wrote Cardinal Mendoza, recounting that he had been preparing to underwrite Colón's quest of the Indies himself, but the queen preempted him entirely, even though her accountant had promised Luis a piece of the voyage. Luis indicated that Colón had found everything he was looking for and asked Mendoza to convince the queen to allow Luis to send some of his own caravels to the Indies each year.

Cristóbal lived at La Rábida while awaiting the sovereigns' reply. He traveled to Puerto de Santa María with Juan de la Cosa to secure the original diagrams and paperwork documenting the specifications of the *Santa María* so Juan might submit a claim to the sovereigns for indemnification of its loss. He made the pilgrimage to the church on the hilltop overlooking Huelva, Nuestra Señora de la Cinta. He sought, without success, to find Martín and the *Pinta*'s gold and institute Martín's prosecution, and Marchena provided no assistance.

The next Sunday, Bakako and Yutowa were invited to don robes and sit to the side in La Rábida's chapel with Admiral's page Pedro so they might observe Holy Communion without participating. They watched as a broken loaf of bread was passed among the natives, including to Pedro, and listened as a behique spoke in another strange tongue.

"We now eat the flesh of Christ," Pedro whispered.

Bakako was startled. He recognized the bread as the natives' cazabi and gazed to the altar, where a large cemí depicted the Christ spirit dying on a cross. He looked to Yutowa and whispered in Taíno, "They believe they're eating the Christ spirit?"

Yutowa shrugged. The behique continued to address the spirits, and a gourd of wine was passed among the worshippers.

When he received the gourd, Pedro whispered, "We now drink the blood of Christ."

Bakako observed Pedro's participation carefully and confirmed for himself that Pedro ate bread and wine, not flesh or blood. Bakako glanced at Yutowa again, and the memory of Father's warning that the pale beings might be Caribes flashed before him. He scrutinized the ceremony intently, seeking to understand if the natives really believed they were eating and drinking the blood of their Christ spirit or were just consciously pretending to do so. The ritual unnerved him, particularly since the thought of even pretending to eat flesh or blood disgusted him.

That night, as they lay in their cell in La Rábida, Yutowa turned to Bakako and asked, "Do you think the natives actually eat flesh and drink blood?"

"No. Like Taínos, they abhor it, including Admiral."

"But why do they do it in their ceremony?"

Bakako had pondered the exotic ritual all day. "I think their beliefs are similar to ours. We believe the fish we eat have come from Yayael's bones after his death. They believe they are fed by their Christ's body after his death." A memory of fishing with Father flickered through his thoughts. "Both understand the living feed upon the remains of the dead."

"That's what they're thinking about?"

"Who knows? Perhaps it just comforts them to eat their spirit."

By March 29, Cristóbal departed by mule for Seville to await the sovereign's approval of his audience in Barcelona. His party included Juan Niño as the Castilian owner and master of the surviving flagship, his three attendants, and the ten Indians led by Guacanagarí's relative Xamabo. He didn't invite Vicente. Prior to departure, Cristóbal instructed Bakako that he and the other Indians should adorn themselves with gold jewelry and body paint appropriate for a great ceremony. The exotic trophies and green parrots, some batey balls, and the store of gold pieces were loaded on the mules. Cristóbal kept the journal and sea charts close at his side. The travelers departed northeast through Moguer and, as in Lisbon, crowds surrounded them in the villages they passed to behold and touch the Indians, now more strikingly attired in fresh paint and plentiful jewelry.

After Colón departed, Vicente and other family members brought Martín to La Rábida for his last days, protected by Marchena from Colón's prosecution.

At the end of March, Fernando and Isabel dispatched a brief letter to Cristóbal, addressing him as the Admiral of the Ocean Sea and commending him for having served the Lord and their kingdoms' benefit. They confirmed he would receive their favors and ordered that he write immediately what needed to be done so that he could return to the new possessions before summer's end. They also dispatched instructions to their ambassador in Rome to obtain the Pope's approval that the lands Colón discovered were theirs.

As the sovereigns' messenger sped overland to Seville to find Colón, Fray Marchena administered Martín's last rites. With Vicente and other family present, he died and was buried at La Rábida's altar. He had first met Colón less than a year before.

TO BARCELONA,
April 1493

Bakako, Yutowa, and two other captives immensely enjoyed the honor of sharing a mule. After departing the fishing villages, they rode through a verdant plain filled with crops and were dazzled by the many uses to which the beast was put, observing mules harnessed to wooden "plows" to cultivate fields, to millstones to grind "flour," and to rope and "pulleys" to lift beams. Their mount's four legs coordinated in a strange, undulating gate of forward yanks and pauses that, by the second day, gave them, and everyone else in Admiral's party, sore backs and buttocks.

On March 31, Bakako and Yutowa observed the native population grow denser as they approached what Admiral's page Pedro called the "city of Seville." Larger crowds gathered to inspect their nakedness, and, as always, many came to poke rather than caress. The riders halted at a great fortress beside a great river,* and the two youths gazed across the water to Seville's tremendous skyline, a wall with towers curling along the river's flood plain enveloping houses packed together—all dominated by a number of churches. Large ships were anchored in the river to the south. Bakako recognized the fortress as an enormous rendition of that designed by Admiral in Guarico, and Juan Niño recognized with contempt that it was a headquarters of the sovereigns' Inquisition. To the youths' amazement, the travelers crossed the river on an immense wood structure Pedro called a "bridge,"† which bustled with innumerable peoples of different colors and both beasts and slaves hauling goods. They arrived and dismounted at a city gate, where a tremendous throng of gaping natives mobbed them.

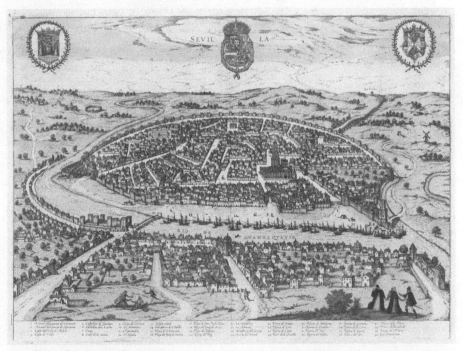

Seville in the sixteenth century.

---

*Castle of St. George, Guadalquivir.
†At the site of the present Puente de Isabel II.

Admiral introduced Xamabo to a number of finely dressed caciques or nitaínos, whom Pedro explained included the "mayor" of Seville, and Admiral asked the "Indians" to exhibit some of their "Indian" items to the natives. Xamabo displayed a face mask. Abasu held a spear. Yutowa posed talking to the parrots. Bakako demonstrated a batey ball, and the onlookers were astounded at its bounce. One of the natives watching—a nineteen-year-old Bartolomé de Las Casas—found the show particularly intriguing. Pedro explained to Bakako and Yutowa that it was "Palm Sunday" and that the "Sevillians" had begun the celebration of "Holy Week." Gaily or penitently dressed pilgrims were surging into the city to parade through the streets to its churches bearing colorful banners and icons of the Virgin and saints.

Cristóbal's triumph had been heralded before his arrival, and he was honored and feted by Andalusian nobility and clergy the entire Holy Week. He met with the leaders of the Genoese community, including Francesco Pinelo and others who had financed the voyage, all of whom were eager to participate in the exploitation of the Indies, which they believed augured tremendous profits in gold, spices, and slaves. Cristóbal was overwhelmed by job seekers and gold hunters who yearned to be selected for the second voyage. He frequently asked his captives to accompany him to meet and be examined by dignitaries and merchants, explaining repeatedly that their skin color proved he had discovered the western route to the Indies.

Pedro escorted Bakako and Yutowa about the city to these audiences. One day, they crossed through Seville's slave market and were stunned to behold not only black-skinned peoples, but many with olive-colored skin much as their own. Pedro explained that these peoples had been enslaved in the "Canary Islands" for resisting the king and queen and denying Christ. Frequently, they encountered pale-skinned natives parading about in exotic attire with lavishly decorated cemís and observed that, as always, hungry and destitute natives congregated near churches and wandered among the marchers, begging for food.

One afternoon, Bakako and Yutowa were fascinated to behold a parade before the city's enormous church,* led by a native dressed

---

*The Cathedral.

as if the Christ spirit, bearing a wooden cross upon his back and a garland of thorns on his head. Bakako turned to Pedro. "What?"

"During Holy Week, we celebrate Christ's death and resurrection." Pedro doubted the two Indians understood. "You know how Christ died?"

"On cross." Bakako and Yutowa nodded.

"You know Jerusalem?"

The youths nodded again, having heard of it many times now and that it lay as Castile across the sea from Guanahaní.

"You remember our Mass at La Rábida?"

"Yes," both replied.

"Christ rode to Jerusalem to die. He ate dinner with his followers—we call it the Last Supper. It was then—the Last Supper—he shared his body and blood with his followers for the first time."

"Last Supper thank Christ crops fish?"

"No." Pedro barely concealed his irritation that the Indians never fully understood and completed his explanation of the pageant regardless of his friends' comprehension. "As Christ foresaw, a follower betrayed him to the Jews, and after dinner they delivered him to the governor. This Friday, many years ago, he died nailed on the cross to save men from their sins. This Sunday, many years ago, he rose to Heaven. The man you see carrying the cross is enacting Christ's last walk to the hillside where he died."

"Christ died. Now eat body, drink blood? Crops good? Fishing good?"

Pedro was startled, and his sense of superiority punctured, by Bakako's untutored perceptivity. "Yes. We believe in Christ and share his body and blood at Mass. Sometimes he hears our prayers and brings rain for the crops—and wind for our sails. Sometimes he punishes lack of faith."

Bakako spoke to Yutowa in Taíno. "The natives consult their Christ spirit for the same reason we consult our spirits—for assistance and protection."

"Maybe to protect each one and his family, but not their neighbors or their people. Everywhere natives go hungry because they don't share food as a people. The only food they share is pretending to share the Christ spirit's flesh and blood."

A vision of the behiques visiting the *Niña* flickered through Baka-ko's memory and he recalled he had heard the word *Jews* a number of times before. He turned to Pedro. "Jews enemy Christians?"

"Yes."

"Why?"

"They deny Christ is the son of the Lord."

"Jews different spirits?"

"Yes. They deny Christ and the Virgin." Pedro reflected on the complexity of the beliefs he held true. "They do worship the Lord in a mistaken manner."

Bakako turned to Yutowa and shrugged. "Pale men who worship different spirits are enemies. Why would they have it so?" Again, they reflected that Admiral's peoples had a singular manner of existence.

Haunted by his own foreboding and a fascination to ascertain their reaction, Pedro led his friends through plazas, alleys, and a gate in the city wall to a field on its southern perimeter, where eventually he spied a flat, burning area with tall, charred logs staked into the ground, removed from the bustle of city life.

Pedro slowly ambled closer to the stakes, apprehensive to keep a healthy distance but bent on getting close enough to inspect the ash scattered about. He pointed at the stakes. "We are on holy ground. You see the stakes? Do you know what is done here?"

Bakako pondered Pedro's fascination and apprehension and sensed it was a place for evil spirits or their worship. He and Yutowa had heard Admiral refer to a Satan spirit more than once—as the root of evil in the pale men's hearts. But he courteously sought another explanation first.

"Kill pig? Kill cow? Cook fire?"

"No."

"Pray Satan?" Bakako responded, venturing what he suspected.

"No."

"Fire slaves death?" asked Yutowa, wincing to intimate he didn't expect that the explanation.

"No." Pedro recognized Bakako and Yutowa would never guess the answer. "Here's where they burn heretics. When a person pretends to believe in Christ but really believes as the Jews, he or she is burned to death here."

Bakako and Yutowa gazed gravely at the ashes, uncertain of the meaning. Pedro tried a second time. "A Christian must believe in Christ. If a Christian doesn't, and secretly believes like the Jews, the Christian is punished—some to be burned here. No Jew may live in Spain."

The Guanahaníans' hearts pounded, fearful that Pedro was revealing critical information they had never understood. Their own people believed in many different spirits, and belief or nonbelief in a particular spirit wasn't cause for a man's harm, no less death. No one killed those who invoked different spirits.

Bakako anxiously probed Pedro's meaning. "No believe Christ die?"

"No. You die only if you pretend to be Christian but deny Christ because you secretly are Jewish." Pedro sensed his friends' incredulity and sought to reassure them. "You, Yutowa, and the others are neither Christian nor secretly Jews. You wouldn't be brought here."

Pedro studied the ashen ground for a moment, realizing Bakako and Yutowa had not truly understood, and his heart now also pounded. In an instant, he asked himself if Bakako and Yutowa were wrong to be incredulous. But, in the same instant, he acknowledged the grave peril of asking that question on the very ground where they stood. He retreated fearfully from further discussion and led them from the field, remorseful to have taken them there. Silently, the three youths returned to the Indians' lodging.

That night, as they lay to sleep, Yutowa turned to Bakako. "The natives are treating us very well here."

"Yes, but they are very different from us," Bakako replied, sensing Yutowa's anxiety and desire to share it.

"Do you think they burn themselves to death often?"

"I don't know."

"Do you think that's our people's fate, but Admiral is just hiding that?" Yutowa whispered hoarsely.

"Admiral doesn't appear to be a savage."

"But the natives are savages! It's one thing to enslave—we could do that if Caribes are captured—it's another thing to burn people to death for the spirits they honor."

"I agree," Bakako responded gravely. "It's astonishing they

do that. It's not as revolting as eating people, but just as savage. Perhaps it's an ancestral rite they continue to observe. Perhaps they're just backward—they've never learned to live in harmony with one another. We've thought of these men as one people, but clearly they think of themselves as many, and entitled to treat others savagely."

Bakako stared into the darkness, trembling to imagine Guacanagarí's horror when he learned how critical a man's belief in the Christ spirit was to the pale men. Guacanagarí had ignored Admiral's promise to teach of the Christ spirit, and Admiral had not divulged any worldly harm of failure to learn.

◻ ◻ ◻

On Easter Sunday, Cristóbal proudly received the sovereigns' letter addressing him as Admiral and ordering a second voyage. He quickly prepared a memorandum summarizing his recommendations for Española's settlement and government, advising that as many as two thousand volunteer colonists should go to secure and manage the island and its trade and that they should be settled in three or four townships built about the island. He believed greed for gold would fuel rapid colonization and proposed that the share a colonist received for the gold gathered would be set by the territory's governor from time to time as development progressed—but that for the first year a colonist's take should be half of that gathered. He indicated that a church should be built staffed with friars to perform divine worship and convert the Indians.

The gold was not his own greatest glory. Cristóbal now believed the Lord had chosen his very name—Cristóbal—to designate him as the one chosen to bring Christ to the heathens across the Ocean Sea. He signed the memorandum with a mystical signature he would use thereafter, ending with the Greco-Latin form of *Cristóbal*, reminding that he was the "Christ bearer."

As Holy Week passed, all the Indians became ill, sniffing, coughing, and growing feverish and weak, their skin breaking into reddish rashes over the entire body.* The extraordinary abnormality of their disorders and pains were terrifying, as was the uncertainty whether

---

*Measles?

they would survive so wrought and suffer indefinitely or quickly die. Bakako and Yutowa desperately consulted Attabeira for guidance and cure. They feared the Christ spirit's punishment for failure of reverence and honored him, as well. Inexplicably, Bakako recovered within days, as did Xamabo and Abasu, but Yutowa and others declined further, with severe earaches, labored breathing, and total incapacity.

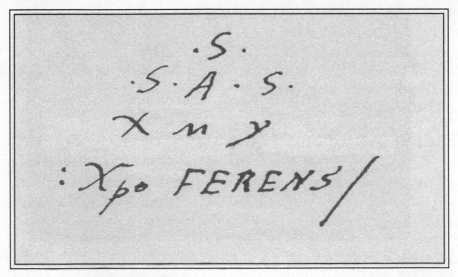

Columbus's signature.

By April 11, Cristóbal departed by mule for Córdoba en route to Barcelona. Yutowa and three other Indians remained too stricken to travel, and Cristóbal left them in Seville under care of friars. Before departing, Bakako tried to hearten Yutowa, reminding they now understood Admiral was returning to Bohío, which gave them hope.

"We came to this new world together, and we'll leave it together," Bakako comforted him.

"Admiral will take us only to Bohío," Yutowa muttered. "We'll never see Guanahaní again. We're doomed to serve as his ears and tongue forever."

Bakako was startled, not by Yutowa's prediction but by his desolateness, as if he didn't care to survive. "Yutowa, you'll recover as I did. We're Lucayans. As Deminán, we'll survive, prevail, and prosper."

⊡ ⊡ ⊡

As he approached Córdoba, Cristóbal's elation was pinched by remorse. Proximity whetted his yearning to reunite with his sons. He anticipated a jubilant reception by Córdoba's nobility and merchant community, as well as the Aranas and his many friends at the apothecary.

But he was now nobility, and Cristóbal felt his stature no longer befit a relationship with Beatriz. His life had become his enterprise, her ignobility had no place in it, and he no longer cared for her because he no longer needed her love and support. He would never marry her, and, when convenient, he would discard her. In a rarest of moments, he felt guilt for the sins of ingratitude and deception—he and the Lord both knew he was born common just as she, and that she had fed, housed, and loved him for seven years and born his child.

Cristóbal's entrance into Córdoba was tumultuous. Andalusia's clergy and nobility met him at the great bridge over the Guadalquivir, together with Diego, little Fernando, Beatriz, and other Aranas. Before all, Cristóbal embraced his sons and Beatriz deeply and explained to the Aranas that their Diego now commanded the first settlement in the Indies and was amassing a fortune of gold. Bakako studied Admiral's natural sons and woman and understood that Admiral indeed was but human. Bakako showed the boys the bounce of the batey ball.

The city council hosted the Admiral to a great feast. That night, after the accolades, Cristóbal returned to Beatriz and the boys in her house. He recounted stories of the naked peoples and their customs, the Caribes who ate human flesh, the weed floating across an enormity of the Ocean Sea, and the tremendous storms. It was hours before the boys slumbered, and then Cristóbal and Beatriz were alone.

Beatriz proudly and passionately embraced him, undressed for him, and drew him into bed. Cristóbal was overcome by her warmth and love and his guilt, and he could not bear or dare to tell her what he intended at that moment. He recalled that Domenico had loyally supported Susanna throughout decades as her husband, whether he had loved her or not. A vision of Filipa's embrace as she lay beneath him on their wedding night scalded his memory, reminding him that she had welcomed him in spite of the very ignobility he now shunned. They made love, Beatriz happily and Cristóbal as if he were outside his body beholding an act by himself that the Lord condemned. When finished, he realized he found neither happiness nor simple pleasure in anything outside the scope of his enterprise.

By April 11, Cristóbal and his party departed for Barcelona, riding west to Murcia and then along the coast to València. The news of Cristóbal's triumph reverberated throughout Spain and crowds flocked to glimpse the entourage in every village, town, and city they passed. An emissary of King João also approached Barcelona, dispatched to advise Fernando and Isabel that the lands discovered were João's.

Lawlessness in Guarico

As the sun rose, Guacanagarí prepared to greet the three lieutenants in the plaza and reflected on the deterioration in the trading settlement the pale men called "Navidad." It barely existed anymore, as the pale men had dispersed into three enclaves in Guarico, apparently under separate rule. Their captain Diego and some dozen men still held the fort and heavier weapons, but Pedro, Rodrigo, and their followers paid no heed to him. A band of crude misfits followed a degenerate rogue named Chachu. Rather than using the fort to store the gold collected, each man kept his own on his person, and it was obvious neither Admiral nor the cacique Fernando would receive it. The pale men's seed had died from neglect, and their only food was that which Guacanagarí supplied or they looted, and they looted daily.

Each pale man now claimed four or five women, there had been no marriages, and it was suspected many women were pregnant. Their husbands, fathers, and brothers were incensed, and Guacanagarí heard bitter harangues for justice and punishment daily. He shuddered that his subjects might resort to their own justice, only to be slaughtered by the garrison's weaponry.

The pale men's reverence for the Christ spirit, so apparent in Admiral, had decayed. Their daily areítos and communal invocations had dwindled to weekly, and now only Diego's band at the fort observed them. Each still wore a cemí of the Christ spirit or his mother about his neck or in his pocket, and most invoked these at dawn and dusk for protection. But few, if any, consulted their spirits frequently during the day as had Admiral, and they lusted for women and gold instead. Guacanagarí considered that his own subjects' frequent spiritual invocations provided tranquility and order, and he suspected the absence of spirituality fueled the pale men's misbehavior. Their fear of spirits had been supplanted by an arrogant celebration of their own flesh.

Many of the pale men now suffered from syphilis, some likely fatally. Guacangari had explained cures to the three lieutenants, but they had dismissed his advice, and it had been obvious they considered his knowledge of remedies inferior. He wondered whether the severity of the pale men's infliction was Yúcahu's design, as vengeance for their abuse of women.

Guacanagarí spotted the lieutenants approaching and resolved to conceal his disdain that pale men were coarse, dirty, untrustworthy, and disrespectful of man, spirit, and nature. He greeted them courteously and invited them to sit with him, his nitaínos, and a youth Guacanagarí had selected to learn to speak their language. The lieutenants responded courteously to Guacanagarí but ignored and insulted the nitaínos as if they were naborias.

Through gestures, Guacanagarí indicated he would select the food allocated to the entire garrison and deliver it to the fort, where it could be divided as the lieutenants wished. He reviewed the cazabi and fish brought by his subjects and, with unease, allocated a disproportionately large amount to the pale men, sensing his nitaínos' irritation.

Diego interrupted and gestured that the garrison should receive more. The nitaínos gazed at the ground, angry and disgusted, as no one ever questioned a caciqual decision on the allocation of food.

"No," Guacanagarí answered, shaking his head. "It will be as I have allocated. Your men have taken food from others already." His youth attempted translation.

Diego, Pedro, and Rodrigo were surprised. Diego touched his stomach and pointed to his mouth. "We need more to eat."

"No. You must stop the looting, both of food and jewelry, and you must stop taking married or unwilling women. Then you may have the food you need."

Rodrigo understood denial and, without waiting translation, replied in a moderate tone, with gestures. "We recognize our men's conduct is not appropriate. But if you give us what we need, we'll prevent the excesses."

Guacanagarí politely listened to his youth's translation and paused as if to think, but he had already decided his plan. "I will give you one more basket of cazabi as a gesture of goodwill. But I will deliver the food to the fort today myself, and I will warn all of your men of the consequence of continued misbehavior." With open disdain, he indicated the lieutenants should leave the plaza. All present, both olive and pale skinned, understood he had signaled his tolerance had reached its limit. Those olive also saw he didn't fear a nonviolent confrontation.

At midday, the garrison's men sauntered to the fort to await Guacanagarí's arrival, lounging in their separate bands in the shade of trees, cautiously eyeing the others. Some brought women to display as trophies or to carry the food obtained as porters. Diego conferred with Pedro and Rodrigo, and, for a moment, they surmounted their mutual contempt to sternly warn all the men to behave.

Diego addressed the entire garrison. "I met this morning with the Lord Guacanagarí. He now will give us food only if we stop looting and abusing the women. The Admiral's orders are clear and must be observed. We can't steal the Indians' food or gold or lie with the married women if we expect to be fed in the future."

Chachu stepped forward and interrupted. "You call the shit he gives us food?" Many snickered, and Chachu was emboldened to continue. "It stinks. Unfortunately, it's the only thing to eat. Your so-called Admiral isn't here to eat it, and he isn't here to police his orders, and if he ever comes back, I'll let him know how much we liked the food."

"Silence! I am your captain!"

"Captain? Captain?!" Chachu spread his arms widely to deride the title. "You've never been a captain of anything, not even a rowboat." The crowd laughed. "You're the captain of a shabby fort among savages on a beach nobody cares about, appointed by a Geno-ese charlatan because he sleeps with your whore sister." Chachu's followers cheered, Diego's were silent, and Pedro and Rodrigo winced at the insult, fearing it would lead to blows. Many lounging sat upright, instinctively resting their hands on daggers belted at the hip or ankle.

"As your captain," said Diego, raising his voice, "I'm the person charged by the Admiral to maintain this garrison and report to him as to each man's conduct—which report he will share with the king and queen. You're violating the Crown's orders if you loot food or jewelry. We can't defame Christianity with the women."

"Defame Christianity? Defame Christianity?!" Chachu gazed to the sky as if to search for the Lord. "I've found some women here, as we all have—including you. But we have fewer women than the king! We have fewer women than Cardinal Mendoza!" There were more cheers. "And we certainly have fewer women than most popes!" The cheers rose to a prolonged applause.

Escobedo raised his voice. "Hold your tongue! We serve the king and queen! Remember the Admiral's instruction that we not anger the Lord Guacanagarí. Our purpose here is to initiate Española's subjugation and colonization. We must treat the Indians kindly so they accept the faith peacefully."

"Accept the faith! Accept the faith?! They worships stones and rocks and idols. They couldn't give a shit about the faith!" Chachu paused and laughed. "The Genoese says we should show them Chris-tian conduct—I agree! Let's enslave 'em like we do the infidels and barbarians from Africa and the Canaries! They're naked, stupid, lazy, and liars, and I don't see any point in showing them the faith. We're here to find gold, every one of us. We should just enslave 'em to dig for it!"

"Your disobedience and insolence to the king has been noted by all present," Escobedo responded. "When the Admiral returns, you will receive swift justice, together with your accomplices. I command you to sit."

"Your mother's a whore." The gathering was silent. Chachu stood his ground, but was silent, as well.

Pedro attempted moderation. "We're here to find gold, for both ourselves and the king, and to show our hosts Christian conduct, so they may be brought to the faith and enrich the sovereigns' kingdoms. If we're able to govern ourselves, we'll all be rich and, for myself and Rodrigo, we will ensure that you leave rich. But we are in Guacanagarí's kingdom and cannot anger him—more than we have already."

"We've spent three months collecting the rubbish they call jewelry," Chachu responded. "I didn't enlist to trade for this. The Genoese said the roofs and bridges were made of gold—bullshit! We need to find the gold mines he pretends to have found."

"We will try to find the mines—as he instructed," Pedro replied. "You'll be rewarded. But those who aren't Christian in their conduct will answer to Fernando."

Jácome el Rico rose and, with hesitation, added a thought. "As Señor Gutiérrez well knows, the king will understand what gold has been gathered as compared to what he receives, and it's best that we gather it first, to be rewarded when we return."

There was silence, and then derisive chuckling at the naïveté to make such a remark.

Guacanagarí then appeared at the forest's edge, followed by nitaínos and naborias bearing baskets of cazabi and fish, and the garrison's men quieted. He arrived at the fort with quiet authority. The three lieutenants greeted him courteously, and even Chachu and his band were respectful. Guacanagarí stood before the crowd and pointed to the food. "I give this to you. I ask that you not take what is not given." His youth translated with gestures.

"I am the ruler of this land. Your king Fernando will receive my relative as emissary on my behalf. I will advise your Admiral when he returns as to your conduct, man by man. I ask that you not steal food. I ask that you not steal gold, jewelry, or anything else. I ask that you not touch married or unwilling women or any girl. That is how my subjects live, and I expect no less of you, my guests." The youth translated some portions.

Escobedo understood little of the words but knew Guacanagarí's message and spoke sternly to the men. "I believe everyone understands what the Lord Guacanagarí wants. It's no more than the Lord's commandments given to Moses on Sinai. We must not steal food or gold or covet other men's women. And remember, this isn't only the Lord Guacanagarí's wish and the Lord's command. It is Colón's direct order to you, rendered as admiral on the authority of the king and queen and violated subject to their stern justice! That justice will reign here upon the Admiral's return!" He turned to Guacanagarí and nodded agreement. "We are Christians and agree."

Guacanagarí surveyed the men and perceived a motley rabble of untrustworthy commoners, fearsome only when armed. He remembered how quickly and assuredly he had offered to be their host and doubted his own wisdom. He nodded sternly to the three lieutenants that there had been agreement and then departed with his people into the forest without further conversation.

The sailors rushed to seize the food baskets. Diego shouted for all to stand back, but none obeyed until Chachu drew his sword, whereupon the three lieutenants and Chachu selected items for their loyalists and all dispersed to their separate camps.

As the moon rose that night, Pedro and Rodrigo dispatched some sailors armed with knives to find Jácome. In the morning, he was found dead with his throat slit by a Castilian knife, the first European casualty in Cristóbal's voyage of discovery. Some crewmen feared the Lord's judgment for the sin, a few felt remorse, and all were sobered that a shipmate had perished at their own hands but none would be punished. They had abandoned the rules of their own civilization.

Guacanagarí carefully observed how the pale men dug a trench and laid Jácome's body within, fully clothed and with the face and eyes gazing upward to the heavens. He examined the burial spot over the following days, seeking to ascertain whether the body lived again as they claimed with respect to the Christ spirit. The grave remained undisturbed and the body presumably within, but he could not ascertain what had happened to the soul.

XIII
SPRING 1493

TRIUMPH IN BARCELONA,
April–May 1493

Isabel and Fernando did not wait upon their admiral's arrival in Barcelona to proclaim the triumph of their sponsorship of the voyage or assert dominion over the lands discovered—wherever they were. They instructed Luis de Santángel to publish Colón's public letter promptly, taking care that it be edited to preclude João's potential claim that the discoveries were Portugal's pursuant the Treaty of Alcáçovas or the related papal bull* because they lay in the Ocean Sea south of the Canaries.

Luis altered Cristóbal's letter to that end, including by adding a notation to indicate that it had been done offshore the Canary Islands, facilitating the argument that Colón's discoveries were newly found Canary Islands on the same latitude and thereby Castile's pursuant to the papal bull. Colón's assertion of Española's possession with a fort was of course retained, as were his descriptions of the peoples discovered—their nakedness, timidity, and inclination to conversion—and the claims of the islands' extraordinary economic potential—gold, spice, mastic, and as many slaves as the sovereigns ordered shipped taken from the idolaters. The edited letter was first published in Castilian in Barcelona on April 1.

---

*Aeterni Regis of 1481.

The sovereigns dispatched instructions to their papal ambassador to obtain promptly the broadest possible papal grant to the lands discovered and to be discovered. In mid-April, they received João's emissary, who did assert that all lands discovered south of Hierro were Portugal's. They dispatched diplomats back to João offering to discuss the matter but warning that he not send a fleet to the lands discovered. Colón's public letter was translated into Latin and published in Rome as the sovereigns' ambassador negotiated with Pope Alexander VI. João also dispatched special emissaries to Alexander, and they sped to intercede in the discussions.

Over the winter, Fernando had recovered partially and returned to participate fully in ceremonial functions. He had beheld and faced death on the battlefield many times and, unlike Isabel, he was neither shocked by his mortality nor worried he had sinned. His royal demeanor and attire fully obscured the physical frailty he yet felt.

As Colón approached Barcelona, the sovereigns prepared a grand reception in the throne room of Barcelona's palace, astride the plaza where the attack had occurred. Cristóbal prepared an equally grand entrance, instructing his Indians to dress themselves with fresh paint and every piece of their gold jewelry. At forty-two, he would wear finery just purchased in Córdoba and comport himself with an authoritative demeanor and airs, confidently exhibiting his sturdy, tall frame and gray hair to cut a figure of a statesman some perceived as august as a Roman senator. Xamabo prepared his finest entrance as well—to bear a large, finely plumed headdress, attended as if a cacique by his younger brethren.

Cristóbal and his entourage arrived Barcelona in mid-April. They were escorted through streets packed with a multitude of gawking onlookers to the plaza, and then through a throng of nobility, ecclesiastics, and city leadership to the throne room, where the sovereigns awaited seated beneath a gold-cloth canopy. Cristóbal approached their dais engulfed with pride that he had achieved the adulation he had sought his entire life. His Indians followed, bearing caged parrots, spears, and other trophies. Fernando eyed them and grasped immediately they were not from Guinea and appeared closer in color to the sovereigns' Canarian vassal Fernando Guanarteme. Xamabo was astounded by the enormity of throne room, the ornate clothing worn by the multitudes of people, and the jewels that bedecked

Fernando's and Isabel's robes and crowns. He fortified himself to be neither cowed nor servile, but proudly sovereign.

Cristóbal fell to his knees at the dais and kissed the hands of the king and queen. They bid him rise and sit beside them, an honor rarely accorded. He gazed directly into Isabel's eyes, thanking her for believing in him, and she gazed directly back, thanking him for achieving for her account yet another astounding victory for the advancement of the sovereigns' realms and reputation. Cristóbal introduced Xamabo, explaining that he was the relative of Española's Lord Guacanagarí, and Fernando and Xamabo embraced.

The sovereigns listened as Cristóbal related the triumphs of his voyage, ballyhooing the rivers and mines of gold discovered, as evident by the Indians' jewelry and some other pieces, and the Indians' receptivity to the faith, as evident by their civility. He professed that Española likely was the Ophir where King Solomon's navy had filled their ships with gold and Juana likely the mainland of Mangi, although the Indians said it an island. Everything he said convinced the sovereigns that their triumph was extraordinary and reinforced their conviction to promptly dispatch a second expedition to preclude João from usurping their dominion. They instructed that the Indians be provided religious instruction and baptized before returning to Española. The choristers from the royal chapel entered, and Isabel and Fernando knelt and raised their hands in devotion as "Te Deum Laudamus" was sung.

The sovereigns afforded their admiral exquisite lodging and favors over the next weeks as they conferred with him on arranging the trading colony and how to resolve the territorial dispute with João. Fernando and Prince Juan took him riding and hunting, and Cardinal Mendoza and other nobility feted, feasted, and claimed to have supported him. Cristóbal basked in the adulation, which exceeded his expectation, but he quickly embraced it as his due entitlement.

Cristóbal delivered his journal to the sovereigns and advised that the best resolution of the territorial dispute would be to replace the papal bull's concept of a latitudinal division of the Ocean Sea at Hierro—where Castile was relegated that north—with a longitudinal division of the Ocean Sea at a point west of the Azores, with Castile taking everything discovered to the west of the line. Cristóbal secretly acknowledged to the sovereigns and their closest advisers that the discoveries were south of Hierro and that he expected further discoveries south, so a latitudinal division favored Portugal. He promised he had attained the Indies and argued that a longitudinal line—such as along the western tips of the Azores and Cape Verde islands— could secure the entirety of the Indies for Spain since João had yet to achieve them from the east by circumventing Guinea. He remembered on the voyage when the weed first appeared to carpet the sea, the compass needles shifted, and a milder temperature prevailed, perceived this area as delineating the known and previously unknown Ocean Sea, and advised that this area—while farther west—could also safely serve as the longitudinal division, estimating it lay one hundred leagues west of the Azores.

As May approached, the Castilian embassy at the Vatican reminded the pope that the sovereigns had fought and shed blood to bring the faith to the Canary Islands, of which these discoveries appeared but an extension, and advanced their proposal for a longitudinal division of the Ocean Sea at the Azores and Cape Verde islands. João's representatives arrived to protest and clamored that Colón had simply found Antillia, to which Portugal's right had been recognized for centuries, and that the papal bull was clear that whatever had been discovered belonged to Portugal if south of Hierro. The Aragonese Alexander listened. He derived substantial support for his papacy from Fernando and Isabel and knew this was an appropriate time to suggest that they could provide even more. Fernando was his friend and, as with all Fernando's friendships, continued friendship relied on doing that which Fernando demanded.

As Alexander reviewed the matter, Isabel and Fernando received information that João had authorized an expedition to investigate Colón's discoveries. With trepidation, they ordered a fleet organized to intercept it. While they expected to prevail with the Aragonese pope, João commanded a larger and considerably more expert navy to take possession of lands, regardless of the pope's declarations. His mathematical and geographical experts might know better that Colón had found the lost Antillia rather than the Indies.

On May 3, Alexander published the papal bull Inter Catera to recognize Castile's right to the islands and mainlands discovered and to be discovered thereafter, provided they were not in the actual possession of another Christian prince. He indicated that no right previously granted another Christian prince was thereby being taken away and that the grant of jurisdiction was on the same terms as the grants of Africa, Guinea, and Mina had been to the Portuguese kings. He also prepared two additional bulls—ultimately to be dated May 3 and 4—providing that a longitudinal line be established one hundred leagues west of any of the Azores and the Cape Verde islands and granting Castile all islands and mainlands found and to be found from that line west or south in the direction of India or toward any other quarter except those possessed by a Christian prince prior to Christmas 1492.

The Portuguese ambassadors despaired they had lost Antillia and any antipodal continent that might exist in the southern hemisphere off Guinea. The Castilian ambassadors rejoiced, but they worried that an ambiguity arose with respect to Castile's entitlement to the Indies themselves in the absence of possession. Fernando and Isabel feared João's ability to take possession and hand the pope a fait accompli.

Regardless of any geographic ambiguities, Pope Alexander VI was absolutely clear on two points. The papacy was supreme in determining and awarding the dominion of Christian princes to newly discovered lands previously unpossessed by Christians. Christian princes owed the pope a duty to bring peoples in lands so awarded to the faith.

Alexander had read Cristóbal's public letter carefully. His bulls noted that it pleased the Lord that barbarous nations be overthrown and brought to the faith and that Christianity's beloved son Christoforum Colon had discovered many unclothed peoples who did not eat meat disposed to embrace the faith and good morals. The bulls recounted that a fortress had already been built and equipped on one of the islands discovered and admonished Fernando and Isabel that it was their duty to lead the peoples discovered to the faith.

Isabel and Fernando spent May intensely engaged in the arrangements necessary to dispatch the fleet to Española promptly. They appointed Juan Rodríguez de Fonseca, then archdeacon of Seville and a protégé of Archbishop Talavera, to administer the project with Colón, as Juan had proven his administrative ability in the conquest of Grenada. They granted Fonseca and Colón broad authority to

commission ships and enlist seamen, soldiers, and tradesmen suitable
for the colony and to provision them with supplies, weapons, and
ammunition, including cannon. Fernando understood the Indians on
Española lacked horses and that a small cavalry would constitute
an overwhelming force, and the sovereigns commissioned twenty
mounted soldiers and their horses to be included among the military
contingent, including five additional mares to replenish the mounts.
The cavalry also would be critical in the event João forced hostilities in the discovered lands, as he had done once in the Canaries.
The sovereigns selected a Catalan Benedictine monk to lead the clerics chosen, Fray Bernaldo Buil. Bernaldo had served on Aragonese
warships and as a secretary to Fernando when younger, and more
recently as ambassador to France, and the sovereigns sought his
designation by Alexander as papal nuncio to the Indies.

The sovereigns' affections for Cristóbal grew stronger, particularly
Isabel's. They reaffirmed the nobility and titles previously conferred
and clarified that the jurisdiction of his admiralship began west of a
line running north to the south through the Azores and the Cape Verde
islands, without the interposition of the one hundred league buffer.
They granted him a coat of arms—a shield heralding his honor and
entitlements—with a quadrant depicting rich gold islands.

Columbus's coat of arms, as painted in La Rábida.

Cristóbal felt it essential that his two brothers, Bartolomé and Giaccomo, return with him to the Indies to assist in governance. The sovereigns awarded them both titles, whereupon Cristóbal dispatched messengers to Paris and Savona, asking them to meet in Seville before the voyage departed. The sovereigns appointed Santángel's partner and a financier of the first voyage, the Sevillian Genoese banker Francesco Pinelo, paymaster for the second.

Isabel and Cristóbal discussed his personal situation and that his elder son, Diego, serve as a page at court when he came of age after living first with sister-in-law Violante. Isabel promised that both sons could become pages to Prince Juan when they came of age, regardless of Fernando's illegitimacy. Isabel arranged that Violante and her husband receive a house in Seville—which the Inquisition had confiscated from a converso—where she and the boys could live. The sovereigns awarded Cristóbal the annual pension of 10,000 marvedis for being the first sailor to sight land on the outward voyage, ignoring the doubts of Rodrigo Sánchez.

On May 29, the sovereigns rendered their written order to Cristóbal for the administration of the lands the Lord had revealed to them through his diligence, aware of Alexander's admonishment as to their duty. The order expressed that their principal concern was the increase of the faith and directed Cristóbal to convert the inhabitants by all ways and means, including through the services of the Indians who had come to Spain. The colony was to be organized similar to Mina, with all merchandise traded and goods obtained being the property of the Crown alone, except Cristóbal would receive of one-tenth of the profits as admiral and an additional one-eighth to the extent he underwrote. The order admonished that the objective of conversion might be better attained if Cristóbal compelled all who voyaged there to treat the Indians very well and lovingly and abstain from doing them any injury, arranging that both peoples hold much conversation and intimacy, each serving the other to the best of their ability. Cristóbal was to give the Indians gifts and punish severely those who maltreated them. Vassalage was contemplated, slavery was not.

But the order didn't address what Cristóbal should do in the event the Indians disagreed with or chose to resist the sovereigns' settlement on their homeland. The pope as the Lord's servant had granted the Indians' homeland to the sovereigns, and there was no misunderstanding whatsoever among people living on terra firma— the pope, King João, the sovereigns' subjects, the Christians, conversos and Jews of Europe, the peoples of the Canary Islands or Guinea, or the infidels at Istanbul or Jerusalem—as to what Queen Isabel and King Fernando expected Cristóbal should then do. Cristóbal was not to graciously withdraw or retreat, but to achieve and maintain the colony by using the weapons provisioned. While they wished the Indians brought into their realm with kindness, education, and love, the sovereigns were to be their supreme rulers—by force if necessary. The order also didn't contemplate what was to be done if the Grand Khan were found and claimed dominion himself.

Xamabo had relished Fernando's embrace but, as the weeks passed, he grew anxious for a substantive discussion of Marien's trading relationship with the sovereigns. Accompanied by Bakako, he advised Admiral that the time for meaningful discussion had come and asked for it to be arranged.

Cristóbal discussed the request with Isabel and Fernando, indicating that he had no intent of establishing an exclusive trading relationship with Guacanagarí and likely would build the first intended settlement at another site. He reminded them that neither Guacanagarí nor the Indians brought to Spain appreciated that Cristóbal would be returning to Española with over a thousand men, including soldiers. The sovereigns understood and said they would give Xamabo kind assurances of friendship. Isabel let Fernando handle the tricky conversation, and Cristóbal summoned Xamabo and Bakako to meet with the king in the throne room.

Fernando waved for the two Indians to enter and invited Xamabo to join him on the dais and sit where Cristóbal had sat. Through Bakako, Fernando and Xamabo pleasantly engaged in courtesies. Fernando inquired whether Castilian food was pleasing and what Xamabo ate in his homeland. After some moments, Fernando obliged his visitor with the audience requested.

"My friend, it's an honor we meet to discuss your Lord Guacanagarí's relationship with myself and the queen." Fernando let Bakako translate as best he could.

"It is my honor, as well. My cacique Guacanagarí asks that you and the queen conduct your trade in the lands Admiral calls the 'Indies' through Guacanagarí. He can provide all the gold you seek."

"You may tell Lord Guacanagarí that we appreciate and recognize his generosity for harboring and protecting our subjects and will always remember and cherish that. The queen and I already consider the Lord Guacanagarí among our most faithful noblemen, and his allegiance to our sovereignty will always be reciprocated." Fernando and Cristóbal watched Bakako translate and doubted that either Indian understood the nature of the intended relationship.

Bakako translated, and Xamabo understood, something—at least enough to recognize that the conversation was tricky. Xamabo replied. "Guacanagarí welcomes your men so we may trade and promises his alliance to you and Queen Isabel to that end." Bakako translated as best he could.

Fernando studied Xamabo and paused, wondering whether Bakako's words were carefully chosen or merely an expression limited to the extent of his Castilian vocabulary. Fernando recalled his meeting with the Canarian Fernando Guanarteme and their express discussions of that native's vassalage to the Crown, and he shied from further discussion, reflecting that his troops were not yet on Española.

Fernando stood. "On behalf of the queen and myself, we have special gifts for the Lord Guacanagarí and yourself." A page stepped forward bearing two satin robes, their collars bedecked with jewels. Fernando helped Xamabo don his and remarked how grandly he appeared, and Xamabo understood the formal discussions were concluded.

As Xamabo was ushered away, Fernando turned to Cristóbal. "I understand the Indian women go as naked as him. How do the men you've left there react to that?"

"It concerns me, very much." Cristóbal paused. "It alone is an important reason that I return promptly." He saw Fernando understood.

⊡   ⊡   ⊡

In early June, the sovereigns convened another solemn, public ceremony, this time for the Indians' baptism. Bakako and Xamabo understood the ceremony was meant as the culmination of their religious instruction, and, as its day approached, the six Taínos discussed it among themselves.

"They say we shall become the children of their Lord, united with their Christ spirit," Bakako explained.

"But I don't trust their Christ spirit or his mother," Abasu objected. "I trust Yúcahu, Attabeira, and our other spirits. I don't want to participate."

Xamabo was uncomfortable. "We're here to further Guacanagarí's objective of trading with the caciques Fernando and Isabel. It's important that we please them, particularly since they believe they are benefiting us by doing this."

"But what will Yúcahu think?" asked a Samanán.

"Yúcahu won't be jealous if you honor him as a superior to their Christ spirit," Xamabo replied. "I will participate in the ceremony intending just that."

"Remember, the pale men say their spirits are the only spirits, and they view this baptism as accepting that," Bakako interjected. "We shouldn't reveal to them that we'll continue to worship our spirits."

"I understand," Abasu answered. "But I'm not concerned with Yúcahu, who'll always be there for us. I fear the Christ spirit himself— what will he do or design for us if we lie to him in this ceremony?"

There was silence.

Xamabo answered. "Yúcahu understands why we are here and what we need to do. He may not be pleased we honor the Christ spirit, but he will protect us from the Christ spirit. He is our spirit, not theirs. We must do what these men expect, but we can honor Yúcahu foremost, and Yúcahu will protect us."

The baptism was held before the sovereigns' nobility, and Fernando, Isabel, and Prince Juan served as the Indians' godparents. Xamabo was christened don Fernando de Aragón and Abasu don Juan de Castilla. Bakako, Cristóbal's favorite, was christened Diego Colón, sharing the name of Cristóbal's younger brother and elder son. Most onlookers, including Prince Juan's fourteen-year-old page Gonzalo Fernández de Oviedo, perceived the Indians received the baptism of their own free will.

As they left the church, Xamabo quietly thanked the other five for their participation. "Now, you may consult Yúcahu and advise that you have not forsaken him."

Caciqual Council in Magua

As winter passed, Haiti's paramount caciques received reports of the pale beings' degenerating conduct in Guarico. Caonabó sought, and Guacanagarí resisted, a caciqual council to discuss the situation, and eventually Guarionex called it. Guacanagarí recognized his attempt to secure a trading advantage with the pale beings was a dismal failure—their conduct was inexcusable and worthy of the severest punishment. But he remained convinced it was an aberration and that upon Admiral's return order and decency would be restored. He resolved not to defend what was occurring, but to argue that Admiral's return would cure it and, regardless, that the other caciques had no authority to review a situation internal to Marien. He suspected the others remained jealous of his relationship with the pale beings regardless of their behavior.

As he welcomed the caciques to Guaricano, Guarionex comported himself with a calmness designed to communicate that the concerns to be discussed were not dire and permitted thoughtful deliberation rather than a hasty decision. Anacaona arrived with Caonabó, suggesting that Caonabó did not intend a gritty denunciation of Guacanagarí and that she and her husband expected measured discourse, as well. Pineapple juice was served, and the caciques sat outside on duhos in the shade cast by Guarionex's ceremonial bohío. Mayobanex brought an interpreter.

"We all know the pale beings' conduct is vile," Guarionex said, opening the meeting. "We or our representatives all have met these men—let me call them that—and traded with them. While I wouldn't have predicted their conduct would be so deplorable, I'm not surprised." He turned to Guacanagarí. "The point of this meeting is to discuss what should be done in Marien by you. It's your cacicazgo, but the presence of these men could affect us all. You should begin by explaining what has occurred so we can advise a solution."

"I thank Guarionex for hosting this council," Behecchio interrupted.

"I do want to hear Guacanagarí's viewpoint. But first I want to express my displeasure with how you've proceeded, Guacanagarí. The rest of us met with these men to trade. But you invited them to stay. You should've consulted us before doing that."

"Behecchio, you misunderstand or distort," Guacanagarí responded. "Unlike canoes, their vessels sink. One did sink, and they had no choice but to leave men with me before returning to their homeland. I never sought their presence, but I allowed them to remain and have assisted them. I wasn't going to throw them in the sea. If their vessel had sunk off Xaraguá, would you have consulted me before you assisted them?"

"You're the one distorting. You've done more than come to their rescue. Your naborias helped them build a structure to store their weapons. You dispatched an emissary to their cacique, seeking an extended relationship."

"What would you have done differently, Behecchio?"

Caonabó addressed Guacanagarí. "You have an utter mess on your hands. It's too late to argue you knew what you were doing. The decision to allow a structure was premature and foolish, an invitation to stay permanently. Their presence could affect us all."

"If these men lived peacefully, as our peoples, they wouldn't need a structure," Anacaona added. "Guacanagarí, their treatment of women is crude and repugnant to every virtue of our people. You must recognize our women's injury is injury to us all, and within the caciqual responsibility of all in this room."

"Quiet, my friends," Guarionex interrupted softly and raised his hands, seeking to dissipate the passions brought to the meeting. "We will discuss these issues today. But first we must understand what has happened. Let's begin by letting Guacanagarí tell us."

Guacanagarí related the vessel's foundering and his meetings with the cacique Admiral, mentioning Admiral's orders to his people to behave and the dismal leaders selected. He itemized the pale men's faults, including their laziness and utter refusal to fish or farm for themselves, the lurid and inappropriate behavior with women and girls, the disrespect of Taíno spirits in favor of their Christ spirit, the insatiable lust for gold, and the dishonesty and vandalism. He observed that these traits were perhaps native to them, but that they had been restrained under good leadership. He mentioned the pale men fought among themselves often and that they had murdered one of their own.

"In their relations with women, is there responsibility and care or any feeling beyond lust?" Anacaona asked.

"This appears to vary by man. There are some who treat their women like wives. But most treat them as servants and concubines. Most are licentious, not caring for contact or relations beyond sex. Remember, they are seafarers, to some extent like our own. There have been no marriages, and I don't foresee any."

"Do they worship their spirits with devotion?" Guarionex asked.

"Admiral did, and most others appeared to when they first arrived. This, too, varies by man. But, as a whole, their worship of their so-called Christ spirit and his mother spirit has substantially declined. When they first arrived, they chanted multiple times daily and frequently sang together. They don't do that anymore. From the beginning, they have denigrated Yúcahu and our spirits. Instinctively, they lust immoderately for women and gold. For the most part, Guarionex, they're not spiritual as you and I would consider spiritual. It may be too harsh a judgment, but I think most of them are too crude to have a significant spiritual existence."

"That's my impression," Guarionex reflected.

"They have fearsome weapons, far more powerful than our own," Guacanagarí continued. "They wear smaller weapons on their body and store the more powerful ones in their structure. There are fewer than forty of them in total, and, regardless of their weaponry, I easily could direct my soldiers to kill them all if that becomes necessary— including as they sleep. But, in my view, it's not necessary. I prefer to wait until Admiral returns to see if their ill behavior is then cured. If not, I will ask Admiral to leave, and to take all his men with him."

Behecchio raised his hands. "A decision that even a single pale man be allowed to remain on Haiti is for this council, given their weapons and conduct. Any future trade through a settlement of them would be for us all."

"Let's spend more time understanding the situation." Guarionex made his irritation evident and turned to Guacanagarí. "What makes you think their conduct will improve when their leader returns?"

"He was a leader capable of enforcing discipline. The men have no leader now."

"I believe I met this leader," said Mayobanex, speaking slowly in Taíno. All turned to him, surprised. He continued in Macorix, translated by his interpreter. "After meeting him, my own decision was to let him pass by without establishing a relationship. He seemed arrogant. He was pursuing, with an assuredness that he would find it, the Guanín and Matininó of our traditions, as well as a 'Grand Kahn' I've never heard of. He captured and presumably enslaved four of my subjects. Worse, his men attacked my subjects with their weapons—which are superior—and wounded two of them, who have since died. I went to meet him on his vessel afterward, and he expressed no remorse whatsoever. He had the attitude of a would-be conqueror."

"Those aren't the only captives taken," Anacaona interjected. "There were Guanahanians seized before he arrived Haiti. The pale men on the northern shore seized men and girls, and the girls were violated." She gazed at Guacanagarí. "I understand there were also male and female captives from Cuba, whom were freed when the vessel sank."

Guarionex raised his eyebrows, and all listened. "Guacanagarí, you may be correct that their leader's return will restore their civility. But Mayobanex's observations hit upon the fundamental issue. What do you really understand of their leader's intent? Does he intend to take the pale men left here back to their homeland? Does he intend to leave them in Guarico? Does he intend to bring more people to live with you or elsewhere in Haiti? Do they want more from Haiti than gold?"

All observed Guacanagarí was uncomfortable with the questions. "My expectation is his people will remain if trading benefits us."

There was silence. Guacanagarí understood all disapproved of his decision to allow the fort to be built. While he concealed emotion, he swelled with humiliation and bitterness at the lifelong disrespect he felt from these colleagues.

Caonabó felt it unproductive to criticize further. "What happened to the body and spirit of the man murdered? My informants say the body of their Christ spirit supposedly returned to life after his death."

Guacanagarí perceived the ultimate focus of Caonabó's inquiry. "They buried the murder victim in the ground, using a different procedure than we use, and I have not seen the victim's body return to life."

"So they can be killed and do not return?"

"It appears so."

Guarionex interrupted. "Caonabó, I don't want to hear a recommendation that we simply kill all of them now—if that's where you're going."

"I've traded with them. I didn't see would-be conquerors in my own brief encounter." Caonabó paused to receive the others' full attention. "But Guacanagarí now has months of contact with them. Based on Guacanagarí's and Mayobanex's observations today, and my own more limited contact, it seems to me these men are of a brutish and incredibly powerful tribe, where force prevails over conscience."

Caonabó turned his gaze to make eye contact with each of his colleagues. "We don't always agree or enjoy each other, and we do have disputes. But our people have enjoyed a general peace for generations. What I fear is these people's weapons and their unknown spirits, particularly their gruesome Christ spirit. There are few of them now, and we can easily destroy them. But if more of them arrive, with more fearsome weapons, it could be difficult to expel them. I'm content, and have been content, to trade with them. But we can't permit them to remain on Haiti. If we do, the misery they've brought to a few in Guarico could become the misery of us all."

"Caonabó, we don't yet know the capability of these people to behave as a good people," Guacanagarí responded. "The men their leader left are commoners, not a nitaíno or cacique among them. The weapons you fear—and rightly fear—are stored in their structure. I could have that overrun and the weapons thrown into the sea at a moment's notice."

"You're too forgiving, Guacanagarí. Their inappropriate conduct has persisted for months and deteriorates. It's very possible their leader will never return." Caonabó shrugged his shoulders and gazed at the sky. "For a moment, hear my thoughts. Assume the leader never returns. These men's conduct will never improve, correct?"

"I can't disagree with that."

"Then you should kill them all right now." Caonabó studied his colleagues' faces. Anacaona looked to the ground, discomforted by her husband's advice but indisposed to disagree publicly with it.

"Assume, on the other hand, that their leader does return. It's also better to kill them all now. You will explain to him the truth—that his men's conduct was entirely unacceptable and they had to be severely punished. If he understands and accepts that, and if he still wishes to trade, we can then trade with him. But he can't have a settlement on Haiti, no matter how small."

"I can't and will not slaughter them indiscriminately. I gave this leader my promise, and, even if I hadn't, this isn't a war."

Behecchio grimaced scornfully. "Caonabó, if you kill them all now, their leader will never understand and will never trade with us again. That's ridiculous."

"Guacanagarí is right," Guarionex interrupted. "Taínos do not slaughter, and this isn't a war like we have with the Caribes." Guarionex sternly glared at Caonabó, and there was more silence. Guarionex turned to Guacanagarí. "But it's your cacicazgo, and your responsibility is to see justice is done. Those pale men guilty of transgressions must be punished, just as you would punish your own subjects. Surely, their leader would understand this."

Mayobanex spoke again, slowly to accommodate precise translation. "If their leader returns, which I doubt, in my view you should indicate you have no interest in trading with him and that he must take his men away. It was easy for me to get rid of him. I just indicated Guanín and Matininó and his 'Gran Khan' were to the east, as were heaps of gold, and he departed like a shark smelling blood."

"My friends, my fear is that gold is not his only objective." Caonabó courteously smiled at Mayobanex. "There was no need for him to build his structure merely to trade for gold. As far as I've heard, the gold they collect isn't even held within the structure. Behecchio and I traded gold with them without their having any structure or permanent settlement. My fear is that these men intend to invade Haiti, or at least that's what we as our people's rulers must assume. Their conduct requires that we assume they are an enemy who has established a foothold from which they might launch an attack. Given their weapons, we can't permit this. They must all be killed now."

Guarionex shook his head in disagreement. "No. Absolutely not. We must seek and fashion a more delicate and harmonious resolution worthy of our spirits."

"For myself and Maguana, I should be clear," Caonabó responded. "If any pale man enters Maguana, I will kill him in Maguana. I will kill all pale men who enter Maguana."

"We don't have a crisis that compels that result," Behecchio interjected. "I take Guarionex's point that miscreants should be punished, severely if necessary. And I take Guacanagarí's point that these men may improve if their leader returns and disciplines them. The goods they have and their know-how is impressive, and trade with them could benefit us if they are content to trade without a settlement. I think we should leave for later a decision to kill them all."

Caonabó turned to Guacanagarí. "Do you have the resolve to punish them individually?"

All waited for Guacanagarí's answer, but there was none.

Anacaona broke the silence to address a separate concern. "Let's remember that there may be women bearing children of the pale men. These women and children will need to be cared for and, as I understand, the pale men haven't entered into a single marriage. If we kill these babies' fathers, we must care for the babies and their mothers nevertheless. We can't let any confusion arise among our subjects otherwise. We are Taíno, not Caribes."

There was silence. Guarionex turned to Guacanagarí. "You've heard us all, and Behecchio is correct. We should've had this conversation before you assisted them in building their structure. But, for the moment, there is no crisis, and this is for you to resolve in Marien, subject to one condition to which I think we all agree. If their leader returns to rescue them, we must then have another conversation about whether the settlement remains."

"I've heard all your views, which I respect, although I don't agree with many of them."

Guarionex gazed up at his ceremonial bohío and was relieved that Father Cacibaquel's cohaba revelation had not been discussed. He wondered whether the other caciques remembered it. He ended the meeting and invited his visitors to watch games of batey.

Haiti's peoples were then well fed and at peace, free from want and blessed with time for leisure and to enjoy friendship. Guarionex recognized that the pale men's presence chilled the harmony and unity of his colleagues. As they watched the games, neither Caonabó nor Behecchio conversed with Guacanagarí.

IN THE PRESENCE OF CHRIST'S MOTHER,
Guadalupe, June 1493

In early June, Isabel and Fernando bade Cristóbal depart for Seville to hasten the preparation and departure of his second voyage. They dispatched more senior envoys to King João to discuss the territorial dispute, and João acquiesced in delaying the departure of his own expedition. But the sovereigns had no intention of agreeing a resolution before their colony was established and Colón reported better geographic information locating the discoveries. Their envoys dithered and bumbled to delay. The sovereigns retained Colón's journal and directed scribes to copy it secretly, hiding its existence from João's spies and envoys, and implored Cristóbal to prepare the chart of the voyage he had promised.

Before Cristóbal's departure, Prince Juan decided to adopt Abasu for the royal household, to be honored as the son of a prominent gentleman. Abasu was distraught and pleaded that Xamabo intercede. Xamabo refused and explained the adoption was an honor and that Abasu couldn't refuse it without insulting the pale men, which would reflect poorly on Guacanagarí. Abasu wept into the night that he would never see his family again, and Bakako lay beside him to offer consolation, understanding how he felt.

Cristóbal and his entourage rode overland to Seville on a difficult route through the mountainous territory of Extremadura, passing through Guadalupe so he could fulfill the first vow of the *Niña*'s crew. Sailing would have been far quicker and easier to meet the urgency of the second voyage, but none doubted the rightness or imperative of satisfying the vow and honoring the Virgin for saving the ship and crew.

Villagers crowded to see the Admiral and his five naked, painted Indians, and word spread through Extremadura's penniless, rustic hamlets that better opportunities might exist in newly discovered lands. In Trujillo, a young bastard swineherd, Francisco Pizarro (b. ca. 1471–1476), marveled at the fortune that might be achieved. In Jerez de los Caballeros, a minor nobleman's third son, Vasco Núñez de Balboa (b. ca. 1475), wondered whether he could possibly fare worse in the Indies than at home. In Medellín, seven-year-old Hernán Cortés (b. 1485) dreamed of growing up to be as the Admiral.

The friars of the Monastery of Santa María de Guadalupe received the Admiral and his Indians warmly with food and water, and Cristóbal paid for the five-pound candle to be molded. It was ready past midnight, and Cristóbal invited Juan Niño and the Indians to join him by torchlight in the pilgrimage vowed.

As they entered the church, Bakako recalled his dread as enormous waves engulfed the *Niña* and that—at the precipice of death—he had honored Yúcahu and Guabancex more fervently than Admiral's spirits. He anguished whether this recourse to Yúcahu and Guabancex had saved the *Niña*, rather than Admiral's prayers to the Christ spirit's mother. He had now taken his first communion and trembled to not honor Virgin. But he feared forsaking the spirits whom he well knew.

Friars led them to the Virgin's chapel and revealed her and they knelt before her. Admiral lit the candle and led a prayer.

Bakako labored to honor Virgin with his fullest devotion and fought to repress unfaithful thoughts that surged uncontrollably within him. He rid Yúcahu and Guabancex from his consciousness. He banished his disrespect of the pale men's assertion that their spirits were the only spirits. He repressed his contempt for the notion that his soul's eternal life was attainable only through belief in the Christ spirit.

But memories of the slave markets in Lisbon and Seville, the behiques who came aboard *Niña* in Palos, and the burning field in Seville overpowered him, and Bakako could not dispatch from the forefront of his consciousness a single, scorching question. If his peoples and Admiral's peoples came to blows, whom would the Christ spirit and Virgin protect?

Chaos in Guarico

Guacanagarí departed with his nitaínos from Guaricano west into the farmlands along the rivers Camú and Yaque. He was moved by the fertility of the great valley, the splendor of the mountains rising north and south, and the enduring labor of farmers tending their fields in the hot sun, as their ancestors had for generations. When

the Yaque permitted, his party boarded small canoes and sped downstream to rendezvous within a day with an enormous canoe waiting
at the ocean, and he asked to be taken to the great cliffs close by
(Cabo del Morro)—where he had camped tracking Caribes years
before—so he might consult Yúcahu.

The view from atop the cliffs also touched him, perhaps as never
before. His cacicazgo stretched west and south beyond the horizons,
and, other than at Guarico, its people were content with their circumstances and the spirits they revered. Through the haze, he identified
the approximate location of Guarico, and a rage momentarily flared
through him. He turned to scan the ocean east to find vessels bearing
Admiral in return, and frustration compounded the rage. He implored
Yúcahu to reveal how the soured relationship with Admiral's men
might be resolved. He realized that Yúcahu was testing his patience to
trust that goodness—rather than evil—could prevail over evil.

When he returned to Guarico, his brother reported that a tremendous altercation had occurred among the pale men the day before,
with many fighting and injured, and one of the injured had died that
morning. Guacanagarí's subjects had not been involved. The pale
men apparently had argued among themselves whether they should
leave Guarico to find more gold in the Cibao in Caonabó's cacicazgo.
Many of them had disparaged Guacanagarí and the gold he brought.

Guacanagarí grimaced contemptuously. "Have their leaders
punished those who fought and the murderers?"

"No. Their leaders participated in the fight themselves. No one
has been punished."

"Is there calm now? Has the body been buried?"

"The body still lies in the plaza. The man was wounded and left
to die and expired during the night. His agony and screams petrified
those living nearby." Brother paused. "No one has dared to touch
or even approach it for fear of evil spirits. Women and children have
been wailing in horror of it."

Guacanagarí was mortified his rule had allowed this to transpire,
and Brother held his hands and spoke gravely. "Some of our subordinate caciques are now critical that you haven't punished these people
as you would our own subjects."

"I understand. That's Guarionex's and Behecchio's view, as well.

Which of our caciques are the most dissatisfied?"

"Mayreni, and others. Mayreni is the most outspoken."

Guacanagarí pondered what to do and momentarily reconsidered Guarionex's advice. But he buried his fury yet again and reluctantly chose—one last time—to reprimand the pale men with a threat that would alter their conduct.

"Fill some baskets with food, and let each of their separate bands know that I will deliver it to the fort this afternoon. Take a few naborias to throw the body into the sea. Tell them I assure the spirits will favor them for doing this. Gather hundreds of warriors to hide undetected in the forest south of the fort, with spears and macanas. I will go to the fort, and after I give the signal, the warriors should charge from the forest, secure the small bohío, and surround the pale men outside the fort. There should be a demonstration of overwhelming force."

Brother and nitaínos were shocked but pleased. Brother asked, "Are we going to fight?"

"No. Not unless I order it. The soldiers should understand that clearly."

As midday approached, the crew gradually gathered outside the fort to await Guacanagarí's food delivery, their knives and swords guardedly sheathed lest another altercation occur. Some grimly pondered the two shipmates lost, musing that the Indians posed less danger than themselves. Pedro and Rodrigo spoke to Diego at a distance, promising to control their loyalists. Chachu and his band arrived last, and, while he displayed neither guilt nor remorse, he indicated he had no intent to resume the previous altercation. There was no further communication, and the men sullenly waited for the food to arrive.

Soon, Guacanagarí entered the clearing before the fort, accompanied by his brother, nitaínos, and naborias bearing the food baskets. He asked the naborias to halt some distance from the fort, and stepped forward with his youthful interpreter to greet the three lieutenants. "I bring food."

Guacanagarí studied the pale men, slowly turned his gaze to make eye contact with many of them, and then pointed to the ground. "This is Guarico, in my cacicazgo Marien. There shall be no fighting, no stealing of food or gold or anything else, and no abuse of women." The interpreter explained by gesture.

Pedro responded. "We understand. We will do better."

Guacanagarí shook his head in displeasure and then spoke in broken Castilian. "Guarico peace. No peace, no gold." He studied the lieutenants' expressions, as well as Chachu's. "No peace, no gold."

Chachu rose and slowly stepped forward, spreading his arms to indicate he would speak for some moments.

"Guacanagarí, or Lord Guacanagarí, if that suits you, you don't have any gold to trade but motley jewelry. I don't care if you don't want to trade gold, because you don't have enough for me and my men in the first place."

Guacanagarí understood the scorn but not the words, and he raised his hand to ask Chachu to stop.

Pedro commanded Chachu to stop, as well, and turned to Guacanagarí. "Ignore him, my lord—he is not of us. We will maintain peace."

Chachu did not stop and raised his voice. "Listen, all of you, it's time I spoke as the only person here capable of leading us." He faced Guacanagarí directly. "You're nothing but a naked buffoon. Kings wear pants, not nose rings. You've been lying to us from the beginning. There're no gold mines here. And if there were, your naked vassals would be too lazy to dig them."

Guacanagarí lowered his hand and flicked his wrist once. He let the savage continue as his troops prepared to rush.

Chachu enjoyed the attention and did continue, facing Diego, Pedro, and Rodrigo. "You're equally as stupid. There's no gold here, at least not enough for me to tolerate this garbage they call food. My men and I are leaving to find it. We've been told by some Indians that Martín Pinzón found it to the southeast."

"The Admiral ordered that we leave this place only in the company of Guacanagarí," Diego retorted.

"I've heard enough of the Genoese and his orders. For the amount of gold we've obtained, each and every one of us would've been better off if we had never met him. He's left and has no say here anymore."

Rodrigo responded. "The Admiral's orders are on behalf of the king and queen, and you will answer to their justice for your disobedience. We must conduct ourselves peacefully so these people can be subjugated peacefully."

"Conduct ourselves peacefully? The sovereigns care that we should conduct ourselves peacefully?!" Chachu laughed. "Bullshit!

If they even knew we were here, the king and queen would expect us to trample over every one of these naked savages who stands in the way of hauling out the gold for their crowns. And they wouldn't give a shit if we maim or kill as many as we want while instilling the faith—the sovereigns burn their own subjects at the stake every day to that end. Neither the king nor queen care if we denigrate this naked buffoon—the Genoese already took his island as the king and queen's kingdom, and the buffoon doesn't even know it."

Chachu's followers cheered.

Chachu reveled in the applause and turned to Guacanagarí. "Look you buffoon, you're not even a man, you're a beast."

The laughter and cheers subsided, as many wondered whether Chachu had gone too far.

Guacanagarí looked directly into Chachu's eyes and, while he did not understand the remark, said in Taíno, "I'm done, you fool."

Guacanagarí flicked his wrist a second time, and hundreds of warriors charged from the forest to surround the fort, the small bohío, and the pale men. The crew trembled in terror to behold the hundreds of spears and macanas poised to kill them and drew their knives and swords to respond.

Slowly, Guacanagarí pointed to Chachu and then the ground, motioning for him to kneel. Chachu hesitated, and Guacanagarí flicked his wrist a third time. A dozen warriors immediately encircled Chachu, the tips of their spears within inches of his throat. Chachu saw death was inevitable if he chose to fight, and he knelt.

The two men glared fiercely at each other, the crowd about them—olive and pale—hushed and breathless in awe of whether mercy or an execution followed. Guacanagarí slowly stared away, and, for an instant, all guessed mercy.

But Guacanagarí pointed to the three lieutenants and then to the ground before him, motioning for them to step forward and kneel, too, and they complied. He spoke in Taíno, knowing they wouldn't understand. "Should I kill all of you now?"

There was silence. Memories of executing Caribes with Mayobanex flashed through Guacanagarí's mind. He had known then that execution was his cacical duty and justice. Caonabó's warning to kill the pale men also passed through his thoughts, and he swelled with rage at the disaster that had befallen Guarico, the malice of these men's conduct, and the unknown insults just delivered. His wrist quivered to snap but once more to order their destruction. Yet he recalled his resolve to achieve a trading relationship and his promise to Admiral, and he feared what Admiral might think of him or do upon returning if the men were killed.

Guacanagarí hesitated a moment further and shut every one of these considerations from consciousness. He surrendered instead solely to his instinctual and unequivocal abhorrence of senseless death, which violated the essential Taíno aspiration of achieving harmony in existence. He relaxed his wrist and spoke to the lieutenants in Taíno. "Peace in Guarico. No fighting, no looting, no abuse of women. My patience has reached its limit."

Rodrigo responded. "Your Lordship, we agree and apologize. We agree and apologize on behalf of King Fernando and Queen Isabel, who would condemn the conduct of these men and severely punish them if they knew of it."

Hearing mention of Fernando and Isabel, Guacanagarí guessed the sense of Rodrigo's remark and looked to Pedro and Diego to ascertain whether each would make the same promise, and they did. He pointed to Chachu and stared at Rodrigo.

"Your Lordship, we will try to maintain order."

Guacanagarí pointed to the food. "That is your allotment. I trust you will honor your agreements." He then turned and departed with his brother and his nitaínos. His warriors remained to watch the pale men allocate the food among themselves, whereupon all disbanded.

Within days, Chachu led his men and boys out of Guarico east along the coast to find gold, or at least the site where some Indians said Pinzón had traded for gold. They discarded most of the women they had slept with, finding new ones in the villages through which they passed, seizing food from the Indians they met and looting their bohíos for jewelry. Guacanagarí instructed some nitaínos to follow them with troops. He remembered Guarionex's admonition to punish miscreants and authorized the nitaínos to execute those engaged in egregious conduct as they would their own people.

XIV
SUMMER 1493

CÓRDOBA,
June 1493

Cristóbal rose in Guadalupe on the morning following the pilgrimage to promise the friars he would name an island in the Indies for their monastery. Bakako and the other Taínos bathed in the fountain in Guadalupe's central plaza.

Cristóbal's entourage then departed for Córdoba, descending along the same route he had traveled with the sovereigns seven years before. After another triumphant entrance and meetings with officials and friends, and after Diego and little Fernando had been put to bed, Cristóbal and Beatriz sat close together on a couch in her bedroom lit only by moonlight. He remembered the storms at sea and the Lord's mercy, and he realized the Lord would desert him now. But the sins of deceiving and discarding women were forgiven daily, and even St. Augustine had done it. He told her they would not marry and their relationship was over.

Beatriz surged with pain, humiliation, and rage and turned furiously upon him. "That has been the promise of seven years and caring for both your children! You're not too important to honor that—no matter what your title!" She burst into tears.

"What were these seven years for?!" she continued. "I have shared my bed, cooked your meals, washed your clothes. I've born your son and raised him as yours. I've been mother to two sons when you sailed, possibly forever if you never returned."

"Beatriz, you have done all that."

"I'm not done! I welcomed and stood with you when you were nothing! You came into my garden nothing but an impoverished agent hawking books and maps—a braggart, rejected by all—and I gave you love time and again while you suffered scorn and despair. I'm the one that lifted your spirits and made your life happy—although that word rarely could describe you!"

"Beatriz, you did all that. We were lovers. But I never promised marriage."

"Promised marriage!" Beatriz recoiled furiously. "We've been married in fact, if not by the church! This wasn't trysts in hideaways. I've raised our son and now both sons and given them a mother's love—far beyond a lover's love! I've been wife to you, Cristóbal, not a lover."

There was silence.

"Beatriz, what you say is true, except we have never been married, by the Lord or the church, and we have both always known that. We are no longer suited."

"No longer suited! You're the greatest pretender and hypocrite that ever lived! You weren't born with nobility, and you walked into my garden lesser status than my own—and we both know that. For years, I listened to you rant and rage how noblemen and their courtiers treated you as an ignorant peasant, lacking title and crest—and I comforted you! And now, when you've found your own title and crest, you turn and say, 'Beatriz, we are no longer suited—I have a crest with gold islands and you're nothing!' The Lord sees all insincerity and self-importance, Cristóbal. Yours are as vast as your Ocean Sea."

Beatriz wept further, and they sat motionless in the moonlight for some moments.

"So you will not marry me. But why is it over?"

"We are no longer suited, Beatriz."

"So you say. But being ill suited for marriage doesn't mean we must part. Countless noblemen have mistresses, most without title or crest, most well beneath my own dignity and education. Some are whores! Your title and crest will not be tarnished if I remain your mistress—albeit the Lord will hold that a sin when he judges you." Beatriz pleaded, "Won't you stay, without marriage?"

"No."

Beatriz was crushed. "I don't please you anymore?"

Cristóbal didn't answer. He knew she didn't, but it would be unjust to tell her so, because the fault was his, not hers. Nothing pleased him anymore but that which furthered his enterprise.

"Is there another?"

"No. There's no other." Cristóbal searched for words and beheld the utter baseness within. He would discard her just as he had been discarded for years. "Beatriz, we loved. But love is beyond me now. I am called by the Lord for another purpose."

Beatriz continued to cry, and, after some moments, Cristóbal continued. "I have made some arrangements. The queen has agreed that Fernando will become a member of the royal household and serve as page to Prince Juan. He will go to court when Diego goes, so the boys will be together."

Beatriz was shocked and dried her tears.

"I've provided well for our son. Before going to court, the boys will live with Violante in Seville, in a house provisioned by the queen. You may visit them whenever you wish."

"You're taking my son from me?!"

Cristóbal angrily drew her to him, and she resisted momentarily and then relented. "Your son—our son—will be a member of the royal household, with education and opportunity far exceeding your wildest imagination."

Beatriz reflected. "But before then, you are taking him?"

"Yes. The boys must live as brothers before they go to court so they well understand and love each other, and their brotherhood and trust become inviolable. You may visit whenever you wish."

Beatriz stood and walked to gaze through the window to her garden, where she and Cristóbal had first kissed. "May I visit him at court?"

"I'm certain the queen understands Fernando will need his mother from time to time."

"So you have planned everything, Cristóbal, as if I had no say."

"You aren't pleased that Fernando will join the royal household?"

"Yes. Yes, I am." Beatriz returned to sit beside Cristóbal. "Everyone will be satisfied but me. That is it, then—we are done?"

"The queen gave me a small pension for life. It's yours."

Into the Cibao
(Summer 1493)

Rodrigo de Escobedo lay on his back on a makeshift cot within a bohío dimly lit by moonlight, surrounded by his harem of women and girls who slept. He ruminated about the conquest of Grenada and how the queen's soldiers and administrators had profited with the booty seized. Other than rape, they had not lain with the infidels' women.

Rodrigo understood conquests relied on ordinary men and that booty was the essential fuel that sustained them, not the queen's faith. He also recognized that the booty yet obtained in Española was insufficient for the hardship endured. He and Pedro had demanded that Guacanagarí bring more raw gold than jewelry, but they rarely received grains larger than sand. Guacanagarí had repeatedly denied entreaties to escort them to the Cibao to see the mines and rivers flowing with gold, and Colón's boasts remained unproven. The only extraordinary reward of the voyage yet achieved was women, a temporary delight without value when they returned home.

Compounding this disappointment, the conditions of daily existence at Navidad amounted to far greater privation than at the battlefront in Andalusia. There was no wine or Spanish food to confiscate, no clothing, shoes, or comforts to plunder, and no proper homes or houses to seize and occupy for shelter. There was, admittedly, no risk of combat death, and men hadn't succumbed to plague. But many had grown ill from frequenting the women, a few so severely they could barely walk. The absence of churches, priests, and military leadership had led to a lawless and debilitating chaos. Distrust and contempt prevailed, both with Arana and his loyalists and toward Guacanagarí and his subjects.

At sunrise, Rodrigo rose to share breakfast with Pedro and they resolved to advise Guacanagarí they would leave for the Cibao with or without him. They found him in Guarico's central plaza, and he invited them to sit and summoned his youth to translate.

"It's been months since the Admiral departed," Rodrigo said and gestured. "The Admiral ordered us to explore for Haiti's gold mines in the Cibao with you, prior to his return. We've asked you to lead us there many times. We must go now, into the Cibao."

Guacanagarí listened to the translation and shook his head no. "As I have said—I'm bringing the Cibao's gold to you."

Rodrigo and Pedro stared at him intently, shaking their heads with disapproval, and Rodrigo continued. "We ask you to escort us. But now we will go ourselves, with or without you. We will take our possessions and award them to those who lead us to the rivers and mines. If necessary, we will find the Lord Caonabó to take us to the mines."

Guacanagarí understood the ultimatum, if not all the words. The threat of trading with Caonabó both angered and amused him. For a moment, he reflected on his promises to Admiral and considered that it was better to lead these lieutenants to the Cibao rather than for Admiral to learn he had refused to do so. He had denied them many times now, and he studied their expressions to confirm their resolve to depart alone.

"If you depart contrary to my advice, I will escort you—as promised Admiral. But I will not take you to Caonabó, and you best not seek him out. His tolerance for your men's conduct is less than mine, and he may kill you." Guacanagarí waited for his youth to explain with gestures.

Rodrigo smiled to indicate gratitude. "Thank you, your Lordship. We will prepare our men to depart. We affirm King Fernando's and Queen Isabel's appreciation for your assistance, and it will be recognized."

Rodrigo and Pedro returned to the bohíos where they and their loyalists lived, glibly deriding Guacanagarí's warning of Caonabó's hostility as but an intrigue to forestall their establishment of a relationship with a competitor. The loyalists—then nine men—applauded the news, jubilant to become the first to locate the Cibao's gold mines. Rodrigo cautioned that, before departing, they needed to retrieve weapons and trifles for trading from the garrison's fort and bohío. That afternoon, Rodrigo, Pedro, and their band gritted themselves for confrontation and strode to the fort, their knives and swords sheathed but openly displayed.

Diego's loyalists—who had dwindled to eleven—studied the band approach and closed ranks outside the fort to defend an attack.

Pedro addressed Diego's loyalists. "We're leaving for the Cibao with Guacanagarí. Those of you who wish to follow Escobedo and myself, rather than Arana, may join us. We come to take truck to trade, as well as arms from the fort. You may waste here with Arana, or come with us to be rich."

"I control the fort and our weapons and trading goods," Diego responded, addressing his loyalists and Pedro's. "It is I, not Gutiérrez or Escobedo, who decides what to trade and with whom. Those loyal to the Admiral and the king and queen must remain with me."

"You're in command of nobody," Pedro responded drily. "Escobedo and I are the Crown's officers, and we are fulfilling the Admiral's command to find the gold mines. We'll take the goods and arms we wish, and I warn you to keep your weapons sheathed as we enter both the bohío and the fort."

"Stand back!" Diego retorted. "My men will deny you entry to both on the king's authority."

But each man of both camps now had but one loyalty, to himself and his survival and enrichment, and each obeyed and ignored his leader's instructions accordingly. Diego's loyalists simply fell back to defend the fort and hoard the weapons within. Pedro and Rodrigo's band took control of the bohío and ransacked it for the best trifles remaining, including a washbasin that Rodrigo envisioned giving to Caonabó if they met him. None of either camp deserted for the other, each man long since having selected the band he believed most likely to survive and profit.

Within days, Guacanagarí escorted Pedro, Rodrigo, and their men southeast into the Cibao, accompanied by nitaínos and a few troops. Most of the band's women also came along, some obediently, some in expectation of marriage, many visibly pregnant.

Guacanagarí entered villages en route with honor, and he introduced Pedro and Rodrigo as nitaínos. The villagers had heard tell of the tensions simmering and erupting in Guarico and were cautious in greeting the pale beings. The sight of pregnant concubines from among their own people made them uneasy. But local caciques freely shared their bohíos, food, and water with both the beings and their concubines.

Pedro and Rodrigo were captivated by the beauty of the foothills and mountains, which reminded them of Andalusia. Their band encountered streams and creeks frequently, and the men pined to stop to dig. But Guacanagarí advised to venture deeper into the mountains before doing so, knowing that the best sites found on gold homages were farther within, and the two lieutenants heeded his advice.

Guacanagarí eventually halted the journey south of a large stream where he had always found gold, confident the lieutenants would be satisfied. The entourage lodged with a local cacique well known to Guacanagarí, and the pale men began to dig with the assistance of local naborias.

As they dined one evening, Guacanagarí decided to teach the lieutenants of the gold homage and its purpose, expecting they would arrogantly dismiss the ritual's significance but curious to explore whether the pale men's lust for gold had any comparable spiritual aspect. With his youthful assistant, he explained that his male subjects purified themselves by vomiting, fasting, and celibacy for three weeks as they dug, honoring the spirits to reveal the gold, and then embedded the gold found in amulets and face masks to animate the spirits of ancestors.

Pedro and Rodrigo listened to the translation, perceiving the mechanic of bodily purification savage and the gold's usage idolatry, but nodded politely that they understood.

Guacanagarí waited for a question, some indication of curiosity to understand more, but there was none. He asked, "Will you use the gold you keep for yourself to honor the Christ spirit?"

Pedro despaired at the tortured journey that had brought him to this moment, place, and question. Gazing at the beauty of Haiti's remote mountains and gorges, he revealed his innermost thoughts—perhaps to reciprocate the spirituality he then grudgingly recognized in Guacanagarí, perhaps simply liberated from the watchful judgment of his church—regardless of whether his thoughts could be translated.

"No. Not I." Pedro shook his head with disgust. "I and other Christians pay too much gold to the church already. We purchase absolution of our sins. We purchase salvation. My king purchases bishoprics for his bastard sons. The church burns heretics to seize their gold. I know—my king has that under his thumb."

Guacanagarí's assistant translated some, and Guacanagarí was startled. He had anticipated the pale men's lust for gold lacked spirituality, but not a contempt for worship of the Christ spirit itself. He mused on it and grew fearful that, at heart, at least some pale men were spiritless.

Outfitting the Second Voyage,
Seville, July and August 1493

When he entered Seville, Cristóbal was handed a letter from the sovereigns entreating that his fleet depart promptly—the king and queen weren't interested in waiting resolution of the negotiations with King João. Cristóbal was gratified by the sovereigns' urgency but recognized more nuanced considerations. He shared the sovereigns' concern to depart before winter's harsh weather, but his precise objective was to achieve the same winds and weather experienced west of Gomera in September on the first voyage. He anxiously worried that his prompt return was necessary to prevent mistrust and hostility arising among the peoples to be subjugated. He also knew, as well as anyone alive, that the Ocean Sea was sovereign to the ships upon it. He could not and would not sail until each ship was ready, regardless of what the king, queen, or any administrator desired, in spite of his fears for the conduct of the crewmen at the garrison.

◻ ◻ ◻

As Admiral reviewed the sovereigns' letter, Bakako learned to his horror that two of the four Taínos left in Seville had died and that the other two barely clung to life and were languishing in a field near the monastery where Admiral lodged.[*] Admiral's page Pedro escorted Bakako there, and they anxiously spied from a distance that Yutowa and another Taíno lay prostrate on cots in the shade of a tree. Their bodies were laced with pocks and emaciated, and Pedro warned they could approach no closer. Bakako called to Yutowa. He heard, sat up slowly, smiled wanly, and faintly replied he was recovering and that the friars left him and their companion food and water generously.

[*]Monasterio de la Cartuja de Santa María de las Cuevas.

A friar heard Bakako's call and emerged from the monastery to recount that the four Indians had succumbed to the plague and been removed from the city to this site, where two had died so far. Yutowa and the other appeared to be recovering. Bakako asked if he could sit with Yutowa and the friar forbade it, indicating that would be death. The friar invited Bakako to stay, together with the other Indians, in the grounds of the monastery itself, and allowed that Bakako could bring Yutowa and his companion food and water by laying it on the ground at a safe distance from them.

▣ ▣ ▣

Diego and little Fernando were escorted to Aunt Violante's new home and were astonished by its elegance and furnishings. Violante had not met Fernando previously and explained to him that she knew his mother lived in Córdoba and that he could see her when he wished. She told him that she and Diego's mother, her sister, had grown up together in Portugal—where the Perestrelo family was nobility—and that his father and she now wanted him and Diego to grow up together just like that, as they were brothers.

▣ ▣ ▣

Cristóbal soon met with the Archdeacon Juan Rodríguez de Fonseca to establish a working relationship and begin commissioning ships and recruiting crews. The two men were the same age but didn't warm naturally. Cristóbal disdained that a Castilian noblemen versed in diplomacy who had never held responsibility for organizing maritime ventures or visited outposts like those at Scio, Thule, Guinea, or the Canary Islands—no less Española—would understand what had to be done. Juan disdained that an uneducated sea captain had the ability to marshal a fleet with over a dozen ships and a crew of over a thousand who would serve not only as crew but then as the settlers to create a permanent colony with its own governing, administrative, commercial, military, and religious functions. But the sovereigns held each with esteem and made each understand cooperation was expected.

The sovereigns dispatched instructions to Francesco Pinelo, now the expedition's paymaster, for financing the voyage. The Duke of

Medina Sidonia provided a loan for a portion of the voyage's cost, and Francesco pledged as collateral jewels and other property confiscated from Jews expelled from the realm and conversos convicted by the Holy Office. Funds were borrowed from the Crown-controlled militia. Cristóbal's friend, the slave trader Juanoto Berardi who had financed Cristóbal's contribution to the first voyage, commissioned a cargo ship for transporting building materials.

◻ ◻ ◻

In Rome, Pope Alexander VI issued a bull[*] recognizing that King Fernando and Queen Isabel were inflamed with devotion to spread the faith to the lands newly discovered and bestowing Fray Buil with authority to do so, including with associates chosen by himself or the sovereigns. Buil was authorized to build churches and monasteries and, so that Christians would be induced to settle, provide confessors to absolve crimes and sins of each man and woman who traveled there with the sovereigns' permission. Fernando relished that he and Isabel would control the church in the new lands more tightly than they did the bishops of the Canary Islands.

King João had been enraged by Alexander's longitudinal division of the Ocean Sea. He dispatched more senior diplomats to Fernando and Isabel in Barcelona to express he found Alexander's pronouncements unacceptable and warn that he would dispatch a fleet westward if Colón's voyage were not suspended. João surmised antipodal lands would be discovered in the southern oceans off Guinea and that the pope's longitudinal division wrongly deprived Portugal of those. The sovereigns promptly dispatched separate instructions to Colón and Fonseca to hasten the fleet's departure. They instructed their papal emissaries to seek yet an additional bull clarifying Castile's right to discoveries in the Indies themselves. They ordered a fleet of warships assembled to protect Colón's ships from Portuguese attack.

◻ ◻ ◻

Cristóbal's ships and crews began to assemble in Cádiz, the westernmost Castilian port large enough to berth them all. Cristóbal selected a nao as his flagship and renamed it the *Santa María*.

---

[*]Pius Fidelium, July 25, 1493.

There were far more applicants to sail on the voyage than needed, most drawn by the siren call of gold. Cristóbal and Juan Fonseca arranged for nearly a thousand to be enlisted to serve as sailors, farmers, laborers, gold diggers, and, if necessary, soldiers, all for fixed salaries. Artisans were enlisted as necessary to service the ships and build the settlement. There were more than two hundred unpaid volunteers, nobility or gentlemen who sought fame and fortune. They included the late Rodrigo Ponce de León's cousin Juan, Diego Velázquez de Cuéllar, and a converso, Pedro de Las Casas.*

Regardless of King Fernando and Queen Isabel's inflammation, there were few volunteers among the clergy, perhaps because of the dangers or hardships involved, an absence of enthusiasm for doing the work of conversion, or scant recruiting effort on behalf of the sovereigns and Fray Buil. Perhaps a dozen clergy enlisted. Fernando had convalesced for a brief period at a secluded monastery in the hills north of Barcelona[†] and held some affection for one of its younger Hieronymite monks, a Catalan Ramón Pané, who was among those chosen.

Most crewmen brought their weapons so they could serve as soldiers. There was a corps of professional foot soldiers commanded by one Francisco de Penalosa, Pedro de Las Casas' brother and a servant to the queen, and the contingent of twenty mounted knights. The soldiers were equipped with chest-armor, crossbow, musket, and a few dogs, as well as the vessels' cannon.

Yutowa and the other sick Taíno did recover. As August waned, Cristóbal rode with his two sons and seven remaining Indians to Cádiz. He began to inspect the ships, men, and provisions intended to establish the first colony under his governorship, in which he would financially participate and by which, as the Lord's chosen servant, he would fulfill his unique destiny to carry Christianity across the Ocean Sea.

INTO MAGUANA
(Late Summer 1493)

Pedro, Rodrigo, and their nine sailors crouched in the streambed to which Guacanagarí had led them and scooped and sifted its gravel

---

*Bartolomé's father.
[†]Monasterio de San Jeronimo de la Murta, Badalona.

and mud by hand. They quickly found grains of gold and, within a day, one of them found a gold nugget the size of a peppercorn, whereupon they exulted that all would be rich. But a week passed before a sailor unearthed another gold peppercorn. Worse, they found that crouching and scooping was exhausting and dirty work, and that flies and mosquitoes swarmed over them when the breeze was slight or died. They bid Guacanagarí provide naborias to do the work and dictated their women do it as well, including those heavy with child. This alleviated the Castilians' discomfort but didn't accelerate the yield.

Soon, Pedro advised Guacanagarí they were disappointed with the stream selected and sought a richer one. Guacanagarí deplored the grand expectations of the pale men and their lack of patience and replied that other streams held the same amount of gold. Pedro curtly retorted that his band would depart to find a richer stream with or without Guacanagarí.

The next day, Guacanagarí thanked the local cacique for his hospitality. Neither Pedro nor Rodrigo did, resentful that the gold achieved had not met expectations. Guacanagarí led the lieutenants and their party east to a larger stream that coursed astride a small village of farmers. He greeted the local cacique and arranged bohíos, food, and naborias to dig the stream. The cacique kindly offered daughters for the lieutenants, but Guacanagarí advised the gesture would be relished but neither appreciated nor reciprocated and not to make it.

This second stream yielded gold, but, within a week, Pedro and Rodrigo realized it held no more than the first. Discontentment grew. One evening, the two lieutenants confronted Guacanagarí and his nitaínos at dinner in the village plaza.

"The gold is lacking," Pedro asserted.

"The homage involves strain and patience, which the spirits acknowledge," Guacanagarí responded through his youth and with gestures. His displeasure grew. "Admiral's original plan was that my people dig and bring the gold to you in your 'Navidad.' You should reconsider that plan. My men can continue to dig here, and transport the gold to you." Guacanagarí abandoned tact, whatever his youth translated. "It's my men who are doing the digging now, anyway. Your men merely watch and burden the local people."

Pedro and Rodrigo scowled, angry that Guacanagarí failed to offer a solution that yielded more gold.

"Admiral instructed that you accompany us to find Haiti's gold," Escobedo retorted. "Many of your people say the gold mines are in Caonabó's territory. Take us to Caonabó."

"No. I've already told you. I won't take you to Caonabó. He will kill you."

"We understand Caonabó has already traded gold with our people," Rodrigo responded. "He didn't kill them." Rodrigo stared directly into Guacanagarí's eyes and shrugged his shoulders. "Why do you say Caonabó will kill us?"

"Don't lie to us," Pedro uttered, rasping his throat. "We'll find the gold mines, with or without you."

"Caonabó will kill you. I know because he told me so." Guacanagarí watched the second thought translated by gestures and, when understood, jar the two pale men. "I, Guacanagarí, am cacique of Marien. Caonabó is cacique of Maguana. We talk. We have both watched you from the first days you came to Haiti."

"When did Caonabó tell you this?" Pedro challenged.

"We spoke over the summer. Haiti's paramount caciques speak occasionally."

There was silence. Pedro addressed Rodrigo. "A total lie. He's been lying from the beginning. Caonabó has the gold, and there's no point in trading with this liar."

Rodrigo grimaced, counseled Pedro to be silent, and turned to Guacanagarí. "Your people say Caonabó has already traded with our people. We've brought him a gift of a basin, much as those you have been given. Admiral can be a friend to both Guacanagarí and Caonabó." Rodrigo smiled to indicate continued friendship. "Admiral wished that you accompany us, and that is what we wish." Rodrigo pointed to all three of them and gestured that together they would journey to Caonabó.

"Caonabó will kill you, whether you give him the basin or not. I will not take you."

"Then we will go without you. We ask that you provide us your soldiers as guides and for protection."

"Neither I nor my soldiers will accompany you."

Pedro scorned his host. "Guacanagarí is afraid Caonabó will harm Guacanagarí."

"Caonabó will not harm me." Guacanagarí laughed, reciprocating the scorn. "We are Haitian caciques. But he will kill you."

Pedro laughed spitefully in return. "You're afraid to enter Caonabó's lands because he will harm you."

There was silence, and Guacanagarí chose to suffer insults no longer and cease further efforts with these lieutenants. He stared at Pedro and responded calmly, unconcerned whether the lieutenants understood or not.

"I could take you to Maguana, but I will not. Caonabó would not harm me because of your people and their conduct. That's ridiculous. After months of living among my subjects, you've learned nothing of us. Your people's arrogance and brutishness is appalling." Turning to Rodrigo, Guacanagarí ended the conversation. "As a Haitian cacique, I will respect Caonabó's wish that your people not enter his cacicazgo. If you enter Maguana, I will advise him that you did so of your own accord, against my wishes and warning, and without my or my subjects' participation."

Guacanagarí and his nitaínos departed for their bohío, leaving Pedro and Rodrigo to decide whether to depart for Caonabó alone. Pedro shook his head in disbelief. "He's jealous and lying. Caonabó will receive us with open arms and be as eager to create a trading relationship as Guacanagarí. The basin will please him, and we may as well promise that he will receive the favors of the king and queen."

"We have few weapons to defend ourselves if Caonabó is hostile."

"That's Arana's fault, and he must die for that."

Rodrigo nodded agreement.

"But we don't need more weapons," Pedro argued. "These people are cowards. The Genoese was correct that the garrison could subdue the entire island." Rodrigo appeared unconvinced, and Pedro continued. "We're not making our fortunes at Navidad or here. We haven't suffered these hardships to return home only a bit richer. Never departing Spain would have been better than shrinking from going forward now."

The next morning, Pedro and Rodrigo advised Guacanagarí they would depart south into Maguana. Guacanagarí replied he was sorry and disheartened and that they could return to Guarico whenever they wished—if they survived.

Parting was not as simple as the three men contemplated. The pale men's concubines were distraught, shocked that they would leave Marien without their cacique Guacanagarí and fearful of what Caonabó might do to the pale men and themselves if they entered Maguana. Many of the women, particularly those pregnant, begged the pale men to stay. Others pleaded with Guacanagarí to accompany them into Maguana, which he refused. The wailing grew louder when it became apparent the pale men didn't care whether the women came or not. Guacanagarí assured the women that they remained, and their unborn children would become, his subjects in every respect, and he invited them to return to Guarico.

The pale men departed south without guide or interpreter, and Guacanagarí returned to Guarico, pondering whether Caonabó's warning would be fulfilled. He chose not to meet his council or Arana, or even confer with his brother, and went instead to think alone by the sea. He rued that his trading relationship with the pale men had injured—rather than aggrandized—his stature among Haiti's paramount caciques and his subordinate caciques. He brooded that, if Admiral did return, Arana still remained and the deaths of the other pale men might then be excused by their own misconduct, perhaps permitting the trading relationship to develop as envisaged and the resuscitation of his honor among caciques.

Yet he now bitterly realized it was just as well if Admiral never returned. He would miss forever exploring a personal relationship with him. They had struck a true friendship bridging the horizon, and Admiral had accorded him greater dignity than did the other paramount caciques. But, if the pale men remaining in Guarico self-destructed like the others, he could then regain the stature lost as memories of the unusual misadventure faded.

Final Instructions,
September 5, 1493

On September 5, the sovereigns dispatched a letter to Cristóbal, informing him of the negotiations with King João and explaining that, to strike the best treaty, they needed to understand the degree coordinates of the route of his first voyage and the Indian discoveries.

They urged his prompt departure and advised he should enlist Fray Marchena or another astronomer who could confirm the geography. They wrote Fonseca separately, again imploring prompt departure.

Isabel also dispatched her own note to Cristóbal, returning a transcript of his journal. She warmly complimented him that he had served the sovereigns well and would receive increasing honor, favor, and wealth as deserved. She gently reminded him to send the sea chart he had repeatedly promised—crucial to the negotiations with João—and asked that he write to inform of everything in the Indies. While she thought the king would resolve the issues with João, with affection she warned Cristóbal to take precaution and not be deceived in any way.

BY A CREEK IN MAGUANA

Caonabó watched Anacaona and her household women bathe in a gentle creek in a lovely mountain gorge north of their village. That morning, they had attended the funeral of an elderly cacique, and there was no rush to return home. The serenity of the gorge pleased Anacaona, and they had decided to relax there for the afternoon.

But Caonabó failed to achieve serenity and relaxation as he pondered the reports received from the Cibao. His scouts were tracking a small band of Guacanagarí's pale men wandering south without a guide and accompanied by concubines—some pregnant— taken of Guacanagarí's people. He had received a messenger from Guacanagarí, who related these men were intent on meeting him even though Guacanagarí had warned them not to enter Maguana and refused to accompany them. The scouts reported that the pale men straggled into villages, brazenly took food from bewildered and frightened villagers, commanded that bohíos be made available for their accommodation, and disrespected the status of local caciques. They also looted jewelry and forced themselves on women and girls. They had defiled a cemí of Yúcahu, stealing it from a sack and then discarding it as if a rock upon the ground.

Anacaona had heard most of the reports and understood the cause of her husband's quandary and discomfort. Neither she nor the other paramount caciques had favored killing the pale men. She rose from the creek, and her attendants offered a cloth and then her nagua. She went to her husband, caressed his shoulders, and sat on a small duho beside him. "You don't look happy. You've enjoyed relaxing in gorges like this for as long as I can remember."

He remained silent.

"What did your scouts report today?"

"The pale men are approaching. Their conduct continues to defile our people and spirits. Yesterday, they ransacked a village, deposed the cacique from his caney, and ripped the gold from face masks they pillaged, destroying them."

"Contemptuous and disgusting." Anacaona shook her head, gravely appalled, and gazed across the creek into the shade of the forest beyond. "What will you do?"

"We know your brother and Guarionex would discipline the conduct but not more. What would you do?"

"I would discipline them and seek a solution that preserves life and harmony."

"That's what one does with friends and strangers, but not with enemies, not on the battlefield."

"I agree, Caonabó. But the question is whether they are enemies."

"I understand the question. Leave me here to think."

Caonabó reached to hold her hand, and she leaned to kiss him. "Maguana is your cacicazgo, I'm your wife, and your decision is mine, as well."

Anacaona gathered the entourage to return home, leaving Caonabó at the creek with two attendants at the trailhead to accompany him home when he wished. As the voices of those departing faded into the distance, Caonabó shut his eyes to slumber and permit the mother beast of Haiti to rejuvenate the gorge with the birds and animals that made it home.

He regained conscious thought some time later but kept his eyes shut to listen more clearly to the birds, which had returned to the trees above. The sun was descending to the west, and shade soon would fall upon the creek, making it easier for the birds to hunt without betrayal by their own shadows.

Caonabó soon opened his eyes and, without shifting his head, scanned the creek. A duck snatched minnows in the shallows, and many smaller birds fed on insects in the mud of the embankment. A

large frog sat on a rock midstream, motionless except for the occasional and barely perceptible lance of its tongue to swipe and devour
unsuspecting mosquitoes. A small, young heron stalked slowly in the
reeds farther upstream, its head lowered so its bill grazed the water's
surface. The frog watched the heron carefully but was satisfied the
bird was hunting fish and was too young and small to attempt prey-
ing on it.

Memories of learning to hunt on Aniyana flickered through
Caonabó's thoughts. He watched the heron pretend to fish and step
from the frog's vision. But the frog remained wary and shifted to
keep the bird in sight.

Caonabó asked Yúcahu what to do with the pale men in Maguana,
and Yúcahu didn't reveal an answer.

When direct sunlight passed from the creek, the frog lanced a care-
less moth and the young heron strutted onto a small boulder beyond
the frog's vision and pivoted to face its prey. Caonabó watched the
bird slowly stretch its head and bill toward the frog and prepare to
leap. The frog feasted on its own prey.

The heron leaped into flight, and the frog jumped into the creek,
belatedly recognizing the peril. But the heron dipped its bill beneath
the water's surface and seized its prey. The young bird struggled to
remain aloft and swallow the frog and achieved both, rising to alight
high in a tree.

Caonabó rose and honored the mother beast of Haiti for reminding him of the consequence of failing to recognize the presence of the
enemy.

PARTICIPANTS, TAÍNO SPIRITS, POPES, AND CONVENTIONS

PARTICIPANTS INTRODUCED PRIOR TO 1492 AND THEIR STATUS IN 1468 OR EARLIER DEATH

Haitian Taíno Caciques (Chiefs) (All historic persons with their historic names):

Anacaona, of Xaraguá's caciqual family, a younger sister to Behecchio

Behecchio, of Xaraguá's caciqual family

Cacibaquel, cacique of Magua and Guarionex's father

Caonabó, Lucayan, of Maguana's caciqual family

Cayacoa, of Higüey's caciqual family

Guacanagarí, of Marien's caciqual family

Guarionex, of Magua's caciqual family, Cacibaquel's son

Mayobanex, of Ciguayo's caciqual family

Other Taínos:

Baisi, Maguan, Guarionex's first wife, historic person with fictitious name

Butiyari, Marien, Guacanagarí's older sister, fictitious person

Heitiana, Marien, Guacanagarí's oldest older sister, fictitious person

Manicoatex, Lucayan, one of Caonabó's younger brothers, historic person with historic name

Onaney, Lucayan, Caonabó's childhood friend, possibly historic person with name accorded in various traditions

Tuobasu, Ciguayan, Mayobanex's first wife, historic person with fictitious name

Castilian Royal Family:

Alfonso, son of King Juan II and Isabel of Portugal, Isabel's younger brother, King Enrique IV's half brother, and claimant to the Castilian throne

King Enrique IV, son of King Juan II and his first wife, crowned 1454

Isabel, daughter of King Juan II and Isabel of Portugal, King Enrique IV's half sister, and an heir to the Castilian throne

Isabel de Barcelos, of the Portuguese royal family, mother of Isabel of Portugal and grandmother of Isabel and Alfonso

Isabel of Portugal, Queen Dowager, King Juan II's second wife and widow, mother of Isabel and Alfonso

King Juan II, died 1454

Princess Juana, Queen Juana's daughter, an heir to the Castilian throne ("La Beltraneja")

Queen Juana, King Enrique IV's second wife and King Afonso V of Portugal's sister

Aragonese Royal Family:

Prince Fernando, King of Sicily and heir to the Aragonese throne

King Juan II, King of Aragón and Prince Fernando's father

Portuguese Royal Family:

King Afonso V, King of Portugal and Prince João's father

Prince Henrique, uncle to King Afonso V ("Henry the Navigator")

Prince João, heir to the Portuguese throne

Leonor, a cousin to Prince João and his future wife

Nobility, Prelates, and Advisers to European Royal Families:

Alfonso Carrillo, Archbishop of Toledo (Castilian)

Enrique de Guzmán, Duke of Medina Sidonia (Castilian)

Hernando de Talavera, Prior of the Monastery of San Leonardo de Alba Torres (near Salamanca) (Castilian)

Luis de la Cerda, a nobleman (to become Duke of Medinaceli in 1479) (Castilian)

Luis de Santángel, member of a leading mercantile family and son of Aragonese crown official (Aragonese)

Pedro González de Mendoza, Bishop of Sigüenza (Castilian)

Rodrigo Ponce de León, nobleman soon to become Marquis of Cádiz (Castilian)

Tomás de Torquemada, Prior of the Dominican Convent of Santa Cruz (Castilian)

Grenadan Royal Family:

Abū l'Hasan 'Alī ben Nasr ben Saad, Emir of Grenada

Al-Zagal, Abū l'Hasan's brother

Boabdil, Abū l'Hasan's son

Ottoman Sultans:

Bayezid II, Mehmed II's son
Mehmed II

Genoese:

Cristoforo Colombo, Domenico and Susanna's eldest child—Columbus

Domenico Colombo, Cristoforo's father

Susanna, Cristoforo's mother

Giovanni Pellegrino, Bartolomeo, Giacomo, and Bianchinetta, Columbus's then-surviving younger brothers and sister (in order of birth)

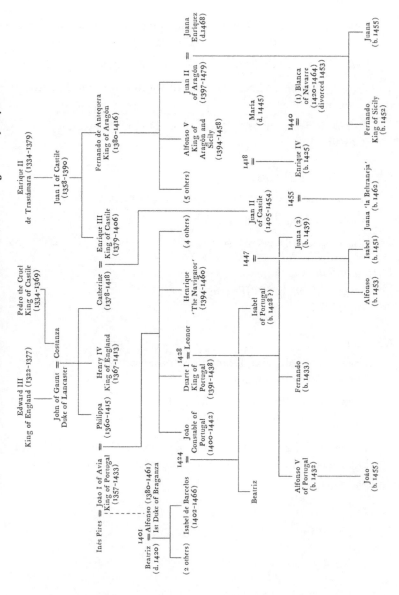

FAMILY TREE FOR CASTILIAN, ARAGONESE AND PORTUGUESE ROYAL FAMILIES AT JUNE, 1468

COLUMBUS'S WIFE AND IN-LAWS, MISTRESS, LOVER, AND CHILDREN

Bartolomeu Perestrelo, Filipa's father, Portuguese nobleman, and governor of Porto Santo, died 1458

Beatriz de Bobadilla, Columbus's Castilian-Canarian lover

Beatriz Enríquez de Arana, Columbus's Córdoban mistress (Castilian)

Diogo (in Portuguese), Columbus's first son, born of Filipa

Fernando, Columbus's second son, born of Beatriz Enríquez de Arana

Filipa Moniz Perestrelo, Cristoforo's wife and daughter of Bartolomeu Perestrelo and Isabel Moniz (Portuguese)

Isabel Moniz, Filipa's mother (Portuguese)

Pêro Correia da Cuhna, a brother-in-law to Columbus

TAÍNO CAPTIVES AND RELATED PERSONS (ALL NAMES FICTITIOUS)

Abana, Guanahanían, Bakako's younger sister, fictitious person

Abasu, Cuban, historic person

Bakako, Guanahanían, historic person

Kamana, Guanahanían, Bakako's friend, fictitious person

Xamabo, Marien, Guacanagarí's relative, historic person

Yomabo, Maguan, Guarionex's son, fictitious person

Yuni, Guanahanían, Bakako's younger brother, fictitious person

Yutowa, Guanahanían, historic person

CREWMEN, ROYAL OFFICIALS, AND CRISTOFORO'S PERSONAL ATTENDANTS ABOARD SANTA MARÍA, PINTA, NIÑA

Chachu, boatswain of *Santa María*

Cristóbal Quintero, owner of and seaman on *Pinta*

Diego de Arana, quartermaster of fleet

Jácome el Rico, Genoese seaman

Juan de la Cosa, owner and master of *Santa María*

Juan Niño, owner and master of *Niña*

Juan Portugués, Columbus's servant

Juan Rodríguez Bermejo, seaman on *Pinta*

Luis de Torres, interpreter

Martín Alonso Pinzón, captain of *Pinta*

Pedro de Terreros, Columbus's steward

Pedro Gutiérrez, sovereigns' observer

Pedro Salcedo, Columbus's page

Pero Alonso Niño, pilot of *Santa María*

Rodrigo de Escobedo, secretary of fleet

Rodrigo Sánchez, comptroller of fleet

Sancho Ruiz de Gama, pilot of *Niña*

Vicente Yáñez Pinzón, captain of *Niña*

Four criminals: Alonso Clavijo, Bartolomé de Torres, Juan de Moguer, Pedro Yzquierdo

CHILDREN TO QUEEN ISABEL AND KING FERNANDO (AND YEAR OF BIRTH)

Isabel	1470
Juan	1478
Juana	1479
María	1482
Catalina	1485

OTHER HISTORIC AFRICAN, CANARIAN, AND EUROPEAN PERSONS

Ansa	Akan king at Mina (Ghana)
Budomel	Wolof chieftain, the Damel (Senegal)
Diogo d'Azambuja	Portuguese nobleman who established Mina
Doramas	Chieftain of Gran Canaria
Alonso de Lugo	Castilian military conqueror, Canary Islands
Fray Antonio de Marchena	Friar at La Rábida
Fray Juan Pérez	Friar at La Rábida
Francesco Pinelo	Genoese merchant in Seville

Tenesor Semidan   Chieftain of Gran Canaria

Pedro de Vera   Castilian military conqueror, Canary Islands

TAÍNO SPIRITS AND ANCESTRAL PERSONS

Yúcahu, the spirit of yuca and male fertility, or more fully Yúcahu Bagua Maórocoti, also being master of the sea, fatherless, and the most important spirit in daily life. The spelling chosen is José Juan Arrom's, but many modern anthropologists use Yucahú or Yocahu or a longer-form Yocahuguamá. See Arrom's *Mitología y artes prehispánicas de las Antillas*.

Attabeira, Yúcahu's mother and the provider of water for crops and other nourishment

Coatrisquie, Guabancex's male assistant who floods the land

Deminán Caracaracol, born into adversity but who learns proper Taíno conduct to prosper

Guabancex, the female spirit of hurricanes and destruction

Guabonito, an ancestral heroine who is rescued from the sea by Guahayona and cures him

Guahayona, the ancestral hero who leads the Taíno women from the Cacibajagua (Cave of the Jagua)

Guataúba, Guabancex's male herald who orders wind and rain

Yaya, the supreme spirit

POPES

Eugenius IV	1431–1447
Nicholas V	1447–1455
Calixtus III	1455–1458
Pius II	1458–1464
Paul II	1464–1471
Sixtus IV	1471–1484
Innocent VIII	1484–1492
Alexander VI	1492–1503

CONVENTIONS

Fictionalization:

My minimum standard for including an event or thought in a story is that I believe it likely could have occurred. This is a combination of fiction and history and, undoubtedly, many events and thoughts depicted may have occurred differently or not at all.

Conversations are fictionalized when possible based on primary sources either relating directly to the conversation (e.g., Las Casas's description of the first meeting between Guacanagarí and Columbus) and/or those discussing or forming the basis of the beliefs and knowledge of the participants (e.g., Pané's account of Taíno religion or the Bible, Ptolemy's *Geography*, and Mandeville's *Travels*).

Names of People:

Names of Spaniards and Portuguese are in Castilian and Portuguese, respectively. For example, Isabella and Ferdinand have their Castilian names Isabel and Fernando and John and Henry are Juan and Enrique in Spain and João and Henrique in Portugal. Names of other Europeans typically are in English translation. Columbus's and his family members' names take a translated form as they move from Genoa to Portugal to Castile.

Names of the paramount Taíno chieftains have spellings currently used by anthropologists, historians, and others writing in English. I have given the principal Taíno captive known to history as Diego Colón a fictitious birth name of Bakako, although some ascribe him the birth name Guaikán (the Taíno word for the remora fish, which attaches itself to sea life and boats). Other historic Taínos generally known to history by their baptized Christian name (i.e., the other captives seized by Columbus) are also given fictitious names, as are some minor fictitious Taíno characters, each as noted in the list of Taíno Captives and Related Persons.

Names of Places:

Names of places are typically the English or Spanish version of the names that would have been used by the persons in the particular passage, usually with the modern spelling. Accordingly, when a narrative is from the Taíno perspective, the Dominican Republic and

Haiti frequently are referred to as Haiti (the English and Spanish spelling of a Taíno name). When a narrative is from the European perspective, they are referred to as Española.

The Roman "Hispania" refers to the entire peninsula of modern Spain and Portugal, and "Spain" refers to the peninsula excluding Portugal, including the fifteenth-century kingdoms or principalities of Castile, Aragón, and Catalonia.

Time:

For uniformity, time is based on Julius Caesar's calendar used by Europeans until 1582, when nine days were added by Pope Gregory XIII in the century before 1500 (ten in the two centuries thereafter) so that October 12, 1492—the Julian date Columbus recorded for his landfall at Guanahaní (likely San Salvador)—would correspond to Gregorian October 21, 1492.

Ages of Taíno Chieftains:

The historical record is unclear or silent as to the birthdates and ages of the Taíno rulers. In the absence of sufficient evidence, I have attributed approximate ages as follows. Caonabó and Guarionex are slightly older than Columbus (born 1451), based on my impression that Columbus or Bartolomé de las Casas perceived they were older, and Guacanagarí is younger than Columbus for the same reason. Anacaona's daughter Higueymota was probably married (after another relationship) in 1499–1500, possibly at approximately fifteen years old, and Anacaona probably reached puberty some years before her birth (Higueymota may not have been her first child), say, approximately 1480–1482, when Anacaona was possibly thirteen to fifteen years old. Anacaona's brother Behecchio was a few years her senior. Mayobanex is approximately the same age as his friend Guarionex.

Distance:

Taínos and Europeans had and thought in their own measures of distance, but for uniformity and simplicity all distances—both actual and as believed or estimated by Taínos and Europeans—are converted to be presented in modern US statutory miles, with one significant exception. Columbus's geographical thinking was sometimes in Roman miles and his *Journal* typically expresses distance in "leagues," and the text use these measures when appropriate to the story. One league equals four Roman miles, one Roman mile equals about 0.92 modern US statutory miles, and a league thereby equals about 3.68 modern US statutory miles.

Taínos, Caribes, Lucayans:

For simplicity, in Taíno passages Taínos sometimes are referred to as Taínos when important to distinguish Taínos (whose civilization was centered in Cuba, Haiti, the Dominican Republic, Puerto Rico, and the Bahamas) from Caribes (who lived in the Lesser Antilles, i.e., Guadeloupe and the islands south). Taínos who lived in the Bahamas—the islands north of Cuba, Haiti, and the Dominican Republic, including the Turks and Caicos—are sometimes referred to as Lucayans. It is doubtful the Taínos conceived of themselves as one people or nation or even used the word *Taíno* to refer to themselves other than to distinguish themselves from Caribes. Instead, they probably referred to themselves in relation to their tribe or the region of their tribe, much as Europeans referred to themselves in relation to their principality.

"Indians":

Fifteenth-century Europeans used the word *Indians* to describe people who lived in the "Indies," which was not uniformly defined, but stretched as far as from modern Japan to modern Ethiopia. Columbus and some Europeans initially believed Columbus's first voyage had reached a place near the Indies and referred to the Taínos as "Indians," which name continued after the realization that the New World had been discovered and gradually assumed an ethnic or racial connotation as opposed to geographic. When a story is from the European perspective, the Taínos typically are referred to as Indians in the fifteenth-century geographical sense except when important to distinguish Taínos from Caribes or Lucayans.

"Infidels, Heretics, Heathens, and Idolaters":

European Christians frequently referred to Jews and Muslims as "infidels," baptized Christians who deviated as "heretics," and others as "heathens" ("pagans") or "idolaters," and believed that none of these peoples could achieve salvation without conversion to Christianity.

GLOSSARY OF TAÍNO WORDS

Spanish spellings of the Taíno words are typically used except for islands, where the likely Taíno phonetic form is sometimes retained. Based upon Julian Granberry and Gary Vescelius's *Languages of the Pre-Columbian Antilles*, William F. Keegan and Lisabeth A. Carlson's *Talking Taíno: Caribbean Natural History from a Native Perspective*, and other sources.

areíto	song, dance
batey	ball game, plaza
behique	shaman (i.e., a priest and doctor)
bohío	house, home, dwelling, shelter
cacicazgo	chiefdom
cacique	chief
caney	house for a chief
Caniba	a Caribe
canoa	canoe
caona	gold
Caribe	fierce, strong, or brave person, and the native people of the Lesser Antilles (i.e., Guadeloupe and the islands south)
cazabi	cassava, a toasted bread made from yucca
cemí	spirit or object that represents spirit, typically of stone, wood, or cotton

chicha	corn beer
cibao	rocky place
cocuyo	firefly
cohaba	narcotic powder used in communication with spirits, or the communication ceremony itself
duho	ceremonial or chief's seat
guanín	a composition of gold, copper, and silver with reddish hue
hutia	cat-size rodent
iguana	iguana
macana	wooden club
mahisi	corn
naboria	servant, the servant class
nagua	married woman's loincloth
nitaíno	nobleman, lord
Taíno	noble or good person, and the native people of Cuba, Haiti, the Dominican Republic, Puerto Rico, the Bahamas, and Turks and Caicos
uici	yucca beer
yuca	yucca, manioc

Islands and Places

Haiti	Dominican Republic and Haiti
Bohío	Lucayans, and sometimes Cubans and Haitians, referred to Haiti (i.e., the Dominican Republic and Haiti) as "Bohío," the word for "home"; Columbus, relying on Lucayan captives, uses "Bohío" in his *Journal* to mean "Haiti" and renames it "La Isla Española"
Amayaúna	Cave without Importance
Aniyana	Middle Caicos, Turks and Caicos
Ba We Ka	Caicos bank
Bajabonico	Bajabonico river
Baneque	Great Iguana?

Boriquén	Puerto Rico
Cacibajugua	Jagua Cave, the Jagua being a tree species from which Taínos extracted dye for body paint
Camú	Camú river
Carib	mythical island of men
Cauta	mountains in "Haiti" containing Cacibajugua
Cibao	rocky, mountainous region in "Haiti"
Ciguayo	Mayobanex's chiefdom
Cuba (an abbr.)	Cuba
Guanahaní	San Salvador?
Guanín	mythical island where Guahayona obtains guanín
Guaricano	Guarionex's village
Guarico	Guacanagarí's village
Higüey	Cayacoa's chiefdom
Lucayans	island people, from the Bahamas or Turks and Caicos
Magua	Guarionex's chiefdom
Maguana	Caonabó's chiefdom
Manigua	Rum Cay
Marien	Guacanagarí's chiefdom
Matininó	mythical island of women
Samana	Samana, Bahamas
Samaná	Samaná, Dominican Republic
Samoete	Crooked, Fortune, and Acklins islands
Utiaquia	Ragged Islands
Wana	East Caicos, Turks and Caicos
Xaraguá	Behecchio's chiefdom
Yamaye	Jamaica
Yaque	Yaque del Norte river
Yasica	Yásica river
Yuma	Long Island

SOURCES

The principal primary (P) and secondary (S) sources considered in writing each story are set forth herein (whether supportive or at variance with the story), including, for primary sources, the chapter, section, paragraph, or date considered (rather than page numbers, in deference to readers with different editions). Stories occasionally quote or paraphrase words from the primary sources so identified (or infrequently, secondary sources) without quotation marks to preserve the novel style.

NOTE ON COLUMBUS'S JOURNAL, RELATED PRIMARY SOURCES, CERTAIN ABBREVIATIONS, AND PERMISSIONS

Columbus's daily ship's log of the first voyage was presented to Isabella at the completion of the voyage and has been lost since her death. Isabella had a copy made and given to Columbus in 1493, which has been lost since the sixteenth century. Before the copy vanished, Columbus's son Ferdinand reviewed it, and Bartolomé de Las Casas prepared an abstract summarizing and sometimes copying portions of it. This abstract has survived, and today we refer to it as the *Journal*. Historians disagree about the extent to which the *Journal* substantively edits or otherwise deviates intentionally or mistakenly from the original log. Portions of the log omitted from Las Casas's abstract, including information for the period from August 9 to September 5, can be found summarized or copied in Ferdinand's biography of his father or, more extensively, Las Casas's *Historia de las Indias*, both of which also add significant detail and color to the days that are presented in the *Journal*.

The *Journal*'s Castilian handwritten text has been transcribed to print a number of times, and these transcriptions or the original text have been translated into English a number of times. For discussion of the various transcriptions and translations, see the prologue to "Fuson *Log*," and, with respect to Las Casas's editing and the *Journal*'s shortcomings as a historical record, the introduction to the "Synoptic Journal," the "Journal Raccolta Notes," and "Zamora," each noted below.

I have considered the following English translations of the *Journal*:

P: *The Journal of Christopher Columbus (During His First Voyage, 1492–93) and Documents Relating the Voyages of John Cabot and Gaspar Corte Real*. Translated by Clements R. Markham. 1893. Reprint, Cambridge: Cambridge University Press, 2010 (referred to herein as the "Hakluyt Journal"). This *Journal*, originally published by the Hakluyt Society in London, is the English translation older readers would have read in their youth. It has been my companion on my investigations in Haiti and the Dominican Republic.

P: Samuel Eliot Morison's translation ("Morison Journal") contained in "Morison *Documents*" noted below.

P: *The Diario of Christopher Columbus's First Voyage to America, 1492–1493*. Translated by Oliver Dunn and James E. Kelley, Jr. Norman: University of Oklahoma Press, 1989 (the "Dunn & Kelley Journal").

P: *Christopher Columbus: The Journal, Account of the First Voyage and Discovery of the Indies, Part 1*. Translated by Marc A. Beckwith and Luciano F. Farina, with an introduction and notes by Paolo Emilio Taviani and Consuelo Varela. Vol. 1, *Nuova Raccolta Colombiana*. Rome: Istituto Poligrafico e Zecca Dello Stato, 1990 (the "Journal Raccolta"). *Part 2* of this volume, identically titled, presents explanatory analysis of the *Journal* reflecting current scholarship (a secondary source, the "Journal Raccolta Notes"). The *Nuova Raccolta Colombiana* is a comprehensive collection of contemporary sources—Spanish texts and Italian and English translations—and analyses sponsored by the Italian Ministry of Cultural and Environmental Assets, National Commission for the Celebration of the Quincentennial of the Discovery of America, with English translations provided by The Ohio State University (the editions I used).

P: *The Log of Christopher Columbus*. Translated by Robert H. Fuson. Camden, ME: International Marine Publishing Company, 1987 ("Fuson *Log*"). This contains modernized language and interpolation of Las Casas's *Historia de las Indias*.

The portions of Las Casas's *Historia de las Indias* corresponding to the *Journal* have been translated into English and presented together with translations of the *Journal* and Ferdinand Columbus's biography—a substantial scholarly effort and achievement—in the following volume, which I have considered for those portions of Las Casas's *Historia de las Indias*:

P: *A Synoptic Edition of the Log of Columbus's First Voyage.* Edited by Francesca Lardicci, with additional editing and translation by Valeria Bertolucci Pizzorusso, Cynthia L. Chamberlin, and Blair Sullivan. Vol. 6, *Repertorium Columbianum.* Turnhout, Belgium: Brepols, 1999 (the "Synoptic Journal" or, as relating to the portions of Las Casas's *Historia de las Indias* alone, the "LC Synoptic Journal"). The *Repertorium Columbianum* is a comprehensive collection of contemporary sources—Spanish or Italian texts and English translations—and analyses relating to Columbus's four voyages published under the auspices of the UCLA Center for Medieval and Renaissance Studies, also undertaken at the time of the quincentenary anniversary of 1492.

As for the remainder of Las Casas's *Historia de las Indias*, which includes information about both the Taínos and Columbus not directly related to the encounter, I have considered:

P: *Las Casas on Columbus: Background and the Second and Fourth Voyages.* Edited and translated by Nigel Griffin. Vol. 7, *Repertorium Columbianum.* Turnhout, Belgium: Brepols Publishers, 1999 ("Las Casas Repertorium"). This work of the *Repertorium Columbianum* translates into English portions of *Historia de las Indias* relating to Columbus other than the *Journal*, as well as some portions of other works of Las Casas.

P: Las Casas, Bartolomé de. *Historia de las Indias.* 3 vols. With prologue, notes, and chronology by André Saint-Lu. Caracas, Venezuela: Biblioteca Ayacucho, 1986 ("Las Casas Historia"). This is the work in Spanish and remains untranslated in its entirety.

As to Ferdinand Columbus's biography, I have used:

P: Columbus, Ferdinand. *The Life of the Admiral Christopher Columbus.* Translated and annotated by Benjamin Keen. New Brunswick, NJ: Rutgers University Press, 1959 ("Ferdinand Columbus").

Readers can refer to any of the foregoing or other versions of the *Journal* for substantially the same basic information, but not the information in Ferdinand Columbus or LC Synoptic Journal. The various texts differ as to details as to what occurred and other nuances, and I have made judgments between them and quoted or paraphrased words, phrases, and portions of sentences selected from some of them, particularly the Hakluyt Journal. There is a substantial translation issue relevant to the ideas presented herein upon which scholars disagree, discussed in Chap. VIII, "From the heavens, Guanahaní, October 13–14, 1492," below. References hereafter to the "Journal" refer to the foregoing translations of the *Journal* collectively due to their similarity, but not to Ferdinand Columbus or Las Casas's *Historia de las Indias* as translated in the LC Synoptic Journal.

In 1985, copies of lost letters purportedly of Columbus were discovered, now known as the "Libro Copiador." Some bear upon the events narrated herein, and I have considered the following translations:

P: *Christopher Columbus: Accounts and Letters of the Second, Third and Fourth Voyages, Part 1.* Edited by Paolo Emilio Taviani, Consuelo Varela, Juan Gil, and María Conti, translated by Marc A. Beckwith and Luciano F. Farina. Vol. 6, *Nuova Raccolta Colombiana.* Rome: Istituto Poligrafico e Zecca Dello Stato, 1994. Section 2 of this *Part 1* includes the lost letters in Spanish and English and is referred to herein as the "Libro Copiador;" and Section 1 contains other Columbian letters previously known, referred to herein as the "Raccolta Letters on Subsequent Voyages." *Part 2* of this *Nuova Raccolta Colombiana* volume, identically titled, presents explanatory analysis of the letters (a secondary source, the "Raccolta Letters Notes").

S: Zamora, Margarita. *Reading Columbus.* Berkeley: University of California Press, 1993 ("Zamora"). This analysis of Columbus's writings includes an English translation of the first lost letter, the Letter to Reyes discussed under Chap. XI. "Letters to the Sovereigns, January–February 1493" below.

Following Columbus's death in 1506, his heirs and the Spanish crown contested Columbus's hereditary entitlements in lawsuits spanning decades, as discussed under Chap. VI, "Christóbal Recruiting Crews to Traverse the Sea of Darkness, Palos, Moguer, Huelva, Summer 1492," below. Some of the lawsuits' testimony bears upon the events narrated herein, and I have considered the following *Repertorium Columbianum* text/translation:

P: Phillips, Jr., William D., ed. and trans. *Testimonies from the Columbian Lawsuits.* Philologist Mark D. Johnston, translated by Anne Marie Wolf. Vol. 8, *Repertorium Columbianum.* Turnhout, Belgium: Brepols Publishers, 2000 (the "Pleitos," i.e., the "lawsuits").

English translations of other documents and records bearing on the events narrated herein include:

S: Nader, Helen, ed. and trans. *The Book of Privileges Issued to Christopher Columbus By King Fernando and Queen Isabel 1492–1502.* Philologist Luciano Formisano. Vol. 2, *Repertorium Columbianum.* Eugene, OR: Wipf & Stock, 1996 ("Nader").

P: Morison, Samuel Eliot, ed. and trans. *Journals and Other Documents on the Life and Voyages of Christopher Columbus.* New York: Heritage, 1963 ("Morison *Documents*").

I thank the following institutions and publishers for the permission to quote or paraphrase words, phrases, and sentence portions from their works, as follows: the UCLA Center for Medieval and Renaissance Studies and Brepols Publishers n.v., with respect to seven volumes of the *Repertorium Columbianum*, the four noted above (Vols. 2, 6, 7, and 8) and three others noted herein below (Vols. 9, 10, and 12); Rutgers, The State University, with respect to Ferdinand Columbus noted above; the University of California Press, with respect to Zamora noted above; and the Hakluyt Society, with respect to the volume relating to Cadamosto cited in the Prologue: 1455 and Chap. IV, "João and King Ansa Mina de Oro (Elmina, Ghana), 1481–1482," below.

In particular, the seven volumes of the *Repertorium Columbianum* include English translations of primary sources that are relevant not only to the period of the *Journal*, but to events occurring over the entire time period of this novel, including translations of works of Las Casas providing information relating to the novel's Taíno participants and the testimonies of members of Columbus's crews and their relatives revealing their viewpoints and understandings; accordingly, I'm especially grateful to both the UCLA Center for Medieval and Renaissance Studies and Brepols for their permission and, more fundamentally, for undertaking the endeavor to make and publish the English translations in the first place.

This book is a novel for which I bear full responsibility, and none of the foregoing institutions or publishers have participated in or bear any responsibility for how I have used their work herein.

PROLOGUE: 1455

Ca' da Mosto
Land of the Budomel (North of Dakar, Senegal, Africa), April–May 1455

P: Ca' da Mosto, Alvise da. *The Voyages of Cadamosto and Other Documents on Western Africa in the Second Half of the Fifteenth Century.* Translated and edited by G. R. Crone. London: Hakluyt Society, 1937 ("Cadamosto"). Chaps. 1–10, 14–22, 25, 26, 29, 31, 33–35, 38.

S: Cipolla, Carlo. *Guns, Sails, and Empires: Technological Innovation and the Early Phases of European Expansion, 1400–1700.* New York: Barnes & Noble Books, 1965.

S: Northrup, David. *Africa's Discovery of Europe, 1450–1850.* Oxford: Oxford University Press, 2002.

S: Russell, Peter. *Prince Henry 'the Navigator': A Life.* New Haven, CT: Yale University Press, 2001.

S: Sallah, Tijan M. *Wolof.* New York: Rosen, 1996 (including for the Wolof proverb, p.42).

S: Saunders, A. C. de C. M. *A Social History of Black Slaves and Freedmen in Portugal, 1441–1555.* Cambridge: Cambridge University Press, 1982.

S: Thomas, Hugh. *The Slave Trade: The Story of the Atlantic Slave Trade, 1440–1870.* New York: Simon & Schuster Paperbacks, 1997 ("Thomas *Slave Trade*").

S: Thornton, John. *Africa and Africans in the Making of the Atlantic World, 1400–1800.* 2nd ed. New York: Cambridge University Press, 1998 ("Thornton *Africans*").

Malik (Pedro) and Ndey are historic persons given fictitious names.

CHAPTER I: 1455 — 1460, CHILDHOOD, LESSONS, LEGACY

Caonabó
Aniyana (Middle Caicos, Turks and Caicos, Caribbean)

P: d'Anghera, Peter Martyr. *De Orbe Novo: The Eight Decades of Peter Martyr d'Anghera.* Translated by Francis Augustus MacNutt. New York: Burt Franklin, 1912 ("Martyr"). Decade 3, bk. 10; decade 7, bk. 1.

P: Las Casas, Bartolomé de. *Apologetica historia de las Indias.* 3 vols. Edition by Vidal Abril Castelló, Jesús A. Barreda, Berta Ares Quieja, and Miguel J. Abril Stoffels. Vols. 6, 7, 8, *Fray Bartolomé de Las Casas: Obras Completas.* Madrid: Alianza Editorial, 1992 ("Las Casas Apologetica"). Chap. 197.

P: Pané, Ramón. *An Account of the Antiquities of the Indians.* New edition by José Juan Arrom, translated by Susan C. Griswold. Durham, NC: Duke University Press, 1999. Preamble; chap. 19.

S: Arrom, José Juan. *Mitología y artes prehispánicos de las Antillas.* 2nd ed. Coyoacán, Mexico: Siglo Veintiuno Editores, 1989.

S: Barreiro, José, "A Note on Tainos: Wither Progress?" In "View from the Shore: American Indian Perspectives on the Quincentenary," edited by José Barriero, Columbus Quincentenary Edition, *Northeast Indian Quarterly.* Vol. 7, no. 3, Fall 1990, pp. 4-22.

S: Granberry, Julian. *The Americas That Might Have Been: Native American Social Systems Through Time.* Tuscaloosa: University of Alabama Press, 2005.

S: Granberry, Julian and Gary Vescelius. *Languages of the Pre-Columbian Antilles.* Tuscaloosa: University of Alabama Press, 2004 ("Granberry *Languages*").

S: Keegan, William F. *The People Who Discovered Columbus: The Prehistory of the Bahamas.* Gainesville: University of Florida Press, 1992 ("Keegan *Prehistory*").

S: Keegan, William F. *Taíno Indian Myth and Practice: The Arrival of the*

Stranger King. Gainesville: University of Florida Press, 2007 ("Keegan *Myth*").

S: Lovén, Sven. 1935. *Origins of the Tainan Culture, West Indies*. Preface by L. Antonio Curet. Tuscaloosa: University of Alabama Press, 2010.

S: Mills, Carlton, gen. ed. *History of the Turks & Caicos Islands*. Oxford: Macmillian, 2008 ("Caicos"). Chap. 7, Josiah Marvel, "Our First Colonists: The Pre-Columbian People of the Turks & Caicos."

S: Rouse, Irving. *The Tainos: Rise and Decline of the People Who Greeted Columbus*. New Haven, CT: Yale University Press, 1992.

S: Sauer, Carl Ortwin. *The Early Spanish Main*. London: Cambridge University Press, 1966.

S: Stevens-Arroyo, Antonio M. *Cave of the Jagua: The Mythological World of the Taínos*. Scranton, PA: University of Scranton Press, 2006.

Historians, anthropologists, and others disagree whether Caonabó was a Caribe or a Lucayan or Haitian Taíno and, if Haitian, whether he might have been of the Macorix or Ciguayo peoples. I have chosen a Lucayan Taíno, born in a Taíno settlement on a Lucayan island, on the basis of Las Casas, Keegan, and Lovén; the presence of brothers in Haiti; and a suspicion that Caonabó's reputation as a warrior led Europeans, including Oviedo, to assume or assert that he was Caribe. In particular, Columbus knew Caonabó, and there is no suggestion by Columbus in the Libro Copiador (see Chap. II, "Caonabó Journey from Aniyana to Haiti," below) that Caonabó was Caribe. Keegan has speculated that Caonabó's homeland was a Taíno settlement on Middle Caicos (i.e., Lucayan)—as presented in the text—but it is unknown.

There are various recurring traditions regarding Onaney as a Haitian born intimate to Caonabó, including that she was of a Ciguayan caciqual family and his lover. I am unaware of primary source evidence validating the traditions, but have speculated—parallel to speculating that Caonabó was Lucayan—that Onaney was an historic person and a Lucayan childhood friend. See introduction to Pedro L. Verges Vidal, Anacaona (1474–1503), Ciudad Trujillo, Dominican Republic: Editora Montalvo, 1947; and Mon González, Lo Feminino en lo Taíno: Religión, Mitología, Sociedad, Sexualidad, Historia, Magia y Poesia, Conferencia dictada en la Biblioteca Nacional de Santo Domingo, August 9, 2005, and en el Centro Cuesta del Libro, October 17, 2005. Special thanks to Lynne Guitar, PhD History and Anthropology.

Cristoforo
Genoa, (March 1460)

P, prev. cit.: Ferdinand Columbus, chap. 1. Las Casas Repertorium, sec. 1.1.

P: Dotson, John ed. and trans. *Christopher Columbus and His Family: The*

Genoese and Ligurian Documents. Vol. 4, *Repertorium Columbianum.* Turnhout, Belgium: Brepols Publishers, 1998 ("Dotson"). Docs. 4 (Domenico has apprentice), 9 and 18 (Domenico named warder of city gate), 26 (Domenico replaced as warder), 30 (Domenico's lease for Genoa home), 41 (Domenico's nephew apprenticed to tailor), 149 (Columbus's first will, 1497, stating born in Genoa).

P: Farina, Luciano F., trans. and ed., and Robert W. Tolf, ed. *Columbus Documents: Summaries of Documents in Genoa.* Detroit: Omnigraphics, 1992.

P: *Oviedo on Columbus.* Edited by Jesús Carrillo, translated by Diane Avalle-Arce. Vol. 9, *Repertorium Columbianum.* Turnhout, Belgium: Brepols Publishers, 2000 ("Oviedo Repertorium"). Sec. 3.3.

P: Palencia, Alonso de. *Crónica de Enrique IV.* Introduction by Antonio Paz y Melia. Vols. 257, 258, and 267, *Biblioteca de Autores Españoles.* Madrid: Ediciones Atlas, 1973–1975 ("Palencia *Cronica*"). Decade 1, bk. 5, chap. 6.

P: Zurita, Jerónimo. *Anales de la Corona de Aragón.* 9 vols. Edition by Angel Canellas Lopez. Zarazoga, Spain: Institucion Fernando el Católico, 1985–2008 ("Zurita *Anales*"). Bk. 16, chaps. 50, 59.

S: Epstein, Steven A. *Genoa and the Genoese, 958–1528.* Chapel Hill: University of North Carolina Press, 1996.

S: Ferro, Gaetano. *Liguria and Genoa at the Time of Columbus.* With contributions from Pietro Barozzi, Daniela Galassi, Stefanella Guardo, and Maria Pia Rota. Translated by Anne Goodrich Heck, revised by Luciano F. Farina. Vol. 3, *Nuova Raccolta Colombiana. 3.* Rome: Instituto Poligrafico e Zecca Dello Stato, 1992.

S: Morison, Samuel Eliot. *Admiral of the Ocean Sea: A Life of Christopher Columbus.* Boston: Little, Brown, 1942 ("Morison *Admiral*").

S: Morison, Samuel Eliot. *The European Discovery of America: The Southern Voyages, AD 1492–1616.* Oxford: Oxford University Press, 1974 ("Morison *Southern*").

S: Taviani, Paolo Emilio. *Christopher Columbus: The Grand Design.* Translated by William Weaver. London: Orbis, 1985 ("Taviani *Grand Design*").

S: Vicens Vives, Jaime. *Fernando el Católico: Principe de Aragón, Rey de Sicilia 1458–1478.* Madrid: Consejo Superior de Investigaciones Cientificas, Biblioteca "Reyes Católicos," 1952.

I have followed Taviani's analysis of the Ligurian notarial documents translated or summarized in Dotson and Farina that Columbus was born in Genoa or environs, most likely between August 25 and October 31, 1451. Antonio is fictitious.

Prince Henrique of Portugal (Henry the Navigator)
Raposeira, Southern Portugal (Spring 1460)

P, prev. cit.: Cadamosto, chap. 1.

P: Acosta, Joseph de. *The Natural and Moral History of the Indies.* Vol. 1. *The Natural History.* Edited by Clements R. Markham. 1880. Reprint, Cambridge: Cambridge University Press, 2009. Chaps. 7–10.

P: Berggren, J. Lennart, and Alexander Jones. *Ptolemy's Geography: An Annotated Translation of the Theoretical Chapters.* Princeton, NJ: Princeton University Press, 2000 ("Ptolemy" or, as to the introduction, "Berggren-Jones"). Ptolemy, bk. 1, sec. 12; bk. 7, sec. 5.

P: Davenport, Frances Gardiner. *European Treaties Bearing on the History of the United States and its Dependencies to 1468.* Translated by William Bollan. Washington, DC: Carnegie Institution of Washington, 1917 ("Davenport"). Romanus Pontifex (January 8, 1455) and Inter Caetera (March 13, 1456).

P: Kritovoulos. *History of Mehmed The Conqueror.* Translated by Charles T. Riggs. Westport, CT: Greenwood, 1954. Pt. 1.

P: Puyol, Julio, ed. *Crónica incompleta de los Reyes Católicos (1469–1476): Según un manuscrito anónimo de la época.* Madrid: Academia de la Historia, 1934 ("Incompleta"). Title 1.

P: Zurara, Gomes Eanes de. *The Chronicle of the Discovery of Guinea.* 2 vols. Translated by Charles R. Beazley and Edgar Prestage for the Hakluyt Society. 1896. Reprint, Cambridge: Cambridge University Press, 2010 ("Zurara" or, as to the introduction in Vol. 2, "Beazley"). Chaps. 2, 4, 5, 7–9, 12, 14–18, 23–26, 31.

P: Genesis 11:1-9. Isaiah 27:1. Job 41:1, 31.

S, prev. cit.: Morison *Admiral*; Russell; Sallah; Saunders; Thomas *Slave Trade*.

S: Babinger, Franz. *Mehmed the Conqueror: and His Time.* Edited by William C. Hickman, translated by Ralph Manheim. Princeton, NJ: Princeton University Press, 1978.

S: Boxer, C. R. *The Portuguese Seaborne Empire, 1415–1825.* Middlesex, UK: Penguin, 1969.

S: Crosby Jr., Alfred W. *The Columbian Exchange: Biological and Cultural Consequences of 1492.* 30th anniv. ed. Westport, CT: Praeger Publishers, 2003 ("Crosby").

S: Disney, A. R. *A History of Portugal and the Portuguese Empire: From Beginnings to 1807.* Vol. I. *Portugal.* Cambridge: Cambridge University Press, 2009.

S: Fernández-Armesto, Felipe. *Before Columbus: Exploration and Colonization from the Mediterranean to the Atlantic, 1229–1492*. Philadelphia: University of Pennsylvania Press, 1987 ("Fernández-Armesto *Before Columbus*").

S: Freely, John. *The Grand Turk Sultan Mehmet II: Conqueror of Constantinople and Master of an Empire*. New York: Overlook. 2009.

S: Hopkins, Donald R. Hopkins. *The Greatest Killer: Smallpox in History*. Chicago: University of Chicago Press, 2002.

S: Mallet, Michael. *The Borgias: The rise and fall of the most infamous family in history*. London: Granada Publishing, 1969.

S: Morison, Samuel Eliot. *The European Discovery of America: The Northern Voyages, AD 500–1600*. Oxford: Oxford University Press, 1971 ("Morison *Northern*").

S: Phillips, Jr., William D., and Carla Rahn Phillips. *The Worlds of Christopher Columbus*. Cambridge: Cambridge University Press, 1992.

S: Rumeu de Armas, Antonio. *La Politica Indigenista de Isabel La Católica*. Valladolid, Spain: Instituto "Isabel La Católica" de Historia Eclesiastica, 1969 ("Rumeu de Armas *Indigenista*").

S: Schwartz, Stuart B., ed. *Implicit Understandings: Observing, Reporting, and Reflecting on the Encounters Between Europeans and Other Peoples in the Early Modern Era*. Cambridge: Cambridge University Press, 1994 ("Schwartz"). Chap. 1, Seymour Phillips, "The outer world of the European Middle Ages."

S: Tozer, Henry Fanshawe. *A History of Ancient Geography*. Cambridge: Cambridge University Press, 1897.

CHAPTER II: 1460S, YOUTH

Caonabó
Journey from Aniyana to Haiti

P, prev. cit.: Journal, 10/13/1492; 12/3/1492; 1/8–9/1493, for descriptions of canoes and Haiti. Libro Copiador, letters 3 (April 1494) and 4 (February 26, 1495), for descriptions of Haiti. Martyr, decade 1, bk. 9 (Haiti's caves); decade 7, bk. 8 (Haiti as beast). Morison *Documents*, Michele de Cuneo's letter on second voyage ("Cuneo"), for descriptions of Haiti. Pané, Preamble; chaps. 1 (the two caves), 2–6, 13.

P: Benzoni, Girolamo. *History of the New World; Shewing His Travels in America, from AD 1541 to 1556: with some Particulars of the Island Canary*. Translated and edited by W. H. Smyth. 1857. Reprint, Cambridge: Cambridge University Press, 2009. Bk. 1.

P: Bernáldez, Andrés. *Historia de los Reyes Católicos D. Fernando y Doña*

Isabel. Seville: D. José María Geofrin, 1870. 2 vols. ("Bernáldez"). Chap. 118.

P: Jane, Cecil, trans. and ed. *The Four Voyages of Columbus: A History in Eight Documents, Including Five by Christopher Columbus, in the Original Spanish, with English Translations.* 2 vols. New York: Dover, 1988 ("Jane"). Dr. Diego Alvarez Chanca's letter on second voyage ("Chanca"), for descriptions of Haiti.

S, prev. cit.: Caicos; Granberry *Languages*; Keegan *Myth*; Keegan *Prehistory*; Rouse; Sauer; Stevens-Arroyo.

S: Alegría, Ricardo E. *Ball Courts and Ceremonial Plazas in the West Indies.* New Haven, CT: Yale University Publications in Anthropology, 1983.

S: Arrom, José Juan. *Estudio de Lexicología Antillana.* 2nd ed. San Juan, Puerto Rico: Editorial de la Universidad de Puerto Rico, 2000 ("Arrom *Lexicología*").

S: Callaghan, Richard T. "Archaeological Views of Caribbean Seafaring." In *The Oxford Handbook of Caribbean Archaeology*, pp. 283-295, edited by William F. Keegan, Corrine L. Hofman, and Reniel Rodríguez Ramos. Oxford: Oxford University Press, 2013.

S: Curet, L. Antonio, and Mark W. Hauser. *Islands at the Crossroads: Migration, Seafaring, and Interaction in the Caribbean.* Tuscaloosa: University of Alabama Press, 2011.

S: Keegan, William F., and Lisabeth A. Carlson. *Talking Taíno: Caribbean Natural History from a Native Perspective.* Tuscaloosa: University of Alabama Press, 2008 ("Keegan *Talking Taíno*").

S: Oliver, José R. *Caciques and Cemí Idols: The Web Spun by Taíno Rulers Between Hispaniola and Puerto Rico.* Tuscaloosa: University of Alabama Press, 2009.

S: Wilson, Samuel M. *Hispaniola: Caribbean Chiefdoms in the Age of Columbus.* Tuscaloosa: University of Alabama Press, 1990.

Primary sources (e.g., Las Casas Historia, bk. 1, chap. 50; Martyr, decade 3, bk. 7; Bernáldez, chap. 118) indicate that the Taínos referred to the entire island of the Dominican Republic and Haiti (i.e., "Española" or the Latinized "Hispaniola") as Haiti and sometimes "Bohío," the latter being the typical Lucayan reference and used by Columbus in the *Journal*. Martyr (decade 3, bk. 7) indicates that the word *Quizqueia* was also used by its "early inhabitants" to describe Hispaniola, and scholars disagree whether *Quizqueia* was a Taíno or pre-Taíno name. While Quizqueia may also be correct, I have used Haiti and sometimes Bohío as the Taíno name for the entire island. See Granberry *Languages* and Arrom *Lexicología*.

Guacanagarí
Marien, Haiti

P, prev. cit.: Ferdinand Columbus, chap. 62, quoting his father's description of the Taíno cohoba ceremony, including dedicated bohio and cemi worship. Journal, 12/23/1492, for description of Guarico. Las Casas Apologetica, chaps. 120 and 166, including English translation thereof in Pané, appendix C. Martyr, decade 1, bk. 9. Morison *Documents*, Nicolò Syllacio's letter to the Duke of Milan, December 13, 1494, relating letter of Guillermo Coma on second voyage ("Syllacio"). Pané, chap. 19.

S: Keegan *Myth*; Journal Raccolta Notes; Oliver; Rouse; Stevens-Arroyo.

S: Deagan, Kathleen, and José María Cruxent. *Columbus's Outpost among the Taínos: Spain and America at La Isabela, 1493–1498*. New Haven, CT: Yale University Press, 2002.

S: Reid, Basil A. *Myths and Realities of Caribbean History*. Tuscaloosa: University of Alabama Press, 2009.

S: Sued-Badillo, Jalil. *Los Caribes: Realidad o Fabula*. Río Piedras, Puerto Rico: Editorial Antillana, 1978 ("Badillo *Caribes*").

S: Wilson, Samuel M., ed. *The Indigenous People of the Caribbean*. Gainesville: University Press of Florida, 1997 ("Indigenous People").

This story depicts Carib wife-raiding, not cannibalism. For discussion of whether Carib cannibalism was mythological or real, see Chap. X. "Ciguayo and Samaná, January 12–16, 1493."

Heitiana and Butiyari are fictitious.

Isabel
Segovia, Castile (January–June 1465)

P, prev. cit.: Bernáldez, chap. 1. Incompleta, title 1. Palencia *Cronica*, decade 1, bk. 1, chaps. 1, 2; bk. 2, chaps. 1, 9, 10; bk. 3, chaps. 1, 2, 6, 9, 10; bk. 4, chap. 2; bk. 6, chaps. 3, 5, 10; bk. 7, chaps. 1, 3, 4, 5, 8. Zurita *Anales*, bk. 16, chaps. 13, 14, 28; bk. 17, chap. 36; bk. 18, chap. 2; bk. 20, chap. 44.

P: Castillo, Diego Enríquez del. *Crónica del Rey D. Enrique el Quarto de Este Nombre*. Madrid: D. Antonio de Sanch, 1787. Chaps. 14, 38–40, 57, 60, 62, 64, 67–70, 77.

P: *Memorias de Don Enrique IV de Castilla*. Vol.2. *Contiene la Colección Diplomatica del Mismo Rey, compuesta y ordenada por la Real Academia de la Historia*. Madrid: Establecimiento Tipográfico de Fortanet, 1835–1913 ("Enrique Colección Diplomatica"). Docs. CI–CV (1464), CIX (1465), CXVIII (1465).

P: Paz y Melia, Antonio, ed. *El Cronista Alonso de Palencia: su vida y sus obras; sus Décadas y las Crónicas contemporáneas; illustraciones de las Décadas y notas varias.* Madrid: Hispanic Society of America, 1914 ("*Palencia Notes*"). Docs. 10 (Real Cedula, September 4, 1464) and 11 (Letter, September 28, 1464).

P: Pulgar, Fernando del. *Crónica de los Reyes Católicos.* 2 vols. Edition by Juan de Mata Carriazo. Granada: Marcial Pons Historia, 2008. Chap. 1.

P: St. Augustine. *Concerning the City of God and the Pagans.* Translated by Henry Bettenson. London: Penguin, 2003 ("Augustine City"). Bk. 5, chap. 11.

P: Sigüenza, José. *Historia de la Orden de San Jerónimo.* Vol. 2. Spain: Junta de Castilla y León, Consejería de Educación y Cultura, 2000. ("Historia Jerónimo"). Pt. 3, bk. 2, chaps. 29, 30, 35.

P: Valera, Diego de. *Memorial de Diversas Hazañas: Crónica de Enrique IV.* Edition by Juan de Mata Carriazo. Madrid: Espasa-Calpe, S. A., 1941. Chaps. 7, 20, 28.

P: Ezekiel 18:20. John 2:14–16; 5:29; 8; 18. Mark 12:29–31. Matthew 5:8, 44–45; 10:34–37; 21:12–13; 27:1–2.

S: Azcona, Tarsicio de. *Isabel La Católica Estudio crítico de su vida y su reinado.* 3rd ed. Madrid: Biblioteca de Autores Christianos, 1993 ("Azcona *Isabel*").

S: Azcona, Tarsicio de. *Juana de Castilla, Mal Llamada La Beltraneja: Vida de la hija de Enrique IV de Castilla y su exilio en Portugal (1462–1530).* Madrid: La Esfera de los Libros, 2007 ("Azcona *Juana*").

S: Caceres, José Miguel Merino de. *The Alcazar of Segovia.* Spain: Edilesa, 2000.

S: Edwards, John. *Torquemada & The Inquisitors.* Gloucestershire, UK: Tempus, 2005.

S: Fernández-Armesto, Felipe. *Ferdinand and Isabella.* New York: Dorsett, 1975 ("Fernández-Armesto *Ferdinand Isabella*").

S: Hays, J. Daniel. *From Every People and Nation a Biblical Theology of Race.* Downers' Grove, IL: InterVarsity Press, 2003.

S: Kamen, Henry. *The Spanish Inquisition: A Historical Revision.* New Haven, CT: Yale University Press, 1997.

S: Liss, Peggy K. *Isabel the Queen: Life and Times.* Rev. ed. Philadelphia: University of Pennsylvania Press, 2004.

S: Martínez Medina, Francisco Javier, and Martín Biersack. *Fray Hernando de Talavera, Primer Arzobispo de Grenada. Hombre de Iglesia, Estado y*

Letras. Granada: Biblioteca Teológica Granadina, 2011.

S: Miller, Townsend. *Henry IV of Castile, 1425–1474*. Philadelphia: J. B. Lippincott, 1972.

S: Netanyahu, B. *The Origins of the Inquisition in Fifteenth Century Spain*. New York: Random House, 1995 ("Netanyahu *Origins*").

S: Pérez, Joseph. *The Spanish Inquisition: A History*. Translated by Janet Llyod. New Haven, CT: Yale University Press, 2004 ("Pérez *Inquisition*").

S: Pérez-Bustamante, Rogelio, and José Manuel Calderon Ortega. *Enrique IV de Castilla, 1454–1474*. Vol. 11, *Corona de España*. Burgos, Spain: Editorial la Olmeda, 1998.

S: Prescott, William H. *History of the Reign of Ferdinand and Isabella*. Vol. 1. New York: J. B. Millar, 1985.

S: Rubin, Nancy. *Isabella of Castile: The First Renaissance Queen*. Lincoln, NE: ASJA Press, 2004.

S: Vicens Vives, Jaime. *Approaches to the History of Spain*. Translated and edited by Joan Connelly Ullman. Berkeley: University of California Press, 1970 ("Vives *Approaches*").

S: Walsh, William Thomas. *Isabella of Spain: The Last Crusader, 1451–1504*. 1930. Reprint, Rockford, IL: Tan Books and Publishers, 1987.

Guarionex
Hurricane, Magua, Haiti

P, prev. cit.: Ferdinand Columbus, chap. 62, quoting his father as to cohaba ceremony and burial. Las Casas Apologetica, chap. 20. Martyr, decade 1, bks. 4, 9; decade 3, bk. 9. Oviedo Repertorium, sec. 3.18.8. Pané, chaps. 15, 16, 23.

P: Las Casas, Bartolomé de. *A Short Account of the Destruction of the Indies*. Edited and translated by Nigel Griffin. London: Penguin, 1992 ("Las Casas Short Account"). Chap. "The Kingdoms of Hispaniola."

S, prev. cit.: Deagan; Oliver; Raccolta Letters Notes; Sauer; Stevens-Arroyo; Wilson.

S: Vega, Bernardo. *Los Cacicazgos de la Hispaniola*. Santo Domingo, Dominican Republic: Museo del Hombre Dominican, 1987 ("Vega *Cacicazgos*").

Baisi is a historic person given a fictitious name. Yomabo is fictitious.

Isabel and Fernando
Death and Marriage in Castile, 1468–1469

P, prev. cit.: Bernáldez, chaps. 1, 7, 105, 108. Castillo, chaps. 114–117, 121–137. Enrique Colección Diplomatico, docs. 152 (1468), 160 (1469),

161 (1469), 163 (1469). Incompleta, titles 2, 3. Palencia *Cronica*, decade 1, bk. 6, chap. 3; bk. 10, chap. 10; decade 2, bk. 1, chaps. 1–5, 7–10; bk. 2, chaps. 1–5. Palencia *Notes*, Isabel's, Queen Juana's, and Fernando's biographies. Pulgar, chaps. 1–9, 23, 24. Valera, chaps. 40-52. Zurita *Anales*, bk. 17, chaps. 3–9, 24–25, 36, 40–41; bk. 18, chaps. 9–11, 16–17, 19–26; bk. 20, chap. 23.

S, prev. cit.: Azcona *Isabel*, including for the text of the Isabel, Ferdinand, Carillo understanding (p. 174); Fernández-Armesto *Ferdinand Isabella*; Liss; Miller; Prescott; Rubin.

S: Clemencín, Diego. *Elogio de la Reina Católica Doña Isabel*. Granada: Universidad de Grenada y Sociedad Estatal de Conmemoraciones Culturales, 2004.

S: Delaney, Carol. *Columbus and the Quest for Jerusalem*. New York: Free Press, 2011.

S: Fernández-Armesto, Felipe. *1492: The Year the World Began*. New York: HarperCollins, 2009 ("Fernández-Armesto *1492*").

S: Nirenberg, David. *Neighboring Faiths: Christianity, Islam, and Judaism in the Middle Ages and Today*. Chicago: University of Chicago Press, 2014.

S: Ryder, Alan. *The Wreck of Catalonia: Civil War in the Fifteenth Century*. Oxford: Oxford University Press, 2007.

S: Vicens Vives, Jaime. *Historia Critica de la Vida y Reinado de Fernando II de Aragón*. Zarazoga: Institución "Fernando el Católico," 2007 ("Vives *Fernando*"). Includes text of Isabel's note, p. 247.

CHAPTER III: 1470S, ASCENSION

Cristoforo
Scio (Chios, Greece), (1470–1474)

P, prev. cit.: Dotson, docs. 47 (Domenico referred to as cheesemonger in addition to weaver), 50 (Domenico referred to as cheesemonger), 65 (Domenico referred to as inn keeper), 86 (Columbus referred to as "wool merchant"). Ferdinand Columbus, chaps. 2, 3, 4. Journal, 11/12/1492, 12/10/1492, as to mastic; 12/21/1492, as to years at sea. Kritovoulos, pt. 4, paras. 67–90. Las Casas Repertorium, sec. 1.2. Journal, Libro Copiador, letter 4 (February 26, 1495), as to years at sea. Mandeville, chap. 4. Oviedo Reportorium, sec. 3.3. Pleitos, doc. 1.12, testimony of Bartolomé Colón, as to his age. Raccolta Letters on Subsequent Voyages, Carta a Los Reyes (February 6, 1502), as to weather. Zurita *Anales*, bk. 18, chaps. 33, 34.

P: *Christopher Columbus's Book of Prophecies: Reproduction of the Original Manuscript With English Translation*. Kay Brigham, translator. Barcelona: Editorial CLIE, 1991 ("Prophecies"). Columbus's letter to King and Queen, 1500–1502(?), as to years at sea.

P: Moseley, C. W. R. D., trans. *The Travels of Sir John Mandeville*. London: Penguin, 2005 ("Mandeville"). Chaps. 18 (heat of Ethiopia), 21 (snake eaters and cannibals).

S, prev. cit.: Babinger; Beazley; Dotson, Introduction; Epstein; Ferro; Jane, vol. 2, Introduction; Journal Raccolta Notes, note on mastic; Morison *Admiral*; Morison *Southern*; Phillips; Russell; Taviani *Grand Design*.

S: Ballesteros Beretta, Antonio. *Cristóbal Colón y el Descubrimiento de América*. 1st ed. Vols. 4,5, *Historia de América y de los Pueblos Americanos*. Barcelona: Salvat Editores, 1945.

S: Fernández-Armesto, Felipe. *Columbus*. London: Gerald Duckworth, 1996 ("Fernández-Armesto *Columbus*").

S: Harrison, Mark. *Contagion: How Commerce Has Spread Disease*. New Haven, CT: Yale University Press, 2012.

S: Larner, John. *Marco Polo and the Discovery of the World*. New Haven, CT: Yale University Press, 1999.

S: Symcox, Geoffrey, and Blair Sullivan. *Christopher Columbus and the Enterprise of the Indies*. New York: Palgrave Macmillan, 2005.

Ferdinand Columbus and Las Casas report that Columbus sailed, inter alia, to Cape Carthage, Chios, Iceland, and Ghana prior to 1492. As to each voyage, historians disagree both if and when it actually occurred. Both Morison and Taviani believe the voyages to Cape Carthage and Chios did occur. I have followed Morison that Carthage occurred first and that Columbus probably was just a common seaman, focusing on what Columbus appreciated from the trick at Cape Carthage, not whether he instigated it (Taviani) or was duped (Morison).

Isabel
Disorder and Hatred in Castile, 1470–1474

P, prev. cit.: Bernáldez, chap. 10. Castillo, chaps. 147, 160, 164. Enrique Colección Diplomatico, doc. 179 (1470). Palencia *Cronica*, decade 2, bk. 2, chap. 7; bk. 3, chaps. 3–6; bk. 7, chap. 9. Palencia *Notes*, Isabel's, Mendoza's, and Queen Juana's biographies. Pulgar, chaps. 10, 15, 16. Valera, chaps. 58, 83. Zurita *Anales*, bk. 18, chaps. 62, 63.

S, prev. cit.: Liss; Netanyahu *Origins*; Rubin, including as to Isabella's veil.

Guarionex
Cacibaquel's Cohaba Ceremony

P, prev. cit.: Benzoni, bk. 1. Ferdinand Columbus, chap. 62. Martyr, decade 1, bk. 9; decade 3, bk. 7. Pané, chaps. 19, 25 (the prophecy), and English translation of Las Casas Apologetica, chaps. 166, 167, in appendix C.

S, prev. cit.: Oliver; Stevens-Arroyo.

Columbus once wrote that the use of a blowpipe to provide Yúcahu a voice was not symbolic, but a trick to make it appear that the cemí was actually talking, and that, on one occasion, a cacique begged Europeans to not disclose the blowpipe's usage to his subjects. I present such usage as accepted symbolism, like communion. See Oliver.

Cohaba ceremonies were regularly and frequently performed in Taíno society with a multitude of learnings and predictions. It is the perspective of the conquerors that led this particular prediction to be recorded by them.

It is unknown whether Cacibaquel was Guarionex's father, uncle, or other relation, and I have relied on Pané in choosing father.

King Afonso V and Prince João of Portugal
Ptolemy, Toscanelli, and Marco Polo, 1474

P, prev. cit.: Ptolemy, bk. 1, secs. 11, 12; bk. 7, sec. 5. Translations of Toscanelli letter to Canon Martins contained in Hakluyt Journal; Morison *Documents*; Ferdinand Columbus, chap. 8.

P: Barros, João de. *Da Asia.* Lisbon: Na Regia Officina Typografica, 1778. Decade 1, bk. 2, chap. 2. English translation of this chapter in Cadamosto.

P: Polo, Marco. *The Travels of Marco Polo.* Translated by W. Marsden, revised by T. Wright and Peter Harris. New York: Everyman's Library, 2008. Bk. 1, chap. 1; bk. 2, chaps. 55, 68, 77; bk. 3, chaps. 2, 3.

S, prev. cit.: Beazley; Berggren-Jones; Morison *Admiral*; Morison *Northern*; Taviani *Grand Design*.

S: Ferro, Gaetano. *The Genoese Cartographic Tradition and Christopher Columbus.* Translated by Hann Heck and Luciano F. Farina. Vol. 12, *Nuova Raccolta Colombiana.* Rome: Instituto Poligrafico e Zecca Dello Stato, 1996 ("Ferro *Cartographic*").

S: Fonseca, Luís Adão da. *D. João II.* Lisbon: Círculo de Leitores e Centro de Estudios dos Poves e Culturas de Expressão Portuguesa, 2011.

S: Fuson, Robert H. *Legendary Islands of the Ocean Sea.* Sarasota, FL: Pineapple Press, 1995 ("Fuson *Islands*").

S: García, José Manuel. *D. João II vs. Colombo: Duas estratégias divergentes na busca das Índias.* Aveleda, Portugal: Quidnovi, 2012.

S: Nunn, George E. *Geographical Conceptions of Columbus.* New York: American Geographical Society, 1992.

S: Vignaud, Henry. *The Columbian Tradition on the Discovery of America and of the part played therein by the Astronomer Toscanelli.* Oxford: Oxford University Press, 1920.

See Chap. IV, "Births of Diogo Colom and an Idea, Porto Santo, (1480–81)" below for discussion of the Toscanelli correspondence.

In his "Geography," Ptolemy measured distance by "stade," with one stade perhaps representing approximately 185 meters. One degree measured 500 stades, 62.5 Roman miles (8 stades per Roman mile) or 57.5 statutory miles, thereby resulting in an estimate of the equatorial circumference of the earth of 180,000 stades, 22,500 Roman miles, or approximately 20,700 statutory miles.

Isabel and Fernando
Succession in Castile, Segovia, 1474–1476

P, prev. cit.: Bernáldez, chaps. 10, 15–19. Historia Jerónimo, pt. 3, bk. 2, chap. 31. Incompleta, titles 10–15. Palencia *Cronica*, decade 2, bk. 10, chaps. 9, 10; decade 3, bk. 1, chaps. 1–9; bk. 2, chap. 1, 4, 7; bk. 3, chap. 7. Palencia *Notes*, Carrillo's, Fernando's, Isabel's, Queen Juana's, and Mendoza's biographies. Pulgar, chaps. 20–22, 26, 38. Valera, chap. 100. Zurita *Anales*, bk. 19, chaps. 13, 16, 18, 19, 23–27.

S, prev. cit.: Azcona *Isabel*; Fernández-Armesto *Ferdinand Isabella*; Liss; Medina; Miller; Prescott; Rubin; Vives *Fernando*, including for terms of Fernando's will, pp. 421–422.

S: Downey, Kirstin. *Isabella: The Warrior Queen.* New York: Nan. A. Talese/ Doubleday, 2014.

S: Harvey, L.P. *Islamic Spain, 1250 to 1500.* Chicago: University of Chicago Press, 1990.

S: Weissberger, Barbara F. *Isabel Rules: Constructing Queenship, Wielding Power.* Minneapolis: University of Minnesota Press, 2004.

Cristoforo
Lagos, Lisbon, London, Galway, Thule, and Vinland, (1476–1477)

P, prev. cit.: Ferdinand Columbus, chaps. 4, 5. Journal, 12/21/1492 (reference to going on route to England). Las Casas Repertorium, secs. 1.2, 1.3. Palencia *Cronica*, decade 3, bk. 24, chap. 7; bk. 26, chap. 5. Zurita *Anales*, bk. 19, chaps. 50, 51; bk. 20, chap. 12.

P: Kunz, Keneva, trans. *The Vinland Sagas: The Icelandic Sagas about the First Documented Voyages across the North Atlantic; The Saga of the Greenlanders and Eirik the Red's Saga.* London: Penguin, 2008.

P: O'Meara, John J., trans. *The Voyage of Saint Brendan: "Journey to the Promised Land."* Buckinghamshire, UK: Colin Smythe, 1991. Chaps. 2–6.

S, prev. cit.: Ballesteros; Boxer; Ferro *Cartographic*; Larner; Morison

Admiral; Morison *Northern*; Morison *Southern*; Tavianni *Grand Design*.

S: Ackroyd, Peter. *Thames: The Biography*. New York: Doubleday, 2007.

S: Black, Jeremy. *London: A History*. Lancaster, UK: Carnegie, 2009.

S: Enterline, James Robert. *Erikson, Eskimos & Columbus: Medieval European Knowledge of America*. Baltimore, MD: Johns Hopkins University Press, 2002.

S: Enterline, James Robert. *Viking America: The Norse Crossings and Their Legacy*. London: New English Library, 1972.

S: Forbes, Jack D. *The American Discovery of Europe*. Urbana: University of Illinois Press, 2007.

S: Jones, Gwyn. *A History of the Vikings*. 2nd ed. Oxford: Oxford University Press, 1984.

S: Karlsson, Gunnar. *The History of Iceland*. Minneapolis: University of Minnesota Press, 2000.

S: Milne, Gustav. *The Port of Medieval London*. Gloucestershire, UK: Tempus, 2003.

S: Sacks, David Harms. *The Widening Gate: Bristol and the Atlantic Economy, 1450–1790*. Berkeley: University of California Press, 1991.

S: Þorsteinsson, Björn. *Enskar heimildir um sögu Íslendinga á 15. og 16. öld*. Reykjavik: Hið íslenzka bókmenntafélag, 1969.

Some historians do not believe that Columbus arrived in Portugal via the pirate attack or that the voyages to England, Ireland, or Iceland occurred. Morison and Taviani suspect each occurred, although Morison would limit England to Bristol. The voyage to Iceland relies on Ferdinand Columbus and then Las Casas, who both purportedly quote Columbus's written notes. Many scholars believe errors in Ferdinand's description of Iceland indicate Columbus traveled elsewhere; some believe Ferdinand and Las Casas invented the voyage to establish a pre-1492 mariner's credential or a "scientific" basis for Columbus's belief the first voyage would reach the Indies; and some believe it occurred and establishes that Columbus knew of Leif Erickson's "discovery of America" (ignoring Native Americans) before Columbus sailed. I don't see sufficient motive for the invention of a voyage to Iceland by Columbus or others, and there is ample evidence of contemporaneous shipping between Bristol and Iceland. I suspect the errors in description do not prove Columbus identified the destination itself incorrectly—Iceland was well known. I suspect that Columbus did not know about Vinland because he did not cite it as evidence to promote his voyage, which would have been in his substantial interest.

Eratosthenes (276–194 BC) is generally credited as being the first to accurately estimate the earth's equitorial circumference at about 25,000 miles.

Modern science measures 24,902 miles. Ptolemy estimated the earth's circumference at about 20,700 miles. His estimate that the known world (i.e., the Canary Islands east to the Indies) stretched 177 degrees implied a distance across the Ocean Sea (without intervening American continents) of at most 183 degrees; this also was too short, as there are 208 degrees west from Lisbon to the coast of Japan. Toscanelli's analysis farther compounded Ptolemy's underestimation.

Scholars disagree whether the man and woman seen at Galway were European (e.g., Lapps or Finns) or Native Americans, such as Inuit from Greenland or from farther south.

Isabel
Guadalupe, Castile, 1477

P, prev. cit.: Bernáldez, chaps. 23–26, 28. Incompleta, titles 27, 44, 51. Palencia *Cronica*, decade 3, bk. 3, chap. 7; bk. 24, chaps. 1, 3, 6–9; bk. 25, chaps. 4, 5, 7–9; bk. 26, chaps. 5, 6; bk. 27, chaps. 5, 7, 8; bk. 29, chaps. 1, 3. Pulgar, chaps. 46, 64, 70, 84–87. Zurita *Anales*, bk. 19, chaps. 30–31, 41–44, 57.

P: Luis Suarez Fernández, ed. *Documentos acerca de la Expulsion de Los Judios*. Valladolid, Spain: Biblioteca Reyes Católicos, 1964 ("Documentos Expulsion"). Docs. 30 (August 30, 1478), 39 (December 24, 1479).

S, prev. cit.: Azcona *Isabel*; Azcona *Juana*; Fernández-Armesto *Ferdinand Isabella*; Liss; Rubin; Vives *Fernando*.

S: Álvarez Álvarez, Arturo. "Guadalupe, devoción predilecta de la Reina Católica." *Historia* 27, no. 334 (February 2004).

S: Beinart, Haim. *The Expulsion of the Jews from Spain*. Translated by Jeffrey M. Green. Oxford: Littman Library of Jewish Civilization, 2002.

S: García, Sebastián. *Real Monasterio de Guadalupe*. Guadalupe, Spain: Ediciones Guadalupe, 2007.

S: Munoz Sanz, Agustin. *Los Hospitales Docentes de Guadalupe*. Guadalupe, Spain: Junta de Extremadura, 2007.

Caonabó
Succession in Maguana

P, prev. cit.: Benzoni, bk. 1. Ferdinand Columbus, chap. 62. Las Casas Historia, bk. 1, chap. 102. Las Casas Apologetica, chap. 197. Las Casas Repertorium, sec. 5.4. Martyr, decade 3, bk. 9. Pané, chaps. 2–6.

P: Oviedo, Gonzalo Fernández de. *Historia General y Natural de Las Indias*. Edition by Juan Pérez de Tudela Bueso. Madrid: Biblioteca de Autores Espanoles, 1959 ("Oviedo"). Bk. 3, chap. 4; bk. 6, chap. 2.

P: Triolo, Gioacchino and Luciano F. Farina, trans. *Christopher Columbus's*

Discoveries in the Testimonials of Diego Alvarez Chanca and Andrés Bernáldez. Vol. 5, *Nuova Raccolta Colombiana.* Rome: Istituto Poligrafico e Zecca Dello Stato, 1992 ("Bernáldez Raccolta"). This contains an English translation of the Bernáldez chapters relating to Columbus. Chap. 131.

S, prev. cit.: Alegría; Granberry *Languages*; Indigenous Peoples; Keegan *Myth*; Lovén; Oliver; Stevens-Arroyo.

Anthropologists disagree whether Taínos produced and drank alcohol prior to the arrival of Europeans. I have assumed they did.

Isabel
Seville, Castile, 1477–1478

P, prev. cit.: Bernáldez, chaps. 29–33, 43. Documentos Expulsion, docs. 21, 33. Palencia *Cronica*, decade 3, bk. 25, chaps. 4, 5; bk. 29, chaps. 7–10 (Guzmán's thoughts, suspicion pregnant); bk. 30, chaps. 1–4. Pulgar, chaps. 89–97. Zurita *Anales*, bk. 20, chaps. 12, 22.

P: Llorca, Bernardino. *Miscellanea Historiae Pontificiae Vol. XV: Bulario Pontificio de la Inquisitión Española en su Periodo Constitutional (1478–1525).* Rome: Pontifica Universita Gregoriana, 1949 ("Inquisition Bulls"). Doc. 3 (Rome, November 1, 1478, and Seville, January 1, 1481).

P: Palencia, Alonso de. *Cuarta Decada.* Madrid: Real Academia de la Historia, 1974 ("Palencia *Cuarta*"). Bk. 32, chap. 1.

P: Talavera, Hernando de. *Católica Impugnacion: del héretico libelo maldito descomulgado que fue divulgado en la ciudad de Sevilla.* Spain: Almuzara, 2012 ("Talavera *Impugnacion*"). Chap. 53.

S, prev. cit.: Azcona *Isabel*; Azcona *Juana*; Beinart; Fernández-Armesto *Ferdinand Isabella*; Harvey; Kamen; Liss; Netanyahu *Origins*; Pérez *Inquisition*; Rubin; Vives *Fernando*.

S: Baer, Yitzhak. *A History of the Jews in Christian Spain.* Philadelphia: Jewish Publication Society, 1966.

S: Benbassa, Esther, and Aron Rodrigue. *Sephardi Jewry: A History of the Judeo-Spanish Community, 14th–20th Centuries.* Berkeley: University of California Press, 2000.

Guacanagarí
Gold Homage, Marien

P, prev. cit.: Bernáldez Raccolta, chap. 130. Chanca. Las Casas Repertorium, sec. 5.3. Libro Copiador, letters 2 (January–February, 1494), 3 (April 1494), and 4 (February 16, 1495), as to gold in Cibao. Martyr, decade 1, bks. 1–3. Pané, chaps. 19 (tree moving roots), 24. Oviedo Repertorium, sec. 3.25. Syllacio.

S, prev. cit.: Oliver; Stevens-Arroyo.

S: Guitar, Lynne. "Cultural Genesis: Relationships among Indians, Africans, and Spaniards in rural Hispaniola, first half of the sixteenth century." PhD diss., Vanderbilt University, Nashville, TN. UMI Microform no. 9915091.

Isabel, Fernando, and João
Treaties at Alcáçovas, Portugal, 1479–1481

P, prev. cit.: Bernáldez, chaps. 49, 50. Davenport, Treaty between Spain and Portugal, concluded at Alcáçovas, September 4, 1479; Aeterni Regis, June 21, 1481. Palencia *Cuarta*, bk. 33, chap. 10; bk. 36, chap. 10. Pulgar, chaps. 81, 104, 107, 109–112. Zurita *Anales*, bk. 20, chaps. 27, 34, 38.

P: Parry, John H. and Robert G. Keith. *New Iberian World A Documentary History of the Discovery and Settlement of Latin America to the Early 17th Century*. Vol. 1. New York: Times Books, 1984. Doc. 5:7, order of Afonso V, 1480.

S, prev. cit.: Azcona *Isabel*; Azcona *Juana*; Fonseca; Morison *Admiral*; Raccolta Letters Notes.

S: Edwards, John. *Ferdinand and Isabella: Profiles in Power*. Harlow, UK: Pearson Education, 2005.

S: Rumeu de Armas, Antonio. *El Tratado de Tordesillas*. Madrid: Editorial MAPFRE, 1992 ("Rumeu de Armas *Tordesillas*").

Anacaona
Succession in Xaraguá

P, prev. cit.: Benzoni, bk. 1. Las Casas Apologetica, chaps. 5, 197. Las Casas Historia, bk. 1, chaps. 102, 114, 116. Las Casas Short Account, chap. "The Kingdoms of Hispaniola." Martyr, decade 1, bk. 5; Decade 3, bks. 7–9; decade 7, bk. 10. Oviedo, bk. 5, chap. 3.

S, prev. cit.: Oliver; Wilson.

S: Sued-Badillo, Jalil. *La mujer indígena y su sociedad*. 6th ed. Río Piedras, Puerto Rico: Editorial Cultural, 2010 ("Badillo *Mujer*").

Cristóvão
Marriage in Lisbon, (1479)

P, prev. cit.: Bernáldez Raccolta, chap. 118. Dotson, doc. 113 (Columbus's declaration as witness in commercial dispute before Genoa's Merchandise Office, August 25, 1479). Ferdinand Columbus, chaps. 2, 5, 11. Las Casas Repertorium, secs. 1.3, 2.2

P: Goís, Damião de. *Lisbon in the Renaissance.* Translated by Jeffery S. Ruth. New York: Italia Press, 1966. Book II.

P: Symcox, Geoffrey, ed., Luciano Formisano, Theodore J. Cachey, Jr., and John C. McLucas, eds. and trans. *Italian Reports on America 1493–1522 Accounts by Contemporary Observers.* Vol. 12, *Repertorium Columbianum.* Turnhout, Belgium: Brepols Publishers, 2002 ("Italian Reports Repertorium"). Docs. 12.1, 12.2 (Agostino Gustiniani, 1516, 1537).

S, prev. cit.: Beazley; Fernández-Armesto *Columbus, 1492*; Fonseca; Morison *Admiral*; Morison *Southern*; Russell; Taviani *Grand Design.*

S: Catz, Rebecca Catz. *Christopher Columbus and the Portuguese, 1476–1478.* Westport, CT: Greenwood Press, 1993.

S: Felicidade Alves, José da. *O Mosteiro dos Jerónimos I—Descrição e Evocação.* Lisbon: Livros Horizonte, 1989.

S: Madariaga, Salvador de. *Christopher Columbus: Being the Life of The Very Magnificent Lord Don Cristóbal Colón.* New York: Christopher Columbus Publishing, 1978.

There is little evidence as to when or how Bartholomew first arrived in Lisbon or how he and Christopher started their mapmaking business. Morison assumed Bartholomew was closer in age to Christopher and arrived in Lisbon before Christopher (i.e., before 1477). Taviani believed Bartholomew would not have arrived before 1479. I have followed Taviani as to the ten-year age difference and Christopher's presence in Lisbon first, but left more time to establish the mapmaking business before Christopher departs Lisbon in 1480.

Salvador de Madariaga has argued that Columbus was born in Genoa of a Spanish-Jewish family that emigrated from Catalonia to Genoa during the repressions of the 1390s; he was raised bilingual (Genoese and Castilian) and brought up in a Spanish atmosphere (explaining his "fluency" in Castilian); thereafter, he engaged in anti-Genoese behavior, fighting with the pirate Coulon against the Genoese; and, while a sincere and devout Catholic, he was influenced by Jewish faith and loyal to that heritage as a descendant of conversos.

Most historians find these particularized arguments unsupported by evidence. A more mainstream view is simply that (i) Columbus was a devout Catholic born in Genoa or its environs (Columbus states he was born in Genoa in his first will, 1497, Dotson, doc. 149)—which, in my view, his writings and the Ligurian record reveal unambiguously, and (ii) he might have had converso (and therefor Jewish) ancestors. In support of the latter view, I believe the historical record shows he was comfortable in relationships with conversos and well versed in the Old Testament (each as presented in the text), and, as discussed under Chap. IX, "To Cueiba (at Bahia de

Gibara) and West, October 26–November 11, 1492," below, he apparently accepts that a converted Jew may become a true Christian—perhaps as his ancestors (similar to Talavera). While the *Journal* acknowledges the sovereigns' expulsion of the Jews from Spain and their effort to eliminate heresy (Prologue) and recommends to the sovereigns that the lands he has discovered be restricted to good Christians (11/27/1492), I suspect this involves some pandering, and it is consistent with the belief a Jew can convert to become a true Christian. I find Columbus devoutly Catholic but that his writings do not evidence the cultural anti-Jewishness prevalent in many of the other primary sources.

For a summary of the debate, see John Noble Wilford, *The Mysterious History of Columbus: An Exploration of the Man, the Myth, the Legacy* (New York: Alfred A. Knopf, 1991). See also Simon Wiesenthal, *Sails of Hope: The Secret Mission of Christopher Columbus*, trans. Richard and Clara Winston (New York: Christopher Columbus Publishing, 1979); and Carlos Esteban Deive, *Heterodoxia e Inquisicion en Santo Domingo 1492–1822* (Santo Domingo, Dominican Republic: Taller, 1983).

CHAPTER IV: 1480—1485, AMBITION

Caonabó and Anacaona
Marriage in Xaraguá

P, prev. cit.: Las Casas Historia, bk. 3, chap. 24. Martyr, decade 7, bk. 8; decade 8, bk. 8. Oviedo, bk. 5, chap. 3; bk. 17, chap. 4.

S, prev. cit.: Arrom *Lexicología*; Badillo *Mujer*; Guitar; Stevens-Arroyo.

Las Casas, Martyr, and Oviedo briefly describe Taíno marriage ceremonies, but the focus is on ordinary (non-caciqual) marriages and none describes this caciqual marriage in Haiti. I have presented Oviedo's description applying to a caciqual Taíno marriage in neighboring Cuba as would be interpreted by Las Casas.

Cristóvão
Births of Diogo Colombo and an Idea, Porto Santo, (1480–1481)

P, prev. cit.: Barros, decade 1, bk. 1, chaps. 2, 3; bk. 2, chap. 1, and English translation of bk. 2, chap. 1, in Cadamosto. Ferdinand Columbus, chaps. 5–9, 11. Las Casas Repertorium, secs. 1.3, 1.4, 2.1. Mandeville, chap. 20. Prophecies, folio 59 rvs., quoting Seneca's Medea. Translations of Toscanelli's letters to Columbus contained in Hakluyt Journal; Morison *Documents*; Ferdinand Columbus, chap. 8.

P: Seneca, Lucius Annaeus. *Natural Questions*. Translated by Harry M. Hine. Chicago: University of Chicago Press, 2010. Book 1, On...Fires.

S, prev. cit.: Ballesteros; Fuson *Islands*; Morison *Admiral*; Morison *Northern*; Morison *Southern*; Nunn; Russell; Taviani *Grand Design*; Vignaud.

S: Gay, Franco, and Cesare Ciano. *The Ships of Christopher Columbus*. Translated by Lucio Bertolazzi and Luciano F. Farina. Vol. 7, *Nuova Raccolta Colombiana*. Rome: Instituto Poligrafico e Zecca Dello Stato, 1996 ("Gay").

S: Greens, Jack P., and Philip D. Morgan, eds. *Atlantic History A Critical Appraisal*. Oxford: Oxford University Press, 2009.

Many scholars believe Columbus, his son Ferdinand, and/or Las Casas invented the correspondence between Columbus and Toscanelli, and a limited minority believe they also invented the correspondence between the Portuguese cleric and Toscanelli; two alleged motivations are (i) to establish that Columbus's aim was to achieve the Indies whereas his true aim simply was to achieve new islands, such as Antilla, or (ii) to attribute the error in not anticipating the American continents to an authority on which Columbus relied.

As Morison, Taviani, and most others, I find the invention of the cleric-Toscanelli correspondence highly improbable because (for me) the content of the original correspondence seems well beyond the perspective of Columbus, Ferdinand, and Las Casas.

As for Columbus's own correspondence with Toscanelli, it reflects the perspective of the cleric-Toscanelli correspondence, which could be copied. Nevertheless, when Ferdinand and Las Casas wrote, the New World's discovery was viewed as a success for Spain, and I do not see the foregoing motives sufficient concerns to induce a fabrication, and, following Taviani and Morison, I have written that the correspondence existed.

More important, in my view, the actual existence of the Columbus-Toscanelli correspondence is a mechanical detail that does not affect the ideas presented in the text. I believe that by 1492 Columbus was aware of the substance of Marco Polo's discussion of Cathay, Mangi, and Cipangu either by (i) direct knowledge of Marco Polo's discussion of them or, at minimum, to the extent discussed by Toscanelli in either (ii) the cleric-Toscanelli correspondence or the (iii) Columbus-Toscanelli correspondence. This awareness—by any one of the three potential sources alone—significantly affects Columbus's perceptions presented in the text after the voyage commences. Although some historians disagree, I find it problematic to refute Columbus's knowledge of Marco Polo's Cathay, Mangi, and Cipangu in 1492.

I have followed most scholars' view that Columbus did not commence reading ancient and current books regarding the earth's geography while in Portugal. However, he would have heard of Marco Polo since youth, and I suspect that he would have heard of Mandeville, Aristotle, and Seneca by virtue of the brothers' mapmaking business and/or sailing on ships and/or his Portuguese relatives.

As Taviani and Morison, I do not credit the story of the "unknown pilot"—whose ship was sailing off Portugal and blown in a storm to the Caribbean, who then returned on the same ship to die as the survivor of the ill-fated voyage in Columbus's house, and who, before dying, revealed to Columbus alone the latitude and longitude of the Caribbean islands (see the accounts in Las Casas Repertorium, sec. 1.4, and Oviedo Repertorium, sec. 3.3). I suspect the account was invented by Columbus detractors among the colonists in Española during the European rebellion against Columbus's rule. But Juan Manzano Manzano believes the account true, as argued in Juan Manzano Manzano, *Colon y su secreto* (Madrid: Ediciones Cultura Hispanica, 1976).

In addition to Porto Santo, Columbus and Filipa probably lived in Madeira and possibly the Canary Islands before 1485. Most historians agree that Columbus sailed to the Canary Islands prior to 1492. Taviani believes he also sailed to the Azores, although the evidence is indirect; I have followed Taviani, although Columbus could merely have heard reports of them.

Isabel, Fernando, Mehmed II, and Abu l'Hassan
Otranto and the Emirate of Grenada, 1480–1481

P, prev. cit.: Bernáldez, chap. 45. Kritovoulos, pt. 1, paras. 234–279; pt. 3, paras. 51–53; pt. 5, paras. 56–60. Palencia *Cuarta*, bk. 36, chap. 9. Pulgar, 119. Zurita *Anales*, bk. 20, chap. 37.

P: Palencia, Alonso de. *Guerra de Granada*. Edicion by Antonio Paz y Melia, preliminary study by Rafael Gerardo Peinado Santaella. Granada: Universidad de Grenada, 1998 ("Palencia *Grenada*"). Bk. 1.

S, prev. cit.: Babinger; Berggren-Jones; Freely; Harvey.

Isabel, Fernando, Doramas, and Tenesor Semidan
Gran Canaria, Canary Islands, 1477–1483

P, prev. cit.: Augustine City, bk. 16, chap. 9. Benzoni, Brief Discourse on Some Remarkable Things in the Canary Islands. Bernáldez, chaps. 35, 64–66. Martyr, decade 1, bk. 1. Palencia *Cuarta*, bk. 31, chaps. 8, 9; bk. 32, chaps. 3, 7; bk. 33, chaps. 5, 8; bk. 34, chap. 8; bk. 35, chaps. 2, 6; bk. 36, chaps. 4, 5. Pulgar, chaps. 81, 145. Zurita *Anales*, bk., 20, chaps. 39, 42.

P: Morales Padrón, Francisco. *Canarias: Crónicas de su Conquista*. 3rd ed. Madrid: Cabildo de Gran Canaria, 2008. Libro de Alferes Alonso Jaimes de Sotomayor ("Ovetense"), chaps. 7, 15, 16, 19–22.

S, prev. cit.: Deagan; Fernández-Armesto *Before Columbus*;

Fernández-Armesto *Ferdinand Isabella*; Fernández-Armesto *1492*; Rumeu de Armas *Indigenista*; Rumeu de Armas *Tordesillas*; Schwartz, Chap. 3, Miguel Angel Ladero Quesada, "Spain, circa 1492: Social values and structures."

S: Castellano Gil, José M., and Fransisco J. Macías Martín. *History of the Canary Islands*. Translated by M. del Pino Minguez Espino. Tenerife, Spain: Centro de la Cultura Popular Canaria, 1993.

S: González Anton, R., and A. Tejera Gaspar. *Los Aborígenes Canarios, Gran Canaria y Tenerife*. Madrid: Colegio Universitario Ediciones Istmo, 1990.

S: Hanke, Lewis. *Aristotle and the American Indians: A Study in Race Prejudice in the Modern World*. Chicago: Henry Regnery Company, 1959.

S: Rumeu de Armas, Antonio. "Introduccion Historica." In *Canarias. La Colección Tierras de España* by Antonio López Gómez, Antonio Rumeu de Armas, Alfonso Armas Ayala, and Jesús Hernández Perera. Madrid: La Fundacion Juan March, 1984, pp. 68-104.

S: Seed, Patricia. *Ceremonies of Possession in Europe's Conquest of the New World, 1492–1640*. New York: Cambridge University Press, 1995.

S: Viera y Clavijo, Joseph de. *Noticias de la Historia General de las islas de Canaria*. Vol. 2. Madrid: Imprenta de Blas Romàn, 1773.

S: Zwemer, Samuel M. *Raymund Lull: First Missionary to the Moslems*. New York: Funk and Wagnalls, 1902.

João and King Ansa
Mina de Oro (Elmina, Ghana), 1481–1482

P, prev. cit.: Barros, decade 1, bk. 3, chaps. 1–3, and English trans. thereof in Cadamosto.

P: Pina, Rui de. *Crónica de el-Rei D. João II*. Coimbra: Atlantida, 1950. Chap. 2.

P: Newitt, Malyn, ed. *The Portuguese in West Africa, 1415–1670: A Documentary History*. Cambridge: Cambridge University Press, 2010. Doc. 22, trans. of Pina, Chronica de El-Rey D. João II.

S, prev. cit.: Boxer; Northrup; Saunders; Thomas *Slave Trade*; Thornton *Africans*.

S: Adoma Perbi, Akosua. *A History of Indigenous Slavery in Ghana: from the 15th to the 19th Century*. Accra, Ghana: Sub-Saharan Publishers, 2004.

Isabel and Fernando
Inquisition, 1480–1483

P, prev. cit.: Bernáldez, chap. 44. Inquisition Bulls, docs. 3 (Rome, November 1, 1481), 4 (Rome, January 29, 1482), 5 (Rome, February 2, 1482), 6

(Rome, April 18, 1482), 7 (Córdoba, May 13, 1482), 8 (Rome, October 10, 1482), 10 (Rome, February 23, 1483). Pulgar, chaps. 96, 120. Talavera *Impugnacion*, chaps. 8, 31, 37, 38, 44, 53, 73–77. Zurita *Anales*, bk. 20, Chap. 49.

S, prev. cit.: Azcona *Isabel*; Baer; Beinart; Documentos Expulsion (preliminary study by Luis Suarez Fernández); Kamen, including for translation and explanation of papal bull of April 18, 1482, p. 49; Liss; Netanyahu *Origins*; Pérez *Inquisition*; Rubin; Walsh.

S: Lea, Henry Charles. *A History of the Inquisition of Spain*. 4 vols. New York: Macmillan, 1922.

S: Netanyahu, B. *The Marranos of Spain*. 3rd ed. Ithaca, NY: Cornell University Press, 1999.

S: Reston, Jr., James. *Dogs of God: Columbus, The Inquisition, and the Defeat of the Moors*. New York: Anchor Books, 2005.

Cristóvão
Voyage to Mina, (1482–1483)

P, prev. cit.: Acosta, chaps. 1–3. Ferdinand Columbus, chap. 4. Journal, 10/28/1492, 11/12/1492, 11/27/1492, 12/21/1492, references to Guinea. Journal Raccolta Notes, n. 30, translation of postils in D'Aily's *Ymago Mundi*. Las Casas Repertorium, sec. 1.2.

P: D'Ailly, Pierre. *Ymago Mundi y otras opúsculos*. Prepared by Antonio Ramírez de Verger, revised by Juan Fernández Valverde y Francisco Socas. *Biblioteca de Colón, Vol. 2*. Madrid: Alianza Editorial, 1992 ("D'Ailly"). This edition includes Columbus's and his brother's postils. Postils 16, 18, 490, 491.

P: *Ymago Mundi de Pierre d'Ailly*. 3 vols. Edmund Buron editor. Paris: Maisonneuve Freres, 1930.

S, prev. cit.: Boxer; Fuson *Islands*; Morison *Admiral*; Morison *Southern*; Nunn; Phillips; Taviani *Grand Design*.

S: Fernández-Armesto, Felipe. *Columbus on Himself*. Indianapolis: Hackett, 2010 ("Fernández-Armesto *Columbus on Himself*").

S: Reséndez, Andrés. *The Other Slavery: The Uncovered Story of Indian Enslavement in America*. Boston: Houghton Mifflin Harcourt, 2016.

Most historians agree Columbus's voyage to Mina occurred. Historians disagree whether, prior to 1492, Columbus had ever "commanded" a ship. Ferdinand Columbus, chap. 4, and Las Casas, Las Casas Repertorim, sec. 1.2, indicate he had, with which Morison and Taviani agree. I believe it is important to distinguish the roles of a "merchant commander," such as Cadamosto, from a "captain," such as Vicente Dias; Prince Henrique looked to Cadamosto to understand Prince Henrique's objectives and to command in that respect, not to command the crew in the operation of the boat. I believe Columbus, at this stage of his life, cared about "command" only in the former sense. Ferdinand's and Las Casas's indications may be exaggerations.

As some other contemporaries, Columbus believed the estimate of 56.67 Roman miles (52.1 statutory miles) to one equatorial degree was consistent with the estimate of 56.67miles by the Arab geographer Al-Farghani (Alfraganus). Columbus later confirmed this when reading Cardinal d'Ailly's *Ymago Mundi*. Columbus (and possibly the cardinal himself) misunderstood, however; Alfraganus's mile was a longer Arabian mile, equivalent to more than 1.2 statutory miles. With a Roman mile equivalent to approximately 0.92 statutory miles, Columbus's estimate of the earth's equatorial circumference was actually 23 percent shorter than Alfragan's, almost 10 percent shorter than Ptolemy's and almost 25 percent shorter than actual.

Isabel and Fernando
Reconquista Resumed, 1482–1485

P, prev. cit.: Bernáldez, chaps. 48, 51–63, 67–71, 75–77. Palencia *Grenada*, bks. 2–5. Pulgar, chaps. 125–138, 141, 147–155, 157–162, 164–173, 194. Zurita *Anales*, bk. 20, chaps. 42–4, 48, 51, 58.

P: Abenhamin. *The Civil Wars of Grenada, and the History of the Factions of the Zegries and Abencerrages, Two Noble Families of that City, To the Final Conquest by Ferdinand and Isabella.* Translated from Arabic into Spanish by Gines Pérez de Hita and into English by Thomas Rodd. London: Thomas Ostell, 1803.

P: Bustani, Alfredo. *Fragmento de la época sobre noticias de los Reyes Nazaritas o Capitulación de Grenada y Emigración de los andaluces a Marruecos.* Larache: Publicaciones del Instituto General Franco para la Investigación Hispano-Árabe, Artes Gráficas Bosca, 1940 ("Fragmento").

S, prev. cit.: Azcona *Isabel*; Harvey; Liss; Rubin; Schwartz, Chap. 3, Miguel Angel Ladero Quesada, "Spain, circa 1492: Social values and structures."

S: Raya Retamero, Salvador. *Guia Historico-Artistica de Alhama de Grenada.* Grenada: Museo Parroquial, 2007.

Anacaona
Birth of Higueymota

P, prev. cit.: Las Casas Historia, bk. 1, chap. 169. Martyr, decade 3, bk. 9; decade 7, bk. 9.

S, prev. cit.: Arrom *Lexicología*; Granberry *Languages*; Wilson.

I have found no primary source addressing whether Higueymota was Caon-abó's child. Some believe Anacaona's marriage to Caonabó occurred close to 1492; if this is correct, Higueymota would have been a child out of wedlock (which carried no moral opprobrium and regularly occurred) or by a prior husband. Anacaona certainly may have had other children with Caonabó or others. I have chosen to present Anacaona's marriage and Higueymo-ta's birth in the chronology and with the father indicated simply on the assumptions that (i) Anacaona would have been married to an important cacique shortly following puberty because of the importance of the alliance to her uncle or Behecchio and (ii) Anacaona's subsequent renown suggests she attained over thirty years by 1500.

Cristóvão and João
Audience and Review, 1484–1485

P, prev. cit.: Barros, decade 1, bk. 3, chap. 11, and English trans. in Catz. Bernáldez, chap. 118. Jane, Letter of Columbus on Third Voyage. Morison *Documents*, Invitation of D. João II to Columbus to Return to Portugal, March 20, 1488. Ferdinand Columbus, chap. 11. Las Casas Repertorium, sec. 2.1. Oviedo Repertorium, sec. 3.5. Pina, chap. 66.

S, prev. cit.: Beazley; Disney; García; Morison *Admiral*; Morison *Northern*; Morison *Southern*; Northrup; Taviani *Grand Design*.

S: Fernández-Armesto, Felipe. *Columbus and the Conquest of the Impossible*. London: Phoenix, 2000 ("Fernández-Armesto *Conquest*").

S: Ravenstein, Ernst Georg, William Brooks Greenlee, and Pero Vaz de Caminha. *Bartolomeu Dias*. Edited by Keith Bridgeman and Tahira Arsham. England: Viartis, 2010 ("Ravenstein").

Columbus met with John and then Ferdinand and Isabella from 1484 to 1492 to convince them to sponsor his first Atlantic voyage. There is no account by a court chronicler of the substance of these meetings written at the time of the meetings—undoubtedly because no one except Columbus thought they were important. Descriptions of Columbus's meetings with royalty prior to 1492 do not have greater foundation than other pre-1492 passages herein. The principal primary source for this story are three para-graphs written by Barros in the sixteenth century. I believe the year and place of this meeting are unknown. García says 1483, Taviani says 1483–1484, Morison says 1484–1485. Columbus handwritten notes indicate he was in Portugal in 1485, so I have followed Morison suspecting Columbus left Lisbon soon after the rejection.

Ferdinand Columbus and Las Casas state, and many historians believe, that Columbus left Portugal secretly because João might have restrained him, possibly because of his knowledge of Toscanelli, Mina, or the potential viability of Columbus's plans. I have not perceived such concern on João's behalf.

CHAPTER V: 1485 — 1490, FAITH

Bakako's Fishing Lesson
Guanahaní (San Salvador?, Bahamas)

P, prev. cit.: Journal, 10/11/1492, 10/13–14/1492, for descriptions of Guanahaní. Las Casas Historia, bk. 1, chap. 86, and Las Casas Repertorium, sec. 5.3, as to Las Casas's acquaintance with "Bakako."

S, prev. cit.: Journal Raccolta Notes; Keegan *Prehistory*; Keegan *Talking Taíno*.

It is undisputed that the inhabitants' name for the first island Columbus visited was Guanahaní and that he named Guanahaní "San Salvador." Geographers and historians continue to disagree whether this Guanahaní/ San Salvador is the island currently named "San Salvador" or another. The text in this story, Chap. VI, "Bakako's Sentry Duty, Guanahaní (San Salvador?, Bahamas)," and Chap. VIII assumes the Guanahaní/San Salvador of 1492 is the island currently named "San Salvador," which accords with my untutored, on-site observation that the current "San Salvador" does well correspond to the *Journal*'s description of San Salvador. This assumption affects the geography described in this passage, Chap. VI, and the route described in Chap. VIII, but the island's current identity is otherwise irrelevant to the story and ideas presented.

Bakako is an historical person given a fictitious name. Yuni is a fictitious person.

Cristóbal, Isabel, Fernando, and Talavera
Palos, Audience with Sovereigns, and Talavera Commission, 1485–1487

P, prev. cit.: D'Ailly, postils 23c-g, 28, 30b, 31, 37, 43, 58, 78, 79, 362, 366, 397, 486, 495, 677, 689. Barros, decade 1, bk. 3, chaps. 3–5. Bernáldez Raccolta, chap. 108. Ferdinand Columbus, chaps. 5, 11–13. Goís, bk. 1. Jane, Columbus's Letter to Sovereigns on Fourth Voyage (July 7, 1503). Journal, 1/14/1493, as to date Columbus began to serve sovereigns. Las Casas Repertorium, secs. 1.4, 2.1–2.3. Marco Polo, bk. 3, chap. 4. Morison *Documents*, Letter of the Duke of Medina Celi to the Grand Cardinal of Spain, March 19, 1493. Oviedo Repertorium, sec. 3.5. Palencia *Cronica*, decade 3, bk. 25, chaps. 4, 5. Pleitos docs. 1.12, 11.2, 19.5, testimonies of Bartolomé Colón, Rodrigo Maldonado, Dr. García Fernández. Prophecies, Columbus's letter to King and Queen, 1500–1502(?), as to mapmaking. Pulgar, chap. 224. Zurita *Anales*, bk. 20, chap. 65.

P: Castanheda, Fernao Lopes de. *Historia do Descobrimento e Conquista da India.* Book I. Lisbon: Na Typographia Rollandiana, 1833. Chap. I.

P: Meyers, Jacob M., trans. *I & II Esdras.* Garden City: Doubleday, 1974 ("Esdras"). Bk. 2, chap. 6, paras. 42–52.

P: Navarrete, Martín Fernández de. *Colección de los Viages y Descubrimientos que Hicieron por Mar Los Españoles Desde Fines del Siglo XV.* Vols. 1–5. Buenos Aires: Editorial Guarania, 1945. Tomo II, Col. Dipl. 2 (disbursements for Columbus).

P: Resende, García de. *Chronica de El-Rei D. João II.* Vols. 1, 3. Lisbon: Bibliotheca de Classicos Portuguezes, 1902. Chap. 61.

P: Zurita, Jerónimo. *Historia del Rey Don Hernando el Católico: de las Empresas y Ligas de Italia.* 6 vols. Edition by Angel Canellas Lopez. Zaragoza, Spain: Diputación General de Aragón, 1989 ("Zurita *Hernando*"). Bk. 1, chap. 13.

S, prev. cit.: Álvarez Álvarez; Baer; Berggren-Jones; Boxer; Catz; Documentos Expulsion (preliminary study by Luis Suarez Fernández); Fernández-Armesto *Columbus*; Fernández-Armesto *Conquest*; Fuson *Islands*; Jane, Introductions; Kamen; Larner; Lea; Liss; Morison *Admiral*; Morison *Portuguese*; Netanyahu *Inquisition*; Phillips; Ravenstein; Rumeu de Armas *Tordesillas*; Seed; Taviani *Grand Design*; Thornton *Africans*.

S: Angel Ortega, P. *La Rábida: Historia Documental Crítica.* Vol 2. Seville: Impr y Editorial de San Antonio, 1880.

S: Kayserling, Meyer, trans. and ed. Charles Gross. *Christopher Columbus and the Participation of the Jews in the Spanish and Portuguese Discoveries.* New York: Longmans, Green, 1894.

S: Manzano Manzano, Juan. *Cristóbal Colón: Siete años decisivos de su vida, 1485–1492.* Madrid: Ediciones Cultura Hispánica, 1964 ("Manzano *Siete*").

S: Morison, Samuel Eliot. *Portuguese Voyages to America in the Fifteenth Century.* Cambridge, MA: Harvard University Press, 1940 ("Morison *Portuguese*").

S: Thomas, Hugh. *Rivers of Gold: The Rise of the Spanish Empire, from Columbus to Magellan.* New York: Random House, 2003 ("Thomas *Rivers*").

Scholars disagree whether Columbus visited La Rábida in 1485, and, if so, why he did, offering various political, mercantile, religious, social, or other connections. Following Ferdinand Columbus, Las Casas, Morison, Taviani, and Manzano, I believe he did. I have assumed the simplest motive: he traveled to Palos to leave Diego with Violante while en route to Seville or Córdoba and, by chance, stopped at La Rábida to honor the Virgin and St.

Francis for the safe voyage.

Scholars disagree where and when Columbus first met Isabella and Ferdinand; whether Columbus offered to sail for the Duke of Medina Sidonia and the Duke of Medinaceli before offering to sail for the sovereigns; and on Bartholomew's whereabouts during this period. Taviani, relying on Manzano's extensive analysis, believes Columbus first met the sovereigns on January 20, 1486, in Alcalá de Henares and, as Ferdinand Columbus and Las Casas indicate, that Columbus's offers to the noblemen were made only after the initial rejection by the sovereigns. Morison believes the first meeting with the sovereigns was in Córdoba and, as Oviedo, followed offers to the noblemen. I have followed Manzano's analysis and Columbus's *Journal* entry of 1/14/1493 and thereby Taviani as to the date and place of the first meeting and as preceding the offers to the noblemen. I have followed Taviani and Manzano placing Bartholomew in Castile. These temporal issues do not affect the ideas presented.

Scholars disagree as to Columbus's precise calculations of, and the resulting mileages for, the breadth of the Ocean Sea and inter island distances. Generally, I have presented mileage consistent with Morison because his is one of the "longer" estimates; even using these "longer" estimates, Columbus grossly underestimated the Ocean Sea's breadth.

Martin Behaim's globe of 1492, in the German Natural History Museum, Nuremberg, and the "Columbus Map," in the National Library, Paris, are perhaps the contemporaneous maps best representing Christopher's and Bartholomew's view of the Ocean Sea, the Indies, and terra firma. The German-born Behaim (ca. 1436–1507) was a geographic adviser to King John and resided in the Azores until 1490, when he returned to Nuremberg. It is possible he met Columbus; regardless, his globe confirms that geographers contemporaneous to Columbus shared d'Ailly's view of the proximity of Cipangu and the Canaries. Most scholars dispute that the "Columbus Map" was drawn by either Columbus brother, but it does reflect Dias's expedition of 1488.

A record of the Talavera commission's members and proceedings has not been found. Historians disagree the extent Columbus had read Marco Polo, Ptolemy, and other authorities cited by this time or even 1492 so as to permit the substance of the discussion I have presented. It may be that Columbus read copies of Ptolemy and Marco Polo only after his first voyage but I suspect a combination of his informal learning and reading of Cardinal d'Ailly by this time permitted the conversation presented.

Guacanagarí, Mayobanex, and Guarionex
On the Border of Marien, Ciguayo, and Magua

P, prev. cit.: Cuneo. Las Casas Historia, bk. 1, chaps. 102, 115, 121. Las Casas Repertorium, sec. 5.4. Martyr, decade 1, bks. 5, 7; decade 3, bks. 7,

8; decade 7, bk. 9. Oviedo, bk. 5, chap. 1. Pané, chap. 18.

S, prev. cit.: Alegría; Deagan; Indigenous Peoples; Keegan *Myth*; Keegan *Talking Taíno*; Lovén; Oliver; Stevens-Arroyo; Wilson.

S: Vega, Bernardo. *Breve historia de Samaná*. Santo Domingo, Dominican Republic: Fundación Cultural Dominicana, 2004 ("Vega *Samaná*").

Tuobasa is an historical person given a fictitious name.

Fernando
Málaga, 1487

P, prev. cit.: Bernáldez, chap. 82–88. Fragmento. Navarrete, vol. 2, Col. Dipl. 2 (disbursements for Columbus). Palencia *Grenada*, chaps. 6, 7. Pulgar, chaps. 197–223. Zurita *Anales*, bk. 20, chaps. 70, 71.

S, prev. cit.: Harvey; Manzano *Siete*; Morison *Admiral*; Prescott; Rubin; Taviani *Grand Design*.

Cristóbal
Beatriz, Dias, Henry VII, and Baby Fernando, 1487–1488

P, prev. cit.: D'Ailly, postil 23b. Barros, decade 1, bk. 3, chap. 4. Ferdinand Columbus, chaps. 11, 13. Goís, bk. 1. Las Casas Historia, bk. 1, chap. 27. Las Casas Repertorium, secs. 2.1, 2.2. Morison *Documents*, Invitation of D. João II to Columbus to Return to Portugal, March 20, 1488. Oviedo Repertorium, sec. 3.5.

S, prev. cit.: Manzano *Siete*; Morison *Admiral*; Morison *Portuguese*; Phillips; Ravenstein; Taviani *Grand Design*; Thomas *Rivers*.

S: Crowley, Roger. *Conquerors: How Portugal Forged the First Global Empire*. New York: Random House, 2015.

S: Subrahmanyam, Sanjay. *The Career and Legend of Vasco de Gama*. Cambridge: Cambridge University Press, 1997.

S: Torre y del Cerro, José de la. *Beatriz Enríquez de Harana y Cristóbal Colón*. Madrid: Compania Iberoamericana de Publicaciones, 1933.

With scant primary source evidence, leading historians disagree as to Bartholomew Columbus's whereabouts from 1485–1494 and, while there is more evidence, Columbus's whereabouts 1487–1491, and whether it was Bartholomew or Christopher (or both or neither) who witnessed Bartholomew Dias's return to Lisbon. Either Christopher or Bartholomew could have recorded the postil in d'Ailly's Ymago Mundi indicating having witnessed the event. Evidence indicates Bartholomew Columbus presented his map to King Henry VII in England in February 1488. I have assumed Bartholomew Columbus was not in Lisbon (and probably in England or

France) in December 1488, and, by process of elimination, Christopher was. The story could be written with Bartholomew in Lisbon in December 1488 and reporting to Christopher without changing the ideas presented.

Isabel and Fernando
Rebellion in Gomera, Canary Islands, 1488–1489

P, prev. cit.: Ovetense, chaps. 24–26.

S, prev. cit.: Fernández-Armesto *Before Columbus, 1492*; Rumeu de Armas *Indigenista*; Viera y Clavijo.

Isabel and Cristóbal
Audience, Jaén, 1489

P, prev. cit.: D'Ailly, postils 374, 397, 398. Bernáldez, chap. 97. Bernáldez Raccolta, chap. 118. Fernando Columbus, chaps. 9, 13. Jane, Columbus's Letters on the Third and Fourth Voyages (October 18, 1498 and July 7, 1503). Las Casas Repertorium, sec. 2.3. Oviedo Repertorium, sec. 3.5. Mandeville, chaps. 20, 22, 30, 33. Marco Polo, bk. 1, chaps. 1, 42, 43, 51–53; bk. 3, chap. 44. Morison *Documents*, Letter of the Duke of Medina Celi to the Grand Cardinal of Spain, March 19, 1493. Navarrete, vol. 2, Col. Dipl. 4 (sovereigns' letter for Columbus's transit). Palencia *Grenada*, chap. 9. Prophecies, Columbus's letter to King and Queen, 1500–1502(?). Pulgar, chap. 260. Zurita *Anales*, bk. 20, chap. 85.

P: Pliny the Elder. *Natural History*. Vol. 2. Translated by H. Rackham. London: The Folio Society, 1940. Bk. 9, paras. 1–3.

P: Genesis 2:9–14. I Kings 9:26–8; 10:11, 22–23.

S: Sánchez González, Antonio. *Medinaceli y Colón: La otra alternativa del Descubrimiento*. Madrid: Editorial MAPFRE, 1995.

S, prev. cit.: Larner; Manzano *Siete*; Morison *Admiral*; Nader, Introduction; Phillips; Taviani *Grand Design*.

The historical record of the substance of this conversation is merely that Isabella gave Columbus certain hope. I have not followed Sánchez González, who believes the Duke of Medinaceli's support occurred during 1490 and the sovereigns' denial of the duke's sponsorship in 1491 (and, by deduction, that the meeting in Jaén had a different pretext).

CHAPTER VI: 1490 — AUGUST 2, 1492, DESTINY

Cristóbal
Forgotten, 1491

P, prev. cit.: Cuneo.Fernando Columbus, chaps. 13, 14. Las Casas Repertorium, sec. 2.3. Oviedo Repertorium, sec. 3.5. Pleitos, docs. 19.5, 22.3, testimonies of García Fernández, Alonso Velez.

S, prev. cit.: Angel Ortega: Fernández-Armesto *Conquest*; Manzano *Siete*; Morison *Admiral*; Phillips; Taviani *Grand Design*.

S: Rumea de Armas, Antonio. *Cristóbal Colón y Beatriz de Bobadilla en las Antevísperas del Descubrimiento*. Las Palmas, Spain: El Museo Canario, 1960.

While not verifiable, many historians believe Columbus had an affair with Beatriz de Bobadilla of the Canary Islands.

Isabel, Fernando, and Cristóbal
Reconquista Completed, 1491–1492

P, prev. cit.: Abenhamin, chap. 17. Bernáldez, chaps. 92–102. Documentos Expulsion, docs. 109, 170. Fragmento. Historia Jerónimo, pt. 3, bk. 2, chap. 32. Palencia *Cuarto*, bk. 36, chap. 3. Palencia *Grenada*, chaps. 7, 9. Pulgar, chaps. 230, 252, 253, 255, 257, 259. Zurita *Anales*, bk. 20, chaps. 49, 79, 81, 84, 87–92.

S, prev. cit.: Azcona *Isabel*; Baer; Beinart; Clavijo; Fernández-Armesto *Conquest*; Harvey; Kamen; Kayserling; Lea; Liss; Netanyahu *Origins*; Peréz; Prescott; Rubin; Rumeu de Armas *Indigenista*; Thomas *Rivers*.

S: Netanyahu, B. *Don Isaac Abravanel Statesman & Philosopher*. 5th ed. Ithaca, NY: Cornell University Press, 1998 ("Netanyahu *Abravanel*").

S: Varela, Consuelo. *Colón y los florentinos*. Madrid: Alianza Editorial, 1988.

S: Vilar Sánchez, Juan Antonio. *1492–1502: Una Década Fraudulenta; Historia del Reino Cristiano de Granada desde su fundación hasta la muerte de la Reina Isabel la Católica*. Grenada: Editorial Alhulia, 2004.

Cristóbal, Isabel, Fernando, and Luis de Santángel
Reconsideration of Colón's Voyage, January–May 1492

P, prev. cit.: Ferdinand Columbus, chaps. 12, 14, 15. Italian Reports Repertorium, doc. 17, Alessandro Geraldini. Journal, 2/14/1493 (two sons living in Córdoba). Journal Raccolta Notes, n. 13, containing translation of Passport and Letter of Credence. Las Casas Repertorium, sec. 2.3. Morison *Documents*, Articles of Agreement, and Nader, Santa Fe Capitulations, April 17, 1492. Morison *Documents*, Conditional Grant of Titles and Honors, and Nader, Grenada Capitulations, April 30, 1492. Morison *Documents*: Letter of Credence, April 30, 1492; Royal Decree Requiring Peoples of Palos to Provide Columbus with Caravels, April 30, 1492; the Passport, in Latin with translation; Royal Decree Ordering the Suspension of Judicial Proceedings Against Criminals, April 30, 1492; Royal Decree Ordering Columbus to be Given Every Facility to Repair His Vessels and Procure Supplies at Reasonable Prices, April 30, 1492; Royal Decree Prohibiting Taxation of Provisions, April 30, 1492. Navarrete, vol. 2, Col. Dipl. 11 (Diego Columbus's appointment as page). Oviedo Repertorium, sec. 3.5.

P: Anghiera, Peter Martyr of. *The Discovery of the New World in the Writings of Peter Martyr of Anghiera.* Edited by Ernesto Lunardi, Elisa Magioncalda, and Rosanna Mazzacane. Translated by Feliz Azzola, revised Luciano F. Farina. Vol. 2, *Nuova Raccolta Colombiana.* Rome: Istituto Poligrafico e Zecca Dello Stato, 1992 ("Martyr Raccolta"). This contains English translations of portions of the Opus Epistolarum in addition to Decadas de Orbo Novo. Letter to John Borromeo, May 14, 1493 (sovereigns' disbelief in Columbus's voyage).

S, prev. cit.: Fernández-Armesto *Before Columbus, Columbus, Conquest*; Journal Raccolta Notes; Manzano *Siete*; Morison *Admiral*; Nader, Introduction; Phillips; Rumeu de Armas *Indigenista*; Taviani *Grand Design*; Thomas *Rivers*; Thomas *Slave Trade*; Torre y del Cerro.

S: Fernández-Armesto, Felipe. *Pathhfinders: A Global History of Exploration.* New York: W.W. Norton, 2006.

S: Gambia García, Mariano. *De Colón a Alonso de Lugo. Las Capitulaciones de Descubrimiento y Conquista a Finales Del Siglo XV: America, Canarias y Africa.* XVIII Coloquio de Historia Canario-Americana, October 2006. Las Palmas de Gran Canaria, Spain: Casa de Colón.

Contemporaneous accounts agree both Isabella and Ferdinand thought the voyage was unlikely to succeed. Historians debate which noblemen, prelates, and other advisers were instrumental in convincing the sovereigns to authorize it. After the voyage's success, many claimed that role. I have limited focus of the narrative to Santángel and the two friars without denying that others may have been instrumental before the fact.

*Isabel, Fernando, Abraham Seneor, and Isaac Abravanel
Expulsion of the Jews, 1492*

P, prev. cit.: Bernáldez, chaps. 110–114. Documentos Expulsion, 177 (Edict of Expulsion, March 31, 1492). Zurita *Hernando*, bk. 1, chap. 6.

P: Pérez, Joseph. *Historia de una tragedia: La expulsión de los judíos de España.* Barcelona: Crítica Grupo Grijalbo-Mondadovi, 1993. Apendices 1 (Torquemada's order of March 20, 1492), 2 (Edict of Expulsion, March 31, 1492), and 3 (Ferdinand's Edict of Expulsion for Aragón, March 31, 1492).

S, prev. cit.: Azcona *Isabel*; Baer; Beinart; Benbassa; Fernández-Armesto *Sovereigns*; Kamen, including translation of Ferdinand's letter to noblemen, p. 21; Kayserling; Lea; Liss; Netanyahu *Abravanel*; Netanyahu *Origins*; Rubin.

I have not trusted Abravenel's (Netanyahu's) account that Isabella might have relented but for Ferdinand.

Cristóbal
Recruiting Crews to Traverse the Sea of Darkness, Palos, Moguer, Huelva,
Summer 1492

P, prev. cit.: Bernáldez, chaps. 111, 112, 117. Ferdinand Columbus, chap. 16. Las Casas Repertorium, sec. 3.1. Marco Polo, bk. 2, chaps. 6, 68, 77; bk. 3, chap. 2. Oviedo Repertorium, sec. 3.6. Pleitos docs. 5.9, 7.2, 7.3, 7.5, 7.6, 8.3, 8.6, 8.7, 9.2, 9.4, 19.8, 20.2, 22.6, 22.7, 22.9, testimonies of Francisco de Morales, Juan Rodríguez Cabezudo, Martín González, Cristóbal de Triana, Alonso Pardo, Bartolomé Colin, Diego Bermudez, Juan Quintero Principe, Gonzalo Alonso Galeote, Juan Rodríguez de Mafra, Diego Fernández Colmenero, Juan Portugues, Fernando Valiente, Pedro Ortiz, Hernan Yáñez Montiel. Raccolta Letters on Subsequent Voyages, Letter to Sovereigns, February 6, 1502 (observations on sailing between Spain and Italy).

P: Gil, Juan. *El Libro de Marco Polo: Las Apostillas a la Historia Natural de Plinio el Viejo*. Vol. 1, *Biblioteca de Colón*. Madrid: Alianza Editorial, 1992 ("Marco Polo Biblioteca"). Bk. 2, chaps. 11, 28, 64, 70; bk. 3, chap. 2.

S, prev. cit.: Angel Ortega; Fernández-Armesto *Conquest*; Gay; Journal Raccolta Notes (including n. 17 as to Juan Portugués); Larner; Manzano *Siete*; Morison *Admiral*; Nunn; Phillips; Taviani *Grand Design*.

S: Fernández Duro, Cesáreo. *Pinzón en el Descubrimiento de las Indias, con Noticias Críticas de Algunas Obras Recientes Relacion*. Madrid: Impreores de la Real Casa, 1892. BiblioLife, LLC reprint.

S: Gould, Alicia B. *Nueva Lista Documentada de los Tripulantes de Colón en 1492*. Madrid: Real Academia de la Historia, 1984.

S: Martínez-Hidalgo, José María. *Las naves de Colón*. Barcelona: Editorial Cadi, 1969.

S: Manzano Manzano, Juan, and Ana María Manzano Fernández-Heredia. *Los Pinzones y el Descubrimiento de America*. Vol. I. Madrid: Ediciones de Cultura Hispanica, 1988 ("Manzano *Pinzón*").

By the time of Columbus's death (1506), the land "discovered or acquired" to which Columbus's titles, authorizations, and profits arguably extended exceeded that envisioned when the agreements were executed in 1492 by gargantuan proportion. Isabella and Ferdinand soon treated the agreements as violated by Columbus's conduct and revoked titles and profit entitlements. Diego Columbus and his heirs contested the crown's revocations in a series of lawsuits—the "Pleitos"—extending in principal part over fifty years. Key issues included which lands Columbus discovered and whether others discovered them first. The parties—the Columbus heirs and the Castilian crown—secured the testimony of witnesses in 1512–1515 and 1535–1536, including Columbus family loyalists and members of the Pinzón family, who aided the crown by giving credit to the discoveries on the first voyage to Martín Alonso Pinzón. While the testimony of many witnesses was infected with self-interest, there are witnesses who may not have had a financial, reputational, or emotional stake in the litigation's outcome, and there is testimony that reflects an admission against interest and/or that must have disappointed the proponent who sought the testimony. The testimony contains factual information as to what occurred in Palos, Moguer, and Huelva in 1492, as analyzed by Manzano in detail, as well as perspectives of seamen and other commoners on the first voyage.

While some historians are persuaded by testimonies of Pinzóns and others that, after delivering the sardines, Martín Alonso Pinzón found documents in the papal library in Rome giving geographic support for his own independently conceived voyage to the Indies, I have found this testimony not credible and it is well controverted. While Pinzóns and others testified that Columbus gave Martín a participation on the voyage, no other evidence establishes that. Las Casas believed that something was offered beyond participating as captain. I have followed Manzano's speculation as to such an offer, finding it the most plausible of many speculations.

In the absence of records, naval historians have debated for centuries the specifications of the three ships. I have relied on Martínez-Hidalgo.

Juan Portugués's Pleitos testimony indicates he was black, Columbus's servant, and from the Canary Islands. Following the Journal Raccolta Notes, I have speculated Juan was a black Guinean who previously had been sold by the Portuguese on the Canaries and then "employed" or purchased by Columbus.

According to Las Casas, Rodrigo de Escobedo was Fray Pérez's nephew. According to Meyer Kayserling, four crew members in addition to Luís de Torres were conversos or Jews.

In the absence of evidence, I have speculated as Taviani that the Genoese seaman Jácome el Rico represented Francesco Pinelo and/or other Italian financiers.

Bakako's Sentry Duty
Guanahaní (San Salvador?, Bahamas)

The same primary and secondary sources listed under Chap. V, "Bakako's Fishing Lesson Guanahaní (San Salvador?, Bahamas)," above.

Kamana is a fictitious person.

CHAPTER VII: CROSSING THE SEA OF DARKNESS

Palos to San Sebastián, Gomera, Canary Islands, August 2–September 9, 1492

P, prev. cit.: Dotson, doc. 140 (Domenico still survives). Ferdinand Columbus, chaps. 16–18. Journal, Prologue; 8/3–9/9/1492; 2/14/1493. LC Synoptic Journal, LC1–6, LC120. Pleitos doc. 7.2, testimony of Juan Rodríguez Cabezudo (muleteer charged with Diego). Oviedo Repertorium, sec. 3.6.

P: Salazar, Eugenio de. *Cartas de Eugenio De Salazar: Vecino y Natural de Madrid, Escritas Á Muy Particulares Amigos Suyos.* Madrid: Imprenta y Estereotipica de M. Rivandeneyra, 1866.

S, prev. cit.: Angel Ortega; Fernández-Armesto *Columbus on Himself*; Fuson *Log*; Gould; Journal Raccolta Notes; Morison *Admiral*; Nader; Nunn; Rumeu de Armas *Tordesillas*; Zamora.

S: Henige, David. *In Search of Columbus: The Sources for the First Voyage.* Tuscon: University of Arizona Press, 1991.

S: Taviani, Paolo Emilio. *The Voyages of Columbus: The Great Discovery.* Translated by Marc A. Beckwith and Luciano F. Farina. Novara: Istituto Geografica de Agostini, 1991 ("Taviani *Voyages*").

Scholars disagree whether Columbus, Columbus's heirs, Las Casas, or another wrote the prologue to the *Journal* and whether the prologue was ever given to Isabella. Since the prologue deals with the voyage's purpose and historical context and bears upon Columbus's and his heirs' claim to land discovered, and since it does not contain nautical information, it is quite possible Columbus did not write it or that the prologue was substantially edited by another—regardless of Las Casas's assertion that he is quoting Columbus's prologue in full. I believe neither Las Casas nor Ferdinand Columbus would have written some of the statements in the prologue in their hindsight; Columbus possessed the thoughts presented in the prologue on August 3, 1492— having argued them to the sovereigns for years as a reason for the voyage, as well as being acutely concerned with his hereditary entitlements; and I have presented the prologue as his work (albeit possibly edited thereafter).

Sea of Darkness,
September 10–October 9, 1492

P, prev. cit.: Bernáldez Raccolta, chap. 118. Ferdinand Columbus, chaps. 18–22. Journal, 9/10–10/9/1492. LC Synoptic Journal, LC6–26. Martyr, decade 1, bk. 1. Oviedo Repertorium, sec. 3.6. Pleitos docs. 17.1, 19.8, 19.11, 20.2, 22.9, testimonies of Manuel de Valdovino, Diego Fernández Colmenero, Francisco García Vallejo, Juan Portugués, Hernán Yáñez de Montiel.

S, prev. cit.: Fernández-Armesto *Conquest*; Fuson *Islands*; Gould; Journal Raccolta Notes; Morison *Admiral*; Nader; Nunn; Phillips; Taviani *Voyages*.

Scholars disagree whether Columbus "kept two logs"—intentionally reporting to the crews shorter distances sailed daily than he actually estimated. While the *Journal* expressly affirms multiple times that he did so, some believe Las Casas or a scribe misinterpreted Columbus's original log in which Columbus was merely converting measurements into Portuguese leagues. Ferdinand Columbus also affirms falsification, and I see ample motive therefor.

The *Journal*, Ferdinand Columbus, and LC Synoptic Journal do not specifically report the conversations on October 9 or that they occurred on board the *Santa María*. Morison believes conversations occurred then and there based largely on testimony in the Pleitos, some noted above, and because the sailing conditions that day permitted transfer between the ships, facilitating the private, frank discussion presented in the text (rather than shouts from ship to ship for all to hear). The Pleitos contain testimony that Columbus wished to return to Spain but the Pinzóns forced him to continue, that Columbus wished to continue but the Pinzóns wanted to return and conceded to proceed only for some days (consistent with Las Casas, Oviedo, and Martyr, as well as Morison), and many accounts in between. I have presented that neither Columbus nor Martín Pinzón wished to return, consistent with the Pleitos testimony of Juan Portugués (Columbus's servant).

Landfall,
October 10–12, 1492

P, prev. cit.: Bernáldez Raccolta, chap. 118. Ferdinand Columbus, chap. 22. Journal, 10/10/1492; 10/11/1492 (which includes 10/12/1492). LC Synoptic Journal, LC24–26. Oviedo Repertorium, sec. 3.6. Pleitos docs. 18.1, 20.2, testimonies of Garcia Fernández (sailor on *Pinta*) and Juan Portuguéz (Columbus's servant, on *Santa María*).

S, prev. cit.: Gould; Morison *Admiral*; Taviani *Voyages*.

Regardless of the assertions by Ferdinand Columbus, Las Casas, Oviedo, and Martyr that a crew's "mutiny" occurred, most scholars agree that the disturbance on the *Santa María* that did occur was more subdued. The *Journal* does not mention a mutiny on October 10, and it is only on February 14 that Columbus or Las Casas so characterizes the events (to be discussed under Chap. XI. "Violent Storm, Off Azores, February 12–15, 1493"). For discussion of Columbus's sighting of firelight, see Chap. VIII. "Possession, Guanahaní, October 12, 1492" below.

CHAPTER VIII: LUCAYAN ISLANDS

Arrival of Unknown, Guanahaní,
October 12, 1492

P, prev. cit.: Ferdinand Columbus, chap. 22. Journal, 10/11/1492 (which includes 10/12/1492). LC Synoptic Journal, LC27–28.

S, prev. cit.: Keegan *Prehistory*; Indigenous People; Journal Raccolta Notes; Morison *Admiral*; Morison *Documents*; Rouse; Schwartz, chap. 5, Peter Hulme, "Tales of Distinction: European ethnography and the Caribbean"; Taviani *Voyages*; Wilson.

S: Craton, Michael, and Gail Saunders. *Islanders in the Stream: A History of the Bahamian People. Vol. 1: From Aboriginal Times to the End of Slavery.* Athens: University of Georgia Press, 1999.

S: Richter, Daniel K. *Facing East from Indian Country: A Native History of Early America.* Cambridge, MA: Harvard University Press, 2001.

It bears repeating that the primary historical record for the encounter was written entirely by Europeans. The text is entirely fictional other than the location of Columbus's ships and their progress to Guanahaní's western coast, as indicated in the primary sources cited. For example, the *Journal* entries for October 12–14, 1492, do not indicate that the Guanahaníans prepared to defend themselves or that Columbus met Guanahaní's paramount cacique or even knowingly identified such person.

Yuni and Abana are fictitious persons.

Possession, Guanahaní,
October 12, 1492

P, prev. cit.: Ferdinand Columbus, chaps. 23, 24. Journal, 10/11/1492 (which includes 10/12/1492); 10/15/1492. LC Synoptic Journal, LC27–29.

S, prev. cit.: Fernández-Armesto *Conquest*; Gay; Keegan *Prehistory*; Journal Raccolta Notes; Morison *Admiral*; Richter; Rouse; Taviani *Voyages*.

S: Deive, Carlos Esteban. *La Española y la Esclavitud del Indio.* Santo Domingo, Dominican Republic: Fundación García Arévalo, 1995.

S: Greenblatt, Stephen. *Marvelous Possessions: The Wonder of the New World.* Chicago: University of Chicago Press, 1991.

S: Restall, Matthew. *Seven Myths of the Spanish Conquest.* Oxford: Oxford University Press, 2003.

S: Todorov, Tzvetan. *The Conquest of America: The Question of the Other.* Translated by Richard Howard. Norman: University of Oklahoma Press, 1939.

S: Weaver, Jace. *The Red Atlantic American Indigenes and the Making of the Modern World, 1000–1927.* Chapel Hill: University of North Carolina Press, 2014.

Most scholars believe Columbus could not have seen firelight on Guanahaní at the estimated distance of the *Santa María* from Guanahaní before midnight on October 11 and that Columbus's sighting was either a lie or wishful thinking. What is known is that the sovereigns' awarded the queen's pension to Columbus, apparently disentitling Juan Rodríguez Bermejo and Pedro Izquierdo. I have assumed that Columbus did not tell his crews of his decision to seek the pension during the voyage—if he had made this decision at this time—because of the rancor it would spawn. The *Journal* entries of October 11 include October 12, and I suspect Columbus wrote them no sooner than at the end of the day on October 12—after landfall and possession. These entries are the key record of Gutiérrez's affirmation of the light and Sánchez's denial, very conveniently establishing both that Columbus's sighting was confirmed and the denial which explains his choice to have the lombard not fired. The *Journal* does not record the independent sighting by Izquierdo, supplied by Oviedo. I suspect Columbus desired and felt justified to take credit and see his lying and wishful thinking both plausible. I also believe there was an additional motivation supporting his lying. See Chap. XIV, "Córdoba, June 1493," below.

It is unclear whether Columbus's crews and the captives referred to him as "Admiral" after landfall, and many historians believe Columbus waited to use that title until the sovereigns confirmed it on his return to Castile. I think otherwise based on Ferdinand Columbus's and Las Casas's narration concerning October 12, Columbus's apparent references to himself as an admiral twice during the return voyage (Journal, 2/19/1493, 3/5/1493), and the text of the Grenada capitulations themselves, which require the "crews" to recognize him as "Admiral" upon the act of possession; while the sovereigns' representatives would have waited the sovereigns' confirmation, I suspect the rest of the crew were concerned more with satisfying Columbus than that protocol.

From the heavens,
Guanahaní, October 13–14, 1492

P, prev. cit.: Bernáldez Raccolta, chap. 118. Ferdinand Columbus, chaps. 24, 25. Journal, 10/13–14/1492, 11/4/1492. LC Synoptic Journal, LC29–30 (including that captives swam to the launch).

P: Genesis 2:25; 3:7, 11.

S, prev. cit.: Manzano *Pinzón*; Morison *Documents*; Phillips; Restall; Richter; Rouse; Wilson.

S: Keegan, William F. "Mobility and Disdain: Columbus and Cannibals in the Land of Cotton." *Ethnohistory* 62, no. 1 (January 2015).

The Castilian text of the *Journal* indicates on October 14 the Taínos then meeting Columbus thought the Europeans came from the "cielo," which can be translated both as "sky" and "heaven" in English. Scholars disagree whether "sky" (a geographic concept), "heavens" (a more encompassing cosmographic concept), or "Heaven" (a religious concept including sacredness) is the correct interpretation of the Taínos' belief, although it seems most contemporaneous Europeans self-righteously interpreted that the Taínos believed the Europeans came from Heaven. Morison and the LC Synoptic Journal translate "sky"; Dunn & Kelley Journal "heavens"; the Hakluyt Journal and Journal Raccolta "heaven"; and Fuson *Log* "Heaven" to capture the European interpretation.

I suspect (i) the "sky" is correct from the point of view of Taíno geographic understanding, but too limited in English translation to capture the Taínos' belief that spirits lived there and their concern that the Europeans might be spirits, and (ii) "Heaven" is wrong, as I doubt the Taínos even had the concept of a Heaven earned by faith and do not read the events related in the *Journal* itself as establishing that, at the time of most initial contacts (i.e., before conflict arose), the Taínos had decided whether the Europeans were friendly as opposed to unfriendly spirits or men, which perhaps was the key question they first confronted. Accordingly, I have presented the Taínos on San Salvador as concluding the Europeans came from the heavens (i.e., the numinous sky, where spirits could travel, if the Eurpopeans were spirits), which most Europeans interpreted as "Heaven."

Search for Gold and Cipangu, October 14–24, 1492

P, prev. cit.: Ferdinand Columbus, chap. 25, 26. Journal, 10/14–25/1492, 11/20/1492. LC Synoptic Journal, LC30–40.

S, prev. cit.: Journal Raccolta Notes; Manzano *Pinzón*; Morison *Documents*.

The *Journal* does not provide Taíno or baptized Christian names for the Guanahanían captives taken, nor does it individually distinguish the captives or their actions. The *Journal* does indicate Columbus gave three captives for use on the *Pinta* and I have deduced one for the *Niña*. This and subsequent volumes will relate Columbus's long-standing use, trust, and affection for one of the younger Guanahanían captives—whom I have fictitiously named "Bakako." Hereafter, when the *Journal* relates Columbus placing special responsibility on a captive, I suspect that would have been "Bakako" and often so written, although it could have been another captive. The *Journal* and LC Synoptic Journal sometimes indicate, suggest, or imply the concurrent active involvement of two captives, one older, and I have fictionally named this second captive "Yutowa." The historical record definitively related to "Bakako" and "Yutowa" as individuals commences in 1493, after the period of the *Journal*.

Caonabó
Maguana

No primary or secondary sources.

CHAPTER IX: CUBA

To Cueiba (at Bahía de Gibara) and West,
October 26–November 11, 1492

P, prev. cit.: Bernáldez Raccolta, chap. 118. Ferdinand Columbus, chaps. 27–29. Journal, 10/26/1492–11/12/1492. LC Synoptic Journal, LC 40–51. See Journal 10/30/1492 and LC Synoptic Journal LC 43 for Bakako's plea and, in the latter, Las Casas's explanation of the word *Cuba*.

S, prev. cit.: Forbes; Gould; Morison *Documents*; Phillips; Reséndez.

S: Harrington, M.R. *Indian Notes & Monographs Cuba Before Columbus*. New York: Museum of the American Indian Heve Foundation, 1921.

S: Hulme, Peter. *Colonial Encounters Europe and the Native Caribbean, 1492–1797*. London: Methuen, 1986.

The discussion of the women captives and the children is based on the translation of Las Casas's *Historia de las Indias* in LC Synoptic Journal, where Las Casas severely criticizes Columbus's intent to force intra-Taíno marriage or concubine relationships on Taínos and relates that the Taíno father brought aboard was the father of the three children already aboard. Dunn and Kelley and some scholars suspect or believe Columbus was arranging concubines for his crew (a criticism beyond Las Casas's criticism, which I suspect is unwarranted) and that the father brought three additional children aboard.

It is here that the *Journal* reveals that Columbus (or perhaps merely Las Casas) is comfortable that a converso can become a genuine Christian: Columbus notes that Luís de Torres had been a Jew (11/2/1492), refers to Torres as a Christian (11/6/1492), and, in an apparent reference to the Jews' expulsion from Spain, refers to the sovereigns' destruction of those Jews who did not convert (11/6/1492). See also Ferdinand Columbus, chaps. 27, 28, and LC Synoptic Journal, LC 46, 50.

East to Baneque (Great Iguana Island?),
November 12–22, 1492

P, prev. cit.: Bernáldez Raccolta, chap. 118. Ferdinand Columbus, chaps. 29, 30, 35. Journal, 11/12–23/1492. LC Synoptic Journal, LC 51–58.

S, prev. cit.: Fernández Duro; Gould; Journal Raccolta Notes; Manzano

Pinzón; Morison *Admiral*; Phillips.

Some historians believe the crews felt the voyage a failure when they failed to find gold and Cipangu at Cuba. I suspect the crew had a lower expectation of quick gratification and were more optimistic. Some historians doubt Baneque was Great Iguana Island.

East to Baracoa, November 23–December 5, 1492

P, prev. cit.: Bernáldez Raccolta, chap. 118. Ferdinand Columbus, chaps. 30, 31. Journal, 11/23/1492–12/5/1492. LC Synoptic Journal, LC 59–70. Martyr, decade 1, bk. 1. Oviedo Repertorium, sec. 3.7.

P: Matthew 6:9–15; 28:16–20.

S, prev. cit.: Forbes; Harrington; Journal Raccolta Notes; Keegan *Myth*; Keegan *Talking Taíno*; Manzano *Pinzón*; Morison *Admiral*; Rouse; Schwartz, chap. 5, Peter Hulme, "Tales of Distinction: European ethnography and the Caribbean"; Wilson.

Primary sources do not discuss or relate facts regarding the transmission in the Caribbean of disease from Europeans to Taínos on Columbus's first voyage other than identifying a Taíno perhaps dying on the return voyage (Oviedo Repertorium, sec. 3.7.12; cf. Bernáldez Raccolta, chap. 118; Martyr Raccolta, bk. 1; Las Casas Repertorium, sec. 3.3). As related in the text hereafter, the captives taken to Spain become ill in Spain.

The substantial weight of epidemiological opinion is that Columbus's observation that his crews had been healthy coupled with (i) the medical fact that the duration of the outward voyage was sufficiently long to preclude the latent, human transmission of many notable infectious diseases, e.g., smallpox, malaria, measles, (ii) the absence of animal cargo other than vermin, (iii) the small number of Europeans involved, and (iv) the brevity of their contacts with Taínos precludes the possibility that disease was transmitted to Taínos in the Carribean on the first voyage. Scholars debate the impact of germs versus guns on Taíno populations after the first voyage, and this horrific topic is for future volumes. But I have not fictionalized epidemics in the Bahamas, Cuba, Haiti, or the Dominican Republic arising from the first voyage. See Crosby and the following:

S: Cook, Noble David. *Born to Die: Disease and New World Conquest, 1492–1650*. Cambridge: Cambridge University Press, 1998.

S: Ramenofsky, Ann F. *Vectors of Death: The Archaeology of European Contact*. Albuquerque, NM: University of New Mexico Press, 1987.

S: Raudzens, George, ed. *Technology, Disease, and Colonial Conquests, Sixteenth to Eighteenth Centuries*. Boston: Brill Academic, 2003.

Barcelona,
December 1492

P, prev. cit.: Bernáldez, chaps. 104, 115, 116. Clemencín, Illustracion 13, Letter de la Reina Doña Isabel a su confessor D. Fr. Hernando de Talavera. Zurita *Hernando*, bk. 1, chaps. 9, 12.

S, prev. cit.: Fernández-Armesto *Ferdinand Isabella*; Liss; Rubin; Ryder.

CHAPTER X: HAITI

Unknown Arrives on Haiti (Bohío),
Late November–Mid-December 1492

P, prev. cit.: Ferdinand Columbus, chap. 35. Journal, 12/27/1492; 1/6 & 10/1493. LC Synoptic Journal, LC101, 104. Las Casas Apologetica, chaps. 1, 2. Pleitos docs. 8.2, 18.1, 19.5, 19.8, 19.11, 19.12, 22.10, testimonies of Pedro Enríquez, García Fernández (sailor on *Pinta*), García Fernández (physician), Diego Fernández Colmenero, Francisco García Vallejo (sailor on *Pinta* or *Niña*), Arias Pérez Pinzón, Gonzalo Martín.

S, prev. cit.: Gould; Journal Raccolta Notes; Manzano *Pinzón*; Morison *Admiral*; Sauer; Wilson.

Martín Alonso Pinzón did not record his voyage separate from Columbus in a journal, and the story is fictionalized from information contained in Columbus's account in the *Journal* (which is contemptuous of Pinzón) and the testimony largely of Crown witnesses in the Pleitos (who are sympathetic to the Pinzón family), including Pinzón's son Arias. As some historians, based on the primary sources I believe Martín Alonso Pinzón arrived at Luperon on the Dominican Republic's northern coast by mid-December 1492. The dates for and the route taken by Pinzón from Baneque to Luperon are unknown.

Cristóbal's First Encounters in Marien (Mole St. Nicholas
to Baie de l'Acul, Haiti),
December 5–22, 1492

P, prev. cit.: Bernáldez Raccolta, chap. 118. Ferdinand Columbus, chaps. 31, 32. Journal, 12/5–22/1492. Las Casas Apologetica, chaps. 1, 2. LC Synoptic Journal, LC70–88.

S, prev. cit.: Journal Raccolta Notes; Morison *Admiral*; Morison *Documents*; Schwartz, Chap. 5, Peter Hulme, "Tales of Distinction: European ethnography and the Caribbean"; Taviani *Voyages*; Wilson.

Bawana is a historical person given a fictitious name. The *Journal* and LC Synoptic Journal are confusing about whether Columbus's caciqual encounters on December 16–18 are with one, two, or three caciques, and scholars disagree. I suspect the first and third encounters were with the same cacique, the intervening encounter with a second cacique (see Wilson).

Guarionex's, Caonabó's, Anacaona's, and Behecchio's First Encounters, Mid-December 1492–Early January 1493

Same sources as "Unknown Arrives on Haiti (Bohío), Late November–Mid-December, 1492" above.

To Guarico, December 23–25, 1492

P, prev. cit.: Ferdinand Columbus, chaps. 33, 34. Journal, 12/23–25/1492. LC Synoptic Journal, LC88–90, 92, 98. Las Casas Apologetica, chaps. 1, 2. Oviedo Repertorium, sec. 3.7.

S, prev. cit.: Journal Raccolta Notes; Morison *Admiral*; Morison *Documents*; Taviani *Voyages*; Wilson.

Guacanagarí's First Encounters, Guarico, December 26–27, 1492

P, prev. cit.: Bernáldez Raccolta, chaps. 118, 126. Ferdinand Columbus, chap. 34. Journal, 12/26–27/1492; 1/2/1493. Las Casas Apologetica, chaps. 1, 2. LC Synoptic Journal, LC91–93, 98. Martyr, decade 1, bk. 1. Oviedo Repertorium, sec. 3.7.

S, prev. cit.: Journal Raccolta Notes; Morison *Admiral*; Wilson.

S: Bergreen, Laurence. *Columbus: The Four Voyages.* New York: Viking, 2011.

The primary sources do not discuss the fate of the Cuban captives, who according to the *Journal* shared the Lucayans fear of "Bohío," other than "Abasu." My speculation is that Guacanagarí would have distributed the unmarried women to his nitaínos for marriage and offered the men work as naborias, allowing the married man to retain his wife and children. This seems harsh by modern standards, but I suspect it quite benign for the fifteenth century and that the arrangements would then have been harsher in each of Seville, Lisbon, Genoa, Rome, Istanbul, the land of the Budomel, and King Ansa's kingdom. For distinctions between the Cuban Taíno peoples, see Rouse.

I believe Abasu is a historical person, and his name is fictitious. See "Ciguayo and Samaná, January 12–16, 1493," below. Xamabo is a historical person with a fictitious name.

In Guacanagarí's Bohío,
December 28, 1492

P, prev. cit.: Benzoni, bk. 1. Journal, 12/28/1492, 1/2/1493. LC Synoptic Journal, LC93. Martyr, decade 1, bks. 3 and 4 as to Bakako's relationship with Columbus.

The *Journal* merely indicates the conversation dealt with what should be "done" and does not indicate that Bakako participated. The primary sources do not explain Guacanagarí's motive for sending his representative to meet the sovereigns, and it is my supposition that it was to establish both a trading relationship and an alliance to augment Guacanagarí's reputation and power as an internal Haitian matter (see Rouse, Wilson).

Final Preparations and Departure,
December 29, 1492–January 4, 1493

P, prev. cit.: Bernáldez Raccolta, chap. 118. Ferdinand Columbus, chaps. 34, 35. Journal, 12/29/1492–1/1/1493. Las Casas Repertorium, sec. 3.3. LC Synoptic Journal, LC93–99. Libro Copiador, letter 2, January–February 1494. Martyr, decade 1, bk. 1. Oviedo Repertorium, secs. 3.7, 3.8.

S, prev. cit.: Gould; Morison *Admiral*; Morison *Documents*; Taviani *Voyages*; Wilson.

Monte Christi,
Early January 1493

P, prev. cit.: Bernáldez Raccolta, chap. 118. Ferdinand Columbus, chap. 35. Journal, 1/5–10/1493. LC Synoptic Journal, LC100–104. Oviedo Repertorium, sec. 3.7. Pleitos doc. 19.11, testimony of Francisco García Vallejo.

S, prev. cit.: Manzano *Pinzón*; Morison *Admiral*; Morison *Documents*.

There is no disinterested record of the Columbus-Pinzón meeting nor any detailed interested record.

Journal translations differ whether Martín's two young captives were girls or boys. I have followed Dunn & Kelley Journal and Las Casas's *Historia* in LC Synoptic Journal as being girls.

Ciguayo and Samaná,
January 12–16, 1493

P, prev. cit.: Ferdinand Columbus, chaps. 36, 37. Journal, 1/12–16/1493. LC Synoptic Journal, LC105–110. Las Casas Apologetica, chap. 3. Mandeville, chap. 17. Marco Polo, bk. 3, chap. 34. Marco Polo Biblioteca, bk. 3, chap. 37. Martyr, decade 1, bk. 5. Oviedo Repertorium, sec. 3.7

S, prev. cit.: Badillo *Caribes*; Fuson *Log*; Hulme; Keegan *Myth*; Morison *Admiral*; Rouse; Vega *Cacicazgos, Samaná*; Wilson.

S: Irving, Washington. *The Life and Voyages of Christopher Columbus.* Hertfordshire, UK: Wordsworth Editions, 2008.

To my knowledge, no primary or secondary source other than Washington Irving identifies Mayobanex as the cacique who meets Columbus on January 14, 1493. Based on Martyr's description, and Rouse's delineation, of Mayobanex's cacicazgo, I speculate as Irving. This identification does not affect the ideas presented in the text (Mayobanex's thoughts could be those of any cacique), but does affect Mayobanex's outlook hereafter.

Historians disagree whether the encounter occurred in Bahía del Rincon or Bahía de Samaná. I suspect the former, but it irrelevant to the encounter and ideas presented.

Anthropologists and historians continue to debate whether Caribes practiced cannibalism. Anthropologists generally do agree that Taíno mythology and belief held that Caribes did practice cannibalism. Historians generally agree that Columbus and subsequent explorers and colonists quickly asserted that cannibalism was justication for enslavement and falsely claimed that many Taínos were eligible for enslavement for that reason. Agreement ends there, and I will return to examine Carib cannibalism in the next novel when Columbus visits a Caribe island. For now, I simply note, as reflected in the text, that Columbus's initial impression that Caribe cannibalism was not real (see Chap. IX, "East to Baracoa, November 23– December 5, 1492," and Journal, 11/26/1492) has—as he leaves Haiti in January 1493—been replaced by an assertion that it is real (see Journal, 1/13/1493). I suspect this assertion is his genuine belief at this time, but it can be argued otherwise.

Primary and secondary sources do not agree the precise number or origin of the captives aboard the *Niña* and *Pinta* when they depart for Spain on January 16, 1493. Bernáldez, Las Casas, Martyr, and Oviedo report, or include as a possible number, ten, which has been my assumption. Based on these sources, as well as the Libro Copiador, I believe the ten includes: "Xamabo," the relative of Guacanagarí, who Oviedo indicates was the leader of the captives (Oviedo Repertorium, sec. 3.8.8); the four Samanáns captured January 15, 1493; "Bakako" and "Yutowa," Guanahanians; "Abasu," the Cuban (see Bernáldez Raccolta, chap. 126); and two others, whom I have assumed were both Guanahanian although one could have been another Haitian relative or nitaíno to Guacanagarí. This implies that, of the original seven Guanahanian captives, one escaped, died, or was released at Navidad before January 4, 1493 (in addition to the two who escaped in October 1492).

Meeting with Admiral's Lieutenants, Guarico, (January, 1493)

P, prev. cit.: Benzoni, bk. 1. Bernáldez Raccolta, chap. 120. Chanca. Cuneo. Ferdinand Columbus, chaps. 49, 50. Las Casas Repertorium, secs. 5.1, 5.2, 5.4. Libro Copiador, letters 2 (undated, summary of second voyage) and 3 (April 1494). Martyr, decade 1, bk. 2. Oviedo Repertorium, secs. 3.9, 3.11. Syllacio.

S, prev. cit.: Morison *Admiral*; Raccolta Letters Notes.

There is no contemporaneous account of what transpired on Haiti after Columbus departed written by the crew members left at Navidad. The foregoing primary sources contain almost all of the limited information known. There is no evidence of this meeting.

CHAPTER XI: NORTHERN CROSSING

Letters to the Sovereigns, January–February 1493

P, prev. cit.: Bernáldez Raccolta, chap. 108. Ferdinand Columbus, chap.37. Journal, 1/16/1493–2/12/1493. LC Synoptic Journal, LC110–119. Letter to Reyes (see below). Letter to Santángel (see below). Martyr Raccolta, I, 1.

S, prev. cit.: Badillo *Caribes*; Ballesteros; Crosby; Fernández-Armesto *Columbus on Himself*; Jane, Introduction; Journal Raccolta Notes; Morison *Admiral*; Phillips; Schwartz, chap. 1, Seymour Phillips, "The outer world of the European Middle Ages"; Stevens-Arroyo; Zamora.

S: Ramos Perez, Demetrio, and Lucio Mijares Perez. *La Carta de Colon Sobre el Descubrimiento*. Granada: Excma. Diputacion Provincial de Granada, 1983.

S: Rumeu de Armas, Antonio. *Libro Copiador de Cristóbal Colón Correspondencia Inedita con Los Reyes Católicos Sobre Los Viajes a America*. Vol. 1. Madrid: Testimonio Compania Editorial, 1989 ("Rumeu de Armas *Libro Copiador*"). This is Rumeu de Armas's analysis of the Libro Copiador. Vol. 2 contains his translations of the letters.

S: Watson, Kelley L. *Insatiable Appetites: Imperial Encounters with Cannibals in the North Atlantic World*. New York: New York University Press, 2015.

Historians disagree about when and where Columbus wrote the "Letter to Santángel"; who edited it in addition to Columbus and when; which version was closest to the original; and its relationship to the drafting of the "Letter to Reyes." I have considered first the translations of the "Letter to Santángel" contained in Jane (dated February 15, 1493, postscript dated March 4,

1493) and Morison *Documents*, as well as other Spanish and English texts. The Letter to Reyes has never been found, but purportedly a copy of it is Libro Copiador, Letter I (dated March 4, 1493), which I have considered as presented in the Libro Copiador and Zamora's translation of the version in Rumeu de Armas *Libro Copiador*, vol. 2 ("Letter to Reyes"). In particular, many scholars believe the qualification that slaves be taken from the "idolaters" was added by Santángel or another in Barcelona. I suspect and have written otherwise, believing the references in the *Journal* to "idolaters" (Preamble, 11/12, 11/27/1492) and to "no religion" or "false religion" (10/11–12, 10/16, 11/1, 11/12, 11/27, 12/26/1492) indicate Columbus had an awareness—which his pre-1492 experience provided—of the sovereigns' concern that enslavement be justified. See Chap. XIII, "Triumph in Barcelona, April 21–May 29, 1493," below.

While disease likely was not transmitted from Europeans to Taínos in the Caribbean on the first voyage, the substantial weight of epidimiological opinion is that the crews were infected in the Caribbean with strains of syphilis unknown in Europe and carried those strains back to Spain. See the secondary sources cited under Chap. IX, "East to Baracoa, November 23–December 5, 1492."

As for Columbus's request that his "son" receive a cardinalate, Consuelo Varela argues the reference is to Fernando, as Diego would inherit Columbus's titles (and I am persuaded), and Antonio Rumeu de Armas argues Diego.

Violent Storm, Off Azores, February 12–15, 1493

P, prev. cit.: Ferdinand Columbus, chaps. 37, 38. Journal, 1/23/1493; 2/12–17/1493. LC Synoptic Journal, LC119–122.

P: Psalm 107:23–30.

S, prev. cit.: Fernández-Armesto *Columbus on Himself, Conquest;* Journal Raccolta Notes; Morison *Admiral;* Phillips.

The Letter to Santángel widely known to history is dated as done "off the Canary Islands." Historians generally agree Columbus knew he was off the Azores but disagree whether Columbus made a mistake by writing the Canaries, simply lied, or wrote nothing, and/or whether the reference to the Canaries was added or changed later by the sovereigns' advisers. Columbus's lying is eminently possible, but I have followed that Santangel added the reference to the Canaries later. While Columbus knew reason to lie that his discoveries were not south of the Canaries' latitude, I suspect he was not focused on the desirability of lying that his return voyage coursed on their latitude.

Santa María, Azores,
February 15–24, 1493

P, prev. cit.: Ferdinand Columbus, chaps. 38, 39. Journal, 2/15–24/1493.
LC Synoptic Journal, LC122–8.

S, prev. cit.: Fernández-Armesto *Conquest*; Journal Raccolta Notes; Morison *Admiral.*

To Bayona, Galicia (Castile),
February 14–Early March 1493

P, prev. cit.: LC Synoptic Journal, LC101. Oviedo Repertorium, sec. 3.7.
Pleitos docs. 8.2, 19.8, 19.11, 19.12, 22.8, 23.1, testimonies of Pedro
Enríquez, Diego Fernández Colmenero, Francisco García Vallejo, Arias
Pérez Pinzón, Fernán Pérez Camacho, Hernan Pérez Mateos. Zurita
Hernando, bk. I, chap. 25.

S, prev. cit.: Manzano *Pinzón.*

Niña, Second Storm,
February 24–March 4, 1493

P, prev. cit.: Ferdinand Columbus, chap. 40. Journal, 2/24/1493–3/4/1493.
LC Synoptic Journal, LC128–133.

S, prev. cit.: Journal Raccolta Notes; Morison *Admiral*; Rumeu de Armas
Libro Copiador.

Alienation, Guarico,
(Winter 1493)

Except as added below, the same primary and secondary sources listed
under Chap. X, "Meeting with Admiral's Lieutenants, Guarico." There is
no evidence of this dinnertime or meeting.

S, prev. cit.: Gould.

CHAPTER XII: LISBON TO BARCELONA

Audience with João,
March 5–13, 1493

P, prev. cit.: Barros, decade 1, bk. 3, chap. 11 (incl. trans. in Catz). Ferdi-
nand Columbus, Chaps. 40–42. Goís, Braun and Hogenberg map (1598).
Journal, 3/5–15/1493. LC Synoptic Journal, LC134–140. Pina, chap. 66.
Pleitos docs. 19.12, 23.1, testimonies of Arias Pérez Pinzón, Hernan Pérez
Mateos. Resende, chap. CLXV. Zurita *Hernando*, bk. 1, chap. 25.

S, prev. cit.: Catz; Gould; Jane, Introduction; Manzano *Pinzón*; Morison

Admiral; Nader, Introduction; Rumeu de Armas *Libro Copiador, Tordesillas*; Saunders; Weaver.

S: Symcox, Geoffrey ed. *Italian Reports on America 1453–1522 Letters, Dispatches and Papal Bulls. Repertorium Columbainum, Vol. X.* Additional editing and translation by Giovanna Rabitti and Peter D. Diehl. Turnhout, Begium: Brepols Publishers, 2001 ("Symcox *Italian Texts*").

S: Thornton, John K. *A Cultural History of the Atlantic World, 1250–1820.* New York: Cambridge University Press, 2012.

Historians agree that Columbus dispatched multiple versions of the Letter to Santángel to publicize his voyage. Historians disagree whether Columbus first dispatched the Letter to Reyes and/or the Letter to Santángel together or separately and/or from Lisbon, Palos, or Seville. I have simply followed Ferdinand Columbus as to a dispatch to the sovereigns from Restelo and assumed the dispatch was of versions of both letters. The letters were designed not to reveal important geographic information for fear third parties (such as King John) would open them. Historians generally agree multiple copies of the Letter to Santángel were dispatched from Palos.

Many historians doubt that the Bartholomew Diaz who meets Columbus was the explorer who rounded South Africa in 1488—with good reason, since neither the *Journal* nor other primary sources make note of that identity or irony. The historical record is slender regarding Diaz's occupations after his historic voyage, but it does point to his having served as the Cristóvão's master. I have found a coincidence that there be two different Bartholomew Diaz's—one who rounded South Africa and the other who served as the Cristóvão's master—unlikely and treated them as the same. If Columbus did not meet Diaz the explorer, he nevertheless was haughty to the other.

Palos, Moguer, and Huelva, March 15–End of March, 1493

P, prev. cit.: Bernáldez Raccolta, chap. 118. Ferdinand Columbus, chap. 42. Las Casas Repertorium, sec. 3.3. Martyr, decade 1, bk. 2. Morison *Documents*, Letter of the Duke of Medina Celi to the Grand Cardinal of Spain, March 19, 1493. Nader, Letter from Fernando and Isabel inviting the admiral to court at Barcelona, March 30, 1493. Oviedo Repertorium, sec. 3.7. Pleitos docs. 4.4, 7.2, 19.12, 23.1, testimonies of Juan Ferrón de Posada (who relates seeing Columbus and Juan de la Cosa together in Puerto de Santa María), Juan Rodríguez Cabezudo (the muleteer, who relates that he received a sliver of gold when Columbus talked to the inquisitors), Arias Pérez Pinzón, Hernan Pérez Mateos.

S, prev. cit.: Angel Ortega; Ballesteros; Manzano *Pinzón, Siete*; Morison *Admiral, Documents*; Nader, Introduction; Phillips; Raccolta Letters Notes; Symcox *Italian Texts*.

With the termination of the *Journal* on March 15, 1493, the historical record for the period until Columbus's arrival in Barcelona reverts to minimal. I am not aware of an accounting for Martín's gold, and speculate as written. There is no contemporaneous record that Columbus or the Taínos resided at La Rábida or how long they remained in Palos.

To Barcelona,
April 1493

P, prev. cit.: Ferdinand Columbus, chap. 42. Las Casas Repertorium, sec. 3.3. Morison *Documents*, Columbus's Memorial to the Sovereigns on Colonial Policy, April 9, 1493, Seville. Oviedo Repertorium, sec. 3.7.

S, prev. cit.: Brigham; Journal Raccolta Notes; Morison *Admiral*; Rumeu de Armas *Tordesillas*.

S: Field, Henry M. *Old and New Spain*. London: Ward & Downey. British Library Historical Collection Reprint, 1988.

S: Friede, Juan and Benjamin Keen, eds. *Bartolomé de Las Casas in History: Toward an Understanding of the Man and His Work*. DeKalb, [IL]: Northern Illinois University Press, 1971.

S: Nash, Elizabeth. *Seville, Córdoba and Granada: A Cultural History*. New York: Oxford University Press, 2008.

For discussion of Columbus's relationship with Beatriz, see Chap. XIV, "Córdoba, June 1493."

Lawlessness in Guarico

P: The same primary and secondary sources listed under Chap. X, "Meeting with Admiral's Lieutenants, Guarico." There is no evidence of this confrontation.

CHAPTER XIII: SPRING 1493

Triumph in Barcelona,
April–May 1493

P, prev. cit.: Barros, decade 1, bk. 3, chap. 11 (including trans. in Catz). Benzoni, bk. 1. Bernáldez Raccolta, chap. 118. Davenport, Inter Caetera (May 3, 1493), Eximiae Devotionis (May 3, 1493), Inter Caetera (May 4, 1493). Ferdinand Columbus, chaps. 42–45. Jane, Columbus's Letter on the Third Voyage, October 18, 1498. Las Casas Repertorium, secs. 3.3, 10.2. Martyr, decade 1, bk. 1. Morison *Documents*, Instructions of the Sovereigns to Columbus for His Second Voyage to the Indies, May 29, 1493. Nader, Warrant to the Admiral and Juan Rodríguez de Fonseca to Outfit the Second Voyage, May 24, 1493; Preface to 1493 Confirmation of the Grenada Capitulations, May 23, 1493;

Appendix to 1493 Confirmation of the Capitulations, May 28, 1493. Navarrette, vol. 2, Col. Dipl. 16 (sovereigns' letter to Duke of Medina Sidonia, May 2, 1493), 20 (sovereigns' grant of coat of arms, May 20, 1493), 26 (sovereigns' letter commissioning cavalry, May 23, 1493), 29 (sovereigns' letter re: Pinelo, May 23, 1493), and 32 (sovereigns' award of annuity to Colón, May 23, 1493). Oviedo Repertorium, secs. 3.8, 3.9. Pina, chap. 66. Resende, chaps. 165, 166. Letter to Santángel. Zurita *Hernando*, bk. 1, chap. 25.

P: I Kings 9:26–28; 10:11.

S, prev. cit.: Catz; Fernández-Armesto *Conquest*; Gould; Journal Raccolta Notes; Morison *Admiral*; Philips; Raccolta Letter Notes; Rumeu de Armas *Tordesillas*; Symcox *Italian Texts* (introduction by Geoffrey Symcox); Thomas *Rivers*; Thomas *Slave Trade*.

S: Myers, Kathleen Ann. *Fernández de Oviedo's Chronicle of America: A New History for a New World*. Translations by Nina M. Scott. Austin: University of Texas Press, 2007.

S: Ramos, Demetrio. *La Primera Noticia de America*. Valladolid, Spain: Casa-Museo de Colón Seminario Americanista de la Universidad de Valladolid, 1986.

There is no evidence of the conversations involving the Taínos.

As previously noted, historians do not agree when, how, or by whom Columbus's public letter was edited. I simply have assumed Santángel made the edits indicated.

Historians do not agree the sequence of events leading to the issuance of the three papal bulls and the text follows Thomas and Raccolta Letter Notes.

The primary sources do not discuss what Xamabo, as Guacanagarí's emissary, did or attempted to achieve in Barcelona other than attend the sovereigns' reception for Columbus and the baptism, and do not mention any special meeting with Fernando.

Caciqual Council in Magua

No primary or secondary sources.

In the Presence of Christ's Mother, Guadalupe, June 1493

P, prev. cit.: Las Casas Repertorium, sec. 3.3. Oviedo Repertorium, sec. 3.8.

S, prev. cit.: Morison *Admiral*.

Chaos in Guarico

The same primary and secondary sources listed under Chap. X, "Meeting with Admiral's Lieutenants, Guarico." The primary sources, written by the

European conquerors, portray Guacanagarí as likely too timid to have this confrontation. I suspect otherwise.

CHAPTER XIV: SUMMER 1493

Córdoba,
June 1493

P, prev. cit.: Ferdinand Columbus, chap. 47, as to Columbus's promise to name an island Santa María de Guadalupe. See also Libro Copiador, letter 2, January–February 1494.

S, prev. cit.: Ballesteros; Manzano *Siete*; Raccolta Letter Notes; Taviani *Grand Design*; Torre y del Cerro.

There is no evidence why Columbus and Beatriz separated and the text presents I believe the most plausible simple explanation (i.e., Columbus left Beatriz because her support was no longer necessary to him and her social status was now below his), which is consistent with the guilt about her Columbus expressed in later years. Some historians argue Columbus discovered that Beatriz had been unfaithful (as Columbus had been) and/or that Columbus' nobility legally precluded marriage.

Into the Cibao
(Summer 1493)

The same primary and secondary sources listed under Chap. X, "Meeting with Admiral's Lieutenants."

Outfitting the Second Voyage,
Seville, July and August 1493

P, prev. cit.: Barros, decade 1, bk. 3, chap. 11 (including trans. in Catz). Benzoni, bk. 1. Bernáldez Raccolta, chap. 118. Clemencín, Illustracion 13, Letter de D. Fr. Hernando de Talavera a la Reina. Davenport, Dudum Siquidem (September 26, 1493). Ferdinand Columbus, chap. 45. Las Casas Repertorium, sec. 4. Martyr, decade 1, bk. 1. Navarrette, vol. 2, Col. Dipl. 21 (financing from Hermandad, May 23, 1493), 25 (instructions to Juanoto Berardi, May 23, 1493), 50 (sovereigns' instructions to Colón, June 12, 1493), 61 (sovereigns' instructions to Pinelo, August 4, 1493), 65 (sovereigns' instructions to Fonseca, August 18, 1493), 67 (sovereigns' instructions to Colón, August 18, 1493). Oviedo Repertorium, sec. 3.9. Pina, chap. 66. Resende, chaps. 165, 166. Zurita *Hernando*, bk. 1, chap. 25.

P: Symcox, Geoffrey, ed. *Italian Reports on America 1493–1522 Letters, Dispatches, and Papal Bulls.* Vol X, *Repertorium Columbianum.* Additional editing and translation by Giovanna Rabitti, Peter D. Diehl. Turnhout, Belgium: Brepols Publishers, 2001. Doc. 11, Piis Fidelium (June 25, 1493).

S, prev. cit.: Deagan; Friede; Manzano *Siete*; Nader; Raccolta Letter Notes; Taviani *Voyages*; Thomas; Weaver.

S: Aymar i Ragolta, Jaume. *Fra Ramón Pané l'Univers Simbòlic Taí.* Barcelona: Facultat de Teologia de Catalunya, 2009.

Libro Copiador, Letter II, expressly states that three of the Samánan captives (out of four) died of "viruelas" or "pocks." As the next volume will relate, the seven Taínos do embark on the second voyage (Chanca) and I doubt the captains of the ships would have permitted a person—European or Taíno—with a visible, deadly communicable disease to board (e.g., smallpox). There is no record of small pox on the second voyage.

Into Maguana
(Late Summer 1493)

The same primary and secondary sources listed under Chap. X. "Meeting with Admiral's Lieutenants, Guarico." There is no evidence of these conversations, other than an indication (Ferdinand Columbus, chap. 50) that a Christian told Guacanagarí that "Christian law" was "vain."

Final Instructions,
September 5, 1493

P, prev. cit.: Nader, Letter from Queen Isabel to Columbus, September 5, 1493. Navarrette, vol. 2, Col. Dipl. 69 (sovereigns' instructions to Fonseca, September 5, 1493), 71 (sovereigns' letter to Colón, September 5, 1493).

S, prev. cit.: Morison *Admiral*; Rumeu de Armas *Tordesillas*; Thomas *Rivers*.

By a Creek in Maguana

No primary or secondary sources.

ACKNOWLEDGMENTS

This book is the result of six years of research in English and Spanish language sources and visits to almost all the Caribbean, European, and Atlantic locations presented, including the archaeological sites or approximate sites where the Taíno chieftains lived in Haiti and the Dominican Republic. It was conceived earlier over many years, on occasional visits to Native American sites or reservations in the United States and Canada or wilderness areas in their close proximity. My inspiration in writing has been to validly depict the encounters of 1492 and 1493 from both Taíno and European viewpoints and to illustrate a civility and tolerance of the society and religion vanquished that are now often lacking in the modern societies and religions we have inherited.

First and foremost, I'm indebted to my esteemed friend Aron Rodrigue, Professor of History at Stanford University, for reviewing and commenting on an early version of the manuscript from the European perspective and, more importantly, for giving me the confidence to explore and interpret history myself. I also thank two Taíno scholars for reviewing portions of a more mature version of the manuscript: William F. Keegan, Professor of Natural History at the University of Florida and Curator of Anthropology at the Florida Museum of Natural History, one of the world's foremost experts on Taíno society and life; and Lynne Guitar, PhD in colonial Latin America history and formerly resident director of the Council on

International Educational Exchange in the Dominican Republic, who accompanied me on visits to Taíno sites in the Dominican Republic. I have benefitted by the insights of these experts, but I haven't incorporated all of their perspectives or comments, and the book remains solely my responsibility.

I believe that understanding the physical environment where events took place is quite important to their comprehension and that, while this environment today is significantly altered from five centuries prior, it still provides clues as to what men and women might have thought or felt five centuries prior. Standing at the beaches of Bord de Mer de Limonade, Haiti, or on San Salvador's west coast; in the open field at the Corral de los Indios in San Juan de la Maguana, Dominican Republic; atop the western cliffs of Porto Santo, Portugal; or on the quay in the tiny harbor at San Sebastián, Gomera, Canary Islands, has shaped my depiction of those thoughts and feelings.

I thank Richard Weber, the founder of Tours, Trips, Treks & Travel of the Dominican Republic, for arranging and assisting my travels in the Dominican Republic and Haiti. Through Richard, I met Domingo Abreu, the director of speleological studies within the Dominican Republic's government, who led me on visits to numerous Taíno sites, including caves, within his country, and Tim Schwartz, PhD in social anthropology, who led me around the Cape Haitien area of Haiti and arranged a small boat to visit the reefs offshore. Special thanks to Carlos Mercedes, my guide in the Dominican Republic, who was my constant companion and kindly drove far off the normal tourist routes, as well as Clark Moore, my guide in Haiti.

Others led me around various sites: Kerri and Rainy Harvey, of the National Trust, Middle Caicos, Cayman Islands, helped me trek about their island; Thomas Karamuslis toured me about the island of Chios, Greece; Birna Þórðardóttir guided me about Iceland; Michael Kojo Orleans and his assistants Francis Dabiagy and Asare Kwakye took me to El Mina, Ghana, and the hills about it. I was guided on walking tours of a number of cities, including: Lisbon, by Jose Antunes; Galway, Ireland, by Conor Riordan; and Barcelona and Gerona, Spain, by Nestor Centelles Duran. I thank my children, Sam, Ben, and Hannah, for assisting my exploration of sites in Spain and the Canary Islands, Portugal and Porto Santo, Genoa, and San Salvador.

From a literary perspective, I'm grateful to a number of editors who critiqued various versions of the manuscript, some of whom are accomplished, published writers themselves, including: Carissa Bluestone, Zach Brown, Samuel Butler, Margaret Crane, Susan Leon, Ernesto Mestre, and Robin O'Dell.

I'm also grateful to David Atkinson of Hand Made Maps, Ltd. for drawing the book's maps and sketches and Robert Hunt for the book's cover. Others who contributed significantly to the book's production include: Glen Edelstein of Hudson Valley Book Design, for the book's layout; Neil Rosini, my lawyer, as well as Rita Carrier; and Angelle Barbazon, Kendall Hinote, and Ellen Zielinski Whitfield for communications.

There have been others with more subtle influences. I thank my grade school teachers at the St. Bernard's school for an appreciation of religion and religious stories. Over years, I've learned from and enjoyed conversations with professors contributing to my alma mater U.C. Berkeley's Center for the Study of Religion, including Anthony Cascardi, Jonathan Sheehan, and Mark Csikszentmihalyi. I thank my mentors when I practiced law, particularly the late Bill Kirby and William Williams, for teaching that analysis precedes advocacy. Some instructors shaped my thoughts on spirituality, including Loren Bassett, Andrea Borrero, and Kiley Holliday. Others gave advice as to writing and publishing generally, including my friends Warren Kozak and Jonathan Mann, and Jonathan's practical guidance and assistance was instrumental, as it's always been.

No influence was greater than that of two ladies. My mother, the late Mary Lee Morey Rowen, was a grade and high school history teacher with a practical knowledge of the world's civilizations since time began that occasionally still surprises me, particularly when I talk with university professors. She liked to pronounce to the effect: "Cecil B. DeMille got it wrong. Other than the Pyramids themselves, most history through the seventeenth century is small, very small— small armies, small battles, small ships. But the thoughts are big, usually bigger than today." My wife, Mary Anne, has been a constant critic of the text and project, reminding that one man's passion may be boredom to others.

ABOUT THE AUTHOR

ANDREW ROWEN is a U.C. Berkeley and Harvard Law grad-
uate who practiced law as a partner of a major New York City law
firm for almost 30 years prior to retiring to write this book. He has
devoted six years to researching *Encounters Unforeseen* and visiting
nearly all the Caribbean, European, and Atlantic locations where the
action takes place, including the archaeological sites where the Taíno
chieftains lived in Haiti and the Dominican Republic. He has long
been interested in the roots of religious intolerance. He lives in New
York City with his wife and three kids.

CPSIA information can be obtained
at www.ICGtesting.com
Printed in the USA
BVHW03*1632120418
513078BV00032B/35/P